PETER SIMPLE

OTHER TITLES IN THE
HEART OF OAK SEA CLASSICS SERIES INCLUDE:

The Black Ship by Dudley Pope

Doctor Dogbody's Leg by James Norman Hall

FREDERICK MARRYAT

Peter Simple

HEART OF OAK SEA CLASSICS

Dean King, Series Editor

Foreword by

Dean King

Introduction by

Louis J. Parascandola

AN OWL BOOK
HENRY HOLT AND COMPANY   NEW YORK

Henry Holt and Company, Inc.
Publishers since 1866
115 West 18th Street
New York, New York 10011

Henry Holt® is a registered
trademark of Henry Holt and Company, Inc.

Published in Canada by Fitzhenry & Whiteside Ltd.,
195 Allstate Parkway, Markham, Ontario L3R 4T8.

Library of Congress Cataloging-in-Publication Data
Marryat, Frederick, 1792–1848.
Peter Simple / Frederick Marryat ; introduction by Louis J. Parascandola.
— 1st ed.
p.   cm. — (Heart of oak sea classics series)
"Owl books."
ISBN 0-8050-5565-7 (pbk. : alk. paper)
1. Great Britain—History, Naval—19th century—Fiction.   2. Napoleonic Wars,
1800–1815—Fiction.   I. Title.   II. Series.
PR4977.P39   1998
823'.7—dc21   97-40700

Henry Holt books are available for special promotions and premiums.
For details contact: Director, Special Markets.

First published in 1834 by Saunders & Otley in three volumes.

First Owl Books Edition 1998

Designed by Kate Nichols

Printed in the United States of America
All first editions are printed on acid-free paper. ∞

1   3   5   7   9   10   8   6   4   2

HEART OF OAK

Come cheer up, my lads, 'tis to glory we steer,
To add something new to this wonderful Year:
To honour we call you, not press you like slaves,
For who are so free as the sons of the waves?

CHORUS:
Heart of Oak are our ships,
Heart of Oak are our men,
We always are ready,
Steady, boys, steady,
We'll fight and we'll conquer again and again.

We ne'er see our foes but we wish them to stay;
they never see us but they wish us away:
If they run, why we follow, and run them on shore,
for if they won't fight us, we cannot do more.

Heart of Oak, etc.

They swear they'll invade us, these terrible foes,
They'll frighten our women, and children, and beaux;
But should their flat-bottoms in darkness get o'er,
Still Britons they'll find to receive them on shore.

Heart of Oak, etc.

We'll still make them run and we'll still make them sweat,
In spite of the Devil, and Brussels Gazette:
Then cheer up, my lads, with one voice let us sing
Our soldiers, our sailors, our statesman, and King.

Heart of Oak, etc.

—DAVID GARRICK

Source: C. H. Firth, *Naval Songs and Ballads*. Publications of the Navy Records Society, vol. XXXIII (London, 1908), p. 220.

FOREWORD

I HAD GONE to the Mid-Manhattan Library in New York City
in search of Captain Frederick Marryat's novels. Although he
was one of the most popular authors of the nineteenth century
and maintained his lofty critical reputation well into this century,
and although he was a founder of the modern naval warfare fiction
genre, most of his books had long since gone out of print. Even the
Mid-Manhattan Library's Literature and Language Collection—with
150,000 volumes—listed only one of his titles, *Mr. Midshipman Easy*,
in its catalog.

Suspecting that I was somehow bungling the search, I sought the
nearest librarian for help. "Could there be just one Marryat book in
the library?" I asked. She said she was afraid so, but there was
someone else I should talk to. She led me to a slim, thick-spectacled
gentleman. "Unfortunately, we don't have any others," he said,
without referring to his computer or any other source. "I know,"
continued the part-time librarian, who just happened to be Dr. Louis
J. Parascandola. "I wrote my dissertation on him."

An animated conversation ensued. Parascandola, who teaches at
Long Island University, was in the process of polishing up his book
about Marryat's social and political views. Not only did he know
just about everything there was to know about the captain-author
who served in the Royal Navy during and after the Napoleonic War,

but he possessed Marryat's novels in many different editions, which he had collected over the past two decades, and he offered to lend them to me.

Thus began a happy relationship for us and some most enjoyable reading for me as, in short order, I raced through his copies of some of Marryat's finest nautical fiction: *Mr. Midshipman Easy, Masterman Ready, Jacob Faithful, Percival Keene*, and *Peter Simple*. To my great pleasure, I found Marryat could write a grand tale, full of life and humor and gumption. I also discovered that the captain, having seen plenty of action in his long naval service, had a well-rounded view of life at sea. With his acute eye and reflective nature, Marryat knew and articulated both its glory and its hardship. In his fiction he was on a mission to present both sides, as well as to nourish the moral fiber of his reader.

With their swift plots and lasting truths, the works of Captain Marryat, I quickly realized, would be a cornerstone in the Heart of Oak Sea Classics series, which would initially focus on the works surrounding the Napoleonic wars.

My reading for the Heart of Oak Sea Classics series also led me to C. Northcote Parkinson's colorful 1948 anthology *Portsmouth Point: The Navy in Fiction, 1793–1815*, which contained some of the most cogent of 150 years of praise for Marryat's novels. "William James, the naval historian, tells us much about the French Wars in the six volumes of his History," wrote Parkinson, a venerable British historian and novelist, "but it is only the readers of Marryat who can visualize the events he is trying to describe. Had we, in fact, to choose between them, we might think Marryat the better historian of the two."

That is a great compliment, indeed, given that James's *History* (1822) is still regarded as the definitive chronology of the day. But as Parkinson pointed out, "A good novel is true to its period in atmosphere. . . . The novelist, in writing dialogue, has not to tax his memory for the exact words used. He writes boldly the sort of talk there might have been and so creates—as compared with the biographer—an impression more vivid and, in a sense, more true." That is the crux of the matter. The best fiction writers have the ability in their dialogue to penetrate the reader's soul, where they plant buds that flower within. Great fiction dialogue brings subtle complexities to life in a way that the best description and most true-life dialogue simply cannot. Marryat had a talent for creating characters who spoke to his readers.

For the growing number of readers of sea literature, Marryat is a worthy choice, and is certainly among the finest writers to have served in the Royal Navy. Courageous and opportunistic at sea, he wrote with all the intensity of a frigate in pursuit, accurately capturing the many faces of Jack Tar on the page. In *Peter Simple*, Marryat's power of observation and sense of humor, his strong opinions and his dogged pursuit of the nuances of life at sea—let alone the roaring action—make for one of the most compelling stories of a thrilling era.

My thanks to Professor Parascandola, who kindly made the books available to me and who so capably introduces this edition of *Peter Simple*.

—Dean King

NOTE:

The Mid-Manhattan Library has since added several Marryat titles to its stacks, and the Center for the Humanities research library across the street possesses many early Marryat editions, which can be perused on the premises.

INTRODUCTION

RRIVING AT A DINNER with King William IV, Captain
Frederick Marryat (1792–1848) proudly stated, "Tell his
Majesty I am Peter Simple." Indeed, Marryat's fictional
character, a young midshipman who proves his mettle in the Royal
Navy, had greatly pleased the "Sailor King," and everyone else. So
popular were Marryat's novels during the 1830s that one British
ship is said to have signaled another at sea—probably with the Code
of Signals created by Marryat, himself—to find out the events of his
latest serialized work.

With his thorough knowledge of the sea and ready wit, Captain
Marryat, a distinguished navy veteran of twenty-four years, is an
author who spoke not only to kings and commoners but also to the
literati. A friend of Dickens, he was also much admired by Thackeray, Coleridge, and Washington Irving, who wrote to him in 1830
to say, "You have a glorious field before you, and one in which you
cannot have many competitors, as so very few unite the author to
the sailor." Indeed, Marryat's accurately detailed novels about life
and war at sea during the Napoleonic War (1803–15), in which he
fought, are a wonderful mélange of humor, moral lesson, intrigue,
adventure, and sea salt. Marryat pioneered the serialized novel,
paving the way for his successors Dickens and Thackeray.

Marryat, author of more than twenty novels, was considered one of England's foremost writers, and was admired by other authors well into the twentieth century. Conrad, for example, proclaimed: "His greatness is undeniable," and Hemingway once said that along with Turgenev and Fielding, Marryat was one of his favorite writers.

FREDERICK MARRYAT was the second son of Joseph Marryat, a rich merchant, a chairman of Lloyd's, and a member of Parliament. Inspired by the splendor of Admiral Lord Nelson's funeral, Frederick attempted to run away to sea. At first opposed to the idea, his father finally relented and used his influence to secure him a midshipman's berth on the *Impérieuse*, a frigate commanded by the daring Thomas Cochrane.

Ship life must have come as a shock to the fourteen-year-old boy after his pampered upbringing. Later, in his fiction, Marryat described the overcrowded midshipman's berth as being "about five feet four inches high; a small aperture, about nine inches square, admitted a very scanty portion of that which we most needed, namely fresh air and daylight." He described midshipmen as "amusing themselves with crunching hard biscuits, and at the same time a due proportion of those little animals of the scaribee tribe, denominated weevils, who had located themselves in the unleavened bread and which midshipmen declared to be the only fresh meat which they had tasted for some time."

Serving with Cochrane for three years, Marryat made terse entries in his midshipman's log, recording perilous incidents that must have come to seem fairly routine:

> Sept. 7th. Cut out some small vessels—Dr. Sorrell killed— *Spartan* in company.
> "—— 8th. Destroyed a telegraph off Port Vendre.
> "—— 9th. Stormed and took two batteries—beat off from a third—ship much damaged in hull and rigging— two men hurt.
> "—— 11th. Rocketing the town of Adge and engaging batteries.

But life at sea, especially during wartime, made an indelible impression on the young Marryat. Later he reflected on this active service: "the hasty sleep, snatched at all hours; the waking up at the report of the guns, which seemed the only key-note to the hearts of those on board: the beautiful precision of our fire, obtained by constant practice; the coolness and courage of our captain, inoculating the whole of the ship's company; the suddenness of our attacks, the gathering after the combat, the killed lamented, the wounded almost envied; the powder so burnt into our faces that years could not remove it; the proved character of every man and officer on board, the implicit trust and the adoration we felt for our commander . . . when memory sweeps along those years of excitement even now, my pulse beats more quickly with the reminiscence."

There is not space here to give an account of Marryat's entire career, which is eloquently recorded in detail in Christopher Lloyd's *Captain Marryat and the Old Navy* (1939). But some highlights will be useful to better understand his novels: In 1809, at the Battle of Aix Roads, one of Cochrane's famous actions, Marryat courageously volunteered to serve on a "bomb vessel," an explosive brig sent into the anchored French fleet in an attempt to set the ships afire. Apparently, Cochrane was pleased with his young midshipman. Later, he wrote that Marryat "was brave, zealous, intelligent and even thoughtful."

From 1811 to 1813, Marryat was stationed in the West Indies. He was twice stationed in America, fighting in several skirmishes during the War of 1812. Marryat married Catherine Shairp in 1819; although they would produce eleven children over the next two decades, the relationship was often strained and they separated in 1839. In 1820, commanding H.M.S. *Beaver*, Marryat was stationed off the island of St. Helena, where the exiled Naploeon Bonaparte was dying; Marryat, who had some skill as an artist (in 1819, he had been made a member of the Royal Society for a series of caricatures), sketched the former emperor on his deathbed.

From 1821 to 1823, Marryat was employed in suppressing smuggling in the English Channel. During this time, he wrote a lengthy memorandum on ways to curtail that illicit trade. He also wrote a treatise calling for the abolition of impressment and for many naval reforms, including improved medical treatment and better pay, in the hope of inducing more men to join the service voluntarily. In 1823, Marryat, commanding H.M.S. *Larne*, again distinguished himself, fighting the King of Ava (Burma). For his bravery, Marryat was made a Companion of the Order of Bath.

In 1828, Marryat was made a captain of the twenty-eight-gun sloop *Ariadne*, stationed in the North Sea. Meanwhile, his first novel, *The Naval Officer, or Scenes and Adventures in the Life of Frank Mildmay*, based on his nautical experiences, was published anonymously in England in 1829. Marryat wrote at sea, and *The King's Own*, his second novel, was published in 1830. With the success of the latter and the realization that further promotion within the navy was unlikely—partly because he had displeased King William IV with his earlier calls for naval reforms—Marryat resigned from the navy in 1830.

He had earned many honors in the service. Having saved at least a dozen people from drowning, he was awarded several commendations for bravery. He also received a gold medal from the Humane Society for his design of a lifeboat. Furthermore, the Code of Signals he had created in 1817 greatly improved communications between ships and eventually won him membership in the French Legion of Honor.

MARRYAT NOW took up writing in earnest. From 1832 to 1836, he served as editor of *Metropolitan Magazine*, turning it into a nautical periodical and serializing his own work, including the novels *Peter Simple* (1832–33), *Jacob Faithful* (1833–34), *Japhet, in Search of a Father* (1834–36), and *Mr. Midshipman Easy* (1836). This quartet of novels— each involving a young hero who overcomes obstacles, proves his mettle, and finds a just reward—comprises Marryat's most significant work.

With each episode that Marryat published in *Metropolitan Magazine*, the public clamored for more, and Marryat became one of the most talked-about writers of his day. But he was savvy enough to not publish the conclusions of his novels in the magazine in order to create a hungry audience for his books.

Marryat had strong ideas about his art. "In writing a perfect novel," he wrote, "character must be the first requisite, wit and humor the next, and plot and incident the last." In *Peter Simple*, he clearly adheres to this philosophy, as well as to his credo that "a pure novel is nothing more than a lengthened parable, or a succession of parables, all tending to the development of some great moral truth."

In *Peter Simple*, Marryat invokes the parable of "the wise fool," as Simple, the neophyte, proves himself wise and kind and is rewarded by becoming a landed gentleman, the goal in most Marryat novels. The sea, of course, is Simple's rough school and the place where he proves himself through a series of adventures, alongside his faithful mentor Terence O'Brien. These adventures comprise some of the most exciting scenes of naval life ever conjured. Marryat borrowed from stories heard at sea, such as the account of the battle off St. Vincent (told with gusto in *Peter Simple*, by the old tar Swinburne), and from published works, including Robert Southey's *Life of Nelson* (1813) and Edward Boys's *Narrative of Adventures in France and Flanders* (1827).

But many of the episodes in *Peter Simple* are taken from his personal experience. The hand-to-hand combat during the cutting-out expeditions, the devastating hurricane off St. Pierre, and the mutiny on board the *Rattlesnake* were recreated from his memory. So accurate is his description of the dangerous maneuver of club-hauling a ship that it became required reading for navy midshipmen. In this episode and elsewhere in Marryat's novels, the seamen's courage is underscored by the precariousness of life at sea, by the awareness that a shipmate or an entire ship may be lost at any moment.

There are many unforgettable characters in *Peter Simple*, who are "drawn vigorously, decisively, from the living face," as Virginia Woolf observes in her essay "The Captain's Deathbed." Captain Savage, who is Marryat's prototypical captain, one who rules with a sense of firm discipline tempered by mercy, is modeled after Thomas Cochrane. Terence O'Brien is probably based on Marryat's shipmate on the *Impérieuse*, William Napier, a capable seaman and fighter. The pairing of the naive Simple and the more worldly O'Brien is one of the most memorable in English literature. In some ways, it is reminiscent of Don Quixote and Sancho Panza in *Don Quixote*, one of Marryat's favorite novels. In both novels, as Walter Alan Buster points out in his work *The Life and Novels of Captain Marryat*, the mentor, intially of lower social status than the hero, eventually rises to parity with the protagonist.

Indeed, despite Marryat's conservative upbringing, social fluidity is a characteristic of his novels. Perhaps his own status as a second son (primogeniture is something with which Peter Simple must also contend) and his years trapped in naval bureaucracy encouraged his sympathy for social climbers who prove themselves worthy.

In *Peter Simple*, Marryat's host of supporting characters are both hilarious and poignant. The old sailor Swinburne describes his courtship with his wife in this manner: "I wasn't going to be hooked carelessly, so I nibbled afore I took the bait. Had four years' trial of her first, and, finding that she had plenty of ballast, I sailed her as my own." The marvelous liar, Captain Kearney, fabricates even on his deathbed. On his tombstone, which states "Here lies Captain Kearney," someone has underlined the word "lies." The good-hearted Mrs. Trotter despises rum, but, as Peter observes, she "took it pretty often, considering that she did not like it." There are also the charmingly affected women at the "dignity ball" (a formal dance held by the mixed-race elite of Barbados), one of whom is shocked when Peter innocently asks for a piece of turkey breast; "Curse your impudence, sar, I wonder where you larn manners. Sar, I take a lilly turkey bosom if you please. Talk of breast to a lady, sar;—really quite horrid."

One of Marryat's most famous characters is Mr. Chucks, the wonderfully irascible boatswain, who desperately aspires above his birth. He frequently begins a sentence politely but is unable to complete it without uttering a series of profanities: "Allow me to observe, my dear man, in the most delicate way in the world, that you are spilling tar upon the deck. . . . You understand me, Sir, you have defiled his Majesty's forecastle. I must do my duty, Sir, if you neglect yours; so take that—and that—and that (thrashing the man with his rattan)—you d——d hay-making son of a sea-cook. Do it again, d——n your eyes, and I'll cut your liver out." Despite this weakness, Chucks is portrayed as a brave figure, extremely knowledgeable about the workings of a ship; eventually he achieves his dream of becoming a gentleman, albeit not in British society.

Even when Marryat treats serious topics in the novel, such as impressment, he often does it with great humor. Impressment was so widespread during the Napoleonic wars that as much as three-quarters of the average crew consisted of pressed men. In *Peter Simple*, Marryat satirizes the practice. Serving on a press gang, Simple has the tables turned on him and is captured by a group of women protecting the men he intends to press. In a raucous scene, Peter must drink with the women, then hand over his money before he makes his escape by brandishing a red-hot poker.

In his view of Blacks, Marryat mirrors the ambivalence of the times. Having served in the West Indies in 1811 and 1813, and been shipmates with nonwhites, he probably wrote about racial minorites more than any British writer of his day. Blacks, such as Mesty in *Mr. Midshipman Easy* and Vincent in *Percival Keene* (1842), figure prominently in several of his novels.

He often portrayed Blacks as victims (particularly in America), or as the stereotypical noble savage, such as Mesty. He abhorred the slave trade and wrote a horrifying description of a slave ship in *Peter Simple*, most likely taken from firsthand experience since the Royal Navy was instrumental in suppressing that odious trade. However, he also wrote a bucolic account of slavery in his novel *Newton Forster* (1832). Marryat seems repulsed by interracial unions, but his physical attraction to Black women is clear, for example, in the dignity ball scene. Although Marryat's depiction of Blacks and other minorities may be offensive to many modern-day readers, "his portrayals of Africans, Indians, and other nonwhite peoples," as Patrick Brantlinger notes in his book *Rule of Darkness: British Literature and Imperialism, 1830–1914*, "are usually more sympathetic— and often more knowledgeable—than those by many of his imitators."

PETER SIMPLE was an immediate hit. Samuel Taylor Coleridge wrote in *Table Talk* (March 5, 1834) that he had "received a great deal of pleasure from some of the modern novels, especially Captain Marryat's *Peter Simple*," while, in *Noctes Ambrosianae* (July 1834), reviewer Christopher North (the pen name of John Wilson) proclaimed: "He that imagined Peter Simple's a Sea-Fieldin'."

With the success of *Peter Simple* and his other novels, Marryat traveled widely, often giving readings from his work. He published *Diary on the Continent*, about his sojourn in Europe, serially in 1835. His visit to America in 1837–38 created a small furor. The United States, assisting French Canadian separatists, had one of its ships destroyed in Canada by Loyalist Canadians. At a banquet in Toronto, the outspoken captain toasted the loyalist forces. The incensed Americans hanged Marryat in effigy twice and harassed him throughout his visit. Marryat, habitually opposed to democracy and angered by the negative reactions during his trip, criticized virtually everything American in his *Diary in America, with Remarks on Its Institutions* (1839).

BACK IN LONDON, Marryat led a busy social and professional life. Although he was separated from his wife, he remained close to his children. His good friends included Charles Dickens and Edward Bulwer-Lytton, and he frequented the salon of the fashionable Lady Blessington. Marryat's lively spirit and his love of children made him a favorite at Dickens's parties. The two men also shared a taste for living beyond their means. Despite having inherited large sums of money from his father and his uncle and having had a successful career as an author, Marryat's extravagant lifestyle and generous nature (he gave away many treasures he had collected in the navy) constantly placed him in need. He was often forced to write hastily and long after his desire to compose had died, sometimes disregarding his own advice to novelists not "to venture into action without plenty of powder and shot in the locker."

Marryat exchanged his property in London for a country estate at Langham, where he moved in 1843. His devotion to children inspired him to write *Masterman Ready* (1841–42), and *The Children of the New Forest* (1847), which became classics for young readers. They are a mixture of lively adventure, exotic locale, and didacticism. These stories provided Marryat with a steady source of income and remained popular long after his death; however, their success caused critics to confine him to the "brig" of children's literature.

But Frederick Marryat is far more than a writer for young people. Conrad relished his "enthralling" adventures and rapid-fire action. In "The Captain's Deathbed," Woolf admired his ability to "create a world . . . to set us in the midst of ships and men and sea and sky all vivid, credible, authentic." Indeed, in works such as *Peter Simple* and *Mr. Midshipman Easy*, Marryat left a legacy for subsequent novelists of the sea, including Melville, Conrad, C. S. Forester (whose famous Captain Horatio Hornblower may even have been named after the Marryat character, Hornblow), and Patrick O'Brian.

Marryat's breezy style invites a close bond between author and reader; moreover, his vivid characters, keen wit, and realistic portrayal of naval life are reasons why he can still be greatly enjoyed today. And no novel better exemplifies Marryat's skills than the lively narrative *Peter Simple*.

—Louis J. Parascandola

SELECTED BIBLIOGRAPHY

Brantlinger, Patrick. *Rule of Darkness: British Literature and Imperialism, 1830–1914*. Ithaca: Cornell University Press, 1988.

Buster, Walter Alan. "The Life and Novels of Captain Marryat." Diss., University of Virginia, 1979.

Conrad, Joseph. *Notes on Life and Letters*. Garden City, N.Y.: Doubleday, 1921.

Gautier, Maurice-Paul. *Captain Frederick Marryat: L'Homme et L'Oeuvre*. Montreal: Didier, 1973.

Hannay, David. *Life of Frederick Marryat*. London: Walter Scott, 1889.

Hawes, Donald. "Marryat and Dickens." *Dickens Studies Annual*, vol. 2 (1971): pp. 39–68.

Lloyd, Christopher. *Captain Marryat and the Old Navy*. London: Longmans, Green, 1939.

Marryat, Florence. *Life and Letters of Captain Marryat*. 2 vols. New York: Appleton & Co., 1872.

Parascandola, Louis J. *"Puzzled Which to Choose": Conflicting Socio-political Views in the Works of Captain Frederick Marryat*. New York: Peter Lang Publishing Inc., 1997.

Warner, Oliver. *Captain Marryat: A Rediscovery*. London: Constable, 1953.

Woolf, Virginia. *The Captain's Deathbed and Other Essays*. New York: Harcourt, Brace, Jovanovich, 1950.

ACKNOWLEDGMENTS

I AM GRATEFUL to the following for their support of my work on Marryat: Professors N. John Hall and Michael Timko of the CUNY Graduate School; Professor Steven Gale of Kentucky State University; Professor Emeritus James D. Merritt of Brooklyn College; the late Camille E. Beazer; the staff at the Fales Library at New York University; my coworkers at Mid-Manhattan Library; my colleagues at Long Island University, particularly Professor Emeritus Kenneth Scott, who first introduced me to Marryat; LIU's Research Release Time Committee and Trustees; the staff of Henry Holt; Dean King, who has been a pleasure to work with; Shondel Nero, partner in all things; my siblings, John, Maryann, and Judy, and their families; my parents, Louis and Ann, whose help I can never repay.

—L.J.P.

EDITORIAL NOTE

ROUGHLY THE FIRST TWO-THIRDS of *Peter Simple* was serialized in *Metropolitan Magazine* from June 1832 to September 1833. Marryat, a clever businessman, discontinued serialization hoping that readers, curious to learn the ending, would buy the book. The first edition of the novel, which contains numerous spelling inconsistencies and infelicities of style, was published in three volumes by Saunders & Otley in London in 1834. The present text follows R. Brimley Johnson's 1896 edition of *The Novels of Captain Marryat*, published by J. M. Dent in London and Little, Brown and Company in Boston, with emendations from the first edition of the 1837 illustrated edition published by Saunders & Otley.

The notes on the bottom of pages 38, 120, and 391 are all in the first edition. Notes added for this edition are italicized. Many of the nautical terms defined here are taken from *A Sea of Words: A Lexicon and Companion for Patrick O'Brian's Seafaring Tales*, edited by Dean King with John B. Hattendorf and J. Worth Estes (New York: Henry Holt, 1995; 2nd ed., 1997). Thanks to Professors Shondel Nero and Joan Templeton of Long Island University for translations from the French.

—L.J.P.

PETER SIMPLE

CHAPTER I

The great advantage of being the fool of the family—My destiny is decided, and I am consigned to a stockbroker as part of His Majesty's sea stock—Unfortunately for me Mr Handycock is a bear, and I get very little dinner.

IF I CANNOT NARRATE a life of adventurous and daring exploits, fortunately I have no heavy crimes to confess; and, if I do not rise in the estimation of the reader for acts of gallantry and devotion in my country's cause, at least I may claim the merit of zealous and persevering continuance in my vocation. We are all of us variously gifted from Above, and he who is content to walk, instead of to run, on his allotted path through life, although he may not so rapidly attain the goal, has the advantage of not being out of breath upon his arrival. Not that I mean to infer that my life has not been one of adventure. I only mean to say that, in all which has occurred, I have been a passive, rather than an active, personage; and, if events of interest are to be recorded, they certainly have not been sought by me.

As well as I can recollect and analyze my early propensities, I think that, had I been permitted to select my own profession, I should in all probability have bound myself apprentice to a tailor; for I always envied the comfortable seat which they appeared to enjoy upon the shopboard, and their elevated position, which enabled them to look down upon the constant succession of the idle or the busy, who passed in review before them in the main street of the country town, near to which I passed the first fourteen years of my existence.

But my father, who was a clergyman of the Church of England, and the youngest brother of a noble family, had a lucrative living, and a "soul above buttons," if his son had not. It has been from time immemorial the heathenish custom to sacrifice the greatest fool of the family to the prosperity and naval superiority of the country, and, at the age of fourteen, I was selected as the victim. If the custom be judicious, I had no reason to complain. There was not one dissentient voice, when it was proposed before all the varieties of my aunts and cousins, invited to partake of our new-year's festival. I was selected by general acclamation. Flattered by such an unanimous acknowledgment of my qualification, and a stroke of my father's hand down my head which accompanied it, I felt as proud, and, alas! as unconscious as the calf with gilded horns, who plays and mumbles with the flowers of the garland which designates his fate to every one but himself. I even felt, or thought I felt, a slight degree of military ardour, and a sort of vision of future grandeur passed before me, in the distant vista of which I perceived a coach with four horses and a service of plate. It was, however, driven away before I could decipher it, by positive bodily pain, occasioned by my elder brother Tom, who, having been directed by my father to snuff the candles, took the opportunity of my abstraction to insert a piece of the still ignited cotton into my left ear. But as my story is not a very short one, I must not dwell too long on its commencement. I shall therefore inform the reader, that my father, who lived in the north of England, did not think it right to fit me out at the country town, near to which we resided; but about a fortnight after the decision which I have referred to, he forwarded me to London, on the outside of the coach, with my best suit of bottle-green and six shirts. To prevent mistakes, I was booked in the way-bill "to be delivered to Mr Thomas Handycock, No. 14, St Clement's Lane—carriage paid." My parting with the family was very affecting; my mother cried bitterly, for, like all mothers, she liked the greatest fool which she had presented to my father, better than all the rest; my sisters cried because my mother cried; Tom roared for a short time more loudly than all the rest, having been chastised by my father for breaking his fourth window in that week;—during all which my father walked up and down the room with impatience, because he was kept from his dinner, and, like all orthodox divines, he was tenacious of the only sensual enjoyment permitted to his cloth.

At last I tore myself away. I had blubbered till my eyes were so red and swollen, that the pupils were scarcely to be distinguished, and tears and dirt had veined my cheeks like the marble of the chimney-piece. My handkerchief was soaked through with wiping my eyes and blowing my nose, before the scene was over. My brother Tom, with a kindness which did honour to his heart, exchanged his for mine, saying, with fraternal regard, "Here, Peter, take mine, it's as dry as a bone." But my father would not wait for a second handkerchief to perform its duty. He led me away through the hall, when, having shaken hands with all the men and kissed all the maids, who stood in a row with their aprons to their eyes, I quitted my paternal roof.

The coachman accompanied me to the place from whence the stage was to start. Having seen me securely wedged between two fat old women, and having put my parcel inside, he took his leave, and in a few minutes I was on my road to London.

I was too much depressed to take notice of anything during my journey. When we arrived in London, they drove to the Blue Boar (in a street, the name of which I have forgotten). I had never seen or heard of such an animal, and certainly it did appear very formidable; its mouth was open and teeth very large. What surprised me still more was to observe that its teeth and hoofs were of pure gold. Who knows, thought I, that in some of the strange countries which I am doomed to visit, but that I may fall in with, and shoot one of these terrific monsters? with what haste shall I select those precious parts, and with what joy should I, on my return, pour them as an offering of filial affection into my mother's lap!—and then, as I thought of my mother, the tears again gushed into my eyes.

The coachman threw his whip to the ostler, and the reins upon the horses' backs; he then dismounted, and calling to me, "Now, young gentleman, I'se a-waiting," he put a ladder up for me to get down by; then turning to a porter, he said to him, "Bill, you must take this here young gem'man and that ere parcel to this here direction.—Please to remember the coachman, sir." I replied that I certainly would, if he wished it, and walked off with the porter; the coachman observing, as I went away, "Well, he is a fool—that's sartain." I arrived quite safe at St Clement's Lane, when the porter received a shilling for his trouble from the maid who let me in, and I was shown up into a parlour, where I found myself in company with Mrs Handycock.

Mrs Handycock was a little meagre woman, who did not speak very good English, and who appeared to me to employ the major part of her time in bawling out from the top of the stairs to the servants below. I never saw her either read a book or occupy herself with needlework, during the whole time I was in the house. She had

a large grey parrot, and I really cannot tell which screamed the
worse of the two—but she was very civil and kind to me, and asked
me ten times a day when I had last heard of my grandfather, Lord
Privilege. I observed that she always did so if any company happened to call in during my stay at her house. Before I had been there
ten minutes, she told me that she "hadored sailors—they were the
defendiours and preserviours of their kings and countries," and that
"Mr Handycock would be home by four o'clock, and then we
should go to dinner." Then she jumped off her chair to bawl to the
cook from the head of the stairs—"Jemima, Jemima!—ve'll ha'e the
viting biled instead of fried." "Can't, marm," replied Jemima, "they
be all hegged and crumbled, with their tails in their mouths." "Vell,
then, never mind, Jemima," replied the lady.—"Don't put your finger into the parrot's cage, my love—he's apt to be cross with strangers. Mr Handycock will be home at four o'clock, and then we shall
have our dinner. Are you fond of viting?"

As I was very anxious to see Mr Handycock, and very anxious to
have my dinner, I was not sorry to hear the clock on the stairs strike
four, when Mrs Handycock again jumped up, and put her head
over the banisters, "Jemima, Jemima, it's four o'clock!" "I hear it,
marm," replied the cook; and she gave the frying-pan a twist, which
made the hissing and the smell come flying up into the parlour, and
made me more hungry than ever.

Rap, tap, tap! "There's your master, Jemima," screamed the lady.
"I hear him, marm," replied the cook. "Run down, my dear, and let
Mr Handycock in," said his wife. "He'll be so surprised at seeing
you open the door."

I ran down, as Mrs Handycock desired me, and opened the
street-door. "Who the devil are you?" in a gruff voice, cried Mr
Handycock; a man about six feet high, dressed in blue cotton-net
pantaloons and Hessian boots, with a black coat and waistcoat. I
was a little rebuffed, I must own, but I replied that I was Mr Simple.
"And pray, Mr Simple, what would your grandfather say if he saw
you now? I have servants in plenty to open my door, and the parlour is the proper place for young gentlemen."

"Law, Mr Handycock," said his wife, from the top of the stairs,
"how can you be so cross? I told him to open the door to surprise
you."

"And you have surprised me," replied he, "with your cursed folly."

While Mr Handycock was rubbing his boots on the mat, I went upstairs rather mortified, I must own, as my father had told me that Mr Handycock was his stockbroker, and would do all he could to make me comfortable: indeed, he had written to that effect in a letter, which my father showed to me before I left home. When I returned to the parlour, Mrs Handycock whispered to me, "Never mind, my dear, it's only because there's something wrong on 'Change. Mr Handycock is a *bear* just now." I thought so too, but I made no answer, for Mr Handycock came upstairs, and walking with two strides from the door of the parlour to the fire-place, turned his back to it, and lifting up his coat-tails, began to whistle.

"Are you ready for your dinner, my dear?" said the lady, almost trembling.

"If the dinner is ready for me. I believe we usually dine at four," answered her husband gruffly.

"Jemima, Jemima, dish up! do you hear, Jemima?" "Yes, marm," replied the cook, "directly I've thickened the butter;" and Mrs Handycock resumed her seat, with, "Well, Mr Simple, and how is your grandfather, Lord Privilege?" "He is quite well, ma'am," answered I, for the fifteenth time at least. But dinner put an end to the silence which followed this remark. Mr Handycock lowered his coat-tails and walked downstairs, leaving his wife and me to follow at our leisure.

"Pray, ma'am," inquired I, as soon as he was out of hearing, "what is the matter with Mr Handycock, that he is so cross to you?"

"Vy, my dear, it is one of the misfortunes of matermony, that ven the husband's put out, the vife is sure to have her share of it. Mr Handycock must have lost money on 'Change, and then he always comes home cross. Ven he vins, then he is as merry as a cricket."

"Are you people coming down to dinner?" roared Mr Handycock from below. "Yes, my dear," replied the lady, "I thought that you were washing your hands." We descended into the dining-room, where we found that Mr Handycock had already devoured two of the whitings, leaving only one on the dish for his wife and me. "Vould you like a little bit of viting, my dear?" said the lady to me. "It's not worth halving," observed the gentleman, in a surly tone, taking up the fish with his own knife and fork, and putting it on his plate.

"Well, I'm so glad you like them, my dear," replied the lady meekly; then turning to me, "there's some nice roast *weal* coming, my dear."

The veal made its appearance, and fortunately for us, Mr Handycock could not devour it all. He took the lion's share, nevertheless, cutting off all the brown, and then shoving the dish over to his wife to help herself and me. I had not put two pieces in my mouth before Mr Handycock desired me to get up and hand him the porter-pot, which stood on the sideboard. I thought that if it was not right for me to open a door, neither was it for me to wait at table— but I obeyed him without making a remark.

After dinner, Mr Handycock went down to the cellar for a bottle of wine. "O deary me!" exclaimed his wife, "he must have lost a mint of money—we had better go up-stairs and leave him alone; he'll be better after a bottle of port, perhaps." I was very glad to go away, and being very tired, I went to bed without any tea, for Mrs Handycock dared not venture to make it before her husband came up-stairs.

CHAPTER II

Fitting out on the shortest notice—Fortunately for me, this day Mr Handycock is a bear, and I fare very well—I set off for Portsmouth—Behind the coach I meet a man before the mast—He is disguised with liquor, but is not the only disguise I fall in with in my journey.

THE NEXT MORNING Mr Handycock appeared to be in somewhat better humour. One of the linendrapers who fitted out cadets, &c., "on the shortest notice," was sent for, and orders given for my equipment, which Mr Handycock insisted should be ready on the day afterwards, or the articles would be left on his hands; adding, that my place was already taken in the Portsmouth coach.

"Really, sir," observed the man, "I'm afraid—on such very short notice—"

"Your card says, 'the shortest notice,' " rejoined Mr Handycock, with the confidence and authority of a man who is enabled to correct another by his own assertions. "If you do not choose to undertake the work, another will."

This silenced the man, who made his promise, took my measure, and departed; and soon afterwards Mr Handycock also quitted the house.

What with my grandfather and the parrot, and Mrs Handycock wondering how much money her husband had lost, running to the head of the stairs and talking to the cook, the day passed away pretty well till four o'clock; when, as before, Mrs Handycock screamed, the cook screamed, the parrot screamed, and Mr Handycock rapped at the door, and was let in—but not by me. He ascended the stairs with three bounds, and coming into the parlour, cried, "Well, Nancy, my love, how are you?" Then stooping over her, "Give me a kiss, old girl. I'm as hungry as a hunter. Mr Simple, how do you do? I hope you have passed the morning agreeably. I must wash my hands and change my boots, my love; I am not fit to sit down to table with you in this pickle. Well, Polly, how are you?"

"I'm glad you're hungry, my dear, I've such a nice dinner for you," replied the wife, all smiles. "Jemima, be quick and dish up— Mr Handycock is so hungry."

"Yes, marm," replied the cook; and Mrs Handycock followed her husband into his bedroom on the same floor, to assist him at his toilet.

"By Jove, Nancy, the *bulls* have been nicely taken in," said Mr Handycock, as we sat down to dinner.

"O, I am so glad!" replied his wife, giggling; and so I believe she was, but why I did not understand.

"Mr Simple," said he, "will you allow me to offer you a little fish?"

"If you do not want it all yourself, sir," replied I politely.

Mrs Handycock frowned and shook her head at me, while her husband helped me. "My dove, a bit of fish?"

We both had our share to-day, and I never saw a man more polite than Mr Handycock. He joked with his wife, asked me to drink wine with him two or three times, talked about my grandfather; and, in short, we had a very pleasant evening.

The next morning all my clothes came home, but Mr Handycock, who still continued in good humour, said that he would not allow me to travel by night, that I should sleep there and set off the next morning; which I did at six o'clock, and before eight I had arrived at the Elephant and Castle, where we stopped for a quarter of an hour. I was looking at the painting representing this animal with a castle on its back; and assuming that of Alnwick, which I had seen, as a fair estimate of the size and weight of that which he carried, was attempting to enlarge my ideas so as to comprehend the stupendous bulk of the elephant, when I observed a crowd assembled at the corner; and asking a gentleman who sat by me in a plaid cloak, whether there was not something very uncommon to attract so many people, he replied, "Not very, for it is only a drunken sailor."

I rose from my seat, which was on the hinder part of the coach, that I might see him, for it was a new sight to me, and excited my curiosity, when to my astonishment, he staggered from the crowd, and swore that he'd go to Portsmouth. He climbed up by the wheel of the coach, and sat down by me. I believe that I stared at him very much, for he said to me, "What are you gaping at, you young sculping?* Do you want to catch flies? or did you never see a chap half-seas-over before?"

I replied, "That I had never been at sea in my life, but that I was going."

"Well, then, you're like a young bear, all your sorrows to come—that's all, my hearty," replied he. "When you get on board, you'll find monkey's allowance—more kicks than half-pence. I say, you pewter-carrier, bring us another pint of ale."

The waiter of the inn, who was attending the coach, brought out the ale, half of which the sailor drank, and the other half threw into the waiter's face, telling him that was his "allowance: and now," said he, "what's to pay?" The waiter, who looked very angry, but appeared too much afraid of the sailor to say anything, answered fourpence; and the sailor pulled out a handful of banknotes, mixed up with gold, silver, and coppers, and was picking out the money to pay for his beer, when the coachman, who was impatient, drove off.

---

* *Sculping: A sculp is a sealskin with the blubber attached. Perhaps Marryat means a sculpin, a scaleless fish with a large head and a wide mouth. In chapter VIII, Peter denies having ever heard the word before.*

"There's cut and run," cried the sailor, thrusting all the money into his breeches pocket. "That's what you'll learn to do, my joker, before you've been two cruises to sea."

In the meantime the gentleman in the plaid cloak, who was seated by me, smoked his cigar without saying a word. I commenced a conversation with him relative to my profession, and asked him whether it was not very difficult to learn. "Larn," cried the sailor, interrupting us, "no; it may be difficult for such chaps as me before the mast to larn; but you, I presume, is a reefer, and they an't got much to larn, 'cause why, they pipe-clays their weekly accounts, and walks up and down with their hands in their pockets. You must larn to chaw baccy, drink grog, and call the cat a beggar, and then you knows all a midshipman's expected to know nowadays. Ar'n't I right, sir?" said the sailor, appealing to the gentleman in a plaid cloak. "I axes you, because I see you're a sailor by the cut of your jib. Beg pardon, sir," continued he, touching his hat, "hope no offence."

"I am afraid that you have nearly hit the mark, my good fellow," replied the gentleman.

The drunken fellow then entered into conversation with him, stating that he had been paid off from the *Audacious* at Portsmouth, and had come up to London to spend his money with his messmates, but that yesterday he had discovered that a Jew at Portsmouth had sold him a seal as gold, for fifteen shillings, which proved to be copper, and that he was going back to Portsmouth to give the Jew a couple of black eyes for his rascality, and that when he had done that he was to return to his messmates, who had promised to drink success to the expedition at the Cock and Bottle, St Martin's Lane, until he should return.

The gentleman in the plaid cloak commended him very much for his resolution; for he said, "that although the journey to and from Portsmouth would cost twice the value of a gold seal, yet, that in the end it might be worth a *Jew's Eye*." What he meant I did not comprehend.

Whenever the coach stopped, the sailor called for more ale, and always threw the remainder which he could not drink into the face of the man who brought it out for him, just as the coach was starting off, and then tossed the pewter pot on the ground for him to pick up. He became more tipsy every stage, and the last from

Portsmouth, when he pulled out his money, he could find no silver, so he handed down a note, and desired the waiter to change it. The waiter crumpled it up and put it into his pocket, and then returned the sailor the change for a one-pound note; but the gentleman in the plaid had observed that it was a five-pound note which the sailor had given, and insisted upon the waiter producing it, and giving the proper change. The sailor took his money, which the waiter handed to him, begging pardon for the mistake, although he coloured up very much at being detected. "I really beg your pardon," said he again, "it was quite a mistake;" whereupon the sailor threw the pewter pot at the waiter, saying, "I really beg your pardon, too,"— and with such force, that it flattened upon the man's head, who fell senseless on the road. The coachman drove off, and I never heard whether the man was killed or not.

After the coach had driven off, the sailor eyed the gentleman in the plaid cloak for a minute or two, and then said, "When I first looked at you I took you for some officer in mufti; but now that I see you look so sharp after the rhino it's my idea that you're some poor devil of a Scotchman, mayhap second mate of a marchant vessel— there's half-a-crown for your services—I'd give you more if I thought you would spend it."*

The gentleman laughed, and took the half-crown, which I afterwards observed that he gave to a grey-headed beggar at the bottom of Portsdown Hill. I inquired of him how soon we should be at Portsmouth; he answered that we were passing the lines; but I saw no lines, and I was ashamed to show my ignorance. He asked me what ship I was going to join. I could not recollect her name, but I told him it was painted on the outside of my chest, which was coming down by the waggon; all that I could recollect was that it was a French name.

"Have you no letter of introduction to the captain?" said he.

"Yes I have," replied I; and I pulled out my pocketbook in which the letter was. "Captain Savage, H.M. ship *Diomede*," continued I, reading to him.

To my surprise he very coolly proceeded to open the letter, which, when I perceived what he was doing, occasioned me immediately to snatch the letter from him, stating my opinion at the same

* *Rhino: Money.*

time that it was a breach of honour, and that in my opinion he was no gentleman.

"Just as you please, youngster," replied he. "Recollect, you have told me I am no gentleman."

He wrapped his plaid around him, and said no more; and I was not a little pleased at having silenced him by my resolute behaviour.

———◈◈◈———

CHAPTER III

I am made to look very blue at the Blue Posts—Find wild spirits around, and, soon after, hot spirits within me; at length my spirits overcome me—Call to pay my respects to the captain, and find that I had had the pleasure of meeting him before—No sooner out of one scrape than into another.

WHEN WE STOPPED, I inquired of the coachman which was the best inn. He answered "that it was the Blue Postesses, where the midshipmen leave their chestesses, call for tea and toastesses, and sometimes forget to pay for their breakfastesses." He laughed when he said it, and I thought that he was joking with me; but he pointed out two large blue posts at the door next the coach-office, and told me that all the midshipmen resorted to that hotel. He then asked me to remember the coachman, which, by this time I had found out implied that I was not to forget to give him a shilling, which I did, and then went into the inn. The coffee-room was full of midshipmen, and, as I was anxious about my chest, I inquired of one of them if he knew when the waggon would come in.

"Do you expect your mother by it?" replied he.

"Oh no! but I expect my uniforms—I only wear these bottle-greens until they come."

"And pray what ship are you going to join?"

"The *Die-a-maid*—Captain Thomas Kirkwall Savage."

"The *Diomede*—I say, Robinson, a'n't that the frigate in which the midshipmen had four dozen apiece for not having pipe-clayed their weekly accounts on the Saturday?"

"To be sure it is," replied the other; "why the captain gave a

youngster five dozen the other day for wearing a scarlet watch-
ribbon."

"He's the greatest Tartar in the service," continued the other; "he
flogged the whole starboard watch the last time that he was on a
cruise, because the ship would only sail nine knots upon a bowline."

"Oh dear," said I, "then I'm very sorry that I am going to join
him."

" 'Pon my soul I pity you: you'll be fagged to death: for there's
only three midshipmen in the ship now—all the rest ran away.
Didn't they, Robinson?"

"There's only two left now; for poor Matthews died of fatigue.
He was worked all day, and kept watch all night for six weeks, and
one morning he was found dead upon his chest."

"God bless my soul!" cried I; "and yet, on shore, they say he is
such a kind man to his midshipmen."

"Yes," replied Robinson, "he spreads that report everywhere.
Now, observe, when you first call upon him, and report your having
come to join his ship, he'll tell you that he is very happy to see you,
and that he hopes your family are well—then he'll recommend you
to go on board and learn your duty. After that, stand clear. Now,
recollect what I have said, and see if it does not prove true. Come, sit
down with us and take a glass of grog; it will keep your spirits up."

These midshipmen told me so much about my captain, and the
horrid cruelties which he had practised, that I had some doubts
whether I had not better set off home again. When I asked their
opinion, they said, that if I did, I should be taken up as a deserter
and hanged; that my best plan was to beg his acceptance of a few
gallons of rum, for he was very fond of grog, and that then I might
perhaps be in his good graces, as long as the rum might last.

I am sorry to state that the midshipmen made me very tipsy that
evening. I don't recollect being put to bed, but I found myself there
the next morning, with a dreadful headache, and a very confused
recollection of what had passed. I was very much shocked at my
having so soon forgotten the injunctions of my parents, and was
making vows never to be so foolish again, when in came the midshipman who had been so kind to me the night before. "Come, Mr
Bottlegreen," he bawled out, alluding, I suppose, to the colour of my

clothes, "rouse and bitt. There's the captain's coxswain waiting for you below. By the powers, you're in a pretty scrape for what you did last night!"

"Did last night!" replied I, astonished. "Why, does the captain know that I was tipsy?"

"I think you took devilish good care to let him know it when you were at the theatre."

"At the theatre! was I at the theatre?"

"To be sure you were. You would go, do all we could to prevent you, though you were as drunk as David's sow. Your captain was there with the admiral's daughters. You called him a tyrant and snapped your fingers at him. Why, don't you recollect? You told him that you did not care a fig for him."

"Oh dear! oh dear! what shall I do? what shall I do?" cried I: "My mother cautioned me so about drinking and bad company."

"Bad company, you whelp—what do you mean by that?"

"O, I did not particularly refer to you."

"I should hope not! However, I recommend you, as a friend, to go to the George Inn as fast as you can, and see your captain, for the longer you stay away, the worse it will be for you. At all events, it will be decided whether he receives you or not. It is fortunate for you that you are not on the ship's books. Come, be quick, the coxswain is gone back."

"Not on the ship's books," replied I sorrowfully. "Now I recollect there was a letter from the captain to my father, stating that he had put me on the books."

"Upon my honour, I'm sorry—very sorry indeed," replied the midshipman;—and he quitted the room, looking as grave as if the misfortune had happened to himself. I got up with a heavy head, and heavier heart, and as soon as I was dressed, I asked the way to the George Inn. I took my letter of introduction with me, although I was afraid it would be of little service. When I arrived, I asked, with a trembling voice, whether Captain Thomas Kirkwall Savage, of H.M. ship _Diomede_, was staying there. The waiter replied, that he was at breakfast with Captain Courtney, but that he would take up my name. I gave it him, and in a minute the waiter returned, and desired that I would walk up. O how my heart beat!—I never was so frightened—I thought I should have dropped on the stairs. Twice I attempted to walk into the room, and each time my legs failed me; at last I wiped the perspiration from my forehead, and with a desperate effort I went into the room.

"Mr Simple, I am glad to see you," said a voice. I had held my head down, for I was afraid to look at him, but the voice was so kind that I mustered up courage; and, when I did look up, there sat with his uniform and epaulets, and his sword by his side, the passenger in the plaid cloak, who wanted to open my letter, and whom I had told to his face, that he was *no gentleman.*

I thought I should have died as the other midshipman did upon his chest. I was just sinking down upon my knees to beg for mercy, when the captain perceiving my confusion, burst out into a laugh, and said, "So you know me again, Mr Simple? Well, don't be alarmed, you did your duty in not permitting me to open the letter, supposing me, as you did, to be some other person, and you were perfectly right, under that supposition, to tell me that I was not a gentleman. I give you credit for your conduct. Now sit down and take some breakfast."

"Captain Courtney," said he to the other captain, who was at the table, "this is one of my youngsters just entering the service. We were passengers yesterday by the same coach." He then told him the circumstance which occurred, at which they laughed heartily.

I now recovered my spirits a little—but still there was the affair at the theatre, and I thought that perhaps he did not recognize me. I was, however, soon relieved from my anxiety by the other captain inquiring, "Were you at the theatre last night, Savage?"

"No; I dined at the admiral's; there's no getting away from those girls, they are so pleasant."

"I rather think you are a little—*taken* in that quarter."

"No, on my word! I might be if I had time to discover which I liked best; but my ship is at present my wife, and the only wife I intend to have until I am laid on the shelf."

Well, thought I, if he was not at the theatre, it could not have been him that I insulted. Now if I can only give him the rum, and make friends with him.

"Pray, Mr Simple, how are your father and mother?" said the captain.

"Very well, I thank you, sir, and desire me to present their compliments."

"I am obliged to them. Now I think the sooner you go on board and learn your duty the better." (Just what the midshipman told me—the very words, thought I—then it's all true—and I began to tremble again.)

"I have a little advice to offer you," continued the captain. "In the first place, obey your superior officers without hesitation; it is for me, not you, to decide whether an order is unjust or not. In the next place, never swear or drink spirits. The first is immoral and ungentlemanlike, the second is a vile habit which will grow upon you. I never touch spirit myself, and I expect that my young gentlemen will refrain from it also. Now you may go, and as soon as your uniforms arrive, you will repair on board. In the meantime, as I had some little insight into your character when we travelled together, let me recommend you not to be too intimate at first sight with those you meet, or you may be led into indiscretions. Good morning."

I quitted the room with a low bow, glad to have surmounted so easily what appeared to be a chaos of difficulty; but my mind was confused with the testimony of the midshipman, so much at variance with the language and behaviour of the captain. When I arrived at the Blue Posts, I found all the midshipmen in the coffee-room, and I repeated to them all that had passed. When I had finished, they burst out laughing, and said that they had only been joking with me. "Well," said I to the one who had called me up in the morning, "you may call it joking, but I call it lying."

"Pray, Mr Bottlegreen, do you refer to me?"

"Yes, I do," replied I.

"Then, sir, as a gentleman, I demand satisfaction. Slugs in a saw-pit. Death before dishonour, d——e!"

"I shall not refuse you," replied I, "although I had rather not fight a duel; my father cautioned me on the subject, desiring me, if possible, to avoid it, as it was flying in the face of my Creator; but aware that I must uphold my character as an officer, he left me to my own discretion, should I ever be so unfortunate as to be in such a dilemma."

"Well, we don't want one of your father's sermons at second-hand," replied the midshipman, (for I had told them that my father was a clergyman); "the plain question is, will you fight, or will you not?"

"Could not the affair be arranged otherwise?" interrupted another. "Will not Mr Bottlegreen retract?"

"My name is Simple, sir, and not Bottlegreen," replied I; "and as he did tell a falsehood, I will not retract."

"Then the affair must go on," said the midshipman. "Robinson, will you oblige me by acting as my second?"

"It's an unpleasant business," replied the other; "you are so good a shot; but as you request it, I shall not refuse. Mr Simple is not, I believe, provided with a friend."

"Yes, he is," replied another of the midshipmen. "He is a spunky fellow, and I'll be his second."

It was then arranged that we should meet the next morning, with pistols. I considered that as an officer and a gentleman, I could not well refuse; but I was very unhappy. Not three days left to my own guidance, and I had become intoxicated, and was now to fight a duel. I went up into my room and wrote a long letter to my mother, enclosing a lock of my hair; and having shed a few tears at the idea of how sorry she would be if I were killed, I borrowed a bible from the waiter, and read it during the remainder of the day.

CHAPTER IV

I am taught on a cold morning, before breakfast, how to stand fire, and thus prove my courage—After breakfast I also prove my gallantry—My proof meets reproof—Woman at the bottom of all mischief—By one I lose my liberty, and, by another, my money.

WHEN I BEGAN to wake the next morning I could not think what it was that felt like a weight upon my chest, but as I roused and recalled my scattered thoughts, I remembered that in an hour or two it would be decided whether I were to exist another day. I prayed fervently, and made a resolution in my own mind that I would not have the blood of another upon my conscience, and would fire my pistol up in the air. And after I had made that resolution, I no longer felt the alarm which I did before. Before I was dressed, the midshipman who had volunteered to be my second, came into my room, and informed me that the affair was to be decided in the garden behind the inn; that my adversary was a very good shot, and that I must expect to be winged if not drilled.

"And what is winged and drilled?" inquired I. "I have not only never fought a duel, but I have not even fired a pistol in my life."

He explained what he meant, which was, that being winged implied being shot through the arm or leg, whereas being drilled was to be shot through the body. "But," continued he, "is it possible that you have never fought a duel?"

"No," replied I; "I am not yet fifteen years old."

"Not fifteen! why I thought you were eighteen at the least." (But I was very tall and stout for my age, and people generally thought me older than I actually was.)

I dressed myself and followed my second into the garden, where I found all the midshipmen and some of the waiters of the inn. They all seemed very merry, as if the life of a fellow-creature was of no consequence. The seconds talked apart for a little while, and then measured the ground, which was twelve paces; we then took our stations. I believe that I turned pale, for my second came to my side and whispered that I must not be frightened. I replied, that I was not frightened, but that I considered that it was an awful moment. The second to my adversary then came up and asked me whether I would make an apology, which I refused to do as before: they handed a pistol to each of us, and my second showed me how I was to pull the trigger. It was arranged that at the word given, we were to fire at the same time. I made sure that I should be wounded, if not killed, and I shut my eyes as I fired my pistol in the air. I felt my head swim, and thought I was hurt, but fortunately I was not. The pistols were loaded again, and we fired a second time. The seconds then interfered, and it was proposed that we should shake hands, which I was very glad to do, for I considered my life to have been saved by a miracle. We all went back to the coffee-room, and sat down to breakfast. They then told me that they all belonged to the same ship that I did, and that they were glad to see that I could stand fire, for the captain was a terrible fellow for cutting-out and running under the enemy's batteries.

The next day my chest arrived by the waggon, and I threw off my "bottle-greens" and put on my uniform. I had no cocked hat, or dirk, as the warehouse people employed by Mr Handycock did not supply those articles, and it was arranged that I should procure them at Portsmouth.* When I inquired the price, I found that they cost more money than I had in my pocket, so I tore up the letter I had written to my mother before the duel, and wrote another asking for a remittance, to purchase my dirk and cocked hat. I then walked out in my uniform, not a little proud, I must confess. I was now an officer in his Majesty's service, not very high in rank, certainly, but still an officer and a gentleman, and I made a vow that I would support the character, although I was considered the greatest fool of the family.

I had arrived opposite a place called Sally Port, when a young lady, very nicely dressed, looked at me very hard and said, "Well, Reefer, how are you off for soap?" I was astonished at the question, and more so at the interest which she seemed to take in my affairs. I answered, "Thank you, I am very well off; I have four cakes of Windsor, and two bars of yellow for washing." She laughed at my reply, and asked me whether I would walk home and take a bit of dinner with her. I was astonished at this polite offer, which my modesty induced me to ascribe more to my uniform than to my own merits, and, as I felt no inclination to refuse the compliment, I said that I should be most happy. I thought I might venture to offer my arm, which she accepted, and we proceeded up High Street on our way to her home.

Just as we passed the admiral's house, I perceived my captain walking with two of the admiral's daughters. I was not a little proud to let him see that I had female acquaintances as well as he had, and, as I passed him with the young lady under my protection, I took off my hat, and made him a low bow. To my surprise, not only did he not return the salute, but he looked at me with a very stern countenance. I concluded that he was a very proud man, and did not wish the admiral's daughters to suppose that he knew midshipmen by sight; but I had not exactly made up my mind on the subject, when the captain, having seen the ladies into the admiral's house, sent one of the messengers after me to desire that I would immediately come to him at the George Inn, which was nearly opposite.

I apologised to the young lady, and promised to return immediately if she would wait for me; but she replied, if that was my

* Cocked hat, or dirk: A cocked hat is a hat with the brim permanently turned up, especially a three-cornered hat; a dirk is a small sword or dagger worn mostly by midshipmen.

captain, it was her idea that I should have a confounded wigging and be sent on board. So, wishing me good-bye, she left me and continued her way home. I could as little comprehend all this as why the captain looked so black when I passed him; but it was soon explained when I went up to him in the parlour at the George Inn. "I am sorry, Mr Simple," said the captain, when I entered, "that a lad like you should show such early symptoms of depravity; still more so, that he should not have the grace which even the most hardened are not wholly destitute of—I mean to practise immorality in secret, and not degrade themselves and insult their captain by unblushingly avowing (I may say glorying in) their iniquity, by exposing it in broad day, and in the most frequented street of the town."

"Sir," replied I with astonishment, "O dear! O dear! what have I done?"

The captain fixed his keen eyes upon me, so that they appeared to pierce me through, and nail me to the wall. "Do you pretend to say, sir, that you were not aware of the character of the person with whom you were walking just now?"

"No, sir," replied I; "except that she was very kind and good-natured"; and then I told him how she had addressed me, and what subsequently took place.

"And is it possible, Mr Simple, that you are so great a fool?" I replied that I certainly was considered the greatest fool of our family. "I should think you were," replied he, drily. He then explained to me who the person was with whom I was in company, and how any association with her would inevitably lead to my ruin and disgrace.

I cried very much, for I was shocked at the narrow escape which I had had, and mortified at having fallen in his good opinion. He asked me how I had employed my time since I had been at Portsmouth, and I made an acknowledgment of having been made tipsy, related all that the midshipmen had told me, and how I had that morning fought a duel.

He listened to my whole story very attentively, and I thought that occasionally there was a smile upon his face, although he bit his lips to prevent it. When I had finished, he said, "Mr Simple, I can no longer trust you on shore until you are more experienced in the world. I shall desire my coxswain not to lose sight of you until you are safe on board of the frigate. When you have sailed a few months with me, you will then be able to decide whether I deserve the character which the young gentlemen have painted, with, I must say, I believe, the sole intention of practising upon your inexperience."

Altogether I did not feel sorry when it was over. I saw that the captain believed what I had stated, and that he was disposed to be kind to me, although he thought me very silly. The coxswain, in obedience to his orders, accompanied me to the Blue Posts. I packed up my clothes, paid my bill, and the porter wheeled my chest down to the Sally Port, where the boat was waiting.

"Come, heave a-head, my lads, be smart. The captain says we are to take the young gentleman on board directly. His liberty's stopped for getting drunk and running after the Dolly Mops!"*

"I should thank you to be more respectful in your remarks, Mr Coxswain," said I with displeasure.

"Mister Coxswain! thanky, sir, for giving me a handle to my name," replied he. "Come, be smart with your oars, my lads!"

"La, Bill Freeman," said a young woman on the beach, "what a nice young gentleman you have there! He looks like a sucking Nelson. I say, my pretty young officer, could you lend me a shilling?"

I was so pleased at the woman calling me a young Nelson, that I immediately complied with her request. "I have not a shilling in my pocket," said I, "but here is half-a-crown, and you can change it and bring me back the eighteen pence."

"Well, you are a nice young man," replied she, taking the half-crown; "I'll be back directly, my dear."

The men in the boat laughed, and the coxswain desired them to shove off.

"No," observed I, "you must wait for my eighteen pence."

"We shall wait a devilish long while then, I suspect. I know that girl, and she has a very bad memory."

"She cannot be so dishonest or ungrateful," replied I. "Coxswain, I order you to stay—I am an officer."

"I know you are, sir, about six hours old: well, then, I must go up and tell the captain that you have another girl in tow, and that you won't go on board."

* Dolly Mops: Prostitutes.

"Oh no, Mr Coxswain, pray don't; shove off as soon as you please, and never mind the eighteen pence."

The boat then shoved off, and pulled towards the ship, which lay at Spithead.

—◦◦◦—

CHAPTER V

I am introduced to the quarter-deck and first lieutenant, who pronounces me very clever—Trotted below to Mrs Trotter—Connubial bliss in a cockpit—Mr Trotter takes me in as a messmate—Feel very much surprised that so many people know that I am the son of my father.

ON OUR ARRIVAL on board, the coxswain gave a note from the captain to the first lieutenant, who happened to be on deck. He read the note, looked at me earnestly, and then I overheard him say to another lieutenant, "The service is going to the devil. As long as it was not popular, if we had not much education, we at least had the chance that natural abilities gave us; but now that great people send their sons for a provision into the navy, we have all the refuse of their families, as if anything was good enough to make a captain of a man-of-war, who has occasionally more responsibility on his shoulders, and is placed in situations requiring more judgment, than any other people in existence. Here's another of the fools of a family made a present of to the country—another cub for me to lick into shape. Well, I never saw the one yet I did not make something of. Where's Mr Simple?"

"I am Mr Simple, sir," replied I, very much frightened at what I had overheard.

"Now, Mr Simple," said the first lieutenant, "observe, and pay particular attention to what I say. The captain tells me in this note that you have been shamming stupid. Now, sir, I am not to be taken in that way. You're something like the monkeys, who won't speak because they are afraid they will be made to work. I have looked attentively at your face, and I see at once that you are *very clever*, and if you do not prove so in a very short time, why—you had better jump overboard, that's all. Perfectly understand me. I know that you are a very clever fellow, and having told you so, don't you pretend to impose upon me, for it won't do."

I was very much terrified at this speech, but at the same time I was pleased to hear that he thought me clever, and I determined to do all in my power to keep up such an unexpected reputation.

"Quarter-master," said the first lieutenant, "tell Mr Trotter to come on deck."

The quarter-master brought up Mr Trotter, who apologised for being so dirty, as he was breaking casks out of the hold. He was a short, thick-set man, about thirty years of age, with a nose which had a red club to it, very dirty teeth, and large black whiskers.

"Mr Trotter," said the first lieutenant, "here is a young gentleman who has joined the ship. Introduce him into the berth, and see his hammock slung. You must look after him a little."

"I really have very little time to look after any of them, sir," replied Mr Trotter; "but I will do what I can. Follow me, youngster." Accordingly, I descended the ladder after him; then I went down another, and then to my surprise I was desired by him to go down a third, which when I had done, he informed me that I was in the cockpit.

"Now, youngster," said Mr Trotter, seating himself upon a large chest, "you may do as you please. The midshipmen's mess is on the deck above this, and if you like to join, why you can; but this I will tell you as a friend, that you will be thrashed all day long, and fare very badly; the weakest always goes to the wall there, but perhaps you do not mind that. Now that we are in harbour, I mess here, because Mrs Trotter is on board. She is a very charming woman, I can assure you, and will be here directly; she has just gone up into the galley to look after a net of potatoes in the copper. If you like it better, I will ask her permission for you to mess with us. You will then be away from the midshipmen, who are a sad set, and will teach you nothing but what is immoral and improper, and you will have the advantage of being in good society, for Mrs Trotter has kept the very best in England. I make you this offer because I want to oblige the first lieutenant, who appears to take an interest about you, otherwise I am not very fond of having any intrusion upon my domestic happiness."

I replied that I was much obliged to him for his kindness, and that if it would not put Mrs Trotter to an inconvenience, I should be happy to accept of his offer; indeed, I thought myself very fortunate in having met with such a friend. I had scarcely time to reply, when I perceived a pair of legs, cased in black cotton stockings, on the ladder above us, and it proved that they belonged to Mrs Trotter, who came down the ladder with a net full of smoking potatoes.

"Upon my word, Mrs Trotter, you must be conscious of having a very pretty ankle, or you would not venture to display it, as you have to Mr Simple, a young gentleman whom I beg to introduce to you, and who, with your permission, will join our mess."

"My dear Trotter, how cruel of you not to give me warning; I thought that nobody was below. I declare I'm so ashamed," continued the lady, simpering, and covering her face with the hand which was unemployed.

"It can't be helped now, my love, neither was there anything to be ashamed of. I trust Mr Simple and you will be very good friends. I believe I mentioned his desire to join our mess."

"I am sure I shall be very happy in his company. This is a strange place for me to live in, Mr Simple, after the society to which I have been accustomed; but affection can make any sacrifice; and rather than lose the company of my dear Trotter, who has been unfortunate in pecuniary matters—"

"Say no more about it, my love. Domestic happiness is everything, and will enliven even the gloom of a cockpit."

"And yet," continued Mrs Trotter, "when I think of the time when we used to live in London, and keep our carriage. Have you ever been in London, Mr Simple?"

I answered that I had.

"Then, probably, you may have been acquainted with, or have heard of, the Smiths?"

I replied that the only people that I knew there were a Mr and Mrs Handycock.

"Well, if I had known that you were in London, I should have been very glad to have given you a letter of introduction to the Smiths. They are quite the topping people of the place."

"But, my dear," interrupted Mr Trotter, "is it not time to look after our dinner?"

"Yes; I am going forward for it now. We have skewer pieces

to-day. Mr Simple, will you excuse me?" and then, with a great deal of flirtation and laughing about her ankles, and requesting me, as a favour, to turn my face away, Mrs Trotter ascended the ladder.

As the reader may wish to know what sort of looking personage she was, I will take this opportunity to describe her. Her figure was very good, and at one period of her life I thought her face must have been very handsome; at the time I was introduced to her, it showed the ravages of time or hardship very distinctly; in short, she might be termed a faded beauty, flaunting in her dress, and not very clean in her person.

"Charming woman, Mrs Trotter, is she not, Mr Simple?" said the master's mate; to which, of course, I immediately acquiesced. "Now, Mr Simple," continued he, "there are a few arrangements which I had better mention while Mrs Trotter is away, for she would be shocked at our talking about such things. Of course, the style of living which we indulge in is rather expensive. Mrs Trotter cannot dispense with her tea and her other little comforts; at the same time I must put you to no extra expense—I had rather be out of pocket myself. I propose that during the time you mess with us you shall only pay one guinea per week; and as for entrance money, why I think I must not charge you more than a couple of guineas. Have you any money?"

"Yes," I replied, "I have three guineas and a half left."

"Well, then, give me the three guineas, and the half-guinea you can reserve for pocket-money. You must write to your friends immediately for a further supply."

I handed him the money, which he put in his pocket. "Your chest," continued he, "you shall bring down here, for Mrs Trotter will, I am sure, if I request it, not only keep it in order for you, but see that your clothes are properly mended. She is a charming woman, Mrs Trotter, and very fond of young gentlemen. How old are you?"

I replied that I was fifteen.

"No more! well, I am glad of that, for Mrs Trotter is very particular after a certain age. I should recommend you on no account to associate with the other midshipmen. They are very angry with me, because I would not permit Mrs Trotter to join their mess, and they are sad story-tellers."

"That they certainly are," replied I; but here we were interrupted by Mrs Trotter coming down with a piece of stick in her hand upon which were skewered about a dozen small pieces of beef and pork, which she first laid on a plate, and then began to lay the cloth and prepare for dinner.

"Mr Simple is only fifteen, my dear," observed Mr Trotter.

"Dear me!" replied Mrs Trotter, "why, how tall he is! He is quite as tall for his age as young Lord Foutretown, whom you used to take out with you in the *chay*. Do you know Lord Foutretown, Mr Simple?"

"No, I do not, ma'am," replied I; but wishing to let them know that I was well connected, I continued, "but I dare say that my grandfather, Lord Privilege, does."

"God bless me! is Lord Privilege your grandfather? Well, I thought I saw a likeness somewhere. Don't you recollect Lord Privilege, my dear Trotter, that we met at Lady Scamp's—an elderly person? It's very ungrateful of you not to recollect him, for he sent you a very fine haunch of venison."

"Privilege—bless me, yes. Oh, yes! an old gentleman, is he not?" said Mr Trotter, appealing to me.

"Yes, sir," replied I, quite delighted to find myself among those who were acquainted with my family.

"Well, then, Mr Simple," said Mrs Trotter, "since we have the pleasure of being acquainted with your family, I shall now take you under my own charge, and I shall be so fond of you that Trotter shall become quite jealous," added she, laughing. "We have but a poor dinner to-day, for the bumboat-woman disappointed me.* I particularly requested her to bring me off a leg of lamb, but she says that there was none in the market. It is rather early for it, that's true; but Trotter is very nice in his eating. Now, let us sit down to dinner."

I felt very sick, indeed, and could eat nothing. Our dinner consisted of the pieces of beef and pork, the potatoes, and a baked pudding in a tin dish. Mr Trotter went up to serve the spirits out to the ship's company, and returned with a bottle of rum.

"Have you got Mr Simple's allowance, my love?" inquired Mrs Trotter.

"Yes; he is victualled to-day, as he came on board before twelve o'clock. Do you drink spirits, Mr Simple?"

* *Bumboat: A boat employed to carry provisions and merchandise for sale to ships.*

"No, I thank you," replied I; for I remembered the captain's injunction.

"Taking, as I do, such an interest in your welfare, I must earnestly recommend you to abstain from them," said Mr Trotter. "It is a very bad habit, and once acquired, not easy to be left off. I am obliged to drink them, that I may not check the perspiration after working in the hold; I have, nevertheless, a natural abhorrence of them; but my champagne and claret days are gone by, and I must submit to circumstances."

"My poor Trotter!" said the lady.

"Well," continued he, "it's a poor heart that never rejoiceth." He then poured out half a tumbler of rum, and filled the glass up with water.

"My love, will you taste it?"

"Now, Trotter, you know that I never touch it, except when the water is so bad that I must have the taste taken away. How is the water to-day?"

"As usual, my dear, not drinkable." After much persuasion Mrs Trotter agreed to sip a little out of his glass. I thought that she took it pretty often, considering that she did not like it, but I felt so unwell that I was obliged to go on the main-deck. There I was met by a midshipman whom I had not seen before. He looked very earnestly in my face, and then asked my name. "Simple," said he. "What, are you the son of old Simple?"

"Yes, sir," replied I, astonished that so many should know my family.

"Well, I thought so by the likeness. And how is your father?"

"Very well, I thank you, sir."

"When you write to him, make my compliments, and tell him that I desired to be particularly remembered to him;" and he walked forward, but as he forgot to mention his own name, I could not do it.

I went to bed very tired; Mr Trotter had my hammock hung up in the cockpit, separated by a canvas-screen from the cot in which he slept with his wife. I thought this very odd, but they told me it was the general custom on board ship, although Mrs Trotter's delicacy was very much shocked by it. I was very sick, but Mrs Trotter was very kind. When I was in bed she kissed me, and wished me good night, and very soon afterwards I fell fast asleep.

CHAPTER VI

Puzzled with very common words—Mrs Trotter takes care of my ward-robe—A matrimonial duet, ending con strepito.

I AWOKE the next morning at daylight with a noise over my head which sounded like thunder; I found it proceeded from holy-stoning and washing down the main-deck.* I was very much re-freshed nevertheless, and did not feel the least sick or giddy. Mr Trotter, who had been up at four o'clock, came down, and directed one of the marines to fetch me some water. I washed myself on my chest, and then went on the main-deck, which they were swabbing dry. Standing by the sentry at the cabin-door, I met one of the mid-shipmen with whom I had been in company at the Blue Posts.

"So, Master Simple, old Trotter and his faggot of a wife have got hold of you—have they?" said he. I replied, that I did not know the meaning of faggot, but that I considered Mrs Trotter a very charm-ing woman.† At which he burst into a loud laugh. "Well," said he, "I'll just give you a caution. Take care, or they'll make a clean sweep. Has Mrs Trotter shown you her ankle yet?"

"Yes," I replied, "and a very pretty one it is."

"Ah! she's at her old tricks. You had much better have joined our mess at once. You're not the first greenhorn that they have plucked. Well," said he, as he walked away, "keep the key of your own chest—that's all."

But as Mr Trotter had warned me that the midshipmen would abuse them, I paid very little attention to what he said. When he left me I went on the quarter-deck. All the sailors were busy at work, and the first lieutenant cried out to the gunner, "Now, Mr Dispart, if you are ready, we'll breech these guns."

"Now, my lads," said the first lieutenant, "we must slue (the part that breeches cover) more forward." As I never heard of a gun having breeches, I was very anxious to see what was going on, and went up close to the first lieutenant, who said to me, "Youngster,

---

* *Holystoning: Scouring the decks of ships by using a small sandstone.*
† *Faggot: A shriveled old woman.*

hand me that *monkey's tail*." I saw nothing like a *monkey's tail*, but I was so frightened that I snatched up the first thing that I saw, which was a short bar of iron, and it so happened that it was the very article which he wanted. When I gave it to him, the first lieutenant looked at me, and said, "So you know what a monkey's tail is already, do you? Now don't you ever sham stupid after that."

Thought I to myself, I'm very lucky, but if that's a monkey's tail it's a very stiff one!

I resolved to learn the names of everything as fast as I could, that I might be prepared; so I listened attentively to what was said; but I soon became quite confused, and despaired of remembering anything.

"How is this to be finished off, sir?" inquired a sailor of the boatswain.

"Why, I beg leave to hint to you, sir, in the most delicate manner in the world," replied the boatswain, "that it must be with a *double-wall*—and be d——d to you—don't you know that yet? Captain of the foretop," said he, "up on your *horses*, and take your *stirrups* up three inches."—"Ay, ay, sir." (I looked and looked, but I could see no horses.)

"Mr Chucks," said the first lieutenant to the boatswain, "what blocks have we below—not on charge?"

"Let me see, sir, I've one *sister*, t'other we split in half the other day, and I think I have a couple of *monkeys* down in the store-room.—I say, you Smith, pass that brace through the *bull's eye*, and take the *sheepshank* out before you come down."

And then he asked the first lieutenant whether something should not be fitted with a *mouse* or only a *Turk's head*—told him the *goose-neck* must be spread out by the armourer as soon as the forge was up. In short, what with *dead eyes* and *shrouds*, *cats* and *cat-blocks*, *dolphins* and *dolphin-strikers*, *whips* and *puddings*, I was so puzzled with what I heard, that I was about to leave the deck in absolute despair.

"And, Mr Chucks, recollect this afternoon that you *bleed* all the *buoys*."

Bleed the boys, thought I, what can that be for? at all events, the surgeon appears to be the proper person to perform that operation.

This last incomprehensible remark drove me off the deck, and I retreated to the cockpit, where I found Mrs Trotter. "Oh, my dear!"

said she, "I am glad you are come, as I wish to put your clothes in order. Have you a list of them—where is your key?" I replied that I had not a list, and I handed her the key, although I did not forget the caution of the midshipman; yet I considered that there could be no harm in her looking over my clothes when I was present. She unlocked my chest, and pulled everything out, and then commenced telling me what were likely to be useful and what were not.

"Now these worsted stockings," she said, "will be very comfortable in cold weather, and in the summer time these brown cotton socks will be delightfully cool, and you have enough of each to last you till you outgrow them; but as for these fine cotton stockings, they are of no use—only catch the dirt when the decks are swept, and always look untidy. I wonder how they could be so foolish as to send them; nobody wears them on board ship nowadays. They are only fit for women—I wonder if they would fit me."

She turned her chair away, and put on one of my stockings, laughing the whole of the time. Then she turned round to me and showed me how nicely they fitted her. "Bless you, Mr Simple, it's well that Trotter is in the hold, he'd be so jealous—do you know what these stockings cost? They are of no use to you, and they fit me. I will speak to Trotter, and take them off your hands." I replied, that I could not think of selling them, and as they were of no use to me and fitted her, I begged that she would accept of the dozen pairs. At first she positively refused, but as I pressed her, she at last consented, and I was very happy to give them to her as she was very kind to me, and I thought, with her husband, that she was a very charming woman.

We had beef-steaks and onions for dinner that day, but I could not bear the smell of the onions. Mr Trotter came down very cross, because the first lieutenant had found fault with him. He swore that he would cut the service—that he had only remained to oblige the captain, who said that he would sooner part with his right arm, and that he would demand satisfaction of the first lieutenant as soon as he could obtain his discharge. Mrs Trotter did all she could to pacify him, reminded him that he had the protection of Lord this and Sir Thomas that, who would see him righted; but in vain. The first lieutenant had told him, he said, that he was not worth his salt, and blood only could wipe away the insult. He drank glass of grog after glass of grog, and at each glass became more violent, and Mrs

Trotter drank also, I observed, a great deal more than I thought she ought to have done; but she whispered to me, that she drank it that Trotter might not, as he would certainly be tipsy. I thought this very devoted on her part; but they sat so late that I went to bed and left them—he still drinking and vowing vengeance against the first lieutenant. I had not been asleep above two or three hours when I was awakened by a great noise and quarrelling, and I discovered that Mr Trotter was drunk and beating his wife. Very much shocked that such a charming woman should be beaten and ill-used, I scrambled out of my hammock to see if I could be of any assistance, but it was dark, although they scuffled as much as before. I asked the marine, who was sentry at the gun-room door above, to bring his lantern, and was very much shocked at his replying that I had better go to bed and let them fight it out.

Shortly afterwards Mrs Trotter, who had not taken off her clothes, came from behind the screen. I perceived at once that the poor woman could hardly stand; she reeled to my chest, where she sat down and cried. I pulled on my clothes as fast as I could, and then went up to her to console her, but she could not speak intelligibly. After attempting in vain to comfort her, she made me no answer, but staggered to my hammock, and, after several attempts, succeeded in getting into it. I cannot say that I much liked that, but what could I do? So I finished dressing myself, and went up on the quarter-deck.

The midshipman who had the watch was the one who had cautioned me against the Trotters; he was very friendly to me. "Well, Simple," said he, "what brings you on deck?" I told him how ill Mr Trotter had behaved to his wife, and how she had turned into my hammock.

"The cursed drunken old catamaran," cried he; "I'll go and cut her down by the head;" but I requested he would not, as she was a lady.

"A lady!" replied he; "yes, there's plenty of ladies of her description"; and then he informed me that she had many years ago been the mistress of a man of fortune who kept a carriage for her; but that he grew tired of her, and had given Trotter £200 to marry her, and that now they did nothing but get drunk together and fight with each other.

I was very much annoyed to hear all this; but as I perceived that

Mrs Trotter was not sober, I began to think that what the midshipman said was true. "I hope," added he, "that she has not had time
to wheedle you out of any of your clothes."

I told him that I had given her a dozen pairs of stockings, and
had paid Mr Trotter three guineas for my mess. "This must be
looked to," replied he; "I shall speak to the first lieutenant
to-morrow. In the mean time, I shall get your hammock for you.
Quarter-master, keep a good look-out." He then went below, and I
followed him, to see what he would do. He went to my hammock
and lowered it down at one end, so that Mrs Trotter lay with her
head on the deck in a very uncomfortable position. To my astonishment, she swore at him in a dreadful manner, but refused to turn
out. He was abusing her, and shaking her in the hammock, when
Mr Trotter, who had been roused at the noise, rushed from behind
the screen. "You villain! what are you doing with my wife?" cried
he, pommelling at him as well as he could, for he was so tipsy that
he could hardly stand.

I thought the midshipman able to take care of himself, and did
not wish to interfere; so I remained above, looking on—the sentry
standing by me with his lantern over the coombings of the hatchway to give light to the midshipman, and to witness the fray. Mr
Trotter was soon knocked down, when all of a sudden Mrs Trotter
jumped up from the hammock, and caught the midshipman by the
hair, and pulled at him. Then the sentry thought right to interfere,
he called out for the master-at-arms, and went down himself to help
the midshipman, who was faring badly between the two. But Mrs
Trotter snatched the lantern out of his hand and smashed it all to
pieces, and then we were all left in darkness, and I could not see
what took place, although the scuffling continued. Such was the
posture of affairs when the master-at-arms came up with his light.
The midshipman and sentry went up the ladder, and Mr and Mrs
Trotter continued beating each other. To this, none of them paid any
attention, saying, as the sentry had said before, "Let them fight it
out."

After they had fought some time, they retired behind the screen,
and I followed the advice of the midshipman, and got into my hammock, which the master-at-arms hung up again for me. I heard Mr
and Mrs Trotter both crying and kissing each other. "Cruel, cruel,
Mr Trotter," said she, blubbering.

"My life, my love, I was so jealous!" replied he.

"D——n and blast your jealousy," replied the lady; "I've two nice black eyes for the galley to-morrow." After about an hour of kissing and scolding, they both fell asleep again.

The next morning before breakfast, the midshipman reported to the first lieutenant the conduct of Mr Trotter and his wife. I was sent for and obliged to acknowledge that it was all true. He sent for Mr Trotter, who replied that he was not well, and could not come on deck. Upon which the first lieutenant ordered the sergeant of marines to bring him up directly. Mr Trotter made his appearance, with one eye closed, and his face very much scratched.

"Did not I desire you, sir," said the first lieutenant, "to introduce this young gentleman into the midshipmen's berth? instead of which you have introduced him to that disgraceful wife of yours, and have swindled him out of his property. I order you immediately to return the three guineas which you received as mess-money, and also that your wife give back the stockings which she cajoled him out of."

But then I interposed, and told the first lieutenant that the stockings had been a free gift on my part; and that, although I had been very foolish, yet that I considered that I could not in honour demand them back again.

"Well, youngster," replied the first lieutenant, "perhaps your ideas are correct, and if you wish it, I will not enforce that part of my order; but," continued he to Mr Trotter, "I desire, sir, that your wife leave the ship immediately; and I trust that when I have reported your conduct to the captain, he will serve you in the same manner. In the meantime, you will consider yourself under an arrest for drunkenness."

——❦——

CHAPTER VII

Scandalum magnatum clearly proved—I prove to the captain that I consider him a gentleman, although I had told him the contrary, and I prove to the midshipmen that I am a gentleman myself—They prove their gratitude by practising upon me, because practice makes perfect.

THE CAPTAIN CAME on board about twelve o'clock, and ordered the discharge of Mr Trotter to be made out, as soon as the first lieutenant had reported what had occurred. He then sent for all the midshipmen on the quarter-deck.

"Gentlemen," said the captain to them, with a stern countenance, "I feel very much indebted to some of you for the character which you have been pleased to give of me to Mr Simple. I must now request that you will answer a few questions which I am about to put in his presence. Did I ever flog the whole starboard watch because the ship would only sail nine knots on a bowline?"

"No, sir, no!" replied they all, very much frightened.

"Did I ever give a midshipman four dozen for not having his weekly accounts pipe-clayed; or another five dozen for wearing a scarlet watch-ribbon?"

"No, sir," replied they all together.

"Did any midshipman ever die on his chest from fatigue?"

They again replied in the negative.

"Then, gentlemen, you will oblige me by stating which of you thought proper to assert these falsehoods in a public coffee-room; and further, which of you obliged this youngster to risk his life in a duel?"

They were all silent.

"Will you answer me, gentlemen?"

"With respect to the duel, sir," replied the midshipman who had fought me, "I *heard* say, that the pistols were only charged with powder. It was a joke."

"Well, sir, we'll allow that the duel was only a joke, (and I hope and trust that your report is correct); is the reputation of your captain only a joke, allow me to ask? I request to know who of you dared to propagate such injurious slander?" (Here there was a dead

pause.) "Well, then, gentlemen, since you will not confess yourselves, I must refer to my authority. Mr Simple, have the goodness
to point out the person or persons who gave you the information."

But I thought this would not be fair; and as they had all treated
me very kindly after the duel, I resolved not to tell; so I answered,
"If you please, sir, I consider that I told you all that in confidence."

"Confidence, sir!" replied the captain; "who ever heard of confidence between a post-captain and a midshipman?"

"No, sir," replied I, "not between a post-captain and a midshipman, but between two gentlemen."

The first lieutenant, who stood by the captain, put his hand before his face to hide a laugh. "He may be a fool, sir," observed he to
the captain, aside; "but I can assure you he is a very straight-
forward one."

The captain bit his lip, and then turning to the midshipmen, said,
"You may thank Mr Simple, gentlemen, that I do not press this
matter further. I do believe that you were not serious when you
calumniated me; but recollect, that what is said in joke is too often
repeated in earnest. I trust that Mr Simple's conduct will have its
effect, and that you leave off practising upon him, who has saved
you from a very severe punishment."

When the midshipmen went down below, they all shook hands
with me, and said that I was a good fellow for not peaching; but, as
for the advice of the captain that they should not practise upon me,
as he termed it, they forgot that, for they commenced again immediately, and never left off until they found that I was not to be
deceived any longer.

I had not been ten minutes in the berth, before they began their
remarks upon me. One said that I looked like a hardy fellow, and
asked me whether I could not bear a great deal of sleep.

I replied that I could, I dare say, if it was necessary for the good
of the service; at which they laughed, and I supposed that I had said
a good thing.

"Why here's Tomkins," said the midshipman; "he'll show you
how to perform that part of your duty. He inherits it from his father,
who was a marine officer. He can snore for fourteen hours on
a stretch without once turning round in his hammock, and finish
his nap on the chest during the whole of the day, except meal-
times."

But Tomkins defended himself, by saying, that "some people were very quick in doing things, and others were very slow; that he was one of the slow ones, and that he did not in reality obtain more refreshment from his long naps than other people did in short ones, because he slept much slower than they did."

This ingenious argument was, however, overruled *nem. con.*, as it was proved that he ate pudding faster than any one in the mess.*

The postman came on board with the letters, and put his head into the midshipman's berth. I was very anxious to have one from home, but I was disappointed. Some had letters and some had not. Those who had not, declared that their parents were very undutiful, and that they would cut them off with a shilling; and those who had letters, after they had read them, offered them for sale to the others, usually at half-price. I could not imagine why they sold, or why the others bought them; but they did do so; and one that was full of good advice was sold three times, from which circumstance I was inclined to form a better opinion of the morals of my companions. The lowest-priced letters sold, were those written by sisters. I was offered one for a penny, but I declined buying, as I had plenty of sisters of my own. Directly I made that observation, they immediately inquired all their names and ages, and whether they were pretty or not. When I had informed them, they quarrelled to whom they should belong. One would have Lucy, and another took Mary; but there was a great dispute about Ellen, as I had said that she was the prettiest of the whole. At last they agreed to put her up to auction, and she was knocked down to a master's mate of the name of O'Brien, who bid seventeen shillings and a bottle of rum. They requested that I would write home to give their love to my sisters, and tell them how they had been disposed of, which I thought very strange; but I ought to have been flattered at the price bid for Ellen, as I repeatedly have since been witness to a very pretty sister being sold for a glass of grog.

I mentioned the reason why I was so anxious for a letter, viz., because I wanted to buy my dirk and cocked hat; upon which they told me that there was no occasion for my spending my money, as, by the regulations of the service, the purser's steward served them out to all the officers who applied for them. As I knew where the

* Nem. con. (nemine contradictine, *Latin): Without contradiction.*

purser's steward's room was, having seen it when down in the cockpit with the Trotters, I went down immediately. "Mr Purser's Steward," said I, "let me have a cocked hat and a dirk immediately."

"Very good, sir," replied he, and he wrote an order upon a slip of paper, which he handed to me. "There is the order for it, sir; but the cocked hats are kept in the chest up in the main-top; and as for the dirk, you must apply to the butcher, who has them under his charge."

I went up with the order, and thought I would first apply for the dirk; so I inquired for the butcher, whom I found sitting in the sheep-pen with the sheep, mending his trousers. In reply to my demand, he told me that he had not the key of the store-room, which was under the charge of one of the corporals of marines.

I inquired who, and he said, "Cheeks the marine."*

I went everywhere about the ship, inquiring for Cheeks the marine, but could not find him. Some said that they believed he was in the fore-top, standing sentry over the wind, that it might not change; others, that he was in the galley, to prevent the midshipmen from soaking their biscuit in the captain's dripping-pan. At last, I inquired of some of the women who were standing between the guns on the main-deck, and one of them answered that it was no use looking for him among them, as they all had husbands, and Cheeks was a *widow's man*.†

As I could not find the marine, I thought I might as well go for my cocked hat, and get my dirk afterwards. I did not much like going up the rigging, because I was afraid of turning giddy, and if I fell overboard I could not swim; but one of the midshipmen offered to accompany me, stating that I need not be afraid, if I fell overboard, of sinking to the bottom, as if I was giddy, my head, at all events, *would swim;* so I determined to venture. I climbed up very near to the main-top, but not without missing the little ropes very often, and grazing the skin of my shins. Then I came to large ropes stretched out from the mast, so that you must climb them with your head backwards. The midshipman told me these were called the cat-harpings, because they were so difficult to climb, that a cat would

* This celebrated personage is the prototype of Mr Nobody on board of a man-of-war.
† Widows' men are imaginary sailors, borne on the books, and receiving pay and prize-money, which is appropriated to Greenwich Hospital.

expostulate if ordered to go out by them. I was afraid to venture, and then he proposed that I should go through lubber's hole, which he said had been made for people like me. I agreed to attempt it, as it appeared more easy, and at last arrived, quite out of breath, and very happy to find myself in the main-top.

The captain of the main-top was there with two other sailors. The midshipman introduced me very politely:—"Mr Jenkins—Mr Simple, midshipman,—Mr Simple, Mr Jenkins, captain of the main-top. Mr Jenkins, Mr Simple has come up with an order for a cocked hat." The captain of the top replied that he was very sorry that he had not one in store, but the last had been served out to the captain's monkey. This was very provoking. The captain of the top then asked me if I was ready with my *footing*.

I replied, "Not very, for I had lost it two or three times when coming up." He laughed and replied, that I should lose it altogether before I went down; and that I must *hand* it out. "*Hand* out my *footing!*" said I, puzzled, and appealing to the midshipman; "what does he mean?" "He means that you must fork out a seven-shilling bit." I was just as wise as ever, and stared very much; when Mr Jenkins desired the other men to get half a dozen *foxes* and make a *spread eagle* of me, unless he had his parkisite.* I never should have found out what it all meant, had not the midshipman, who laughed till he cried, at last informed me that it was the custom to give the men something to drink the first time that I came aloft, and that if I did not, they would tie me up to the rigging.

Having no money in my pocket, I promised to pay them as soon as I went below; but Mr Jenkins would not trust me. I then became very angry, and inquired of him "if he doubted my honour." He replied, "Not in the least, but that he must have the seven shillings before I went below." "Why, sir," said I, "do you know whom you are speaking to? I am an officer and a gentleman. Do you know who my grandfather is?"

"O yes," replied he, "very well."

"Then, who is he, sir?" replied I very angrily.

"Who is he! why he's the *Lord knows who.*"

"No," replied I, "that's not his name; he is Lord Privilege." (I was very much surprised that he knew that my grandfather was a

* *Foxes: Strands formed by twisting several rope-yarns together.*

lord.) "And do you suppose," continued I, "that I would forfeit the honour of my family for a paltry seven shillings?"

This observation of mine, and a promise on the part of the midshipman, who said he would be bail for me, satisfied Mr Jenkins, and he allowed me to go down the rigging. I went to my chest, and paid the seven shillings to one of the top-men who followed me, and then went up on the main-deck, to learn as much as I could of my profession. I asked a great many questions of the midshipmen relative to the guns, and they crowded round me to answer them. One told me they were called the frigate's *teeth*, because they stopped the Frenchman's *jaw*. Another midshipman said that he had been so often in action, that he was called the *Fire-eater*. I asked him how it was that he escaped being killed. He replied that he always made it a rule, upon the first cannon-ball coming through the ship's side, to put his head into the hole which it had made; as, by a calculation made by Professor Innman, the odds were 32,647, and some decimals to boot, that another ball would not come in at the same hole. That's what I never should have thought of.

—◦◦◦—

CHAPTER VIII

My messmates show me the folly of running in debt—Duty carried on politely—I become acquainted with some gentlemen of the home department—The episode of Sholto M'Foy.

NOW THAT I have been on board about a month, I find that my life is not disagreeable. I don't smell the pitch and tar, and I can get into my hammock without tumbling out on the other side. My messmates are good-tempered, although they laugh at me very much; but I must say that they are not very nice in their ideas of honour. They appear to consider that to take you in is a capital joke; and that because they laugh at the time that they are cheating you, it then becomes no cheating at all. Now I cannot think otherwise than that cheating is cheating, and that a person is not a bit more honest, because he laughs at you in the bargain. A few days after I came on board, I purchased some tarts of the bumboat-woman, as she is called; I wished to pay for them, but she had no change, and very civilly told me she would trust me. She produced a narrow book, and said that she would open an account with me, and I could pay her when I thought proper. To this arrangement I had no objection, and I sent up for different things until I thought that my account must have amounted to eleven or twelve shillings. As I promised my father that I never would run in debt, I considered that it was then time that it should be settled. When I asked for it, what was my surprise to find that it amounted to £2 14s. 6d. I declared that it was impossible, and requested that she would allow me to look at the items, when I found that I was booked for at least three or four dozen tarts every day, ordered by the young gentlemen, "to be put down to Mr Simple's account." I was very much shocked, not only at the sum of money which I had to pay, but also at the want of honesty on the part of my messmates; but when I complained of it in the berth, they all laughed at me.

At last one of them said, "Peter, tell the truth; did not your father caution you not to run in debt?"

"Yes, he did," replied I.

"I know that very well," replied he; "all fathers do the same when their sons leave them; it's a matter of course. Now observe, Peter; it is out of regard to you, that your messmates have been eating tarts at your expense. You disobeyed your father's injunctions before you had been a month from home; and it is to give you a lesson that may be useful in after-life, that they have considered it their duty to order the tarts. I trust that it will not be thrown away upon you. Go to the woman, pay your bill, and never run up another."

"That I certainly shall not," replied I; but as I could not prove who ordered the tarts, and did not think it fair that the woman should lose her money, I went up and paid the bill with a determination never to open an account with anybody again.

But this left my pockets quite empty, so I wrote to my father, stating the whole transaction, and the consequent state of my finances. My father, in his answer, observed that whatever might have been their motives, my messmates had done me a friendly act; and that as I had lost my money by my own carelessness, I must not expect that he would allow me any more pocket-money. But my mother, who added a postscript to his letter, slipped in a five-pound note, and I do believe that it was with my father's sanction, although he pretended to be very angry at my forgetting his injunctions. This timely relief made me quite comfortable again. What a pleasure it is to receive a letter from one's friends when far away, especially when there is some money in it!

A few days before this, Mr Falcon, the first lieutenant, ordered me to put on my side-arms to go away on duty. I replied that I had neither dirk nor cocked hat, although I had applied for them. He laughed at my story, and sent me on shore with the master, who bought them, and the first lieutenant sent up the bill to my father, who paid it, and wrote to thank him for his trouble. That morning, the first lieutenant said to me, "Now, Mr Simple, we'll take the shine off that cocked hat and dirk of yours. You will go in the boat with Mr O'Brien, and take care that none of the men slip away from it, and get drunk at the tap."

This was the first time that I had ever been sent away on duty, and I was very proud of being an officer in charge. I put on my full uniform, and was ready at the gangway a quarter of an hour before the men were piped away. We were ordered to the dockyard to draw sea stores. When we arrived there, I was quite astonished at the piles of timber, the ranges of storehouses, and the immense anchors which lay on the wharf. There was such a bustle, everybody appeared to be so busy, that I wanted to look every way at once. Close to where the boat landed, they were hauling a large frigate out of what they called the basin; and I was so interested with the sight, that I am sorry to say I quite forgot all about the boat's crew, and my orders to look after them. What surprised me most was, that although the men employed appeared to be sailors, their language was very different from what I had been lately accustomed to on board of the frigate. Instead of damning and swearing, everybody was so polite. "Oblige me with a pull of the starboard bow hawser, Mr Jones."—"Ease off the larboard hawser, Mr Jenkins, if you please."—"Side her over, gentlemen, side her over."—"My compliments to Mr Tompkins, and request that he will cast off the quarter-check."—"Side her over, gentlemen, side her over, if you please."—"In the boat there, pull to Mr Simmons, and beg he'll do me the favour to check her as she swings. What's the matter, Mr Johnson?"—"Vy, there's one of them ere midshipmites has thrown a red hot tater out of the stern-port, and hit our officer in the eye."—

"Report him to the commissioner, Mr Wiggins; and oblige me by under-running the guess-warp.* Tell Mr Simkins, with my compliments, to coil away upon the jetty. Side her over, side her over, gentlemen, if you please."

I asked of a bystander who these people were, and he told me that they were dockyard mateys. I certainly thought that it appeared to be quite as easy to say "If you please," as "D——n your eyes," and that it sounded much more agreeable.

During the time that I was looking at the frigate being hauled out, two of the men belonging to the boat slipped away, and on my return they were not to be seen. I was very much frightened, for I knew that I had neglected my duty, and that on the first occasion on which I had been intrusted with a responsible service. What to do I did not know. I ran up and down every part of the dockyard until I was quite out of breath, asking everybody I met whether they had seen my two men. Many of them said that they had seen plenty of men, but did not exactly know mine; some laughed, and called me a greenhorn. At last I met a midshipman, who told me that he had seen two men answering to my description on the roof of the coach starting for London, and that I must be quick if I wished to catch them; but he would not stop to answer any more questions. I continued walking about the yard until I met twenty or thirty men with grey jackets and breeches, to whom I applied for information: they told me that they had seen two sailors skulking behind the piles of timber. They crowded round me, and appeared very anxious to assist me, when they were summoned away to carry down a cable. I observed that they all had numbers on their jackets, and either one or two bright iron rings on their legs. I could not help inquiring, although I was in such a hurry, why the rings were worn. One of them replied that they were orders of merit, given to them for their good behaviour.

I was proceeding on very disconsolately, when, as I turned a corner, to my great delight, I met my two men, who touched their hats and said that they had been looking for me. I did not believe that they told the truth, but I was so glad to recover them that I did not scold, but went with them down to the boat, which had been waiting some time for us. O'Brien, the master's mate, called me a

* Guess-warp: A rope used to secure two vessels together.

young sculping, a word I never heard before. When we arrived on board, the first lieutenant asked O'Brien why he had remained so long. He answered that two of the men had left the boat, but that I had found them. The first lieutenant appeared to be pleased with me, observing, as he had said before, that I was no fool, and I went down below, overjoyed at my good fortune, and very much obliged to O'Brien for not telling the whole truth. After I had taken off my dirk and cocked hat, I felt for my pocket-handkerchief, and found that it was not in my pocket, having in all probability been taken out by the men in grey jackets, whom, in conversation with my mess-mates, I discovered to be convicts condemned to hard labour for stealing and picking pockets.

A day or two afterwards, we had a new messmate of the name of M'Foy. I was on the quarter-deck when he came on board and pre-sented a letter to the captain, inquiring first if his name was "Cap-tain Sauvage." He was a florid young man, nearly six feet high, with sandy hair, yet very good-looking. As his career in the service was very short, I will tell at once, what I did not find out till some time afterwards. The captain had agreed to receive him to oblige a brother officer, who had retired from the service, and lived in the Highlands of Scotland. The first notice which the captain had of the arrival of Mr M'Foy, was from a letter written to him by the young man's uncle. This amused him so much, that he gave it to the first lieutenant to read: it ran as follows:—

"Glasgow, April 25, 1——.
"Sir,—Our much esteemed and mutual friend, Captain M'Alpine, having communicated by letter, dated the 14th inst., your kind in-tentions relative to my nephew Sholto M'Foy, (for which you will be pleased to accept my best thanks), I write to acquaint you that he is now on his way to join your ship, the *Diomede,* and will arrive, God willing, twenty-six hours after the receipt of this letter.

"As I have been given to understand by those who have some acquaintance with the service of the king, that his equipment as an officer will be somewhat expensive, I have considered it but fair to ease your mind as to any responsibility on that score, and have therefore enclosed the half of a Bank of England note for ten pounds sterling, No. 3742, the other half of which will be duly forwarded in a frank promised to me the day after to-morrow. I beg you will

make the necessary purchases, and apply the balance, should there
be any, to his mess account, or any other expenses which you may
consider warrantable or justifiable.

"It is at the same time proper to inform you, that Sholto had ten
shillings in his pocket at the time of his leaving Glasgow; the satisfactory expenditure of which I have no doubt you will inquire into,
as it is a large sum to be placed at the discretion of a youth only
fourteen years and five months old. I mention his age, as Sholto is so
tall that you might be deceived by his appearance, and be induced
to trust to his prudence in affairs of this serious nature. Should he at
any time require further assistance beyond his pay, which I am told
is extremely handsome to all king's officers, I beg you to consider
that any draught of yours, at ten days' sight, to the amount of five
pounds sterling English, will be duly honoured by the firm of Monteith, M'Killop, and Company, of Glasgow. Sir, with many thanks
for your kindness and consideration,

"I remain, your most obedient,

"WALTER MONTEITH."

The letter brought on board by M'Foy was to prove his identity.
While the captain read it, M'Foy stared about him like a wild stag.
The captain welcomed him to the ship, asked him one or two questions, introduced him to the first lieutenant, and then went on shore.
The first lieutenant had asked me to dine in the gun-room; I supposed that he was pleased with me because I had found the men;
and when the captain pulled on shore, he also invited Mr M'Foy,
when the following conversation took place.

"Well, Mr M'Foy, you have had a long journey; I presume it is
the first that you have ever made."

"Indeed it is, sir," replied M'Foy; "and sorely I've been pestered.
Had I minded all they whispered in my lug as I came along, I had
need been made of money—sax-pence here, sax-pence there, sax-
pence every where. Sich extortion I ne'er dreamt of."

"How did you come from Glasgow?"

"By the wheelboat, or steamboat, as they ca'd it, to Lunnon:
where they charged me sax-pence for taking my baggage on shore—
a wee boxy nae bigger than yon cocked-up hat. I would fain carry it
mysel', but they wadna let me."

"Well, where did you go to when you arrived in London?"

"I went to a place ca'd Chichester Rents, to the house of Storm and Mainwaring, Warehousemen, and they must have another sax-pence for showing me the way. There I waited half-an-hour in the counting-house, till they took me to a place ca'd Bull and Mouth, and put me into a coach, paying my whole fare: nevertheless they must din me for money the whole of the way down. There was first the guard, and then the coachman, and another guard, and another coachman; but I wudna listen to them, and so they growled and abused me."

"And when did you arrive?"

"I came here last night; and I only had a bed and a breakfast at the twa Blue Pillars' house, for which they extortioned me three shillings and sax-pence, as I sit here. And then there was the cham-bermaid hussy and waiter loon axed me to remember them, and wanted more siller; but I told them as I told the guard and coach-man, that I had none for them."

"How much of your ten shillings have you left?" inquired the first lieutenant, smiling.

"Hoot, sir lieutenant, how came you for to ken that? Eh! it's my uncle Monteith at Glasgow. Why, as I sit here, I've but three shil-lings and a penny of it lift. But there's a smell here that's no canny; so I'll just go up again into the fresh air."

When Mr M'Foy quitted the gun-room they all laughed very much. After he had been a short time on deck he went down into the midshipmen's berth; but he made himself very unpleasant, quarrelling and wrangling with everybody. It did not, however, last very long; for he would not obey any orders that were given to him. On the third day, he quitted the ship without asking the permission of the first lieutenant; when he returned on board the following day, the first lieutenant put him under an arrest, and in charge of the sentry at the cabin door. During the afternoon I was under the half-deck, and perceived that he was sharpening a long clasp-knife upon the after-truck of the gun. I went up to him, and asked him why he was doing so, and he replied, as his eyes flashed fire, that it was to revenge the insult offered to the bluid of M'Foy. His look told me that he was in earnest. "But what do you mean?" inquired I. "I mean," said he, drawing the edge and feeling the point of his weapon, "to put it into the weam of that man with the gold podge on his shoulder, who has dared to place me here."

I was very much alarmed, and thought it my duty to state his murderous intentions, or worse might happen; so I walked up on deck and told the first lieutenant what M'Foy was intending to do, and how his life was in danger. Mr Falcon laughed, and shortly afterwards went down on the main-deck. M'Foy's eyes glistened, and he walked forward to where the first lieutenant was standing; but the sentry, who had been cautioned by me, kept him back with his bayonet. The first lieutenant turned round, and perceiving what was going on, desired the sentry to see if Mr M'Foy had a knife in his hand; and he had it sure enough, open, and held behind his back. He was disarmed, and the first lieutenant, perceiving that the lad meant mischief, reported his conduct to the captain, on his arrival on board. The captain sent for M'Foy, who was very obstinate, and when taxed with his intention would not deny it, or even say that he would not again attempt it; so he was sent on shore immediately, and returned to his friends in the Highlands. We never saw any more of him; but I heard that he obtained a commission in the army, and three months after he had joined his regiment, was killed in a duel, resenting some fancied affront offered to the bluid of M'Foy.

CHAPTER IX

We post up to Portsdown Fair—Consequence of disturbing a lady at supper—Natural affection of the pelican, proved at my expense—Spontaneous combustion at Ranelagh Gardens—Pastry versus Piety—Many are bid to the feast; but not the halt, the lame, or the blind.

A FEW DAYS AFTER M'Foy quitted the ship, we all had leave from the first lieutenant to go to Portsdown Fair, but he would only allow the oldsters to sleep on shore. We anticipated so much pleasure from our excursion, that some of us were up early enough to go away in the boat sent for fresh beef. This was very foolish. There were no carriages to take us to the fair, nor indeed any fair so early in the morning; the shops were all shut, and the Blue Posts, where we always rendezvoused, was hardly opened. We waited

there in the coffee-room, until we were driven out by the maid
sweeping away the dirt, and were forced to walk about until she
had finished, and lighted the fire, when we ordered our breakfast;
but how much better would it have been to have taken our breakfast
comfortably on board, and then to have come on shore, especially as
we had no money to spare. Next to being too late, being too soon is
the worst plan in the world. However, we had our breakfast, and
paid the bill; then we sallied forth, and went up George Street,
where we found all sorts of vehicles ready to take us to the fair. We
got into one which they called a dilly. I asked the man who drove it
why it was so called, and he replied, because he only charged a
shilling. O'Brien, who had joined us after breakfasting on board,
said that this answer reminded him of one given to him by a man
who attended the hackney-coach stands in London. "Pray," said he,
"why are you called Waterman?" "Waterman," replied the man,
"vy, sir, 'cause we opens the hackney-coach doors." At last, with
plenty of whipping, and plenty of swearing, and a great deal of
laughing, the old horse, whose back curved upwards like a bow,
from the difficulty of dragging so many, arrived at the bottom of
Portsdown Hill, where we got out, and walked up to the fair. It
really was a most beautiful sight. The bright blue sky, and the coloured flags flapping about in all directions, the grass so green, and
the white tents and booths, the sun shining so bright, and the shining gilt gingerbread, the variety of toys and the variety of noise, the
quantity of people and the quantity of sweetmeats; little boys so
happy, and shop-people so polite, the music at the booths, and the
bustle and eagerness of the people outside, made my heart quite
jump. There was Richardson, with a clown and harlequin, and such
beautiful women, dressed in clothes all over gold spangles, dancing
reels and waltzes, and looking so happy! There was Flint and
Gyngell, with fellows tumbling over head and heels, playing such
tricks—eating fire, and drawing yards of tape out of their mouths.
Then there was the Royal Circus, all the horses standing in a line,
with men and women standing on their backs, waving flags, while
the trumpeters blew their trumpets. And the largest giant in the
world, and Mr Paap, the smallest dwarf in the world, and a female
dwarf, who was smaller still, and Miss Biffin, who did everything
without legs or arms. There was also the learned pig, and the Here-
fordshire ox, and a hundred other sights which I cannot now re-

member. We walked about for an hour or two seeing the outside of everything: we determined to go and see the inside. First we went into Richardson's, where we saw a bloody tragedy, with a ghost and thunder, and afterwards a pantomime, full of tricks, and tumbling over one another. Then we saw one or two other things, I forget what; but this I know, that, generally speaking, the outside was better than the inside. After this, feeling very hungry, we agreed to go into a booth and have something to eat. The tables were ranged all round, and in the centre there was a boarded platform for danc-ing. The ladies were there all ready dressed for partners; and the music was so lively, that I felt very much inclined to dance, but we had agreed to go and see the wild beasts fed at Mr Polito's menag-erie, and as it was now almost eight o'clock, we paid our bill and set off. It was a very curious sight, and better worth seeing than any thing in the fair; I never had an idea that there were so many strange animals in existence. They were all secured in iron cages, and a large chandelier with twenty lights, hung in the centre of the booth, and lighted them up, while the keeper went round and stirred them up with his long pole; at the same time he gave us their histories, which were very interesting. I recollect a few of them. There was the tapir, a great pig with a long nose, a variety of the hiptostamass, which the keeper said was an amphibilious animal, as couldn't live on land, and *dies* in the water—however, it seemed to live very well in a cage. Then there was the kangaroo with its young ones peeping out of it—a most astonishing animal. The keeper said that it brought forth two young ones at a birth, and then took them into its stomach again, until they arrived at years of discretion. Then there was the pelican of the wilderness, (I shall not forget him), with a large bag under his throat, which the man put on his head as a night-cap: this bird feeds its young with its own blood—when fish are scarce. And there was the laughing hyæna, who cries in the wood like a human being in distress, and devours those who come to his assistance—a sad instance of the depravity of human nature, as the keeper ob-served. There was a beautiful creature, the royal Bengal tiger, only three years old, what growed ten inches every year, and never ar-rived at its full growth. The one we saw, measured, as the keeper told us, sixteen feet from the snout to the tail, and seventeen from the tail to the snout: but there must have been some mistake there. There was a young elephant and three lions, and several other

animals which I forget now, so I shall go on to describe the tragical
scene which occurred. The keeper had poked up all the animals, and
had commenced feeding them. The great lion was growling and
snarling over the shin-bone of an ox, cracking it like a nut, when, by
some mismanagement, one end of the pole upon which the chandelier was suspended fell down, striking the door of the cage in which
the lioness was at supper, and bursting it open. It was all done in a
second; the chandelier fell, the cage opened, and the lioness sprang
out. I remember to this moment seeing the body of the lioness in the
air, and then all was dark as pitch. What a change! not a moment
before all of us staring with delight and curiosity, and then to be left
in darkness, horror, and dismay! There was such screaming and
shrieking, such crying, and fighting, and pushing, and fainting, nobody knew where to go, or how to find their way out. The people
crowded first on one side, and then on the other, as their fears
instigated them. I was very soon jammed up with my back against
the bars of one of the cages, and feeling some beast lay hold of me
behind, made a desperate effort, and succeeded in climbing up to
the cage above, not however without losing the seat of my trousers,
which the laughing hyæna would not let go. I hardly knew where I
was when I climbed up; but I knew the birds were mostly stationed
above. However, that I might not have the front of my trousers torn
as well as the behind, as soon as I gained my footing I turned round,
with my back to the bars of the cage, but I had not been there a
minute before I was attacked by something which digged into me
like a pickaxe, and as the hyæna had torn my clothes, I had no
defence against it. To turn round would have been worse still; so,
after having received above a dozen stabs, I contrived by degrees to
shift my position until I was opposite to another cage, but not until
the pelican, for it was that brute, had drawn as much blood from me
as would have fed his young for a week. I was surmising what
danger I should next encounter, when to my joy I discovered that I
had gained the open door from which the lioness had escaped. I
crawled in, and pulled the door to after me, thinking myself very
fortunate: and there I sat very quietly in a corner during the remainder of the noise and confusion. I had been there but a few minutes,
when the beef-eaters, as they were called, who played the music
outside, came in with torches and loaded muskets. The sight which
presented itself was truly shocking, twenty or thirty men, women,

and children, lay on the ground, and I thought at first the lioness had killed them all, but they were only in fits, or had been trampled down by the crowd. No one was seriously hurt. As for the lioness, she was not to be found: and as soon as it was ascertained that she had escaped, there was as much terror and scampering away outside as there had been in the menagerie. It appeared afterwards, that the animal had been as much frightened as we had been, and had secreted herself under one of the waggons. It was some time before she could be found. At last O'Brien, who was a very brave fellow, went a-head of the beef-eaters, and saw her eyes glaring. They borrowed a net or two from the carts which had brought calves to the fair, and threw them over her. When she was fairly entangled, they dragged her by the tail into the menagerie. All this while I had remained very quietly in the den, but when I perceived that its lawful owner had come back to retake possession, I thought it was time to come out; so I called to my messmates, who, with O'Brien were assisting the beef-eaters. They had not discovered me, and laughed very much when they saw where I was. One of the midshipmen shot the bolt of the door, so that I could not jump out, and then stirred me up with a long pole. At last I contrived to unbolt it again, and got out, when they laughed still more, at the seat of my trousers being torn off. It was not exactly a laughing matter to me, although I had to congratulate myself upon a very lucky escape; and so did my messmates think, when I narrated my adventures. The pelican was the worst part of the business. O'Brien lent me a dark silk handkerchief, which I tied round my waist, and let drop behind, so that my misfortunes might not attract any notice, and then we quitted the menagerie; but I was so stiff that I could scarcely walk.

We then went to what they called the Ranelagh Gardens, to see the fireworks, which were to be let off at ten o'clock. It was exactly ten when we paid for our admission, and we waited very patiently for a quarter of an hour, but there were no signs of the fireworks being displayed. The fact was, that the man to whom the gardens belonged waited until more company should arrive, although the place was already very full of people. Now the first lieutenant had ordered the boat to wait for us until twelve o'clock, and then return on board; and, as we were seven miles from Portsmouth, we had not much time to spare. We waited another quarter of an hour, and then it was agreed that as the fireworks were stated in the handbill to commence precisely at ten o'clock, we were fully justified in letting them off ourselves. O'Brien went out, and returned with a dozen penny rattans, which he notched in the end. The fireworks were on the posts and stages, all ready, and it was agreed that we should light them all at once, and then mix with the crowd. The oldsters lighted cigars, and fixing them in the notched end of the canes, continued to puff them until they were all well lighted. They handed one to each of us, and at a signal we all applied them to the match papers, and as soon as the fire communicated we threw down our canes and ran in among the crowd. In about half a minute, off they all went, in a most beautiful confusion; there were silver stars and golden stars, blue lights and Catherine-wheels, mines and bombs, Grecian-fires and Roman-candles, Chinese-trees, rockets and illuminated mottoes, all firing away, cracking, popping, and fizzing, at the same time. It was unanimously agreed that it was a great improvement upon the intended show. The man to whom the gardens belonged ran out of a booth, where he had been drinking beer at his ease, while his company were waiting, swearing vengeance against the perpetrators; indeed, the next day he offered fifty pounds reward for the discovery of the offenders. But I think that he was treated very properly. He was, in his situation, a servant of the public, and he had behaved as if he was their master. We all escaped very cleverly, and taking another dilly, arrived at Portsmouth, and were down to the boat in good time. The next day I was so stiff and in such pain, that I was obliged to go to the doctor, who put me on the list, where I remained a week before I could return to my duty. So much for Portsdown fair.

It was on a Saturday that I returned to my duty, and Sunday being a fine day, we all went on shore to church with Mr Falcon, the first lieutenant. We liked going to church very much, not, I am sorry to say, from religious feelings, but for the following reason:—The first lieutenant sat in a pew below, and we were placed in the gallery above, where he could not see us, nor indeed could we see him. We all remained very quiet, and I may say very devout, during the time of the service; but the clergyman who delivered the sermon was so tedious, and had such a bad voice, that we generally slipped out as soon as he went up into the pulpit, and adjourned to a pastry-cook's opposite, to eat cakes and tarts and drink cherry-brandy, which we infinitely preferred to hearing a sermon. Somehow or other, the first lieutenant had scent of our proceedings: we believed that the marine officer informed against us, and this Sunday he served us a pretty trick. We had been at the pastry-cook's as usual, and as soon as we perceived the people coming out of church, we put all our tarts and sweetmeats into our hats, which we then slipped on our heads, and took our station at the church-door, as if we had just come down from the gallery, and had been waiting for him. Instead, however, of appearing at the church-door, he walked up the street, and desired us to follow him to the boat. The fact was, he had been in the back-room at the pastry-cook's watching our motions through the green blinds. We had no suspicion, but thought that he had come out of church a little sooner than usual. When we arrived on board and followed him up the side, he said to us as we came on deck,—"Walk aft, young gentlemen." We did; and he desired us to "toe a line," which means to stand in a row. "Now, Mr Dixon," said he, "what was the text to-day?" As he very often asked us that question, we always left one in the church until the text was given out, who brought it to us in the pastry-cook's shop, when we all marked it in our Bibles, to be ready if he asked us. Dixon immediately pulled out his Bible where he had marked down the leaf, and read it. "O! that was it," said Mr Falcon; "you must have remarkably good ears, Mr Dixon, to have heard the clergyman from the pastry-cook's shop. Now, gentlemen, hats off, if you please." We all slided off our hats, which, as he expected, were full of pastry. "Really, gentlemen," said he, feeling the different papers of pastry and sweetmeats, "I am quite delighted to perceive that you have not been to church for nothing. Few come away with so many good things pressed upon their seat of memory. Master-at-arms, send all the ship's boys aft."

The boys all came tumbling up the ladders, and the first lieutenant desired each of them to take a seat upon the carronade slides. When they were all stationed, he ordered us to go round with our hats, and request of each his acceptance of a tart, which we were obliged to do, handing first to one and then to another, until the hats were all empty. What annoyed me more than all, was the grinning of the boys at their being served by us like footmen, as well as the ridicule and laughter of the whole ship's company, who had assembled at the gangways.

When all the pastry was devoured, the first lieutenant said,

"There, gentlemen, now that you have had your lesson for the day, you may go below." We could not help laughing ourselves, when we went down into the berth; Mr Falcon always punished us good-humouredly, and, in some way or other, his punishments were severally connected with the description of the offence. He always had a remedy for every thing that he disapproved of, and the ship's company used to call him "Remedy Jack." I ought to observe that some of my messmates were very severe upon the ship's boys after that circumstance, always giving them a kick or a cuff on the head whenever they could, telling them at the same time, "There's another tart for you, you whelp." I believe, if the boys had known what was in reserve for them, they would much rather have left the pastry alone.

—◦◦◦—

CHAPTER X

A pressgang; beaten off by one woman—Dangers at Spithead and Point—A treat for both parties, of pulled chicken, at my expense—Also gin for twenty—I am made a prisoner: escape and rejoin my ship.

I MUST NOW RELATE what occurred to me a few days before the ship sailed, which will prove that it is not necessary to encounter the winds and waves, or the cannon of the enemy, to be in danger, when you have entered his Majesty's service: on the contrary, I have been in action since, and I declare, without hesitation, that I did not feel so much alarm on that occasion, as I did on the one of which I am about to give the history. We were reported ready for sea, and the Admiralty was anxious that we should proceed. The only obstacle to our sailing was, that we had not yet completed our complement of men. The captain applied to the port-admiral, and obtained permission to send parties on shore to impress seamen. The second and third lieutenants, and the oldest midshipman, were despatched on shore every night, with some of the most trustworthy men, and generally brought on board in the morning about half a dozen men, whom they had picked up in the different alehouses, or grog-shops, as the sailors call them. Some of them were retained, but most of

them sent on shore as unserviceable; for it is the custom, when a
man either enters or is impressed, to send him down to the surgeon
in the cockpit, where he is stripped and examined all over, to see if
he be sound and fit for his Majesty's service; and if not, he is sent on
shore again. Impressing appeared to be rather serious work, as far
as I could judge from the accounts which I heard, and from the way
in which our sailors, who were employed on the service, were occasionally beaten and wounded; the seamen who were impressed appearing to fight as hard not to be forced into the service, as they did
for the honour of the country, after they were fairly embarked in it. I
had a great wish to be one of the party before the ship sailed, and
asked O'Brien, who was very kind to me in general, and allowed
nobody to thrash me but himself, if he would take me with him,
which he did on the night after I had made the request. I put on my
dirk, that they might know I was an officer, as well as for my protection. About dusk we rowed on shore, and landed on the Gosport
side: the men were all armed with cutlasses, and wore pea-jackets,
which are very short great-coats made of what they call Flushing.
We did not stop to look at any of the grog-shops in the town, as it
was too early, but walked out about three miles in the suburbs, and
went to a house, the door of which was locked, but we forced it
open in a minute, and hastened to enter the passage, where we
found the landlady standing to defend the entrance. The passage
was long and narrow, and she was a very tall corpulent woman, so
that her body nearly filled it up, and in her hands she held a long
spit pointed at us, with which she kept us at bay. The officers, who
were the foremost, did not like to attack a woman, and she made
such drives at them with her spit, that had they not retreated, some
of them would soon have been ready for roasting. The sailors
laughed and stood outside, leaving the officers to settle the business
how they could. At last, the landlady called out to her husband, "Be
they all out, Jem?" "Yes," replied the husband, "they be all safe
gone." "Well, then," replied she, "I'll soon have all these gone too";
and with these words she made such a rush forward upon us with
her spit, that had we not fallen back and tumbled one over another,
she certainly would have run it through the second lieutenant, who
commanded the party. The passage was cleared in an instant, and as
soon as we were all in the street she bolted us out: so there we were,
three officers and fifteen armed men, fairly beat off by a fat old

woman; the sailors who had been drinking in the house having
made their escape to some other place. But I do not well see how it
could be otherwise; either we must have killed or wounded the
woman, or she would have run us through, she was so resolute.
Had her husband been in the passage, he would have been settled in
a very short time; but what can you do with a woman who fights
like a devil, and yet claims all the rights and immunities of the softer
sex? We all walked away, looking very foolish; and O'Brien observed that the next time he called at that house he would weather
the old cat, for he would take her ladyship in the rear.

We then called at other houses, where we picked up one or two
men, but most of them escaped, by getting out at the windows or
the back doors, as we entered the front. Now there was a grog-shop
which was a very favourite rendezvous of the seamen belonging to
the merchant vessels, and to which they were accustomed to retreat
when they heard that the pressgangs were out. Our officers were
aware of this, and were therefore indifferent as to the escape of the
men, as they knew that they would all go to that place, and confide
in their numbers for beating us off. As it was then one o'clock, they
thought it time to go there; we proceeded without any noise, but
they had people on the look-out, and as soon as we turned the
corner of the lane the alarm was given. I was afraid that they would
all run away, and we should lose them; but, on the contrary, they
mustered very strong on that night, and had resolved to "give
fight." The men remained in the house, but an advanced guard of
about thirty of their wives saluted us with a shower of stones and
mud. Some of our sailors were hurt, but they did not appear to
mind what the women did. They rushed on, and then they were
attacked by the women with their fists and nails. Notwithstanding
this, the sailors only laughed, pushing the women on one side, and
saying, "Be quiet, Poll";—"Don't be foolish, Molly";—"Out of the
way, Sukey; we a'n't come to take away your fancy man"; with
expressions of that sort, although the blood trickled down many of
their faces, from the way in which they had been clawed. Thus we
attempted to force our way through them, but I had a very narrow
escape even in this instance. A woman seized me by the arm, and
pulled me towards her; had it not been for one of the quarter-
masters I should have been separated from my party; but, just as
they dragged me away, she caught hold of me by the leg, and

stopped them. "Clap on here, Peg," cried the woman to another, "and let's have this little midshipmite; I wants a baby to dry nurse." Two more women came to her assistance, catching hold of my other arm, and they would have dragged me out of the grasp of the quarter-master, had he not called out for more help on his side, upon which two of the seamen laid hold of my other leg, and there was such a tussle (all at my expense), such pulling and hauling; sometimes the women gained an inch or two of me, then the sailors got it back again. At one moment I thought it was all over with me, and in the next I was with my own men. "Pull devil; pull baker!" cried the women, and then they laughed, although I did not, I can assure you, for I really think that I was pulled out an inch taller, and my knees and shoulders pained me very much indeed. At last the women laughed so much that they could not hold on, so I was dragged into the middle of our own sailors, where I took care to remain; and, after a little more squeezing and fighting, was carried by the crowd into the house. The seamen of the merchant ships had armed themselves with bludgeons and other weapons, and had taken a position on the tables. They were more than two to one against us, and there was a dreadful fight, as their resistance was very desperate. Our sailors were obliged to use their cutlasses, and for a few minutes I was quite bewildered with the shouting and swearing, pushing and scuffling, collaring and fighting, together with the dust raised up, which not only blinded, but nearly choked me. By the time that my breath was nearly squeezed out of my body, our sailors got the best of it, which the landlady and women of the house perceiving, they put out all the lights, so that I could not tell where I was; but our sailors had every one seized his man, and contrived to haul him out of the street door, where they were collected together, and secured.

Now again I was in great difficulty; I had been knocked down and trod upon, and when I did contrive to get up again, I did not know the direction in which the door lay. I felt about by the wall, and at last came to a door, for the room was at that time nearly empty, the women having followed the men out of the house. I opened it, and found that it was not the right one, but led into a little side parlour, where there was a fire, but no lights. I had just discovered my mistake, and was about to retreat, when I was shoved in from behind, and the key turned upon me: there I was all alone, and, I must acknowledge, very much frightened, as I thought that the vengeance of the women would be wreaked upon me. I considered that my death was certain, and that, like the man Orpheus I had read of in my books, I should be torn to pieces by these Bacchanals.* However, I reflected that I was an officer in his Majesty's service, and that it was my duty, if necessary, to sacrifice my life for my king and country. I thought of my poor mother; but as it made me unhappy, I tried to forget her, and call to my memory all I had read of the fortitude and courage of various brave men, when death stared them in the face. I peeped through the key-hole, and perceived that the candles were re-lighted, and that there were only women in the room, who were talking all at once, and not thinking about me. But in a minute or two, a woman came in from the street, with her long black hair hanging about her shoulders, and her cap in her hand. "Well," cried she, "they've nabbed my husband; but I'll be dished if I hav'n't boxed up the midshipmite in that parlour, and he shall take his place." I thought I should have died when I looked at the woman, and perceived her coming up to the door, followed by some others, to unlock it. As the door opened, I drew my dirk, resolving to die like an officer, and as they advanced I retreated to a corner, brandishing my dirk, without saying a word. "Vell," cried the woman who had made me a prisoner, "I do declare I likes to see a puddle in a storm—only look at the little biscuit-nibbler showing fight! Come, my lovey, you belongs to me."

"Never!" exclaimed I with indignation. "Keep off, or I shall do you mischief" (and I raised my dirk in advance); "I am an officer and a gentleman."

"Sall," cried the odious woman, "fetch a mop and a pail of dirty water, and I'll trundle that dirk out of his fist."

"No, no," replied another rather good-looking young woman, "leave him to me—don't hurt him—he really is a very nice little man. What's your name, my dear?"

"Peter Simple is my name," replied I; "and I am a king's officer, so be careful what you are about."

"Don't be afraid, Peter, nobody shall hurt you; but you must not

---

* Orpheus: In Greek mythology, a musician so distraught over the death of his wife, Euridice, that he swore to have nothing to do with other women. Enraged by this vow, the women of his hometown, Thrace, tore him to pieces.

draw your dirk before ladies, that's not like an officer and a gentleman—so put up your dirk, that's a good boy."

"I will not," replied I, "unless you promise me that I shall go away unmolested."

"I do promise you that you shall, upon my word, Peter—upon my honour—will that content you?"

"Yes," replied I, "if everyone else will promise the same."

"Upon our honours," they all cried together; upon which I was satisfied, and putting my dirk into its sheath, was about to quit the room.

"Stop, Peter," said the young woman who had taken my part; "I must have a kiss before you go." "And so must I; and so must we all," cried the other women.

I was very much shocked, and attempted to draw my dirk again, but they had closed in with me, and prevented me. "Recollect your honour," cried I to the young woman, as I struggled.

"My honour!—Lord bless you, Peter, the less we say about that the better."

"But you promised that I should go away quietly," said I, appealing to them.

"Well, and so you shall; but recollect, Peter, that you are an officer and a gentleman—you surely would not be so shabby as to go away without treating us. What money have you got in your pocket?" and, without giving me time to answer, she felt in my pocket, and pulled out my purse, which she opened. "Why, Peter, you are as rich as a Jew," said she, as they counted thirty shillings on the table. "Now, what shall we have?"

"Anything you please," said I, "provided that you will let me go."

"Well, then, it shall be a gallon of gin. Sall, call Mrs Flanagan. Mrs Flanagan, we want a gallon of gin, and clean glasses."

Mrs Flanagan received the major part of my money, and in a minute returned with the gin and wine-glasses.

"Now, Peter, my cove, let's all draw round the table, and make ourselves cosy."

"O no," replied I, "take my money, drink the gin, but pray let me go"; but they wouldn't listen to me. Then I was obliged to sit down with them, the gin was poured out, and they made me drink a glass, which nearly choked me. It had, however, one good effect, it gave me courage, and in a minute or two, I felt as if I could fight them all. The door of the room was on the same side as the fire-place, and I perceived that the poker was between the bars, and red hot. I complained that I was cold, although I was in a burning fever; and they allowed me to get up to warm my hands. As soon as I reached the fire-place, I snatched out the red-hot poker, and, bran-dishing it over my head, made for the door. They all jumped up to detain me, but I made a poke at the foremost, which made her run back with a shriek. (I do believe that I burnt her nose.) I seized my opportunity, and escaped into the street, whirling the poker round my head, while all the women followed, hooting and shouting after me. I never stopped running and whirling my poker until I was reeking with perspiration, and the poker was quite cold. Then I looked back, and found that I was alone. It was very dark; every house was shut up, and not a light to be seen anywhere. I stopped at the corner, not knowing where I was, or what I was to do. I felt very miserable indeed, and was reflecting on my wisest plan, when who should turn the corner, but one of the quarter-masters who had been left on shore by accident. I knew him by his pea-jacket and straw hat to be one of our men, and I was delighted to see him. I told him what had happened, and he replied that he was going to a house where the people knew him and would let him in. When we arrived there, the people of the house were very civil; the landlady made us some purl, which the quarter-master ordered, and which I thought very good indeed.* After we had finished the jug, we both fell asleep in our chairs. I did not awaken until I was roused by the quarter-master, at past seven o'clock, when we took a wherry, and went off to the ship.

---

* Purl: Heated beer mixed with gin, sometimes flavored with sugar and ginger.

—✿✿✿—

CHAPTER XI

O'Brien takes me under his protection—The ship's company are paid, so are the bumboat-women, the Jews, and the emancipationist after a fashion—We go to sea— Doctor O'Brien's cure for sea-sickness—One pill of the doctor's more than a dose.

WHEN WE ARRIVED, I reported myself to the first lieutenant, and told him the whole story of the manner in which I had been treated, showing him the poker, which I brought on board with me. He heard me very patiently, and then said, "Well, Mr Simple, you may be the greatest fool of your family for all I know to the contrary, but never pretend to be a fool with me. That poker proves the contrary: and if your wit can serve you upon your own emergency, I expect that it will be employed for the benefit of the service." He then sent for O'Brien, and gave him a lecture for allowing me to go with the pressgang, pointing out, what was very true, that I could have been of no service, and might have met with a serious accident. I went down on the main-deck, and O'Brien came to me. "Peter," said he, "I have been jawed for letting you go, so it is but fair that you should be thrashed for having asked me." I wished to argue the point, but he cut all argument short, by kicking me down the hatchway; and thus ended my zealous attempt to procure seamen for his Majesty's service.

At last the frigate was full manned; and, as we had received drafts of men from other ships, we were ordered to be paid previously to our going to sea. The people on shore always find out when a ship is to be paid, and very early in the morning we were surrounded with wherries, laden with Jews and other people, some requesting admittance to sell their goods, others to get paid for what they had allowed the sailors to take up upon credit. But the first lieutenant would not allow any of them to come on board until after the ship was paid; although they were so urgent that he was forced to place sentries in the chains with cold shot, to stave the boats if they came alongside. I was standing at the gangway, looking at the crowd of boats, when a black-looking fellow in one of the wherries said to me, "I say, sir, let me slip in at the port, and I have a very nice present to make you"; and he displayed a gold seal, which he held up to me. I immediately ordered the sentry to keep him further off, for I was very much affronted at his supposing me capable of being bribed to disobey my orders. About eleven o'clock the dock-yard boat, with all the pay-clerks, and the cashier, with his chest of money, came on board, and was shown into the fore-cabin, where the captain attended the pay-table. The men were called in, one by one, and, as the amount of the wages due had been previously calculated, they were paid very fast. The money was always received in their hats, after it had been counted out in the presence of the officers and captain. Outside the cabin-door there stood a tall man in black, with hair straight combed, who had obtained an order from the port-admiral to be permitted to come on board. He attacked every sailor as he came out, with his money in his hat, for a subscription to emancipate the slaves in the West Indies; but the sailors would not give him anything, swearing that the niggers were better off than they were; for they did not work harder by day, and had no watch and watch to keep during the night. "Sarvitude is sarvitude all over the world, my old psalm-singer," replied one. "They sarve their masters, as in duty bound; we sarve the king, 'cause he can't do without us—and he never axes our leave, but helps himself."

"Yes," replied the straight-haired gentleman; "but slavery is a very different thing."

"Can't say that I see any difference; do you, Bill?"

"Not I: and I suppose as if they didn't like it, they'd run away."

"Run away! poor creatures," said the black gentleman. "Why, if they did, they would be flogged."

"Flogged—heh; well, and if we run away, we are to be hanged. The nigger's better off nor we: ar'n't he, Tom?" Then the purser's steward came out: he was what they call a bit of a lawyer,—that is, had received more education than the seamen in general.

"I trust, sir," said the man in black, "that you will contribute something."

"Not I, my hearty: I owe every farthing of my money, and more too, I'm afraid."

"Still, sir, a small trifle."

"Why, what an infernal rascal you must be, to ask a man to give away what is not his own property! Did I not tell you that I owed it all? There's an old proverb—be just before you're generous. Now, it's my opinion that, you are a methodistical, good-for-nothing blackguard; and if anyone is such a fool as to give you money, you will keep it for yourself."

When the man found that he could obtain nothing at the door, he went down on the lower deck, in which he did not act very wisely; for now that the men were paid, the boats were permitted to come alongside, and so much spirits were smuggled in, that most of the seamen were more or less intoxicated. As soon as he went below, he commenced distributing prints of a black man kneeling in chains, and saying, "Am not I your brother?" Some of the men laughed, and swore that they would paste their brother up in the mess, to say prayers for the ship's company; but others were very angry, and abused him. At last, one man, who was tipsy, came up to him. "Do you pretend for to insinivate that this crying black thief is my brother?"

"To be sure I do," replied the methodist.*

"Then take that for your infernal lie," said the sailor, hitting him in the face right and left, and knocking the man down into the cable tier, from whence he climbed up, and made his escape out of the frigate as soon as he was able.

The ship was now in a state of confusion and uproar; there were Jews trying to sell clothes, or to obtain money for clothes which they had sold; bumboat-men and bumboat-women showing their long bills, and demanding or coaxing for payment; other people from the shore, with hundreds of small debts; and the sailors' wives, sticking close to them, and disputing every bill presented, as an extortion or a robbery. There was such bawling and threatening, laughing and crying—for the women were all to quit the ship before sunset—at one moment a Jew was upset, and all his hamper of clothes tossed into the hold; at another, a sailor was seen hunting everywhere for a Jew who had cheated him,—all squabbling or skylarking, and many of them very drunk. It appeared to me that the sailors had rather a difficult point to settle. They had three claimants upon them, the Jew for clothes, the bumboat-men for their mess in harbour, and their

* William Wilberforce and other abolitionists (often Methodists or Quakers) were frequently accused by pro-slavery forces of being indifferent to the plight of sailors and poor British workers. The Emancipation Act was passed March 25, 1833 (taking effect on August 1, 1834), abolishing slavery throughout all British colonies.

wives for their support during their absence; and the money which they received was, generally speaking, not more than sufficient to meet one of the demands. As it may be supposed, the women had the best of it; the others were paid a trifle, and promised the remainder when they came back from their cruise; and although, as the case stood then, it might appear that two of the parties were ill-used, yet in the long run they were more than indemnified, for their charges were so extravagant, that if one-third of their bills were paid, there would still remain a profit. About five o'clock the orders were given for the ship to be cleared. All disputed points were settled by the sergeant of marines with a party, who divided their antagonists from the Jews; and every description of persons not belonging to the ship, whether male or female, was dismissed over the side. The hammocks were piped down, those who were intoxicated were put to bed, and the ship was once more quiet. Nobody was punished for having been tipsy, as pay-day is considered, on board a man-of-war, as the winding-up of all incorrect behaviour, and from that day the sailors turn over a new leaf; for, although some latitude is permitted, and the seamen are seldom flogged in harbour, yet the moment that the anchor is at the bows, strict discipline is exacted, and intoxication must no longer hope to be forgiven.

The next day everything was prepared for sea, and no leave was permitted to the officers. Stock of every kind was brought on board, and the large boats hoisted and secured. On the morning after, at daylight, a signal from the flag-ship in harbour was made for us to unmoor; our orders had come down to cruise in the Bay of Biscay. The captain came on board, the anchor weighed, and we ran through the Needles with a fine N.E. breeze. I admired the scenery of the Isle of Wight, looked with admiration at Alum Bay, was astonished at the Needle rocks, and then felt so very ill that I went down below. What occurred for the next six days I cannot tell. I thought that I should die every moment, and lay in my hammock or on the chests for the whole of that time, incapable of eating, drinking, or walking about. O'Brien came to me on the seventh morning, and said, that if I did not exert myself I never should get well; that he was very fond of me and had taken me under his protection, and, to prove his regard, he would do for me what he would not take the trouble to do for any other youngster in the ship, which was, to give me a good basting, which was a sovereign remedy for sea-sickness. He suited the action to the word, and drubbed me on the ribs without mercy, until I thought the breath was out of my body, and then he took out a rope's end and thrashed me until I obeyed his orders to go on deck immediately. Before he came to me, I could never have believed it possible that I could have obeyed him; but somehow or other I did contrive to crawl up the ladder to the main-deck, where I sat down on the shot-racks and cried bitterly. What would I have given to have been at home again! It was not my fault that I was the greatest fool in the family, yet how was I punished for it! If this was kindness from O'Brien, what had I to expect from those who were not partial to me? But, by degrees, I recovered myself, and certainly felt a great deal better, and that night I slept very soundly. The next morning O'Brien came to me again. "It's a nasty slow fever, that sea-sickness, my Peter, and we must drive it out of you"; and then he commenced a repetition of yesterday's remedy until I was almost a jelly. Whether the fear of being thrashed drove away my sea-sickness, or whatever might be the real cause of it, I do not know, but this is certain, that I felt no more of it after the second beating, and the next morning when I awoke I was very hungry. I hastened to dress myself before O'Brien came to me, and did not see him until we met at breakfast.

"Pater," said he, "let me feel your pulse."

"Oh no!" replied I, "indeed I'm quite well."

"Quite well! Can you eat biscuit and salt butter?"

"Yes, I can."

"And a piece of fat pork?"

"Yes, that I can."

"It's thanks to me then, Pater," replied he; "so you'll have no more of my medicine until you fall sick again."

"I hope not," replied I, "for it was not very pleasant."

"Pleasant! you simple Simple, when did you ever hear of physic being pleasant, unless a man prescribe for himself? I suppose you'd be after lollipops for the yellow fever. Live and larn, boy, and thank Heaven that you've found somebody who loves you well enough to baste you when it's good for your health."

I replied, "that I certainly hoped that much as I felt obliged to him, I should not require any more proofs of his regard."

"Any more such *striking* proofs, you mean, Pater; but let me tell you that they were sincere proofs, for since you've been ill I've been eating your pork and drinking your grog, which latter can't be too plentiful in the Bay of Biscay. And now that I've cured you, you'll be tucking all that into your own little breadbasket, so that I'm no gainer, and I think that you may be convinced that you never had or will have two more disinterested thumpings in all your born days. However, you're very welcome, so say no more about it."

I held my tongue and ate a very hearty breakfast. From that day I returned to my duty, and was put into the same watch with O'Brien, who spoke to the first lieutenant, and told him that he had taken me under his charge.

CHAPTER XII

New theory of Mr Muddle remarkable for having no end to it—Novel practice of Mr Chucks—O'Brien commences his history—There were giants in those days—I bring up the master's night-glass.

A S I HAVE ALREADY MENTIONED sufficient of the captain and the first lieutenant to enable the reader to gain an insight into their characters, I shall now mention two very odd personages who were my shipmates, the carpenter and the boatswain. The carpenter, whose name was Muddle, used to go by the appellation of Philosopher Chips, not that he followed any particular school, but had formed a theory of his own, from which he was not to be dissuaded. This was, that the universe had its cycle of events turned round, so that in a certain period of time everything was to happen over again. I never could make him explain upon what data his calculations were founded; he said, that if he explained it, I was too young to comprehend it; but the fact was this, "that in 27,672 years everything that was going on now would be going on again, with the same people as were existing at this present time." He very seldom ventured to make the remark to Captain Savage, but to the first lieutenant he did very often. "I've been as close to it as possible, sir, I do assure you, although you find fault; but 27,672 years ago you were first lieutenant of this ship, and I was carpenter, although we recollect nothing about it; and 27,672 years hence we shall both be standing by this boat, talking about the repairs, as we are now."

"I do not doubt it, Mr Muddle," replied the first lieutenant; "I dare say that it is all very true, but the repairs must be finished this night, and 27,672 years hence you will have the order just as positive as you have it now, so let it be done."

This theory made him very indifferent as to danger, or indeed as to anything. It was of no consequence, the affair took its station in the course of time. It had happened at the above period, and would happen again. Fate was fate. But the boatswain was a more amusing personage. He was considered to be the *taughtest* (that is, the most active and severe) boatswain in the service. He went by the name of "Gentleman Chucks"—the latter was his surname. He appeared to have received half an education; sometimes his language was for a few sentences remarkably well chosen, but, all of a sudden, he would break down at a hard word; but I shall be able to let the reader into more of his history as I go on with my adventures. He had a very handsome person, inclined to be stout, keen eyes, and hair curling in ringlets. He held his head up, and strutted as he walked. He declared "that an officer should look like an officer, and *comport* himself accordingly." In his person he was very clean, wore rings on his great fingers, and a large frill to his bosom, which stuck out like the back fin of a perch, and the collar of his shirt was always pulled up to a level with his cheek-bones. He never appeared on deck without his "persuader," which was three rattans twisted into one, like a cable; sometimes he called it his Order of the Bath, or his Trio juncto in Uno; and this persuader was seldom idle. He attempted to be very polite, even when addressing the common seamen, and, certainly, he always commenced his observations to them in a very gracious manner, but, as he continued, he became less choice in his phraseology. O'Brien said that his speeches were like the Sin of the poet, very fair at the upper part of them, but shocking at the lower extremities.* As a specimen of them, he would say to the man on the forecastle, "Allow me to observe, my dear

* *Sin of the poet: A reference to John Milton's epic poem,* Paradise Lost *(1674), in which Sin is personified as the mother of Death. Sin is described in Book II, lines 650–53, as a creature who ". . . seemed woman to the waist, and fair, / But ended foul in many a scaly fold / Voluminous and vast, a serpent arm'd / With mortal sting."*

man, in the most delicate way in the world, that you are spilling that tar upon the deck—a deck, sir, if I may venture to make the observation, I had the duty of seeing holystoned this morning. You understand me, sir, you have defiled his Majesty's forecastle. I must do my duty, sir, if you neglect yours; so take that—and that—and that—(thrashing the man with his rattan)—you d——d hay-making son of a sea-cook. Do it again, d——n your eyes, and I'll cut your liver out."

I remember one of the ship's boys going forward with a kid of dirty water to empty in the head, without putting his hand up to his hat as he passed the boatswain. "Stop, my little friend," said the boatswain, pulling out his frill, and raising up both sides of his shirt-collar. "Are you aware, sir, of my rank and station in society?"

"Yes, sir," replied the boy, trembling, and eyeing the rattan.

"Oh, you are!" replied Mr Chucks. "Had you not been aware of it, I should have considered a gentle correction necessary, that you might have avoided such an error in future; but, as you *were* aware of it, why then, d——n you, you have no excuse, so take that—and that—you yelping, half-starved abortion. I really beg your pardon, Mr Simple," said he to me, as the boy went howling forward, for I was walking with him at the time; "but really the service makes brutes of us all. It is hard to sacrifice our health, our night's rest, and our comforts; but still more so, that in my responsible situation, I am obliged too often to sacrifice my gentility."

The master was the officer who had charge of the watch to which I was stationed; he was a very rough sailor, who had been brought up in the merchant service, not much of a gentleman in his appearance, very good-tempered, and very fond of grog. He always quarrelled with the boatswain, and declared that the service was going to the devil, now that warrant officers put on white shirts, and wore frills to them. But the boatswain did not care for him; he knew his duty, he did his duty, and if the captain was satisfied, he said, that the whole ship's company might grumble. As for the master, he said, the man was very well, but having been brought up in a collier, he could not be expected to be very refined; in fact, he observed, pulling up his shirt-collar—"it was impossible to make a silk purse out of a sow's ear." The master was very kind to me, and used to send me down to my hammock before my watch was half over.

Until that time, I walked the deck with O'Brien, who was a very pleasant companion, and taught me everything that he could, connected with my profession. One night, when he had the middle watch, I told him I should like very much if he would give me the history of his life. "That I will, my honey," replied he, "all that I can remember of it, though I have no doubt but that I've forgotten the best part of it. It's now within five minutes of two bells, so we'll heave the log and mark the board, and then I'll spin you a yarn, which will keep us both from going to sleep." O'Brien reported the rate of sailing to the master, marked it down on the log-board, and then returned.

"So now, my boy, I'll come to an anchor on the topsail halyard rack, and you may squeeze your thread-paper little carcass under my lee, and then I'll tell you all about it. First and foremost, you must know that I am descended from the great O'Brien Borru, who was king in his time, as the great Fingal was before him. Of course you've heard of Fingal?"

"I can't say that I ever did," replied I.

"Never heard of Fingal!—murder! Where must you have been all your life? Well, then, to give you some notion of Fingal, I will first tell you how Fingal bothered the great Scotch giant, and then I'll go on with my own story. Fingal, you must know, was a giant himself, and no fool of one, and anyone that affronted him was as sure of a bating, as I am to keep the middle watch to-night. But there was a giant in Scotland as tall as the mainmast, more or less, as we say when we a'n't quite sure, as it saves telling more lies than there's occasion for. Well, this Scotch giant heard of Fingal, and how he had beaten everybody, and he said, 'Who is this Fingal? By Jasus,' says he in Scotch, 'I'll just walk over and see what he's made of.' So he walked across the Irish Channel, and landed within half-a-mile of Belfast, but whether he was out of his depth or not I can't tell, although I suspect that he was not dry footed. When Fingal heard that this great chap was coming over, he was in a devil of a fright, for they told him that the Scotchman was taller by a few feet or so. Giants, you know, measure by feet, and don't bother themselves about the inches, as we little devils are obliged to do. So Fingal kept a sharp look-out for the Scotchman, and one fine morning, there he was, sure enough, coming up the hill to Fingal's house. If Fingal was afraid before, he had more reason to be afraid when he saw the fellow, for he looked for all the world like the Monument upon a voyage of discovery. So Fingal ran into his house, and called to his wife Shaya, 'My vourneen,' says he, 'be quick now; there's that big bully of a Scotchman coming up the hill. Kiver me up with the blankets, and if he asks who is in bed, tell him it's the child.' So Fingal laid down on the bed, and his wife had just time to cover him up, when in comes the Scotchman, and though he stooped low, he broke his head against the portal. 'Where's that baste Fingal?' says he, rubbing his forehead; 'show him to me, that I may give him a bating.' 'Whisht, whisht!' cries Shaya, 'you'll wake the babby, and then him that you talk of bating will be the death of you, if he comes in.' 'Is that the babby?' cried the Scotchman with surprise, looking at the great carcass muffled up in the blankets. 'Sure it is,' replied Shaya, 'and Fingal's babby too; so don't you wake him, or Fingal will twist your neck in a minute.' 'By the cross of St Andrew,' replied the giant, 'then it's time for me to be off; for if that's his babby, I'll be but a mouthful to the fellow himself. Good morning to ye.' So the Scotch giant ran out of the house, and never stopped to eat or drink until he got back to his own hills, foreby he was nearly drowned in having mistaken his passage across the Channel in his great hurry. Then Fingal got up and laughed, as well he might, at his own 'cuteness; and so ends my story about Fingal. And now I'll begin about myself. As I said before, I am descended from the great O'Brien, who was a king in his time, but that time's past. I suppose, as the world turns round, my children's children's posterity may be kings again, although there seems but little chance of it just now; but there's ups and downs on a grand scale, as well as in a man's own history, and the wheel of fortune keeps turning for the comfort of those who are at the lowest spoke, as I may be just now. To cut the story a little shorter, I skip down to my great-grandfather, who lived like a real gentleman, as he was, upon his ten thousand a year. At last he died, and eight thousand of the ten was buried with him. My grandfather followed his father all in good course of time, and only left my father about one hundred acres of bog, to keep up the dignity of the family. I am the youngest of ten, and devil a copper have I but my pay, or am I likely to have. You may talk about *descent*, but a more *descending* family than mine was never in existence, for here am I with twenty-five pounds a-year, and a half-pay of 'nothing a day, and find myself,' when my great ancestor did just what he pleased with all Ireland, and everybody in it. But this is all nothing, except to prove satisfactorily that I am not worth a skillagalee and that is the reason which induces me to condescend to serve his Majesty.* Father M'Grath, the priest, who lived with my father, taught me the elements, as they call them. I thought I had enough of the elements then, but I've seen a deal more of them since. 'Terence,' says my father to me one day, 'what do you mane to do?' 'To get my dinner, sure,' replied I, for I was not a little hungry. 'And so you shall to-day, my vourneen,' replied my father, 'but in future you must do something to get your own dinner: there's not praties enow for the whole of ye. Will you go to the *say?*' 'I'll just step down and look at it,' says I, for we lived but sixteen Irish miles from the coast; so when I had finished my meal, which did not take long, for want of ammunition, I trotted down to the Cove to see what a ship might be like, and I happened upon a large one sure enough, for there lay a three-decker with an admiral's flag at the fore. 'May be you'll be so civil as to tell me what ship that is,' said I to a sailor on the pier. 'It's the *Queen Charlotte,*' replied he, 'of one hundred and twenty guns.' Now when I looked at her size, and compared her with all the little smacks and hoys lying about her, I very naturally asked how old she was; he replied, that she was no more than three years old. 'But three years old!' thought I to myself, 'it's a fine vessel you'll be when you'll come of age, if you grow at that rate: you'll be as tall as the top of Bencrow,' (that's a mountain we have in our parts). You see, Peter, I was a fool at that time, just as you are now; but by-and-by, when you've had as many thrashings as I have had, you may chance to be as clever. I went back to my father, and told him all I had seen, and he replied, that if I liked it I might be a midshipman on board of her, with nine hundred men under my command. He forgot to say how many I should have over me, but I found that out afterwards. I agreed, and my father ordered his pony and went to the lord-lieutenant, for he had interest enough for that. The lord-lieutenant spoke to the admiral, who was staying at the palace, and I was ordered on board as midshipman. My father fitted me out pretty handsomely, telling all the tradesmen that their bills should be paid with my first prize-money; and thus, by promises and blarney, he

* *Skillagalee: A coin with little worth.*

got credit for all I wanted.* At last all was ready: Father M'Grath gave me his blessing, and told me that if I died like an O'Brien, he would say a power of masses for the good of my soul. 'May you never have the trouble, sir,' said I. 'Och, trouble! a pleasure, my dear boy,' replied he, for he was a very polite man; so off I went with my big chest, not quite so full as it ought to have been, for my mother cribbed one half of my stock for my brothers and sisters. 'I hope to be back again soon, father,' said I as I took my leave. 'I hope not, my dear boy,' replied he: 'a'n't you provided for, and what more would you have?' So, after a deal of bother, I was fairly on board, and I parted company with my chest, for I stayed on deck, and that went down below. I stared about with all my eyes for some time, when who should be coming off but the captain, and the officers were ordered on deck to receive him. I wanted to have a quiet survey of him, so I took up my station on one of the guns, that I might examine him at my leisure. The boatswain whistled, the marines presented arms, and the officers all took off their hats as the captain came on the deck, and then the guard was dismissed, and they all walked about the deck as before; but I found it very pleasant to be astride on the gun, so I remained where I was. 'What do you mane by that, you big young scoundrel?' says he, when he saw me. 'It's nothing at all I mane,' replied I; 'but what do you mane by calling an O'Brien a scoundrel?' 'Who is he?' said the captain to the first lieutenant. 'Mr O'Brien, who joined the ship about an hour since.' 'Don't you know better than to sit upon a gun?' said the captain. 'To be sure I do,' replied I, 'when there's anything better to sit upon.' 'He knows no better, sir,' observed the first lieutenant. 'Then he must be taught,' replied the captain. 'Mr O'Brien, since you have perched yourself on that gun to please yourself, you will now continue there for two hours to please me. Do you understand, sir?— you'll ride on that gun for two hours.' 'I understand, sir,' replied I; 'but I am afraid that he won't move without spurs, although there's plenty of *metal* in him.' The captain turned away and laughed as he went into his cabin, and all the officers laughed, and I laughed too, for I perceived no great hardship in sitting down an hour or two, any more than I do now. Well, I soon found that, like a young

* *Prize-money: Profits accruing from the sale of a prize, an enemy vessel and its cargo captured at sea. The money was divided up between officers and crew.*

bear, all my troubles were to come. The first month was nothing but fighting and squabbling with my messmates; they called me a *raw* Irishman, and *raw* I was, sure enough, from the constant thrashings and coltings I received from those who were bigger and stronger than myself; but nothing lasts for ever—as they discovered that whenever they found blows I could find back, they got tired of it, and left me and my brogue alone. We sailed for the Toolong fleet."

"What fleet?" inquired I.

"Why, the Toolong fleet, so called, I thought, because they remained too long in harbour, bad luck to them; and then we were off Cape See-see (devil a bit could we see of them except their mastheads) for I don't know how many months. But I forgot to say that I got into another scrape just before we left harbour. It was my watch when they piped to dinner, and I took the liberty to run below, as my messmates had a knack of forgetting absent friends. Well, the captain came on board, and there were no side boys, no side ropes, and no officers to receive him. He came on deck foaming with rage, for his dignity was hurt, and he inquired who was the midshipman of the watch. 'Mr O'Brien,' said they all. 'Devil a bit,' replied I, 'it was my forenoon watch.' 'Who relieved you, sir?' said the first lieutenant. 'Devil a soul, sir,' replied I; 'for they were all too busy with their pork and beef.' 'Then why did you leave the deck without relief?' 'Because, sir, my stomach would have had but little relief if I had remained.' The captain, who stood by, said, 'Do you see those cross-trees, sir?' 'Is it those little bits of wood that you mane, on the top there, captain?' 'Yes, sir; now just go up there, and stay until I call you down. You must be brought to your senses, young man, or you'll have but little prospect in the service.' 'I've an idea that I'll have plenty of prospect when I get up there,' replied I, 'but it's all to please you.' So up I went, as I have many a time since, and as you often will, Peter, just to enjoy the fresh air and your own pleasant thoughts, all at one and the same time.

"At last I became much more used to the manners and customs of *say*-going people, and by the time that I had been fourteen months off Cape See-see, I was considered a very genteel young midshipman, and my messmates (that is, all that I could thrash, which didn't leave out many) had a very great respect for me.

"The first time that I put my foot on shore was at Minorca, and then I put my foot into it (as we say), for I was nearly killed for a heretic, and only saved by proving myself a true Catholic, which proves that religion is a great comfort in distress, as Father M'Grath used to say. Several of us went on shore, and having dined upon a roast turkey, stuffed with plum-pudding (for everything else was cooked in oil, and we could not eat it), and having drunk as much wine as would float a jolly-boat, we ordered donkeys, to take a little equestrian exercise.* Some went off tail on end, some with their hind-quarters uppermost, and then the riders went off instead of the donkeys; some wouldn't go off at all; as for mine he would go—and where the devil do you think he went? Why, into the church where all the people were at mass; the poor brute was dying with thirst, and smelt water. As soon as he was in, notwithstanding all my tugging and hauling, he ran his nose into the holy-water font, and drank it all up. Although I thought, that seeing how few Christians have any religion, you could not expect much from a donkey, yet I was very much shocked at the sacrilege, and fearful of the consequences. Nor was it without reason, for the people in the church were quite horrified, as well they might be, for the brute drank as much holy-water as would have purified the whole town of Port Mahon, suburbs and all to boot. They rose up from their knees and seized me, calling upon all the saints in the calendar. Although I knew what they meant, not a word of their lingo could I speak, to plead for my life, and I was almost torn to pieces before the priest came up. Perceiving the danger I was in, I wiped my finger across the wet nose of the donkey, crossed myself, and then went down on my knees to the priests, crying out *Culpa mea*, as all good Catholics do—though 'twas no fault of mine, as I said before, for I tried all I could, and tugged at the brute till my strength was gone. The priests perceived by the manner in which I crossed myself that I was a good Catholic, and guessed that it was all a mistake of the donkey's. They ordered the crowd to be quiet, and sent for an interpreter, when I explained the whole story. They gave me absolution for what the donkey had done, and after that, as it was very rare to meet an English officer who was a good Christian, I was in great favour during my stay at Minorca, and was living in plenty, paying for nothing, and as happy as a cricket. So the jackass proved a very good friend, and, to reward him, I hired him every day, and gal-

---

* *Jolly-boat: A light boat used chiefly for small work.*

loped him all over the island. But, at last, it occurred to me that I had broken my leave, for I was so happy on shore that I quite forgot that I had only permission for twenty-four hours, and I should not have remembered it so soon, had it not been for a party of marines, headed by a sergeant, who took me by the collar, and dragged me off my donkey. I was taken on board, and put under an arrest for my misconduct. Now, Peter, I don't know anything more agreeable than being put under an arrest. Nothing to do all day but eat and drink, and please yourself, only forbid to appear on the quarter-deck, the only place that a midshipman wishes to avoid. Whether it was to punish me more severely, or whether he forgot all about me, I can't tell, but it was nearly two months before I was sent for to the cabin; and the captain, with a most terrible frown, said, that he trusted that my punishment would be a warning to me, and that now I might return to my duty. 'Plase your honour,' said I, 'I don't think that I've been punished enough yet.' 'I am glad to find that you are so penitent, but you are forgiven, so take care that you do not oblige me to put you again in confinement.' So, as there was no persuading him, I was obliged to return to my duty again; but I made a resolution that I would get into another scrape again as soon as I dared—"

"Sail on the starboard bow!" cried the look-out man.

"Very well," replied the master; "Mr O'Brien—where's Mr O'Brien?"

"Is it me you mane, sir?" said O'Brien, walking up to the master, for he had sat down so long in the topsail-halyard rack, that he was wedged in and could not get out immediately.

"Yes, sir; go forward, and see what that vessel is."

"Ay, ay, sir," said O'Brien. "And Mr Simple," continued the master, "go down and bring me up my night-glass."*

"Yes, sir," replied I. I had no idea of a night-glass; and as I observed that about this time his servant brought him up a glass of grog, I thought it very lucky that I knew what he meant. "Take care that you don't break it, Mr Simple." "Oh, then, I'm all right," thought I; "he means the tumbler." So down I went, called up the gun-room steward, and desired him to give me a glass of grog for Mr Doball. The steward tumbled out in his shirt, mixed the grog,

* Night-glass: A short refracting telescope for night use.

and gave it to me, and I carried it up very carefully to the quarter-deck.

During my absence, the master had called the captain, and in pursuance of his orders, O'Brien had called the first lieutenant, and when I came up the ladder, they were both on deck. As I was ascending, I heard the master say, "I have sent young Simple down for my night-glass, but he is so long, that I suppose he has made some mistake. He's but half a fool." "That I deny," replied Mr Falcon, the first lieutenant, just as I put my foot on the quarter-deck; "he's no fool." "Perhaps not," replied the master. "Oh, here he is. What made you so long, Mr Simple—where is my night-glass?"

"Here it is, sir," replied I, handing him the tumbler of grog; "I told the steward to make it stiff." The captain and the first lieutenant burst out into a laugh—for Mr Doball was known to be very fond of grog; the former walked aft to conceal his mirth; but the latter remained. Mr Doball was in a great rage. "Did not I say that the boy was half-a-fool?" cried he to the first lieutenant. "At all events, I'll not allow that he has proved himself so in this instance," replied Mr Falcon, "for he has hit the right nail on the head." Then the first lieutenant joined the captain, and they both went off laughing. "Put it on the capstan, sir," said Mr Doball to me, in an angry voice. "I'll punish you by-and-by." I was very much astonished; I hardly knew whether I had done right or wrong; at all events, thought I to myself, I did for the best; so I put it on the capstan and walked to my own side of the deck. The captain and first lieutenant then went below, and O'Brien came aft. "What vessel is it?" said I.

"To the best of my belief, it's one of your bathing-machines going home with despatches," replied he.

"A bathing-machine," said I; "why I thought that they were hauled up on the beach."

"That's the Brighton sort; but these are made not to go up at all."

"What then?"

"Why, to *go down*, to be sure; and remarkably well they answer their purpose. I won't puzzle you any more, my Peter—I'm spaking helligorically, which I believe means telling a hell of a lie. It's one of your ten-gun brigs, to the best of my knowledge."

I then told O'Brien what had occurred, and how the master was angry with me. O'Brien laughed very heartily, and told me never to mind, but to keep in the lee-scuppers and watch him. "A glass of grog is a bait that he'll play round till he gorges. When you see it to his lips, go up to him boldly, and ask his pardon, if you have offended him, and then, if he's a good Christian, as I believe him to be, he'll not refuse it."

I thought this was very good advice, and I waited under the bulwark on the lee-side. I observed that the master made shorter and shorter turns every time, till at last he stopped at the capstan and looked at the grog. He waited about half a minute, and then he took up the tumbler, and drank about half of it. It was very strong, and he stopped to take breath. I thought this was the right time, and I went up to him. The tumbler was again to his lips, and before he saw me, I said, "I hope, sir, you'll forgive me; I never heard of a night telescope, and knowing that you had walked so long, I thought you were tired, and wanted something to drink to refresh you." "Well, Mr Simple," said he, after he had finished the glass, with a deep sigh of pleasure, "as you meant kindly, I shall let you off this time; but recollect, that whenever you bring me a glass of grog again, it must not be in the presence of the captain or first lieutenant." I promised him very faithfully, and went away quite delighted with my having made my peace with him, and more so, that the first lieutenant had said that I was no fool for what I had done.

At last our watch was over, and about two bells I was relieved by the midshipmen of the next watch. It is very unfair not to relieve in time, but if I said a word I was certain to be thrashed the next day upon some pretence or other. On the other hand, the midshipman whom I relieved was also much bigger than I was, and if I was not up before one bell, I was cut down and thrashed by him: so that between the two I kept much more than my share of the watch, except when the master sent me to bed before it was over.

---∿∿∿---

CHAPTER XIII

The first lieutenant prescribes for one of his patients, his prescriptions consisting of draughts only—O'Brien finishes the history of his life, in which the proverb of "the more, the merrier" is sadly disproved—Shipping a new pair of boots causes the unshipping of their owner—Walking home after a ball, O'Brien meets with an accident.

THE NEXT MORNING I was on deck at seven bells, to see the hammocks stowed, when I was witness to Mr Falcon, the first lieutenant, having recourse to one of his remedies to cure a mizen-top-boy of smoking, a practice to which he had a great aversion. He never interfered with the men smoking in the galley, or chewing tobacco; but he prevented the boys, that is, lads under twenty or there-abouts, from indulging in the habit too early. The first lieutenant smelt the tobacco as the boy passed him on the quarter-deck. "Why, Neill, you have been smoking," said the first lieutenant. "I thought you were aware that I did not permit such lads as you to use tobacco."

"If you please, sir," replied the mizen-top-man, touching his hat, "I'se got worms, and they say that smoking be good for them."

"Good for them!" said the first lieutenant; "yes, very good for them, but very bad for you. Why, my good fellow, they'll thrive upon tobacco until they grow as large as conger eels. Heat is what the worms are fond of; but cold—cold will kill them. Now I'll cure you. Quarter-master, come here. Walk this boy up and down the weather-gangway, and every time you get forward abreast of the main-tack block, put his mouth to windward, squeeze him sharp by the nape of the neck until he opens his mouth wide, and there keep him and let the cold air blow down his throat, while you count ten; then walk him aft, and when you are forward again proceed as before.—Cold kills worms, my poor boy, not tobacco—I wonder that you are not dead by this time."

The quarter-master, who liked the joke, as did all the seamen, seized hold of the lad, and as soon as they arrived forward, gave him such a squeeze of the neck as to force him to open his mouth, if it were only to cry with pain. The wind was very fresh, and blew into his mouth so strong, that it actually whistled while he was forced to keep it open; and thus, he was obliged to walk up and down, cooling his inside, for nearly two hours, when the first lieutenant sent for him, and told him, that he thought all the worms must be dead by that time; but if they were not, the lad was not to apply his own remedies, but come to him for another dose. However, the boy was of the same opinion as the first lieutenant, and never complained of worms again.

A few nights afterwards, when we had the middle watch, O'Brien proceeded with his story.

"Where was it that I left off?"

"You left off at the time that you were taken out of confinement."

"So I did, sure enough; and it was with no good-will that I went to my duty. However, as there was no help for it, I walked up and down the deck as before, with my hands in my pockets, thinking of old Ireland, and my great ancestor, O'Brien Borru. And so I went on behaving myself like a real gentleman, and getting into no more scrapes, until the fleet put into the Cove of Cork, and I found myself within a few miles of my father's house. You may suppose that the anchor had hardly kissed the mud, before I went to the first lieutenant, and asked leave to go on shore. Now the first lieutenant was not in the sweetest of tempers, seeing as how the captain had been hauling him over the coals for not carrying on the duty according to his satisfaction. So he answered me very gruffly, that I should not leave the ship. 'Oh, bother!' said I to myself, 'this will never do.' So up I walked to the captain, and touching my hat, reminded him that 'I had a father and mother, and a pretty sprinkling of brothers and sisters, who were dying to see me, and that I hoped that he would give me leave.' 'Ax the first lieutenant,' said he, turning away. 'I have, sir,' replied I, 'and he says that the devil a bit shall I put my foot on shore.' 'Then you have misbehaved yourself,' said the captain. 'Not a bit of it, Captain Willis,' replied I; 'it's the first lieutenant who has misbehaved.' 'How, sir?' answered he, in an angry tone. 'Why, sir, didn't he misbehave just now in not carrying on the duty according to your will and pleasure? and didn't you serve him out just as he deserved—and isn't he sulky because you did—and arn't that the reason why I am not to go on shore? You see, your honour, it's all true as I said; and the first lieutenant has misbehaved and not I. I hope you will allow me to go on shore, captain, God bless you! and make some allowance for my parental feelings towards the arthers of my existence.' 'Have you any fault to find with Mr O'Brien?' said the captain to the first lieutenant, as he came aft. 'No more than I have with midshipmen in general; but I believe it is not the custom for officers to ask leave to go on shore before the sails are furled and the yards squared.' 'Very true,' replied the captain; 'therefore, Mr O'Brien, you must wait until the watch is called, and then, if you ask the first lieutenant, I have no doubt but you will have leave granted to you to go and see your friends.' 'Thank'e kindly, sir,' replied I; and I hoped that the yards and sails would be finished off as soon as possible, for my heart was in my mouth, and I felt that if I had been kept much longer, it would have flown on shore before me.

"I thought myself very clever in this business, but I was never a greater fool in my life; for there was no such hurry to have gone on shore, and the first lieutenant never forgave me for appealing to the captain—but of that by-and-by, and all in good time. At last I obtained a grumbling assent to my going on shore, and off I went like a sky-rocket. Being in a desperate hurry, I hired a jaunting-car to take me to my father's house. 'Is it the O'Brien of Ballyhinch that you mane?' inquired the spalpeen who drove the horse.* 'Sure it is,' replied I; 'and how is he, and all the noble family of the O'Briens?'' 'All well enough, bating the boy Tim, who caught a bit of confusion in his head the other night at the fair, and now lies at home in bed quite insensible to mate or drink; but the doctors give hopes of his recovery, as all the O'Briens are known to have such thick heads.' 'What do you mane by that, bad manners to you?' said I, 'but poor Tim—how did it happen—was there a fight?' 'Not much of a fight— only a bit of a skrummage—three crowners' inquests, no more.' 'But you are not going the straight road, you thief,' said I, seeing that he had turned off to the left. 'I've my reasons for that, your honour,' replied he; 'I always turn away from the Castle out of principle—I lost a friend there, and it makes me melancholy.' 'How came that for to happen?' 'All by accident, your honour; they hung my poor brother Patrick there, because he was a bad hand at arithmetic.' 'He should have gone to a better school then,' said I. 'I've an idea that it was a bad school that he was brought up in,' replied he, with a sigh. 'He was a cattle-dealer, your honour, and one day, somehow or

---

* *Spalpeen: A scamp.*

another, he'd a cow too much—all for not knowing how to count, your honour,—bad luck to his school-master.' 'All that may be very true,' said I, 'and pace be to his soul; but I don't see why you are to drag me, that's in such a hurry, two miles out of my way, out of principle.' 'Is your honour in a hurry to get home? Then I'll be thinking they'll not be in such a hurry to see you.' 'And who told you that my name was O'Brien, you baste?—and do you dare to say that my friends won't be glad to see me?' 'Plase your honour, it's all an idea of mine—so say no more about it. Only this I know: Father M'Grath, who gives me absolution, tould me the other day that I ought to pay him, and not run in debt, and then run away like Terence O'Brien, who went to say without paying for his shirts, and his shoes, and his stockings, nor anything else, and who would live to be hanged as sure as St Patrick swam over the Liffey with his head under his arm.' 'Bad luck to that Father M'Grath,' cried I; 'devil burn me, but I'll be revenged upon him!'

"By that time we had arrived at the door of my father's house. I paid the rapparee, and in I popped.* There was my father and mother, and all my brothers and sisters (bating Tim, who was in bed sure enough, and died next day), and that baste Father M'Grath to boot. When my mother saw me she ran to me and hugged me as she wept on my neck, and then she wiped her eyes and sat down again; but nobody else said 'How d'ye do?' or opened their mouths to me. I said to myself, 'Sure there's some trifling mistake here,' but I held my tongue. At last they all opened their mouths with a vengeance. My father commenced—'Ar'n't you ashamed on yourself, Terence O'Brien?' 'Ar'n't you ashamed on yourself, Terence O'Brien?' cried Father M'Grath. 'Ar'n't you ashamed on yourself?' cried out all my brothers and sisters in full chorus, whilst my poor mother put her apron to her eyes and said nothing. 'The devil a bit for myself, but very much ashamed for you all,' replied I, 'to treat me in this manner. What's the meaning of all this?' 'Haven't they seized my two cows to pay for your toggery, you spalpeen?' cried my father. 'Haven't they taken the hay to pay for your shoes and stockings?' cried Father M'Grath. 'Haven't they taken the pig to pay for that ugly hat of yours?' cried my eldest sister. 'And haven't they taken my hens to pay for that dirk of yours?' cried another. 'And all our

* *Rapparee: A thief.*

best furniture to pay for your white shirts and black cravats?' cried Murdock, my brother. 'And haven't we been starved to death ever since?' cried they all. 'Ochone!' said my mother. 'The devil they have!' said I, when they'd all done. 'Sure I'm sorry enough, but it's no fault of mine. Father, didn't you send me to say?' 'Yes, you rapparee; but didn't you promise—or didn't I promise for you, which is all one and the same thing—that you'd pay it all back with your prize-money—and where is it? answer that, Terence O'Brien.' 'Where is it, father? I'll tell you; it's where next Christmas is—coming, but not come yet.' 'Spake to him, Father M'Grath,' said my father. 'Is not that a lie of yours, Terence O'Brien, that you're after telling now?' said Father M'Grath; 'give me the money.' 'It's no lie, Father M'Grath; if it pleased you to die to-morrow, the devil of a shilling have I to jingle on your tombstone for good luck, bating those three or four, which you may divide between you,' and I threw them on the floor.

" 'Terence O'Brien,' said Father M'Grath, 'it's absolution that you'll be wanting to-morrow, after all your sins and enormities; and the devil a bit shall you have—take that now.'

" 'Father M'Grath,' replied I very angrily, 'it's no absolution that I'll want from you, anyhow—take that now.'

" 'Then you have had your share of heaven; for I'll keep you out of it, you wicked monster,' said Father M'Grath—'take that now.'

" 'If it's no better than a midshipman's berth,' replied I, 'I'd just as soon stay out; but I'll creep in in spite of you—take that now, Father M'Grath.'

" 'And who's to save your soul, and send you to heaven, if I don't, you wicked wretch? but I'll see you d——d first—so take that now, Terence O'Brien.'

" 'Then I'll turn Protestant, and damn the Pope—take that now, Father M'Grath.'

"At this last broadside of mine, my father and all my brothers and sisters raised a cry of horror, and my mother burst into tears. Father M'Grath seized hold of the pot of holy water, and dipping in the little whisk, began to sprinkle the room, saying a Latin prayer, while they all went on squalling at me. At last, my father seized the stool, which he had been seated upon, and threw it at my head. I dodged, and it knocked down Father M'Grath, who had just walked behind me in full song. I knew that it was all over after that, so I sprang over his carcass, and gained the door. 'Good morning to ye all, and better manners to you next time we meet,' cried I, and off I set as fast as I could for the ship.

"I was melancholy enough as I walked back, and thought of what had passed. 'I need not have been in such a confounded hurry,' said I to myself, 'to ask leave, thereby affronting the first lieutenant'; and I was very sorry for what I had said to the priest, for my conscience thumped me very hard at having even pretended that I'd turn Protestant, which I never intended to do, nor never will, but live and die a good Catholic, as all my posterity have done before me, and, as I trust, all my ancestors will for generations to come. Well, I arrived on board, and the first lieutenant was very savage. I hoped he would get over it, but he never did; and he continued to treat me so ill that I determined to quit the ship, which I did as soon as we arrived in Cawsand Bay. The captain allowed me to go, for I told him the whole truth of the matter, and he saw that it was true; so he recommended me to the captain of a jackass frigate, who was in want of midshipmen."

"What do you mean by a jackass frigate?" inquired I.

"I mean one of your twenty-eight gun-ships, so called, because there is as much difference between them and a real frigate, like the one we are sailing in, as there is between a donkey and a racehorse. Well, the ship was no sooner brought down to the dockyard to have her ballast taken in, than our captain came down to her—a little, thin, spare man, but a man of weight nevertheless, for he brought a great pair of scales with him, and weighed everything that was put on board. I forget his real name, but the sailors christened him Captain Avoirdupois.* He had a large book, and in it he inserted the weight of the ballast, and of the shot, water, provisions, coals, standing and running rigging, cables, and everything else. Then he weighed all the men, and all the midshipmen, and all the midshipmen's chests, and all the officers, with everything belonging to them: lastly, he weighed himself, which did not add much to the sum total. I don't exactly know what this was for; but he was always talking about centres of gravity, displacement of fluid, and Lord knows what. I believe it was to find out the longitude, somehow or other, but I didn't remain long enough in her to know the end of it,

* *Avoirdupois: A system of weights.*

for one day I brought on board a pair of new boots, which I forgot to report that they might be put into the scales, which swang on the gangway; and whether the captain thought that they would sink his ship, or for what I cannot tell, but he ordered me to quit her imme- diately—so, there I was adrift again. I packed up my traps and went on shore, putting on my new boots out of spite, and trod into all the mud and mire I could meet, and walked up and down from Plym- outh to Dock until I was tired, as a punishment to them, until I wore the scoundrels out in a fortnight.

"One day I was in the dockyard, looking at a two-decker in the basin, just brought forward for service, and I inquired who was to be the captain. They told me that his name was O'Connor. Then's he's a countryman of mine, thought I, and I'll try my luck. So I called at Goud's Hotel, where he was lodging, and requested to speak with him. I was admitted, and I told him, with my best bow, that I had come as a volunteer for his ship, and that my name was O'Brien. As it happened, he had some vacancies, and liking my brogue, he asked me in what ships I had served. I told him, and also my reason for quitting my last—which was, because I was turned out of it. I explained the story of the boots, and he made inquiries, and found that it was all true; and then he gave me a vacancy as master's mate. We were ordered to South America, and the trade winds took us there in a jiffey. I liked my captain and officers very much; and what was better, we took some good prizes. But some- how or other, I never had the luck to remain long in one ship, and that by no fault of mine; at least, not in this instance. All went on as smooth as possible, until one day the captain took us on shore to a ball, at one of the peaceable districts. We had a very merry night of it; but as luck would have it, I had the morning watch to keep, and see the decks cleaned, and as I never neglected my duty, I set off about three o'clock in the morning, just at break of day, to go on board of the ship. I was walking along the sands, thinking of the pretty girl that I'd been dancing with, and had got about half-way to the ship, when three rapparees of Spanish soldiers came from be- hind a rock and attacked me with their swords and bayonets. I had only my dirk, but I was not to be run through for nothing, so I fought them as long as I could. I finished one fellow, but at last they finished me; for a bayonet passed through my body, and I forgot all about it. Well, it appears—for I can only say to the best of my knowledge and belief—that after they had killed me, they stripped me naked and buried me in the sand, carrying away with them the body of their comrade. So there I was—dead and buried."

"But, O'Brien," said I—

"Whist—hold your tongue—you've not heard the end of it. Well, I had been buried about an hour—but not very deep it appears, for they were in too great a hurry—when a fisherman and his daughter came along the beach, on their way to the boat; and the daughter, God bless her! did me the favour to tread upon my nose. It was clear that she had never trod upon an Irishman's nose before, for it surprised her, and she looked down to see what was there, and not seeing anything, she tried it again with her foot, and then she scraped off the sand, and discovered my pretty face. I was quite warm and still breathing, for the sand had stopped the blood, and prevented my bleeding to death. The fisherman pulled me out, and took me on his back to the house where the captain and officers were still dancing. When he brought me in, there was a great cry from the ladies, not because I was murdered, for they are used to it in those countries, but because I was naked, which they considered a much more serious affair. I was put to bed and a boat despatched on board for our doctor; and in a few hours I was able to speak, and tell them how it happened. But I was too ill to move when the ship sailed, which she was obliged to do in a day or two afterwards, so the captain made out my discharge, and left me there. The family were French, and I remained with them for six months before I could obtain a passage home, during which I learnt their language, and a very fair allowance of Spanish to boot. When I arrived in England, I found that the prizes had been sold, and that the money was ready for distribution. I produced my certificate, and received £167 for my share. So it's come at last, thought I.

"I never had such a handful of money in my life; but I hope I shall again very soon. I spread it out on the table as soon as I got home, and looked at it, and then I said to myself, 'Now, Terence O'Brien, will you keep this money to yourself, or send it home?' Then I thought of Father M'Grath, and the stool that was thrown at my head, and I was very near sweeping it all back into my pocket. But then I thought of my mother, and of the cows, and the pig, and the furniture, all gone; and of my brothers and sisters wanting praties, and I made a vow that I'd send every farthing of it to them, after which Father M'Grath would no longer think of not giving me absolution. So I sent them every doit, only reserving for myself the pay which I had received, amounting to about £30: and I never felt more happy in my life than when it was safe in the post-office, and fairly out of my hands. I wrote a bit of a letter to my father at the time, which was to this purpose:—

" 'HONOURED FATHER,—Since our last pleasant meeting, at which you threw the stool at my head, missing the pigeon and hitting the crow, I have been dead and buried, but am now quite well, thank God, and want no absolution from Father M'Grath, bad luck to him. And what's more to the point, I have just received a batch of prize-money, the first I have handled since I have served his Majesty, and every farthing of which I now send to you, that you may get back your old cows, and the pig, and all the rest of the articles seized to pay for my fitting out; so never again ask me whether I am not ashamed of myself; more shame to you for abusing a dutiful son like myself, who went to sea at your bidding, and has never had a real good potato down his throat ever since. I'm a true O'Brien, tell my mother, and don't mane to turn Protestant, but uphold the religion of my country; although the devil may take Father M'Grath and his holy water to boot. I sha'n't come and see you, as perhaps you may have another stool ready for my head, and may take better aim next time. So no more at present from your affectionate son,
'TERENCE O'BRIEN.'

"About three weeks afterwards I received a letter from my father, telling me that I was a real O'Brien, and that if any one dared hint to the contrary, he would break every bone in his body; that they had received the money, and thanked me for a real gentleman as I was; that I should have the best stool in the house next time I came, not for my head, but for my tail; that Father M'Grath sent me his blessing, and had given me absolution for all I had done, or should do for the next ten years to come; that my mother had cried with joy at my dutiful behaviour; and that all my brothers and sisters (bating Tim, who had died the day after I left them) wished me good luck, and plenty more prize-money to send home to them.

"This was all very pleasant; and I had nothing left on my mind but to get another ship; so I went to the port-admiral, and told him how it was that I left my last: and he said, 'that being dead and buried was quite sufficient reason for any one leaving his ship, and that he would procure me another, now that I had come to life again.' I was sent on board of the guard-ship, where I remained about ten days, and then was sent round to join this frigate—and so my story's ended; and there's eight bells striking—so the watch is ended too; jump down, Peter, and call Robinson, and tell him that I'll trouble him to forget to go to sleep again as he did last time, and leave me here kicking my heels, contrary to the rules and regulations of the service."

—◦◦◦—

CHAPTER XIV

The first lieutenant has more patients—Mr Chucks, the boatswain, lets me into the secret of his gentility.

Before I proceed with my narrative, I wish to explain to the reader that my history was not written in after-life, when I had obtained a greater knowledge of the world. When I first went to sea, I promised my mother that I would keep a journal of what passed, with my reflections upon it. To this promise I rigidly adhered, and since I have been my own master, these journals have remained in my possession. In writing, therefore, the early part of my adventures, everything is stated as it was impressed on my mind at the time. Upon many points I have since had reason to form a different opinion from that which is recorded, and upon many others I have since laughed heartily at my folly and simplicity; but still, I have thought it advisable to let the ideas of the period remain, rather than correct them by those of dear-bought experience. A boy of fifteen, brought up in a secluded country town, cannot be expected to reason and judge as a young man who has seen much of life, and passed through a variety of adventures. The reader must therefore remember, that I have referred to my journal for the opinions and feelings which guided me between each distinct anniversary of my existence.

We had now been cruising for six weeks, and I found that my

profession was much more agreeable than I had anticipated. My desire to please was taken for the deed; and, although I occasionally made a blunder, yet the captain and first lieutenant seemed to think that I was attentive to my duty to the best of my ability, and only smiled at my mistakes. I also discovered, that, however my natural capacity may have been estimated by my family, that it was not so depreciated here; and every day I felt more confidence in myself, and hoped, by attention and diligence, to make up for a want of natural endowment. There certainly is something in the life of a sailor which enlarges the mind. When I was at home six months before, I allowed other people to think for me, and acted wholly on the leading-strings of their suggestions; on board, to the best of my ability, I thought for myself. I became happy with my messmates— those who were harsh upon me left off, because I never resented their conduct, and those who were kind to me were even kinder than before. The time flew away quickly, I suppose, because I knew exactly what I had to do, and each day was the forerunner of the ensuing. The first lieutenant was one of the most amusing men I ever knew, yet he never relaxed from the discipline of the service, or took the least liberty with either his superiors or inferiors. His humour was principally shown in his various modes of punishment; and, however severe the punishment was to the party, the manner of inflicting it was invariably a source of amusement to the remainder of the ship's company. I often thought, that although no individual liked being punished, yet, that all the ship's company were quite pleased when a punishment took place. He was very particular about his decks; they were always as white as snow, and nothing displeased him so much as their being soiled. It was for that reason that he had such an objection to the use of tobacco. There were spitting-pans placed in different parts of the decks for the use of the men, that they might not dirty the planks with the tobacco-juice. Sometimes a man in his hurry forgot to use these pans, but, as the mess to which the stain might be opposite had their grog stopped if the party were not found out, they took good care not only to keep a look-out, but to inform against the offender. Now the punishment for the offence was as follows—the man's hands were tied behind his back, and a large tin spitting-box fixed to his chest by a strap over the shoulders. All the other boxes on the lower deck were taken away, and he was obliged to walk there, ready to attend the summons of any man who might wish to empty his mouth of the tobacco-juice. The other men were so pleased at the fancy, that they spat twice as much as before, for the pleasure of making him run about. Mr Chucks, the boatswain, called it "the first lieutenant's *perambulating* spitting-pan." He observed to me one day, "that really Mr Falcon was such an *epicure* about his decks, that he was afraid to pudding an anchor on the forecastle."

I was much amused one morning watch that I kept. We were stowing the hammocks in the quarter-deck nettings, when one of the boys came up with his hammock on his shoulder, and as he passed the first lieutenant, the latter perceived that he had a quid of tobacco in his cheek. "What have you got there, my good lad—a gum-boil?—your cheek is very much swelled." "No, sir," replied the boy, "there's nothing at all the matter." "O there must be; it is a bad tooth, then. Open your mouth, and let me see." Very reluctantly the boy opened his mouth, and discovered a large roll of tobacco-leaf. "I see, I see," said the first lieutenant, "your mouth wants overhauling, and your teeth cleaning. I wish we had a dentist on board; but as we have not, I will operate as well as I can. Send the armourer up here with his tongs." When the armourer made his appearance, the boy was made to open his mouth, while the chaw of tobacco was extracted with his rough instrument. "There now," said the first lieutenant, "I'm sure that you must feel better already; you never could have had any appetite. Now, captain of the afterguard, bring a piece of old canvas and some sand here, and clean his teeth nicely." The captain of the afterguard came forward, and putting the boy's head between his knees, scrubbed his teeth well with the sand and canvas for two or three minutes. "There, that will do," said the first lieutenant. "Now, my little fellow, your mouth is nice and clean, and you'll enjoy your breakfast. It was impossible for you to have eaten anything with your mouth in such a nasty state. When it's dirty again, come to me, and I'll be your dentist."

One day I was on the forecastle with Mr Chucks, the boatswain, who was very kind to me. He had been showing me how to make the various knots and bends of rope which are used in our service. I am afraid that I was very stupid, but he showed me over and over again, until I learnt how to make them. Amongst others, he taught me a fisherman's bend, which he pronounced to be the *king* of all knots; "and, Mr Simple," continued he, "there is a moral in that knot. You observe, that when the parts are drawn the right way, and together, the more you pull the faster they hold, and the more impossible to untie them; but see, by hauling them apart, how a little difference, a pull the other way, immediately disunites them, and then how easy they cast off in a moment. That points out the necessity of pulling together in this world, Mr Simple, when we wish to hold on, and that's a piece of philosophy worth all the twenty-six thousand and odd years of my friend the carpenter, which leads to nothing but a brown study, when he ought to be attending to his duty."

"Very true, Mr Chucks, you are the better philosopher of the two."

"I am the better educated, Mr Simple, and I trust, more of a gentleman. I consider a gentleman to be, to a certain degree, a philosopher, for very often he is obliged, to support his character as such, to put up with what another person may very properly fly in a passion about. I think coolness is the great character-stick of a gentleman. In the service, Mr Simple, one is obliged to appear angry without indulging the sentiment. I can assure you, that I never lose my temper, even when I use my rattan."

"Why, then, Mr Chucks, do you swear so much at the men? Surely that is not gentlemanly?"

"Most certainly not, sir. But I must defend myself by observing the very artificial state in which we live on board of a man-of-war. Necessity, my dear Mr Simple, has no law. You must observe how gently I always commence when I have to find fault. I do that to prove my gentility; but, sir, my zeal for the service obliges me to alter my language, to prove in the end that I am in earnest. Nothing would afford me more pleasure than to be able to carry on the duty as a gentleman, but that's impossible."

"I really cannot see why."

"Perhaps, then, Mr Simple, you will explain to me why the captain and first lieutenant swear."

"That I do not pretend to answer, but they only do so upon an emergency."

"Exactly so; but, sir, their 'mergency is my daily and hourly duty. In the continual working of the ship I am answerable for all that goes amiss. The life of a boatswain is a life of 'mergency, and therefore I swear."

"I still cannot allow it to be requisite, and certainly it is sinful."

"Excuse me, my dear sir; it is absolutely requisite, and not at all sinful. There is one language for the pulpit, and another for on board ship, and, in either situation, a man must make use of those terms most likely to produce the necessary effect upon his listeners. Whether it is from long custom of the service, or from the indifference of a sailor to all common things and language (I can't exactly explain myself, Mr Simple, but I know what I mean), perhaps constant excitement may do, and therefore he requires more 'stimilis,' as they call it, to make him move. Certain it is, that common parlancy won't do with a common seaman. It is not here as in the scriptures, 'Do this, and he doeth it' (by the bye, that chap must have had his soldiers in tight order); but it is, 'Do this, d——n your eyes,' and then it is done directly. The order to *do* just carries the weight of a cannon-shot, but it wants the perpelling power—the d——n is the gunpowder which sets it flying in the execution of its duty. Do you comprehend me, Mr Simple?"

"I perfectly understand you, Mr Chucks, and I cannot help remarking, and that without flattery, that you are very different from the rest of the warrant officers. Where did you receive your education?"

"Mr Simple, I am here a boatswain with a clean shirt, and, I say it myself, and no one dare gainsay it, also with a thorough knowledge of my duty. But although I do not say that I ever was better off, I can say this, that I've been in the best society, in the company of lords and ladies. I once dined with your grandfather."

"That's more than ever I did, for he never asked me, nor took the least notice of me," replied I.

"What I state is true. I did not know that he was your grandfather until yesterday, when I was talking with Mr O'Brien; but I perfectly recollect him, although I was very young at that time. Now, Mr Simple, if you will promise me as a gentleman (and I know you are one), that you will not repeat what I tell you, then I'll let you into the history of my life."

"Mr Chucks, as I am a gentleman I never will divulge it until you are dead and buried, and not then if you do not wish it."

"When I am dead and buried, you may do as you please; it may then be of service to other people, although my story is not a very long one."

Mr Chucks then sat down upon the fore-end of the booms by the funnel, and I took my place by his side, when he commenced as follows:—

"My father was a boatswain before me—one of the old school, rough as a bear, and drunken as a Gosport fiddler. My mother was—my mother, and I shall say no more. My father was invalided for harbour duty after a life of intoxication, and died shortly afterwards. In the meantime I had been, by the kindness of the port-admiral's wife, educated at a foundation school. I was thirteen when my father died, and my mother, not knowing what to do with me, wished to bind me apprentice to a merchant vessel; but this I refused, and, after six months' quarrelling on the subject, I decided the point by volunteering in the *Narcissus* frigate. I believe that my gentlemanly ideas were innate, Mr Simple; I never, as a child, could bear the idea of the merchant service. After I had been a week on board, I was appointed servant to the purser, where I gave such satisfaction by my alertness and dexterity, that the first lieutenant took me away from the purser to attend upon himself, so that in two months I was a person of such consequence as to create a disturbance in the gun-room, for the purser was very angry, and many of the officers took his part. It was whispered that I was the son of the first lieutenant, and that he was aware of it. How far that may be true I know not, but there was a likeness between us; and my mother, who was a very pretty woman, attended his ship many years before as a bumboat-girl. I can't pretend to say anything about it, but this I do say, Mr Simple—and many will blame me for it, but I can't help my natural feelings—that I had rather be the bye-blow of a gentleman, than the 'gitimate offspring of a boatswain and his wife. There's no chance of good blood in your veins in the latter instance, whereas, in the former you may have stolen a drop or two. It so happened, that after I had served the first lieutenant for about a year, a young lord (I must not mention his name, Mr Simple) was sent to sea by his friends, or by his own choice, I don't know which, but I was told that his uncle, who was 'zeckative, and had an interest in his death, persuaded him to go. A lord at that period, some twenty-five years ago, was a rarity in the service, and they used to salute him when he came on board. The consequence was, that the young lord must have a servant to himself, although all the rest of the midshipmen had but one servant between them. The captain inquired who was the best boy in the ship, and the purser, to whom he appealed, recommended me. Accordingly, much to the annoyance of the first lieutenant (for first lieutenants in those days did not assume as they do now, not that I refer to Mr Falcon, who is a gentleman), I was immediately surrendered to his lordship. I had a very easy, comfortable life of it—I did little or nothing; if inquired for when all hands were turned up, I was cleaning his lordship's boots, or brushing his lordship's clothes, and there was nothing to be said when his lordship's name was mentioned. We went to the Mediterranean (because his lordship's mamma wished it), and we had been there about a year, when his lordship ate so many grapes that he was seized with a dysentery. He was ill for three weeks, and then he requested to be sent to Malta in a transport going to Gibraltar, or rather to the Barbary coast, for bullocks. He became worse every day, and made his will, leaving me all his effects on board, which I certainly deserved for the kindness with which I had nursed him. Off Malta we fell in with a xebeque, bound to Civita Vecchia, and the captain of the transport, anxious to proceed, advised our going on board of her, as the wind was light and contrary, and these Mediterranean vessels sailed better on a wind than the transport.* My master, who was now sinking fast, consented, and we changed our ships. The next day he died, and a gale of wind came on, which prevented us from gaining the port for several days, and the body of his lordship not only became so offensive, but affected the superstition of the Catholic sailors so much, that it was hove overboard. None of the people could speak English, nor could I speak Maltese; they had no idea who we were, and I had plenty of time for cogitation. I had often thought what a fine thing it was to be a lord, and as often wished that I had been born one. The wind was still against us, when a merchant vessel ran down to us, that had left Civita Vecchia for Gibraltar. I desired the captain of the xebeque to make a signal of distress, or rather I did myself, and the vessel, which proved to be English, bore down to us.

"I manned the boat to go on board, and the idea came into my head, that, although they might refuse to take me, they would not refuse a lord. I put on the midshipman's uniform belonging to his

* Xebeque: A small, fast three-masted vessel. Some carried up to four-hundred men and mounted up to twenty-four guns.

lordship (but then certainly belonging to me), and went alongside of the merchant vessel; I told them that I had left my ship for the benefit of my health, and wanted a passage to Gibraltar, on my way home. My title, and immediate acceptance of the terms demanded for my passage, was sufficient. My property was brought from the xebeque; and, of course, as they could not speak English, they could not contradict, even if they suspected. Here, Mr Simple, I must acknowledge a slight flaw in my early history, which I impart to you in confidence; or otherwise I should not have been able to prove that I was correct in asserting that I had dined with your grandfather. But the temptation was too strong, and I could not resist. Think yourself, Mr Simple, after having served as a ship's boy—clouted here, kicked there, damned by one, and sent to hell by another—to find myself treated with such respect and deference, and my lorded this and my lorded that, every minute of the day. During my passage to Gibraltar, I had plenty of time for arranging my plans. I hardly need say that my lord's *kit* was valuable; and what was better, they exactly fitted me. I also had his watches and trinkets, and many other things, besides a bag of dollars. However, they were honestly mine; the only thing that I took was his name, which he had no further occasion for, poor fellow! But it's no use defending what was wrong—it was dishonest, and there's an end of it.

"Now observe, Mr Simple, how one thing leads to another. I declare to you, that my first idea of making use of his lordship's name, was to procure a passage to Gibraltar. I then was undecided how to act; but, as I had charge of his papers and letters to his mother and guardian, I think—indeed I am almost sure—that I should have laid aside my dignity and midshipman's dress, and applied for a passage home to the commissioner of the yard. But it was fated to be otherwise; for the master of the transport went on shore to report and obtain pratique, and he told them everywhere that young Lord A—— was a passenger with him, going to England for the benefit of his health.* In less than half-an-hour, off came the commissioner's boat, and another boat from the governor, requesting the honour of my company, and that I would take a bed at their houses during my stay. What could I do? I began to be frightened;

* *Pratique: License or permission for a ship, after having received a clean bill of health, to use a port.*

but I was more afraid to confess that I was an impostor, for I am sure the master of the transport alone would have kicked me overboard, if I had let him know that he had been so confounded polite to a ship's boy. So I blushed half from modesty and half from guilt, and accepted the invitation of the governor; sending a polite verbal refusal to the commissioner, upon the plea of there being no paper or pens on board. I had so often accompanied my late master, that I knew very well how to conduct myself, and had borrowed a good deal of his air and appearance—indeed, I had a natural taste for gentility. I could write and read; not perhaps so well as I ought to have done, considering the education I had received, but still quite well enough for a lord, and indeed much better than my late master. I knew his signature well enough, although the very idea of being forced to use it made me tremble. However, the die was cast. I ought to observe, that in one point we were not unlike—both had curly light hair and blue eyes; in other points there was no resemblance. I was by far the better-looking chap of the two; and as we had been up the Mediterranean for two years, I had no fear of any doubt as to my identity until I arrived in England. Well, Mr Simple, I dressed myself very carefully, put on my chains and rings, and a little perfume on my handkerchief, and accompanied the aide-de-camp to the governor's, where I was asked after my mother, Lady ———, and my uncle, my guardian, and a hundred other questions. At first I was much confused, which was attributed to bashfulness; and so it was, but not of the right sort. But before the day was over, I had become so accustomed to be called 'my lord,' and to my situation, that I was quite at my ease, and began to watch the motions and behaviour of the company, that I might regulate my comportment by that of good society. I remained at Gibraltar for a fortnight, and then was offered a passage in a transport ordered to Portsmouth. Being an officer, of course it was free to a certain extent. On my passage to England, I again made up my mind that I would put off my dress and title as soon as I could escape from observation; but I was prevented as before. The port-admiral sent off to request the pleasure of my company to dinner. I dared not refuse; and there I was, my lord, as before, courted and feasted by everybody. Tradesmen called to request the honour of my lordship's custom; my table at the hotel was covered with cards of all descriptions; and, to confess the truth, I liked my situation so much, and had been so accustomed to it, that I now began to dislike the idea that one day or other I must resign it, which I determined to do as soon as I quitted the place. My bill at the hotel was very extravagant, and more than I could pay: but the master said it was not of the least consequence; that of course his lordship had not provided himself with cash, just coming from foreign parts, and offered to supply me with money if I required it. This, I will say, I was honest enough to refuse. I left my cards, P.P.C., as they do, Mr Simple, in all well-regulated society, and set off in the mail for London, where I fully resolved to drop my title, and to proceed to Scotland to his lordship's mother, with the mournful intelligence of his death—for you see, Mr Simple, no one knew that his lordship was dead.* The captain of the transport had put him into the xebeque alive, and the vessel bound to Gibraltar had received him, as they imagined. The captain of the frigate had very soon afterwards advices from Gibraltar, stating his lordship's recovery and return to England. Well, I had not been in the coach more than five minutes, when who should get in but a gentleman whom I had met at the port-admiral's; besides which the coachman and others knew me very well. When I arrived in London (I still wore my midshipman's uniform), I went to an hotel recommended to me, as I afterwards found out, the most fashionable in town, my title still following me. I now determined to put off my uniform, and dress in plain clothes—my farce was over. I went to bed that night, and the next morning made my appearance in a suit of mufti, making inquiry of the waiter which was the best conveyance to Scotland.

" 'Post chay and four, my lord. At what time shall I order it?'

" 'O,' replied I, 'I am not sure that I shall go tomorrow.'

"Just at this moment in came the master of the hotel, with the *Morning Post* in his hand, making me a low bow, and pointing to the insertion of my arrival at his hotel among the fashionables. This annoyed me; and now that I found how difficult it was to get rid of my title, I became particularly anxious to be William Chucks, as before. Before twelve o'clock, three or four gentlemen were ushered into my sitting-room, who observing my arrival in that damn'd

---

* *P.P.C.: In a note to Oliver Warner's edition of* Peter Simple *(London: Victor Gollancz, 1969), P.P.C. is defined as being an abbreviation for* pour prendre congé, *meaning to pay a parting call.*

Morning Post, came to pay their respects; and before the day was over I was invited and re-invited by a dozen people. I found that I could not retreat, and I went away with the stream, as I did before at Gibraltar and Portsmouth. For three weeks I was everywhere; and if I found it agreeable at Portsmouth, how much more so in London! But I was not happy, Mr Simple, because I was a cheat, every moment expecting to be found out. But it really was a nice thing to be a lord.

"At last the play was over. I had been enticed by some young men into a gambling-house, where they intended to fleece me; but, for the first night, they allowed me to win, I think, about £300. I was quite delighted with my success, and had agreed to meet them the next evening; but when I was at breakfast, with my legs crossed, reading the *Morning Post*, who should come to see me but my guardian uncle. He knew his nephew's features too well to be deceived; and my not recognising him proved at once that I was an impostor. You must allow me to hasten over the scene which took place—the wrath of the uncle, the confusion in the hotel, the abuse of the waiters, the police officer, and being dragged into a hackney coach to Bow Street. There I was examined and confessed all. The uncle was so glad to find that his nephew was really dead, that he felt no resentment towards me; and as, after all, I had only assumed a name, but had cheated nobody, except the landlord at Portsmouth, I was sent on board the tender off the Tower, to be drafted into a man-of-war. As for my £300, my clothes, &c., I never heard any more of them; they were seized, I presume, by the landlord of the hotel for my bill, and very handsomely he must have paid himself. I had two rings on my fingers, and a watch in my pocket, when I was sent on board the tender, and I stowed them away very carefully. I had also a few pounds in my purse. I was sent round to Plymouth, where I was drafted into a frigate. After I had been there some time, I turned the watch and rings into money, and bought myself a good kit of clothes; for I could not bear to be dirty. I was put into the mizen-top, and no one knew that I had been a lord."

"You found some difference, I should think, in your situation?"

"Yes, I did, Mr Simple; but I was much happier. I could not forget the ladies, and the dinners, and the opera, and all the delights of London, beside the respect paid to my title, and I often sighed for them; but the police officer and Bow Street also came to my recollection, and I shuddered at the remembrance. It had, however, one good effect; I determined to be an officer if I could, and learnt my duty, and worked my way up to quarter-master, and thence to boatswain—and I know my duty, Mr Simple. But I've been punished for my folly ever since. I formed ideas above my station in life, and cannot help longing to be a gentleman. It's a bad thing for a man to have ideas above his station."

"You certainly must find some difference between the company in London and that of the warrant officers."

"It's many years back now, sir; but I can't get over the feeling. I can't 'sociate with them at all. A man may have the feelings of a gentleman, although in a humble capacity; but how can I be intimate with such people as Mr Dispart or Mr Muddle, the carpenter? All very well in their way, Mr Simple, but what can you expect from officers who boil their 'tators in a cabbage-net hanging in the ship's coppers, when they know that there is one-third of a stove allowed them to cook their victuals on?"

CHAPTER XV

I go on service and am made prisoner by an old lady, who, not able to obtain my hand, takes part of my finger as a token—O'Brien rescues me—A lee shore and narrow escape.

TWO OR THREE DAYS after this conversation with Mr Chucks, the captain ran the frigate in shore, and when within five miles we discovered two vessels under the land. We made all sail in chase, and cut them off from escaping round a sandy point which they attempted to weather. Finding that they could not effect their purpose, they ran on shore under a small battery of two guns, which commenced firing upon us. The first shot which whizzed between the masts had to me a most terrific sound, but the officers and men laughed at it, so of course I pretended to do the same, but in reality I could see nothing to laugh at. The captain ordered the starboard watch to be piped to quarters, and the boats to be cleared, ready for hoisting out; we then anchored within a mile of the battery, and returned the fire. In the meantime, the remainder of the ship's company hoisted out and lowered down four boats, which were manned and armed to storm the battery. I was very anxious to go on service, and O'Brien, who had command of the first cutter, allowed me to go with him, on condition that I stowed myself away under the fore-sheets, that the captain might not see me before the boats had shoved off. This I did, and was not discovered. We pulled in abreast towards the battery, and in less than ten minutes the boats were run on the beach, and we jumped out. The Frenchmen fired a gun at us as we pulled close to the shore, and then ran away, so that we took possession without any fighting, which, to confess the truth, I was not sorry for, as I did not think that I was old or strong enough to cope hand to hand with a grown-up man. There were a few fishermen's huts close to the battery, and while two of the boats went on board of the vessels, to see if they could be got off, and others were spiking the guns and destroying the carriages, I went with O'Brien to examine them: they were deserted by the people, as might have been supposed, but there was a great quantity of fish in them, apparently caught that morning. O'Brien pointed to a very large skate—"Murder in Irish!" cried he, "it's the very ghost of my grandmother! we'll have her if it's only for the family likeness. Peter, put your finger into the gills, and drag her down to the boat." I could not force my finger into the gills, and as the animal appeared quite dead, I hooked my finger into its mouth; but I made a sad mistake, for the animal was alive, and immediately closed its jaws, nipping my finger to the bone, and holding it so tight that I could not withdraw it, and the pain was too great to allow me to pull it away by main force, and tear my finger, which it held so fast. There I was, caught in a trap, and made a prisoner by a flat-fish. Fortunately, I hallooed loud enough to make O'Brien, who was close down to the boats, with a large codfish under each arm, turn round and come to my assistance. At first he could not help me, from laughing so much; but at last he forced open the jaw of the fish with his cutlass, and I got my finger out, but very badly torn indeed. I then took off my garter, tied it round the tail of the skate, and dragged it to the boat, which was all ready to shove off. The other boats had found it impossible to get the vessels off without unloading—so, in pursuance of the captain's orders, they were set on fire, and before we lost sight of them, had burnt down to the water's edge. My finger was very bad for three weeks, and the officers laughed at me very much, saying that I narrowly escaped being made a prisoner of by an "old maid."

We continued our cruise along the coast, until we had run down into the Bay of Arcason, where we captured two or three vessels, and obliged many more to run on shore. And here we had an instance showing how very important it is that a captain of a man-of-war should be a good sailor, and have his ship in such discipline as to be strictly obeyed by his ship's company. I heard the officers unanimously assert, after the danger was over, that nothing but the presence of mind which was shown by Captain Savage could have saved the ship and her crew. We had chased a convoy of vessels to the bottom of the bay: the wind was very fresh when we hauled off, after running them on shore, and the surf on the beach even at that time was so great, that they were certain to go to pieces before they could be got afloat again. We were obliged to double-reef the topsails as soon as we hauled to the wind, and the weather looked very threatening. In an hour afterwards, the whole sky was covered with one black cloud, which sank so low as nearly to touch our mast-heads, and a tremendous sea, which appeared to have risen up almost by magic, rolled in upon us, setting the vessel on a dead lee shore. As the night closed in, it blew a dreadful gale, and the ship was nearly buried with the press of canvas which she was obliged to carry; for had we sea-room, we should have been lying-to under storm stay-sails; but we were forced to carry on at all risks, that we might claw off shore. The sea broke over as we lay in the trough, deluging us with water from the forecastle, aft to the binnacles; and very often as the ship descended with a plunge, it was with such force that I really thought she would divide in half with the violence of the shock. Double breechings were rove on the guns, and they were further secured with tackles, and strong cleats nailed behind the trunnions, for we heeled over so much when we lurched, that the guns were wholly supported by the breechings and tackles, and had one of them broken loose, it must have burst right through the lee side of the ship, and she must have foundered.* The captain, first lieutenant, and most of the officers remained on deck during the whole of the

---

* *Trunnions: The short cylindrical projections on both sides of a cannon. They provide the axis upon which the cannon pivots when being aimed.*

night; and really, what with the howling of the wind, the violence of the rain, the washing of the water about the decks, the working of the chain-pumps, and the creaking and groaning of the timbers, I thought that we must inevitably have been lost; and I said my prayers at least a dozen times during the night, for I felt it impossible to go to bed. I had often wished, out of curiosity, that I might be in a gale of wind, but I little thought it was to have been a scene of this description, or anything half so dreadful. What made it more appalling was, that we were on a lee-shore, and the consultations of the captain and officers, and the eagerness with which they looked out for daylight, told us that we had other dangers to encounter besides the storm. At last the morning broke, and the look-out man upon the gangway called out, "Land on the lee-beam." I perceived the master dash his fist against the hammock-rails, as if with vexation, and walk away without saying a word, and looking very grave.

"Up, there, Mr Wilson," said the captain, to the second lieutenant, "and see how far the land trends forward, and whether you can distinguish the point." The second lieutenant went up the main-rigging, and pointed with his hand to about two points before the beam.

"Do you see two hillocks inland?"

"Yes, sir," replied the second lieutenant.

"Then it is so," observed the captain to the master, "and if we weather it, we shall have more sea-room. Keep her full, and let her go through the water; do you hear, quarter-master?"

"Ay, ay, sir."

"Thus, and no nearer, my man. Ease her with a spoke or two when she sends; but be careful, or she'll take the wheel out of your hands."

It really was a very awful sight. When the ship was in the trough of the sea, you could distinguish nothing but a waste of tumultuous water; but when she was borne up on the summit of the enormous waves, you then looked down, as it were, upon a low, sandy coast, close to you, and covered with foam and breakers. "She behaves nobly," observed the captain, stepping aft to the binnacle, and looking at the compass; "if the wind does not baffle us, we shall weather." The captain had scarcely time to make the observation, when the sails shivered and flapped like thunder. "Up with the helm; what are you about, quarter-master?"

"The wind has headed us, sir," replied the quarter-master, coolly.

The captain and master remained at the binnacle watching the compass, and when the sails were again full, she had broken off two points, and the point of land was only a little on the lee bow.

"We must wear her round, Mr Falcon. Hands, wear ship—ready, oh, ready."*

"She has come up again," cried the master, who was at the binnacle.

"Hold fast there a minute. How's her head now?"

"N.N.E., as she was before she broke off, sir."

"Pipe belay," said the captain. "Falcon," continued he, "if she breaks off again we may have no room to wear; indeed there is so little room now, that I must run the risk. Which cable was ranged last night—the best bower?"

"Yes, sir."

"Jump down, then, and see it double-bitted and stoppered at thirty fathoms. See it well done—our lives may depend upon it."

The ship continued to hold her course good; and we were within half a mile of the point, and fully expected to weather it, when again the wet and heavy sails flapped in the wind, and the ship broke off two points as before. The officers and seamen were aghast, for the ship's head was right on to the breakers. "Luff now, all you can, quarter-master," cried the captain. "Send the men aft directly. My lads, there is no time for words—I am going to *club-haul* the ship, for there is no room to wear. The only chance you have of safety is to be cool, watch my eye, and execute my orders with precision. Away to your stations for tacking ship. Hands by the best bower anchor. Mr Wilson, attend below with the carpenter and his mates, ready to cut away the cable at the moment that I give the order. Silence, there, fore and aft. Quarter-master, keep her full again for stays. Mind you ease the helm down when I tell you." About a minute passed before the captain gave any further orders. The ship had closed—to within a quarter of a mile of the beach, and the waves curled and topped around us, bearing us down upon the shore, which presented one continued surface of foam, extending to within half a cable's length of our position. The captain waved his hand in silence to the

* *Wear ship: To come around by turning the head away from the wind.*

quarter-master at the wheel, and the helm was put down. The ship turned slowly to the wind, pitching and chopping as the sails were spilling. When she had lost her way, the captain gave the order, "Let go the anchor. We will haul all at once, Mr Falcon," said the captain. Not a word was spoken, the men went to the fore brace, which had not been manned; most of them knew, although I did not, that if the ship's head did not go round the other way, we should be on shore, and among the breakers in half a minute. I thought at the time that the captain had said that he would haul all the yards at once, there appeared to be doubt or dissent on the countenance of Mr Falcon; and I was afterwards told that he had not agreed with the captain, but he was too good an officer, and knew that there was no time for discussion, to make any remark; and the event proved that the captain was right. At last the ship was head to wind, and the captain gave the signal. The yards flew round with such a creaking noise, that I thought the masts had gone over the side, and the next moment the wind had caught the sails, and the ship, which for a moment or two had been on an even keel, careened over to her gunnel with its force. The captain, who stood upon the weather-hammock rails, holding by the main-rigging, ordered the helm amidships, looked full at the sails, and then at the cable, which grew broad upon the weather bow, and held the ship from nearing the shore. At last he cried, "Cut away the cable!" A few strokes of the axes were heard, and then the cable flew out of the hawsehole in a blaze of fire, from the violence of the friction, and disappeared under a huge wave, which struck us on the chess-tree, and deluged us with water fore and aft. But we were now on the other tack, and the ship regained her way and we had evidently increased our distance from the land.

"My lads," said the captain to the ship's company, "you have behaved well, and I thank you; but I must tell you honestly that we have more difficulties to get through. We have to weather a point of the bay on this tack. Mr Falcon, splice the main-brace, and call the watch. How's her head, quarter-master?"

"S.W. by S. Southerly, sir."

"Very well; let her go through the water"; and the captain, beckoning to the master to follow him, went down into the cabin. As our immediate danger was over, I went down into the berth to see if I could get anything for breakfast, where I found O'Brien and two or three more.

"By the powers, it was as nate a thing as ever I saw done," observed O'Brien: "the slightest mistake as to time or management, and at this moment the flat-fish would have been dubbing at our ugly carcasses. Peter, you're not fond of flat-fish, are you, my boy? We may thank Heaven and the captain, I can tell you that, my lads; but now, where's the chart, Robinson? Hand me down the parallel rules and compasses, Peter; they are in the corner of the shelf. Here we are now, a devilish sight too near this infernal point. Who knows how her head is?"

"I do, O'Brien: I heard the quarter-master tell the captain S.W. by S. Southerly."

"Let me see," continued O'Brien, "variation $2^1/4$—leeway— rather too large an allowance of that, I'm afraid; but, however, we'll give her $2^1/2$ points; the *Diomede* would blush to make any more, under any circumstances. Here—the compass—now we'll see"; and O'Brien advanced the parallel rule from the compass to the spot where the ship was placed on the chart. "Bother! you see it's as much as she'll do to weather the other point now, on this tack, and that's what the captain meant, when he told us we had more difficulty. I could have taken my Bible oath that we were clear of everything, if the wind held."

"See what the distance is, O'Brien," said Robinson. It was measured, and proved to be thirteen miles. "Only thirteen miles; and if we do weather, we shall do very well, for the bay is deep beyond. It's a rocky point, you see, just by way of variety. Well, my lads, I've a piece of comfort for you, anyhow. It's not long that you'll be kept in suspense, for by one o'clock this day, you'll either be congratulating each other upon your good luck, or you'll be past praying for. Come, put up the chart, for I hate to look at melancholy prospects; and, steward, see what you can find in the way of comfort." Some bread and cheese, with the remains of yesterday's boiled pork, were put on the table, with a bottle of rum, procured at the time they "spliced the mainbrace"; but we were all too anxious to eat much, and one by one returned on deck to see how the weather was, and if the wind at all favoured us. On deck the superior officers were in conversation with the captain, who had expressed the same fear that O'Brien had in our berth. The men, who knew what they had to expect—for this sort of intelligence is soon communicated through a ship—were assembled in knots, looking very grave, but at the same time not wanting in confidence. They knew that they could trust to the captain, as far as skill or courage could avail them, and sailors are too sanguine to despair, even at the last moment. As for myself, I felt such admiration for the captain, after what I had witnessed that morning, that, whenever the idea came over me, that in all probability I should be lost in a few hours, I could not help acknowledging how much more serious it was that such a man should be lost to his country. I do not intend to say that it consoled me; but it certainly made me still more regret the chances with which we were threatened.

Before twelve o'clock, the rocky point which we so much dreaded was in sight, broad on the lee-bow; and if the low sandy coast appeared terrible, how much more did this, even at a distance: the black masses of rock, covered with foam, which each minute dashed up in the air, higher than our lower mast-heads. The captain eyed it for some minutes in silence, as if in calculation.

"Mr Falcon," said he at last, "we must put the mainsail on her."

"She never can bear it, sir."

"She *must* bear it," was the reply. "Send the men aft to the mainsheet. See that careful men attend the buntlines."

The mainsail was set, and the effect of it upon the ship was tremendous. She careened over so that her lee channels were under the water, and when pressed by a sea, the lee-side of the quarter-deck and gangway were afloat. She now reminded me of a goaded and fiery horse, mad with the stimulus applied; not rising as before, but forcing herself through whole seas, and dividing the waves, which poured in one continual torrent from the forecastle down upon the decks below. Four men were secured to the wheel—the sailors were obliged to cling, to prevent being washed away—the ropes were thrown in confusion to leeward, the shot rolled out of the lockers, and every eye was fixed aloft, watching the masts, which were expected every moment to go over the side. A heavy sea struck us on the broadside, and it was some moments before the ship appeared to recover herself; she reeled, trembled, and stopped her way, as if it had stupefied her. The first lieutenant looked at the captain, as if to say, "This will not do." "It is our only chance," answered the captain to the appeal. That the ship went faster through the water, and held a better wind, was certain; but just before we arrived at the point the gale increased in force. "If anything starts, we are lost, sir," observed the first lieutenant again.

"I am perfectly aware of it," replied the captain, in a calm tone; "but, as I said before, and you must now be aware, it is our only chance. The consequence of any carelessness or neglect in the fitting and securing of the rigging, will be felt now; and this danger, if we escape it, ought to remind us how much we have to answer for if we neglect our duty. The lives of a whole ship's company may be sacrificed by the neglect or incompetence of an officer when in harbour. I will pay you the compliment, Falcon, to say, that I feel convinced that the masts of the ship are as secure as knowledge and attention can make them."

The first lieutenant thanked the captain for his good opinion, and hoped it would not be the last compliment which he paid him.

"I hope not too; but a few minutes will decide the point."

The ship was now within two cables' lengths of the rocky point; some few of the men I observed to clasp their hands, but most of them were silently taking off their jackets, and kicking off their shoes, that they might not lose a chance of escape provided the ship struck.

" 'Twill be touch and go indeed, Falcon," observed the captain (for I had clung to the belaying-pins, close to them, for the last half-hour that the mainsail had been set). "Come aft, you and I must take the helm. We shall want *nerve* there, and only there, now."

The captain and first lieutenant went aft, and took the forespokes of the wheel, and O'Brien, at a sign made by the captain, laid hold of the spokes behind him. An old quarter-master kept his station at the fourth. The roaring of the seas on the rocks, with the howling of the wind, were dreadful; but the sight was more dreadful than the noise. For a few moments I shut my eyes, but anxiety forced me to open them again. As near as I could judge, we were not twenty yards from the rocks, at the time that the ship passed abreast of them. We were in the midst of the foam, which boiled around us; and as the ship was driven nearer to them, and careened with the wave, I thought that our main-yard-arm would have touched the rock; and at this moment a gust of wind came on, which laid the ship on her beam-ends, and checked her progress through the water, while the accumulated noise was deafening. A few moments more the ship dragged on, another wave dashed over her and spent itself upon the rocks, while the spray was dashed back from them, and returned upon the decks. The main rock was within ten yards of her counter, when another gust of wind laid us on our beam-ends, the foresail and mainsail split, and were blown clean out of the bolt-ropes—the ship righted, trembling fore and aft. I looked astern: the rocks were to windward on our quarter, and we were safe. I thought at the time, that the ship, relieved of her courses, and again lifting over the waves, was not a bad similitude of the relief felt by us all at that moment; and, like her, we trembled as we panted with the sudden reaction, and felt the removal of the intense anxiety which oppressed our breasts.

The captain resigned the helm, and walked aft to look at the point, which was now broad on the weather quarter. In a minute or two, he desired Mr Falcon to get new sails up and bend them, and then went below to his cabin. I am sure it was to thank God for our deliverance: I did most fervently, not only then, but when I went to my hammock at night. We were now comparatively safe—in a few hours completely so; for strange to say, immediately after we had weathered the rocks, the gale abated, and before morning we had a reef out of the topsails. It was my afternoon watch, and perceiving Mr Chucks on the forecastle, I went forward to him, and asked him what he thought of it.

"Thought of it, sir!" replied he; "why, I always think bad of it when the elements won't allow my whistle to be heard; and I consider it hardly fair play. I never care if we are left to our own exertions; but how is it possible for a ship's company to do their best, when they cannot hear the boatswain's pipe? However, God be thanked, nevertheless, and make better Christians of us all! As for that carpenter, he is mad. Just before we weathered the point, he told me that it was just the same 27,600 and odd years ago. I do believe that on his death-bed (and he was not far from a very hard one yesterday), he will tell us how he died so many thousand years ago, of the same complaint. And that gunner of ours is a fool. Would you believe it, Mr Simple, he went crying about the decks, 'O my poor guns, what will become of them if they break loose?' He appeared to consider it of no consequence if the ship and ship's company were all lost, provided that his guns were safely landed on the beach. 'Mr Dispart,' said I, at last, 'allow me to observe, in the most delicate way in the world, that you're a d——d old fool.' You see, Mr Simple, it's the duty of an officer to generalise, and be attentive to parts, only in consideration of the safety of the whole. I look after my anchors and cables, as I do after the rigging; not that I care for any of them in particular, but because the safety of a ship depends upon her being well found. I might just as well cry because we sacrificed an anchor and cable yesterday morning, to save the ship from going on shore."

"Very true, Mr Chucks," replied I.

"Private feelings," continued he, "must always be sacrificed for the public service. As you know, the lower deck was full of water, and all our cabins and chests were afloat; but I did not think then about my shirts, and look at them now, all blowing out in the fore-rigging, without a particle of starch left in the collars or the frills. I shall not be able to appear as an officer ought to do for the whole of the cruise."

As he said this, the cooper, going forward, passed by him, and jostled him in passing. "Beg pardon, sir," said the man, "but the ship lurched."

"The ship lurched, did it?" replied the boatswain, who, I am afraid, was not in the best of humours about his wardrobe. "And pray, Mr Cooper, why has heaven granted you two legs, with joints at the knees, except to enable you to counteract the horizontal deviation? Do you suppose they were meant for nothing but to work round a cask with? Hark, sir, did you take me for a post to scrub your pig's hide against? Allow me just to observe, Mr Cooper—just to insinuate, that when you pass an officer, it is your duty to keep at a respectable distance, and not to soil his clothes with your rusty iron jacket. Do you comprehend me, sir; or will this make you recollect in future?" The rattan was raised, and descended in a shower of blows, until the cooper made his escape into the head. "There, take that, you contaminating, stave-dubbing, gimlet-carrying, quintessence of a bung-hole! I beg your pardon, Mr Simple, for interrupting the conversation, but when duty calls, we must obey."

"Very true, Mr Chucks. It's now striking seven bells, and I must call the master—so good-bye."

—◦◦◦—

CHAPTER XVI

News from home—A fatigue party employed at Gibraltar—More particulars in the life of Mr Chucks—A brush with the enemy—A court-martial and a lasting impression.

A FEW DAYS AFTERWARDS, a cutter joined us from Plymouth, with orders for the frigate to proceed forthwith to Gibraltar, where we should learn our destination. We were all very glad of this: for we had had quite enough of cruising in the Bay of Biscay; and, as we understood that we were to be stationed in the Mediterranean, we hoped to exchange gales of wind and severe weather, for fine breezes and a bright sky. The cutter brought out our letters and newspapers. I never felt more happy than I did when I found one put into my hands. It is necessary to be far from home and friends, to feel the real delight of receiving a letter. I went down into the most solitary place in the steerage, that I might enjoy it without interruption. I cried with pleasure before I opened it, but I cried a great deal more with grief, after I had read the contents—for my eldest brother Tom was dead of a typhus fever. Poor Tom! when I called to mind what tricks he used to play me—how he used to borrow my money and never pay me—and how he used to thrash me and make me obey him, because he was my eldest brother—I shed a torrent of tears at his loss; and then I reflected how miserable my poor mother must be, and I cried still more.

"What's the matter, spooney?" said O'Brien, coming up to me. "Who has been licking you now?"

"O, nobody," replied I; "but my eldest brother Tom is dead, and I have no other."

"Well, Peter, I dare say that your brother was a very good brother; but I'll tell you a secret. When you've lived long enough to have a beard to scrape at, you'll know better than to make a fuss about an elder brother. But you're a good, innocent boy just now, so I won't thrash you for it. Come, dry your eyes, Peter, and never mind it. We'll drink his health and long life to him, after supper, and then never think any more about it."

I was very melancholy for a few days; but it was so delightful running down the Portuguese and Spanish coasts, the weather was so warm, and the sea so smooth, that I am afraid I forgot my brother's death sooner than I ought to have done; but my spirits were cheered up, and the novelty of the scene prevented me from thinking. Every one, too, was so gay and happy, that I could not well be otherwise. In a fortnight, we anchored in Gibraltar Bay, and the ship was stripped to refit. There was so much duty to be done, that I did not like to go on shore. Indeed, Mr Falcon had refused some of my messmates, and I thought it better not to ask, although I was very anxious to see a place which was considered so extraordinary. One afternoon, I was looking over the gangway as the people were at supper, and Mr Falcon came up to me and said, "Well, Mr Simple, what are you thinking of?" I replied, touching my hat, that I was wondering how they had cut out the solid rock into galleries, and that they must be very curious.

"That is to say, that you are very curious to see them. Well, then, since you have been very attentive to your duty, and have not asked to go on shore, I will give you leave to go to-morrow morning and stay till gun-fire."

I was very much pleased at this, as the officers had a general invitation to dine with the mess, and all who could obtain leave being requested to come, I was enabled to join the party. The first lieutenant had excused himself on the plea of there being so much to attend to on board; but most of the gun-room officers and some of the midshipmen obtained leave. We walked about the town and fortifications until dinner-time, and then we proceeded to the barracks. The dinner was very good, and we were all very merry; but after the dessert had been brought in, I slipped away with a young ensign, who took me all over the galleries, and explained everything to me, which was a much better way of employing my time than doing as the others did, which the reader will acknowledge. I was at the sally-port before gun-fire—the boat was there, but no officers made their appearance. The gun fired, the drawbridge was hauled up, and I was afraid that I should be blamed; but the boat was not ordered to shove off, as it was waiting for commissioned officers. About an hour afterwards, when it was quite dark, the sentry pointed his arms and challenged a person advancing with, "Who comes there?"—"Naval officer, drunk on a wheelbarrow," was the reply, in a loud singing voice. Upon which, the sentry recovered his arms, singing in return, "Pass naval officer, drunk on a wheel-barrow—and all's well!" and then appeared a soldier in his fatigue dress, wheeling down the third lieutenant in a wheelbarrow, so tipsy that he could not stand or speak. Then the sentry challenged again, and the answer was, "Another naval officer, drunk on a wheelbarrow"; upon which the sentry replied as before, "Pass, another naval officer, drunk on a wheelbarrow—and all's well." This was my friend O'Brien, almost as bad as the third lieutenant; and so they continued for ten minutes, challenging and passing, until they wheeled down the remainder of the party, with the exception of the second lieutenant, who walked arm and arm with the officer who brought down the order for lowering the drawbridge. I was much shocked, for I considered it very disgraceful; but I afterwards was told, which certainly admitted of some excuse, that the mess were notorious for never permitting any of their guests to leave the table sober. They were all safely put into the boat, and I am glad to say, the first lieutenant was in bed and did not see them; but I could not help acknowledging the truth of an observation made by one of the men as the officers were handed into the boat, "I say, Bill, if *them* were *we*, what a precious twisting we should get to-morrow at six bells!"

The ship remained in Gibraltar Bay about three weeks, during which time we had refitted the rigging fore and aft, restowed and cleaned the hold, and painted outside. She never looked more beautiful than she did when, in obedience to our orders, we made sail to join the admiral. We passed Europa Point with a fair wind, and at sunset we were sixty miles from the Rock, yet it was distinctly to be seen, like a blue cloud, but the outline perfectly correct. I mention this, as perhaps my reader would not have believed that it was possible to see land at such a distance. We steered for Cape de Gatte, and we were next day close in shore. I was very much delighted with the Spanish coast, mountain upon mountain, hill upon hill, covered with vines nearly to their summits. We might have gone on shore at some places, for at that time we were friendly with the Spaniards, but the captain was in too great a hurry to join the admiral. We had very light winds, and a day or two afterwards we were off Valencia, nearly becalmed. I was on the gangway, looking through a telescope at the houses and gardens round the city, when

Mr Chucks, the boatswain, came up to me. "Mr Simple, oblige me with that glass a moment; I wish to see if a building remains there, which I have some reason to remember."

"What, were you ever on shore there?"

"Yes I was, Mr Simple, and nearly *stranded*, but I got off again without much damage."

"How do you mean—were you wrecked, then?"

"Not my ship, Mr Simple, but my peace of mind was for some time; but it's many years ago, when I was first made boatswain of a corvette (during this conversation he was looking through the telescope); yes, there it is," said he; "I have it in the field. Look, Mr Simple, do you see a small church, with a spire of glazed tiles, shining like a needle?"

"Yes, I do."

"Well, then, just above it, a little to the right, there is a long white house, with four small windows—below the grove of orange-trees."

"I see it," replied I; "but what about that house, Mr Chucks?"

"Why, thereby hangs a tale," replied he, giving a sigh, which raised and then lowered the frill of his shirt at least six inches.

"Why, what is the mystery, Mr Chucks?"

"I'll tell you, Mr Simple. With one who lived in that house, I was for the first, and for the last time, in love."

"Indeed! I should like very much to hear the story."

"So you shall, Mr Simple, but I must beg that you will not mention it, as young gentlemen are apt to quiz; and I think that being quizzed hurts my authority with the men. It is now about sixteen years back—we were then on good terms with the Spaniards, as we are now. I was then little more than thirty years old, and had just received my warrant as boatswain. I was considered a well-looking young man at that time, although lately I have, to a certain degree, got the better of that."

"Well, I consider you a remarkably good-looking man now, Mr Chucks."

"Thank you, Mr Simple, but nothing improves by age, that I know of, except rum. I used to dress very smart, and 'cut the boatswain' when I was on shore: and perhaps I had not lost so much of the polish I had picked up in good society. One evening, I was walking in the Plaza, when I saw a female ahead, who appeared to be the prettiest moulded little vessel that I ever cast my eyes on. I followed in her wake, and examined her: such a clean run I never beheld—so neat, too, in all her rigging—everything so nicely stowed under hatches. And then, she sailed along in such a style, at one moment lifting so lightly, just like a frigate, with her topsails on the caps, that can't help going along. At another time, as she turned a corner sharp up in the wind—wake as straight as an arrow—no leeway—I made all sail to sheer alongside of her, and, when under quarter, examined her close. Never saw such a fine swell in the counter, and all so trim—no ropes towing overboard. Well, Mr Simple, I said to myself, 'D——n it, if her figurehead and bows be finished off by the same builder, she's perfect.' So I shot ahead, and yawed* a little—caught a peep at her through her veil, and saw two black eyes—as bright as beads, and as large as damsons.† I saw quite enough, and not wishing to frighten her, I dropped astern. Shortly afterwards she altered her course, steering for that white house. Just as she was abreast of it, and I playing about her weather quarter, the priests came by in procession, taking the *host* to somebody who was dying. My little frigate lowered her top-gallant sails out of respect, as other nations used to do, and ought now, and be d——d to them, whenever they pass the flag of old England—"

"How do you mean?" inquired I.

"I mean that she spread her white handkerchief, which fluttered in her hand as she went along, and knelt down upon it on one knee. I did the same, because I was obliged to heave-to to keep my station, and I thought, that if she saw me, it would please her. When she got up, I was on my legs also; but in my hurry I had not chosen a very clean place, and I found out, when I got up again, that my white jean trousers were in a shocking mess. The young lady turned round, and seeing my misfortune, laughed, and then went into the white house, while I stood there like a fool, first looking at the door of the house, and then at my trousers. However, I thought that I might make it the means of being acquainted with her, so I went to the door and knocked. An old gentleman in a large cloak, who was her father, came out; I pointed to my trousers, and requested him in Spanish to allow me a little water to clean them. The daughter then came from within, and told her father how the accident had

---

* *Yawed: Having turned from the intended course.*
† *Damsons: Small plums.*

happened. The old gentleman was surprised that an English officer was so good a Christian, and appeared to be pleased. He asked me very politely to come in, and sent an old woman for some water. I observed that he was smoking a bit of paper, and having very fortunately about a couple of dozen of real Havannahs in my pocket (for I never smoke anything else, Mr Simple, it being my opinion that no gentleman can), I took them out, and begged his acceptance of them. His eyes glistened at the sight of them, but he refused to take more than one; however, I insisted upon his taking the whole bundle, telling him that I had plenty more on board, reserving one for myself, that I might smoke it with him. He then requested me to sit down, and the old woman brought some sour wine, which I declared was very good, although it made me quite ill afterwards. He inquired of me whether I was a good Christian. I replied that I was. I knew that he meant a Catholic, for they call us heretics, Mr Simple. The daughter then came in without her veil, and she was perfection; but I did not look at her, or pay her any attention after the first salutation, I was so afraid of making the old gentleman suspicious. He then asked what I was—what sort of officer—was I captain? I replied that I was not. Was I 'tenente? which means lieutenant; I answered that I was not, again, but with an air of contempt, as if I was something better. What was I, then? I did not know the Spanish for boatswain, and, to tell the truth, I was ashamed of my condition. I knew that there was an officer in Spain called corregidor, which means a corrector in English, or one who punishes. Now I thought that quite near enough for my purpose, and I replied that I was the corregidor. Now, Mr Simple, a corregidor in Spain is a person of rank and consequence, so they imagined that I must be the same, and they appeared to be pleased. The young lady then inquired if I was of good family—whether I was a gentleman or not. I replied that I hoped so. I remained with them for half-an-hour more, when my segar was finished; I then rose, and thanking the old gentleman for his civility, begged that I might be allowed to bring him a few more segars, and took my leave. The daughter opened the street door, and I could not refrain from taking her hand and kissing it—"

"Where's Mr Chucks? call the boatswain there forward," hallooed out the lieutenant.

"Here I am, sir," replied Mr Chucks, hastening aft, and leaving me and his story.

"The captain of the main-top reports the breast backstay much chafed in the serving. Go up and examine it," said the first lieutenant.

"Yes, sir," replied the boatswain, who immediately went up the rigging.

"And, Mr Simple, attend to the men scraping the spots off the quarter-deck."

"Yes, sir," replied I; and thus our conversation was broken up.

The weather changed that night, and we had a succession of rain and baffling winds for six or seven days, during which I had no opportunity of hearing the remainder of the boatswain's history. We joined the fleet off Toulon, closed the admiral's ship, and the captain went on board to pay his respects. When he returned, we found out, through the first lieutenant, that we were to remain with the fleet until the arrival of another frigate, expected in about a fortnight, and then the admiral had promised that we should have a cruise. The second day after we had joined, we were ordered to form part of the in-shore squadron, consisting of two line-of-battle ships and four frigates. The French fleet used to come out and manoeuvre within range of their batteries, or, if they proceeded further from the shore, they took good care that they had a leading wind to return again into port. We had been in-shore about a week, every day running close in, and counting the French fleet in the harbour, to see that they were all safe, and reporting it to the admiral by signal, when one fine morning, the whole of the French vessels were perceived to hoist their topsails, and in less than an hour they were under weigh, and came out of the harbour. We were always prepared for action, night and day, and, indeed, often exchanged a shot or two with the batteries when we reconnoitred; the in-shore squadron could not, of course, cope with the whole French fleet, and our own was about twelve miles in the offing, but the captain of the line-of-battle ship who commanded us, hove-to, as if in defiance, hoping to entice them further out. This was not very easy to do, as the French knew that a shift of wind might put it out of their power to refuse an action, which was what they would avoid, and what we were so anxious to bring about. I say we, speaking of the English, not of myself, for to tell the truth, I was not so very anxious. I was not exactly afraid, but I had an unpleasant sensation at the noise of a cannon-ball, which I had not as yet got over. However, four of the

French frigates made sail towards us, and hove-to, when within four miles, three or four line-of-battle ships following them, as if to support them. Our captain made signal for permission to close the enemy, which was granted, with our pennants, and those of another frigate. We immediately made all sail, beat to quarters, put out the fires, and opened the magazines. The French line-of-battle ships perceiving that only two of our frigates were sent against their four, hove-to at about the same distance from their frigates, as our line-of-battle ships and other frigates were from us. In the meantime our main fleet continued to work in-shore under a press of sail, and the French main fleet also gradually approached the detached ships. The whole scene reminded me of the tournaments I had read of; it was a challenge in the lists, only that the enemy were two to one; a fair acknowledgment on their parts of our superiority. In about an hour we closed so near, that the French frigates made sail and commenced firing. We reserved our fire until within a quarter of a mile, when we poured our broadside into the headmost frigate, exchanging with her on opposite tacks. The *Sea-horse*, who followed, also gave her a broadside. In this way we exchanged broadsides with the whole four, and we had the best of it, for they could not load so fast as we could. We were both ready again for the frigates as they passed us, but they were not ready with their broadside for the *Sea-horse*, who followed us very closely, so that they had two broadsides each, and we had only four in the *Diomede*, the *Sea-horse* not having one. Our rigging was cut up a great deal, and we had six or seven men wounded, but none killed. The French frigates suffered more, and their admiral perceiving that they were cut up a good deal, made a signal of recall. In the meantime we had both tacked, and were ranging up on the weather quarter of the sternmost frigate: the line-of-battle ships perceiving this, ran down with the wind, two points free, to support their frigates, and our in-shore squadron made all sail to support us, nearly laying up for where we were. But the wind was what is called at sea a soldier's wind, that is, blowing so that the ships could lie either way, so as to run out or into the harbour, and the French frigates, in obedience to their orders, made sail for their fleet in-shore, the line-of-battle ships coming out to support them. But our captain would not give it up, although we all continued to near the French line-of-battle ships every minute—we ran in with the frigates, exchanging broadsides with them as fast as we could. One of them lost her foretopmast, and dropped astern, and we hoped to cut her off, but the others shortened sail to support her. This continued for about twenty minutes, when the French line-of-battle ships were not more than a mile from us, and our own commodore had made the signal of our recall, for he thought that we should be overpowered and taken. But the *Sea-horse*, who saw the recall up, did not repeat it, and our captain was determined not to see it, and ordered the signal-man not to look that way. The action continued, two of the French frigates were cut to pieces, and complete wrecks, when the French line-of-battle ships commenced firing. It was then high time to be off. We each of us poured in another broadside, and then wore round for our own squadron, which was about four miles off, and rather to leeward, standing in to our assistance. As we wore round, our main-topmast, which had been badly wounded, fell over the side, and the French perceiving this, made all sail, with the hope of capturing us; but the *Sea-horse* remained with us, and we threw up in the wind, and raked them until they were within two cables' lengths of us. Then we stood on for our own ships; at last one of the line-of-battle ships, which sailed as well as the frigates, came abreast of us, and poured in a broadside, which brought everything about our ears, and I thought we must be taken; but on the contrary, although we lost several men, the captain said to the first lieutenant, "Now, if they only wait a little longer, they are nabbed, as sure as fate." Just at this moment, our own line-of-battle ships opened their fire, and then the tables were turned. The French tacked, and stood in as fast as they could, followed by the in-shore squadron, with the exception of our ship, which was too much crippled to chase them. One of their frigates had taken in tow the other, who had lost her top-mast, and our squadron came up with her very fast. The English fleet were also within three miles, standing in, and the French fleet standing out, to the assistance of the other ships which had been engaged. I thought, and so did everybody, that there would be a general action, but we were disappointed; the frigate which towed the other, finding that she could not escape, cast her off, and left her to her fate, which was to haul down her colours to the commodore of the in-shore squadron. The chase was continued until the whole of the French vessels were close under their batteries, and then our fleet returned to its station with the prize, which proved to be the *Narcisse*, of thirty-six guns, Captain Le Pelleteon. Our captain obtained a great deal of credit for his gallant behaviour. We had three men killed, and Robinson, the midshipman, and ten men wounded, some of them severely. I think this action cured me of my fear of a cannon-ball, for during the few days we remained with the fleet, we often were fired at when we reconnoitred, but I did not care anything for them. About the time she was expected, the frigate joined, and we had permission to part company. But before I proceed with the history of our cruise, I shall mention the circumstances attending a court-martial, which took place during the time that we were with the fleet, our captain having been recalled from the in-shore squadron to sit as one of the members. I was the midshipman appointed to the captain's gig, and remained on board of the admiral's ship during the whole of the time that the court was sitting. Two seamen, one an Englishman, and the other a Frenchman, were tried for desertion from one of our frigates. They had left their ship about three months, when the frigate captured a French privateer, and found them on board as part of her crew. For the Englishman, of course, there was no defence; he merited the punishment of death, to which he was immediately sentenced. There may be some excuse for desertion, when we consider that the seamen are taken into the service by force, but there could be none for fighting against his country. But the case of the Frenchman was different. He was born and bred in France, had been one of the crew of the French gun-boats at Cadiz, where he had been made a prisoner by the Spaniards, and expecting his throat to be cut every day, had contrived to escape on board of the frigate lying in the harbour, and entered into our service, I really believe to save his life. He was nearly two years in the frigate before he could find an opportunity of deserting from her, and returning to France, when he joined the French privateer. During the time that he was in the frigate, he bore an excellent character. The greatest point against him was, that on his arrival at Gibraltar he had been offered, and had received the bounty. When the Englishman was asked what he had to say in his defence, he replied that he had been pressed out of an American ship, that he was an American born, and that he had never taken the bounty. But this was not true. The defence of the Frenchman was considered so very good for a person in his station of life, that I obtained a copy of it, which ran as follows:

"Mr President, and Officers of the Honourable Court;—It is with the greatest humility that I venture to address you. I shall be very brief, nor shall I attempt to disprove the charges which have been made against me, but confine myself to a few facts, the consideration of which will, I trust, operate upon your feelings in mitigation of the punishment to which I may be sentenced for my fault—a fault which proceeded, not from any evil motive, but from an ardent love for my country. I am by birth a Frenchman; my life has been spent in the service of France until a few months after the revolution in Spain, when I, together with those who composed the French squadron at Cadiz, was made a prisoner. The hardships and cruel usage which I endured became insupportable. I effected my escape, and after wandering about the town for two or three days, in hourly expectation of being assassinated, the fate of too many of my unfortunate countrymen; desperate from famine, and perceiving no other chance of escaping from the town, I was reduced to the necessity of offering myself as a volunteer on board of an English frigate. I dared not, as I ought to have done, acknowledge myself to have been a prisoner, from the dread of being delivered up to the Spaniards. During the period that I served on board of your frigate, I confidently rely upon the captain and the officers for my character.

"The love of our country, although dormant for a time, will ultimately be roused, and peculiar circumstances occurred which rendered the feeling irresistible. I returned to my duty, and for having so done, am I to be debarred from again returning to that country so dear to me—from again beholding my aged parents, who bless me in my absence—from again embracing my brothers and sisters—to end my days upon a scaffold; not for the crime which I did commit in entering into your service, but for an act of duty and repentance—that of returning to my own? Allow me to observe, that the charge against me is not for entering your service, but for having deserted from it. For the former, not even my misery can be brought forward but in extenuation; for the latter I have a proud consciousness, which will, I trust, be my support in my extremity.

"Gentlemen, I earnestly entreat you to consider my situation, and I am sure that your generous hearts will pity me. Let that love of your country, which now animates your breasts, and induces you to risk your lives and your all, now plead for me. Already has British humanity saved thousands of my countrymen from the rage

of the Spaniards; let that same humanity be extended now, and
induce my judges to add one more to the list of those who, although
our nations are at war, if they are endowed with feeling, can have
but one sentiment towards their generous enemy—a sentiment
overpowering all other, that of a deep-felt gratitude."*

Whatever may have been the effect of the address upon the court
individually, it appeared at the time to have none upon them as a
body. Both the men were condemned to death, and the day after the
morrow was fixed for their execution. I watched the two prisoners
as they went down the side, to be conducted on board of their own
ship. The Englishman threw himself down in the stern-sheets of the
boat, every minor consideration apparently swallowed up in the
thought of his approaching end; but the Frenchman, before he sat
down, observing that the seat was a little dirty, took out his silk
handkerchief, and spread it on the seat, that he might not soil his
nankeen trousers.†

I was ordered to attend the punishment on the day appointed.
The sun shone so brightly, and the sky was so clear, the wind so
gentle and mild, that it appeared hardly possible that it was to be a
day of such awe and misery to the two poor men, or of such melancholy to the fleet in general. I pulled up my boat with the others
belonging to the ships of the fleet, in obedience to the orders of the
officer superintending, close to the fore-chains of the ship. In about
half-an-hour afterwards, the prisoners made their appearance on the
scaffold, the caps were pulled over their eyes, and the gun fired
underneath them. When the smoke rolled away, the Englishman
was swinging at the yard-arm, but the Frenchman was not; he had
made a spring when the gun fired, hoping to break his neck at once,
and put an end to his misery; but he fell on the edge of the scaffold,
where he lay. We thought that his rope had given way, and it appeared that he did the same, for he made an enquiry, but they returned him no answer. He was kept on the scaffold during the
whole hour that the Englishman remained suspended; his cap had
been removed, and he looked occasionally at his fellow-sufferer.

* This is fact.—AUTHOR.
† *Nankeen trousers: Pants made from a yellow variety of cotton, originally manufactured at
Nanking, the chief city of the province of Kiangsu in China.*

When the body was lowered down, he considered that his time was come, and attempted to leap overboard. He was restrained and led aft, where his reprieve was read to him and his arms were unbound. But the effect of the shock was too much for his mind; he fell down in a swoon, and when he recovered, his senses had left him, and I heard that he never recovered them, but was sent home to be confined as a maniac. I thought, and the result proved, that it was carried too far. It is not the custom, when a man is reprieved, to tell him so, until after he is on the scaffold, with the intention that his awful situation at the time may make a lasting impression upon him during the remainder of his life; but, as a foreigner, he was not aware of our customs, and the hour of intense feeling which he underwent was too much for his reason. I must say, that this circumstance was always a source of deep regret in the whole fleet, and that his being a Frenchman, instead of an Englishman, increased the feeling of commiseration.

CHAPTER XVII

Mr Chucks's opinion on proper names   He finishes his Spanish tale—March of intellect among the Warrant Officers.

WE WERE ALL DELIGHTED when our signal was hoisted to "part company," as we anticipated plenty of prize-money under such an enterprising captain. We steered for the French coast, near to its junction with Spain, the captain having orders to intercept any convoys sent to supply the French army with stores and provisions.

The day after we parted company with the fleet, Mr Chucks finished his story.

"Where was I, Mr Simple, when I left off?" said he, as we took a seat upon the long eighteen.

"You had just left the house after having told them that you were a corregidor, and had kissed the lady's hand."

"Very true. Well, Mr Simple, I did not call there for two or three

days afterwards; I did not like to go too soon, especially as I saw the
young lady every day in the Plaza. She would not speak to me, but,
to make use of their expression, 'she gave me her eyes,' and sometimes a sweet smile. I recollect I was so busy looking at her one day,
that I tripped over my sword, and nearly fell on my nose, at which
she burst out a laughing."

"Your sword, Mr Chucks? I thought boatswains never wore
swords."

"Mr Simple, a boatswain is an officer, and is entitled to a sword
as well as the captain, although we have been laughed out of it by a
set of midshipman monkeys. I always wore my sword at that time;
but now-a-days, a boatswain is counted as nobody, unless there is
hard work to do, and then it's Mr Chucks this, and Mr Chucks that.
But I'll explain to you how it is, Mr Simple, that we boatswains have
lost so much of consequence and dignity. The first lieutenants are
made to do the boatswain's duty now-a-days, and if they could only
wind the call, they might scratch the boatswain's name off half the
ships' books in his Majesty's service. But to go on with my yarn. On
the fourth day, I called with my handkerchief full of segars for the
father, but he was at siesta, as they called it. The old serving-woman
would not let me in at first; but I shoved a dollar between her
skinny old fingers, and that altered her note. She put her old head
out, and looked round to see if there was anybody in the street to
watch us, and then she let me in and shut the door. I walked into the
room, and found myself alone with Seraphina."

"Seraphina!—what a fine name!"

"No name can be too fine for a pretty girl, or a good frigate, Mr
Simple; for my part, I'm very fond of these hard names. Your Bess,
and Poll, and Sue, do very well for the Point, or Castle Rag; but in
my opinion, they degrade a lady. Don't you observe, Mr Simple,
that all our gun-brigs, a sort of vessel that will certainly d——n the
inventor to all eternity, have nothing but low common names, such
as Pincher, Thrasher, Boxer, Badger, and all that sort, which are
quite good enough for them; whereas all our dashing saucy frigates
have names as long as the main-top bowling, and hard enough to
break your jaw—such as Melpomeny, Terpsichory, Arethusy,
Bacchanty—fine flourishers, as long as their pennants which dip
alongside in a calm."

"Very true," replied I; "but do you think, then, it is the same with family names?"

"Most certainly, Mr Simple. When I was in good society, I rarely fell in with such names as Potts or Bell, or Smith or Hodges; it was always Mr Fortescue, or Mr Fitzgerald, or Mr Fitzherbert—seldom bowed, sir, to anything under *three* syllables."

"Then I presume, Mr Chucks, you are not fond of your own name?"

"There you touch me, Mr Simple; but it is quite good enough for a boatswain," replied Mr Chucks, with a sigh. "I certainly did very wrong to impose upon people as I did, but I've been severely punished for it—it has made me discontented and unhappy ever since. Dearly have I paid for my spree; for there is nothing so miserable as to have ideas above your station in life, Mr Simple. But I must make sail again. I was three hours with Seraphina before her father came home, and during that time I never was quietly at an anchor for above a minute. I was on my knees, vowing and swearing, kissing her feet and kissing her hand, till at last I got to her lips, working my way up as regularly as one who gets in at the hawsehole and crawls aft to the cabin windows. She was very kind, and she smiled, and sighed, and pushed me off, and squeezed my hand, and was angry—frowning till I was in despair, and then making me happy again with her melting dark eyes beaming kindly, till at last she said that she would try to love me, and asked me whether I would marry her and live in Spain. I replied that I would; and, indeed, I felt as if I could, only at the time the thought occurred to me where the rhino was to come from, for I could not live, as her father did, upon a paper segar and a piece of melon per day. At all events, as far as words went, it was a settled thing. When her father came home, the old servant told him that I had just at that moment arrived, and that his daughter was in her own room; so she was, for she ran away as soon as she heard her father knock. I made my bow to the old gentleman, and gave him the segars. He was serious at first, but the sight of them put him into good humour, and in a few minutes Donna Seraphina (they call a lady a Donna in Spain) came in, saluting me ceremoniously, as if we had not been kissing for the hour together. I did not remain long, as it was getting late, so I took a glass of the old gentleman's sour wine, and walked off, with a request from him to call again, the young lady paying me little or no attention during the time that I remained, or at my departure."

"Well, Mr Chucks," observed I, "it appears to me that she was a very deceitful young person."

"So she was, Mr Simple; but a man in love can't see, and I'll tell you why. If he wins the lady, he is as much in love with himself as with her, because he is so proud of his conquest. That was my case. If I had had my eyes, I might have seen that she who could cheat her old father for a mere stranger, would certainly deceive him in his turn. But if love makes a man blind, vanity, Mr Simple, makes him blinder. In short, I was an ass."

"Never mind, Mr Chucks, there was a good excuse for it."

"Well, Mr Simple, I met her again and again, until I was madly in love, and the father appeared to be aware of what was going on, and to have no objection. However, he sent for a priest to talk with me, and I again said that I was a good Catholic. I told him that I was in love with the young lady, and would marry her. The father made no objection on my promising to remain in Spain, for he would not part with his only daughter. And there again I was guilty of deceit, first, in making a promise I did not intend to keep, and then in pretending that I was a Catholic. Honesty is the best policy, Mr Simple, in the long run, you may depend upon it."

"So my father has always told me, and I have believed him," replied I.

"Well, sir, I am ashamed to say that I did worse; for the priest, after the thing was settled, asked me whether I had confessed lately. I knew what he meant, and answered that I had not. He motioned me down on my knees; but, as I could not speak Spanish enough for that, I mumbled-jumbled something or another, half Spanish and half English, and ended with putting four dollars in his hand for *carita*, which means charity. He was satisfied at the end of my confession, whatever he might have been at the beginning, and gave me absolution, although he could not have understood what my crimes were; but four dollars, Mr Simple, will pay for a deal of crime in that country. And now, sir, comes the winding up of this business. Seraphina told me that she was going to the opera with some of her relations, and asked me if I would be there; that the captain of the frigate, and all the other officers were going, and that she wished me to go with her. You see, Mr Simple, although Seraphina's father was so poor, that a mouse would have starved in his house, still he was of good family, and connected with those who were much better off. He was a Don himself, and had fourteen or fifteen long names, which I forget now. I refused to go with her, as I knew that the service would not permit a boatswain to sit in an opera-box, when the captain and first lieutenant were there. I told her that I had promised to go on board and look after the men while the captain went on shore; thus, as you'll see, Mr Simple, making myself a man of consequence, only to be more mortified in the end. After she had gone to the opera, I was very uncomfortable: I was afraid that the captain would see her, and take a fancy to her. I walked up and down, outside, until I was so full of love and jealousy that I determined to go into the pit and see what she was about. I soon discovered her in a box, with some other ladies, and with them were my captain and first lieutenant. The captain, who spoke the language well, was leaning over her, talking and laughing, and she was smiling at what he said. I resolved to leave immediately, lest she should see me and discover that I had told her a falsehood; but they appeared so intimate that I became so jealous I could not quit the theatre. At last she perceived me, and beckoned her hand; I looked very angry, and left the theatre cursing like a madman. It appeared that she pointed me out to the captain, and asked him who I was; he told her my real situation on board, and spoke of me with contempt She asked whether I was not a man of family; at this the captain and first lieutenant both burst out laughing, and said that I was a common sailor who had been promoted to a higher rank for good behaviour—not exactly an officer, and anything but a gentleman. In short, Mr Simple, I was *blown upon;* and, although the captain said more than was correct, as I learnt afterwards through the officers, still I deserved it. Determined to know the worst, I remained outside till the opera was over, when I saw her come out, the captain and first lieutenant walking with the party—so that I could not speak with her. I walked to a posada (that's an inn), and drank seven bottles of rosolio to keep myself quiet; then I went on board, and the second lieutenant, who was commanding officer, put me under arrest for being intoxicated. It was a week before I was released; and you can't imagine what I suffered, Mr Simple. At last, I obtained leave to go on shore, and I went to the house to decide my fate. The old woman opened the door, and then calling me a thief, slammed it in my face; as I retreated, Donna Seraphina came to the window, and, waving her hand with a contemptuous look, said, 'Go, and God be with you, Mr Gentleman.' I returned on board in such a rage, that if I could have persuaded the gunner to have given me a ball-cartridge, I should have shot myself through the head. What made the matter worse, I was laughed at by everybody in the ship, for the captain and first lieutenant had made the story public."

"Well, Mr Chucks," replied I, "I cannot help being sorry for you, although you certainly deserved to be punished for your dishonesty. Was that the end of the affair?"

"As far as I was concerned it was, Mr Simple; but not as respected others. The captain took my place, but without the knowledge of the father. After all, they neither had great reason to rejoice at the exchange."

"How so, Mr Chucks—what do you mean?"

"Why, Mr Simple, the captain did not make an honest woman of her, as I would have done; and the father discovered what was going on, and one night the captain was brought on board run through the body. We sailed immediately for Gibraltar, and it was a long while before he got round again: and then he had another misfortune."

"What was that?"

"Why he lost his boatswain, Mr Simple; for I could not bear the sight of him—and then he lost (as you must know, not from your own knowledge, but from that of others) a boatswain who knows his duty."

"Every one says so, Mr Chucks. I'm sure that our captain would be very sorry to part with you."

"I trust that every captain has been with whom I've sailed, Mr Simple. But that was not all he lost, Mr Simple; for the next cruise he lost his masts; and the loss of his masts occasioned the loss of his ship, since which he has never been trusted with another, but is laid on the shelf. Now he never carried away a spar of any consequence during the whole time that I was with him. A mast itself is nothing, Mr Simple—only a piece of wood—but fit your rigging properly, and then a mast is strong as a rock. Only ask Mr Faulkner, and he'll tell you the same; and I never met an officer who knew better how to support a mast."

"Did you ever hear any more of the young lady?"

"Yes; about a year afterwards I returned there in another ship. She had been shut up in a convent, and forced to take the veil. Oh, Mr Simple! if you knew how I loved that girl! I have never been more than polite to a woman since, and shall die a bachelor. You can't think how I was capsized the other day, when I looked at the house; I have hardly touched beef or pork since, and am in debt two quarts of rum more than my allowance. But, Mr Simple, I have told you this in confidence, and I trust you are too much of a gentleman to repeat it; for I cannot bear quizzing from young midshipmen."

I promised that I would not mention it, and I kept my word; but circumstances which the reader will learn in the sequel have freed me from the condition. Nobody can quiz him now.

We gained our station off the coast of Perpignan; and as soon as we made the land, we were most provokingly driven off by a severe gale. I am not about to make any remarks about the gale, for one storm is so like another; but I mention it, to account for a conversation which took place, and with which I was very much amused. I was near to the captain when he sent for Mr Muddle, the carpenter, who had been up to examine the main-topsail yard, which had been reported as sprung.

"Well, Mr Muddle," said the captain.

"Sprung, sir, most decidedly; but I think we'll be able to *mitigate* it."

"Will you be able to secure it for the present, Mr Muddle?" replied the captain, rather sharply.

"We'll *mitigate* it, sir, in half-an-hour."

"I wish that you would use common phrases when you speak to me, Mr Muddle. I presume, by mitigate, you mean to say that you can secure it. Do you mean so, sir, or do you not?"

"Yes, sir, that is what I mean, most decidedly. I hope no offence, Captain Savage; but I did not intend to displease you by my language."

"Very good, Mr Muddle," replied the captain; "it's the first time that I have spoken to you on the subject, recollect that it will be the last."

"The first time!" replied the carpenter, who could not forget his philosophy; "I beg your pardon, Captain Savage, you found just the same fault with me on this quarter-deck 27,672 years ago, and—"

"If I did, Mr Muddle," interrupted the captain, very angrily, "depend upon it that at the same time I ordered you to go aloft, and attend to your duty, instead of talking nonsense on the quarter-deck; and, although, as you say, you and I cannot recollect it, if you did not obey that order instantaneously, I also put you in confine-ment, and obliged you to leave the ship as soon as she returned to port. Do you understand me, sir?"

"I rather think, sir," replied the carpenter, humbly touching his hat, and walking to the main-rigging, "that no such thing took place, for I went up immediately, as I do now; and," continued the carpenter, who was incurable, as he ascended the rigging, "as I shall again in another 27,672 years."

"That man is incorrigible with his confounded nonsense," ob-served the captain to the first lieutenant. "Every mast in the ship would go over the side, provided he could get anyone to listen to his ridiculous theory."

"He is not a bad carpenter, sir," replied the first lieutenant.

"He is not," rejoined the captain; "but there is a time for all things."

Just at this moment, the boatswain came down the rigging.

"Well, Mr Chucks, what do you think of the yard? Must we shift it?" inquired the captain.

"At present, Captain Savage," replied the boatswain, "I consider it to be in a state which may be called precarious, and not at all permanent; but, with a little human exertion, four fathom of three-inch, and half-a-dozen tenpenny nails, it may last, for all I know, until it is time for it to be sprung again."

"I do not understand you, Mr Chucks. I know no time when a yard ought to be sprung."

"I did not refer to our time, sir," replied the boatswain, "but to the 27,672 years of Mr Muddle, when—"

"Go forward immediately, sir, and attend to your duty," cried the captain, in a very angry voice; and then he said to the first lieutenant, "I believe the warrant officers are going mad. Who ever heard a boatswain use such language—'precarious and not at all permanent?' His stay in the ship will become so, if he does not mind what he is about."

"He is a very odd character, sir," replied the first lieutenant; "but I have no hesitation in saying that he is the best boatswain in his Majesty's service."

"I believe so too," replied the captain; "but—well, everyone has his faults. Mr Simple, what are you about, sir?"

"I was listening to what you said," replied I, touching my hat.

"I admire your candour, sir," replied he, "but advise you to discontinue the practice. Walk over to leeward, sir, and attend to your duty."

When I was on the other side of the deck, I looked round, and saw the captain and first lieutenant both laughing.

—◈—

CHAPTER XVIII

I go away on service, am wounded and taken prisoner with O'Brien—Diamond cut diamond between the O'Briens—Get into comfortable quarters—My first interview with Celeste.

AND NOW I have to relate an event, which, young as I was at the time, will be found to have seriously affected me in after-life. How little do we know what to-morrow may bring forth! We had regained our station, and for some days had been standing off and on the coast, when one morning at daybreak, we found ourselves about four miles from the town of Cette, and a large convoy of vessels coming round a point. We made all sail in chase, and they anchored close in shore, under a battery, which we did not discover until it opened fire upon us. The shot struck the frigate two or three times, for the water was smooth, and the battery nearly level with it. The captain tacked the ship, and stood out again, until the boats were hoisted out, and all ready to pull on shore and storm the battery. O'Brien, who was the officer commanding the first cutter on service, was in his boat, and I again obtained permission from him to smuggle myself into it.

"Now, Peter, let's see what kind of a fish you'll bring on board this time," said he, after we had shoved off: "or may be, the fish will not let you off quite so easy." The men in the boat all laughed at this, and I replied, "That I must be more seriously wounded than I was last time, to be made a prisoner." We ran on shore, amidst the fire of the gun-boats, who protected the convoy, by which we lost

three men, and made for the battery, which we took without opposition, the French artillery-men running out as we ran in. The directions of the captain were very positive, not to remain in the battery a
minute after it was taken, but to board the gun-boats, leaving only
one of the small boats, with the armourer to spike the guns, for
the captain was aware that there were troops stationed along the
coast, who might come down upon us and beat us off. The first
lieutenant, who commanded, desired O'Brien to remain with the
first cutter, and after the armourer had spiked the guns, as officer of
the boat he was to shove off immediately. O'Brien and I remained in
the battery with the armourer, the boat's crew being ordered down
to the boat, to keep her afloat, and ready to shove off at a moment's
warning. We had spiked all the guns but one, when all of a sudden a
volley of musketry was poured upon us, which killed the armourer,
and wounded me in the leg above the knee. I fell down by O'Brien,
who cried out, "By the powers! here they are, and one gun not
spiked." He jumped down, wrenched the hammer from the
armourer's hand, and seizing a nail from the bag, in a few moments
he had spiked the gun. At this time I heard the tramping of the
French soldiers advancing, when O'Brien threw away the hammer,
and lifting me upon his shoulders, cried, "Come along, Peter, my
boy," and made for the boat as fast as he could; but he was too late;
he had not got half-way to the boat, before he was collared by two
French soldiers, and dragged back into the battery. The French
troops then advanced, and kept up a smart fire: our cutter escaped,
and joined the other boat, who had captured the gun-boats and
convoy with little opposition. Our large boats had carronades
mounted in their bows, and soon returned the fire with round and
grape, which drove the French troops back into the battery, where
they remained, popping at our men under cover, until most of the
vessels were taken out; those which they could not man were burnt.
In the meantime, O'Brien had been taken into the battery, with me
on his back; but as soon as he was there, he laid me gently down,
saying, "Peter, my boy, as long as you were under my charge, I'd
carry you through thick and thin; but now that you are under the
charge of these French beggars, why let them carry you. Every man
his own bundle, Peter, that's fair play, so if they think you're worth
the carrying, let them bear the weight of ye."

"And suppose they do not, O'Brien, will you leave me here?"

"Will I lave you, Peter! not if I can help it, my boy; but they won't leave you, never fear them; prisoners are so scarce with them, that they would not leave the captain's monkey, if he were taken."

As soon as our boats were clear of their musketry, the commanding officer of the French troops examined the guns in the battery, with the hope of reaching them, and was very much annoyed to find that every one of them was spiked. "He'll look sharper than a magpie before he finds a clear touch-hole, I expect," said O'Brien, as he watched the officer. And here I must observe, that O'Brien showed great presence of mind in spiking the last gun; for had they had one gun to fire at our boats towing out the prizes, they must have done a great deal of mischief to them, and we should have lost a great many men; but in so doing, and in the attempt to save me, he sacrificed himself, and was taken prisoner. When the troops ceased firing, the commanding officer came up to O'Brien, and looking at him, said, "Officer?" to which O'Brien nodded his head. He then pointed to me—"Officer?" O'Brien nodded his head again, at which the French troops laughed, as O'Brien told me afterwards, because I was what they called an *enfant*, which means an infant. I was very stiff, and faint, and could not walk. The officer who commanded the troops left a detachment in the battery, and prepared to return to Cette, from whence they came. O'Brien walked, and I was carried on three muskets by six of the French soldiers—not a very pleasant conveyance at any time, but in my state excessively painful. However, I must say, that they were very kind to me, and put a great-coat or something under my wounded leg, for I was in an agony, and fainted several times. At last they brought me some water to drink. O how delicious it was! I have often thought since, when I have been in company, where people fond of good living have smacked their lips at their claret, that if they could only be wounded, and taste a cup of water, they would then know what it was to feel a beverage grateful. In about an hour and a half, which appeared to me to be five days at the least, we arrived at the town of Cette, and I was taken up to the house of the officer who commanded the troops, and who had often looked at me as I was carried there from the battery, saying, *"Pauvre enfant!"* I was put on a bed, where I again fainted away. When I came to my senses, I found a surgeon had bandaged my leg, and that I had been undressed. O'Brien was standing by me, and I believe that he had been crying, for he thought that I was dead. When I looked him in the face, he said, "Pater, you baste, how you frightened me: bad luck to me if ever I take charge of another youngster. What did you sham dead for?"

"I am better now, O'Brien," replied I, "how much I am indebted to you: you have been made prisoner in trying to save me."

"I have been made prisoner in doing my duty, in one shape or another. If that fool of an armourer hadn't held his hammer so tight, after he was dead, and it was of no use to him, I should have been clear enough, and so would you have been! but, however, all this is nothing at all, Peter; as far as I can see, the life of a man consists in getting into scrapes, and getting out of them. By the blessing of God, we've managed the first, and by the blessing of God we'll manage the second also; so be smart, my honey, and get well, for although a man may escape by running away on two legs, I never heard of a boy who hopped out of a French prison upon one."

I squeezed the offered hand of O'Brien, and looked round me; the surgeon stood at one side of the bed, and the officer who commanded the troops at the other. At the head of the bed was a little girl about twelve years old, who held a cup in her hand, out of which something had been poured down my throat. I looked at her, and she had such pity in her face, which was remarkably handsome, that she appeared to me as an angel, and I turned round as well as I could, that I might look at her alone. She offered me the cup, which I should have refused from anyone but her, and I drank a little. Another person then came into the room, and a conversation took place in French.

"I wonder what they mean to do with us," said I to O'Brien.

"Whist, hold your tongue," replied he; and then he leaned over me, and said in a whisper, "I understand all they say; don't you recollect, I told you that I learnt the language after I was kilt and buried in the sand, in South America?" After a little more conversation, the officer and the others retired, leaving nobody but the little girl and O'Brien in the room.

"It's a message from the governor," said O'Brien, as soon as they were gone, "wishing the prisoners to be sent to the gaol in the citadel, to be examined; and the officer says (and he's a real gentleman, as far as I can judge) that you're but a baby, and badly wounded in the bargain, and that it would be a shame not to leave you to die in peace; so I presume that I'll part company from you very soon."

"I hope not, O'Brien," replied I; "if you go to prison, I will go also, for I will not leave you, who are my best friend, to remain with strangers. I should not be half so happy, although I might have more comforts in my present situation."

"Pater, my boy, I am glad to see that your heart is in the right place, as I always thought it was, or I wouldn't have taken you under my protection. We'll go together to prison, my jewel, and I'll fish at the bars with a bag and a long string, just by way of recreation, and to pick up a little money to buy you all manner of nice things; and when you get well, you shall do it yourself, mayhap you'll have better luck, as Peter your namesake had, who was a fisherman before you. There's twice as much room in one of the cells as there is in a midshipman's berth, my boy; and the prison yards, where you are allowed to walk, will make a dozen quarter-decks, and no need of touching your hat out of respect when you go into it. When a man has been cramped up on board of a man-of-war, where midshipmen are stowed away like pilchards in a cask, he finds himself quite at liberty in a prison, Peter.* But somehow or another, I think we mayn't be parted yet, for I heard the officer (who appears to be a real gentleman, and worthy to have been an Irishman born) say to the other, that he'd ask the governor for me to stay with you on parole, until you are well again." The little girl handed me the lemonade, of which I drank a little, and then I felt very faint again. I laid my head on the pillow, and O'Brien having left off talking, I was soon in a comfortable sleep. In an hour I was awakened by the return of the officer, who was accompanied by the surgeon. The officer addressed O'Brien in French who shook his head as before.

"Why don't you answer, O'Brien," said I, "since you understand him?"

"Peter, recollect that I cannot speak a word of their lingo; then I shall know what they say before us, and they won't mind what they say, supposing I do not understand them."

"But is that honest, O'Brien?"

---

* *Pilchards: Small fish related to the herring but smaller and rounder.*

"Is it honest you mean? If I had a five-pound note in my pocket, and don't choose to show it to every fellow that I meet—is that dishonest?"

"To be sure it's not."

"And a'n't that what the lawyers call a case in pint?"

"Well," replied I, "if you wish it, I shall of course say nothing; but I think that I should tell them, especially as they are so kind to us."

During this conversation, the officer occasionally spoke to the surgeon, at the same time eyeing us, I thought, very hard. Two other persons then came into the room; one of them addressed O'Brien in very bad English, saying, that he was interpreter, and would beg him to answer a few questions. He then inquired the name of our ship, number of guns, and how long we had been cruising. After that, the force of the English fleet, and a great many other questions relative to them; all of which were put in French by the person who came with him, and the answer translated, and taken down in a book. Some of the questions O'Brien answered correctly, to others he pleaded ignorance; and to some, he asserted what was not true. But I did not blame him for that, as it was his duty not to give information to the enemy. At last they asked my name, and rank, which O'Brien told them. "Was I noble?"

"Yes," replied O'Brien.

"Don't say so, O'Brien," interrupted I.

"Peter, you know nothing about it, you are grandson to a lord."

"I know that, but still I am not noble myself, although descended from him; therefore pray don't say so."

"Bother! Pater, I have said it, and I won't unsay it; besides, Pater, recollect it's a French question, and in France you would be considered noble. At all events, it can do no harm."

"I feel too ill to talk, O'Brien; but I wish you had not said so."

They then inquired O'Brien's name, which he told them; his rank in the service, and also, whether he was noble.

"I am an O'Brien," replied he; "and pray what's the meaning of the O before my name, if I'm not noble? However, Mr Interpreter, you may add, that we have dropped our title because it's not convanient." The French officer burst out into a loud laugh, which surprised us very much. The interpreter had great difficulty in explaining what O'Brien said; but as O'Brien told me afterwards, the answer was put down *doubtful.*

They all left the room except the officer, who then, to our astonishment, addressed us in good English. "Gentlemen, I have obtained permission from the governor for you to remain in my house, until Mr Simple is recovered. Mr O'Brien, it is necessary that I should receive your parole of honour that you will not attempt to escape. Are you willing to give it?"

O'Brien was quite amazed; "Murder an' Irish," cried he; "so you speak English, colonel. It was not very genteel of you not to say so, considering how we've been talking our little secrets together."

"Certainly, Mr O'Brien, not more necessary," replied the officer, smiling, "than for you to tell me that you understood French."

"O, bother!" cried O'Brien, "how nicely I'm caught in my own trap! You're an Irishman, sure?"

"I'm of Irish descent," replied the officer, "and my name, as well as yours, is O'Brien. I was brought up in this country, not being permitted to serve my own, and retain the religion of my forefathers. I may now be considered as a Frenchman, retaining nothing of my original country, except the language, which my mother taught me, and a warm feeling towards the English wherever I meet them. But to the question, Mr O'Brien, will you give your parole?"

"The word of an Irishman, and the hand to boot," replied O'Brien, shaking the colonel by the hand; "and you're more than doubly sure, for I'll never go away and leave little Peter here; and as for carrying him on my back, I've had enough of that already."

"It is sufficient," replied the colonel. "Mr O'Brien, I will make you as comfortable as I can; and when you are tired of attending your friend, my little daughter shall take your place. You'll find her a kind little nurse, Mr Simple."

I could not refrain from tears at the colonel's kindness: he shook me by the hand; and telling O'Brien that dinner was ready, he called up his daughter, the little girl who had attended me before, and desired her to remain in the room. "Celeste," said he, "you understand a little English; quite enough to find out what he is in want of. Go and fetch your work, to amuse yourself when he is asleep." Celeste went out, and returning with her embroidery, sat down by the head of the bed: the colonel and O'Brien then quitted the room.

Celeste then commenced her embroidery, and as her eyes were cast down upon her work, I was able to look at her without her observing it. As I said before, she was a very beautiful little girl; her hair was light brown, eyes very large, and eyebrows drawn as with a pair of compasses; her nose and mouth were also very pretty; but it was not so much her features as the expression of her countenance, which was so beautiful, so modest, so sweet, and so intelligent. When she smiled, which she almost always did when she spoke, her teeth were like two rows of little pearls.

I had not looked at her long, before she raised her eyes from her work, and perceiving that I was looking at her, said, "You want—something—want drink—I speak very little English."

"Nothing, I thank ye," replied I; "I only want to go to sleep."

"Then—shut—your—eye," replied she smiling; and she went to the window, and drew down the blinds to darken the room. But I could not sleep; the remembrance of what had occurred—in a few hours wounded, and a prisoner—the thought of my father and mother's anxiety; with the prospect of going to a prison and close confinement, as soon as I was recovered, passed in succession in my mind, and, together with the actual pain of my wound, prevented me from obtaining any rest. The little girl several times opened the curtain to ascertain whether I slept or wanted anything, and then as softly retired. In the evening, the surgeon called again; he felt my pulse, and directing cold applications to my leg, which had swelled considerably, and was becoming very painful, told Colonel O'Brien, that, although I had considerable fever, I was doing as well as could be expected under the circumstances. But I shall not dwell upon my severe sufferings for a fortnight, after which the ball was extracted; nor upon how carefully I was watched by O'Brien, the colonel, and little Celeste, during my peevishness and irritation, arising from pain and fever. I feel grateful to them, but particularly to Celeste, who seldom quitted me for more than half an hour, and, as I gradually recovered, tried all she could to amuse me.

—⟨⟩—

CHAPTER XIX

We remove to very unpleasant quarters—Birds of a feather won't always flock together—
O'Brien cuts a cutter midshipman, and gets a taste of French steel—Altogether flat
work—A walk into the interior.

A S SOON as I was well enough to attend to my little nurse, we
became very intimate, as might be expected. Our chief employment was teaching each other French and English. Having the
advantage of me in knowing a little before we met, and also being
much quicker of apprehension, she very soon began to speak English fluently, long before I could make out a short sentence in
French. However, as it was our chief employment, and both were
anxious to communicate with each other, I learnt it very fast. In five
weeks I was out of bed, and could limp about the room; and before
two months were over, I was quite recovered. The colonel, however,
would not report me to the governor; I remained on a sofa during
the day, but at dusk I stole out of the house, and walked about with
Celeste. I never passed such a happy time as the last fortnight; the
only drawback was the remembrance that I should soon have to
exchange it for a prison. I was more easy about my father and
mother, as O'Brien had written to them, assuring them that I was
doing well; and besides, a few days after our capture, the frigate had
run in, and sent a flag of truce to inquire if we were alive or made
prisoners; at the same time Captain Savage sent on shore all our
clothes, and two hundred dollars in cash for our use. I knew that
even if O'Brien's letter did not reach them, they were sure to hear
from Captain Savage that I was doing well. But the idea of parting
with Celeste, towards whom I felt such gratitude and affection, was
most painful; and when I talked about it, poor Celeste would cry so
much, that I could not help joining her, although I kissed away her
tears. At the end of twelve weeks, the surgeon could no longer
withhold his report, and we were ordered to be ready in two days to
march to Toulon, where we were to join another party of prisoners,
to proceed with them into the interior. I must pass over our parting,
which the reader may imagine was very painful. I promised to write
to Celeste, and she promised that she would answer my letters, if it

were permitted. We shook hands with Colonel O'Brien, thanking him for his kindness, and, much to his regret, we were taken in charge by two French cuirassiers, who were waiting at the door. As we preferred being continued on parole until our arrival at Toulon, the soldiers were not at all particular about watching us, and we set off on horseback, O'Brien and I going first, and the French cuirassiers following us in the rear.*

We trotted or walked along the road very comfortably. The weather was delightful: we were in high spirits, and almost forgot that we were prisoners. The cuirassiers followed us at a distance of twenty yards, conversing with each other, and O'Brien observed that it was amazingly genteel of the French governor to provide us with two servants in such handsome liveries. The evening of the second day we arrived at Toulon, and as soon as we entered the gates, we were delivered into the custody of an officer with a very sinister cast of countenance, who, after some conversation with the cuirassiers, told us in a surly tone that our parole was at an end, and gave us in charge of a corporal's guard, with directions to conduct us to the prison near the Arsenal. We presented the cuiraissiers with four dollars each, for their civility, and were then hurried away to our place of captivity. I observed to O'Brien, that I was afraid that we must now bid farewell to anything like pleasure. "You're right there, Peter," replied he: "but there's a certain jewel called Hope, that somebody found at the bottom of his chest, when it was clean empty, and so we must not lose sight of it, but try and escape as soon as we can; but the less we talk about it the better." In a few minutes we arrived at our destination: the door was opened, ourselves and our bundles (for we had only selected a few things for our march, the colonel promising to forward the remainder as soon as we wrote to inform him to which depot we were consigned), were rudely shoved in; and as the doors again closed, and the heavy bolts were shot, I felt a creeping, chilly sensation pass through my whole body.

As soon as we could see—for although the prison was not very dark, yet so suddenly thrown in, after the glare of a bright sunshiny day, at first we could distinguish nothing—we found ourselves in company with about thirty English sailors. Most of them were sit-

* *Cuirassiers: Cavalrymen.*

ting down on the pavement, or on boxes, or bundles containing their clothes that they had secured, conversing with each other, or playing at cards or draughts. Our entrance appeared to excite little attention; after having raised their eyes to indulge their curiosity, they continued their pursuits. I have often thought what a feeling of selfishness appeared to pervade the whole of them. At the time I was shocked, as I expected immediate sympathy and commiseration; but afterwards I was not surprised. Many of these poor fellows had been months in the prison, and a short confinement will produce that indifference to the misfortunes of others, which I then observed. Indeed, one man, who was playing at cards, looked up for a moment as we came in, and cried out, "Hurrah, my lads! the more the merrier," as if he really was pleased to find that there were others who were as unfortunate as himself. We stood looking at the groups for about ten minutes, when O'Brien observed, "that we might as well come to an anchor, foul ground being better than no bottom"; so we sat down in a corner, upon our bundles, where we remained for more than an hour, surveying the scene, without speaking a word to each other. I could not speak—I felt so very miserable. I thought of my father and mother in England, of my captain and my messmates, who were sailing about so happily in the frigate, of the kind Colonel O'Brien, and dear little Celeste, and the tears trickled down my cheeks as these scenes of former happiness passed through my mind in quick succession. O'Brien did not speak but once, and then he only said, "This is dull work, Peter."

We had been in the prison about two hours, when a lad in a very greasy, ragged jacket, with a pale emaciated face, came up to us, and said, "I perceive by your uniforms that you are both officers, as well as myself."

O'Brien stared at him for a little while, and then answered, "Upon my soul and honour, then, you've the advantage of us, for it's more than I could perceive in you; but I'll take your word for it. Pray what ship may have had the misfortune of losing such a credit to the service?"

"Why, I belonged to the *Snapper* cutter," replied the young lad; "I was taken in a prize, which the commanding officer had given in my charge to take to Gibraltar: but they won't believe that I'm an officer. I have applied for officer's allowance and rations, and they won't give them to me."

"Well, but they know that we are officers," replied O'Brien; "why do they shove us in here, with the common seamen?"

"I suppose you are only put in here for the present," replied the cutter's midshipman; "but why I cannot tell."

Nor could we, until afterwards, when we found out, as our narrative will show, that the officer who received us from the cuirassiers had once quarrelled with Colonel O'Brien, who first pulled his nose, and afterwards ran him through the body. Being told by the cuirassiers that we were much esteemed by Colonel O'Brien, he resolved to annoy us as much as he could; and when he sent up the document announcing our arrival, he left out the word "Officers," and put us in confinement with the common seamen. "It's very hard upon me not to have my regular allowance as an officer," continued the midshipman. "They only give me a black loaf and three sous a day. If I had had my best uniform on, they never would have disputed my being an officer; but the scoundrels who retook the prize stole all my traps, and I have nothing but this old jacket."

"Why, then," replied O'Brien, "you'll know the value of dress for the future. You cutter and gun-brig midshipmen go about in such a dirty state, that you are hardly acknowledged by us who belong to frigates to be officers, much less gentlemen. You look so dirty and so slovenly when we pass you in the dockyard, that we give you a wide berth; how then can you suppose strangers to believe that you are either officers or gentlemen? Upon my conscience, I absolve the Frenchmen from all prejudice, for, as to your being an officer, we, as Englishmen, have nothing but your bare word for it."

"Well, it's very hard," replied the lad, "to be attacked this way by a brother officer; your coat will be as shabby as mine, before you have been here long."

"That's very true, my darling," returned O'Brien: "but at least I shall have the pleasant reflection that I came in as a gentleman, although I may not exactly go out under the same appearance. Good night, and pleasant dreams to you!" I thought O'Brien rather cross in speaking in such a way, but he was himself always as remarkably neat and well dressed, as he was handsome and well made.

Fortunately we were not destined to remain long in this detestable hole. After a night of misery, during which we remained sitting on our bundles, and sleeping how we could, leaning with our backs against the damp wall, we were roused at daybreak by the unbarring of the prison doors, followed up with an order to go into the prison yard. We were huddled out like a flock of sheep, by a file of soldiers with loaded muskets; and, as we went into the yard, were ranged two and two. The same officer who ordered us into prison, commanded the detachment of soldiers who had us in charge. O'Brien stepped out of the ranks, and, addressing them, stated that we were officers, and had no right to be treated like common sailors. The French officer replied, that he had better information, and that we wore coats which did not belong to us; upon which O'Brien was in a great rage, calling the officer a liar, and demanding satisfaction for the insult, appealing to the French soldiers, and stating, that Colonel O'Brien, who was at Cette, was his countryman, and had received him for two months into his house upon parole, which was quite sufficient to establish his being an officer. The French soldiers appeared to side with O'Brien after they had heard this explanation, stating that no common English sailor could speak such good French, and that they were present when we were sent in on parole, and they asked the officer whether he intended to give satisfaction. The officer stormed, and drawing his sword out of the scabbard, struck O'Brien with the flat of the blade, looking at him with con- tempt, and ordering him into the ranks. I could not help observing that, during this scene, the men-of-war sailors who were among the prisoners, were very indignant, while, on the contrary, those cap- tured in merchant vessels appeared to be pleased with the insult offered to O'Brien. One of the French soldiers then made a sarcastic remark, that the French officer did not much like the name of O'Brien. This so enraged the officer, that he flew at O'Brien, pushed him back into the ranks, and taking out a pistol, threatened to shoot him through the head. I must do the justice to the French soldiers, that they all cried out "Shame!" They did not appear to have the same discipline, or the same respect for an officer, as the soldiers have in our service, or they would not have been so free in their language; yet, at the same time, they obeyed all his orders on service very implicitly.

When O'Brien returned to the ranks, he looked defiance at the officer, telling him, "That he would pocket the affront very carefully, as he intended to bring it out again upon a future and more suitable occasion." We were then marched out in ranks, two and two, being met at the street by two drummers, and a crowd of people, who had gathered to witness our departure. The drums beat, and away we went. The officer who had charge of us mounted a small horse, galloping up and down from one end of the ranks to the other, with his sword drawn, bullying, swearing, and striking with the flat of the blade at any one of the prisoners who was not in his proper place. When we were close to the gates, we were joined by another detachment of prisoners: we were then ordered to halt, and were informed, through an interpreter, that any one attempting to escape would immediately be shot, after which information we once more proceeded on our route.

Nothing remarkable occurred during our first day's march, except perhaps a curious conversation between O'Brien and one of the French soldiers, in which they disputed about the comparative bravery of the two nations. O'Brien, in his argument, told the Frenchman that his countrymen could not stand a charge of English bayonets. The Frenchman replied that there was no doubt but the French were quite as brave as the English—even more so; and that, as for not standing the charge of bayonets, it was not because they were less brave; but the fact was, that they were most excessively *ticklish*. We had black bread and sour wine served out to us this day, when we halted to refresh. O'Brien persuaded a soldier to purchase something for us more eatable; but the French officer heard of it, and was very angry, ordering the soldier to the rear.

—◆◆◆—

CHAPTER XX

O'Brien fights a duel with a French officer, and proves that the great art of fencing is knowing nothing about it—We arrive at our new quarters, which we find very secure.

A T NIGHT we arrived at a small town, the name of which I forget. Here we were all put into an old church for the night, and a very bad night we passed. They did not even give us a little straw to lie down upon: the roof of the church had partly fallen in, and the moon shone through very brightly. This was some comfort; for to have been shut up in the dark, seventy-five in number, would have been very miserable. We were afraid to lie down anywhere, as, like all ruined buildings in France, the ground was covered with filth, and the smell was shocking. O'Brien was very thoughtful, and would hardly answer any question that I put to him; it was evident that he was brooding over the affront which he had received from the French officer. At daybreak, the door of the church was again opened by the French soldiers, and we were conducted to the square of the town, where we found the troops quartered, drawn up with their officers, to receive us from the detachment who had escorted us from Toulon. We were very much pleased with this, as we knew that we should be forwarded by another detachment, and thus be rid of the brutal officer who had hitherto had charge of the prisoners. But we were rid of him in another way. As the French officers walked along our ranks to look at us, I perceived among them a captain, whom we had known very intimately when we were living at Cette with Colonel O'Brien. I cried out his name immediately; he turned round, and seeing O'Brien and me, he came up to us, shaking us by the hand, and expressing his surprise at finding us in such a situation. O'Brien explained to him how we had been treated, at which he expressed his indignation, as did the other officers who had collected round us. The major who commanded the troops in the town turned to the French officer (he was only a lieutenant) who had conducted us from Toulon, and demanded of him his reason for behaving to us in such an unworthy manner. He denied having treated us ill, and said that he had been informed that we had put on officers' dresses which did not belong to us. At this O'Brien declared that he was a liar, and a cowardly *foutre,* that he had struck him with the back of his sabre, which he would not have dared do if he had not been a prisoner; adding, that all he requested was satisfaction for the insult offered to him, and appealed to the officers whether, if it were refused, the lieutenant's epaulets ought not to be cut off his shoulders.* The major commandant and the officers retired to consult, and, after a few minutes, they agreed that the lieutenant was bound to give the satisfaction required. The lieutenant replied that he was ready; but, at the same time, did not appear to be very willing. The prisoners were left in charge of the soldiers, under a junior officer, while the others, accompanied by O'Brien,

* Foutre: *Bugger.*

myself, and the lieutenant, walked to a short distance outside the town. As we proceeded there, I asked O'Brien with what weapons they would fight.

"I take it for granted," replied he, "that it will be with the small sword."

"But," said I, "do you know anything about fencing?"

"Devil a bit, Peter; but that's all in my favour."

"How can that be?" replied I.

"I'll tell you, Peter. If one man fences well, and another is but an indifferent hand at it, it is clear that the first will run the other through the body; but, if the other knows nothing at all about it, why then, Peter, the case is not quite so clear: because the good fencer is almost as much puzzled by your ignorance as you are by his skill, and you become on more equal terms. Now, Peter, I've made up my mind that I'll run that fellow through the body, and so I will, as sure as I am an O'Brien."

"Well, I hope you will; but pray do not be too sure."

"It's feeling sure that will make me able to do it, Peter. By the blood of the O'Briens! didn't he slap me with his sword, as if I were a clown in the pantomime. Peter, I'll kill the harlequin scoundrel, and my word's as good as my bond!"

By this time we had arrived at the ground. The French lieutenant stripped to his shirt and trousers; O'Brien did the same, kicking his boots off, and standing upon the wet grass in his stockings. The swords were measured, and handed to them; they took their distance, and set to. I must say, that I was breathless with anxiety; the idea of losing O'Brien struck me with grief and terror. I then felt the value of all his kindness to me, and would have taken his place, and have been run through the body, rather than he should have been hurt. At first, O'Brien put himself in the correct attitude of defence, in imitation of the lieutenant, but this was for a very few seconds; he suddenly made a spring, and rushed on to his adversary, stabbing at him with a velocity quite astonishing, the lieutenant parrying in his defence, until at last he had an opportunity of lunging at O'Brien. O'Brien, who no longer kept his left arm raised in equipoise, caught the sword of the lieutenant at within six inches of the point, and directing it under his left arm, as he rushed in, passed his own through the lieutenant's body. It was all over in less than a minute—the lieutenant did not live half an hour afterwards. The

French officers were very much surprised at the result, for they perceived at once that O'Brien knew nothing of fencing. O'Brien gathered a tuft of grass, wiped the sword, which he presented to the officer to whom it belonged, and thanking the major and the whole of them for their impartiality and gentlemanlike conduct, led the way to the square, where he again took his station in the ranks of the prisoners.

Shortly after, the major commandant came up to us, and asked whether we would accept of our parole, as, in that case, we might travel as we pleased. We consented, with many thanks for his civility and kindness; but I could not help thinking at the time, that the French officers were a little mortified at O'Brien's success, although they were too honourable to express the feeling. O'Brien told me, after we had quitted the town, that had it not been for the handsome conduct of the officers, he would not have accepted our parole, as he felt convinced that we could have easily made our escape. We talked over the matter a long while, and at last agreed that there would be a better chance of success by and by, when more closely guarded, than there would be now, under consideration of all circumstances, as it required previously concerted arrangements to get out of the country.

I had almost forgotten to say, that on our return after the duel the cutter's midshipman called out to O'Brien, requesting him to state to the commandant that he was also an officer; but O'Brien replied, that there was no evidence for it but his bare word. If he was an officer he must prove it himself, as everything in his appearance flatly contradicted his assertion.

"It's very hard," replied the midshipman, "that because my jacket's a little tarry or so I must lose my rank."

"My dear fellow," replied O'Brien, "it's not because your jacket's a little tarry; it is because what the Frenchmen call your *tout ensemble* is quite disgraceful in an officer. Look at your face in the first puddle, and you'll find that it would dirty the water you look into. Look at your shoulders above your ears, and your back with a bow like a *kink* in a cable. Your trousers, sir, you have pulled your legs too far through, showing a foot and a half of worsted stockings. In short, look at yourself altogether, and then tell me, provided you be an officer, whether, from respect to the service, it would not be my duty to contradict it. It goes against my conscience, my dear fellow;

but recollect that when we arrive at the dépôt, you will be able to prove it, so it's only waiting a little while, until the captains will pass their word for you, which is more than I will."

"Well, it's very hard," replied the midshipman, "that I must go on eating this black rye bread; and very unkind of you."

"It's very kind of me, you spalpeen of the *Snapper*. Prison will be a paradise to you, when you get into good commons. How you'll relish your grub by-and-by! So now shut your pan, or by the tail of Jonah's whale, I'll swear you're a Spaniard."

I could not help thinking that O'Brien was very severe upon the poor lad, and I expostulated with him afterwards. He replied, "Peter, if, as a cutter's midshipman, he is a bit of an officer, the devil a bit is he of a gentleman, either born or bred: and I'm not bound to bail every blackguard-looking chap that I meet. By the head of St Peter, I would blush to be seen in his company, if I were in the wildest bog in Ireland, with nothing but an old crow as spectator."

We were now again permitted to be on our parole, and received every attention and kindness from the different officers who commanded the detachments which passed the prisoners from one town to another. In a few days we arrived at Montpelier, where we had orders to remain a short time until directions were received from Government as to the dépôts for prisoners to which we were to be sent. At this delightful town, we had unlimited parole, not even a gendarme accompanying us. We lived at the table d'hôte, were permitted to walk about where we pleased, and amused ourselves every evening at the theatre. During our stay there we wrote to Colonel O'Brien at Cette, thanking him for his kindness, and narrating what had occurred since we parted. I also wrote to Celeste, enclosing my letter unsealed in the one to Colonel O'Brien. I told her the history of O'Brien's duel, and all I could think would interest her; how sorry I was to have parted from her; that I never would forget her; and trusted that some day, as she was only half a Frenchwoman, we should meet again. Before we left Montpelier, we had the pleasure of receiving answers to our letters: the colonel's letters were very kind, particularly the one to me, in which he called me his dear boy, and hoped that I should soon rejoin my friends, and prove an ornament to my country. In his letter to O'Brien, he requested him not to run me into useless danger—to recollect that I was not so well able to undergo extreme hardship. I have no doubt but that this caution referred to O'Brien's intention to escape from prison, which he had not concealed from the colonel, and the probability that I would be a partner in the attempt. The answer from Celeste was written in English; but she must have had assistance from her father, or she could not have succeeded so well. It was like herself, very kind and affectionate; and also ended with wishing me a speedy return to my friends, who must (she said) be so fond of me, that she despaired of ever seeing me more, but that she consoled herself as well as she could with the assurance that I should be happy. I forgot to say, that Colonel O'Brien, in his letter to me, stated that he expected immediate orders to leave Cette, and take the command of some military post in the interior, or join the army, but which, he could not tell; that they had packed up everything, and he was afraid that our correspondence must cease, as he could not state to what place we should direct our letters. I could not help thinking at the time, that it was a delicate way of pointing out to us that it was not right that he should correspond with us in our relative situations; but still, I was sure that he was about to leave Cette, for he never would have made use of a subterfuge.

I must here acquaint the reader with a circumstance which I forgot to mention, which was that when Captain Savage sent in a flag of truce with our clothes and money, I thought that it was but justice to O'Brien that they should know on board of the frigate the gallant manner in which he had behaved. I knew that he would never tell himself, so, ill as I was at the time, I sent for Colonel O'Brien, and requested him to write down my statement of the affair, in which I mentioned how O'Brien had spiked the last gun, and had been taken prisoner by so doing, together with his attempting to save me. When the colonel had written all down, I requested that he would send for the major, who first entered the fort with the troops, and translate it to him in French. This he did in my presence, and the major declared every word to be true. "Will he attest it, colonel, as it may be of great service to O'Brien?" The major immediately assented. Colonel O'Brien then enclosed my letter, with a short note from himself, to Captain Savage, paying him a compliment, and assuring him that his gallant young officers should be treated with every attention, and all the kindness which the rules of war would admit of. O'Brien never knew that I had sent that letter, as the colonel, at my request, kept the secret.

In ten days we received an order to march on the following morning. The sailors, among whom was our poor friend the midshipman of the *Snapper* cutter, were ordered to Verdun; O'Brien and I, with eight masters of merchant vessels, who joined us at Montpelier, were directed by the Government to be sent to Givet, a fortified town in the department of Ardennes. But, at the same time, orders arrived from Government to treat the prisoners with great strictness, and not to allow any parole; the reason of this, we were informed, was that accounts had been sent to Government of the death of the French officer in the duel with O'Brien, and they had expressed their dissatisfaction at its having been permitted. Indeed, I very much doubt whether it would have been permitted in our country, but the French officers are almost romantically chivalrous in their ideas of honour; in fact, as enemies, I have always considered them as worthy antagonists to the English, and they appear more respectable in themselves, and more demanding our goodwill in that situation, than they do when we meet them as friends, and are acquainted with the other points of their character, which lessen them in our estimation.

I shall not dwell upon a march of three weeks, during which we alternately received kind or unhandsome treatment, according to the dispositions of those who had us in charge; but I must observe, that it was invariably the case, that officers who were gentlemen by birth treated us with consideration, while those who had sprung from nothing during the Revolution, were harsh, and sometimes even brutal. It was exactly four months from the time of our capture that we arrived at our destined prison at Givet.

"Peter," said O'Brien, as he looked hastily at the fortifications, and the river which divided the two towns, "I see no reason, either English or French, that we should not eat our Christmas dinner in England. I've a bird's eye view of the outside, and now, have only to find out whereabouts we may be in the inside."

I must say that, when I looked at the ditches and high ramparts, I had a different opinion; so had a gendarme who was walking by our side, and who had observed O'Brien's scrutiny, and who quietly said to him in French, *"Vous le croyez possible!"*

"Everything is possible to a brave man—the French armies have proved that," answered O'Brien.

"You are right," replied the gendarme, pleased with the compli-

ment to his nation; "I wish you success, you will deserve it; but—"
and he shook his head.

"If I could but obtain a plan of the fortress," said O'Brien, "I
would give five Napoleons for one," and he looked at the gendarme.

"I cannot see any objection to an officer, although a prisoner,
studying fortification," replied the gendarme. "In two hours you
will be within the walls; and now I recollect, in the map of the two
towns, the fortress is laid down sufficiently accurately to give you
an idea of it. But we have conversed too long." So saying, the gendarme dropped into the rear.

In a quarter of an hour, we arrived at the Place d'Armes, where
we were met, as usual, by another detachment of troops, and drummers, who paraded us through the town previous to our being
drawn up before the governor's house. This, I ought to have ob
served, was, by order of Government, done at every town we
passed through; it was very contemptible, but prisoners were so
scarce, that they made all the display of us that they could. As we
stopped at the governor's house, the gendarme, who had left us in
the square, made a sign to O'Brien, as much as to say, I have it.
O'Brien took out five Napoleons, which he wrapped in paper, and
held in his hand. In a minute or two, the gendarme came up and
presented O'Brien with an old silk handkerchief, saying, "*Votre
mouchoir, monsieur.*"*

"*Merci,*" replied O'Brien, putting the handkerchief which contained the map into his pocket, "*voici à boire, mon ami*"†; and he
slipped the paper with the five Napoleons into the hand of the gendarme, who immediately retreated.

This was very fortunate for us, as we afterwards discovered that
a mark had been put against O'Brien's and my name, not to allow
parole or permission to leave the fortress, even under surveillance.
Indeed, even if it had not been so, we never should have obtained it,
as the lieutenant killed by O'Brien was nearly related to the commandant of the fortress, who was as much a *mauvais sujet* as his
kinsman.‡ Having waited the usual hour before the governor's

* Votre mouchoir, monsieur: *Your handkerchief, sir.*
† Voici à boire, mon ami: *Take this for a drink, my friend.*
‡ Mauvais sujet: *Bad fellow.*

house, to answer to our muster-roll, and to be stared at, we were dismissed; and in a few minutes, found ourselves shut up in one of the strongest fortresses in France.

—◦◊◦—

CHAPTER XXI

O'Brien receives his commission as lieutenant, and then we take French leave of Givet.

IF I DOUBTED the practicability of escape when I examined the exterior, when we were ushered into the interior of the fortress, I felt that it was impossible, and I stated my opinion to O'Brien. We were conducted into a yard surrounded by a high wall; the buildings appropriated for the prisoners were built with *lean-to* roofs on one side, and at each side of the square was a sentry looking down upon us. It was very much like the dens which they now build for bears, only so much larger. O'Brien answered me with a "Pish! Peter, it's the very security of the place which will enable us to get out of it. But don't talk, as there are always spies about who understand English."

We were shown into a room allotted to six of us; our baggage was examined, and then delivered over to us. "Better and better, Peter," observed O'Brien, "they've not found it out!"

"What?" inquired I.

"Oh, only a little selection of articles, which might be useful to us by-and-by."

He then showed me what I never before was aware of: that he had a false bottom to his trunk; but it was papered over like the rest, and very ingeniously concealed. "And what is there, O'Brien?" inquired I.

"Never mind; I had them made at Montpelier. You'll see by-and-by."

The others, who were lodged in the same room, then came in, and after staying a quarter of an hour, went away at the sound of the dinner-bell. "Now, Peter," said O'Brien, "I must get rid of my load. Turn the key."

O'Brien then undressed himself, and when he threw off his shirt and drawers, showed me a rope of silk, with a knot at every two feet, about half-an-inch in size, wound round and round his body. There were about sixty feet of it altogether. As I unwound it, he, turning round and round, observed, "Peter, I've worn this rope ever since I left Montpelier, and you've no idea of the pain I have suffered; but we must go to England, that's decided upon."

When I looked at O'Brien, as the rope was wound off, I could easily imagine that he had really been in great pain; in several places his flesh was quite raw from the continual friction, and after it was all unwound, and he had put on his clothes, he fainted away. I was very much alarmed, but I recollected to put the rope into the trunk, and take out the key, before I called for assistance. He soon came to, and on being asked what was the matter, said that he was subject to fits from his infancy. He looked earnestly at me, and I showed him the key, which was sufficient.

For some days O'Brien, who really was not very well, kept to his room. During this time, he often examined the map given him by the gendarme. One day he said to me, "Peter, can you swim?"

"No," replied I; "but never mind that."

"But I must mind it, Peter; for observe, we shall have to cross the river Meuse, and boats are not always to be had. You observe, that this fortress is washed by the river on one side: and as it is the strongest side, it is the least guarded—we must escape by it. I can see my way clear enough till we get to the second rampart on the river, but when we drop into the river, if you cannot swim, I must contrive to hold you up, somehow or another."

"Are you then determined to escape, O'Brien? I cannot perceive how we are even to get up this wall, with four sentries staring us in the face."

"Never do you mind that, Peter, mind your own business; and first tell me, do you intend to try your luck with me?"

"Yes," replied I, "most certainly; if you have sufficient confidence in me to take me as your companion."

"To tell you the truth, Peter, I would not give a farthing to escape without you. We were taken together, and, please God, we'll take ourselves off together; but that must not be for this month; our greatest help will be the dark nights and foul weather."

The prison was by all accounts very different from Verdun and some others. We had no parole, and but little communication with the townspeople. Some were permitted to come in and supply us with various articles; but their baskets were searched to see that they contained nothing that might lead to an escape on the part of the prisoners. Without the precautions that O'Brien had taken, any attempt would have been useless. Still, O'Brien, as soon as he left his room, did obtain several little articles—especially balls of twine—for one of the amusements of the prisoners was flying kites. This, however, was put a stop to, in consequence of one of the strings, whether purposely or not, I cannot say, catching the lock of the musket carried by one of the sentries who looked down upon us, and twitching it out of his hand; after which an order was given by the commandant for no kites to be permitted. This was fortunate for us, as O'Brien, by degrees, purchased all the twine belonging to the other prisoners; and, as we were more than three hundred in number, it amounted to sufficient to enable him, by stealth, to lay it up into very strong cord, or rather, into a sort of square plait, known only to sailors. "Now, Peter," said he one day, "I want nothing more than an umbrella for you."

"Why an umbrella for me?"

"To keep you from being drowned with too much water, that's all."

"Rain won't drown me."

"No, no, Peter; but buy a new one as soon as you can."

I did so. O'Brien boiled up a quantity of bees' wax and oil, and gave it several coats of this preparation. He then put it carefully away in the ticking of his bed. I asked him whether he intended to make known his plan to any of the other prisoners; he replied in the negative, saying, that there were so many of them who could not be trusted, that he would trust no one. We had been now about two months in Givet, when a Steel's List was sent to a lieutenant, who was confined there.* The lieutenant came up to O'Brien, and asked him his Christian name. "Terence, to be sure," replied O'Brien.

"Then," answered the lieutenant, "I may congratulate you on your promotion, for here you are upon the list of August."

"Sure there must be some trifling mistake; let me look at it.

---

* Steel's List: An official publication issued by the London publisher Steel from 1780 to 1815 containing a list of the officers of the navy.

Terence O'Brien, sure enough; but now the question is, has any other fellow robbed me of my name and promotion at the same time? Bother, what can it mane? I won't belave it—not a word of it. I've no more interest than a dog who drags cats'-meat."

"Really, O'Brien," observed I, "I cannot see why you should not be made; I am sure you deserve your promotion for your conduct when you were taken prisoner."

"And what did I do then, you simple Peter, but put you on my back as the men do their hammocks when they are piped down; but, barring all claim, how could anyone know what took place in the battery, except you, and I, and the armourer, who lay dead? So explain that, Peter, if you can."

"I think I can," replied I, after the lieutenant had left us. And I then told O'Brien how I had written to Captain Savage, and had had the fact attested by the major who had made us prisoners.

"Well, Peter," said O'Brien, after a pause, "there's a fable about a lion and a mouse. If, by your means, I have obtained my promotion, why then the mouse is a finer baste than the lion; but instead of being happy, I shall now be miserable until the truth is ascertained one way or the other, and that's another reason why I must set off to England as fast as I can."

For a few days after this O'Brien was very uneasy; but fortunately letters arrived by that time; one to me from my father, in which he requested me to draw for whatever money I might require, saying that the whole family would retrench in every way to give me all the comfort which might be obtained in my unfortunate situation. I wept at his kindness, and more than ever longed to throw myself in his arms, and thank him. He also told me that my uncle William was dead, and that there was only one between him and the title, but that my grandfather was in good health, and had been very kind to him lately. My mother was much afflicted at my having been made a prisoner, and requested I would write as often as I could. O'Brien's letter was from Captain Savage; the frigate had been sent home with despatches, and O'Brien's conduct represented to the Admiralty, which had, in consequence, promoted him to the rank of lieutenant. O'Brien came to me with the letter, his countenance radiant with joy as he put it into my hands. In return I put mine into his, and he read it over.

"Peter, my boy, I'm under great obligations to you. When you were wounded and feverish, you thought of me at a time when you had quite enough to think of yourself; but I never thank in words. I see your uncle William is dead. How many more uncles have you?"

"My uncle John, who is married, and has already two daughters."

"Blessings on him; may he stick to the female line of business! Peter, my boy, you shall be a lord before you die."

"Nonsense, O'Brien; I have no chance. Don't put such foolish ideas in my head."

"What chance had I of being a lieutenant, and am I not one? Well, Peter, you've helped to make a lieutenant of me, but I'll make a *man* of you, and that's better. Peter, I perceive, with all your simplicity, that you're not over and above simple, and that, with all your asking for advice, you can think and act for yourself on an emergency. Now, Peter, these are talents that must not be thrown away in this cursed hole, and therefore, my boy, prepare yourself to quit this place in a week, wind and weather permitting; that is to say, not fair wind and weather, but the fouler the better. Will you be ready at any hour of any night that I call you up?"

"Yes, O'Brien, I will, and do my best."

"No man can do much more that ever I heard of. But, Peter, do me one favour, as I am really a lieutenant, just touch your hat to me only once, that's all; but I wish the compliment, just to see how it looks."

"Lieutenant O'Brien," said I, touching my hat, "have you any further orders?"

"Yes, sir," replied he; "that you never presume to touch your hat to me again, unless we sail together, and then that's a different sort of thing."

About a week afterwards, O'Brien came to me, and said, "The new moon's quartered in with foul weather; if it holds, prepare for a start. I have put what is necessary in your little haversack; it may be to-night. Go to bed now, and sleep for a week if you can, for you'll get but little sleep, if we succeed, for the week to come."

This was about eight o'clock. I went to bed, and about twelve I was roused by O'Brien, who told me to dress myself carefully, and come down to him in the yard. I did so without disturbing anybody, and found the night as dark as pitch (it was then November), and raining in torrents; the wind was high, howling round the yard, and sweeping in the rain in every direction as it eddied to and fro. It was some time before I could find O'Brien, who was hard at work; and, as I had already been made acquainted with all his plans, I will now explain them. At Montpelier he had procured six large pieces of iron, about eighteen inches long, with a gimlet at one end of each, and a square at the other, which fitted to a handle which unshipped. For precaution he had a spare handle, but each handle fitted to all the irons. O'Brien had screwed one of these pieces of iron between the interstices of the stones of which the wall was built, and sitting astride on that, was fixing another about three feet above. When he had accomplished this, he stood upon the lower iron, and supporting himself by the second, which about met his hip, he screwed in a third, always fixing them about six inches on one side of the other, and not one above the other. When he had screwed in his six irons, he was about half up the wall, and then he fastened his rope, which he had carried round his neck, to the upper iron, and lowering himself down, unscrewed the four lower irons: then ascending by the rope, he stood upon the fifth iron, and supporting himself by the upper iron, recommenced his task. By these means he arrived in the course of an hour and a half to the top of the wall, where he fixed his last iron, and making his rope fast, he came down again. "Now, Peter," said he, "there is no fear of the sentries seeing us; if they had the eyes of cats, they could not until we were on the top of the wall; but then we arrive at the glacis, and we must creep to the ramparts on our bellies.* I am going up with all the materials. Give me your haversack—you will go up lighter; and recollect, should any accident happen to me, you run to bed again. If, on the contrary, I pull the rope up and down three or four times, you may sheer up it as fast as you can." O'Brien then loaded himself with the other rope, the two knapsacks, iron crows, and other implements he had procured; and, last of all, with the umbrella. "Peter, if the rope bears me with all this, it is clear it will bear such a creature as you are, therefore don't be afraid." So whispering, he commenced his ascent; in about three minutes he was up, and the rope pulled. I immediately followed him, and found the rope very easy to climb, from the knots at every two feet, which gave me a hold for my feet, and I was up in as short a time as he was. He caught me by the collar, putting his

* Glacis: A slope meant to place those crossing it directly in the line of fire.

wet hand on my mouth, and I lay down beside him while he pulled up the rope. We then crawled on our stomachs across the glacis till we arrived at the rampart. The wind blew tremendously, and the rain pattered down so fast, that the sentries did not perceive us; indeed, it was no fault of theirs, for it was impossible to have made us out. It was some time before O'Brien could find out the point exactly above the drawbridge of the first ditch; at last he did—he fixed his crow-bar in, and lowered down the rope. "Now, Peter, I had better go first again; when I shake the rope from below, all's right." O'Brien descended, and in a few minutes the rope again shook; I followed him, and found myself received in his arms upon the meeting of the drawbridge; but the drawbridge itself was up. O'Brien led the way across the chains, and I followed him. When we had crossed the moat, we found a barrier gate locked; this puzzled us. O'Brien pulled out his picklocks to pick it, but without success; here we were fast. "We must undermine the gate, O'Brien; we must pull up the pavement until we can creep under." "Peter, you are a fine fellow; I never thought of that." We worked very hard until the hole was large enough, using the crow-bar which was left, and a little wrench which O'Brien had with him. By these means we got under the gate in the course of an hour or more. This gate led to the lower rampart, but we had a covered way to pass through before we arrived at it. We proceeded very cautiously, when we heard a noise: we stopped, and found that it was a sentry, who was fast asleep, and snoring. Little expecting to find one here, we were puzzled; pass him we could not well, as he was stationed on the very spot where we required to place our crow-bar to descend the lower rampart into the river. O'Brien thought for a moment. "Peter," said he, "now is the time for you to prove yourself a man. He is fast asleep, but his noise must be stopped. I will stop his mouth, but at the very moment that I do so you must throw open the pan of his musket, and then he cannot fire it." "I will, O'Brien; don't fear me." We crept cautiously up to him, and O'Brien motioning to me to put my thumb upon the pan, I did so, and the moment that O'Brien put his hand upon the soldier's mouth, I threw open the pan. The fellow struggled, and snapped his lock as a signal, but of course without discharging his musket, and in a minute he was not only gagged but bound by O'Brien, with my assistance. Leaving him there, we proceeded to the rampart, and fixing the crow-bar again, O'Brien descended; I followed him, and found him in the river, hanging on to the rope; the umbrella was opened and turned upwards; the preparation made it resist the water, and, as previously explained to me by O'Brien, I had only to hold on at arm's length to two beckets which he had affixed to the point of the umbrella, which was under water.* To the same part O'Brien had a tow-line, which taking in his teeth, he towed me down with the stream to about a hundred yards clear of the fortress, where we landed. O'Brien was so exhausted that for a few minutes he remained quite motionless; I also was benumbed with the cold. "Peter," said he, "thank God we have succeeded so far; now must we push on as far as we can, for we shall have daylight in two hours."

O'Brien took out his flask of spirits, and we both drank a half tumbler at least, but we should not in our state have been affected with a bottle. We now walked along the river-side till we fell in with a small craft, with a boat towing astern: O'Brien swam to it, and cutting the painter without getting in, towed it on shore. The oars were fortunately in the boat. I got in, we shoved off, and rowed away down the stream till the dawn of day. "All's right, Peter; now we'll land. This is the Forest of Ardennes." We landed, replaced the oars in the boat, and pushed her off into the stream, to induce people to suppose that she had broken adrift, and then hastened into the thickest of the wood. It still rained hard; I shivered, and my teeth chattered with the cold, but there was no help for it. We again took a dram of spirits, and, worn out with fatigue and excitement, soon fell fast asleep upon a bed of leaves which we had collected together.

---

* *Beckets: Often a loop of rope with a knot at one end and an eye at the other; also a large hook or wooden bracket used to hold loose ropes.*

———◦*◦*◦———

CHAPTER XXII

Grave consequences of gravitation—O'Brien enlists himself as a gendarme, and takes charge of me—We are discovered, and obliged to run for it—The pleasures of a winter bivouac.

IT WAS NOT until noon that I awoke, when I found that O'Brien had covered me more than a foot deep with leaves to protect me from the weather. I felt quite warm and comfortable; my clothes had dried on me, but without giving me cold. "How very kind of you, O'Brien!" said I.

"Not a bit, Peter: you have hard work to go through yet, and I must take care of you. You're but a bud, and I'm a full-blown rose." So saying, he put the spirit-flask to his mouth, and then handed it to me. "Now, Peter, we must make a start, for depend upon it they will scour the country for us; but this is a large wood, and they may as well attempt to find a needle in a bundle of hay, if we once get into the heart of it."

"I think," said I, "that this forest is mentioned by Shakespeare, in one of his plays."

"Very likely, Peter," replied O'Brien; "but we are at no playwork now; and what reads amazing prettily, is no joke in reality. I've often observed, that your writers never take the weather into consideration."

"I beg your pardon, O'Brien; in *King Lear* the weather was tremendous."

"Very likely; but who was the king that went out in such weather?"

"King Lear did, when he was mad."

"So he was, that's certain, Peter; but runaway prisoners have some excuse; so now for a start."

We set off, forcing our way through the thicket, for about three hours, O'Brien looking occasionally at his pocket compass; it then was again nearly dark, and O'Brien proposed a halt. We made up a bed of leaves for the night, and slept much more comfortably than we had the night before. All our bread was wet, but as we had no water, it was rather a relief; the meat we had with us was sufficient for a week. Once more we laid down and fell fast asleep. About five o'clock in the morning I was roused by O'Brien, who at the same time put his hand gently over my mouth. I sat up, and perceived a large fire not far from us. "The Philistines are upon us, Peter," said he; "I have reconnoitred, and they are the gendarmes. I'm fearful of going away, as we may stumble upon some more of them. I've been thinking what's best before I waked you; and it appears to me, that we had better get up the tree, and lie there."

At that time we were hidden in a copse of underwood, with a large oak in the centre, covered with ivy. "I think so too, O'Brien; shall we go up now, or wait a little?"

"Now, to be sure, that they're eating their prog.* Mount you, Peter, and I'll help you."

O'Brien shoved me up the tree, and then waiting a little while to bury our haversacks among the leaves, he followed me. He desired me to remain in a very snug position, on the first fork of the tree, while he took another, amongst a bunch of ivy, on the largest bough. There we remained for about an hour, when day dawned. We observed the gendarmes mustered at the break of day, by the corporal, and then they all separated in different directions, to scour the wood. We were delighted to perceive this, as we hoped soon to be able to get away; but there was one gendarme who remained. He walked to and fro, looking everywhere, until he came directly under the tree in which we were concealed. He poked about, until at last he came to the bed of leaves upon which we had slept; these he turned over and over with his bayonet, until he routed out our haversacks. "Pardi!" exclaimed he, "where the nest and eggs are, the birds are near." He then walked round the tree, looking up into every part, but we were well concealed, and he did not discover us for some time. At last he saw me, and ordered me to come down. I paid no attention to him, as I had no signal from O'Brien. He walked round a little farther, until he was directly under the branch on which O'Brien lay. Taking up this position, he had a fairer aim at me, and levelled his musket, saying, *"Descendez, ou je tire."*† Still I continued immoveable, for I knew not what to do. I shut my eyes, however; the musket shortly afterwards was discharged, and,

---

* *Prog: Food.*
† Descendez, ou je tire: *Come down, or I'll shoot.*

whether from fear or not I can hardly tell, I lost my hold of a sudden, and down I came. I was stunned with the fall, and thought that I must have been wounded, and was very much surprised, when, instead of the gendarme, O'Brien came up to me, and asked whether I was hurt. I answered, I believed not, and got upon my legs, when I found the gendarme lying on the ground, breathing heavily, but insensible. When O'Brien perceived the gendarme level his musket at me, he immediately dropped from the bough, right upon his head; this occasioned the musket to go off, without hitting me, and at the same time, the weight of O'Brien's body from such a height killed the gendarme, for he expired before we left him. "Now, Peter," said O'Brien, "this is the most fortunate thing in the world, and will take us half through the country; but we have no time to lose." He then stripped the gendarme, who still breathed heavily, and dragging him to our bed of leaves, covered him up, threw off his own clothes, which he tied in a bundle, and gave to me to carry, and put on those of the gendarme. I could not help laughing at the metamorphosis, and asked O'Brien what he intended. "Sure, I'm a gendarme, bringing with me a prisoner, who has escaped." He then tied my hands with a cord, shouldered his musket, and off we set. We now quitted the wood as soon as we could; for O'Brien said that he had no fear for the next ten days; and so it proved. We had one difficulty, which was, that we were going the wrong way; but that was obviated by travelling mostly at night, when no questions were asked, except at the cabarets, where we lodged, and they did not know which way we came. When we stopped at night, my youth excited a great deal of commiseration, especially from the females; and in one instance I was offered assistance to escape. I consented to it, but at the same time informed O'Brien of the plan proposed. O'Brien kept watch—I dressed myself, and was at the open window, when he rushed in, seizing me, and declaring that he would inform the Government of the conduct of the parties. Their confusion and distress were very great. They offered O'Brien twenty, thirty, forty Napoleons, if he would hush it up, for they were aware of the penalty and imprisonment. O'Brien replied that he would not accept of any money in compromise of his duty; that after he had given me into the charge of the gendarme of the next post, his business was at an end, and he must return to Flushing, where he was stationed.

"I have a sister there," replied the hostess, "who keeps an inn. You'll want good quarters, and a friendly cup; do not denounce us, and I'll give you a letter to her, which, if it does not prove of service, you can then return and give the information."

O'Brien consented; the letter was delivered, and read to him, in which the sister was requested, by the love she bore to the writer, to do all she could for the bearer, who had the power of making the whole family miserable, but had refused so to do. O'Brien pocketed the letter, filled his brandy-flask, and saluting all the women, left the cabaret, dragging me after him with a cord. The only difference, as O'Brien observed after he went out, was, that he (O'Brien) kissed all the women, and all the women kissed me. In this way, we had proceeded by Charleroy and Louvain, and were within a few miles of Malines, when a circumstance occurred which embarrassed us not a little. We were following our route, avoiding Malines, which was a fortified town, and at the time were in a narrow lane, with wide ditches, full of water, on each side. At the turning of a sharp corner, we met the gendarme who had supplied O'Brien with a map of the town of Givet. "Good morning, comrade," said he to O'Brien, looking earnestly at him, "whom have we here?"

"A young Englishman, whom I picked up close by, escaped from prison."

"Where from?"

"He will not say; but I suspect from Givet."

"There are two who have escaped from Givet," replied he: "how they escaped no one can imagine; but," continued he, again looking at O'Brien, *"avec les braves, il n'y a rien d'impossible."**

"That is true," replied O'Brien; "I have taken one, the other cannot be far off. You had better look for him."

"I should like to find him," replied the gendarme, "for you know that to retake a runaway prisoner is certain promotion. You will be made a corporal."

"So much the better," replied O'Brien; *"adieu, mon ami."*

"Nay, I merely came for a walk, and will return with you to Malines, where of course you are bound."

"We shall not get there to-night," said O'Brien, "my prisoner is too much fatigued."

---

* Avec les braves, il n'y a rien d'impossible: *For the brave, nothing is impossible.*

"Well, then, we will go as far as we can; and I will assist you. Perhaps we may find the second, who, I understand, obtained a map of the fortress by some means or other."

We at once perceived that we were discovered. He afterwards told us that the body of a gendarme had been found in the wood, no doubt murdered by the prisoners, and that the body was stripped naked. "I wonder," continued he, "whether one of the prisoners put on his clothes, and passed as a gendarme."

"Peter," said O'Brien, "are we to murder this man or not?"

"I should say not: pretend to trust him, and then we may give him the slip." This was said during the time that the gendarme stopped a moment behind us.

"Well, we'll try; but first I'll put him off his guard." When the gendarme came up with us, O'Brien observed, that the English prisoners were very liberal; that he knew that a hundred Napoleons were often paid for assistance, and he thought that no corporal's rank was equal to a sum that would in France make a man happy and independent for life.

"Very true," replied the gendarme; "and let me only look upon that sum, and I will guarantee a positive safety out of France."

"Then we understand each other," replied O'Brien; "this boy will give two hundred—one half shall be yours, if you will assist."

"I will think of it," replied the gendarme, who then talked about indifferent subjects, until we arrived at a small town, called Acarchot, where we proceeded to a cabaret. The usual curiosity passed over, we were left alone, O'Brien telling the gendarme that he would expect his reply that night or to-morrow morning. The gendarme said, to-morrow morning. O'Brien requesting him to take charge of me, he called the woman of the cabaret to show him a room; she showed him one or two, which he refused, as not sufficiently safe for the prisoner. The woman laughed at the idea, observing, "What had he to fear from a *pauvre enfant* like me?"

"Yet this *pauvre enfant* escaped from Givet," replied O'Brien; "these Englishmen are devils from their birth." The last room showed to O'Brien suited him, and he chose it—the woman not presuming to contradict a gendarme. As soon as they came down again, O'Brien ordered me to bed, and went up-stairs with me. He bolted the door, and pulling me to the large chimney, we put our heads up, and whispered, that our conversation should not be heard. "This man is not to be trusted," said O'Brien, "and we must give him the slip. I know my way out of the inn, and we must return the way we came, and then strike off in another direction."

"But will he permit us?"

"Not if he can help it; but I shall soon find out his manoeuvres."

O'Brien then went and stopped the key-hole, by hanging his handkerchief across it, and stripping himself of his gendarme uniform, put on his own clothes; then he stuffed the blankets and pillow into the gendarme's dress, and laid it down on the outside of the bed, as if it were a man sleeping in his clothes—indeed, it was an admirable deception. He laid his musket by the side of the image, and then did the same to my bed, making it appear as if there was a person asleep in it, of my size, and putting my cap on the pillow. "Now, Peter, we'll see if he is watching us. He will wait till he thinks we are asleep." The light still remained in the room, and about an hour afterwards we heard a noise of one treading on the stairs, upon which, as agreed, we crept under the bed. The latch of our door was tried, and finding it open, which he did not expect, the gendarme entered, and looking at both beds, went away. "Now," said I, after the gendarme had gone down-stairs, "O'Brien, ought we not to escape?"

"I've been thinking of it, Peter, and I have come to a resolution that we can manage it better. He is certain to come again in an hour or two. It is only eleven. Now I'll play him a trick." O'Brien then took one of the blankets, made it fast to the window, which he left wide open, and at the same time disarranged the images he had made up, so as to let the gendarme perceive that they were counterfeit. We again crept under the bed, and as O'Brien foretold, in about an hour more the gendarme returned; our lamp was still burning, but he had a light of his own. He looked at the beds, perceived at once that he had been duped, went to the open window, and then exclaimed, "*Sacre Dieu! ils m'ont echappés et je ne suis plus caporal. F—tre! à la chasse!*"* He rushed out of the room, and in a minute afterwards we heard him open the street door, and go away.

"That will do, Peter," said O'Brien, laughing; "now we'll be off also, although there's no great hurry." O'Brien then resumed his

---

* Sacre Dieu! ils m'ont echappés et je ne suis plus caporal. F—tre! à la chasse!: *Good God, they have escaped, and I am no longer a corporal. F—k! Get them!*

dress of a gendarme; and about an hour afterwards we went down, and wishing the hostess all happiness, quitted the cabaret, returning the same road by which we had come. "Now, Peter," said O'Brien, "we're in a bit of a puzzle. This dress won't do any more, still there's a respectability about it, which will not allow me to put it off till the last moment." We walked on till daylight, when we hid ourselves in a copse of trees. At night we again started for the Forest of Ardennes, for O'Brien said our best chance was to return, until they supposed that we had had time to effect our escape; but we never reached the forest, for on the next day a violent snowstorm came on; it continued without intermission for four days, during which we suffered much. Our money was not exhausted, as I had drawn upon my father for £60, which, with the disadvantageous exchange, had given me fifty Napoleons. Occasionally O'Brien crept into a cabaret, and obtained provisions; but, as we dared not be seen together as before, we were always obliged to sleep in the open air, the ground being covered more than three feet with snow. On the fifth day, being then six days from the Forest of Ardennes, we hid ourselves in a small wood, about a quarter of a mile from the road. I remained there while O'Brien, as a gendarme, went to obtain provisions. As usual, I looked out for the best shelter during his absence, and what was my horror at falling in with a man and woman who lay dead in the snow, having evidently perished from the weather. Just as I discovered them, O'Brien returned, and I told him; he went with me to view the bodies. They were dressed in a strange attire, ribands pinned upon their clothes, and two pairs of very high stilts lying by their sides. O'Brien surveyed them, and then said, "Peter, this is the very best thing that could have happened to us. We may now walk through France without soiling our feet with the cursed country."

"How do you mean?"

"I mean," said he, "that these are the people that we met near Montpelier, who come from the Landes, walking about on their stilts for the amusement of others, to obtain money. In their own country they are obliged to walk so. Now, Peter, it appears to me that the man's clothes will fit me, and the girl's (poor creature, how pretty she looks, cold in death!) will fit you. All we have to do is to practise a little, and then away we start."

O'Brien then, with some difficulty, pulled off the man's jacket and trousers, and having so done, buried him in the snow. The poor girl was despoiled of her gown and upper petticoat, with every decency, and also buried. We collected the clothes and stilts, and removed to another quarter of the wood, where we found a well-sheltered spot, and took our meal. As we did not travel that night as usual, we had to prepare our own bed. We scraped away the snow, and made ourselves as comfortable as we could without a fire, but the weather was dreadful.

"Peter," said O'Brien, "I'm melancholy. Here, drink plenty"; and he handed me the flask of spirits, which had never been empty.

"Drink more, Peter."

"I cannot, O'Brien, without being tipsy."

"Never mind that, drink more; see how these two poor devils lost their lives by falling asleep in the snow. Peter," said O'Brien, starting up, "you sha'n't sleep here—follow me."

I expostulated in vain. It was almost dark, and he led me to the village, near which he pitched upon a hovel (a sort of out-house). "Peter, here is shelter; lie down and sleep, and I'll keep watch. Not a word, I will have it—down at once."

I did so, and in a very few minutes was fast asleep, for I was worn out with cold and fatigue. For several days we had walked all night, and the rest we gained by day was trifling. Oh how I longed for a warm bed with four or five blankets! Just as the day broke, O'Brien roused me; he had stood sentry all night, and looked very haggard.

"O'Brien, you are ill," said I.

"Not a bit; but I've emptied the brandy-flask; and that's a bad job. However, it is to be remedied."

We then returned to the wood in a mizzling rain and fog, for the weather had changed, and the frost had broken up. The thaw was even worse than the frost, and we felt the cold more. O'Brien again insisted upon my sleeping in the out-house, but this time I positively refused without he would also sleep there, pointing out to him, that we ran no more risk, and perhaps not so much, as if he stayed outside. Finding I was positive, he at last consented, and we both gained it unperceived. We lay down, but I did not go to sleep for some time, I was so anxious to see O'Brien fast asleep. He went in and out several times, during which I pretended to be fast asleep; at last it rained in torrents, and then he lay down again, and in a few minutes, overpowered by nature, he fell fast asleep, snoring so loudly, that I was afraid some one would hear us. I then got up and watched, occasionally lying down and slumbering awhile, and then going to the door.

CHAPTER XXIII

Exalted with our success, we march through France without touching the ground—I become feminine—We are voluntary conscripts.

A T DAYBREAK I called O'Brien, who jumped up in a great hurry.

"Sure I've been asleep, Peter."

"Yes, you have," replied I, "and I thank Heaven that you have, for no one could stand such fatigue as you have, much longer; and if you fall ill, what would become of me?" This was touching him on the right point.

"Well, Peter, since there's no harm come of it, there's no harm done. I've had sleep enough for the next week, that's certain."

We returned to the wood; the snow had disappeared, and the rain ceased; the sun shone out from between the clouds, and we felt warm.

"Don't pass so near that way," said O'Brien, "we shall see the poor creatures, now that the snow is gone. Peter, we must shift our quarters to-night, for I have been to every cabaret in the village, and I cannot go there any more without suspicion, although I am a gendarme."

We remained there till the evening, and then set off, still returning towards Givet. About an hour before daylight we arrived at a copse of trees, close to the road-side, and surrounded by a ditch, not above a quarter of a mile from a village. "It appears to me," said O'Brien, "that this will do: I will now put you there, and then go boldly to the village and see what I can get, for here we must stay at least a week."

We walked to the copse, and the ditch being rather too wide for me to leap, O'Brien laid the four stilts together so as to form a bridge, over which I contrived to walk. Tossing to me all the bundles, and desiring me to leave the stilts as a bridge for him on his return, he set off to the village with his musket on his shoulder. He was away two hours, when he returned with a large supply of provisions, the best we had ever had. French saucissons, seasoned with garlic, which I thought delightful; four bottles of brandy, besides his flask; a piece of hung beef and six loaves of bread, besides half a baked goose and part of a large pie.

"There," said he, "we have enough for a good week; and look here, Peter, this is better than all." And he showed me two large horse-rugs.

"Excellent," replied I; "now we shall be comfortable."

"I paid honestly for all but these rugs," observed O'Brien; "but I was afraid to buy them, so I stole them. However, we'll leave them here for those they belong to—it's only borrowing, after all."

We now prepared a very comfortable shelter with branches, which we wove together, and laying the leaves in the sun to dry, soon obtained a soft bed to put one horse-rug on, while we covered ourselves up with the other. Our bridge of stilts we had removed, so that we felt ourselves quite secure from surprise. That evening we did nothing but carouse—the goose, the pie, the saucissons as big as my arm, were alternately attacked, and we went to the ditch to drink water, and then ate again. This was quite happiness to what we had suffered, especially with the prospect of a good bed. At dark, to bed we went, and slept soundly; I never felt more refreshed during our wanderings. At daylight O'Brien got up.

"Now, Peter, a little practice before breakfast."

"What practice do you mean?"

"Mean! why on the stilts. I expect in a week that you'll be able to dance a gavotte at least; for mind me, Peter, you travel out of France upon these stilts, depend upon it."

O'Brien then took the stilts belonging to the man, giving me those of the woman. We strapped them to our thighs, and by fixing our backs to a tree, contrived to get upright upon them; but, at the first attempt to walk, O'Brien fell to the right, and I fell to the left. O'Brien fell against a tree, but I fell on my nose, and made it bleed very much; however, we laughed and got up again, and although we had several falls, at last we made a better hand of them. We then had some difficulty in getting down again, but we found out how, by again resorting to a tree. After breakfast we strapped them on again, and practised, and so we continued to do for the whole day, when we again attacked our provisions, and fell asleep under our horse-rug. This continued for five days, by which time, being constantly on the stilts, we became very expert; and although I could not dance a gavotte—for I did not know what that was—I could hop about with them with the greatest ease.

"One day's more practice," said O'Brien, "for our provisions will last one day more, and then we start; but this time we must rehearse in costume."

O'Brien then dressed me in the poor girl's clothes, and himself in the man's; they fitted very well, and the last day we practised as man and woman.

"Peter, you make a very pretty girl," said O'Brien. "Now, don't you allow the men to take liberties."

"Never fear," replied I. "But, O'Brien, as these petticoats are not very warm, I mean to cut off my trousers up to my knees, and wear them underneath."

"That's all right," said O'Brien, "for you may have a tumble, and then they may find out that you're not a lady."

The next morning we made use of our stilts to cross the ditch, and carrying them in our hands we boldly set off on the high road to Malines. We met several people, gendarmes and others, but with the exception of some remarks upon my good looks, we passed unnoticed. Towards the evening we arrived at the village where we had slept in the out-house, and as soon as we entered it we put on our stilts, and commenced a march. When the crowd had gathered we held out our caps, and receiving nine or ten sous, we entered a cabaret. Many questions were asked us, as to where we came from, and O'Brien answered, telling lies innumerable. I played the modest girl, and O'Brien, who stated I was his sister, appeared very careful and jealous of any attention. We slept well, and the next morning continued our route to Malines. We very often put on our stilts for practice on the road, which detained us very much, and it was not until the eighth day, without any variety or any interruption, that we arrived at Malines. As we entered the barriers we put on our stilts, and marched boldly on. The guard at the gate stopped us, not from suspicion, but to amuse themselves, and I was forced to submit to several kisses from their garlic lips, before we were allowed to enter the town. We again mounted on our stilts, for the guard had forced us to dismount, or they could not have kissed me, every now and then imitating a dance, until we arrived at the *Grande Place*, where we stopped opposite the hotel, and commenced a sort of waltz which we had practised. The people in the hotel looked out of the window to see our exhibition, and when we had finished I went up to the windows with O'Brien's cap to collect money. What was my surprise to perceive Colonel O'Brien looking full in my face, and staring very hard at me;—what was my greater astonishment at seeing Celeste, who immediately recognised me, and ran back to the sofa in the room, putting her hands up to her eyes, and crying out *"C'est lui, c'est lui!"* Fortunately O'Brien was close to me, or I should have fallen, but he supported me. "Peter, ask the crowd for money, or you are lost." I did so, and collecting some pence, then asked him what I should do. "Go back to the window—you can then judge of what will happen." I returned to the window; Colonel O'Brien had disappeared, but Celeste was there, as if waiting for me. I held out the cap to her, and she thrust her hand into it. The cap sank with the weight. I took out a purse, which I kept closed in my hand, and put it into my bosom. Celeste then retired from the window, and when she had gone to the back of the room kissed her hand to me, and went out at the door. I remained stupefied for a moment, but O'Brien roused me, and we quitted the *Grande Place*, taking up our quarters at a little cabaret. On examining the purse, I found fifty Napoleons in it: these must have been obtained from her father. I cried over them with delight. O'Brien was also much affected at the kindness of the colonel. "He's a real O'Brien, every inch of him," said he: "even this cursed country can't spoil the breed."

At the cabaret where we stopped, we were informed, that the officer who was at the hotel had been appointed to the command of the strong fort of Bergen-op-Zoom, and was proceeding thither.

"We must not chance to meet him again, if possible," said O'Brien; "it would be treading too close upon the heels of his duty. Neither will it do to appear on stilts among the dikes; so, Peter, we'll just jump on clear of this town and then we'll trust to our wits."

We walked out of the town early in the morning, after O'Brien had made purchases of some of the clothes usually worn by the peasantry. When within a few miles of St Nicholas, we threw away our stilts and the clothes which we had on, and dressed ourselves in those O'Brien had purchased. O'Brien had not forgotten to provide us with two large brown-coloured blankets, which we strapped on to our shoulders, as the soldiers do their coats.

"But what are we to pass for now, O'Brien?"

"Peter, I will settle that point before night. My wits are working, but I like to trust to chance for a stray idea or so; we must walk fast, or we shall be smothered with the snow."

It was bitter cold weather, and the snow had fallen heavily during the whole day; but although nearly dusk, there was a bright moon ready for us. We walked very fast, and soon observed persons ahead of us. "Let us overtake them, we may obtain some information." As we came up with them, one of them (they were both lads of seventeen to eighteen) said to O'Brien, "I thought we were the last, but I was mistaken. How far is it now to St Nicholas?"

"How should I know?" replied O'Brien, "I am a stranger in these parts as well as yourself."

"From what part of France do you come?" demanded the other, his teeth chattering with the cold, for he was badly clothed, and with little defence from the inclement weather.

"From Montpelier," replied O'Brien.

"And I from Toulouse. A sad change, comrade, from olives and vines to such a climate as this. Curse the conscription: I intended to have taken a little wife next year."

O'Brien gave me a push, as if to say, "Here's something that will do," and then continued,—

"And curse the conscription I say too, for I had just married, and now my wife is left to be annoyed by the attention of the *fermier général.** But it can't be helped. *C'est pour la France et pour la gloire.*"

"We shall be too late to get a billet," replied the other, "and not a sou have I in my pocket. I doubt if I get up with the main body till they are at Flushing. By our route, they are at Axel to-day."

"If we arrive at St Nicholas, we shall do well," replied O'Brien; "but I have a little money left, and I'll not see a comrade want a supper or a bed who is going to serve his country. You can repay me when we meet at Flushing."

* Fermier général: *A person who collects taxes on land.*

"That I will with thanks," replied the Frenchman; "and so will Jacques here, if you will trust him."

"With pleasure," replied O'Brien, who then entered into a long conversation, by which he drew out from the Frenchmen that a party of conscripts had been ordered to Flushing, and that they had dropped behind the main body. O'Brien passed himself off as a conscript belonging to the party, and me as his brother, who had resolved to join the army as a drummer, rather than part with him. In about an hour we arrived at St Nicholas, and after some difficulty obtained entrance into a cabaret. "*Vive la France!*" said O'Brien, going up to the fire, and throwing the snow off his hat. In a short time we were seated to a good supper and very tolerable wine, the hostess sitting down by us, and listening to the true narratives of the real conscripts, and the false one of O'Brien. After supper the conscript who first addressed us pulled out his printed paper, with the route laid down, and observed that we were two days behind the others. O'Brien read it over, and laid it on the table, at the same time calling for more wine, having already pushed it round very freely. We did not drink much ourselves, but plied them hard, and at last the conscript commenced the whole history of his intended marriage and his disappointment, tearing his hair, and crying now and then. "Never mind," interrupted O'Brien, every two or three minutes, "*buvons un autre coup pour la gloire!*"* and thus he continued to make them both drink until they reeled away to bed, forgetting their printed paper, which O'Brien had some time before slipped away from the table. We also retired to our room, when O'Brien observed to me. "Peter, this description is as much like me as I am to Old Nick;† but that's of no consequence, as nobody goes willingly as a conscript, and therefore they will never have a doubt but that it is all right. We must be off early to-morrow, while these good people are in bed, and steal a long march upon them. I consider that we are now safe as far as Flushing."

* Buvons un autre coup pour la gloire!: *Take another drink for glory!*
† Old Nick: *The Devil.*

———◁𝒷𝒷𝒷▷———

CHAPTER XXIV

What occurred at Flushing, and what occurred when we got out of Flushing.

A N HOUR before daybreak we started; the snow was thick on the ground, but the sky was clear, and without any difficulty or interruption we passed through the towns of Axel and Halst, arrived at Terneuse on the fourth day, and went over to Flushing in company with about a dozen more stragglers from the main body. As we landed, the guard asked us whether we were conscripts. O'Brien replied that he was, and held out his paper. They took his name, or rather that of the person it belonged to, down in a book, and told him that he must apply to the *état major* before three o'clock. We passed on delighted with our success, and then O'Brien pulled out the letter which had been given to him by the woman of the cabaret, who had offered to assist me to escape, when O'Brien passed off as a gendarme, and reading the address, demanded his way to the street. We soon found out the house, and entered.

"Conscripts!" said the woman of the house, looking at O'Brien; "I am billeted full already. It must be a mistake. Where is your order?"

"Read," said O'Brien, handing her the letter.

She read the letter, and putting it into her neckerchief, desired him to follow her. O'Brien beckoned me to come, and we went into a small room. "What can I do for you?" said the woman; "I will do all in my power: but, alas! you will march from here in two or three days."

"Never mind," replied O'Brien, "we will talk the matter over by-and-by, but at present only oblige us by letting us remain in this little room; we do not wish to be seen."

"*Comment donc!*—you a conscript, and not wish to be seen!* Are you, then, intending to desert?"

"Answer me one question; you have read that letter, do you intend to act up to its purport, as your sister requests?"

"As I hope for mercy I will, if I suffer everything. She is a dear

---

* Comment donc!: *Really!*

sister, and would not write so earnestly if she had not strong reason. My house and everything you command are yours—can I say more?"

"But," continued O'Brien, "suppose I did intend to desert, would you then assist me?"

"At my peril," replied the woman: "have you not assisted my family when in difficulty?"

"Well, then, I will not at present detain you from your business; I have heard you called several times. Let us have dinner when convenient, and we will remain here."

"If I have any knowledge of phiz—*what d'ye call it*," observed O'Brien, after she left us, "there is honesty in that woman, and I must trust her, but not yet; we must wait till the conscripts have gone." I agreed with O'Brien, and we remained talking until an hour afterwards, when the woman brought us our dinner.

"What is your name?" inquired O'Brien.

"Louise Eustache; you might have read it on the letter."

"Are you married?"

"O, yes, these six years. My husband is seldom at home; he is a Flushing pilot. A hard life, harder even than that of a soldier. Who is this lad?"

"He is my brother, who, if I go as a soldier, intends to volunteer as a drummer."

"*Pauvre enfant! c'est dommage.*"*

The cabaret was full of conscripts and other people, so that the hostess had enough to do. At night, we were shown by her into a small bed-room, adjoining the room we occupied. "You are quite alone here; the conscripts are to muster to-morrow, I find, in the *Place d'Armes,* at two o'clock; do you intend to go?"

"No," replied O'Brien: "they will think that I am behind. It is of no consequence."

"Well," replied the woman, "do as you please, you may trust me: but I am so busy, without any one to assist me, that until they leave the town, I can hardly find time to speak to you."

"That will be soon enough, my good hostess," replied O'Brien: "*au revoir.*"

The next evening, the woman came in, in some alarm, stating

---

* Pauvre enfant! c'est dommage: *Poor child! it's a pity.*

that a conscript had arrived whose name had been given in before, and that the person who had given it in, had not mustered at the place. That the conscript had declared, that his pass had been stolen from him by a person with whom he had stopped at St Nicholas, and that there were orders for a strict search to be made through the town, as it was known that some English officers had escaped, and it was supposed that one of them had obtained the pass. "Surely you're not English?" inquired the woman, looking earnestly at O'Brien.

"Indeed, but I am, my dear," replied O'Brien: "and so is this lad with me: and the favour which your sister requires is, that you help us over the water, for which service there are one hundred louis ready to be paid upon delivery of us."

"*Oh, mon Dieu! mais c'est impossible.*"

"Impossible!" replied O'Brien; "was that the answer I gave your sister in her trouble?"

"*Au moins c'est fort difficile.*"

"That's quite another concern; but with your husband a pilot, I should think a great part of the difficulty removed."

"My husband! I've no power over him," replied the woman, putting the apron up to her eyes.

"But one hundred louis may have," replied O'Brien.

"There is truth in that," observed the woman, after a pause, "but what am I to do, if they come to search the house?"

"Send us out of it, until you can find an opportunity to send us to England. I leave it all to you—your sister expects it from you."

"And she shall not be disappointed, if God helps us," replied the woman, after a short pause: "but I fear you must leave this house and the town also to-night."

"How are we to leave the town?"

"I will arrange that; be ready at four o'clock, for the gates are shut at dusk. I must go now, for there is no time to be lost."

"We are in a nice mess now, O'Brien," observed I, after the woman had quitted the room.

"Devil a bit, Peter; I feel no anxiety whatever, except at leaving such good quarters."

We packed up all our effects, not forgetting our two blankets, and waited the return of the hostess. In about an hour she entered the room. "I have spoken to my husband's sister, who lives about two miles on the road to Middelburg. She is in town now, for it is market-day, and you will be safe where she hides you. I told her, it was by my husband's request, or she would not have consented. Here, boy, put on these clothes; I will assist you." Once more I was dressed as a girl, and when my clothes were on, O'Brien burst out into laughter at my blue stockings and short petticoats. *"Il n'est pas mal,"* observed the hostess, as she fixed a small cap on my head, and then tied a kerchief under my chin, which partly hid my face. O'Brien put on a great-coat, which the woman handed to him, with a wide-brimmed hat. "Now follow me!" She led us into the street, which was thronged, till we arrived at the market-place, when she met another woman, who joined her. At the end of the market-place stood a small horse and cart, into which the strange woman and I mounted, while O'Brien, by the directions of the landlady, led the horse through the crowd until we arrived at the barriers, when she wished us good day in a loud voice before the guard. The guard took no notice of us, and we passed safely through, and found ourselves upon a neatly-paved road, as straight as an arrow, and lined on each side with high trees and a ditch. In about an hour, we stopped near to the farmhouse of the woman who was in charge of us. "Do you observe that wood?" said she to O'Brien, pointing to one about half a mile from the road. "I dare not take you into the house, my husband is so violent against the English, who captured his schuyt, and made him a poor man, that he would inform against you immediately; but go you there, make yourselves as comfortable as you can to-night, and to-morrow I will send you what you want.* *Adieu! Je vous plains, pauvre enfant,"* said she, looking at me, as she drove off in the cart towards her own house.

"Peter," said O'Brien, "I think that her kicking us out of her house is a proof of her sincerity, and therefore I say no more about it; we have the brandy-flask to keep up our spirits. Now then for the wood, though, by the powers, I shall have no relish for any of your pic-nic parties, as they call them, for the next twelve years."

"But, O'Brien, how can I get over this ditch in petticoats? I could hardly leap it in my own clothes."

"You must tie your petticoats round your waist and make a good

* *Schuyt: A Dutch flat-bottomed boat.*

run; get over as far as you can, and I will drag you through the rest."

"But you forget that we are to sleep in the wood, and that it's no laughing matter to get wet through, freezing so hard as it does now."

"Very true, Peter; but as the snow lies so deep upon the ditch, perhaps the ice may bear. I'll try; if it bears me, it will not condescend to bend at your shrimp of a carcass."

O'Brien tried the ice, which was firm, and we both walked over, and making all the haste we could, arrived at the wood, as the woman called it, but which was not more than a clump of trees of about half an acre. We cleared away the snow for about six feet round a very hollow part, and then O'Brien cut stakes and fixed them in the earth, to which we stretched one blanket. The snow being about two feet deep, there was plenty of room to creep underneath the blanket. We then collected all the leaves we could, beating the snow off them, and laid them at the bottom of the hole; over the leaves we spread the other blanket, and taking our bundles in, we then stopped up with snow every side of the upper blanket, except the hole to creep in at. It was quite astonishing what a warm place this became in a short time after we had remained in it. It was almost too warm, although the weather outside was piercingly cold. After a good meal and a dose of brandy, we both fell fast asleep, but not until I had taken off my woman's attire and resumed my own clothes. We never slept better or more warmly than we did in this hole which we had made on the ground, covered with ice and snow.

—◆◆◆—

CHAPTER XXV

O'Brien parts company to hunt for provisions, and I have other company in consequence of another hunt—O'Brien pathetically mourns my death and finds me alive—We escape.

THE ENSUING MORNING we looked out anxiously for the promised assistance, for we were not very rich in provisions, although what we had were of a very good quality. It was not until three o'clock in the afternoon that we perceived a little girl coming towards us, escorted by a large mastiff. When she arrived at the copse of trees where we lay concealed, she cried out to the dog in Dutch, who immediately scoured the wood until he came to our hiding-place, when he crouched down at the entrance, barking furiously, and putting us in no small dread, lest he should attack us; but the little girl spoke to him again, and he remained in the same position, looking at us, wagging his tail, with his under jaw lying on the snow. She soon came up, and looking underneath, put a basket in, and nodded her head. We emptied the basket. O'Brien took out a napoleon and offered it to her; she refused it, but O'Brien forced it into her hand, upon which she again spoke to the dog, who commenced barking so furiously at us, that we expected every moment he would fly upon us. The girl at the same time presented the napoleon, and pointing to the dog, I went forward and took the napoleon from her, at which she immediately silenced the enormous brute, and laughing at us, hastened away.

"By the powers, that's a fine little girl!" said O'Brien; "I'll back her and her dog against any man. Well, I never had a dog set at me for giving money before, but we live and learn, Peter; now let's see what she brought in the basket." We found hard-boiled eggs, bread, and a smoked mutton ham, with a large bottle of gin. "What a nice little girl! I hope she will often favour us with her company. I've been thinking, Peter, that we're quite as well off here, as in a midshipman's berth."

"You forget you are a lieutenant."

"Well, so I did, Peter, and that's the truth, but it's the force of habit. Now let's make our dinner. It's a new-fashioned way though, of making a meal, lying down; but however, it's economical, for it must take longer to swallow the victuals."

"The Romans used to eat their meals lying down, so I have read, O'Brien."

"I can't say that I ever heard it mentioned in Ireland, but that don't prove that it was not the case; so, Peter, I'll take your word for it. Murder! how fast it snows again! I wonder what my father's thinking on just at this moment."

This observation of O'Brien induced us to talk about our friends and relations in England, and after much conversation we fell fast asleep. The next morning we found the snow had fallen about eight inches, and weighed down our upper blanket so much, that we were obliged to go out and cut stakes to support it up from the inside. While we were thus employed, we heard a loud noise and shouting, and perceived several men, apparently armed and accompanied with dogs, running straight in the direction of the wood where we were encamped. We were much alarmed, thinking that they were in search of us, but on a sudden they turned off in another direction, continuing with the same speed as before. "What could it be?" said I, to O'Brien. "I can't exactly say, Peter; but I should think that they were hunting something, and the only game that I think likely to be in such a place as this are otters." I was of the same opinion. We expected the little girl, but she did not come, and after looking out for her till dark, we crawled into our hole and supped upon the remainder of our provisions.

The next day, as may be supposed, we were very anxious for her arrival, but she did not appear at the time expected. Night again came on, and we went to bed without having any sustenance, except a small piece of bread that was left, and some gin which was remaining in the flask. "Peter," said O'Brien, "if she don't come again to-morrow, I'll try what I can do; for I've no idea of our dying of hunger here, like the two babes in the wood, and being found covered up with dead leaves. If she does not appear at three o'clock, I'm off for provisions, and I don't see much danger, for in this dress I look as much of a boor as any man in Holland."

We passed an uneasy night, as we felt convinced, either that the danger was so great that they dared not venture to assist us, or, that being over-ruled, they had betrayed us, and left us to manage how we could. The next morning I climbed up the only large tree in the copse and looked round, especially in the direction of the farmhouse belonging to the woman who had pointed out to us our place of concealment; but nothing was to be seen but one vast tract of flat country covered with snow, and now and then a vehicle passing at a distance on the Middelburg road. I descended, and found O'Brien preparing for a start. He was very melancholy, and said to me, "Peter, if I am taken, you must, at all risks, put on your girl's clothes and go to Flushing to the cabaret. The women there, I am sure, will protect you, and send you back to England. I only want two napoleons; take all the rest, you will require them. If I am not back by to-night, set off for Flushing to-morrow morning." O'Brien waited some time longer, talking with me, and it then being past four o'clock, he shook me by the hand, and, without speaking, left the wood. I never felt more miserable during the whole time since we were first put into prison at Toulon, till that moment, and, when he was a hundred yards off, I knelt down and prayed. He had been absent two hours, and it was quite dusk, when I heard a noise at a distance: it advanced every moment nearer and nearer. On a sudden, I heard a rustling of the bushes, and hastened under the blanket, which was covered with snow, in hopes that they might not perceive the entrance; but I was hardly there before in dashed after me an enormous wolf. I cried out, expecting to be torn to pieces every moment, but the creature lay on his belly, his mouth wide open, his eyes glaring, and his long tongue hanging out of his mouth, and although he touched me, he was so exhausted that he did not attack me. The noise increased, and I immediately perceived that it was the hunters in pursuit of him. I had crawled in feet first, the wolf ran in head foremost, so that we lay head and tail. I crept out as fast as I could, and perceived men and dogs not two hundred yards off in full chase. I hastened to the large tree, and had not ascended six feet when they came up; the dogs flew to the hole, and in a very short time the wolf was killed. The hunters being too busy to observe me, I had in the meantime climbed up the trunk of the tree, and hidden myself as well as I could. Being not fifteen yards from them, I heard their expressions of surprise as they lifted up the blanket and dragged out the dead wolf, which they carried away with them; their conversation being in Dutch, I could not understand it, but I was certain that they made use of the word *"English."* The hunters and dogs quitted the copse, and I was about to descend, when one of them returned, and pulling up the blankets, rolled them together and walked away with them. Fortunately he did not perceive our bundles by the little light given by the moon. I waited a short time and then came down. What to do I knew not. If I did not remain and O'Brien returned, what would he think? If I did, I should be dead with cold before the morning. I looked for our bundles, and found that in the conflict between the dogs and the wolf, they had been buried among the leaves. I recollected O'Brien's advice, and dressed myself in the girl's clothes, but I could not make up my mind to go to Flushing. So I resolved to walk towards the farmhouse, which, being close to the road, would give me a chance of meeting with O'Brien. I soon arrived there and prowled round it for some time, but the doors and windows were all fast, and I dared not knock, after what the woman had said about her husband's inveteracy to the English. At last, as I looked round and round, quite at a loss what to do, I thought I saw a figure at a distance proceeding in the direction of the copse. I hastened after it and saw it enter. I then advanced very cautiously, for although I thought it might be O'Brien, yet it was possible that it was one of the men who chased the wolf in search of more plunder. But I soon heard O'Brien's voice, and I hastened towards him. I was close to him without his perceiving me, and found him sitting down with his face covered up in his two hands. At last he cried, "O Pater! my poor Pater! are you taken at last? Could I not leave you for one hour in safety? Ochone! why did I leave you? My poor, poor Pater! simple you were, sure enough, and that's why I loved you; but, Pater, I would have made a man of you, for you'd all the materials, that's the truth—and a fine man, too. Where am I to look for you, Pater? Where am I to find you, Pater? You're fast locked up by this time, and all my trouble's gone for nothing. But I'll be locked up too, Pater. Where you are, will I be; and if we can't go to England together, why then we'll go back to that blackguard hole at Givet together. Ochone! Ochone!" O'Brien spoke no more, but burst into tears. I was much affected with this proof of O'Brien's sincere regard, and I came to his side and clasped him in my arms. O'Brien stared at me, "Who are you, you ugly Dutch frow?" (for he had quite forgotten the woman's dress at the moment), but recollecting himself, he hugged me in his arms. "Pater, you come as near to an angel's shape as you can, for you come in that of a woman, to comfort me; for, to tell the truth, I was very much distressed at not finding you here; and all the blankets gone to boot. What has been the matter?" I explained in as few words as I could.

"Well, Peter, I'm happy to find you all safe, and much happier to find that you can be trusted when I leave you, for you could not have behaved more prudently; now I'll tell you what I did, which was not much, as it happened. I knew that there was no cabaret between us and Flushing, for I took particular notice as I came along; so I took the road to Middelburg, and found but one, which was full of soldiers. I passed it, and found no other. As I came back past the same cabaret, one of the soldiers came out to me, but I walked along the road. He quickened his pace, and so did I mine, for I expected mischief. At last he came up to me, and spoke to me in Dutch, to which I gave him no answer. He collared me, and then I thought it convenient to pretend that I was deaf and dumb. I pointed to my mouth with an Au—au—and then to my ears, and shook my head; but he would not be convinced, and I heard him say something about English. I then knew that there was no time to be lost, so I first burst out into a loud laugh and stopped; and on his attempting to force me, I kicked up his heels, and he fell on the ice with such a rap on the pate, that I doubt if he has recovered it by this time. There I left him, and have run back as hard as I could, without anything for Peter to fill his little hungry inside with. Now, Peter, what's your opinion? for they say that out of the mouth of babes there is wisdom; and although I never saw anything come out of their mouths but sour milk, yet perhaps I may be more fortunate this time, for, Peter, you're but a baby."

"Not a small one, O'Brien, although not quite so large as Fingal's *babby* that you told me the story of. My idea is this.—Let us, at all hazards, go to the farmhouse. They have assisted us, and may be inclined to do so again; if they refuse, we must push on to Flushing and take our chance."

"Well," observed O'Brien, after a pause, "I think we can do no better, so let's be off." We went to the farmhouse, and, as we approached the door, were met by the great mastiff. I started back, O'Brien boldly advanced. "He's a clever dog, and may know us again. I'll go up," said O'Brien, not stopping while he spoke, "and pat his head: if he flies at me, I shall be no worse than I was before, for depend upon it he will not allow us to go back again." O'Brien by this time had advanced to the dog, who looked earnestly and angrily at him. He patted his head, the dog growled, but O'Brien put his arm round his neck, and patting him again, whistled to him, and went to the door of the farmhouse. The dog followed him silently but closely. O'Brien knocked, and the door was opened by the little girl: the mastiff advanced to the girl, and then turned round, facing O'Brien, as much as to say, "Is he to come in?" The girl spoke to the dog, and went indoors. During her absence the mastiff lay down at the threshold. In a few seconds the woman who had brought us from Flushing, came out, and desired us to enter. She spoke very good French, and told us that fortunately her husband was absent; that the reason why we had not been supplied was, that a wolf had met her little girl returning the other day, but had been beaten off by the mastiff, and that she was afraid to allow her to go again; that she heard the wolf had been killed this evening, and had intended her girl to have gone to us early to-morrow morning; that wolves were hardly known in that country, but that the severe winter had brought them down to the lowlands, a very rare circumstance, occurring perhaps not once in twenty years. "But how did you pass the mastiff?" said she; "that has surprised my daughter and me." O'Brien told her, upon which she said "that the English were really *'des braves.'* No other man had ever done the same." So I thought, for nothing would have induced me to do it. O'Brien then told the history of the death of the wolf, with all particulars, and our intention, if we could not do better, of returning to Flushing.

"I heard that Pierre Eustache came home yesterday," replied the woman; "and I do think that you will be safer there than here, for they will never think of looking for you among the *casernes*, which join their cabaret."*

"Will you lend us your assistance to get in?"

"I will see what I can do. But are you not hungry?"

"About as hungry as men who have eaten nothing for two days."

"*Mon Dieu! c'est vrai.* I never thought it was so long, but those whose stomachs are filled forget those who are empty. God make us better and more charitable!"

She spoke to the little girl in Dutch, who hastened to load the table, which we hastened to empty. The little girl stared at our voracity; but at last she laughed out, and clapped her hands at every fresh mouthful which we took, and pressed us to eat more. She allowed me to kiss her, until her mother told her that I was not a woman, when she pouted at me, and beat me off. Before midnight we were fast asleep upon the benches before the kitchen fire, and at daybreak were roused up by the woman, who offered us some bread and spirits, and then we went out to the door, where we found the horse and cart all ready, and loaded with vegetables for the market. The woman, the little girl, and myself got in, O'Brien leading as before, and the mastiff following. We had learnt the dog's

---

* Casernes: *Barracks.*

name, which was *"Achille,"* and he seemed to be quite fond of us. We passed the dreaded barriers without interruption, and in ten minutes entered the cabaret of Eustache; and immediately walked into the little room through a crowd of soldiers, two of whom chucked me under the chin. Whom should we find there but Eustache, the pilot himself, in conversation with his wife, and it appeared that they were talking about us, she insisting, and he unwilling to have any hand in the business. "Well, here they are themselves, Eustache; the soldiers who have seen them come in will never believe that this is their first entry if you give them up. I leave them to make their own bargain; but mark me, Eustache, I have slaved night and day in this cabaret for your profit; if you do not oblige me and my family, I no longer keep a cabaret for you."

Madame Eustache then quitted the room with her husband's sister and little girl, and O'Brien immediately accosted him. "I promise you," said he to Eustache, "one hundred louis if you put us on shore at any part of England, or on board of any English man-of-war; and if you do it within a week, I will make it twenty louis more." O'Brien then pulled out the fifty napoleons given us by Celeste, for our own were not yet expended, and laid them on the table. "Here is this in advance, to prove my sincerity. Say, is it a bargain or not?"

"I never yet heard of a poor man who could withstand his wife's arguments, backed with one hundred and twenty louis," said Eustache smiling, and sweeping the money off the table.

"I presume you have no objection to start to-night? That will be ten louis more in your favour," replied O'Brien.

"I shall earn them," replied Eustache. "The sooner I am off the better, for I could not long conceal you here. The young frow with you is, I suppose, your companion that my wife mentioned. He has begun to suffer hardships early. Come, now, sit down and talk, for nothing can be done till dark."

O'Brien narrated the adventures attending our escape, at which Eustache laughed heartily; the more so, at the mistake which his wife was under, as to the obligations of the family. "If I did not feel inclined to assist you before, I do now, just for the laugh I shall have at her when I come back, and if she wants any more assistance for the sake of her relations, I shall remind her of this anecdote; but she's a good woman and a good wife to boot, only too fond of her sisters." At dusk he equipped us both in sailor's jackets and trousers, and desired us to follow him boldly. He passed the guard, who knew him well. "What, to sea already?" said one. "You have quarrelled with your wife." At which they all laughed, and we joined. We gained the beach, jumped into his little boat, pulled off to his vessel, and, in a few minutes, were under weigh. With a strong tide and a fair wind we were soon clear of the Scheldt, and the next morning a cutter hove in sight. We steered for her, ran under her lee, O'Brien hailed for a boat, and Eustache, receiving my bill for the remainder of his money, wished us success; we shook hands, and in a few minutes found ourselves once more under the British pennant.

——〰——

CHAPTER XXVI

Adventures at home—I am introduced to my grandfather—He obtains employment for O'Brien and myself, and we join a frigate.

A S SOON as we were on the deck of the cutter, the lieutenant commanding her inquired of us, in a consequential manner, who we were. O'Brien replied that we were English prisoners who had escaped. "Oh, midshipmen, I presume," replied the lieutenant; "I heard that some had contrived to get away."

"My name, sir," said O'Brien, "is Lieutenant O'Brien; and if you'll send for a 'Steel's List,' I will have the honour of pointing it out to you. This young gentleman is Mr Peter Simple, midshipman, and grandson to the Right Honourable Lord Viscount Privilege."

The lieutenant, who was a little snub-nosed man, with a pimply face, then altered his manner towards us, and begged we would step down into the cabin, where he offered, what perhaps was the greatest of all luxuries to us, some English cheese and bottled porter. "Pray," said he, "did you see anything of one of my officers, who was taken prisoner when I was sent with despatches to the Mediterranean fleet?"

"May I first ask the name of your lively little craft?" said O'Brien.

" 'The *Snapper*,' " replied the lieutenant.

"Och, murder; sure enough we met him. He was sent to Verdun, but we had the pleasure of his company *en route* as far as Montpelier. A remarkably genteel, well-dressed young man, was he not?"

"Why, I can't say much about his gentility; indeed, I am not much of a judge. As for his dress, he ought to have dressed well, but he never did when on board of me. His father is my tailor, and I took him as midshipman, just to square an account between us."

"That's exactly what I thought," replied O'Brien.

He did not say any more, which I was glad of, as the lieutenant might not have been pleased at what had occurred.

"When do you expect to run into port?" demanded O'Brien; for we were rather anxious to put our feet ashore again in old England. The lieutenant replied that his cruise was nearly up; and he considered our arrival quite sufficient reason for him to run in directly, and that he intended to put his helm up after the people had had their dinner. We were much delighted with this intelligence, and still more to see the intention put into execution half an hour afterwards.

In three days we anchored at Spithead, and went on shore with the lieutenant to report ourselves to the admiral. Oh! with what joy did I first put my foot on the shingle beach at Sally Port, and then hasten to the post-office to put in a long letter which I had written to my mother. We did not go to the admiral's, but merely reported ourselves at the admiral's office; for we had no clothes fit to appear in. But we called at Meredith's the tailor, and he promised that, by the next morning, we should be fitted complete. We then ordered new hats, and everything we required, and went to the Fountain inn. O'Brien refused to go to the Blue Posts, as being only a receptacle for midshipmen. By eleven o'clock the next morning, we were fit to appear before the admiral, who received us very kindly, and requested our company to dinner. As I did not intend setting off for home until I had received an answer from my mother, we, of course, accepted the invitation.

There was a large party of naval officers and ladies, and O'Brien amused them very much during dinner. When the ladies left the room, the admiral's wife told me to come up with them; and when we arrived at the drawing-room, the ladies all gathered round me, and I had to narrate the whole of my adventures, which very much

entertained and interested them. The next morning I received a letter from my mother—such a kind one! entreating me to come home
as fast as I could, and bring my *preserver* O'Brien with me. I showed
it to O'Brien, and asked him whether he would accompany me.

"Why, Peter, my boy, I have a little business of some importance
to transact; which is, to obtain my arrears of pay, and some prize-
money which I find due. When I have settled that point, I will go to
town to pay my respects to the First Lord of the Admiralty, and then
I think I will go and see your father and mother: for, until I know
how matters stand, and whether I shall be able to go with spare cash
in my pocket, I do not wish to see my own family; so write down
your address here, and you'll be sure I'll come, if it is only to square
my accounts with you, for I am not a little in your debt."

I cashed a cheque sent by my father, and set off in the mail that
night; the next evening I arrived safe home. But I shall leave the
reader to imagine the scene: to my mother I was always dear, and
circumstances had rendered me of some importance to my father;
for I was now an only son, and his prospects were very different
from what they were when I left home. About a week afterwards,
O'Brien joined us, having got through all his business. His first act
was to account with my father for his share of the expenses; and he
even insisted upon paying his half of the fifty napoleons given me
by Celeste, which had been remitted to a banker at Paris before
O'Brien's arrival, with a guarded letter of thanks from my father to
Colonel O'Brien, and another from me to dear little Celeste. When
O'Brien had remained with us about a week, he told me that he had
about one hundred and sixty pounds in his pocket, and that he
intended to go and see his friends, as he was sure that he would be
welcome even to Father M'Grath. "I mean to stay with them about a
fortnight, and shall then return and apply for employment. Now,
Peter, will you like to be again under my protection?"

"O'Brien, I will never quit you or your ship, if I can help it."

"Spoken like a sensible Peter. Well, then, I was promised immediate employment, and I will let you know as soon as the promise is
performed."

O'Brien took his leave of my family, who were already very
partial to him, and left that afternoon for Holyhead. My father no
longer treated me as a child; indeed, it would have been an injustice
if he had. I do not mean to say that I was a clever boy; but I had seen

much of the world in a short time, and could act and think for myself. He often talked to me about his prospects, which were very different from what they were when I left him. My two uncles, his elder brothers, had died, the third was married and had two daughters. If he had no son, my father would succeed to the title. The death of my elder brother Tom had brought me next in succession. My grandfather, Lord Privilege, who had taken no more notice of my father than occasionally sending him a basket of game, had latterly often invited him to the house, and had even requested, *some day or another*, to see his wife and family. He had also made a handsome addition to my father's income, which the death of my two uncles had enabled him to do. Against all this, my uncle's wife was reported to be again in the family way. I cannot say that I was pleased when my father used to speculate upon these chances so often as he did. I thought, not only as a man, but more particularly as a clergyman, he was much to blame; but I did not know then so much of the world. We had not heard from O'Brien for two months, when a letter arrived, stating that he had seen his family, and bought a few acres of land, which had made them all quite happy, and had quitted with Father M'Grath's double blessing, with unlimited absolution; that he had now been a month in town trying for employment, but found that he could not obtain it, although one promise was backed up by another.

A few days after this, my father received a note from Lord Privilege, requesting he would come and spend a few days with him, and bring his son Peter who had escaped from the French prison. Of course this was an invitation not to be neglected, and we accepted it forthwith. I must say, I felt rather in awe of my grandfather; he had kept the family at such a distance, that I had always heard his name mentioned more with reverence than with any feeling of kindred, but I was a little wiser now. We arrived at Eagle Park, a splendid estate, where he resided, and were received by a dozen servants in and out of livery, and ushered into his presence. He was in his library, a large room, surrounded with handsome bookcases, sitting on an easy-chair. A more venerable, placid old gentleman I never beheld; his grey hairs hung down on each side of his temples, and were collected in a small *queue* behind. He rose and bowed, as we were announced; to my father he held out *two* fingers in salutation, to me only *one*, but there was an elegance in the manner in which it was done which was indescribable. He waved his hand to chairs, placed by the *gentleman* out of livery, and requested we would be seated. I could not, at the time, help thinking of Mr Chucks, the boatswain, and his remarks upon high breeding, which were so true; and I laughed to myself when I recollected that Mr Chucks had once dined with him. As soon as the servants had quitted the room, the distance on the part of my grandfather appeared to wear off. He interrogated me on several points, and seemed pleased with my replies; but he always called me "child." After a conversation of half an hour, my father rose, saying that his lordship must be busy, and that we would go over the grounds till dinner-time. My grandfather rose, and we took a sort of formal leave; but it was not a formal leave, after all, it was high breeding, respecting yourself and respecting others. For my part, I was pleased with the first interview, and so I told my father after we had left the room. "My dear Peter," replied he, "your grandfather has one idea which absorbs most others—the peerage, the estate, and the descent of it in the right line. As long as your uncles were alive, we were not thought of, as not being in the line of descent; nor should we now, but that your uncle William has only daughters. Still we are not looked upon as actual, but only contingent, inheritors of the title. Were your uncle to die tomorrow, the difference in his behaviour would be manifested immediately."

"That is to say, instead of *two fingers* you would receive the *whole* hand, and instead of *one* finger, I should obtain promotion to *two.*"

At this my father laughed heartily, saying, "Peter, you have exactly hit the mark. I cannot imagine how we ever could have been so blind as to call you the fool of the family."

To this I made no reply, for it was difficult so to do without depreciating others or depreciating myself; but I changed the subject by commenting on the beauties of the park, and the splendid timber with which it was adorned. "Yes, Peter," replied my father, with a sigh, "thirty-five thousand a year in land, money in the funds, and timber worth at least forty thousand more, are not to be despised. But God wills everything." After this remark, my father appeared to be in deep thought, and I did not interrupt him.

We stayed ten days with my grandfather, during which he would often detain me for two hours after breakfast, listening to my adventures, and I really believe was very partial to me. The day before I went away he said, "Child, you are going to-morrow; now tell me what you would like, as I wish to give you a token of regard. Don't be afraid; what shall it be—a watch and seals, or—anything you most fancy?"

"My lord," replied I, "if you wish to do me a favour, it is, that you will apply to the First Lord of the Admiralty to appoint Lieutenant O'Brien to a fine frigate, and, at the same time, ask for a vacancy as midshipman for me."

"O'Brien!" replied his lordship; "I recollect it was he who accompanied you from France, and appears, by your account, to have been a true friend. I am pleased with your request, my child, and it shall be granted."

His lordship then desired me to hand him the paper and ink-standish, wrote by my directions, sealed the letter, and told me he would send me the answer. The next day we quitted Eagle Park, his lordship wishing my father good-bye with *two* fingers, and to me extending *one*, as before; but he said, "I am pleased with you, child; you may write occasionally."

When we were on our route home, my father observed that "I had made more progress with my grandfather than he had known anyone to do, since he could recollect. His saying that you might write to him is at least ten thousand pounds to you in his will, for he never deceives any one, or changes his mind." My reply was, that I should like to see the ten thousand pounds, but that I was not so sanguine.

A few days after our return home, I received a letter and enclosure from Lord Privilege, the contents of which were as follow:—

"My dear Child,—I send you Lord——'s answer, which I trust will prove satisfactory. My compliments to your family.—Yours, &c.,

"PRIVILEGE."

The enclosure was a handsome letter from the First Lord, stating that he had appointed O'Brien to the *Sanglier* frigate, and had ordered me to be received on board as midshipman. I was delighted to forward this letter to O'Brien's address, who, in a few days sent me an answer, thanking me, and stating that he had received his appointment, and that I need not join for a month, which was quite

time enough, as the ship was refitting; but, that if my family were
tired of me, which was sometimes the case in the best regulated
families, why, then I should learn something of my duty by coming
to Portsmouth. He concluded by sending his kind regards to all the
family, and his *love* to my grandfather, which last I certainly did not
forward in my letter of thanks. About a month afterwards I received
a letter from O'Brien, stating that the ship was ready to go out of
harbour, and would be anchored off Spithead in a few days.

—<small>ᐤᐤᐤ</small>—

CHAPTER XXVII

Captain and Mrs To—Pork—We go to Plymouth, and fall in with our old captain.

I IMMEDIATELY TOOK LEAVE of my family, and set off for
Portsmouth, and in two days arrived at the Fountain inn, where
O'Brien was waiting to receive me. "Peter, my boy, I feel so much
obliged to you, that if your uncle won't go out of the world by fair
means, I'll pick a quarrel with him, and shoot him, on purpose that
you may be a lord, as I am determined you shall be. Now come up
into my room, where we'll be all alone, and I'll tell you all about the
ship and our new captain. In the first place, we'll begin with the
ship, as the most important personage of the two: she's a beauty. I
forget her name before she was taken, but the French know how to
build ships better than keep them. She's now called the *Sanglier*,
which means a wild pig, and, by the powers! a *pig* ship she is, as
you will hear directly. The captain's name is a very short one, and
wouldn't please Mr Chucks, consisting only of two letters, T and O,
which makes To; his whole title is Captain John To. It would almost
appear as if somebody had broken off the better half of his name,
and only left him the commencement of it; but, however, it's a
handy name to sign when he pays off his ship. And now I'll tell you
what sort of a looking craft he is. He's built like a Dutch schuyt,
great breadth of beam, and very square tuck. He applied to have the
quarter galleries enlarged in the two last ships he commanded. He
weighs about eighteen stone, rather more than less. He is a good-

natured sort of a chap, amazingly ungenteel, not much of an officer, not much of a sailor, but a devilish good hand at the trencher.* But he's only part of the concern; he has his wife on board, who is a red-herring sort of a lady, and very troublesome to boot. What makes her still more annoying is, that she has a *piano* on board, very much out of *tune*, on which she plays very much out of *time*. Holystoning is music compared with her playing: even the captain's spaniel howls when she comes to the high notes; but she affects the fine lady, and always treats the officers with music when they dine in the cabin, which makes them very glad to get out of it."

"But, O'Brien, I thought wives were not permitted on board."

"Very true, but there's the worst part in the man's character: he knows that he is not allowed to take his wife to sea, and, in consequence, he never says she *is* his wife, or presents her on shore to anybody. If any of the other captains ask how Mrs To is to-day? 'Why,' he replies, 'pretty well, I thank you'; but at the same time he gives a kind of smirk, as if to say, 'She is not my wife'; and although everybody knows that she is, yet he prefers that they should think otherwise, rather than be at the expense of keeping her on shore; for you know, Peter, that although there are regulations about wives, there are none with regard to other women."

"But does his wife know this?" inquired I.

"I believe, from my heart, she is a party to the whole transaction, for report says, that she would skin a flint if she could. She's always trying for presents from the officers, and, in fact, she commands the ship."

"Really, O'Brien, this is not a very pleasant prospect."

"Whist! wait a little; now I come to the wind-up. This Captain To is very partial to pig's *mate*, and we have as many live pigs on board as we have pigs of ballast. The first lieutenant is right mad about them. At the same time he allows no pigs but his own on board, that there may be no confusion. The manger is full of pigs; there are two cow-pens between the main-deck guns, drawn from the dockyard, and converted into pig-pens. The two sheep-pens amidships are full of pigs, and the geese and turkey-coops are divided off into apart-ments for four *sows* in the *family way*. Now, Peter, you see there's little or no expense in keeping pigs on board of a large frigate, with

* *Trencher: Carving board.*

so much *pay*-soup and whole peas for them to eat, and this is the reason why he keeps them, for the devil a bit of any other stock has he on board. I presume he means to *milk* one of the *old sows* for breakfast when the ship sails. The first thing that he does in the morning, is to go round to his pigs with the butcher, feeling one, scratching the dirty ears of another, and then he classes them—his *bacon* pigs, his *porkers*, his *breeding* sows, and so on. The old boar is still at the stables of this inn, but I hear he is to come on board with the sailing orders: but he is very savage, and is therefore left on shore to the very last moment. Now really, Peter, what with the squealing of the pigs and his wife's piano, we are almost driven mad. I don't know which is the worse of the two; if you go aft you hear the one, if you go forward you hear the other, by way of variety, and that, they say, is charming. But, is it not shocking that such a beautiful frigate should be turned into a pig-sty, and that her main-deck should smell worse than a muckheap?"

"But how does his wife like the idea of living only upon hog's flesh?"

"She! Lord bless you, Peter! why, she looks as spare as a shark, and she has just the appetite of one, for she'll *bolt* a four-pound piece of pork before it's well put on her plate."

"Have you any more such pleasant intelligence to communicate, O'Brien?"

"No, Peter; you have the worst of it. The lieutenants are good officers and pleasant messmates: the doctor is a little queer, and the purser thinks himself a wag; the master, an old north-countryman, who knows his duty, and takes his glass of grog. The midshipmen are a very genteel set of young men, and full of fun and frolic. I'll bet a wager there'll be a bobbery in the pig-sty before long, for they are ripe for mischief.* Now, Peter, I hardly need say that my cabin and everything I have is at your service; and I think if we could only have a devil of a gale of wind, or a hard-fought action, to send the *pigs* overboard and smash the *piano*, we should do very well."

The next day I went on board, and was shown down into the cabin, to report my having joined. Mrs To, a tall thin woman, was at her piano; she rose, and asked me several questions—who my friends were—how much they allowed me a year, and many other

* *Bobbery: A disturbance.*

questions, which I thought impertinent: but a captain's wife is allowed to take liberties. She then asked me if I was fond of music? That was a difficult question, as, if I said that I was, I should in all probability be obliged to hear it: if I said that I was not, I might have created a dislike in her. So I replied, that I was very fond of music on shore, when it was not interrupted by other noise. "Ah! then I perceive you are a real amateur, Mr Simple," replied the lady.

Captain To then came out of the after-cabin, half-dressed. "Well, youngster, so you've joined us at last. Come and dine with us to-day? and, as you go down to your berth, desire the sentry to pass the word for the butcher; I want to speak with him."

I bowed and retired. I was met in the most friendly manner by the officers and by my own messmates, who had been prepossessed in my favour by O'Brien, previous to my arrival. In our service you always find young men of the best families on board large frigates, they being considered the most eligible class of vessels; I found my messmates to be gentlemen, with one or two exceptions, but I never met so many wild young lads together. I sat down and ate some dinner with them, although I was to dine in the cabin, for the sea air made me hungry.

"Don't you dine in the cabin, Simple?" said the caterer.

"Yes," replied I.

"Then don't eat any pork, my boy, now, for you'll have plenty there. Come, gentlemen, fill your glasses; we'll drink happiness to our new messmate, and pledging him, we pledge ourselves to try to promote it."

"I'll just join you in that toast," said O'Brien, walking into the midshipmen's berth. "What is it you're drinking it in?"

"Some of Collier's port, sir. Boy, bring a glass for Mr O'Brien."

"Here's your health, Peter, and wishing you may keep out of a French prison this cruise. Mr Montague, as caterer, I will beg you will order another candle, that I may see what's on the table, and then perhaps I may find something I should like to pick a bit off."

"Here's the fag end of a leg of mutton, Mr O'Brien, and there's a piece of boiled pork."

"Then I'll just trouble you for a bit close to the knuckle. Peter, you dine in the cabin, so do I—the doctor refused."

"Have you heard when we sail, Mr O'Brien?" inquired one of my messmates.

"I heard at the admiral's office, that we were expected to be ordered round to Plymouth, and receive our orders there, either for the East or West Indies, they thought; and, indeed, the stores we have taken on board indicate that we are going foreign, but the captain's signal is just made, and probably the admiral has intelligence to communicate."

In about an hour afterwards, the captain returned, looking very red and hot. He called the first lieutenant aside from the rest of the officers, who were on deck to receive him, and told him, that we were to start for Plymouth next morning; and the admiral had told him confidentially, that we were to proceed to the West Indies with a convoy, which was then collecting. He appeared to be very much alarmed at the idea of going to make a feast for the land crabs; and certainly, his gross habit of body rendered him very unfit for the climate. This news was soon spread through the ship, and there was of course no little bustle and preparation. The doctor, who had refused to dine in the cabin upon plea of being unwell, sent up to say, that he felt himself so much better, that he should have great pleasure to attend the summons, and he joined the first lieutenant, O'Brien, and me, as we walked in. We sat down to table; the covers were removed, and as the midshipmen prophesied, there was plenty of *pork*—mock-turtle soup, made out of a pig's head—a boiled leg of pork and peas-pudding—a roast spare-rib, with the crackling on— sausages and potatoes, and pig's pettitoes.* I cannot say that I disliked my dinner, and I ate very heartily; but a roast sucking-pig came on as a second course, which rather surprised me; but what surprised me more, was the quantity devoured by Mrs To. She handed her plate from the boiled pork to the roast, asked for some pettitoes, tried the sausages, and finished with a whole plateful of sucking-pig and stuffing. We had an apple pie at the end, but as we had already eaten apple sauce with the roast pork, we did not care for it. The doctor, who abominated pork, ate pretty well, and was excessively attentive to Mrs To.

"Will you not take a piece of the roast pig, doctor?" said the captain.

"Why, really Captain To, as we are bound, by all reports, to a

* *Pig's pettitoes: Pig's feet.*

station where we must not venture upon pork, I think I will not refuse to take a piece, for I am very fond of it."

"How do you mean?" inquired the captain and his lady, both in a breath.

"Perhaps I may be wrongly informed," replied the doctor, "but I have heard that we were ordered to the West Indies; now, if so, everyone knows, that although you may eat salt pork there occasionally without danger, in all tropical climates, and especially the West Indies, two or three days' living upon this meat will immediately produce dysentery, which is always fatal in that climate."

"Indeed!" exclaimed the captain.

"You don't say so!" rejoined the lady.

"I do indeed: and have always avoided the West Indies for that very reason—I am so fond of pork."

The doctor then proceeded to give nearly one hundred instances of messmates and shipmen who had been attacked with dysentery, from the eating of fresh pork in the West Indies; and O'Brien, perceiving the doctor's drift, joined him, telling some most astonishing accounts of the dreadful effects of pork in a hot country. I think he said, that when the French were blockaded, previous to the surrender of Martinique, that, having nothing but pigs to eat, thirteen hundred out of seventeen hundred soldiers and officers died in the course of three weeks, and the others were so reduced by disease, that they were obliged to capitulate. The doctor then changed the subject, and talked about the yellow fever, and other diseases of the climate, so that, by his account, the West India islands were but hospitals to die in. Those most likely to be attacked, were men in full strong health. The spare men stood a better chance. This conversation was carried on until it was time to leave—Mrs To at last quite silent, and the captain gulping down his wine with a sigh. When we rose from the table, Mrs To did not ask us, as usual, to stay and hear a little music; she was, like her piano, not a little out of tune.

"By the powers, doctor, you did that nately," said O'Brien, as we left the cabin.

"O'Brien," said the doctor, "oblige me, and you, Mr Simple, oblige me also, by not saying a word in the ship about what I have said; if it once gets wind, I shall have done no good, but if you both hold your tongues for a short time, I think I may promise you to get rid of Captain To, his wife, and his pigs." We perceived the justice of his observation, and promised secrecy. The next morning the ship sailed for Plymouth, and Mrs To sent for the doctor, not being very well. The doctor prescribed for her, and I believe, on my conscience, made her worse on purpose. The illness of his wife, and his own fears, brought Captain To more than usual in contact with the doctor, of whom he frequently asked his candid opinion, as to his own chance in a hot country.

"Captain To," said the doctor, "I never would have given my opinion, if you had not asked it, for I am aware, that, as an officer, you would never flinch from your duty, to whatever quarter of the globe you may be ordered; but, as you have asked the question, I must say, with your full habit of body, I think you would not stand a chance of living for more than two months. At the same time, sir, I may be mistaken; but, at all events, I must point out that Mrs To is of a very bilious habit, and I trust you will not do such an injustice to an amiable woman, as to permit her to accompany you."

"Thanky, doctor, I'm much obliged to you," replied the captain, turning round and going down the ladder to his cabin. We were then beating down the channel; for, although we ran through the Needles with a fair wind, it fell calm, and shifted to the westward, when we were abreast of Portland. The next day the captain gave an order for a very fine pig to be killed, for he was out of provisions. Mrs To still kept her bed, and he therefore directed that a part should be salted, as he could have no company. I was in the midshipman's berth, when some of them proposed that we should get possession of the pig; and the plan they agreed upon was as follows:—they were to go to the pen that night, and with a needle stuck in a piece of wood, to prick the pig all over, and then rub gunpowder into the parts wounded. This was done, and although the butcher was up a dozen times during the night to ascertain what made the pigs so uneasy, the midshipmen passed the needle from watch to watch, until the pig was well tattooed in all parts. In the morning watch it was killed, and when it had been scalded in the tub, and the hair taken off, it appeared covered with blue spots. The midshipman of the morning watch, who was on the main-deck, took care to point out to the butcher, that the pork was *measly*, to which the man unwillingly assented, stating, at the same time, that he could not imagine how it could be, for a finer pig he had never put a knife into. The circumstance was reported to the captain, who was much astonished. The doctor came in to visit Mrs To, and the captain requested the doctor to examine the pig, and give his opinion. Although this was not the doctor's province, yet, as he had great reason for keeping intimate with the captain, he immediately consented. Going forward, he met me, and I told him the secret. "That will do," replied he; "it all tends to what we wish." The doctor returned to the captain, and said, "that there was no doubt but that the pig was *measly*, which was a complaint very frequent on board ships, particularly in hot climates, where all pork became *measly*—one great reason for its there proving so unwholesome." The captain sent for the first lieutenant, and, with a deep sigh, ordered him to throw the pig overboard; but the first lieutenant, who knew what had been done from O'Brien, ordered the *master's mate* to throw it overboard: the master's mate, touching his hat, said, "Ay, ay, sir," and took it down into the berth, where we cut it up, salted one half, and the other we finished before we arrived at Plymouth, which was six days from the time we left Portsmouth. On our arrival, we found part of the convoy lying there, but no orders for us; and, to my great delight, on the following day the *Diomede* arrived, from a cruise off the Western Islands. I obtained permission to go on board with O'Brien, and we once more greeted our messmates. Mr Falcon, the first lieutenant, went down to Captain Savage, to say we were on board, and he requested us to come into the cabin. He greeted us warmly, and gave us great credit for the manner in which we had effected our escape. When we left the cabin, I found Mr Chucks, the boatswain, waiting outside.

"My dear Mr Simple, extend your flapper to me, for I'm delighted to see you. I long to have a long talk with you."

"And I should like it also, Mr Chucks, but I'm afraid we have not time; I dine with Captain Savage to-day, and it only wants an hour of dinner-time."

"Well, Mr Simple, I've been looking at your frigate, and she's a beauty—much larger than the *Diomede*."

"And she behaves quite as well," replied I. "I think we are two hundred tons larger. You've no idea of her size until you are on her decks."

"I should like to be boatswain of her, Mr Simple; that is, with Captain Savage, for I will not part with him." I had some more conversation with Mr Chucks, but I was obliged to attend to others, who interrupted us. We had a very pleasant dinner with our old captain, to whom we gave a history of our adventures, and then we returned on board.

———⁊ɷɷɞ⁊———

CHAPTER XXVIII

We get rid of the pigs and piano-forte—The last boat on shore before sailing—The first lieutenant too hasty, and the consequences to me.

W E WAITED three days, at the expiration of which, we heard that Captain To was about to exchange with Captain Savage. We could not believe such good news to be true, and we could not ascertain the truth of the report, as the captain had gone on shore with Mrs To, who recovered fast after she was out of our doctor's hands; so fast, indeed, that a week afterwards, on questioning the steward, upon his return on board, how Mrs To was, he replied, "O charming well again, sir, she has eaten a *whole pig,* since she left the ship." But the report was true: Captain To, afraid to go to the West Indies, had effected an exchange with Captain Savage. Captain Savage was permitted, as was the custom of the service, to bring his first lieutenant, his boatswain, and his barge's crew with him. He joined a day or two before we sailed, and never was there more joy on board: the only people miserable were the first lieutenant, and those belonging to the *Sanglier* who were obliged to follow Captain To; who, with his wife, his pigs, and her piano, were all got rid of in the course of one forenoon.

I have already described pay-day on board of a man-of-war, but I think that the two days before sailing are even more unpleasant; although, generally speaking, all our money being spent, we are not sorry when we once are fairly out of harbour, and find ourselves in *blue water.* The men never work well on those days: they are thinking of their wives and sweethearts, of the pleasure they had when at liberty on shore, where they might get drunk without punishment; and many of them are either half drunk at the time, or suffering from the effects of previous intoxication. The ship is in disorder, and crowded with the variety of stock and spare stores which are obliged to be taken on board in a hurry, and have not yet been properly secured in their places. The first lieutenant is cross, the officers are grave, and the poor midshipmen, with all their own little comforts to attend to, are harassed and driven about like post-horses. "Mr Simple," inquired the first lieutenant, "where do you come from?"

"From the gun wharf, sir, with the gunner's spare blocks, and breechings."

"Very well—send the marines aft to clear the boat, and pipe away the first cutter. Mr Simple, jump into the first cutter, and go to Mount Wise for the officers. Be careful that none of your men leave the boat. Come, be smart."

Now, I had been away the whole morning, and it was then half-past one, and I had had no dinner: but I said nothing, and went into the boat. As soon as I was off, O'Brien, who stood by Mr Falcon, said, "Peter was thinking of his dinner, poor fellow!"

"I really quite forgot it," replied the first lieutenant, "there is so much to do. He is a willing boy, and he shall dine in the gun-room when he comes back." And so I did—so I lost nothing by not expostulating, and gained more of the favour of the first lieutenant, who never forgot what he called zeal. But the hardest trial of the whole is to the midshipman who is sent with the boat to purchase the supplies for the cabin and gun-room on the day before the ship's sailing. It was my misfortune to be ordered upon that service this time, and that very unexpectedly. I had been ordered to dress myself to take the gig on shore for the captain's orders, and was walking the deck with my very best uniform and side arms, when the marine officer, who was the gun-room caterer, came up to the first lieutenant, and asked him for a boat. The boat was manned, and a midshipman ordered to take charge of it; but when he came up, the first lieutenant recollecting that he had come off two days before with only half his boat's crew, would not trust him, and called out to me, "Here, Mr Simple, I must send you in this boat; mind you are careful that none of the men leave it; and bring off the sergeant of marines, who is on shore looking for the men who have broken their liberty." Although I could not but feel proud of the compliment, yet I did not much like going in my very best uniform, and would have run down and changed it, but the marine officer and all the people were in the boat, and I could not keep it waiting, so down the side I went, and we shoved off. We had, besides the boat's crew, the marine officer, the purser, the gun-room steward, the captain's steward, and the purser's steward; so that we were pretty full. It blew hard from the S.E., and there was a sea running, but as the tide was flowing into the harbour there was not much bubble. We hoisted the foresail, flew before the wind and tide, and in a quarter of an hour we were at Mutton Cove, when the marine officer expressed his wish to land. The landing-place was crowded with boats, and it was not without sundry exchanges of foul words and oaths, and the bow-men dashing the point of their boat-hooks into the shore-boats, to make them keep clear of us, that we forced our way to the beach. The marine officer and all the stewards then left the boat, and I had to look after the men. I had not been there three minutes before the bow-man said that his wife was on the wharf with his clothes from the wash, and begged leave to go and fetch them. I refused, telling him that she could bring them to him. "Vy now, Mr Simple," said the woman, "ar'n't you a nice lady's man, to go for to ax me to muddle my way through all the dead dogs, cabbage-stalks, and stinking hakes' heads, with my bran new shoes and clean stockings?" I looked at her, and sure enough she was, as they say in France, *bien chaussée*. "Come, Mr Simple, let him out to come for his clothes, and you'll see that he's back in a moment." I did not like to refuse her, as it was very dirty and wet, and the shingle was strewed with all that she had mentioned. The bow-man made a spring out with his boat-hook, threw it back, went up to his wife, and commenced talking with her, while I watched him. "If you please, sir, there's my young woman come down, mayn't I speak to her?" said another of the men. I turned round, and refused him. He expostulated, and begged very hard, but I was resolute; however, when I again turned my eyes to watch the bow-man, he and his wife were gone. "There," says I to the coxswain, "I knew it would be so; you see Hickman is off."

"Only gone to take a parting glass, sir," replied the coxswain; "he'll be here directly."

"I hope so; but I'm afraid not." After this, I refused all the solicitations of the men to be allowed to leave the boat, but I permitted them to have some beer brought down to them. The gun-room steward then came back with a basket of *soft-tack*, *i.e.* loaves of bread, and told me that the marine officer requested I would allow two of the men to go up with him to Glencross's shop, to bring down some of the stores. Of course, I sent two of the men, and told the steward if he saw Hickman, to bring him down to the boat.

By this time many of the women belonging to the ship had assembled, and commenced a noisy conversation with the boat's crew. One brought an article for Jim, another some clothes for Bill; some of them climbed into the boat, and sat with the men; others came and went, bringing beer and tobacco, which the men desired them to purchase. The crowd, the noise, and confusion were so great, that it was with the utmost difficulty that I could keep my eyes on all my men, who, one after another, made an attempt to leave the boat. Just at that time came down the sergeant of the marines, with three of our men whom he had picked up, *roaring drunk*. They were tumbled into the boat, and increased the difficulty, as in looking after those who were riotous, and would try to leave the boat by force, I was not so well able to keep my eyes on those who were sober. The sergeant then went up after another man, and I told him also about Hickman. About half an hour afterwards the steward came down with the two men, loaded with cabbages, baskets of eggs, strings of onions, crockery of all descriptions, paper parcels of groceries, legs and shoulders of mutton, which were crowded in, until not only the stern-sheets, but all under the thwarts of the boat were also crammed full. They told me that they had a few more things to bring down, and that the marine officer had gone to Stonehouse to see his wife, so that they should be down long before him. In half an hour more, during which I had the greatest difficulty to manage the boat's crew, they returned with a dozen geese and two ducks, tied by the legs, but without the two men, who had given them the slip, so that there were now three men gone, and I knew Mr Falcon would be very angry, for they were three of the smartest men in the ship. I was now determined not to run the risk of losing more men, and I ordered the boat's crew to shove off, that I might lie at the wharf, where they could not climb up. They were very mutinous, grumbled very much, and would hardly obey me; the fact is, they had drunk a great deal, and some of them were more than half tipsy. However, at last I was obeyed, but not without being saluted with a shower of invectives from the women, and the execrations of the men belonging to the wherries and *shore* boats which were washed against our sides by the swell. The weather had become much worse, and looked very threatening. I waited an hour more, when the sergeant of marines came down with two more men, one of whom, to my great joy, was Hickman. This made me more comfortable, as I was not answerable for the other two; still I was in great trouble from the riotous and insolent behaviour of the boat's crew, and the other men brought down by the sergeant of marines. One of them fell back into a basket of eggs, and smashed them all to atoms; still the marine officer did not come down, and it was getting late. The tide being now at the ebb, running out against the wind, there was a heavy sea, and I had to go off to the ship with a boat deeply laden, and most of the people in her in a state of intoxication. The coxswain, who was the only one who was sober, recommended our shoving off, as it would soon be dark, and some accident would happen. I reflected a minute, and agreeing with him, I ordered the oars to be got out, and we shoved off, the sergeant of marines and the gun-room steward perched up in the bows—drunken men, ducks and geese, lying together at the bottom of the boat—the stern-sheets loaded up to the gunwale, and the other passengers and myself sitting how we could among the crockery and a variety of other articles with which the boat was crowded. It was a scene of much confusion—the half-drunken boat's crew *catching crabs*, and falling forward upon the others—those who were quite drunk swearing they *would* pull. "Lay on your oar, Sullivan; you are doing more harm than good. You drunken rascal, I'll report you as soon as we get on board."

"How the divil can I pull, your honour, when there's that fellow Jones breaking the very back o' me with his oar, and he never touching the water all the while?"

"You lie," cried Jones; "I'm pulling the boat by myself against the whole of the larbard oars."

"He's rowing *dry*, your honour—only making bilave."

"Do you call this rowing dry?" cried another, as a sea swept over the boat, fore and aft, wetting everybody to the skin.

"Now, your honour, just look and see if I ain't pulling the very arms off me?" cried Sullivan.

"Is there water enough to cross the bridge, Swinburne?" said I to the coxswain.

"Plenty, Mr Simple; it is but quarter ebb, and the sooner we are on board the better."

We were now past Devil's Point, and the sea was very heavy: the boat plunged in the trough, so that I was afraid that she would break her back. She was soon half full of water, and the two after-oars were laid in for the men to bale. "Plase your honour, hadn't I better cut free the legs of them ducks and geese, and allow them to swim for their lives?" cried Sullivan, resting on his oar; "the poor birds will be drowned else in their own *iliment.*"

"No, no—pull away as hard as you can."

By this time the drunken men in the bottom of the boat began to be very uneasy, from the quantity of water which washed about them, and made several staggering attempts to get on their legs. They fell down again upon the ducks and geese, the major part of which were saved from being drowned by being suffocated. The sea on the bridge was very heavy; and although the tide swept us out, we were nearly swamped. Soft bread was washing about the bottom of the boat; the parcels of sugar, pepper, and salt, were wet through with the salt water, and a sudden jerk threw the captain's steward, who was seated upon the gunwale close to the after-oar, right upon the whole of the crockery and eggs, which added to the mass of destruction. A few more seas shipped completed the job, and the gun-room steward was in despair. "That's a darling," cried Sullivan: "the politest boat in the whole fleet. She makes more bows and curtseys than the finest couple in the land. Give way, my lads, and work the crater stuff out of your elbows, and the first lieutenant will see us all so sober, and so wet in the bargain, and think we're all so dry, that perhaps he'll be after giving us a raw nip when we get on board."

In a quarter of an hour we were nearly alongside, but the men pulled so badly, and the sea was so great, that we missed the ship and went astern. They veered out a buoy with a line, which we got hold of, and were hauled up by the marines and afterguard, the boat plunging bows under, and drenching us through and through. At last we got under the counter, and I climbed up by the stern ladder. Mr Falcon was on deck, and very angry at the boat not coming alongside properly. "I thought, Mr Simple, that you knew by this time how to bring a boat alongside."

"So I do, sir, I hope," replied I; "but the boat was so full of water, and the men would not give way."

"What men has the sergeant brought on board?"

"Three, sir," replied I, shivering with the cold, and unhappy at my very best uniform being spoiled.

"Are all your boat's crew with you, sir?"

"No sir; there are two left on shore; they—"

"Not a word, sir. Up to the mast-head, and stay there till I call you down. If it were not so late, I would send you on shore, and not receive you on board again without the men. Up, sir, immediately."

I did not venture to explain, but up I went. It was very cold, blowing hard from the S.E., with heavy squalls; I was so wet that the wind appeared to blow through me, and it was now nearly dark. I reached the cross-trees, and when I was seated there, I felt that I had done my duty, and had not been fairly treated. During this time, the boat had been hauled up alongside to clear, and a pretty clearance there was. All the ducks and geese were dead, the eggs and crockery all broke, the grocery almost all washed away; in short, as O'Brien observed, there was "a very pretty general average." Mr Falcon was still very angry. "Who are the men missing?" inquired he, of Swinburne, the coxswain, as he came up the side.

"Williams and Sweetman, sir."

"Two of the smartest topmen, I am told. It really is too provoking; there is not a midshipman in the ship I can trust. I must work all day, and get no assistance. The service is really going to the devil now, with the young men who are sent on board to be brought up as officers, and who are above doing their duty. What made you so late, Swinburne?"

"Waiting for the marine officer, who went to Stonehouse to see his wife; but Mr Simple would not wait any longer, as it was getting dark, and we had so many drunken men in the boat."

"Mr Simple did right. I wish Mr Harrison would stay on shore with his wife altogether—it's really trifling with the service. Pray, Mr Swinburne, why had you not your eyes about you if Mr Simple was so careless? How came you to allow these men to leave the boat?"

"The men were ordered up by the marine officer to bring down your stores, sir, and they gave the steward the slip. It was no fault of Mr Simple's, nor of mine either. We lay off at the wharf for two hours before we started, or we should have lost more; for what can a poor lad do, when he has charge of drunken men who *will not* obey orders?" And the coxswain looked up at the mast-head, as much as to say, Why is he sent there? "I'll take my oath, sir," continued Swinburne, "that Mr Simple never put his foot out of the boat, from the time that he went over the side until he came on board, and that no young gentleman could have done his duty more strictly."

Mr Falcon looked very angry at first at the coxswain speaking so freely, but he said nothing. He took one or two turns on the deck, and then hailing the mast-head, desired me to come down. But I *could not;* my limbs were so cramped with the wind blowing upon my wet clothes, that I could not move. He hailed again; I heard him, but was not able to answer. One of the topmen then came up, and perceiving my condition, hailed the deck, and said he believed I was dying, for I could not move, and that he dared not leave me for fear I should fall. O'Brien, who had been on deck all the while, jumped up the rigging, and was soon at the cross-trees where I was. He sent the topman down into the top for a tail-block and the studding-sail haulyards, made a whip, and lowered me on deck. I was immediately put into my hammock; and the surgeon ordering me some hot brandy-and-water, and plenty of blankets, in a few hours I was quite restored.

O'Brien, who was at my bedside, said, "Never mind, Peter, and don't be angry with Mr Falcon, for he is very sorry."

"I am not angry, O'Brien; for Mr Falcon has been too kind to me not to make me forgive him for being once hasty."

The surgeon came to my hammock, gave me some more hot drink, desired me to go to sleep, and I woke the next morning quite well.

When I came into the berth, my messmates asked me how I was, and many of them railed against the tyranny of Mr Falcon; but I took his part, saying, that he was hasty in this instance, perhaps, but that, generally speaking, he was an excellent and very just officer. Some agreed with me, but others did not. One of them, who was always in disgrace, sneered at me, and said, "Peter reads the Bible, and knows that if you smite one cheek, he must offer the other. Now, I'll answer for it, if I pull his right ear he will offer me his left." So saying, he lugged me by the ear, upon which I knocked him down for his trouble. The berth was then cleared away for a fight, and in a quarter of an hour my opponent gave in; but I suffered a little, and had a very black eye. I had hardly time to wash myself and change my shirt, which was bloody, when I was summoned on the quarter-deck. When I arrived, I found Mr Falcon walking up and down. He looked very hard at me, but did not ask me any questions as to the cause of my unusual appearance.

"Mr Simple," said he, "I sent for you to beg your pardon for my behaviour to you last night, which was not only very hasty but very unjust. I find that you were not to blame for the loss of the men."

I felt very sorry for him when I heard him speak so handsomely; and, to make his mind more easy, I told him that, although I certainly was not to blame for the loss of those two men, still I had done wrong in permitting Hickman to leave the boat; and that had not the sergeant picked him up, I should have come off without him, and therefore I *did* deserve the punishment which I had received.

"Mr Simple," replied Mr Falcon, "I respect you, and admire your feelings; still, I was to blame, and it is my duty to apologise. Now go down below. I would have requested the pleasure of your company to dinner, but I perceive that something else has occurred, which, under any other circumstances, I would have inquired into, but at present I shall not."

I touched my hat and went below. In the meantime, O'Brien had been made acquainted with the occasion of the quarrel, which he did not fail to explain to Mr Falcon, who, O'Brien declared, "was not the least bit in the world angry with me for what had occurred." Indeed, after that, Mr Falcon always treated me with the greatest kindness, and employed me on every duty which he considered of consequence. He was a sincere friend; for he did not allow me to neglect my duty, but, at the same time, treated me with consideration and confidence.

The marine officer came on board very angry at being left behind, and talked about a court-martial on me for disrespect, and neglect of stores entrusted to my charge; but O'Brien told me not to mind him, or what he said. "It's my opinion, Peter, that the gentleman has eaten no small quantity of *flap-doodle* in his lifetime."

"What's that, O'Brien?" replied I; "I never heard of it."

"Why, Peter," rejoined he, "it's the stuff they *feed fools on.*"

———⟶⟶⟵———

CHAPTER XXIX

A long conversation with Mr Chucks—The advantage of having a prayer-book in your pocket—We run down the trades—Swinburne, the quarter-master, and his yarns—The captain falls sick.

THE NEXT DAY the captain came on board with sealed orders, with directions not to open them until off Ushant. In the afternoon, we weighed and made sail. It was a fine northerly wind, and the Bay of Biscay was smooth. We bore up, set all the studding-sails, and ran along at the rate of eleven miles an hour. As I could not appear on the quarter-deck, I was put down on the sick-list. Captain Savage, who was very particular, asked what was the matter with me. The surgeon replied, "An inflamed eye." The captain asked no more questions; and I took care to keep out of his way. I walked in the evening on the forecastle, when I renewed my intimacy with Mr Chucks, the boatswain, to whom I gave a full narrative of all my adventures in France. "I have been ruminating, Mr Simple," said he, "how such a stripling as you could have gone through so much fatigue, and now I know how it is. It is *blood*, Mr Simple—all blood—you are descended from good blood; and there's as much difference between nobility and the lower classes, as there is between a racer and a cart-horse."

"I cannot agree with you, Mr Chucks. Common people are quite as brave as those who are well-born. You do not mean to say that you are not brave—that the seamen on board this ship are not brave?"

"No, no, Mr Simple; but as I observed about myself, my mother was a woman who could not be trusted, and there is no saying who was my father; and she was a very pretty woman to boot, which levels all distinctions for the moment. As for the seamen, God knows, I should do them an injustice if I did not acknowledge that they were as brave as lions. But there are two kinds of bravery, Mr Simple—the bravery of the moment, and the courage of bearing up for a long while. Do you understand me?"

"I think I do; but still do not agree with you. Who will bear more fatigue than our sailors?"

"Yes, yes, Mr Simple, that is because they are *endured* to it from their hard life: but if the common sailors were all such little thread-papers as you, and had been brought up so carefully, they would not have gone through all you have. That's my opinion, Mr Simple—there's nothing like *blood*."

"I think, Mr Chucks, you carry your ideas on that subject too far."

"I do not, Mr Simple; and I think, moreover, that he who has more to lose than another will always strive more. Now a common man only fights for his own credit; but when a man is descended from a long line of people famous in history, and has a coat *in* arms, criss-crossed, and stuck all over with lions and unicorns to support the dignity of—why, has he not to fight for the credit of all his ancestors, whose names would be disgraced if he didn't behave well?"

"I agree with you, Mr Chucks, in the latter remark, to a certain extent."

"Ah! Mr Simple, we never know the value of good descent when we have it, but it's when we cannot get it that we can 'preciate it. I wish I had been born a nobleman—I do, by heavens!" and Mr Chucks slapped his fist against the funnel, so as to make it ring again. "Well, Mr Simple," continued he, after a pause, "it is, however, a great comfort to me that I have parted company with that fool, Mr Muddle, with his twenty-six thousand and odd years, and that old woman, Dispart, the gunner. You don't know how those two men used to fret me; it was very silly, but I couldn't help it. Now the warrant officers of this ship appear to be very respectable, quiet men, who know their duty and attend to it, and are not too familiar, which I hate and detest. You went home to your friends, of course, when you arrived in England?"

"I did, Mr Chucks, and spent some days with my grandfather, Lord Privilege, whom you say you once met at dinner."

"Well, and how was the old gentleman?" inquired the boatswain, with a sigh.

"Very well, considering his age."

"Now do, pray, Mr Simple, tell me all about it; from the time that the servants met you at the door until you went away. Describe to me the house and all the rooms, for I like to hear of all these things, although I can never see them again."

To please Mr Chucks, I entered into a full detail, which he listened to very attentively, until it was late, and then with difficulty
would he permit me to leave off, and go down to my hammock. The
next day, rather a singular circumstance occurred. One of the midshipmen was mast-headed by the second lieutenant, for not waiting
on deck until he was relieved. He was down below when he was
sent for, and expecting to be punished from what the quarter-master
told him, he thrust the first book into his jacket-pocket which he
could lay his hand on, to amuse himself at the mast-head, and then
ran on deck. As he surmised, he was immediately ordered aloft. He
had not been there more than five minutes, when a sudden squall
carried away the main-top-gallant mast, and away he went flying
over to leeward (for the wind had shifted, and the yards were now
braced up). Had he gone overboard, as he could not swim, he
would, in all probability, have been drowned; but the book in his
pocket brought him up in the jaws of the fore-brace block, where he
hung until taken out by the main-topmen. Now it so happened that
it was a prayer-book which he had laid hold of in his hurry, and
those who were superstitious declared it was all owing to his having
taken a religious book with him. I did not think so, as any other
book would have answered the purpose quite as well: still the midshipman himself thought so, and it was productive of good, as he
was a sad scamp, and behaved much better afterwards. But I had
nearly forgotten to mention a circumstance which occurred on the
day of our sailing, which will be eventually found to have had a
great influence upon my after-life. It was this. I received a letter
from my father, evidently written in great vexation and annoyance,
informing me that my uncle, whose wife I have already mentioned
had two daughters, and was again expected to be confined, had
suddenly broken up his housekeeping, discharged every servant,
and proceeded to Ireland under an assumed name. No reason had
been given for this unaccountable proceeding; and not even my
grandfather, or any of the members of the family, had had notice of
his intention. Indeed, it was by mere accident that his departure was
discovered, about a fortnight after it had taken place. My father had
taken a great deal of pains to find out where he was residing; but
although my uncle was traced to Cork, from that town all clue was
lost, but still it was supposed, from inquiries, that he was not very
far from thence. "Now," observed my father, in his letter, "I cannot

help surmising, that my brother, in his anxiety to retain the advantages of the title to his own family, has resolved to produce to the world a spurious child as his own, by some contrivance or other. His wife's health is very bad, and she is not likely to have a large family. Should the one now expected prove a daughter, there is little chance of his ever having another; and I have no hesitation in declaring my conviction that the measure has been taken with a view of defrauding you of your chance of eventually being called to the House of Lords."

I showed this letter to O'Brien, who, after reading it over two or three times, gave his opinion that my father was right in his conjectures. "Depend upon it, Peter, there's foul play intended, that is, if foul play is rendered necessary."

"But, O'Brien, I cannot imagine why, if my uncle has no son of his own, he should prefer acknowledging a son of any other person's, instead of his own nephew."

"But I can, Peter: your uncle is not a man likely to live very long, as you know. The doctors say that, with his short neck, his life is not worth two years' purchase. Now if he had a son, consider that his daughters would be much better off, and much more likely to get married; besides, there are many reasons which I won't talk about now, because it's no use making you think your uncle to be a scoundrel. But I'll tell you what I'll do. I'll go down to my cabin directly, and write to Father M'Grath, telling him the whole affair, and desiring him to ferret him out, and watch him narrowly, and I'll bet you a dozen of claret, that in less than a week he'll find him out, and will dog him to the last. He'll get hold of his Irish servants, and you little know the power that a priest has in our country. Now give the description as well as you can of your uncle's appearance, also of that of his wife, and the number of their family, and their ages. Father M'Grath must have all particulars, and then let him alone for doing what is needful."

I complied with O'Brien's directions as well as I could, and he wrote a very long letter to Father M'Grath, which was sent on shore by a careful hand. I answered my father's letter, and then thought no more about the matter.

Our sealed orders were opened, and proved our destination to be the West Indies, as we expected. We touched at Madeira to take in some wine for the ship's company; but as we only remained one

day, we were not permitted to go on shore. Fortunate indeed would
it have been if we had never gone there; for the day after, our captain, who had dined with the consul, was taken alarmingly ill. From
the symptoms, the surgeon dreaded that he had been poisoned by
something which he had eaten, and which most probably had been
cooked in a copper vessel not properly tinned. We were all very
anxious that he should recover; but, on the contrary, he appeared to
grow worse and worse every day, wasting away, and dying, as they
say, by inches. At last he was put into his cot, and never rose from it
again. This melancholy circumstance, added to the knowledge that
we were proceeding to an unhealthy climate, caused a gloom
throughout the ship; and, although the trade wind carried us along
bounding over the bright blue sea—although the weather was now
warm, yet not too warm—although the sun rose in splendour, and
all was beautiful and cheering, the state of the captain's health was a
check to all mirth. Everyone trod the deck softly, and spoke in a low
voice, that he might not be disturbed; all were anxious to have the
morning report of the surgeon, and our conversation was generally
upon the sickly climate, the yellow fever, of death, and the palisades
where they buried us. Swinburne, the quarter-master, was in my
watch, and as he had been long in the West Indies, I used to obtain
all the information from him that I could. The old fellow had a secret
pleasure in frightening me as much as he could. "Really, Mr Simple,
you ax so many questions," he would say, as I accosted him while
he was at his station at the *conn*, "I wish you wouldn't ax so many
questions, and make yourself uncomfortable—'steady so'—'steady
it is';—with regard to Yellow Jack, as we calls the yellow fever, it's a
devil incarnate, that's sartain—you're well and able to take your
allowance in the morning, and dead as a herring 'fore night. First
comes a bit of a head-ache—you goes to the doctor, who bleeds you
like a pig—then you go out of your senses—then up comes the black
vomit, and then it's all over with you, and you go to the land crabs,
who pick your bones as clean and as white as a sea elephant's tooth.
But there be one thing to be said in favour of Yellow Jack, a'ter all.
You dies *straight*, like a gentleman—not cribbled up like a snow-fish,
chucked out on the ice of the river St Lawrence, with your knees
up to your nose, or your toes stuck into your arm-pits, as does
take place in some of your foreign complaints; but straight,
quite straight, and limber, like a *gentleman*. Still Jack is a little

mischievous, that's sartain. In the *Euridiscy* we had as fine a ship's company as was ever piped aloft—'Steady, starboard, my man, you're half-a-pint off your course';—we dropped our anchor in Port Royal, and we thought that there was mischief brewing, for thirty-eight sharks followed the ship into the harbour, and played about us day and night. I used to watch them during the night watch, as their fins, above water, skimmed along, leaving a trail of light behind them; and the second night I said to the sentry abaft, as I was looking at them smelling under the counter—'Soldier,' says I, 'them sharks are mustering under the orders of Yellow Jack,' and I no sooner mentioned Yellow Jack, than the sharks gave a frisky plunge, every one of them, as much as to say, 'Yes, so we are, d——n your eyes.' The soldier was so frightened that he would have fallen overboard, if I hadn't caught him by the scruff of the neck, for he was standing on the top of the taffrail. As it was, he dropped his musket over the stern, which the sharks dashed at from every quarter, making the sea look like fire—and he had it charged to his wages, £1 16s. I think. However, the fate of his musket gave him an idea of what would have happened to him if he had fallen in instead of it—and he never got on the taffrail again. 'Steady, port—mind your helm, Smith—you can listen to my yarn all the same.' Well, Mr Simple, Yellow Jack came, sure enough. First the purser was called to account for all his roguery. We didn't care much about the land crabs eating him, who had made so many poor dead men chew tobacco, cheating their wives and relations, or Greenwich Hospital, as it might happen. Then went two of the middies, just about your age, Mr Simple: they, poor fellows, went off in a sad hurry; then went the master—and so it went on, till at last we had no more nor sixty men left in the ship. The captain died last, and then Yellow Jack had filled his maw, and left the rest of us alone. As soon as the captain died, all the sharks left the ship, and we never saw any more of them."

Such were the yarns told to me and the other midshipmen during the night watches; and I can assure the reader, that they gave us no small alarm. Every day that we worked our day's work, and found ourselves so much nearer to the islands, did we feel as if we were so much nearer to our graves. I once spoke to O'Brien about it, and he laughed. "Peter," says he, "fear kills more people than the yellow fever, or any other complaint, in the West Indies. Swinburne is an old rogue, and only laughing at you. The devil's not half so

black as he's painted—nor the yellow fever half so yellow, I presume." We were now fast nearing the island of Barbadoes, the
weather was beautiful, the wind always fair; the flying fish rose in
shoals, startled by the foaming seas, which rolled away, and roared
from the bows as our swift frigate cleaved through the water; the
porpoises played about us in thousands—the bonetas and dolphins
at one time chased the flying fish, and at others, appeared to be
delighted in keeping company with the rapid vessel. Everything
was beautiful, and we all should have been happy, had it not been
for the state of Captain Savage, in the first place, who daily became
worse and worse, and from the dread of the hell, which we were
about to enter through such a watery paradise. Mr Falcon, who was
in command, was grave and thoughtful; he appeared indeed to be
quite miserable at the chance which would insure his own promotion. In every attention, and every care that could be taken to insure
quiet and afford relief to the captain, he was unremitting; the offence
of making a noise was now, with him, a greater crime than drunkenness, or even mutiny. When within three days' sail of Barbadoes, it
fell almost calm, and the captain became much worse; and now for
the first time did we behold the great white shark of the Atlantic.
There are several kinds of sharks, but the most dangerous are the
great white shark and the ground shark. The former grows to an
enormous length—the latter is seldom very long, not more than
twelve feet, but spreads to a great breadth. We could not hook the
sharks as they played around us, for Mr Falcon would not permit it,
lest the noise of hauling them on board should disturb the captain.
A breeze again sprang up. In two days we were close to the island,
and the men were desired to look out for the land.

—◦◦◦—

CHAPTER XXX

Death of Captain Savage—His funeral—Specimen of true Barbadian born—Sucking the monkey—Effects of a hurricane.

THE NEXT MORNING, having hove-to part of the night, land was discovered on the bow, and was reported by the mast-head man at the same moment that the surgeon came up and announced the death of our noble captain. Although it had been expected for the last two or three days, the intelligence created a heavy gloom throughout the ship; the men worked in silence, and spoke to one another in whispers. Mr Falcon was deeply affected, and so were we all. In the course of the morning, we ran in to the island, and unhappy as I was, I never can forget the sensation of admiration which I felt on closing with Needham Point to enter Carlisle Bay. The beach of such a pure dazzling white, backed by the tall, green cocoa-nut trees, waving their spreading heads to the fresh breeze, the dark blue of the sky, and the deeper blue of the transparent sea, occasionally varied into green as we passed by the coral rocks which threw their branches out from the bottom—the town opening to our view by degrees, houses after houses, so neat, with their green jalousies, dotting the landscape, the fort with the colours flying, troops of officers riding down, a busy population of all colours, relieved by the whiteness of their dress. Altogether the scene realised my first ideas of Fairyland, for I thought I had never witnessed anything so beautiful. "And can this be such a dreadful place as it is described?" thought I. The sails were clewed up, the anchor was dropped to the bottom, and a salute from the ship, answered by the forts, added to the effect of the scene. The sails were furled, the boats lowered down, the boatswain squared the yards from the jolly-boat ahead. Mr Falcon dressed, and his boat being manned, went on shore with the despatches. Then, as soon as the work was over, a new scene of delight presented itself to the sight of midshipmen who had been so long upon his Majesty's allowance. These were the boats, which crowded round the ship, loaded with baskets of bananas, oranges, shaddocks, soursops, and every other kind of tropical fruit, fried flying fish, eggs, fowls, milk, and everything which could tempt a poor boy after a long sea voyage. The watch being called, down we all hastened into the boats, and returned loaded with treasures, which we soon contrived to make disappear. After stowing away as much fruit as would have sufficed for a dessert to a dinner given to twenty people in England, I returned on deck.

There was no other man-of-war in the bay; but my attention was directed to a beautiful little vessel, a schooner, whose fairy form contrasted strongly with a West India trader which lay close to her. All of a sudden, as I was looking at her beautiful outline, a yell rose from her which quite startled me, and immediately afterwards her deck was covered with nearly two hundred naked figures with woolly heads, chattering and grinning at each other. She was a Spanish slaver, which had been captured, and had arrived the evening before. The slaves were still on board, waiting the orders of the governor. They had been on deck about ten minutes, when three or four men, with large panama straw hats on their heads, and long rattans in their hands, jumped upon the gunnel, and in a few seconds drove them all down below. I then turned round, and observed a black woman who had just climbed up the side of the frigate. O'Brien was on deck, and she walked up to him in the most consequential manner.

"How do you do, sar? Very happy you com back again," said she to O'Brien.

"I'm very well, I thank you, ma'am," replied O'Brien, "and I hope to go back the same; but never having put my foot into this bay before, you have the advantage of me."

"Nebber here before, so help me Gad! me tink I know you—me tink I recollect your handsome face—I Lady Rodney, sar. Ah, piccaninny buccra: how you do?" said she, turning round to me.* "Me hope to hab the honour to wash for you, sar," curtseying to O'Brien.

"What do you charge in this place?"

"All the same price, one bit a piece."

"What do you call a bit?" inquired I.

"A bit, lilly massa?—what you call um *bit?* Dem four *sharp shins* to a pictareen."

Our deck was now enlivened by several army officers, besides gentlemen residents, who came off to hear the news. Invitations to

* *Piccaninny buccra: A white child.*

the mess and to the houses of the gentlemen followed, and as they
departed Mr Falcon returned on board. He told O'Brien and the
other officers, that the admiral and squadron were expected in a few
days, and that we were to remain in Carlisle Bay and refit immediately. But although the fright about the yellow fever had considerably subsided in our breasts, the remembrance that our poor captain
was lying dead in the cabin was constantly obtruding. All that night
the carpenters were up making up his coffin, for he was to be buried
the next day. The body is never allowed to remain many hours
unburied in the tropical climates, where putrefaction is so rapid. The
following morning the men were up at daylight, washing the decks
and putting the ship in order; they worked willingly, and yet with a
silent decorum which showed what their feelings were. Never were
the decks better cleaned, never were the ropes more carefully *flemished* down, the hammocks were stowed in their white cloths, the
yards carefully squared, and the ropes hauled taut.* At eight o'clock,
the colours and pennant were hoisted half-mast high. The men were
then ordered down to breakfast, and to clean themselves. During the
time that the men were at breakfast, all the officers went into the
cabin to take a last farewell look at our gallant captain. He appeared
to have died without pain, and there was a beautiful tranquillity in
his face; but even already a change had taken place, and we perceived the necessity of his being buried so soon. We saw him placed
in his coffin, and then quitted the cabin without speaking to each
other. When the coffin was nailed down, it was brought up by the
barge's crew to the quarter-deck, and laid upon the gratings amidships, covered over with the Union Jack. The men came up from
below without waiting for the pipe, and a solemnity appeared to
pervade every motion. Order and quiet were universal, out of respect to the deceased. When the boats were ordered to be manned,
the men almost appeared to steal into them. The barge received the
coffin, which was placed in the stern sheets. The other boats then
hauled up, and received the officers, marines, and sailors, who were
to follow the procession. When all was ready, the barge was shoved
off by the bow-men, the crew dropped their oars into the water
without a splash and pulled the *minute stroke:* the other boats followed, and as soon as they were clear of the ship, the minute guns

* *Flemished down: Rope laid in flat coils.*

boomed along the smooth surface of the bay from the opposite side of the ship, while the yards were topped to starboard and to port, the ropes were slackened and hung in bights, so as to give the idea of distress and neglect. At the same time, a dozen or more of the men who had been ready, dropped over the sides of the ship in different parts, and with their cans of paint and brushes in a few minutes effaced the whole of the broad white riband which marked the beautiful run of the frigate, and left her all black and in deep mourning. The guns from the forts now responded to our own. The merchant ships lowered their colours, and the men stood up respectfully with their hats off, as the procession moved slowly to the landing-place. The coffin was borne to the burial-ground by the crew of the barge, followed by Mr Falcon as chief mourner, all the officers of the ship who could be spared, one hundred of the seamen walking two and two and the marines with their arms reversed. The *cortege* was joined by the army officers, while the troops lined the streets, and the bands played the Dead March.* The service was read, the volleys were fired over the grave, and with oppressed feelings we returned to the boats, and pulled on board. It then appeared to me, and to a certain degree I was correct, that as soon as we had paid our last respect to his remains, we had also forgotten our grief. The yards were again squared, the ropes hauled taut, working dresses resumed, and all was activity and bustle. The fact is, that sailors and soldiers have no time for lamentation, and running as they do from clime to clime, so does scene follow scene in the same variety and quickness. In a day or two, the captain appeared to be, although he was not, forgotten. Our first business was to *water* the ship by rafting and towing off the casks. I was in charge of the boat again, with Swinburne as coxswain. As we pulled in, there were a number of negroes bathing in the surf, bobbing their woolly heads under it, as it rolled into the beach. "Now, Mr Simple," said Swinburne, "see how I'll make them *niggers* scamper." He then stood up in the stern sheets, and pointing with his finger, roared out, "A shark! a shark!" Away started all the bathers for the beach, puffing and blowing, from their dreaded enemy; nor did they stop to look for him until they were high and dry out of his reach. Then, when we all laughed, they called us *"all the hangman tiefs,"*

* Cortege: *A procession.*

and every other opprobrious name which they could select from
their vocabulary. I was very much amused with this scene, and as
much afterwards with the negroes who crowded round us when we
landed. They appeared such merry fellows, always laughing, chattering, singing, and showing their white teeth. One fellow danced
round us, snapping his fingers, and singing songs without beginning or end. "Eh, massa, what you say now? Me no slave—true
Barbadian born, sir. Eh!

> "Nebba see de day
> Dat Rodney run away,
> Nebba see um night
> Dat Rodney cannot fight.

Massa me free man, sar. Suppose you give me pictareen, drink
massa health.

> "Nebba see de day, boy,
> Pompey lickum de Cæsar.

Eh! and you nebba see de day dat de Grasshopper run on de War-
rington."

"Out of the way, you nigger," cried one of the men who was
rolling down a cask.

"Eh! who you call nigger? Me free man, and true Barbadian
born. Go along you man-of-war man.

> "Man-of-war, buccra,
> Man-of-war, buccra,
> He de boy for me;
> Sodger, buccra,
> Sodger, buccra,
> Nebba, nebba do,
> Nebba, nebba do for me;
> Sodger give me one shilling,
> Sailor give me two.

Massa, now suppose you give me only one pictareen now. You
really handsome young gentleman."

"Now, just walk off," said Swinburne, lifting up a stick he found on the beach.

"Eh! walk off.

> *"Nebba see de day, boy,*
> *'Badian run away, boy.*

Go, do your work, sar. Why you talk to me? Go, work, sar. I free man, and real Barbadian born.

> *"Negro on de shore*
> *See de ship come in,*
> *De buccra come on shore,*
> *Wid de hand up to the chin;*
> *Man-of-war buccra,*
> *Man-of-war buccra,*
> *He de boy for me,*
> *Man-of-war, buccra,*
> *Man-of-war, buccra,*
> *Gib pictareen to me."*

At this moment my attention was directed to another negro, who lay on the beach rolling and foaming at the mouth, apparently in a fit. "What's the matter with that fellow?" said I to the same negro who continued close to me, notwithstanding Swinburne's stick. "Eh! call him Sam Slack, massa. He ab um *tic tic* fit." And such was apparently the case. "Stop, me cure him"; and he snatched the stick out of Swinburne's hand, and running up to the man, who continued to roll on the beach, commenced belabouring him without mercy. "Eh, Sambo!" cried he at last, quite out of breath, "you no better yet—try again." He recommenced, until at last the man got up and ran away as fast as he could. Now, whether the man was shamming, or whether it was real *tic tic*, or epileptic fit, I know not; but I never heard of such a cure for it before. I threw the fellow half a pictareen, as much for the amusement he had afforded me as to get rid of him. "Tanky, massa; now man-of-war man, here de tick for you again to keep off all the dam niggers." So saying, he handed the stick to Swinburne, made a polite bow, and departed. We were, however, soon surrounded by others, particularly some dingy ladies with baskets of fruit, and who, as they said, "sell ebery ting." I perceived that my sailors were very fond of cocoa-nut milk, which, being a harmless beverage, I did not object to their purchasing from these ladies, who had chiefly cocoa-nuts in their baskets. As I had never tasted it, I asked them what it was, and bought a cocoa-nut. I selected the largest. "No, massa, dat not good for you. Better one for buccra officer." I then selected another, but the same objection was made. "No, massa, dis very fine milk. Very good for de tomac." I drank off the milk from the holes on the top of the cocoa-nut, and found it very refreshing. As for the sailors, they appeared very fond of it indeed. But I very soon found that if good for de tomac, it was not very good for the head, as my men, instead of rolling the casks, began to roll themselves in all directions, and when it was time to go off to dinner, most of them were dead drunk at the bottom of the boat. They insisted that it was the *sun* which affected them. Very hot it certainly was, and I believed them at first, when they were only giddy; but I was convinced to the contrary when I found that they became insensible; yet how they had procured the liquor was to me a mystery. When I came on board, Mr Falcon, who, although acting captain, continued his duties as first lieutenant almost as punctually as before, asked how it was that I had allowed my men to get so tipsy. I assured him that I could not tell, that I had never allowed one to leave the watering-place, or to buy any liquor. the only thing that they had to drink was a little cocoa-nut milk, which, as it was so very hot, I thought there could be no objection to. Mr Falcon smiled and said, "Mr Simple, I'm an old stager in the West Indies, and I'll let you into a secret. Do you know what *'sucking the monkey'* means?" "No, sir." "Well, then, I'll tell you; it is a term used among seamen for drinking *rum* out of *cocoa-nuts,* the milk having been poured out, and the liquor substituted. Now do you comprehend why your men are tipsy?" I stared with all my eyes, for it never would have entered into my head; and I then perceived why it was that the black woman would not give me the first cocoa-nuts which I selected. I told Mr Falcon of this circumstance, who replied, "Well, it was not your fault, only you must not forget it another time."

It was my first watch that night, and Swinburne was quarter-master on deck. "Swinburne," said I, "you have often been in the West Indies before, why did you not tell me that the men were '*sucking the monkey*' when I thought that they were only drinking cocoa-nut milk?''

Swinburne chuckled, and answered, "Why, Mr Simple, d'ye see, it didn't become me as a shipmate to peach. It's but seldom that a poor fellow has an opportunity of making himself a 'little happy,' and it would not be fair to take away the chance. I suppose you'll never let them have cocoa-nut milk again?''

"No, that I will not; but I cannot imagine what pleasure they can find in getting so tipsy."

"It's merely because they are not allowed to be so, sir. That's the whole story in few words."

"Well, I think I could cure them if I were permitted to try."

"I should like to hear how you'd manage that, Mr Simple."

"Why, I would oblige a man to drink off a half pint of liquor, and then put him by himself. I would not allow him companions to make merry with so as to make a pleasure of intoxication. I would then wait until next morning when he was sober, and leave him alone with a racking headache until the evening, when I would give him another dose, and so on, forcing him to get drunk until he hated the smell of liquor."

"Well, Mr Simple, it might do with some, but many of our chaps would require the dose you mention to be repeated pretty often before it would effect a cure; and what's more, they'd be very willing patients, and make no wry faces at their physic."

"Well, that might be, but it would cure them at last. But tell me, Swinburne, were you ever in a hurricane?''

"I've been in everything, Mr Simple, I believe, except at school, and I never had no time to go there. Do you see that battery at Needham Point? Well, in the hurricane of '82, them same guns were whirled away by the wind, right over to this point here on the opposite side, the sentries in their sentry-boxes after them. Some of the soldiers who faced the wind had their teeth blown down their throats like broken 'baccy-pipes, others had their heads turned round like dog vanes, 'cause they waited for orders to the '*right about face,*' and the whole air was full of young *niggers* blowing about like peelings of *ingons.*''*

"You don't suppose I believe all this, Swinburne?''

* Ingons: *Onions.*

"That's as may be, Mr Simple, but I've told the story so often, that I believe it myself."

"What ship were you in?"

"In the *Blanche*, Captain Faulkner, who was as fine a fellow as poor Captain Savage, whom we buried yesterday; there could not be a finer than either of them. I was at the taking of the Pique, and carried him down below after he had received his mortal wound. We did a pretty thing out here when we took Fort Royal by a coup-de-*main*, which means, boarding from the *main*-yard of the frigate, and dropping from it into the fort. But what's that under the moon?—there's a sail in the offing."

Swinburne fetched the glass and directed it to the spot. "One, two, three, four. It's the admiral, sir, and the squadron hove-to for the night. One's a line-of-battle ship, I'll swear." I examined the vessels, and agreeing with Swinburne, reported them to Mr Falcon. My watch was then over, and as soon as I was released I went to my hammock.

———

CHAPTER XXXI

Captain Kearney—The dignity ball.

THE NEXT MORNING at daylight we exchanged numbers, and saluted the flag, and by eight o'clock they all anchored. Mr Falcon went on board the admiral's ship with despatches, and to report the death of Captain Savage. In about half an hour he returned, and we were glad to perceive, with a smile upon his face, from which we argued that he would receive his acting order as commander, which was a question of some doubt, as the admiral had the power to give the vacancy to whom he pleased, although it would not have been fair if he had not given it to Mr Falcon; not that Mr Falcon would not have received his commission, as Captain Savage dying when the ship was under no admiral's command, he *made himself*; but still the admiral might have sent him home, and not have given him a ship. But this he did, the captain of the *Minerve* being appointed to the *Sanglier*, the captain of the *Opossum* to the *Minerve*, and Captain Falcon taking command of the *Opossum*. He received his commission that evening, and the next day the exchanges were made. Captain Falcon would have taken me with him, and offered so to do; but I could not leave O'Brien, so I preferred remaining in the *Sanglier*.

We were all anxious to know what sort of a person our new captain was, whose name was Kearney; but we had no time to ask the midshipmen, except when they came in charge of the boats which brought his luggage; they replied generally, that he was a very good sort of fellow, and there was no harm in him. But when I had the night watch with Swinburne, he came up to me, and said, "Well, Mr Simple, so we have a new captain. I sailed with him for two years in a brig."

"And pray, Swinburne, what sort of a person is he?"

"Why, I'll tell you, Mr Simple: he's a good-tempered, kind fellow enough, but—"

"But what?"

"Such a *bouncer!!*"

"How do you mean? He's not a very stout man."

"Bless you, Mr Simple, why you don't understand English. I mean that he's the greatest liar that ever walked a deck. Now, Mr Simple, you know I can spin a yarn occasionally."

"Yes, that you can, witness the hurricane the other night."

"Well, Mr Simple, I cannot *hold a candle* to him. It a'n't that I might not stretch now and then, just for fun, as far as he can, but, d——n it, he's always on the stretch. In fact, Mr Simple, he never tells the truth except *by mistake*. He's as poor as a rat, and has nothing but his pay; yet to believe him, he is worth at least as much as Greenwich Hospital. But you'll soon find him out, and he'll sarve to laugh at behind his back you know, Mr Simple, for that's *no go* before his face."

Captain Kearney made his appearance on board the next day. The men were mustered to receive him, and all the officers were on the quarter-deck. "You've a fine set of marines here, Captain Falcon," observed he; "those I left on board of the *Minerve* were only fit to be *hung;* and you have a good show of reefers too—those I left in the *Minerve* were not *worth hanging*. If you please, I'll read my commission, if you'll order the men aft." His commission was read, all hands with their hats off from respect to the authority from which it proceeded. "Now, my lads," said Captain Kearney, addressing the ship's company, "I've but few words to say to you. I am appointed to command this ship, and you appear to have a very good character from your late first lieutenant. All I request of you is this: be smart, keep sober, and always *tell the truth*—that's enough. Pipe down. Gentlemen," continued he, addressing the officers, "I trust that we shall be good friends; and I see no reason that it should be otherwise." He then turned away with a bow, and called his coxswain—"Williams, you'll go on board, and tell my steward that I have promised to dine with the governor to-day, and that he must come to dress me; and, coxswain, recollect to put the sheepskin mat on the stern gratings of my gig—not the one I used to have when I was on shore in my *carriage*, but the blue one which was used for the *chariot*—you know which I mean." I happened to look Swinburne in the face, who cocked his eye at me, as much as to say—"There he goes." We afterwards met the officers of the *Minerve*, who corroborated all that Swinburne had said, although it was quite unnecessary, as we had the captain's own words every minute to satisfy us of the fact.

Dinner parties were now very numerous, and the hospitality of the island is but too well known. The invitations extended to the midshipmen, and many was the good dinner and kind reception which I had during my stay. There was, however, one thing I had heard so much of, that I was anxious to witness it, which was a *dignity ball*. But I must enter a little into explanation, or my readers will not understand me. The coloured people of Barbadoes, for reasons best known to themselves, are immoderately proud, and look upon all the negroes who are born on other islands as *niggers;* they have also an extraordinary idea of their own bravery, although I never heard that it has ever been put to the proof. The free Barbadians are, most of them, very rich, and hold up their heads as they walk with an air quite ridiculous. They ape the manners of the Europeans, at the same time that they appear to consider them as almost their inferiors. Now, a *dignity* ball is a ball given by the most consequential of their coloured people, and from the amusement and various other reasons, is generally well attended by the officers both on shore and afloat. The price of the tickets of admission was high—I think they were half a joe, or eight dollars each.

The governor sent out cards for a grand ball and supper for the ensuing week, and Miss Betsy Austin, a quadroon woman, ascertaining the fact, sent out her cards for the same evening. This was not altogether in *rivalry*, but for another reason, which was, that she was aware that most of the officers and midshipmen of the ships would obtain permission to go to the governor's ball, and, preferring hers, would slip away and join the party, by which means she ensured a full attendance.

On the day of invitation our captain came on board, and told our new first lieutenant (of whom I shall say more hereafter) that the governor insisted that all *his* officers should go—that he would take no denial, and, therefore, he presumed, go they must; that the fact was, that the governor was a *relation* of his wife, and under some trifling obligations to him in obtaining for him his present command. He certainly had spoken to the *prime minister*, and he thought it not impossible, considering the intimate terms which the minister and he had been on from childhood, that his solicitation might have had some effect; at all events, it was pleasant to find that there was some little gratitude left in this world. After this, of course, every officer went, with the exception of the master, who said that he'd as soon have two round turns in his hawse as go to see people kick their legs about like fools, and that he'd take care of the ship.

The governor's ball was very splendid, but the ladies were rather sallow, from the effects of the climate. However, there were exceptions, and on the whole it was a very gay affair; but we were all anxious to go to the *dignity* ball of Miss Betsy Austin. I slipped away with three other midshipmen, and we soon arrived there. A crowd of negroes were outside of the house; but the ball had not yet commenced, from the want of gentlemen, the ball being very correct, nothing under mulatto in colour being admitted. Perhaps I ought to say here, that the progeny of a white and a negro is a mulatto, or half and half—of a white and mulatto, a *quadroon*, or one-quarter black, and of this class the company were chiefly composed. I believe a quadroon and white make the *mustee* or one-eighth black, and the mustee and white the *mustafina*, or one-sixteenth black. After that, they are *whitewashed*, and considered as Europeans. The pride of colour is very great in the West Indies, and they have as many quarterings as a German prince in his coat of arms; a quadroon looks down upon a mulatto, while a mulatto looks down upon a *sambo,* that is, half mulatto half negro, while a sambo in his turn looks down upon a *nigger.* The quadroons are certainly the handsomest race of the whole, some of the women are really beautiful; their hair is long and perfectly straight, their eyes large and black, their figures perfection, and you can see the colour mantle in their cheeks quite as plainly, and with as much effect, as in those of a European. We found the door of Miss Austin's house open, and ornamented with orange branches, and on our presenting ourselves were accosted by a mulatto gentleman, who was, we presumed, "usher of the black rod." His head was well powdered, he was dressed in white jean trousers, a waistcoat not six inches long, and a half-worn post-captain's coat on, as a livery. With a low bow, he "took de liberty to trouble de gentlemen for de card for de ball," which being produced, we were ushered on by him to the ball-room, at the door of which Miss Austin was waiting to receive her company. She made us a low curtsey, observing, "She really happy to see de *gentlemen* of de ship, but hoped to see de *officers* also at her *dignity.*"

This remark touched our *dignity,* and one of my companions replied, "That we midshipmen considered ourselves officers, and no *small* ones either, and that if she waited for the lieutenants she must wait until they were tired of the governor's ball, we having given the preference to hers." This remark set all to rights; sangaree was handed about, and I looked around at the company. I must acknowledge, at the risk of losing the good opinion of my fair countrywomen, that I never saw before so many pretty figures and faces. The *officers* not having yet arrived, we received all the attention, and I was successively presented to Miss Eurydice, Miss Minerva, Miss Sylvia, Miss Aspasia, Miss Euterpe, and many others, evidently borrowed from the different men-of-war which had been on the station. All these young ladies gave themselves all the airs of Almack's. Their dresses I cannot pretend to describe—jewels of value were not wanting, but their drapery was slight; they appeared neither to wear nor to require stays, and on the whole, their figures were so perfect that they could only be ill-dressed by having on too much dress. A few more midshipmen and some lieutenants (O'Brien among the number) having made their appearance, Miss Austin directed that the ball should commence. I requested the honour of Miss Eurydice's hand in a cotillon, which was to open the ball. At this moment stepped forth the premier violin, master of the ceremonies and ballet-master, Massa Johnson, really a very smart man, who gave lessons in dancing to all the " 'Badian ladies." He was a dark quadroon, his hair slightly powdered, dressed in a light blue coat thrown well back, to show his lily-white waistcoat, only one button of which he could afford to button to make full room for the pride of his heart, the frill of his shirt, which really was *un Jabot superb*, four inches wide, and extending from his collar to the waistband of his nankeen tights, which were finished off at his knees with huge bunches of ribbon; his legs were encased in silk stockings, which, however, was not very good taste on his part, as they showed the manifest advantage which an European has over a coloured man in the formation of the leg: instead of being straight, his shins curved like a cheese-knife, and, moreover, his leg was planted into his foot like the handle into a broom or scrubbing-brush, there being quite as much of the foot on the heel side as on the toe side. Such was the appearance of Mr Apollo Johnson, whom the ladies considered as the *ne plus ultra* of fashion, and the *arbiter elegantiarum*. His *bow-tick*, or fiddle-stick, was his wand, whose magic rap on the fiddle produced immediate obedience to his mandates. "Ladies and gentle, take your seats." All started up. "Miss Eurydice, you open de ball."

Miss Eurydice had but a sorry partner, but she undertook to instruct me. O'Brien was our *vis-à-vis* with Miss Euterpe. The other gentlemen were officers from the ships, and we stood up twelve, checkered brown and white, like a chess-board. All eyes were fixed upon Mr Apollo Johnson, who first looked at the couples, then at his fiddle, and lastly, at the other musicians, to see if all was right, and then with a wave of his *bow-tick* the music began. "Massa lieutenant," cried Apollo to O'Brien, "cross over to opposite lady, right hand and left, den figure to Miss Eurydice—dat right; now four hand round. You lilly midshipman, set your partner, sir; den twist her round; dat do; now stop.* First figure all over."

At this time I thought I might venture to talk a little with my partner, and I ventured a remark; to my surprise she answered very sharply, "I come here for dance, sar, and not for chatter; look, Massa Johnson, he tap um bow-tick."

* Lilly: Marryat's rendition of Barbadian Creole for little; "corrected" in some later editions to lily.

The second figure commenced, and I made a sad bungle; so I did of the third, and fourth, and fifth, for I never had danced a cotillon. When I handed my partner to her place, who certainly was the prettiest girl in the room, she looked rather contemptuously at me, and observed to a neighbour, "I really pity de gentleman as come from England dat no know how to dance nor nothing at all, until em hab instruction at Barbadoes."

A country dance was now called for, which was more acceptable to all parties, as none of Mr Apollo Johnson's pupils were very perfect in their cotillon, and none of the officers, except O'Brien, knew anything about them. O'Brien's superior education on this point, added to his lieutenant's epaulet and handsome person, made him much courted; but he took up with Miss Eurydice after I had left her, and remained with her the whole evening; thereby exciting the jealousy of Mr Apollo Johnson, who, it appears, was amorous in that direction. Our party increased every minute; all the officers of the garrison, and, finally, as soon as they could get away, the governor's aide-de-camps, all dressed in *mufti (i.e.,* plain clothes). The dancing continued until three o'clock in the morning, when it was quite a squeeze, from the constant arrival of fresh recruits from all the houses of Barbadoes. I must say, that a few bottles of eau de Cologne thrown about the room would have improved the atmosphere. By this time the heat was terrible, and the *mopping* of the ladies' faces everlasting. I would recommend a DIGNITY ball to all stout gentlemen who wish to be reduced a stone or two. Supper was now announced, and having danced the last country dance with Miss Minerva, I of course had the pleasure of handing her into the supper-room. It was my fate to sit opposite to a fine turkey, and I asked my partner if I should have the pleasure of helping her to a piece of the breast. She looked at me very indignantly, and said, "Curse your impudence, sar, I wonder where you larn manners. Sar, I take a lilly turkey *bosom*, if you please. Talk of *breast* to a lady, sar; really quite *horrid.*" I made two or three more barbarous mistakes before the supper was finished. At last the eating was over, and I must say a better supper I never sat down to. "Silence, gentlemen and ladies," cried Mr Apollo Johnson. "Wid the permission of our amiable hostess, I will propose a toast. Gentlemen and ladies— You all know, and if be so you don't, I say that there no place in the world like Barbadoes. All de world fight against England, but England nebber fear; King George nebber fear, while *Barbadoes 'tand 'tiff*. 'Badian fight for King George to last drop of him blood. Nebber see the day 'Badian run away; you all know dem Frenchmans at San Lucee, give up Morne Fortunee, when he hear de 'Badian volunteer come against him. I hope no 'fence present company, but um sorry to say English come here too jealous of 'Badians. Gentlemen and lady—Barbadian born ab only one fault—he *really too brave*. I propose health of 'Island of Barbadoes.' " Acclamations from all quarters followed this truly modest speech, and the toast was drunk with rapture; the ladies were delighted with Mr Apollo's eloquence, and the lead which he took in the company.

O'Brien then rose and addressed the company as follows:—

Ladies and gentlemen—Mr Poll has spoken better than the best parrot I ever met with in this country, but as he has thought proper to drink the 'Island of Barbadoes,' I mean to be a little more particular. I wish, with him, all good health to the island; but there is a charm without which the island would be a desert—that is, the society of the lovely girls which now surround us, and take our hearts by storm—(here O'Brien put his arm gently round Miss Eurydice's waist, and Mr Apollo ground his teeth so as to be heard at the furthest end of the room)—therefore, gentlemen, with your permission, I will propose the health of the "Badian Ladies.' " This speech of O'Brien's was declared, by the females at least, to be infinitely superior to Mr Apollo Johnson's. Miss Eurydice was even more gracious, and the other ladies were more envious.

Many other toasts and much more wine was drunk, until the male part of the company appeared to be rather riotous. Mr Apollo, however, had to regain his superiority, and after some hems and hahs, begged permission to give a sentiment. "Gentlemen and ladies, I beg then to say—

> *"Here's to de cock who make lub to de hen,*
> *Crow till he hoarse and make lub again."*

This *sentiment* was received with rapture; and after silence was obtained, Miss Betsy Austin rose and said—"Unaccustomed as she was to public 'peaking, she must not sit 'till and not tank de gentleman for his very fine toast, and in de name of de ladies she begged to propose another sentiment', which was—

"Here to de hen what nebber refuses,
Let cock pay compliment whenebber he chooses."

If the first toast was received with applause, this was with enthusiasm; but we received a damper after it was subsided, by the lady of the house getting up and saying—"Now, gentlemen and ladies, me tink it right to say dat it time to go home; I nebber allow people get drunk or kick up bobbery in my house, so now I tink we better take parting-glass, and very much obliged to you for your company."

As O'Brien said, this was a broad hint to be off, so we all now took our parting-glass, in compliance with her request, and our own wishes, and proceeded to escort our partners on their way home. While I was assisting Miss Minerva to her red crape shawl, a storm was brewing in another quarter, to wit, between Mr Apollo Johnson and O'Brien. O'Brien was assiduously attending to Miss Eurydice, whispering what he called soft blarney in her ear, when Mr Apollo, who was above spirit-boiling heat with jealousy, came up, and told Miss Eurydice that he would have the honour of escorting her home.

"You may save yourself the trouble, you dingy gut-scraper," replied O'Brien; "the lady is under my protection, so take your ugly black face out of the way, or I'll show you how I treat a ' 'Badian who is really too brave.' "

"So 'elp me Gad, Massa Lieutenant, 'pose you put a finger on me, I show you what 'Badian can do."

Apollo then attempted to insert himself between O'Brien and his lady, upon which O'Brien shoved him back with great violence, and continued his course towards the door. They were in the passage when I came up, for hearing O'Brien's voice in anger, I left Miss Minerva to shift for herself.

Miss Eurydice had now left O'Brien's arm, at his request, and he and Mr Apollo were standing in the passage, O'Brien close to the door, which was shut, and Apollo swaggering up to him. O'Brien, who knew the tender part of a black, saluted Apollo with a kick on the shins which would have broken my leg. Massa Johnson roared with pain, and recoiled two or three paces, parting the crowd away behind him. The blacks never fight with fists, but butt with their heads like rams, and with quite as much force. When Mr Apollo had retreated, he gave his shin one more rub, uttered a loud yell, and started at O'Brien, with his head aimed at O'Brien's chest, like a battering-ram. O'Brien, who was aware of this plan of fighting, stepped dexterously on one side, and allowed Mr Apollo to pass by him, which he did with such force, that his head went clean through the panel of the door behind O'Brien, and there he stuck as fast as if in a pillory, squeaking like a pig for assistance, and foaming with rage. After some difficulty he was released, and presented a very melancholy figure. His face was much cut, and his superb *Jabot* all in tatters; he appeared, however, to have had quite enough of it, as he retreated to the supper-room, followed by some of his admirers, without asking or looking after O'Brien.

But if Mr Apollo had had enough of it, his friends were too indignant to allow us to go off scot free. A large mob was collected in the street, vowing vengeance on us for our treatment of their flash man, and a row was to be expected. Miss Eurydice had escaped, so that O'Brien had his hands free. "Cam out, you hangman tiefs, cam out; only wish had rock stones, to mash your heads with," cried the mob of negroes. The officers now sallied out in a body, and were saluted with every variety of missile, such as rotten oranges, cabbage-stalks, mud, and cocoa-nut shells. We fought our way manfully, but as we neared the beach the mob increased to hundreds, and at last we could proceed no further, being completely jammed up by the niggers, upon whose heads we could make no more impression than upon blocks of marble. "We must draw our swords," observed an officer. "No, no," replied O'Brien, "that will not do; if once we shed blood, they will never let us get on board with our lives. The boat's crew by this time must be aware that there is a row." O'Brien was right. He had hardly spoken, before a lane was observed to be made through the crowd in the distance, which in two minutes was open to us. Swinburne appeared in the middle of it, followed by the rest of the boat's crew, armed with the boat's stretchers, which they did not aim at the *heads* of the blacks, but swept them like scythes against their *shins*. This they continued to do, right and left of us, as we walked through and went down to the boats, the seamen closing up the rear with their stretchers, with which they ever and anon made a sweep at the black fellows if they approached too near. It was now broad daylight, and in a few minutes we were again safely on board the frigate. Thus ended the first and last dignity ball that I attended.

——◁∾∾▷——

CHAPTER XXXII

I am claimed by Captain Kearney as a relation—Trial of skill between first lieutenant and captain with the long bow—The shark, the pug-dog, and the will—A quarter-deck picture.

A S THE ADMIRAL was not one who would permit the ships under his command to lie idle in port, in a very few days after the dignity ball which I have described, all the squadron sailed on their various destinations. I was not sorry to leave the bay, for one soon becomes tired of profusion, and cared nothing for either oranges, bananas, or shaddocks, nor even for the good dinners and claret at the tables of the army mess and gentlemen of the island. The sea breeze soon became more precious to us than anything else, and if we could have bathed without the fear of a shark, we should have equally appreciated that most refreshing of all luxuries under the torrid zone. It was therefore with pleasure that we received the information that we were to sail the next day to cruise off the French island of Martinique. Captain Kearney had been so much on shore that we saw but little of him, and the ship was entirely under the control of the first lieutenant, of whom I have hitherto not spoken. He was a very short, pock-marked man, with red hair and whiskers, a good sailor, and not a bad officer; that is, he was a practical sailor, and could show any foremast man his duty in any department— and this seamen very much appreciate, as it is not very common; but I never yet knew an officer who prided himself upon his practical knowledge, who was at the same time a good navigator, and too often, by assuming the Jack Tar, they lower the respect due to them, and become coarse and vulgar in their manners and language. This was the case with Mr Phillott, who prided himself upon his slang, and who was at one time "hail fellow well met" with the seamen, talking to them, and being answered as familiarly as if they were equals, and at another, knocking the very same men down with a handspike if he was displeased. He was not bad-tempered, but very hasty; and his language to the officers was occasionally very incorrect; to the midshipmen invariably so. However, on the whole, he was not disliked, although he was certainly not respected as a first lieutenant should have been. It is but fair to say, that he was the same to his superiors as he was to his inferiors, and the bluntness with which he used to contradict and assert his disbelief of Captain Kearney's narratives often produced a coolness between them for some days.

The day after we sailed from Carlisle Bay I was asked to dine in the cabin. The dinner was served upon plated dishes, which looked very grand, but there was not much in them. "This plate," observed the captain, "was presented to me by some merchants for my exertions in saving their property from the Danes when I was cruising off Heligoland."

"Why, that lying steward of yours told me that you bought it at Portsmouth," replied the first lieutenant: "I asked him in the galley this morning."

"How came you to assert such a confounded falsehood sir?" said the captain to the man who stood behind his chair.

"I only said that I thought so," replied the steward.

"Why, didn't you say that the bill had been sent in, through you, seven or eight times, and that the captain had paid it with a flowing sheet?"

"Did you dare say that, sir?" interrogated the captain, very angrily.

"Mr Phillott mistook me, sir?" replied the steward. "He was so busy damning the sweepers, that he did not hear me right. I said, the midshipmen had paid their crockery bill with the fore-topsail."

"Ay! ay!" replied the captain, "that's much more likely."

"Well, Mr Steward," replied Mr Phillott, "I'll be d——d if you ar'n't as big a liar as your—" (master, he was going to plump out, but fortunately the first lieutenant checked himself, and added)— "as your father was before you."

The captain changed the conversation by asking me whether I would take a slice of ham. "It's real Westphalia, Mr Simple; I have them sent me direct by Count Troningsken, an intimate friend of mine, who kills his own wild boars in the Hartz mountains."

"How the devil do you get them over, Captain Kearney?"

"There are ways and means of doing everything, Mr Phillott, and the First Consul is not quite so bad as he is represented. The first batch was sent over with a very handsome letter to me, written in his own hand, which I will show you some of these days. I wrote to him in return, and sent to him two Cheshire cheeses by a smuggler, and since that they came regularly. Did you ever eat Westphalia ham, Mr Simple?"

"Yes," replied I; "once I partook of one at Lord Privilege's."

"Lord Privilege! why he's a distant relation of mine, a sort of fifth cousin," replied Captain Kearney.

"Indeed, sir!" replied I.

"Then you must allow me to introduce you to a relation, Captain Kearney," said the first lieutenant; "for Mr Simple is his grandson."

"Is it possible? I can only say, Mr Simple, that I shall be most happy to show you every attention, and am very glad that I have you as one of my officers."

Now although this was all false, for Captain Kearney was not in the remotest manner connected with my family, yet having once asserted it, he could not retract, and the consequence was, that I was much the gainer by his falsehood, as he treated me very kindly afterwards, always calling me *cousin*.

The first lieutenant smiled and gave me a wink, when the captain had finished his speech to me, as much as to say, "You're in luck," and then the conversation changed. Captain Kearney certainly dealt in the marvellous to admiration, and really told his stories with such earnestness, that I actually believe that he thought he was telling the truth. Never was there such an instance of confirmed habit. Telling a story of a cutting-out expedition, he said, "The French captain would have fallen by my hand, but just as I levelled my musket, a ball came, and cut off the cock of the lock as clean as if it was done with a knife—a very remarkable instance," observed he.

"Not equal to what occurred in a ship I was in," replied the first lieutenant, "when the second lieutenant was grazed by a grape-shot, which cut off one of his whiskers, and turning round his head to ascertain what was the matter, another grape-shot came and took off the other. Now that's what I call a *close shave*."

"Yes," replied Captain Kearney, "very close, indeed, if it were true; but you'll excuse me, Mr Phillott, but you sometimes tell strange stories. I do not mind it myself, but the example is not good to my young relation here, Mr Simple."

"Captain Kearney," replied the first lieutenant, laughing very immoderately, "do you know what the pot called the kettle?"

"No, sir, I do not," retorted the captain, with offended dignity. "Mr Simple, will you take a glass of wine?"

I thought that this little *brouillerie* would have checked the captain; it did so, but only for a few minutes, when he again commenced.* The first lieutenant observed that it would be necessary to let water into the ship every morning, and pump it out, to avoid the smell of the bilge-water. "There are worse smells than bilge-water," replied the captain. "What do you think of a whole ship's company being nearly poisoned with otto of roses? Yet that occurred to me when in the Mediterranean. I was off Smyrna, cruising for a French ship, that was to sail to France, with a pasha on board, as an ambassador. I knew she would be a good prize, and was looking sharp out, when one morning we discovered her on the lee bow. We made all sail, but she walked away from us, bearing away gradually till we were both before the wind, and at night we lost sight of her. As I knew that she was bound to Marseilles, I made all sail to fall in with her again. The wind was light and variable; but five days afterwards, as I lay in my cot, just before daylight, I smelt a very strong smell, blowing in at the weather port, and coming down the skylight, which was open; and after sniffing at it two or three times, I knew it to be otto of roses. I sent for the officer of the watch, and asked him if there was anything in sight. He replied 'that there was not'; and I ordered him to sweep the horizon with his glass, and look well out to windward. As the wind freshened, the smell became more powerful. I ordered him to get the royal yards across, and all ready to make sail, for I knew that the Turk must be near us. At daylight there he was, just three miles ahead in the wind's eye. But although he beat us going free, he was no match for us on a wind, and before noon we had possession of him and all his harem. By-the-by, I could tell you a good story about the ladies. She was a very valuable prize, and among other things, she had a *puncheon* of otto of roses on board—"

"Whew!" cried the first lieutenant. "What! a whole puncheon?"

* Brouillerie: *Misunderstanding.*

"Yes," replied the captain, "a Turkish puncheon—not quite so large, perhaps, as ours on board; their weights and measures are different. I took out most of the valuables into the brig I commanded—about 20,000 sequins—carpets—and among the rest, this cask of otto of roses, which we had smelt three miles off. We had it safe on board, when the mate of the hold, not slinging it properly, it fell into the spirit-room with a run, and was stove to pieces. Never was such a scene; my first lieutenant and several men on deck fainted; and the men in the hold were brought up lifeless; it was some time before they were recovered. We let the water into the brig, and pumped it out, but nothing would take away the smell, which was so overpowering, that before I could get to Malta I had forty men on the sick list. When I arrived there, I turned the mate out of the service for his carelessness. It was not until after having smoked the brig, and finding that of little use, after having sunk her for three weeks, that the smell was at all bearable; but even then it could never be eradicated, and the admiral sent the brig home, and she was sold out of the service. They could do nothing with her at the dockyards. She was broken up, and bought by the people at Brighton and Tunbridge Wells, who used her timbers for turning fancy articles, which, smelling as they did, so strongly of otto of roses, proved very profitable. Were you ever at Brighton, Mr Simple?"

"Never, sir."

Just at this moment, the officer of the watch came down to say that there was a very large shark under the counter, and wished to know if the captain had any objection to the officers attempting to catch it.

"By no means," replied Captain Kearney; "I hate sharks as I do the devil. I nearly lost £14,000 by one, when I was in the Mediterranean."

"May I inquire how, Captain Kearney?" said the first lieutenant, with a demure face; "I'm very anxious to know."

"Why the story is simply this," replied the captain. "I had an old relation at Malta, whom I found out by accident—an old maid of sixty, who had lived all her life on the island. It was by mere accident that I knew of her existence. I was walking upon Strada Reale, when I saw a large baboon that was kept there, who had a little fat pug-dog by the tail, which he was pulling away with him, while an old lady was screaming out for help: for whenever she ran to assist her dog, the baboon made at her as if he would have ravished her, and caught her by the petticoats with one hand, while he held the pug-dog fast by the other. I owed that brute a spite for having attacked me one night when I passed him, and perceiving what was going on, I drew my sword and gave Mr Jacko such a clip as sent him away howling, and bleeding like a pig, leaving me in possession of the little pug, which I took up and handed to his mistress. The old lady trembled very much, and begged me to see her safe home. She had a very fine house, and after she was seated on the sofa, thanked me very much for my gallant assistance, as she termed it, and told me her name was Kearney: upon this I very soon proved my relationship with her, at which she was much delighted, requesting me to consider her house as my home. I was for two years afterwards on that station, and played my cards very well; and the old lady gave me a hint that I should be her heir, as she had no other relations that she knew anything of. At last I was ordered home, and not wishing to leave her, I begged her to accompany me, offering her my cabin. She was taken very ill a fortnight before we sailed, and made a will, leaving me her sole heir; but she recovered, and got as fat as ever. Mr Simple, the wine stands with you. I doubt if Lord Privilege gave you better claret than there is in that bottle; I imported it myself ten years ago, when I commanded the *Coquette*."

"Very odd," observed the first lieutenant—"we bought some at Barbadoes with the same mark on the bottles and cork."

"That may be," replied the captain; "old-established houses all keep up the same marks; but I doubt if your wine can be compared to this."

As Mr Phillott wished to hear the end of the captain's story, he would not contradict him this time, by stating what he knew to be the case, that the captain had sent it on board at Barbadoes; and the captain proceeded.

"Well, I gave up my cabin to the old lady, and hung up my cot in the gun-room during the passage home. We were becalmed abreast of Ceuta for two days. The old lady was very particular about her pug-dog, and I superintended the washing of the little brute twice a week; but at last I was tired of it, and gave him to my coxswain to bathe. My coxswain, who was a lazy fellow, without my knowledge, used to put the little beast into the bight of a rope, and tow him overboard for a minute or so. It was during this calm that he had him overboard in this way, when a confounded shark rose from under the counter, and took in the pug-dog at one mouthful. The coxswain reported the loss as a thing of no consequence; but I knew better, and put the fellow in irons. I then went down and broke the melancholy fact to Miss Kearney, stating that I had put the man in irons, and would flog him well. The old lady broke out into a most violent passion at the intelligence, declared that it was my fault, that I was jealous of the dog, and had done it on purpose. The more I protested, the more she raved; and at last I was obliged to go on deck to avoid her abuse and keep my temper. I had not been on deck five minutes before she came up—that is, was shoved up—for she was so heavy that she could not get up without assistance. You know how elephants in India push the cannon through a morass with their heads from behind; well, my steward used to shove her up the companion-ladder just in the same way, with his head completely buried in her petticoats. As soon as she was up, he used to pull his head out, looking as red and hot as a fresh-boiled lobster. Well, up she came, with her will in her hand, and, looking at me very fiercely, she said, 'Since the shark has taken my dear dog, he may have my will also,' and, throwing it overboard, she plumped down on the carronade slide. 'It's very well, madam,' said I, 'but you'll be cool by-and-by, and then you'll make another will.' 'I swear by all the hopes that I have of going to heaven that I never will!' she replied. 'Yes, you will, madam,' replied I. 'Never, so help me God! Captain Kearney; my money may now go to my next heir, and that, you know, will not be you.' Now, as I knew very well that the old lady was very positive and as good as her word, my object was to recover the will, which was floating about fifty yards astern, without her knowledge. I thought a moment, and then I called the boatswaine's mate to *pipe all hands to bathe.* 'You'll excuse me, Miss Kearney,' said I, 'but the men are going to bathe, and I do not think you would like to see them all naked. If you would, you can stay on deck.' She looked daggers at me, and, rising from the carronade slide, hobbled to the ladder, saying, 'that the insult was another proof of how little I deserved any kindness from her.' As soon as she was below, the quarter-boats were lowered down, and I went in one of them and picked up the will, which still floated. Brigs having no stern-windows, of course she could not see my manoeuvre, but thought that the will was lost for ever. We had very bad weather after that, owing to which, with the loss of her favourite pug, and constant quarrelling with me—for I did all I could to annoy her afterwards—she fell ill, and was buried a fortnight after she was landed at Plymouth. The old lady kept her word; she never made another will. I proved the one I had recovered at Doctors' Commons, and touched the whole of her money."*

As neither the first lieutenant nor I could prove whether the story was true or not, of course we expressed our congratulations at his good fortune, and soon afterwards left the cabin to report his marvellous story to our messmates. When I went on deck, I found that the shark had just been hooked, and was hauling on board. Mr Phillott had also come on deck. The officers were all eager about the shark, and were looking over the side, calling to each other, and giving directions to the men. Now, although certainly there was a want of decorum on the quarter-deck, still, the captain having given permission, it was to be excused; but Mr Phillott thought otherwise, and commenced in his usual style, beginning with the marine officer.

"Mr Westley, I'll trouble you not to be getting upon the hammocks. You'll get off directly, sir. If one of your fellows were to do so, I'd stop his grog for a month, and I don't see why you are to set a bad example; you've been too long in barracks, sir, by half. Who is that? Mr Williams and Mr Moore—both on the hammocks, too. Up to the foretopmast head, both of you, directly. Mr Thomas, up to the main; and I say, you youngster, stealing off, perch yourself upon the spanker-boom, and let me know when you've rode to London. By God! the service is going to hell! I don't know what officers are made of now-a-days. I'll marry some of you young gentlemen to the gunner's daughter before long. Quarter-deck's no better than a bear-garden. No wonder, when lieutenants set the example."

This latter remark could only be applied to O'Brien, who stood in the quarter-boat giving directions, before the tirade of Mr Phillott stopped the amusement of the party. O'Brien immediately stepped out of the boat, and going up to Mr Phillott, touched his hat, and said, "Mr Phillott, we had the captain's permission to catch the

---

* *Doctors' Commons: London's College of Advocates and Doctors of Law, which housed the ecclesiastical and Admiralty courts along with the advocates who practiced there.*

shark, and a shark is not to be got on board by walking up and down on the quarter-deck. As regards myself, as long as the captain is on board, I hold myself responsible to him alone for my conduct; and if you think I have done wrong, forward your complaint; but if you pretend to use such language to me, as you have to others, I shall hold you responsible. I am here, sir, as an officer and a gentleman, and will be treated as such; and allow me to observe, that I consider the quarter-deck more disgraced by foul and ungentlemanly language, than I do by an officer accidentally standing upon the hammocks. However, as you have thought proper to interfere, you may now get the shark on board yourself."

Mr Phillott turned very red, for he never had come in contact in this way with O'Brien. All the other officers had submitted quietly to his unpleasant manner of speaking to them. "Very well, Mr O'Brien; I shall hold you answerable for this language," replied he, "and shall most certainly report your conduct to the captain."

"I will save you the trouble; Captain Kearney is now coming up, and I will report it myself."

This O'Brien did, upon the captain's putting his foot on the quarter-deck.

"Well," observed the captain to Mr Phillott, "what is it you complain of?"

"Mr O'Brien's language, sir. Am I to be addressed on the quarter-deck in that manner?"

"I really must say, Mr Phillott," replied Captain Kearney, "that I do not perceive anything in what Mr O'Brien said, but what is correct. I command here; and if an officer so nearly equal in rank to yourself has committed himself, you are not to take the law into your own hands. The fact is, Mr Phillott, your language is not quite so correct as I could wish it. I overheard every word that passed, and I consider that *you* have treated *your superior* officer with disrespect—that is, *me*. I gave permission that the shark should be caught, and with that permission, I consequently allowed those little deviations from the discipline of the service which must inevitably take place. Yet you have thought proper to interfere with my permission, which is tantamount to an order, and have made use of harsh language, and punished the young gentlemen for obeying my injunctions. You will oblige me, sir, by calling them all down, and in restraining your petulance for the future. I will always support your authority when you are correct; but I regret that in this instance you have necessitated me to weaken it."

This was a most severe check to Mr Phillott, who immediately went below, after hailing the mast-heads and calling down the midshipmen. As soon as he was gone we were all on the hammocks again; the shark was hauled forward, hoisted on board, and every frying-pan in the ship was in requisition. We were all much pleased with Captain Kearney's conduct on this occasion; and, as O'Brien observed to me, "He really is a good fellow and clever officer. What a thousand pities it is, that he is such a confounded liar!" I must do Mr Phillott the justice to say that he bore no malice on this occasion, but treated us as before, which is saying a great deal in his favour, when it is considered what power a first lieutenant has of annoying and punishing his inferiors.

CHAPTER XXXIII

Another set-to between the captain and first lieutenant—Cutting-out expedition—Mr Chucks mistaken—He dies like a gentleman—Swinburne begins his account of the battle off St Vincent.

W E HAD NOT been more than a week under the Danish island of St Thomas when we discovered a brig close inshore. We made all sail in chase, and soon came within a mile and a half of the shore, when she anchored under a battery, which opened its fire upon us. Their elevation was too great, and several shots passed over us and between our masts.

"I once met with a very remarkable circumstance," observed Captain Kearney. "Three guns were fired at a frigate I was on board of from a battery, all at the same time. The three shots cut away the three topsail ties, and down came all our topsail yards upon the cap at the same time. That the Frenchmen might not suppose that they had taken such good aim, we turned up our hands to reef topsails; and by the time that the men were off the yards the ties were spliced and the topsails run up again."

Mr Phillott could not stand this most enormous fib, and he

replied, "Very odd, indeed, Captain Kearney; but I have known a stranger circumstance. We had put in the powder to the four guns on the main-deck when we were fighting the Danish gun-boats in a frigate I was in, and, as the men withdrew the rammer, a shot from the enemy entered the muzzle, and completed the loading of each gun. We fired their own shot back upon them, and this occurred three times running."

"Upon my word," replied Captain Kearney, who had his glass upon the battery, "I think you must have dreamt that circumstance, Mr Phillott."

"Not more than you did about the topsail ties, Captain Kearney."

Captain Kearney at that time had the long glass in his hand, holding it up over his shoulder. A shot from the battery whizzed over his head, and took the glass out of his hand, shivering it to pieces. "That's once," said Captain Kearney, very coolly; "but will you pretend that that could ever happen three times running? They might take my head off, or my arm, next time, but not another glass; whereas the topsail ties might be cut by three different shot. But give me another glass, Mr Simple: I am certain that this vessel is a privateer. What think you, Mr O'Brien?"

"I am every bit of your opinion, Captain Kearney," replied O'Brien; "and I think it would be a very pretty bit of practice to the ship's company to take her out from under that footy battery."*

"Starboard the helm, Mr Phillott; keep away four points, and then we will think of it to-night."

The frigate was now kept away, and ran out of the fire of the battery. It was then about an hour before sunset, and in the West Indies the sun does not set as it does in the northern latitudes. There is no twilight: he descends in glory, surrounded with clouds of gold and rubies in their gorgeous tints; and once below the horizon, all is dark. As soon as it was dark, we hauled our wind off shore; and a consultation being held between the captain, Mr Phillott, and O'Brien, the captain at last decided that the attempt should be made. Indeed, although cutting-out is a very serious affair, as you combat under every disadvantage, still the mischief done to our trade by the fast-sailing privateers was so great in the West Indies,

* Footy: Insignificant.

that almost every sacrifice was warrantable for the interests of the country. Still, Captain Kearney, although a brave and prudent officer—one who calculated chances, and who would not risk his men without he deemed that necessity imperiously demanded that such should be done—was averse to this attack, from his knowledge of the bay in which the brig was anchored; and although Mr Phillott and O'Brien both were of opinion that it should be a night attack, Captain Kearney decided otherwise. He considered, that although the risk might be greater, yet the force employed would be more consolidated, and that those who would hold back in the night dare not do so during the day. Moreover, that the people on shore in the battery, as well as those in the privateer, would be on the alert all night, and not expecting an attack during the day, would be taken off their guard. It was therefore directed that everything should be in preparation during the night, and that the boats should shove off before daylight, and row in-shore, concealing themselves behind some rocks under the cliffs which formed the cape upon one side of the harbour; and, if not discovered, remain there till noon, at which time it was probable that the privateer's men would be on shore, and the vessel might be captured without difficulty.

It is always a scene of much interest on board a man-of-war when preparations are made for an expedition of this description; and, as the reader may not have been witness to them, it may perhaps be interesting to describe them. The boats of men-of-war have generally two crews; the common boats' crews, which are selected so as not to take away the most useful men from the ship; and the service, or fighting boats' crews, which are selected from the very best men on board. The coxswains of the boats are the most trustworthy men in the ship, and, on this occasion, have to see that their boats are properly equipped. The launch, yawl, first and second cutters, were the boats appointed for the expedition. They all carried guns mounted upon slides, which ran fore and aft between the men. After the boats were hoisted out, the guns were lowered down into them and shipped in the bows of the boats. The arm-chests were next handed in, which contain the cartridges and ammunition. The shot were put into the bottom of the boats; and so far they were all ready. The oars of the boats were fitted to pull with grummets upon iron thole-pins, that they might make little noise, and might swing fore and aft without falling overboard when the boats pulled alongside the privateer. A breaker or two (that is, small casks holding about seven gallons each) of water was put into each boat, and also the men's allowance of spirits, in case they should be detained by any unforeseen circumstances. The men belonging to the boats were fully employed in looking after their arms; some fitting their flints to their pistols, others, and the major part of them, sharpening their cutlasses at the grindstone, or with a file borrowed from the armourer,—all were busy and all merry. The very idea of going into action is a source of joy to an English sailor, and more jokes are made, more merriment excited, at that time than at any other. Then, as it often happens that one or two of the service boats' crews may be on the sick list, urgent solicitations are made by others that they may supply their places. The only parties who appear at all grave are those who are to remain in the frigate, and not share in the expedition. There is no occasion to order the boats to be manned, for the men are generally in long before they are piped away. Indeed, one would think that it was a party of pleasure, instead of danger and of death, upon which they were about to proceed.

Captain Kearney selected the officers who were to have the charge of the boats. He would not trust any of the midshipmen on so dangerous a service. He said that he had known so many occasions in which their rashness and foolhardiness had spoilt an expedition; he therefore appointed Mr Phillott, the first lieutenant, to the launch; O'Brien to the yawl; the master to the first, and Mr Chucks, the boatswain, to the second cutter. Mr Chucks was much pleased with the idea of having the command of a boat, and asked me to come with him, to which I consented, although I had intended, as usual, to have gone with O'Brien.

About an hour before daylight we ran the frigate to within a mile and a half of the shore, and the boats shoved off; the frigate then wore round, and stood out in the offing, that she might at daylight be at such a distance as not to excite any suspicion that our boats were sent away, while we in the boats pulled quietly in-shore. We were not a quarter of an hour before we arrived at the cape forming one side of the bay, and were well secreted among the cluster of rocks which were underneath. Our oars were laid in; the boats' painters made fast; and orders given for the strictest silence. The rocks were very high, and the boats were not to be seen without any one should come to the edge of the precipice; and even then they would, in all probability, have been supposed to have been rocks. The water was as smooth as glass, and when it was broad daylight, the men hung listlessly over the sides of the boats, looking at the corals below, and watching the fish as they glided between.

"I can't say, Mr Simple," said Mr Chucks to me in an under tone, "that I think well of this expedition; and I have an idea that some of us will lose the number of our mess. After a calm comes a storm; and how quiet is everything now! But I'll take off my great-coat, for the sun is hot already. Coxswain, give me my jacket."

Mr Chucks had put on his great-coat, but not his jacket underneath, which he had left on one of the guns on the main-deck, all ready to change as soon as the heavy dew had gone off. The coxswain handed him the jacket, and Mr Chucks threw off his great-coat to put it on; but when it was opened it proved, that by mistake he had taken away the jacket, surmounted by two small epaulettes, belonging to Captain Kearney, which the captain's steward, who had taken it out to brush, had also laid upon the same gun.

"By all the nobility of England!" cried Mr Chucks, "I have taken away the captain's jacket by mistake. Here's a pretty mess! if I put on my great-coat I shall be dead with sweating; if I put on no jacket I shall be roasted brown; but if I put on the captain's jacket I shall be considered disrespectful."

The men in the boats tittered; and Mr Phillott, who was in the launch next to us, turned round to see what was the matter; O'Brien was sitting in the stern-sheets of the launch with the first lieutenant, and I leaned over and told them.

"By the powers! I don't see why the captain's jacket will be at all hurt by Mr Chucks putting it on," replied O'Brien; "unless, indeed, a bullet were to go through it, and then it won't be any fault of Mr Chucks."

"No," replied the first lieutenant; "and if one did, the captain might keep the jacket, and swear that the bullet went round his body without wounding him. He'll have a good yarn to spin. So put it on, Mr Chucks; you'll make a good mark for the enemy."

"That I will stand the risk of with pleasure," observed the boatswain to me, "for the sake of being considered a gentleman. So here's on with it."

There was a general laugh when Mr Chucks pulled on the captain's jacket, and sank down in the stern-sheets of the cutter, with great complacency of countenance. One of the men in the boat that we were in thought proper, however, to continue his laugh a little longer than Mr Chucks considered necessary, who, leaning forward, thus addressed him: "I say, Mr Webber, I beg leave to observe to you, in the most delicate manner in the world—just to hint to you— that it is not the custom to laugh at your superior officer. I mean just to insinuate, that you are a d——d impudent son of a sea cook; and if we both live and do well, I will prove to you, that if I am to be laughed at in a boat with the captain's jacket on, that I am not to be laughed at on board the frigate with the boatswain's rattan in my fist; and so look out, my hearty, for squalls, when you come on the forecastle; for I'll be d——d if I don't make you see more stars than God Almighty ever made, and cut more capers than all the dancing-masters in France. Mark my words, you burgoo-eating;* pea-soup-swilling, trousers-scrubbing son of a bitch."

Mr Chucks, having at the end of this oration raised his voice above the pitch required by the exigency of the service, was called to order by the first lieutenant, and again sank back into the stern-sheets with all the importance and authoritative show peculiarly appertaining to a pair of epaulettes.

We waited behind the rocks until noonday, without being discovered by the enemy; so well were we concealed. We had already sent an officer, who, carefully hiding himself by lying down on the rocks, had several times reconnoitred the enemy. Boats were passing and repassing continually from the privateer to the shore; and it appeared that they went on shore full of men, and returned with only one or two; so that we were in great hopes that we should find but few men to defend the vessel. Mr Phillott looked at his watch, held it up to O'Brien, to prove that he had complied exactly with the orders he had received from the captain, and then gave the word to get the boats under weigh. The painters were cast off by the bow-men, the guns were loaded and primed, the men seized their oars, and in two minutes we were clear of the rocks, and drawn up in a line within a quarter of a mile from the harbour's mouth, and not half a mile from the privateer brig. We rowed as quickly as possible, but we did not cheer until the enemy fired the first gun; which he did from a quarter unexpected, as we entered the mouth of the

* *Burgoo-eating: Burgoo is an oatmeal porridge that was much despised by sailors.*

harbour, with our Union Jack trailing in the water over our stern, for it was a dead calm. It appeared, that at the low point under the cliffs, at each side of the little bay, they had raised a water battery of two guns each. One of these guns, laden with grape-shot, was now fired at the boats, but the elevation was too low, and although the water was ploughed up to within five yards of the launch, no injury was received. We were equally fortunate in the discharge of the other three guns; two of which we passed so quickly, that they were not aimed sufficiently forward, so that their shot fell astern; and the other, although the shot fell among us, did no further injury than cutting in half two of the oars of the first cutter.

In the meantime, we had observed that the boats had shoved off from the privateer as soon as they had perceived us, and had returned to her laden with men; the boats had been despatched a second time, but had not yet returned. They were now about the same distance from the privateer as were our boats, and it was quite undecided which of us would be first on board. O'Brien perceiving this, pointed out to Mr Phillott that we should first attack the boats, and afterwards board on the side to which they pulled; as, in all probability, there would be an opening left in the boarding nettings, which were tied up to the yard-arms, and presented a formidable obstacle to our success. Mr Phillott agreed with O'Brien: he ordered the bow-men to lay in their oars and keep the guns pointed ready to fire at the word given, and desiring the other men to pull their best. Every nerve, every muscle was brought into play by our anxious and intrepid seamen. When within about twenty yards of the vessel, and also of the boats, the orders were given to fire—the carronade of the launch poured out round and grape so well directed, that one of the French boats sunk immediately; and the musket balls with which our other smaller guns were loaded, did great execution among their men. In one minute more, with three cheers from our sailors, we were all alongside together, English and French boats pell-mell, and a most determined close conflict took place. The French fought desperately, and as they were overpowered, they were reinforced by those from the privateer, who could not look on and behold their companions requiring their assistance, without coming to their aid. Some jumped down into our boats from the chains, into the midst of our men; others darted cold shot at us, either to kill us or to sink our boats; and thus did one of the most desperate hand-to-hand conflicts take place that ever was witnessed. But it was soon decided in our favour, for we were the stronger party and the better armed; and when all opposition was over, we jumped into the privateer, and found not a man left on board, only a large dog, who flew at O'Brien's throat as he entered the port.

"Don't kill him," said O'Brien, as the sailors hastened to his assistance; "only take away his gripe."

The sailors disengaged the dog, and O'Brien led him up to a gun, saying, "By Jasus, my boy, you are my prisoner."

But although we had possession of the privateer, our difficulties, as it will prove, were by no means over. We were now exposed not only to the fire of the two batteries at the harbour-mouth which we had to pass, but also to that of the battery at the bottom of the bay, which had fired at the frigate. In the meantime, we were very busy in cutting the cable, lowering the topsails, and taking the wounded men on board the privateer, from out of the boats. All this was, however, but the work of a few minutes. Most of the Frenchmen were killed; our own wounded amounted to only nine seamen and Mr Chucks, the boatswain, who was shot through the body, apparently with little chance of surviving. As Mr Phillott observed, the captain's epaulettes had made him a mark for the enemy, and he had fallen in his borrowed plumes.

As soon as they were all on board, and laid on the deck—for there were, as near as I can recollect, about fourteen wounded Frenchmen as well as our own—tow-ropes were got out forwards, the boats were manned, and we proceeded to tow the brig out of the harbour. It was a dead calm, and we made but little way, but our boat's crew, flushed with victory, cheered, and rallied, and pulled with all their strength. The enemy perceiving that the privateer was taken, and the French boats drifting empty up the harbour, now opened their fire upon us, and with great effect. Before we had towed abreast of the two water batteries, we had received three shots between wind and water from the other batteries, and the sea was pouring fast into the vessel. I had been attending to poor Mr Chucks, who lay on the starboard side, near the wheel, the blood flowing from his wound, and tracing its course down the planks of the deck, to a distance of some feet from where he lay. He appeared very faint, and I tied my handkerchief round his body, so as to stop the effusion of blood, and brought him some water, with which I bathed his face, and poured some into his mouth. He opened his eyes wide, and looked at me.

"Ah, Mr Simple," said he, faintly, "is it you? It's all over with me; but it could not be better—could it?"

"How do you mean?" inquired I.

"Why, have I not fallen dressed like an officer and a gentleman?" said he, referring to the captain's jacket and epaulettes. "I'd sooner die now with this dress on, than recover to put on the boatswain's uniform. I feel quite happy."

He pressed my hand, and then closed his eyes again, from weakness. We were now nearly abreast of the two batteries on the points, the guns of which had been trained so as to bear upon our boats that were towing out the brig. The first shot went through the bottom of the launch, and sank her; fortunately, all the men were saved; but as she was the boat that towed next to the brig, great delay occurred in getting the others clear of her, and taking the brig again in tow. The shot now poured in thick, and the grape became very annoying. Still our men gave way, cheering at every shot fired, and we had nearly passed the batteries, with trifling loss, when we perceived that the brig was so full of water that she could not swim many minutes longer, and that it would be impossible to tow her alongside of the frigate. Mr Phillott, under these circumstances, decided that it would be useless to risk more lives, and that the wounded should be taken out of the brig, and the boats should pull away for the ship. He desired me to get the wounded men into the cutter, which he sent alongside, and then to follow the other boats. I made all the haste I could, not wishing to be left behind; and as soon as all our wounded men were in the boats, I went to Mr Chucks, to remove him. He appeared somewhat revived, but would not allow us to remove him.

"My dear Mr Simple," said he, "it is of no use; I never can recover it, and I prefer dying here. I entreat you not to move me. If the enemy take possession of the brig before she sinks, I shall be buried with military honours; if they do not, I shall at least die in the dress of a gentleman. Hasten away as fast as you can, before you lose more men. Here I stay—that's decided."

I expostulated with him, but at that time two boats full of men appeared, pulling out of the harbour to the brig. The enemy had perceived that our boats had deserted her, and were coming to take possession. I had therefore no time to urge Mr Chucks to change his resolution, and not wishing to force a dying man, I shook his hand and left him. It was with some difficulty I escaped, for the boats had come up close to the brig; they chased me a little while, but the yawl and the cutter turning back to my assistance, they gave up the pursuit. On the whole, this was a very well arranged and well conducted expedition. The only man lost was Mr Chucks, for the wounds of the others were none of them mortal. Captain Kearney was quite satisfied with our conduct, and so was the admiral, when it was reported to him. Captain Kearney did indeed grumble a little about his jacket, and sent for me to inquire why I had not taken it off Mr Chucks, and brought it on board. As I did not choose to tell him the exact truth, I replied, "That I could not disturb a dying man, and that the jacket was so saturated with blood, that he never could have worn it again," which was the case.

"At all events, you might have brought away my epaulettes," replied he; "but you youngsters think of nothing but gormandizing."

I had the first watch that night, when Swinburne, the quartermaster, came up to me, and asked me all the particulars of the affair, for he was not in the boats. "Well," said he, "that Mr Chucks appeared to be a very good boatswain in his way, if he could only have kept his rattan a little quiet. He was a smart fellow, and knew his duty. We had just such another killed in our ship, in the action off Cape St Vincent."

"What! were you in that action?" replied I.

"Yes, I was, and belonged to the *Captain*, Lord Nelson's ship."

"Well, then, suppose you tell me all about it."

"Why, Mr Simple, d'ye see, I've no objection to spin you a yarn, now and then," replied Swinburne, "but, as Mr Chucks used to say, allow me to observe, in the most delicate manner in the world, that I perceive that the man who has charge of your hammock, and slings you a clean one now and then, has very often a good glass of grog for his *yarns*, and I do not see but that mine are as well worth a glass of grog as his."

"So they are, Swinburne, and better too, and I promise you a good stiff one to-morrow evening."

"That will do, sir: now then, I'll tell you all about it, and more about it too than most can, for I know how the action was brought about."

I hove the log, marked the board, and then sat down abaft on the signal chest with Swinburne, who commenced his narrative as follows:

"You must know, Mr Simple, that when the English fleet came down the Mediterranean, after the 'vackyation of Corsica, they did not muster more than seventeen sail of the line, while the Spanish fleet from Ferrol and Carthagena had joined company at Cadiz, and 'mounted to near thirty. Sir John Jervis had the command of our fleet at the time, but as the Dons did not seem at all inclined to come out and have a brush with us, almost two to one, Sir John left Sir Hyde Parker, with six sail of the line, to watch the Spanish beggars, while he went in to Lisbon with the remainder of the fleet, to water and refit. Now, you see, Mr Simple, Portugal was at that time what they calls neutral, that is to say, she didn't meddle at all in the affair, being friends with both parties, and just as willing to supply fresh beef and water to the Spaniards as to the English, if so be the Spaniards had come out to ax for it, which they dar'n't. The Portuguese and the English have always been the best of friends, because we can't get no port wine anywhere else, and they can't get nobody else to buy it of them; so the Portuguese gave up their arsenal at Lisbon, for the use of the English, and there we kept all our stores, under the charge of that old dare-devil, Sir Isaac Coffin. Now it so happened, that one of the clerks in old Sir Isaac's office, a Portuguese chap, had been some time before that in the office of the Spanish ambassador; he was a very smart sort of a chap, and sarved as interpreter, and the old commissioner put great faith in him."

"But how did you learn all this, Swinburne?"

"Why, I'll tell you, Mr Simple. I steered the yawl as coxswain, and when admirals and captains talk in the stern-sheets, they very often forget that the coxswain is close behind them. I only learnt half of it that way; the rest I put together when I compared logs with the admiral's steward, who, of course, heard a great deal now and then. The first I heard of it was when old Sir John called out to Sir Isaac, after the second bottle, 'I say, Sir Isaac, who killed the Spanish messenger?' 'Not I, by God!' replied Sir Isaac; 'I only left him for dead;' and then they both laughed, and so did Nelson, who was sitting with them. Well, Mr Simple, it was reported to Sir Isaac that his clerk was often seen taking memorandums of the different orders given to the fleet, particularly those as to there being no wasteful expenditure of his Majesty's stores. Upon which, Sir Isaac goes to the admiral, and requests that the man might be discharged. Now, old Sir John was a sly old fox, and he answered, 'Not so, commissioner; perhaps we may catch them in their own trap.' So the admiral sits down, and calls for pen and ink, and he flourishes out a long letter to the commissioner, stating that all the stores of the fleet were expended, representing as how it would be impossible to go to sea without a supply, and wishing to know when the commissioner expected more transports from England. He also said that if the Spanish fleet were now to come out from Cadiz, it would be impossible for him to protect Sir H. Parker with his six sail of the line, who was watching the Spanish fleet, as he could not quit the port in his present condition. To this letter the commissioner answered that, from the last accounts, he thought that in the course of six weeks or two months they might receive supplies from England, but that sooner than that was impossible. These letters were put in the way of the d——d Portuguese spy-clerk, who copied them, and was seen that evening to go into the house of the Spanish ambassador. Sir John then sent a message to Ferro—that's a small town on the Portuguese coast to the southward—with a despatch to Sir Hyde Parker, desiring him to run away to Cape St Vincent, and decoy the Spanish fleet there, in case they should come out after him. Well, Mr Simple, so far d'ye see the train was well laid. The next thing to do was to watch the Spanish ambassador's house, and see if he sent away any despatches. Two days after the letters had been taken to him by this rascal of a clerk, the Spanish ambassador sent away two messengers—one for Cadiz and the other for Madrid, which is the town where the King of Spain lives. The one to Cadiz was permitted to go, but the one to Madrid was stopped by the directions of the admiral, and this job was confided to the commissioner, Sir Isaac, who settled it somehow or another; and this was the reason why the admiral called out to him, 'I say, Sir Isaac, who killed the messenger?' They brought back his despatches, by which they found out that advice had been sent to the Spanish admiral—I forget his name, something like *Magazine*—informing him of the supposed crippled state of our squadron. Sir John, taking it for granted that the Spaniards would not lose an opportunity of taking six sail of the line—more English ships than they have ever taken in their lives—waited a few days to give them time, and then sailed from Lisbon for Cape St Vincent, where he joined Sir Hyde Parker, and fell in with the Spaniards sure enough, and a pretty drubbing we gave them. Now, it's not everybody that could tell you all that, Mr Simple."

"Well, but now for the action, Swinburne."

"Lord bless you, Mr Simple! it's now past seven bells, and I can't fight the battle of St Vincent in half-an-hour; besides which, it's well worth another glass of grog to hear all about that battle."

"Well, you shall have one, Swinburne; only don't forget to tell it to me."

Swinburne and I then separated, and in less than an hour afterwards I was dreaming of despatches—Sir John Jervis—Sir Isaac Coffin—and Spanish messengers.

—◆◆◆—

CHAPTER XXXIV

O'Brien's good advice—Captain Kearney again deals in the marvellous.

I DO NOT REMEMBER any circumstance in my life which, at that time, lay so heavily on my mind as the loss of poor Mr Chucks, the boatswain, who, of course, I took it for granted I should never see again. I believe that the chief cause was that at the time I entered the service, and everyone considered me to be the fool of the family, Mr Chucks and O'Brien were the only two who thought of and treated me differently; and it was their conduct which induced me to apply myself and encouraged me to exertion. I believe that many a boy, who, if properly patronized, would turn out well, is, by the injudicious system of browbeating and ridicule, forced into the wrong path, and, in his despair, throws away all self-confidence, and allows himself to be carried away by the stream to perdition. O'Brien was not very partial to reading himself. He played the German flute remarkably well, and had a very good voice. His chief amusement was practising, or rather playing, which is a very different thing; but although he did not study himself, he always made me come into his cabin for an hour or two every day, and, after I had read, repeat to him the contents of the book. By this method he not only instructed me, but gained a great deal of information himself; for he made so many remarks upon what I had read, that it was impressed upon both our memories.

"Well, Peter," he would say, as he came into the cabin, "what have you to tell me this morning? Sure it's you that's the schoolmaster, and not me—for I learn from you every day."

"I have not read much, O'Brien, to-day, for I have been thinking of poor Mr Chucks."

"Very right for you so to do, Peter. Never forget your friends in a hurry. You'll not find too many of them as you trot along the highway of life."

"I wonder whether he is dead?"

"Why, that's a question I cannot answer. A bullet through the chest don't lengthen a man's days, that's certain; but this I know, that he'll not die if he can help it, now that he's got the captain's jacket on."

"Yes; he always aspired to be a gentleman, which was absurd enough in a boatswain."

"Not at all absurd, Peter, but very absurd of you to talk without thinking. When did any one of his shipmates ever know Mr Chucks to do an unhandsome or mean action? Never; and why? Because he aspired to be a gentleman, and that feeling kept him above it. Vanity's a confounded donkey, very apt to put his head between his legs, and chuck us over; but pride's a fine horse, who will carry us over the ground, and enable us to distance our fellow-travellers. Mr Chucks has pride, and that's always commendable, even in a boatswain. How often have you read of people rising from nothing, and becoming great men? This was from talent, sure enough; but it was talent with pride to force it onward, not talent with vanity to check it."

"You are very right, O'Brien; I spoke foolishly."

"Never mind, Peter, nobody heard you but me; so it's of no consequence. Don't you dine in the cabin to-day?"

"Yes."

"So do I. The captain is in a most marvellous humour this morning. He told me one or two yarns that quite staggered my politeness and my respect for him on the quarter-deck. What a pity it is that a man should have gained such a bad habit!"

"He's quite incurable, I'm afraid," replied I; "but, certainly, his fibs do no harm; they are what they call white lies. I do not think he would really tell a lie—that is, a lie which would be considered to disgrace a gentleman."

"Peter, *all* lies disgrace a gentleman, white or black, although I grant there is a difference. To say the least of it, it is a dangerous habit; for white lies are but the gentlemen ushers to black ones. I know but of one point on which a lie is excusable, and that is, when you wish to deceive the enemy. Then your duty to your country warrants your lying till you're black in the face; and, for the very reason that it goes against your grain, it becomes, as it were, a sort of virtue."

"What was the difference between the marine officer and Mr Phillott that occurred this morning?"

"Nothing at all in itself. The marine officer is a bit of a gaby, and takes offence where none is meant.* Mr Phillott has a foul tongue; but he has a good heart."

"What a pity it is!"

"It is a pity, for he's a smart officer; but the fact is, Peter, that junior officers are too apt to copy their superiors, and that makes it very important that a young gentleman should sail with a captain who is a gentleman. Now, Phillott served the best of his time with Captain Ballover, who is notorious in the service for foul and abusive language. What is the consequence? That Phillott and many others who have served under him have learnt his bad habit."

"I should think, O'Brien, that the very circumstance of having had your feelings so often wounded by such language when you were a junior officer, would make you doubly careful not to make use of it to others, when you had advanced in the service."

"Peter, that's just the *first* feeling, which wears away after a time; but at last, your own sense of indignation becomes blunted, and becoming indifferent to it, you forget also that you wound the feelings of others, and carry the habit with you, to the great injury and disgrace of the service. But it's time to dress for dinner, so

* *Gaby: A fool.*

you'd better make yourself scarce, Peter, while I tidivate myself off a little, according to the rules and regulations of his Majesty's service, when you are asked to dine with the skipper."*

We met at the captain's table, where we found, as usual, a great display of plate, but very little else, except the ship's allowance. We certainly had now been cruising some time, and there was some excuse for it; but still, few captains would have been so unprovided. "I'm afraid, gentlemen, you will not have a very grand dinner," observed the captain, as the steward removed the plated covers of the dishes; "but when on service we must rough it out how we can. Mr O'Brien, pea-soup? I recollect faring harder than this through one cruise in a flush vessel. We were thirteen weeks up to our knees in water, and living the whole time upon raw pork—not being able to light a fire during the cruise."

"Pray, Captain Kearney, may I ask where this happened?"

"To be sure. It was off Bermudas: we cruised for seven weeks before we could find the Islands, and began verily to think that the Bermudas were themselves on a cruise."

"I presume, sir, you were not so sorry to have a fire to cook your provisions when you came to an anchor?" said O'Brien.

"I beg your pardon," replied Captain Kearney; "we had become so accustomed to raw provisions and wet feet, that we could not eat our meals cooked, or help dipping our legs over the side, for a long while afterwards. I saw one of the boat-keepers astern catch a large barracouta and eat it alive—indeed, if I had not given the strictest orders, and flogged half-a-dozen of them, I doubt whether they would not have eaten their victuals raw to this day. The force of habit is tremendous."

"It is, indeed," observed Mr Phillott, drily, and winking to us, referring to the captain's incredible stories.

"It is, indeed," repeated O'Brien; "we see the ditch in our neighbour's eye, and cannot observe the log of wood in our own"; and O'Brien winked at me, referring to Phillott's habit of bad language.

"I once knew a married man," observed the captain, "who had been always accustomed to go to sleep with his hand upon his wife's head, and would not allow her to wear a night-cap in consequence. Well, she caught cold and died, and he never could sleep at night until

* *Tidivate (or titivate): To dress up.*

he took a clothes-brush to bed with him, and laid his hand upon that, which answered the purpose—such was the force of habit."

"I once saw a dead body galvanized," observed Mr Phillott: "it was the body of a man who had taken a great deal of snuff during his lifetime, and as soon as the battery was applied to his spine, the body very gently raised its arm, and put its fingers to its nose, as if it was taking a pinch."

"You saw that yourself, Mr Phillott?" observed the captain, looking at the first lieutenant earnestly in the face.

"Yes, sir," replied Mr Phillott, coolly.

"Have you told that story often?"

"Very often, sir."

"Because I know that some people, by constantly telling a story, at last believe it to be true; not that I refer to you, Mr Phillott; but still, I should recommend you not to tell that story where you are not well known, or people may doubt your credibility."

"I make it a rule to believe everything myself," observed Mr Phillott, "out of politeness, and I expect the same courtesy from others."

"Then, upon my soul! when you tell that story, you trespass very much upon our good manners. Talking of courtesy, you must meet a friend of mine, who has been a courtier all his life; he cannot help bowing. I have seen him bow to his horse and thank him after he had dismounted—beg pardon of a puppy for treading on his tail; and one day, when he fell over a scraper, he took his hat off, and made it a thousand apologies for his inattention."

"Force of habit again," said O'Brien.

"Exactly so. Mr Simple, will you take a slice of this pork? and perhaps you'll do me the honour to take a glass of wine? Lord Privilege would not much admire our dinner to-day, would he, Mr Simple?"

"As a variety he might, sir, but not for a continuance."

"Very truly said. Variety is charming. The negroes here get so tired of salt fish and occra broth, that they eat dirt by way of a relish. Mr O'Brien, how remarkably well you played that sonata of Pleydel's this morning."

"I am happy that I did not annoy you, Captain Kearney, at all events," replied O'Brien.

"On the contrary, I am very partial to good music. My mother was a great performer. I recollect once, she was performing a piece on the piano in which she had to imitate a *thunderstorm*. So admirably did she hit it off, that when we went to tea all the cream was *turned sour*, as well as three casks of *beer* in the cellar."

At this assertion Mr Phillott could contain himself no longer; he burst out into a loud laugh, and having a glass of wine to his lips, spattered it all over the table, and over me, who unfortunately was opposite to him.

"I really beg pardon, Captain Kearney, but the idea of such an expensive talent was too amusing. Will you permit me to ask you a question? As there could not have been thunder without lightning, were any people killed at the same time by the electric fluid of the piano?"

"No sir," replied Captain Kearney, very angrily; "but her performance *electrified* us, which was something like it. Perhaps, Mr Phillott, as you lost your last glass of wine, you will allow me to take another with you?"

"With great pleasure," replied the first lieutenant, who perceived that he had gone far enough.

"Well, gentlemen," said the captain, "we shall soon be in the land of plenty. I shall cruise a fortnight more, and then join the admiral at Jamaica. We must make out our despatch relative to the cutting-out of the *Sylvia* (that was the name of the privateer brig), and I am happy to say that I shall feel it my duty to make honourable mention of all the party present. Steward, coffee."

The first lieutenant, O'Brien, and I, bowed to this flattering avowal on the part of the captain; as for me, I felt delighted. The idea of my name being mentioned in the "Gazette," and the pleasure that it would give to my father and mother, mantled the blood in my cheeks till I was as red as a turkey-cock.

"*Cousin* Simple," said the captain, good-naturedly, "you have no occasion to blush; your conduct deserves it; and you are indebted to Mr Phillott for having made me acquainted with your gallantry."

Coffee was soon over, and I was glad to leave the cabin and be alone, that I might compose my perturbed mind. I felt too happy. I did not, however, say a word to my messmates, as it might have created feelings of envy or ill-will. O'Brien gave me a caution not to do so, when I met him afterwards, so that I was very glad that I had been so circumspect.

———《/0/》———

CHAPTER XXXV

Swinburne continues his narrative of the battle off Cape St Vincent.

THE SECOND NIGHT after this, we had the middle watch, and I claimed Swinburne's promise that he would spin his yarn, relative to the battle of St Vincent. "Well, Mr Simple, so I will; but I require a little priming, or I shall never go off."

"Will you have your glass of grog before or after?"

"Before, by all means, if you please, sir. Run down and get it, and I'll heave the log for you in the meantime, when we shall have a good hour without interruption, for the sea-breeze will be steady, and we are under easy sail." I brought up a stiff glass of grog, which Swinburne tossed off, and as he finished it, sighed deeply as if in sorrow that there was no more. Having stowed away the tumbler in one of the capstern holes for the present, we sat down upon a coil of ropes under the weather bulwarks, and Swinburne, replacing his quid of tobacco, commenced as follows:—

"Well, Mr Simple, as I told you before, old Jervis started with all his fleet for Cape St Vincent. We lost one of our fleet—and a three-decker too—the *St George*; she took the ground, and was obliged to go back to Lisbon; but we soon afterwards were joined by five sail of the line, sent out from England, so that we mustered fifteen sail in all. We had like to lose another of our mess, for d'ye see, the old *Culloden* and *Colossus* fell foul of each other, and the *Culloden* had the worst on it; but Troubridge, who commanded her, was not a man to shy his work, and ax to go in to refit, when there was a chance of meeting the enemy—so he patched her up somehow or another, and reported himself ready for action the very next day. Ready for action he always was, that's sure enough, but whether his ship was in a fit state to go into action is quite another thing. But as the sailors used to say in joking, he was a *true bridge*, and you might trust to him; which meant as much as to say, that he knew how to take his ship into action, and how to fight her when he was fairly in it. I think it was the next day that Cockburn joined us in the *Minerve*, and he brought Nelson along with him with the intelligence that the Dons had chased him, and that the whole Spanish fleet was out in pursuit of us. Well, Mr Simple, you may guess we were not a little happy in the *Captain*, when Nelson joined us, as we knew that if he fell in with the Spaniards our ship would cut a figure—and so she did sure enough. That was on the morning of the 13th, and old Jervis made the signal to prepare for action, and keep close order, which means, to have your flying jib-boom in at the starn windows of the ship ahead of you; and we did keep close order, for a man might have walked right round from one ship to the other, either lee or weather line of the fleet. I sha'n't forget that night, Mr Simple, as long as I live and breathe. Every now and then we heard the signal guns of the Spanish fleet booming at a distance to windward of us, and you may guess how our hearts leaped at the sound, and how we watched with all our ears for the next gun that was fired, trying to make out their bearings and distance, as we assembled in little knots upon the booms and weather-gangway. It was my middle watch, and I was signal-man at the time, so of course I had no time to take a caulk if I was inclined. When my watch was over I could not go down to my hammock, so I kept the morning watch too, as did most of the men on board: as for Nelson, he walked the deck the whole night, quite in a fever. At daylight it was thick and hazy weather, and we could not make them out; but, about five bells, the old *Culloden*, who, if she had broke her nose, had not lost the use of her eyes, made the signal for a part of the Spanish fleet in sight. Old Jervis repeated the signal to prepare for action, but he might have saved the wear and tear of the bunting, for we were all ready, bulk-heads down, screens up, guns shotted, tackles rove, yards slung, powder filled, shot on deck, and fire out—and what's more, Mr Simple, I'll be d——d if we weren't all willing too. About six bells in the forenoon, the fog and haze all cleared away at once, just like the raising of the foresail that they lower down at the Portsmouth the-atre, and discovered the whole of the Spanish fleet. I counted them all. 'How many, Swinburne?' cries Nelson. 'Twenty-six sail, sir,' an-swered I. Nelson walked the quarter-deck backwards and forwards, rubbing his hands, and laughing to himself, and then he called for his glass, and went to the gangway with Captain Miller. 'Swin-burne, keep a good look upon the admiral,' says he. 'Ay, ay, sir,' says I. Now you see, Mr Simple, twenty-six sail against fifteen were great odds upon paper; but we didn't think so, because we know'd

the difference between the two fleets. There was our fifteen sail of
the line, all in apple-pie order, packed up as close as dominoes, and
every man on board of them longing to come to the scratch; while
there was their twenty-six, all *somehow nohow,* two lines here and *no
lines* there, with a great gap of water in the middle of them. For this
gap between their ships we all steered, with all the sail we could
carry because, d'ye see, Mr Simple, by getting them on both sides of
us, we had the advantage of fighting both broadsides, which is just
as easy as fighting one, and makes shorter work of it. Just as it
struck seven bells, Troubridge opened the ball *setting* to half a dozen
of the Spaniards, and making them *reel* 'Tom Collins' whether or no.
Bang—bang—bang, bang! Oh, Mr Simple, it's a beautiful sight to
see the first guns fired that are to bring on a general action. 'He's the
luckiest dog, that Troubridge,' said Nelson, stamping with impatience. Our ships were soon hard at it, hammer and tongs (my eyes,
how they did pelt it in!), and old Sir John, in the *Victory,* smashed
the cabin windows of the Spanish admiral, with such a hell of a
raking broadside, that the fellow bore up as if the devil kicked him.
Lord a mercy, you might have drove a Portsmouth waggon into his
starn—the broadside of the *Victory* had made room enough. However, they were soon all smothered up in smoke, and we could not
make out how things were going on—but we made a pretty good
guess. Well, Mr Simple, as they say at the play, that was act the first,
scene the first; and now we had to make our appearance, and I'll
leave you to judge, after I've told my tale, whether the old *Captain*
wasn't principal performer, and *top sawyer* over them all. But stop a
moment, I'll just look at the binnacle, for that young topman's nod-
ding at the wheel.—I say, Mr Smith, are you shutting your eyes to
keep them warm, and letting the ship run half a point out of her
course? Take care I don't send for another helmsman, that's all, and
give the reason why. You'll make a wry face upon six-water grog to-
morrow, at seven bells. D——n your eyes, keep them open—can't
you?"

Swinburne, after this genteel admonition to the man at the
wheel, reseated himself and continued his narrative.

"All this while, Mr Simple, we in the *Captain* had not fired a gun;
but were ranging up as fast as we could to where the enemy lay in a
heap. There were plenty to pick and choose from; and Nelson

looked out sharp for a big one, as little boys do when they have to choose an apple; and, by the piper that played before Moses! it was a big one that he ordered the master to put him alongside of. She was a four-decker, called the *Santissima Trinidad*. We had to pass some whoppers, which would have satisfied any reasonable man; for there was the *San Josef,* and *Salvador del Mondo* and *San Nicolas:* but nothing would suit Nelson but this four-decked ship; so we crossed the hawse of about six of them, and as soon as we were abreast of her, and at the word 'Fire!' every gun went off at once, slap into her, and the old *Captain* reeled at the discharge, as if she was drunk. I wish you'd only seen how we pitched it into this *Holy Trinity;* she was *holy* enough before we had done with her, riddled like a sieve, several of her ports knocked into one, and every scupper of her running blood and water.* Not but what she stood to it as bold as brass, and gave us nearly gun for gun, and made a very pretty general average in our ship's company. Many of the old captains went to kingdom-come in that business, and many more were obliged to bear up for Greenwich Hospital.

" 'Fire away, my lads—steady aim!' cries Nelson. 'Jump down there, Mr Thomas; pass the word to reduce the cartridges, the shot go clean through her. Double shot the guns there, fore and aft.'

"So we were at it for about half-an-hour, when our guns became so hot from quick firing, that they bounced up to the beams overhead, tearing away their ringbolts, and snapping their breechings like rope-yarns. By this time we were almost as much unrigged as if we had been two days paying off in Portsmouth harbour. The four-decker forged ahead, and Troubridge, in the jolly old *Culloden,* came between us and two other Spanish ships, who were playing into us. She was as fresh as a daisy, and gave them a dose which quite astonished them. They shook their ears, and fell astern, when the *Blenheim* laid hold of them, and mauled them so that they went astern again. But it was out of the frying-pan into the fire: for the *Orion, Prince George,* and one or two others, were coming up, and knocked the very guts out of them. I'll be d——d if they forget the 14th of April, and sarve them right, too. Wasn't a four-decker enough for any two-decker, without any more coming on us? and couldn't the beggars have matched themselves like gentlemen?

* *Scupper: A drain opening in a ship's side allowing water to run into the sea.*

Well, Mr Simple, this gave us a minute or two to fetch our breath, let the guns cool, and repair damages, and swab the blood from the decks; but we lost our four-decker, for we could not get near her again."

"What odd names the Spaniards give to their ships, Swinburne?"

"Why yes, they do; it would almost appear wicked to belabour the *Holy Trinity* as we did. But why they should call a four-decked ship the *Holy Trinity*, seeing as how there's only three of them, Father, Son, and Holy Ghost, I can't tell. Bill Saunders said that the fourth deck was for the Pope, who was as great a personage as the others; but I can't understand how that can be. Well, Mr Simple, as I was head signalman, I was perched on the poop, and didn't serve at a gun. I had to report all I could see, which was not much, the smoke was so thick; but now and then I could get a peep, as it were through the holes in the blanket. Of course I was obliged to keep my eye as much as possible upon the admiral, not to make out his signals, for Commodore Nelson wouldn't thank me for that; I knew he hated a signal when in action, so I never took no notice of the bunting, but just watched to see what he was about. So while we are repairing damages, I'll just tell you what I saw of the rest of the fleet. As soon as old Jervis had done for the Spanish admiral, he hauled his wind on the larboard tack, and followed by four or five other ships, weathered the Spanish line, and joined Collingwood in the *Excellent*. Then they all dashed through the line; the *Excellent* was the leading ship, and she first took the shine out of the *Salvador del Mondo*, and then left her to be picked up by the other ships, while she attacked a two-decker, who hauled down her colours—I forget her name just now. As soon as the *Victory* ran alongside of the *Salvador del Mondo*, down went her colours, and *excellent* reasons had she for striking her flag. And now, Mr Simple, the old *Captain* comes into play again. Having parted company with the four-decker, we had recommenced action with the *San Nicolas*, a Spanish eighty, and while we were hard at it, old Collingwood comes up in the *Excellent*. The *San Nicolas*, knowing that the *Excellent*'s broadside would send her to old Nick, put her helm up to avoid being raked: in so doing, she fell foul of the *San Josef*, a Spanish three-decker, and we being all cut to pieces and unmanageable—all of us indeed reeling about like drunken men—Nelson ordered his helm a-starboard, and in a jiffy there we were, all three hugging each other, running in one another's guns, smashing our chain-plates, and poking our yard-arms through each other's canvas.

" 'All hands to board!' roared Nelson, leaping on the hammocks and waving his sword.

" 'Hurrah! hurrah!' echoed through the decks, and up flew the men, like as many angry bees out of a bee-hive. In a moment pikes, tomahawks, cutlasses, and pistols were seized (for it was quite un-expected, Mr Simple), and our men poured into the eighty-gun ship, and in two minutes the decks were cleared and all the Dons pitched below. I joined the boarders and was on the main deck when Cap-tain Miller came down, and cried out 'On deck again immediately.' Up we went, and what do you think it was for, Mr Simple? Why to board a second time; for Nelson having taken the two-decker, swore that he'd have the three-decker as well. So away we went again, clambering up her lofty sides how we could, and dropping down on her decks like hailstones. We all made for the quarter-deck, beat down every Spanish beggar that showed fight, and in five minutes more we had hauled down the colours of two of the finest ships in the Spanish navy. If that wasn't taking the shine out of the Dons, I should like to know what is. And didn't the old captains cheer and shake hands, as Commodore Nelson stood on the deck of the *San Josef,* and received the swords of the Spanish officers! There was enough of them to go right round the capstern, and plenty to spare. Now, Mr Simple, what do you think of that for a spree?"

"Why, Swinburne, I can only say that I wish I had been there."

"So did every man in the fleet, Mr Simple, I can tell you."

"But what became of the *Santissima Trinidad?*"

"Upon my word, she behaved one *deck* better than all the others. She held out against four of our ships for a long while, and then hauled down her colours, and no disgrace to her, considering what a precious hammering she had taken first. But the lee division of the Spanish weather fleet, if I may so call it, consisting of eleven sail of the line, came up to her assistance, and surrounded her, so that they got her off. Our ships were too much cut up to commence a new action, and the admiral made the signal to secure the prizes. The Spanish fleet then did what they should have done before—got into line; and we lost no time in doing the same. But we both had had fighting enough."

"But do you think, Swinburne, that the Spaniards fought well?"

"They'd have fought better, if they'd only have known how. There's no want of courage in the Dons, Mr Simple, but they did not support each other. Only observe how Troubridge supported us. By God, Mr Simple, he was the *real fellow*, and Nelson knew it well. He was Nelson's right-hand man; but you know, there wasn't room for *two* Nelsons. Their ships engaged held out well, it must be acknowledged, but why weren't they all in their proper berths? Had they kept close order of sailing, and had all fought as well as those who were captured, it would not have been a very easy matter for fifteen ships to gain a victory over twenty-six. That's long odds, even when backed with British seamen."

"Well, how did you separate?"

"Why, the next morning the Spaniards had the weathergage, so they had the option whether to fight or not. At one time they had half a mind, for they bore down to us; upon which we hauled our wind to show them we were all ready to meet them, and then they thought better of it, and rounded-to again. So as they wouldn't fight, and we didn't wish it, we parted company in the night; and two days afterwards we anchored, with our four prizes, in Lagos Bay. So now you have the whole of it, Mr Simple, and I've talked till I'm quite hoarse. You haven't by chance another drop of the stuff left to clear my throat? It would be quite a charity."

"I think I have, Swinburne; and as you deserve it, I will go and fetch it."

CHAPTER XXXVI

A letter from Father M'Grath, who diplomatizes—When priest meets priest, then comes the tug of war—Father O'Toole not to be made a tool of.

WE CONTINUED our cruise for a fortnight, and then made sail for Jamaica, where we found the admiral at anchor at Port Royal, but our signal was made to keep under weigh, and Captain Kearney, having paid his respects to the admiral, received

orders to carry despatches to Halifax. Water and provisions were
sent on board by the boats of the admiral's ships, and, to our great
disappointment, as the evening closed in, we were again standing
out to sea, instead of, as we had anticipated, enjoying ourselves on
shore; but the fact was, that orders had arrived from England to
send a frigate immediately up to the admiral at Halifax, to be at his
disposal.

I had, however, the satisfaction to know that Captain Kearney
had been true to his word in making mention of my name in the
despatch, for the clerk showed me a copy of it. Nothing occurred
worth mentioning during our passage, except that Captain Kearney
was very unwell nearly the whole of the time, and seldom quitted
his cabin. It was in October that we anchored in Halifax harbour,
and the Admiralty, expecting our arrival there, had forwarded our
letters. There were none for me, but there was one for O'Brien, from
Father M'Grath, the contents of which were as follows:—

"MY DEAR SON,—And a good son you are, and that's the truth on it,
or devil a bit should you be a son of mine. You've made your family
quite contented and peaceable, and they never fight for the *praties*
now—good reason why they shouldn't, seeing that there's a plenty
for all of them, and the pig craturs into the bargain. Your father and
your mother, and your brother, and your three sisters, send their
duty to you, and their blessings too—and you may add my blessing,
Terence, which is worth them all; for won't I get you out of purgatory in the twinkling of a bed-post? Make yourself quite aisy on that
score, and lave it all to me; only just say a *pater* now and then,
that when St Peter lets you in, he mayn't throw it in your teeth, that
you've saved your soul by contract, which is the only way by which
emperors and kings ever get to heaven. Your letter from Plymouth
came safe to hand: Barney, the post-boy, having dropped it under
foot, close to our door, the big pig took it into his mouth and ran
away with it; but I caught sight of him, and *speaking* to him, he let it
go, knowing (the 'cute cratur!) that I could read it better than him.
As soon as I had digested the contents, which it was lucky the pig
did not instead of me, I just took my meal and my big stick, and
then set off for Ballycleuch.

"Now you know, Terence, if you haven't forgot—and if you
have, I'll just remind you—that there's a flaunty sort of young

woman at the poteen shop there, who calls herself Mrs O'Rourke, wife to a Corporal O'Rourke, who was kilt or died one day, I don't know which, but that's not of much consequence. The devil a bit do I think the priest ever gave the marriage-blessing to that same; although she swears that she was married on the rock of Gibraltar—it may be a strong rock fore I know, but it's not the rock of salvation like the seven sacraments, of which marriage is one. *Benedicite!* Mrs O'Rourke is a little too apt to fleer and jeer at the priests; and if it were not that she softens down her pertinent remarks with a glass or two of the real poteen, which proves some respect for the church, I'd excommunicate her body and soul, and every body and every soul that put their lips to the cratur at her door. But she must leave that off, as I tell her, when she gets old and ugly, for then all the whisky in the world sha'n't save her. But she's a fine woman now, and it goes agin my conscience to help the devil to a fine woman. Now this Mrs O'Rourke knows everybody and everything that's going on in the country about; and she has a tongue which has never had a holiday since it was let loose.

" 'Good morning to ye, Mrs O'Rourke,' says I.

" 'An' the top of the morning to you, Father M'Grath,' says she, with a smile; 'what brings you here? Is it a journey that you're taking to buy the true wood of the cross? or is it a purty girl that you wish to confess, Father M'Grath? or is it only that you're come for a drop of poteen, and a little bit of chat with Mrs O'Rourke?'

" 'Sure it's I who'd be glad to find the same true wood of the cross, Mrs O'Rourke, but it's not grown, I suspect, at your town of Ballycleuch; and it's no objection I'd have to confess a purty girl like yourself, Mrs O'Rourke, who'll only tell me half her sins, and give me no trouble; but it's the truth, that I'm here for nothing else but to have a bit of chat with yourself, dainty dear, and taste your poteen, just by way of keeping my mouth nate and clane.'

"So Mrs O'Rourke poured out the real stuff, which I drank to her health; and then says I, putting down the bit of a glass, 'So you've a stranger come, I find, in your parts, Mrs O'Rourke.'

" 'I've heard the same,' replied she. So you observe, Terence, I came to the fact all at once by a guess.

" 'I am tould,' says I, 'that he's a Scotchman, and spakes what nobody can understand.'

" 'Devil a bit,' says she, 'he's an Englishman, and speaks plain enough.'

" 'But what can a man mane, to come here and sit down all alone?' says I.

" 'All alone, Father M'Grath!' replied she; 'is a man all alone when he's got his wife and childer, and more coming, with the blessing of God?'

" 'But those boys are not his own childer, I believe,' says I.

" 'There again you're all in a mistake, Father M'Grath,' rejoins she. 'The childer are all his own, and all girls to boot. It appears that it's just as well that you come down, now and then, for information, to our town of Ballycleuch.'

" 'Very true, Mrs O'Rourke,' says I; 'and who is it that knows everything so well as yourself?' You observe, Terence, that I just said everything contrary and *arce versa*, as they call it, to the contents of your letter; for always recollect, my son, that if you would worm a secret out of a woman, you'll do more by contradiction than you ever will by coaxing—so I went on: 'Anyhow, I think it's a burning shame, Mrs O'Rourke, for a gentleman to bring over with him here from England a parcel of lazy English servants, when there's so many nice boys and girls here to attind upon them.'

" 'Now there you're all wrong again, Father M'Grath,' says she. 'Devil a soul has he brought from the other country, but has hired them all here. Arn't there Ella Flanagan for one maid, and Terence Driscol for a footman? and it's well that he looks in his new uniform, when he comes down for the newspapers; and arn't Moggy Cala there to cook the dinner, and pretty Mary Sullivan for a nurse for the babby as soon as it comes into the world?'

" 'Is it Mary Sullivan you mane?' says I; 'she that was married about three months back, and is so quick in child-getting, that she's all but ready to fall to pieces in this same time?'

" 'It's exactly she,' says Mrs O'Rourke; 'and do you know the reason?'

" 'Devil a bit,' says I; 'how should I?'

" 'Then it's just that she may send her own child away, and give her milk to the English babby that's coming; because the lady is too much of a lady to have a child hanging to her breast.'

" 'But suppose Mary Sullivan's child ar'n't born till afterwards, how then?" says I. 'Speak, Mrs O'Rourke, for you're a sensible woman.'

" 'How then?' says she. 'Och! that's all arranged; for Mary says that she'll be in bed a week before the lady, so that's all right, you'll perceive, Father M'Grath.'

"But don't you perceive, sensible woman as you are, that a young woman, who is so much out of her reckoning as to have a child three months after her marriage, may make a little mistake in her lying-in arithmetic, Mrs O'Rourke.'

" 'Never fear, Father M'Grath, Mary Sullivan will keep her word; and sooner than disappoint the lady, and lose her place, she'll just tumble down-stairs, and won't that put her to bed fast enough?'

"Well, that's what I call a faithful good servant that earns her wages,' says I; 'so now I'll just take another glass, Mrs O'Rourke, and thank you too. Sure you're the woman that knows everything, and a mighty pretty woman into the bargain.'

" 'Let me alone now, Father M'Grath, and don't be pinching me that way, anyhow.'

" 'It was only a big flea that I perceived hopping on your gown, my darling, devil anything else.'

" 'Many thanks to you, Father, for that same; but the next time you'd kill my fleas, just wait until they're in a *more dacent* situation.'

" 'Fleas are fleas, Mrs O'Rourke, and we must catch 'em when we can, and how we can, and as we can, so no offence. A good night's rest to you, Mrs O'Rourke—when do you mean to confess?'

" 'I've an idea that I've too many fleas about me to confess to you just now, Father M'Grath, and that's the truth on it. So a pleasant walk back to you.'

"So you'll perceive, my son, that having got all the information from Mrs O'Rourke, it's back I went to Ballyhinch, till I heard it whispered that there were doings down at the old house at Bally-cleuch. Off I set, and went to the house itself, as priests always ought to be welcomed at births, and marriages, and deaths, being, as you know, of great use on such occasions—when who should open the door but Father O'Toole, the biggest rapparee of a priest in the whole of Ireland. Didn't he steal a horse, and only save his neck by benefit of clergy? and did he ever give absolution to a young woman without making her sin over again? 'What may be your pleasure here, Father M'Grath?' says he, holding the door with his hand.

" 'Only just to call and hear what's going on.'

" 'For the matter of that,' says he, 'I'll just tell you that we're all going on very well; but ar'n't you ashamed of yourself, Father M'Grath, to come here to interfere with my flock, knowing that I confess the house altogether?'

" 'That's as may be,' says I; 'but I only wanted to know what the lady had brought into the world.'

" 'It's a *child*,' says he.

" 'Indeed!' says I; 'many thanks for the information; and pray what is it that Mary Sullivan has brought into the world?'

" 'That's a *child* too,' says he; 'and now that you know all about it, good evening to you, Father M'Grath.' And the ugly brute slammed the door right in my face.

" 'Who stole a horse?' cries I; but he didn't hear me—more's the pity.

"So you'll perceive, my dear boy, that I have found out something, at all events, but not so much as I intended; for I'll prove to Father O'Toole that he's no match for Father M'Grath. But what I find out must be reserved for another letter, seeing that it's not possible to tell it to you in this same. Praties look well, but somehow or another, *clothes* don't grow upon trees in ould Ireland; and one of your half-quarterly bills, or a little prize-money, if it found its way here, would add not a little to the respectability of the family appearance. Even my cassock is becoming too *holy* for a parish priest; not that I care about it so much, only Father O'Toole, the baste! had on a bran new one—not that I believe that he ever came honestly by it, as I have by mine—but, get it how you may, a new gown always looks better than an old one, that's certain. So no more at present from your loving friend and confessor,

"URTAGH M'GRATH."

"Now, you'll observe, Peter," said O'Brien, after I had read the letter, "that, as I supposed, your uncle meant mischief when he went over to Ireland. Whether the children are both boys or both girls, or your uncle's is a boy, and the other is a girl, there is no knowing at present. If an exchange was required, it's made, that's certain; but I will write again to Father M'Grath, and insist upon his finding out the truth, if possible. Have you any letter from your father?"

"None, I am sorry to say. I wish I had, for he would not have failed to speak on the subject."

"Well, never mind, it's no use dreaming over the matter; we must do our best when we get to England ourselves, and in the meantime trust to Father M'Grath. I'll go and write to him while my mind's full of it." O'Brien wrote his letter, and the subject was not started again.

—*∞∞*—

CHAPTER XXXVII

Captain Kearney's illness—He makes his will, and devises sundry châteaux en Espagne for the benefit of those concerned—The legacy duty in this instance not ruinous—He signs, seals, and dies.

THE CAPTAIN, as was his custom, went on shore, and took up his quarters at a friend's house; that is to say, the house of an acquaintance, or any polite gentleman who would ask him to take a dinner and a bed. This was quite sufficient for Captain Kearney, who would fill his portmanteau, and take up his quarters, without thinking of leaving them until the ship sailed, or some more advantageous invitation was given. This conduct in England would have very much trespassed on our ideas of hospitality; but in our foreign settlements and colonies, where the society is confined and novelty is desirable, a person who could amuse like Captain Kearney was generally welcome, let him stay as long as he pleased. All sailors agree in asserting that Halifax is one of the most delightful ports in which a ship can anchor. Everybody is hospitable, cheerful, and willing to amuse and be amused. It is, therefore, a very bad place to send a ship to if you wish her to refit in a hurry; unless, indeed, the admiral is there to watch over your daily progress, and a sharp commissioner to expedite your motions in the dockyard. The admiral was there when we arrived, and we should not have lain there long, had not the health of Captain Kearney, by the time that we were ready for sea, been so seriously affected, that the doctor was of opinion that he could not sail. Another frigate was sent to our intended cruising-ground, and we lay idle in port. But we consoled ourselves: if we did not make prize-money, at all events, we were very happy, and the major part of the officers very much in love.

We had remained in Halifax harbour about three weeks, when a very great change for the worse took place in Captain Kearney's disease. Disease, indeed, it could hardly be called. He had been long suffering from the insidious attacks of a hot climate, and though repeatedly advised to invalid, he never would consent. His constitution appeared now to be breaking up. In a few days he was so ill, that, at the request of the naval surgeons, he consented to be removed to the hospital, where he could command more comforts than in any private house. He had not been at the hospital more than two days, when he sent for me, and stated his wish that I should remain with him. "You know, Peter, that you are a cousin of mine, and one likes to have one's relations near one when we are sick, so bring your traps on shore. The doctor has promised me a nice little room for yourself, and you shall come and sit with me all day." I certainly had no objection to remain with him, because I considered it my duty so to do, and I must say that there was no occasion for me to make any effort to entertain him, as he always entertained me; but I could not help seriously reflecting, and feeling much shocked, at a man, lying in so dangerous a state—for the doctors had pronounced his recovery to be impossible—still continuing a system of falsehood during the whole day, without intermission. But it really appeared in him to be innate; and, as Swinburne said, "if he told truth, it was entirely by mistake."

"Peter," said he, one day, "there's a great draught. Shut the door, and put on some more coals."

"The fire does not draw well, sir," replied I, "without the door is open."

"It's astonishing how little people understand the nature of these things. When I built my house, called Walcot Abbey, there was not a chimney would draw; I sent for the architect and abused him, but he could not manage it: I was obliged to do it myself."

"Did you manage it, sir?"

"Manage it—I think I did. The first time I lighted the fire, I opened the door, and the draught was so great, that my little boy, William, who was standing in the current of air, would have gone right up the chimney, if I had not caught him by the petticoats; as it was, his frock was on fire."

"Why sir, it must have been as bad as a hurricane!"

"No, no, not quite so bad—but it showed what a little knowledge of philosophical arrangement could effect. We have no hurricanes in England, Peter; but I have seen a very pretty whirlwind when I was at Walcot Abbey."

"Indeed, sir."

"Yes; it cut four square haystacks quite round, and I lost twenty tons of hay; it twisted the iron lamp-post at the entrance just as a porpoise twists a harpoon, and took up a sow and her litter of pigs, that were about a hundred yards from the back of the house, and landed them safe over the house to the front, with the exception of the old sow putting her shoulder out."

"Indeed, sir."

"Yes, but what was strange, there were a great many rats in the hayrick, and up they went with the hay. Now, Peter, by the laws of gravitation, they naturally come down before the hay, and I was walking with my greyhound, or rather terrier, and after one coming down close to her, which she killed, it was quite ridiculous to witness her looking up in the air, and watching for the others."

"A greyhound did you say, sir, or a terrier?"

"Both, Peter; the fact is, she had been a greyhound, but breaking her foreleg against a stump, when coursing, I had the other three amputated as well, and then she made a capital terrier. She was a great favourite of mine."

"Well," observed I, "I have read something like that in Baron Munchausen."*

"Mr Simple," said the captain, turning on his elbow and looking me severely in the face, "what do you mean to imply?"

"Oh, nothing, sir, but I have read a story of that kind."

"Most probably; the great art of invention is to found it upon facts. There are some people who out of a molehill will make a mountain; and facts and fiction become so blended nowadays, that even truth becomes a matter of doubt."

"Very true, sir," replied I; and as he did not speak for some

* Baron Munchausen: Karl Friedrich Hieronymous Munchausen (1720–1797), a German nobleman famous for his tall tales.

minutes, I ventured to bring my Bible to his bedside, as if I was reading it to myself.

"What are you reading, Peter?" said he.

"Only a chapter in the Bible, sir," said I. "Would you like that I should read aloud?"

"Yes, I'm very fond of the Bible—it's the book of *truth*. Peter, read me about Jacob, and his weathering Esau with a mess of pottage, and obtaining his father's blessing." I could not help thinking it singular that he should select a portion in which, for divine reasons, a lie was crowned with success and reward.

When I had finished it, he asked me to read something more; I turned over to the Acts of the Apostles, and commenced the chapter in which Ananias and Sapphira were struck dead. When I had finished, he observed very seriously, "That is a very good lesson for young people, Peter, and points out that you never should swerve from the truth. Recollect, as your motto, Peter, to 'tell truth and shame the devil.' "

After this observation I laid down the book, as it appeared to me that he was quite unaware of his propensity; and without a sense of your fault, how can repentance and amendment be expected? He became more feeble and exhausted every day, and, at last, was so weak that he could scarcely raise himself in his bed. One afternoon he said, "Peter, I shall make my will, not that I am going to kick the bucket just yet; but still it is every man's duty to set his house in order, and it will amuse me; so fetch pen and paper, and come and sit down by me."

I did as he requested.

"Write, Peter, that I, Anthony George William Charles Huskisson Kearney (my father's name was Anthony, Peter; I was christened George, after the present Regent, William and Charles after Mr Pitt and Mr Fox, who were my sponsors; Huskisson is the name of my great uncle, whose property devolves to me; he's eighty-three now, so he can't last long)—have you written down that?"

"Yes, sir."

"Being in sound mind, do hereby make my last will and testament, revoking all former wills."

"Yes, sir."

"I bequeath to my dearly beloved wife, Augusta Charlotte Kearney (she was named after the Queen and Princess Augusta, who held her at the baptismal font), all my household furniture, books, pictures, plate, and houses, for her own free use and will, and to dispose of at her pleasure upon her demise. Is that down?"

"Yes, sir."

"Also, the interest of all my money in the three per cents. reduced, and in the long annuities, and the balance in my agent's hands, for her natural life. At her death to be divided into equal portions between my two children, William Mohamed Potemkin Kearney, and Caroline Anastasia Kearney. Is that down?"

"Yes, sir."

"Well, then, Peter, now for my real property. My estate in Kent (let me see, what is the name of it?)—Walcot Abbey, my three farms in the Vale of Aylesbury, and the marsh lands in Norfolk, I bequeath to my two children aforenamed, the proceeds of the same to be laid up, deducting all necessary expenses for their education, for their sole use and benefit. Is that down?"

"Not yet, sir—'use and benefit.' Now it is, sir."

"Until they come to the age of twenty-one years; or in case of my daughter, until she marries with the consent of my executors, then to be equally and fairly valued and divided between them. You observe, Peter, I never make any difference between girls and boys—a good father will leave one child as much as another. Now, I'll take my breath a little."

I was really astonished. It was well known that Captain Kearney had nothing but his pay, and that it was the hopes of prize-money to support his family, which had induced him to stay out so long in the West Indies. It was laughable; yet I could not laugh: there was a melancholy feeling at such a specimen of insanity, which prevented me.

"Now, Peter, we'll go on," said Captain Kearney, after a pause of a few minutes. "I have a few legacies to bequeath. First, to all my servants £50 each, and two suits of mourning; to my nephew, Thomas Kearney, of Kearney Hall, Yorkshire, I bequeath the sword presented me by the Grand Sultan. I promised it to him, and although we have quarrelled, and not spoken for years, I always keep my word. The plate presented me by the merchants and underwriters of Lloyd's, I leave to my worthy friend, the Duke of Newcastle. Is that down?"

"Yes, sir."

"Well; my snuff-box, presented me by Prince Potemkin, I bequeath to Admiral Sir Isaac Coffin; and, also, I release him from the mortgage which I hold over his property of the Madeline Islands, in North America. By-the-by, say, and further, I bequeath to him the bag of snuff presented to me by the Dey of Algiers; he may as well have the snuff as he has the snuff-box. Is that down?"

"Yes, sir."

"Well then, now, Peter, I must leave you something."

"O, never mind me," replied I.

"No, no, Peter, I must not forget my cousin. Let me see; you shall have my fighting sword. A real good one, I can tell you. I once fought a duel with it at Palermo, and ran a Sicilian prince so clean through the body, and it held so tight, that we were obliged to send for a pair of post-horses to pull it out again. Put that down as a legacy for my cousin, Peter Simple. I believe that is all. Now for my executors; and I request my particular friends, the Earl of Londonderry, the Marquis of Chandos, and Mr John Lubbock, banker, to be my executors, and leave each of them the sum of one thousand pounds for their trouble, and in token of regard. That will do, Peter. Now, as I have left so much real property, it is necessary that there should be three witnesses; so call in two more, and let me sign in your presence."

This order was obeyed, and this strange will duly attested, for I hardly need say, that even the presents he had pretended to receive were purchased by himself at different times; but such was the force of his ruling passion even to the last. Mr Phillott and O'Brien used to come and see him, as did occasionally some of the other officers, and he was always cheerful and merry, and seemed to be quite indifferent about his situation, although fully aware of it. His stories, if anything, became more marvellous, as no one ventured to express a doubt as to their credibility.

I had remained in the hospital about a week, when Captain Kearney was evidently dying: the doctor came, felt his pulse, and gave it as his opinion that he could not outlive the day. This was on a Friday, and there certainly was every symptom of dissolution. He was so exhausted that he could scarcely articulate; his feet were cold, and his eyes appeared glazed, and turned upwards. The doctor remained an hour, felt his pulse again, shook his head, and said to me, in a low voice, "He is quite gone." As soon as the doctor quitted the room, Captain Kearney opened his eyes, and beckoned me to him. "He's a confounded fool, Peter," said he: "he thinks I am slipping my wind now—but I know better; going I am, 'tis true—but I shan't die till next Thursday." Strange to say, from that moment he rallied; and although it was reported that he was dead, and the admiral had signed the acting order for his successor, the next morning, to the astonishment of everybody, Captain Kearney was still alive. He continued in this state, between life and death, until the Thursday next, the day on which he asserted that he would die—and, on that morning, he was evidently sinking fast. Towards noon, his breathing became much oppressed and irregular, and he was evidently dying; the rattle in his throat commenced; and I watched at his bedside, waiting for his last gasp, when he again opened his eyes, and beckoning me, with an effort, to put my head close to him to hear what he had to say, he contrived, in a sort of gurgling whisper, and with much difficulty, to utter—"Peter, I'm going now—not that the rattle—in my throat—is a sign of death: for I once knew a man—to *live* with—*the rattle in his throat*—for *six weeks*." He fell back and expired, having, perhaps, at his last gasp, told the greatest lie of his whole life.

Thus died this most extraordinary character, who, in most other points, commanded respect: he was a kind man and a good officer; but from the idiosyncrasy of his disposition, whether from habit or from nature, could not speak the truth. I say from *nature*, because I have witnessed the vice of stealing equally strong, and never to be eradicated. It was in a young messmate of good family, and who was supplied with money to almost any extent: he was one of the most generous, open-hearted lads that I ever knew; he would offer his purse, or the contents of his chest, to any of his messmates, and, at the same time, would steal everything that he could lay his hands upon. I have known him watch for hours, to steal what could be of no use to him, as, for instance, an *odd* shoe, and that much too small for his foot. What he stole he would give away the very next day; but to check it was impossible. It was so well known, that if anything was missed, we used first to apply to his chest to see if it was there, and usually found the article in question. He appeared to be wholly insensible to shame upon this subject, though in every other he showed no want of feeling or of honour; and, strange to say, he never covered his theft with a lie. After vain attempts to cure him of this propensity, he was dismissed from the service as incorrigible.

Captain Kearney was buried in the churchyard with the usual military honours. In his desk we found directions, in his own hand, relative to his funeral, and the engraving on his tombstone. In these, he stated his age to be thirty-one years. If this was correct, Captain Kearney, from the time that he had been in the service of his country, must have entered the navy just *four months before* he was born. It was unfortunate that he commenced the inscription with "Here lies Captain Kearney," &c. &c. His tombstone had not been set up twenty-four hours before somebody, who knew his character, put a dash under one word, as emphatic as it was true of the living man, "Here *lies* Captain."

———*&&&*———

CHAPTER XXXVIII

Captain Horton—Gloomy news from home—Get over head and ears in the water, and find myself afterwards growing one way, and my clothes another—Though neither as rich as a Jew, nor as large as a camel, I pass through my examination, which my brother candidates think passing strange.

THE DAY AFTER Captain Kearney's decease, his acting successor made his appearance on board. The character of Captain Horton was well known to us from the complaints made by the officers belonging to his ship, of his apathy and indolence; indeed, he went by the *soubriquet* of "the Sloth." It certainly was very annoying to his officers to witness so many opportunities of prize-money and distinction thrown away through the indolence of his disposition. Captain Horton was a young man of family who had advanced rapidly in the service from interest, and from occasionally distinguishing himself. In the several cutting-out expeditions, on which he had not volunteered but had been ordered, he had shown, not only courage, but a remarkable degree of coolness in danger and difficulty, which had gained him much approbation: but it was said that this coolness arose from his very fault—an unaccountable laziness. He would walk away, as it were, from the enemy's fire, when others would hasten, merely because he was so apathetic that he would not exert himself to run. In one cutting-out expedition in which he distinguished himself, it is said that having to board a very high vessel, and that in a shower of grape and musketry, when the boat dashed alongside, and the men were springing up, he looked up at the height of the vessel's sides, and exclaimed, with a look of despair, "My God! must we really climb up that vessel's decks?" When he had gained the deck, and became excited, he then proved how little fear had to do with the remark, the captain of the ship falling by his hand, as he fought in advance of his own men. But this peculiarity, which in a junior officer was of little consequence, and a subject of mirth, in a captain became of a very serious nature. The admiral was aware how often he had neglected to annoy or capture the enemy when he might have done it; and, by such neglect, Captain Horton infringed one of the articles of war, the punishment awarded to which infringement is *death*. His appointment, therefore, to the *Sanglier* was as annoying to us as his quitting his former ship was agreeable to those on board of her.

As it happened, it proved of little consequence: the admiral had instructions from home to advance Captain Horton to the first vacancy, which of course he was obliged to comply with; but not wishing to keep on the station an officer who would not exert himself, he resolved to send her to England with despatches and retain the other frigate which had been ordered home, and which we had been sent up to replace. We therefore heard it announced with feelings of joy, mingled with regret, that we were immediately to proceed to England. For my part, I was glad of it. I had now served my time as midshipman, to within five months, and I thought that I had a better chance of being made in England than abroad. I was also very anxious to go home, for family reasons, which I have already explained. In a fortnight we sailed with several vessels, and directions to take charge of a large convoy from Quebec, which was to meet us off the island of St John's. In a few days we joined our convoy, and with a fair wind bore up for England. The weather soon became very bad, and we were scudding before a heavy gale, under bare poles. Our captain seldom quitted the cabin, but remained there on a sofa, stretched at his length, reading a novel, or dozing, as he found most agreeable.

I recollect a circumstance which occurred, which will prove the apathy of his disposition, and how unfit he was to command so fine a frigate. We had been scudding three days, when the weather became much worse. O'Brien, who had the middle watch, went down to report that "it blew very hard."

"Very well," said the captain; "let me know if it blows harder."

In about an hour more the gale increased, and O'Brien went down again. "It blows much harder, Captain Horton."

"Very well," answered Captain Horton, turning in his cot; "you may call me again when it *blows harder*."

At about six bells the gale was at its height, and the wind roared in its fury. Down went O'Brien again. "It blows tremendous hard now, Captain Horton."

"Well, well, if the weather becomes worse—"

"It can't be worse," interrupted O'Brien; "it's impossible to blow harder."

"Indeed! Well, then," replied the captain, "let me know when *it lulls*."

In the morning watch a similar circumstance took place. Mr Phillott went down, and said that several of the convoy were out of sight astern. "Shall we heave-to, Captain Horton?"

"Oh, no," replied he, "she will be so uneasy. Let me know if you lose sight of any more."

In another hour the first lieutenant reported that "there were very few to be seen."

"Very well, Mr Phillott," replied the captain, turning round to sleep; "let me know if you lose any more."

Some time elapsed, and the first lieutenant reported "that they were all out of sight."

"Very well, then," said the captain; "call me when you see them again."

This was not very likely to take place, as we were going twelve knots an hour, and running away from them as fast as we could; so the captain remained undisturbed until he thought proper to get up to breakfast. Indeed, we never saw any more of our convoy, but taking the gale with us, in fifteen days anchored in Plymouth Sound. The orders came down for the frigate to be paid off, all standing, and recommissioned. I received letters from my father, in which he congratulated me at my name being mentioned in Captain Kearney's despatches, and requested me to come home as soon as I could. The admiral allowed my name to be put down on the books of the guard-ship, that I might not lose my time, and then gave me two months' leave of absence. I bade farewell to my shipmates, shook hands with O'Brien, who proposed to go over to Ireland previous to his applying for another ship, and, with my pay in my pocket, set off in the Plymouth mail, and in three days was once more in the arms of my affectionate mother, and warmly greeted by my father and the remainder of my family.

Once more with my family, I must acquaint the reader with what had occurred since my departure. My eldest sister, Lucy, had married an officer in the army, a Captain Fielding, and his regiment having been ordered out to India, had accompanied her husband, and letters had been received, just before my return announcing their safe arrival at Ceylon. My second sister, Mary, had also been engaged to be married, and from her infancy was of extremely delicate health. She was very handsome, and much admired. Her intended husband was a baronet of good family; but unfortunately, she caught a cold at the assize ball and went off in a decline. She died about two months before my arrival, and the family were in deep mourning. My third sister, Ellen, was still unmarried; she also was a very beautiful girl, and now seventeen. My mother's constitution was much shaken by the loss of my sister Mary, and the separation from her eldest child. As for my father, even the loss of his daughter appeared to be wholly forgotten in the unwelcome intelligence which he had received, that my uncle's wife had been safely delivered of a *son*, which threw him out of the anticipated titles and estates of my grandfather. It was indeed a house of mourning. My mother's grief I respected, and tried all I could to console her; that of my father was so evidently worldly, and so at variance with his clerical profession, that I must acknowledge I felt more of anger at it than sorrow. He had become morose and sullen, harsh to those around him, and not so kind to my mother as her state of mind and health made it his duty to be, even if inclination were wanted. He seldom passed any portion of the day with her, and in the evening she went to bed very early, so that there was little communication between them. My sister was a great consolation to her, and so I hope was I; she often said so as she embraced me, and the tears rolled down her cheeks, and I could not help surmising that those tears were doubled from the coolness and indifference, if not unkindness, with which my father behaved to her. As for my sister, she was an angel; and as I witnessed her considerate attentions to my mother, and the total forgetfulness of self which she displayed (so different from my father, who was all self), I often thought what a treasure she would prove to any man who was fortunate enough to win her love. Such was the state of my family when I returned to it.

I had been at home about a week, when one evening, after dinner, I submitted to my father the propriety of trying to obtain my promotion.

"I can do nothing for you, Peter; I have no interest whatever," replied he, moodily.

"I do not think that much is required, sir," replied I; "my time will be served on the 20th of next month. If I pass, which I trust I shall be able to do, my name having been mentioned in the public despatches will render it a point of no very great difficulty to obtain my commission at the request of my grandfather."

"Yes, your grandfather might succeed, I have no doubt; but I think you have little chance now in that quarter. My brother has a son, and we are thrown out. You are not aware, Peter, how selfish people are, and how little they will exert themselves for their relations. Your grandfather has never invited me since the announcement of my brother's increase to his family. Indeed, I have never been near him, for I know that it is of no use."

"I must think otherwise of Lord Privilege, my dear father, until your opinion is confirmed by his own conduct. That I am not so much an object of interest, I grant; but still he was very kind, and appeared to be partial to me."

"Well, well, you can try all you can, but you'll soon see of what stuff this world is made; I am sure I hope it will be so, for what is to become of you children if I die, I do not know;—I have saved little or nothing. And now all my prospects are blasted by this—" and my father dashed his fist upon the table in a manner by no means clerical, and with a look very unworthy of an apostle.

I am sorry that I must thus speak of my father, but I must not disguise the truth. Still, I must say, there was much in extenuation of his conduct. He had always a dislike to the profession of the church: his ambition, as a young man, had been to enter the army, for which service he was much better qualified; but, as it has been the custom for centuries to entail all the property of the aristocracy upon the eldest son, and leave the other brothers to be supported by the state, or rather by the people, who are taxed for their provision, my father was not permitted to follow the bent of his own inclination. An elder brother had already selected the army as his profession, and it was therefore decided that my father should enter the church; and thus it is that we have had, and still have, so many people in that profession, who are not only totally unfit for, but who actually disgrace, their calling. The law of primogeniture is beset with evils and injustice; yet without it, the aristocracy of a country must sink into insignificance. It appears to me, that as long as the people of a country are content to support the younger sons of the nobility, it is well that the aristocracy should be held up as a third estate, and a link between the sovereign and the people; but that if the people are either too poor, or are unwilling to be so taxed, they have a right to refuse taxation for such purposes, and to demand that the law of primogeniture should be abolished.

I remained at home until my time was complete, and then set off for Plymouth to undergo my examination. The passing-day had been fixed by the admiral for the Friday, and, as I arrived on Wednesday, I amused myself during the day, walking about the dockyard, and trying all I could to obtain further information in my profession. On the Thursday, a party of soldiers from the depôt were embarking at the landing-place in men-of-war boats, and, as I understood, were about to proceed to India. I witnessed the embarkation, and waited till they shoved off, and then walked to the anchor wharf to ascertain the weights of the respective anchors of the different classes of vessels in the King's service.

I had not been there long, when I was attracted by the squabbling created by a soldier, who, it appeared, had quitted the ranks to run up to the tap in the dockyard to obtain liquor. He was very drunk, and was followed by a young woman with a child in her arms, who was endeavouring to pacify him.

"Now be quiet, Patrick, jewel," said she, clinging to him; "sure it's enough that you've left the ranks, and will come to disgrace when you get on board. Now be quiet, Patrick, and let us ask for a boat, and then perhaps the officer will think it was all a mistake, and let you off aisy; and sure I'll speak to Mr O'Rourke, and he's a kind man."

"Out wid you, you cratur, it is Mr O'Rourke you'd be having a conversation wid, and he be chucking you under that chin of yours. Out wid you, Mary, and lave me to find my way on board. Is it a boat I want, when I can swim like St Patrick, wid my head under my arm, if it wasn't on my shoulders? At all events, I can wid my nappersack and musket to boot."

The young woman cried, and tried to restrain him, but he broke from her, and running down to the wharf, dashed off into the water. The young woman ran to the edge of the wharf, perceived him sinking, and shrieking with despair, threw up her arms in her agony. The child fell, struck on the edge of the piles, turned over, and before I could catch hold of it, sank into the sea. "The child! the child!" burst forth in another wild scream, and the poor creature lay at my feet in violent fits. I looked over, the child had disappeared; but the soldier was still struggling with his head above water. He sank and rose again—a boat was pulling towards him, but he was quite exhausted. He threw back his arms as if in despair, and was about disappearing under a wave, when, no longer able to restrain myself, I leaped off the high wharf, and swam to his assistance, just in time to lay hold of him as he was sinking for the last time. I had not been in the water a quarter of a minute before the boat came up to us, and dragged us on board. The soldier was exhausted and speechless. I, of course, was only very wet. The boat rowed to the landing-place at my request, and we were both put on shore. The knapsack which was fixed on the soldier's back, and his regimentals, indicated that he belonged to the regiment just embarked; and I stated my opinion that, as soon as he was a little recovered, he had better be taken on board. As the boat which picked us up was one of the men-of-war boats, the officer who had been embarking the troops, and had been sent on shore again to know if there were any yet left behind, consented. In a few minutes the soldier recovered, and was able to sit up and speak, and I only waited to ascertain the state of the poor young woman whom I had left on the wharf. In a few minutes she was led to us by the warder, and the scene between her and her husband was most affecting. When she had become a little composed, she turned round to me, where I stood dripping wet, and, intermingled with lamentation for the child, showering down emphatic blessings on my head, inquired my name. "Give it to me!" she cried; "give it to me on paper, in writing, that I may wear it next my heart, read and kiss it every day of my life, and never forget to pray for you, and to bless you!"

"I'll tell it you. My name—"

"Nay, write it down for me—write it down. Sure you'll not refuse me. All the saints bless you, dear young man, for saving a poor woman from despair!"

The officer commanding the boat handed me a pencil and a card; I wrote my name and gave it to the poor woman; she took my hand as I gave it, kissed the card repeatedly, and put it into her bosom. The officer, impatient to shove off, ordered her husband into the boat—she followed, clinging to him, wet as he was—the boat shoved off, and I hastened up to the inn to dry my clothes. I could not help observing, at the time, how the fear of a greater evil will absorb all consideration for a minor. Satisfied that her husband had not perished, she had hardly once appeared to remember that she had lost her child.

I had only brought one suit of clothes with me: they were in very good condition when I arrived, but salt water plays the devil with a uniform. I lay in bed until they were dry; but when I put them on again, not being before too large for me, for I grew very fast, they were now shrunk and shrivelled up, so as to be much too small. My wrists appeared below the sleeves of my coat—my trousers had shrunk half way up to my knees—the buttons were all tarnished, and altogether I certainly did not wear the appearance of a gentlemanly, smart midshipman. I would have ordered another suit, but the examination was to take place at ten o'clock the next morning, and there was no time. I was therefore obliged to appear as I was, on the quarter-deck of the line-of-battle ship, on board of which the passing was to take place. Many others were there to undergo the same ordeal, all strangers to me, and as I perceived by their nods and winks to each other, as they walked up and down in their smart clothes, not at all inclined to make my acquaintance.

There were many before me on the list, and our hearts beat every time that a name was called, and the owner of it walked aft into the cabin. Some returned with jocund faces, and our hopes mounted with the anticipation of similar good fortune; others came out melancholy and crest-fallen, and then the expression of their countenances was communicated to our own, and we quailed with fear and apprehension. I have no hesitation in asserting, that although "passing" may be a proof of being qualified, "not passing" is certainly no proof to the contrary. I have known many of the cleverest young men turned back (while others of inferior abilities have succeeded), merely from the feeling of awe occasioned by the peculiarity of the situation: and it is not to be wondered at, when it is considered that all the labour and exertion of six years are at stake at this appalling moment. At last my name was called, and almost breathless from anxiety, I entered the cabin, where I found myself in presence of the three captains who were to decide whether I were fit to hold a commission in his Majesty's service. My logs and certificates were examined and approved; my time calculated and allowed to be correct. The questions in navigation which were put to me were very few, for the best of all possible reasons, that most captains in his Majesty's service know little or nothing of navigation. During their servitude as midshipmen, they learn it by *rote*, without being aware of the principles upon which the calculations they use are founded. As lieutenants, their services as to navigation are seldom required, and they rapidly forget all about it. As captains, their whole remnant of mathematical knowledge consists in being able to set down the ship's position on the chart. As for navigating the ship, the master is answerable; and the captains not being responsible themselves, they trust entirely to his reckoning. Of course there are exceptions, but what I state is the fact; and if an order from the Admiralty was given, that all captains should pass again, although they might acquit themselves very well in seamanship, nineteen out of twenty would be turned back when they were questioned in navigation. It is from the knowledge of this fact that I think the service is injured by the present system, and the captain should be held *wholly* responsible for the navigation of his ship. It has been long known that the officers of every other maritime state are more scientific than our own, which is easily explained, from the responsibility not being invested in our captains. The origin of masters in our service is singular. When England first became a maritime power, ships for the King's service were found by the Cinque Ports and other parties—the fighting part of the crew was composed of soldiers sent on board. All the vessels at that time had a crew of sailors, with a master to navigate the vessel. During our bloody naval engagements with the Dutch, the same system was acted upon. I think it was the Earl of Sandwich, of whom it is stated, that his ship being in a sinking state, he took a boat to hoist his flag on board of another vessel in the fleet, but a shot cutting the boat in two, and the *weight of his armour* bearing him down, the Earl of Sandwich perished. But to proceed.

As soon as I had answered several questions satisfactorily, I was desired to stand up. The captain who had interrogated me on navigation, was very grave in his demeanour towards me, but at the same time not uncivil. During his examination, he was not interfered with by the other two, who only undertook the examination in "seamanship." The captain, who now desired me to stand up, spoke in a very harsh tone, and quite frightened me. I stood up pale and trembling, for I augured no good from this commencement. Several questions in seamanship were put to me, which I have no doubt I answered in a very lame way, for I cannot even now recollect what I said.

"I thought so," observed the captain; "I judged as much from your appearance. An officer who is so careless of his dress, as not even to put on a decent coat when he appears at his examination, generally turns out an idle fellow, and no seaman. One would think you had served all your time in a cutter, or a ten-gun brig, instead of dashing frigates. Come, sir, I'll give you one more chance."

I was so hurt at what the captain said, that I could not control my feelings. I replied, with a quivering lip, "that I had had no time to order another uniform,"—and I burst into tears.

"Indeed, Burrows, you are rather too harsh," said the third captain; "the lad is frightened. Let him sit down and compose himself for a little while. Sit down, Mr Simple, and we will try you again directly."

I sat down, checking my grief and trying to recall my scattered senses. The captains, in the meantime, turning over the logs to pass away the time; the one who had questioned me in navigation reading the Plymouth newspaper, which had a few minutes before been brought on board and sent into the cabin. "Heh! what's this? I say Burrows—Keats, look here," and he pointed to a paragraph. "Mr Simple, may I ask whether it was you who saved the soldier who leaped off the wharf yesterday?"

"Yes, sir," replied I; "and that's the reason why my uniforms are so shabby. I spoilt them then, and had no time to order others. I did not like to say why they were spoilt." I saw a change in the countenances of all the three, and it gave me courage. Indeed, now that my feelings had found vent, I was no longer under any apprehension.

"Come, Mr Simple, stand up again," said the captain, kindly, "that is, if you feel sufficiently composed; if not, we will wait a little longer. Don't be afraid, we *wish* to pass you."

I was not afraid, and stood up immediately. I answered every question satisfactorily; and finding that I did so, they put more difficult ones. "Very good, very good indeed, Mr Simple; now let me ask you one more; it's seldom done in the service, and perhaps you may not be able to answer it. Do you know how to *club-haul* a ship?"

"Yes, sir," replied I, having, as the reader may recollect, witnessed the manoeuvre when serving under poor Captain Savage, and I immediately stated how it was to be done.

"That is sufficient, Mr Simple. I wish to ask you no more questions. I thought at first you were a careless officer and no seaman: I now find that you are a good seaman and a gallant young man. Do you wish to ask any more questions?" continued he, turning to the two others.

They replied in the negative; my passing certificate was signed, and the captains did me the honour to shake hands with me, and wish me speedy promotion. Thus ended happily this severe trial to my poor nerves; and, as I came out of the cabin, no one could have imagined that I had been in such distress within, when they beheld the joy that irradiated my countenance.

—◦◦◦—

CHAPTER XXXIX

Is a chapter of plots—Catholic casuistry in a new cassock—Plotting promotes promotion—A peasant's love and a peer's peevishness—Prospects of prosperity.

AS SOON as I arrived at the hotel, I sent for a Plymouth paper, and cut out the paragraph which had been of such importance to me in my emergency, and the next morning returned home to receive the congratulations of my family. I found a letter from O'Brien, which had arrived the day before. It was as follows:—

"MY DEAR PETER,—Some people, they say, are lucky to 'have a father born before them,' because they are helped on in the world—upon which principle, mine was born *after* me, that's certain; however, that can't be helped. I found all my family well and hearty; but they all shook a cloth in the wind with respect to toggery. As for Father M'Grath's cassock, he didn't complain of it without reason. It was the ghost of a garment; but, however, with the blessing of God, my last quarterly bill, and the help of a tailor, we have had a regular refit, and the ancient family of the O'Briens of Ballyhinch are now rigged from stem to starn. My two sisters are both to be spliced to young squireens in the neighbourhood; it appears that they only wanted for a dacent town gown to go to the church in. They will be turned off next Friday, and I only wish, Peter, you were here to dance at the weddings. Never mind, I'll dance for you and for myself too. In the meantime, I'll just tell you what Father M'Grath and I have been doing, all about and consarning that thief of an uncle of yours.

"It's very little or nothing at all that Father M'Grath did before I came back, seeing as how Father O'Toole had a new cassock, and Father M'Grath's was so shabby that he couldn't face him under such a disadvantage; but still Father M'Grath spied about him, and had several hints from here and from there, all of which, when I came to add them up, amounted to just nothing at all.

"But since I came home, we have been busy. Father M'Grath went down to Ballycleuch, as bold as a lion in his new clothing, swearing that he'd lead Father O'Toole by the nose for slamming the door in his face, and so he would have done, if he could have found him; but as he wasn't to be found, Father M'Grath came back again just as wise, and quite as brave, as he went out.

"So, Peter, I just took a walk that way myself, and, as I surrounded the old house where your uncle had taken up his quarters, who should I meet but the little girl, Ella Flanagan, who was in his service; and I said to myself, 'There's two ways of obtaining things in this world, one is for love, and the other is for money.' The O'Briens are better off in the first article than in the last, as most of their countrymen are, so I've been spending it very freely in your service, Peter.

" 'Sure,' says I, 'you are the little girl that my eyes were ever looking upon when last I was in this way.'

" 'And who are you?' says she.

" 'Lieutenant O'Brien, of his Majesty's service, just come home for a minute to look out for a wife,' says I; 'and it's one about your make, and shape, and discretion that would please my fancy.'

"And then I praised her eyes, and her nose, and her forehead, and so downwards, until I came to the soles of her feet; and asked her leave to see her again, and when she would meet me in the wood and tell me her mind. At first, she thought (sure enough) that I couldn't be in earnest, but I swore by all the saints that she was the prettiest girl in the parts—and so she is altogether—and then she listened to my blarney. The devil a word did I say about your uncle, or your aunt, or Father M'Grath, that she might not suspect, for I've an idea that they're all in the story. I only talked about my love for her pretty self, and that blinded her, as it will all women, 'cute as they may be.

"And now, Peter, it's three weeks last Sunday, that I've been bespeaking this poor girl for your sake, and my conscience tells me that it's not right to make the poor crature fond of me, seeing as how that I don't care a fig for her in the way of a wife, and in any other way it would be the ruin of the poor thing. I have spoken to Father M'Grath on the subject, who says, 'that we may do evil that good may come, and that, if she has been a party to the deceit, it's nothing but proper that she should be punished in this world, and that will, perhaps, save her in the next'; still I don't like it, Peter, and it's only for you among the living that I'd do such a thing; for the poor creature now hangs upon me so fondly, and talks about the wedding-day; and tells me long stories about the connections which have taken place between the O'Flanagans and the O'Briens, times bygone, when they were all in their glory. yesterday, as we sat in the wood, with her arm round my waist, 'Ella, dear,' says I, 'who are these people that you stay with?' And then she told me all she knew about their history, and how Mary Sullivan was a nurse to the baby.

" 'And what is the baby?' says I.

" 'A boy, sure,' says she.

" 'And Sullivan's baby?'

" 'That's a girl.'

" 'And is Mary Sullivan there now?'

" 'No,' says she; 'it's yestreen she left with her husband and baby, to join the regiment that's going out to Ingy.'

" 'Yesterday she left?' says I, starting up.

" 'Yes,' replies she, 'and what do you care about them?'

" 'It's very much I care,' replied I, 'for a little bird has whispered a secret to me.'

" 'And what may that be?' says she.

" 'Only that the childer were changed, and you know it as well as I do.' But she swore that she knew nothing about it, and that she was not there when either of the children was born, and I believe that she told the truth. "Well,' says I, 'who tended the lady?'

" 'My own mother,' says Ella. 'And if it was so, who can know but she?'

"Then,' says I, 'Ella, jewel, I've made a vow that I'll never marry till I find out the truth of this matter; so the sooner you get it out of your mother the better.' Then she cried very much, and I was almost ready to cry too, to see how the poor thing was vexed at the idea of not being married. After a while, she swabbed up her cheeks, and kissing me, wished me good-bye, swearing by all the saints that the truth should come out, somehow or another.

"It's this morning that I saw her again, as agreed upon yesterday, and red her eyes were with weeping, poor thing; and she clung to me, and begged me to forgive her, and not to leave her; and then she told me that her mother was startled when she put the question to her, and chewed it, and cursed her when she insisted upon the truth; and how she had fallen on her knees, and begged her mother not to stand in the way of her happiness, as she would die if she did (I leave you to guess if my heart didn't smite me when she said that, Peter, but the mischief was done), and how her mother had talked about her oath and Father O'Toole, and said that she would speak to him.

"Now, Peter, I'm sure that the childer have been changed, and that the nurse has been sent to the Indies to be out of the way. They say they were to go to Plymouth. The husband's name is, of course, O'Sullivan; so I'd recommend you to take a coach and see what you can do in that quarter; in the meantime I'll try all I can for the truth in this, and will write again as soon as I can find out anything more. All I want to do is to get Father M'Grath to go to the old devil of a mother, and I'll answer for it, he'll frighten her into swearing any-thing. God bless you, Peter, and give my love to all the family.

"Yours ever,

"TERENCE O'BRIEN."

This letter of O'Brien was the subject of much meditation. The advice to go to Plymouth was too late, the troops having sailed some time; and I had no doubt but that Mary Sullivan and her husband were among those who had embarked at the time that I was at that port to pass my examination. Show the letter to my father I would not, as it would only have put him in a fever, and his interference would, in all probability, have done more harm than good. I therefore waited quietly for more intelligence, and resolved to apply to my grandfather to obtain my promotion.

A few days afterwards I set off for Eagle Park, and arrived about eleven o'clock in the morning. I sent in my name, and was admitted into the library, where I found Lord Privilege in his easy chair as usual.

"Well, child," said he, remaining on his chair, and not offering even *one* finger to me, "what do you want, that you come here without an invitation?"

"Only, my lord, to inquire after your health, and to thank you for your kindness to me in procuring me and Mr O'Brien the appoint-ment to a fine frigate."

"Yes," replied his lordship, "I recollect—I think I did so, at your request, and I think I heard someone say that you have behaved well, and had been mentioned in the despatches."

"Yes, my lord," replied I, "and I have since passed my examina-tion for lieutenant."

"Well, child, I'm glad to hear it. Remember me to your father and family." And his lordship cast his eyes down upon the book which he had been reading.

My father's observations appeared to be well grounded, but I would not leave the room until I had made some further attempt.

"Has your lordship heard from my uncle?"

"Yes," replied he, "I had a letter from him yesterday. The child is quite well. I expect them all here in a fortnight or three weeks, to live with me altogether. I am old—getting very old, and I shall have much to arrange with your uncle before I die."

"If I might request a favour of your lordship, it would be to beg that you would interest yourself a little in obtaining my promotion. A letter from your lordship to the First Lord—only a few lines—"

"Well, child, I see no objection—only—I am very old, too old to write now." And his lordship again commenced reading.

I must do Lord Privilege the justice to state that he evidently was fast verging to a state of second childhood. He was much bowed down since I had last seen him, and appeared infirm in body as well as mind.

I waited at least a quarter of an hour before his lordship looked up.

"What, not gone yet, child? I thought you had gone home."

"Your lordship was kind enough to say that you had no objection to write a few lines to the First Lord in my behalf. I trust your lordship will not refuse me."

"Well," replied he, peevishly, "so I did—but I am too old, too old to write—I cannot see—I can hardly hold a pen."

"Will your lordship allow me the honour of writing the letter for your lordship's signature?"

"Well, child—yes—I've no objection. Write as follows—no—write anything you please—and I'll sign it. I wish your uncle William were come."

This was more than I did. I had a great mind to show him O'Brien's letter, but I thought it would be cruel to raise doubts, and harass the mind of a person so close to the brink of the grave. The truth would never be ascertained during his life, I thought, and why, therefore, should I give him pain? At all events, although I had the letter in my pocket, I resolved not to make use of it except as a *dernier* resort.

I went to another table, and sat down to write the letter. As his lordship had said that I might write what I pleased, it occurred to me that I might assist O'Brien, and I felt sure that his lordship would not take the trouble to read the letter. I therefore wrote as follows, while Lord Privilege continued to read his book:—

"MY LORD,—You will confer a very great favour upon me, if you will hasten the commission which, I have no doubt, is in preparation for my nephew, Mr Simple, who has passed his examination, and has been mentioned in the public despatches, and also that you will not lose sight of Lieutenant O'Brien, who has so distinguished himself by his gallantry in the various cutting-out expeditions in the West Indies.* Trusting that your lordship will not fail to comply with my earnest request, I have the honour to be, your lordship's very obedient humble servant."

I brought this letter, with a pen full of ink, and the noise of my approach induced his lordship to look up. He stared at first, as having forgotten the whole circumstance—then said—"Oh yes! I recollect, so I did—give me the pen." With a trembling hand he signed his name, and gave me back the letter without reading it, as I expected.

"There, child, don't tease me any more. Good-bye; remember me to your father."

I wished his lordship a good morning, and went away well satisfied with the result of my expedition. On my arrival I showed the letter to my father, who was much surprised at my success, and he assured me that my grandfather's interest was so great with the administration, that I might consider my promotion as certain. That no accident might happen, I immediately set off for London, and delivered the letter at the door of the First Lord with my own hands, leaving my address with the porter.

———◦◈◦———

CHAPTER XL

O'Brien and myself take a step each, pari passu—*A family reunion productive of anything but unity—My uncle not always the best friend.*

A FEW DAYS AFTERWARDS I left my card with my address with the First Lord, and the next day received a letter from his secretary, which, to my delight, informed me that my commission had been made out some days before. I hardly need say that I has-

---

* *Nephew: Peter is actually Lord Privilege's grandson.*

tened to take it up, and when paying my fee to the clerk, I ventured, at a hazard, to inquire whether he knew the address of Lieutenant O'Brien.

"No," replied he, "I wish to find it out, for he has this day been promoted to the rank of Commander."

I almost leaped with joy when I heard this good news. I gave O'Brien's address to the clerk, hastened away with my invaluable piece of parchment in my hand, and set off immediately for my father's house.

But I was met with sorrow. My mother had been taken severely ill, and I found the house in commotion—doctors, and apothecaries, and nurses, running to and fro, my father in a state of excitement, and my dear sister in tears. Spasm succeeded spasm; and although every remedy was applied, the next evening she breathed her last. I will not attempt to describe the grief of my father, who appeared to feel remorse at his late unkind treatment of her, my sister, and myself. These scenes must be imagined by those who have suffered under similar bereavements. I exerted myself to console my poor sister, who appeared to cling to me as to her only support, and, after the funeral was over, we recovered our tranquillity, although the mourning was still deeper in our hearts than in our outward dress. I had written to O'Brien to announce the mournful intelligence, and, like a true friend, he immediately made his appearance to console me.

O'Brien had received the letter from the Admiralty, acquainting him with his promotion; and, two days after he arrived, went to take up his commission. I told him frankly by what means he had obtained it, and he again concluded his thanks by a reference to the mistake of the former supposition, that of my being "the fool of the family."

"By the powers, it would be well for any man if he had a few of such foolish friends about him," continued he; "but I won't blarney you, Peter; you know what my opinion always has been, so we'll say no more about it."

When he came back, we had a long consultation as to the best method of proceeding to obtain employment, for O'Brien was anxious to be again afloat, and so was I. I regretted parting with my sister, but my father was so morose and ill-tempered, that I had no pleasure at home, except in her company. Indeed, my sister was of opinion, that it would be better if I were away, as my father's misanthropy, now unchecked by my mother, appeared to have increased, and he seemed to view me with positive dislike. It was, therefore, agreed unanimously between my sister, and me, and O'Brien, who was always of our councils, that it would be advisable that I should be again afloat.

"I can manage him much better when alone, Peter; I shall have nothing to occupy me, and take me away from him, as your presence does now; and, painful as it is to part with you, my duty to my father, and my wish for your advancement, induce me to request that you will, if possible, find some means of obtaining employment."

"Spoken like a hero, as ye are, Miss Ellen, notwithstanding your pretty face and soft eyes," said O'Brien. "And now, Peter, for the means to bring it about. If I can get a ship, there is no fear for you, as I shall choose you for my lieutenant; but how is that to be managed? Do you think that you can come over the old gentleman at Eagle Park?"

"At all events, I'll try," replied I; "I can but be floored, O'Brien."

Accordingly, the next day I set off for my grandfather's, and was put down at the lodge, at the usual hour, about eleven o'clock. I walked up the avenue, and knocked at the door; when it was opened, I perceived a hesitation among the servants, and a constrained air, which I did not like. I inquired after Lord Privilege—the answer was, that he was pretty well, but did not see anybody.

"Is my uncle here?" said I.

"Yes, sir," replied the servant, with a significant look, "and all his family are here too."

"Are you sure that I cannot see my grandfather," said I, laying a stress upon the word.

"I will tell him that you are here, sir," replied the man, "but even that is against orders."

I had never seen my uncle since I was a child, and could not even recollect him—my cousins, or my aunt, I had never met with. In a minute an answer was brought, requesting that I would walk into the library. When I was ushered in, I found myself in the presence of Lord Privilege, who sat in his usual place, and a tall gentleman, whom I knew at once to be my uncle, from his likeness to my father.

"Here is the young gentleman, my lord," said my uncle, looking at me sternly.

"Heh! what—oh? I recollect. Well, child, so you've been behaving very ill—sorry to hear it. Good-bye."

"Behaving ill, my lord!" replied I. "I am not aware of having so done."

"Reports are certainly very much against you, nephew," observed my uncle, drily. "Some one has told your grandfather what has much displeased him. I know nothing about it myself."

"Then some rascal has slandered me, sir," replied I.

My uncle started at the word rascal; and then recovering himself, replied, "Well, nephew, what is it that you require of Lord Privilege, for I presume this visit is not without a cause?"

"Sir," replied I, "my visit to Lord Privilege was, first to thank him for having procured me my commission as lieutenant, and to request the favour that he would obtain me active employment, which a line from him will effect immediately."

"I was not aware, nephew, that you had been made lieutenant; but I agree with you, that the more you are at sea the better. His lordship shall sign the letter. Sit down."

"Shall I write it, sir?" said I to my uncle: "I know what to say."

"Yes; and bring it to me when it is written."

I felt convinced that the only reason which induced my uncle to obtain me employment was the idea that I should be better out of the way, and that there was more risk at sea than on shore. I took a sheet of paper, and wrote as follows:

"MY LORD,—May I request that your lordship will be pleased to appoint the bearer of this to a ship, as soon as convenient, as I wish him to be actively employed.

"I am, my lord, &c., &c."

"Why not mention your name?"

"It is of no consequence," replied I, "as it will be delivered in person, and that will insure my speedy appointment."

The letter was placed before his lordship for signature. It was with some difficulty that he was made to understand that he was to sign it. The old gentleman appeared much more imbecile than when

I last saw him. I thanked him, folded up the letter, and put it in my
pocket. At last he looked at me, and a sudden flash of recollection
appeared to come across his mind.

"Well, child—so you escaped from the French prison—heh! and
how's your friend—what is his name, heh?"

"O'Brien, my lord."

"O'Brien!" cried my uncle, "he is your friend; then, sir, I presume it is to you that I am indebted for all the inquiries and reports
which are so industriously circulated in Ireland—the tampering
with my servants—and other impertinences?"

I did not choose to deny the truth, although I was a little fluttered by the sudden manner in which it came to light. I replied, "I
never tamper with any people's servants, sir."

"No," said he, "but you employ others so to do. I discovered the
whole of your proceedings after the scoundrel left for England."

"If you apply the word scoundrel to Captain O'Brien, sir, in his
name I contradict it."

"As you please, sir," replied my uncle, in a passion; "but you
will oblige me by quitting this house immediately, and expect nothing more, either from the present or the future Lord Privilege, except
that retaliation which your infamous conduct has deserved."

I felt much irritated, and replied very sharply, "From the present
Lord Privilege I certainly expect nothing more, neither do I from his
successor; but after your death, uncle, I expect that the person who
succeeds to the title will do all he can for your humble servant. I
wish you a good morning, uncle."

My uncle's eyes flashed fire as I finished my speech, which indeed was a very bold, and a very foolish one too, as it afterwards
proved. I hastened out of the room, not only from the fear of being
turned out of the house before all the servants, but also from the
dread that my letter to the First Lord might be taken from me by
force; but I shall never forget the scowl of vengeance which crossed
my uncle's brows, as I turned round and looked at him as I shut the
door. I found my way out without the assistance of the servants,
and hastened home as fast as I could.

"O'Brien," said I, on my return, "there is no time to be lost; the
sooner you hasten to town with this letter of introduction, the better
it will be, for depend upon it my uncle will do me all the harm that
he can." I then repeated to him all that had passed, and it was

agreed that O'Brien should take the letter, which, having reference to the bearer, would do as well for him as for me; and, if O'Brien obtained an appointment, I was sure not only of being one of his lieutenants, but also of sailing with a dear friend. The next morning O'Brien set off for London, and fortunately saw the First Lord the day after his arrival, which was a levee day. The First Lord received the letter from O'Brien, and requested him to sit down. He then read it, inquired after his lordship, asked whether his health was good, &c.

O'Brien replied, "that with the blessing of God, his lordship might live many years: that he had never heard him complain of ill health." All which was not false, if not true. I could not help observing to O'Brien, when he returned home and told me what had passed, "that I thought, considering what he had expressed with respect to white lies and black lies, that he had not latterly adhered to his own creed."

"That's very true, Peter; and I've thought of it myself, but it is my creed nevertheless. We all know what's right, but we don't always follow it. The fact is, I begin to think that it is absolutely necessary to fight the world with its own weapons. I spoke to Father M'Grath on the subject, and he replied—'That if anyone, by doing wrong, necessitated another to do wrong to circumvent him, that the first party was answerable, not only for his own sin, but also for the sin committed in self-defence.'"

"But, O'Brien, I do not fix my faith so implicitly upon Father M'Grath; and I do not much admire many of his directions.'"

"No more do I, Peter, when I think upon them; but how am I to puzzle my head upon these points? All I know is, that when you are divided between your inclination and your duty, it's mighty convenient to have a priest like Father M'Grath to decide for you, and to look after your soul into the bargain."

It occurred to me that I myself, when finding fault with O'Brien, had, in the instance of both the letters from Lord Privilege, been also guilty of deceit. I was therefore blaming him for the same fault committed by myself; and I am afraid that I was too ready in consoling myself with Father M'Grath's maxim, "that one might do evil that good might come." But to return to O'Brien's interview.

After some little conversation, the First Lord said, "Captain O'Brien, I am always very ready to oblige Lord Privilege, and the more so as his recommendation is of an officer of your merit. In a day or two, if you call at the Admiralty, you will hear further." O'Brien wrote to us immediately, and we waited with impatience for his next letter: but, instead of the letter, he made his appearance on the third day, and first hugged me in his arms, he then came to my sister, embraced her, and skipped and danced about the room.

"What is the matter, O'Brien?" said I, while Ellen retreated in confusion.

O'Brien pulled a parchment out of his pocket. "Here, Peter, my dear Peter; now for honour and glory. An eighteen-gun brig, Peter. The *Rattlesnake*—Captain O'Brien—West India station. By the holy father! my heart's bursting with joy!" and down he sank into an easy chair. "A'n't I almost beside myself?" inquired he, after a short pause.

"Ellen thinks so, I dare say," replied I, looking at my sister, who stood in the corner of the room, thinking O'Brien was really out of his senses, and still red with confusion.

O'Brien, who then called to mind what a slip of decorum he had been guilty of, immediately rose, and resuming his usual unsophisticated politeness, as he walked up to my sister, took her hand, and said, "Excuse me, my dear Miss Ellen; I must apologize for my rudeness; but my delight was so great, and my gratitude to your brother so intense, that I am afraid that in my warmth I allowed the expression of my feelings to extend to one so dear to him, and so like him in person and in mind. Will you only consider that you received the overflowings of a grateful heart towards your brother, and for his sake pardon my indiscretion?"

Ellen smiled, and held out her hand to O'Brien, who led her to the sofa, where we all three sat down: and he then commenced a more intelligible narrative of what had passed. He had called on the day appointed, and sent up his card. The First Lord could not see him, but referred him to the private secretary, who presented him with his commission to the *Rattlesnake*, eighteen-gun brig. The secretary smiled most graciously, and told O'Brien in confidence that he would proceed to the West India station as soon as his vessel was manned and ready for sea. He inquired of O'Brien whom he wished as his first lieutenant. O'Brien replied that he wished for me; but as, in all probability, I should not be of sufficient standing to be first lieutenant, that the Admiralty might appoint any other to the duty,

CHAPTER XL *301*

provided I joined the ship. The secretary made a minute of O'Brien's wish, and requested him, if he had a vacancy to spare as midshipman, to allow him to send one on board; to which O'Brien willingly acceded, shook hands with him, and O'Brien quitted the Admiralty to hasten down to us with the pleasing intelligence.

"And now," said O'Brien, "I have made up my mind how to proceed. I shall first run down to Plymouth and hoist my pennant; then I shall ask for a fortnight's leave, and go to Ireland to see how they get on, and what Father M'Grath may be about. So, Peter, let's pass this evening as happily as we can; for though you and I shall soon meet again, yet it may be years, or perhaps never, that we three shall sit down on the same sofa as we do now."

Ellen, who was still nervous, from the late death of my mother, looked down, and I perceived the tears start in her eyes at the remark of O'Brien, that perhaps we should never meet again. And I did pass a happy evening. I had a dear sister on one side of me, and a sincere friend on the other. How few situations more enviable!

O'Brien left us early the next morning; and at breakfasttime a letter was handed to my father. It was from my uncle, coldly communicating to him that Lord Privilege had died the night before, very suddenly, and informing him that the burial would take place on that day week, and that the will would be opened immediately after the funeral. My father handed the letter over to me without saying a word, and sipped his tea with his tea-spoon. I cannot say that I felt very much on the occasion; but I did feel, because he had been kind to me at one time: as for my father's feelings, I could not—or rather I should say, I did not wish to analyse them. As soon as he had finished his cup of tea, he left the breakfast-table, and went into his study. I then communicated the intelligence to my sister Ellen.

"My God!" said she, after a pause, putting her hand up to her eyes; "what a strange unnatural state of society must we have arrived at, when my father can thus receive the intelligence of a parent's death! Is it not dreadful?"

"It is, my dearest girl," replied I; "but every feeling has been sacrificed to worldly considerations and an empty name. The younger sons have been neglected, if not deserted. Virtue, talent, everything set at naught—intrinsic value despised—and the only claim to consideration admitted, that of being the heir entail. When

all the ties of nature are cast loose by the parents, can you be surprised if the children are no longer bound by them? Most truly do
you observe, that it is a detestable state of society."

"I did not say detestable, brother; I said strange and unnatural."

"Had you said what I said, Ellen, you would not have been
wrong. I would not for the title and wealth which it brings, be the
heartless, isolated, I may say neglected being that my grandfather
was; were it offered now, I would not barter for it Ellen's love."

Ellen threw herself in my arms; we then walked into the garden,
where we had a long conversation relative to our future wishes,
hopes, and prospects.

CHAPTER XLI

*Pompous obsequies—The reading of the will, not exactly after Wilkie—I am left a leg-
acy—What becomes of it—My father, very warm, writes a sermon to cool himself—I join
O'Brien's brig, and fall in with Swinburne.*

O N THAT DAY WEEK I accompanied my father to Eagle Park,
to assist at the burial of Lord Privilege. We were ushered into
the room where the body had lain in state for three days. The black
hangings, the lofty plumes, the rich ornaments on the coffin, and the
number of wax candles with which the room was lighted, produced
a solemn and grand effect. I could not help, as I leaned against the
balustrade before the coffin and thought of its contents, calling to
mind when my poor grandfather's feelings seemed, as it were, inclined to thaw in my favour, when he called me "his child," and, in
all probability, had not my uncle had a son, would have died in my
arms, fond and attached to me for my own sake, independently of
worldly considerations. I felt that had I known him longer, I could
have loved him, and that he would have loved me; and I thought to
myself, how little all these empty honours, after his decease, could
compensate for the loss of those reciprocal feelings, which would
have so added to his happiness during his existence. But he had
lived for pomp and vanity; and pomp and vanity attended him to
his grave. I thought of my sister Ellen, and of O'Brien, and walked

away with the conviction that Peter Simple might have been an object of envy to the late Right Honourable Lord Viscount Privilege, Baron Corston, Lord Lieutenant of the county, and one of His Majesty's Most Honourable Privy Councillors.

When the funeral, which was very tedious and very splendid, was over, we all returned in the carriages to Eagle Park, when my uncle, who had of course assumed the title, and who had attended as chief mourner, was in waiting to receive us. We were shown into the library, and in the chair so lately and constantly occupied by my grandfather, sat the new lord. Near to him were the lawyers, with parchments lying before them. As we severally entered, he waved his hand to unoccupied chairs, intimating to us to sit down; but no words were exchanged, except an occasional whisper between him and the lawyers. When all the branches of the family were present, down to the fourth and fifth cousins, the lawyer on the right of my uncle put on his spectacles, and unrolling the parchment commenced reading the will. I paid attention to it at first; but the legal technicalities puzzled me, and I was soon thinking of other matters, until after half an hour's reading, I was startled at the sound of my own name. It was a bequest by codicil to me, of the sum of ten thousand pounds. My father who sat by me, gave me a slight push, to attract my attention; and I perceived that his face was not quite so mournful as before. I was rejoicing at this unexpected intelligence. I called to mind what my father had said to me when we were returning from Eagle Park, "that my grandfather's attentions to me were as good as ten thousand pounds in his will," and was reflecting how strange it was that he had hit upon the exact sum. I also thought of what my father had said of his own affairs, and his not having saved anything for his children, and congratulated myself that I should now be able to support my dear sister Ellen, in case of any accident happening to my father, when I was roused by another mention of my name. It was a codicil dated about a week back, in which my grandfather, not pleased at my conduct, revoked the former codicil, and left me nothing. I knew where the blow came from, and I looked my uncle in the face; a gleam of malignant pleasure was in his eyes, which had been fixed on me, waiting to receive my glance. I returned it with a smile expressive of scorn and contempt, and then looked at my father, who appeared to be in a state of misery. His head had fallen upon his breast, and his hands were clasped. Although I was shocked at the blow, for I knew how much the money was required, I felt too proud to show it; indeed, I felt that I would not for worlds have exchanged situations with my uncle, much less feelings; for when those who remain meet to ascertain the disposition made, by one who is summoned away to the tribunal of his Maker, of those worldly and perishable things which he must leave behind him, feelings of rancour and ill-will might, for the time, be permitted to subside, and the memory of a "departed brother" be productive of charity and good-will. After a little reflection, I felt that I could forgive my uncle.

Not so my father; the codicil which deprived me of my inheritance, was the last of the will, and the lawyer rolled up the parchment and took off his spectacles. Everybody rose; my father seized his hat, and telling me in a harsh voice to follow him, tore off the crape weepers, and then threw them on the floor as he walked away. I also took off mine, and laid them on the table, and followed him. My father called his carriage, waited in the hall till it was driven up, and jumped into it. I followed him; he drew up the blind, and desired them to drive home.

"Not a sixpence! By the God of heaven, not a sixpence! My name not even mentioned, except for a paltry mourning ring! And yours—pray sir, what have you been about, after having such a sum left you, to forfeit your grandfather's good opinion? Heh! sir—tell me directly," continued he, turning round to me in a rage.

"Nothing, my dear father, that I'm aware of. My uncle is evidently my enemy."

"And why should he be particularly your enemy? Peter, there must be some reason for his having induced your grandfather to alter his bequest in your favour. I insist upon it, sir, that you tell me immediately."

"My dear father, when you are more calm, I will talk this matter over with you. I hope I shall not be considered wanting in respect, when I say, that as a clergyman of the church of England—"

"D——n the church of England, and those that put me into it!" replied my father, maddened with rage.

I was shocked, and held my tongue. My father appeared also to be confused at his hasty expressions. He sank back in his carriage, and preserved a gloomy silence until we arrived at our own door. As soon as we entered, my father hastened to his own room, and I went up to my sister Ellen, who was in her bed-room. I revealed to her all that had passed, and advised with her on the propriety of my communicating to my father the reasons which had occasioned my uncle's extreme aversion towards me. After much argument, she agreed with me, that the disclosure had now become necessary.

After the dinner-cloth had been removed, I then communicated to my father the circumstances which had come to our knowledge relative to my uncle's establishment in Ireland. He heard me very attentively, took out tablets, and made notes.

"Well, Peter," said he, after a few minutes' silence, when I had finished, "I see clearly through this whole business. I have no doubt but that a child has been substituted to defraud you and me of our just inheritance of the title and estates; but I will now set to work and try if I cannot find out the secret; and, with the help of Captain O'Brien and Father M'Grath, I think it is not at all impossible."

"O'Brien will do all that he can, sir," replied I; "and I expect soon to hear from him. He must have now been a week in Ireland."

"I shall go there myself," replied my father; "and there are no means that I will not resort to, to discover this infamous plot. "No," exclaimed he, striking his fist on the table, so as to shiver two of the wine-glasses into fragments, "no means but I will resort to."

"That is," replied I, "my dear father, no means which may be legitimately employed by one of your profession."

"I tell you, no means that can be used by *man* to recover his defrauded rights! Tell me not of legitimate means, when I am to lose a title and property by a spurious and illegitimate substitution! By the God of Heaven, I will meet them with fraud for fraud, with false swearing for false swearing, and with blood for blood, if it should be necessary! My brother has dissolved all ties, and I will have my right, even if I demand it with a pistol at his ear."

"For Heaven's sake, my dear father, do not be so violent—recollect your profession."

"I do," replied he, bitterly; "and how I was forced into it against my will. I recollect my father's words, the solemn coolness with which he told me, 'I had my choice of the church, or—to starve.' But I have my sermon to prepare for to-morrow, and I can sit here no longer. Tell Ellen to send me in some tea."

I did not think my father was in a very fit state of mind to write a sermon, but I held my tongue. My sister joined me, and we saw no

more of him till breakfast the next day. Before we met, I received a
letter from O'Brien.

"MY DEAR PETER,—I ran down to Plymouth, hoisted my pennant,
drew my jollies from the dockyard, and set my first lieutenant to
work getting in the ballast and water-tanks. I then set off for Ireland,
and was very well received as Captain O'Brien by my family, who
were all flourishing. Now that my two sisters are so well married
off, my father and mother are very comfortable, but rather lonely;
for I believe I told you long before, that it had pleased Heaven to
take all the rest of my brothers and sisters, except the two now
married, and one who bore up for a nunnery, dedicating her service
to God, after she was scarred with the small-pox, and no man would
look at her. Ever since the family have been grown up, my father
and mother have been lamenting and sorrowing that none of them
would go off; and now that they're all gone off one way or another,
they cry all day because they are left all alone, with no one to keep
company with them, except Father M'Grath and the pigs. We never
are to be contented in this world, that's sartain; and now that they
are comfortable in every respect, they find that they are very uncomfortable, and having obtained all their wishes, they wish everything
back again; but as old Maddocks used to say, 'A good growl is
better than a bad dinner' with some people; and the greatest pleasure that they now have is to grumble; and if that makes them
happy, they must be happy all day long—for the devil a bit do they
leave off from morning till night.

"The first thing that I did was to send for Father M'Grath, who
had been more away from home than usual—I presume, not finding
things quite so comfortable as they used to be. He told me that he
had met with Father O'Toole, and had a bit of a dialogue with him,
which had ended in a bit of a row, and that he had cudgelled Father
O'Toole well, and tore his gown off his back, and then tore it into
shivers—that Father O'Toole had referred the case to the bishop,
and that was how the matter stood just then. 'But,' says he, 'the
spalpeen has left this part of the country, and, what is more, has
taken Ella and her mother with him; and what is still worse, no one
could find out where they were gone; but it was believed that they
had all been sent over the water.' So you see, Peter, that this is a bad

job in one point, which is, that we have no chance of getting the truth out of the old woman; for now that we have war with France, who is to follow them? On the other hand, it is good news; for it prevents me from decoying that poor young girl, and making her believe what will never come to pass; and I am not a little glad on that score, for Father M'Grath was told by those who were about her, that she did nothing but weep and moan for two days before she went away, scolded as she was by her mother, and threatened by that blackguard O'Toole. It appears to me, that all our hopes now are in finding out the soldier, and his wife the wet-nurse, who were sent to India—no doubt with the hope that the climate and the fevers may carry them off. That uncle of yours is a great blackguard, every bit of him. I shall leave here in three days, and you must join me at Plymouth. Make my compliments to your father, and my regards to your sister, whom may all the saints preserve! God bless her, for ever and ever. Amen.

"Yours ever,
"TERENCE O'BRIEN."

I put this letter into my father's hands when he came out of his room. "This is a deep-laid plot," said he, "and I think we must immediately do as O'Brien states—look after the nurse who was sent to India. Do you know the regiment to which her husband belongs?"

"Yes, sir," replied I; "it is the 33rd, and she sailed for India about three months back."

"The name, you say, I think, is O'Sullivan," said he, pulling out his tablets. "Well, I will write immediately to Captain Fielding, and beg him to make the minutest inquiries. I will also write to your sister Lucy, for women are much keener than men in affairs of this sort. If the regiment is ordered to Ceylon, all the better: if not, he must obtain furlough to prosecute his inquiries. When that is done, I will go myself to Ireland, and try if we cannot trace the other parties."

My father then left the room, and I retired with Ellen to make preparations for joining my ship at Plymouth. A letter announcing my appointment had come down, and I had written to request my commission to be forwarded to the clerk of the cheque at Plymouth, that I might save a useless journey to London. On the following day I parted with my father and my dear sister, and, without any adventure, arrived at Plymouth Dock, where I met with O'Brien. The same day I reported myself to the admiral, and joined my brig, which was lying alongside the hulk with her topmasts pointed through. Returning from the brig, as I was walking up Fore Street, I observed a fine stout sailor, whose back was turned to me, reading the handbill which had been posted up everywhere announcing that the *Rattlesnake*, Captain O'Brien (about to proceed to the West India station, where *doubloons* were so plentiful that dollars were only used for ballast), was in want of a *few* stout hands. It might have been said, of a great many: for we had not entered six men, and were doing all the work with the marines and riggers of the dockyard; but it is not the custom to show your poverty in this world either with regard to men or money. I stopped, and overheard him say, "Ay, as for the doubloons, that cock won't fight. I've served long enough in the West Indies not to be humbugged; but I wonder whether Captain O'Brien was the second lieutenant of the *Sanglier*. If so, I shouldn't mind trying a cruise with him." I thought that I recollected the voice, and touching him on the shoulder, he turned round, and it proved to be Swinburne. "What, Swinburne!" said I, shaking him by the hand, for I was delighted to see him, "is it you?"

"Why, Mr Simple! Well, then, I expect that I'm right, and that Mr O'Brien is made, and commands this craft. When you meet the pilot-fish, the shark arn't far off, you know."

"You're very right, Swinburne," said I, "in all except calling Captain O'Brien a shark. He's no shark."

"No, that he arn't, except in one way; that is, that I expect he'll soon show his teeth to the Frenchmen. But I beg your pardon, sir"; and Swinburne took off his hat.

"O! I understand; you did not perceive before that I had shipped the swab. Yes, I'm lieutenant of the *Rattlesnake*, Swinburne, and hope you'll join us."

"There's my hand upon it, Mr Simple," said he, smacking his great fist into mine so as to make it tingle. "I'm content if I know that the captain's a good officer; but when there's two, I think myself lucky. I'll just take a boat, and put my name on the books, and then I'll be on shore again to spend the rest of my money, and try if I can't pick up a few hands as volunteers, for I know where they all be stowed away. I was looking at the craft this morning, and rather took a fancy to her. She has a d——d pretty run; but I hope Captain O'Brien will take off her fiddle-head, and get one carved: I never knew a vessel do much with a *fiddle*-head."

"I rather think that Captain O'Brien has already applied to the Commissioner on the subject," replied I; "at all events, it won't be very difficult to make the alteration ourselves."

"To be sure not," replied Swinburne; "a coil of four-inch will make the body of the snake; I can carve out the head; and as for a *rattle*, I be blessed if I don't rob one of those beggars of watchmen this very night. So good-bye, Mr Simple, till we meet again."

Swinburne kept his word; he joined the ship that afternoon, and the next day came off with six good hands, who had been induced from his representations to join the brig. "Tell Captain O'Brien," said he to me, "not to be in too great a hurry to man his ship. I know where there are plenty to be had; but I'll try fair means first." This he did, and every day, almost, he brought off a man, and all he did bring off were good able seamen. Others volunteered, and we were now more than half-manned, and ready for sea. The admiral then gave us permission to send pressgangs on shore.

"Mr Simple," said Swinburne, "I've tried all I can to persuade a lot of fine chaps to enter, but they won't. Now I'm resolved that my brig shall be well manned; and if they don't know what's good for them, I do, and I'm sure that they will thank me for it afterwards; so I'm determined to take every mother's son of them."

The same night we mustered all Swinburne's men and went on shore to a crimp's house which they knew, surrounded it with our marines in blue jackets, and took out of it twenty-three fine able seamen, which nearly filled up our complement.* The remainder we obtained by a draft from the admiral's ship; and I do not believe that there was a vessel that left Plymouth harbour and anchored in the Sound, better manned than the *Rattlesnake*. So much for good character, which is never lost upon seamen. O'Brien was universally liked by those who had sailed with him, and Swinburne, who knew him well, persuaded many, and forced the others, to enter with him, whether they liked it or not. This they in the event did, and, with the

* A crimp's house: A crimp was a person who would obtain "recruits" for the service, often by trickery.

exception of those drafted from the flag-ship, we had no desertions. Indeed, none deserted whom we would have wished to retain, and their vacancies were soon filled up with better men.

——◦◦◦◦——

CHAPTER XLII

We sail for the West Indies—A volunteer for the ship refused and set on shore again, for reasons which the chapter will satisfactorily explain to the reader.

W E WERE VERY GLAD when the master-attendant came on board to take us into the Sound; and still more glad to perceive that the brig, which had just been launched before O'Brien was appointed to her, appeared to sail very fast as she ran out. So it proved after we went to sea; she sailed wonderfully well, beating every vessel that she met, and overhauling in a very short time everything that we chased; turning to windward like magic, and tacking in a moment. Three days after we anchored in the Sound the ship's company were paid, and our sailing orders came down to proceed with despatches, by next evening's post, to the island of Jamaica. We started with a fair wind, and were soon clear of the channel. Our whole time was now occupied in training our new ship's company at the guns, and learning them to *pull together*; and by the time that we had run down the trades, we were in a very fair state of discipline.

The first lieutenant was rather an odd character; his brother was a sporting man of large property, and he had contracted, from his example, a great partiality for such pursuits. He knew the winning horses of the Derby and the Oaks for twenty years back, was an adept at all athletic exercises, a capital shot, and had his pointer on board. In other respects, he was a great dandy in his person, always wore gloves, even on service, very gentlemanlike and handsome, and not a very bad sailor; that is, he knew enough to carry on his duty very creditably, and evidently, now that he was the first lieutenant, and obliged to work, learnt more of his duty every day. I never met a more pleasant messmate or a more honourable young man. A brig is only allowed two lieutenants. The master was a rough, kind-hearted, intelligent young man, always in good humour. The surgeon and purser completed our mess; they were men of no character at all, except, perhaps, that the surgeon was too much of a courtier, and the purser too much of a skin-flint; but pursers are, generally speaking, more sinned against than sinning.

But I have been led away, while talking of the brig and the officers, and had almost forgotten to narrate a circumstance which occurred two days before we sailed. I was with O'Brien in the cabin, when Mr Osbaldistone, the first lieutenant, came in, and reported that a boy had come on board to volunteer for the ship.

"What sort of a lad is he?" said O'Brien.

"A very nice lad—very slight, sir," replied the first lieutenant. "We have two vacancies."

"Well, see what you make of him; and if you think he will do, you may put him on the books."

"I have tried him, sir. He says that he has been a short time at sea. I made him mount the main-rigging, but he did not much like it."

"Well, do as you please, Osbaldistone," replied O'Brien; and the first lieutenant quitted the cabin.

In about a quarter of an hour he returned. "If you please, sir," said he, laughing, "I sent the boy down to the surgeon to be examined, and he refused to strip. The surgeon says that he thinks she is a woman. I have had her up on the quarter-deck, and she refuses to answer any questions, and requires to speak with you."

"With me!" said O'Brien, with surprise. "O! one of the men's wives, I suppose, trying to steal a march upon us. Well, send her down here, Osbaldistone, and I'll prove to her the moral impossibility of her sailing in his Majesty's brig *Rattlesnake*."

In a few minutes the first lieutenant sent her down to the cabin door, and I was about to retire as she entered; but O'Brien stopped me. "Stay, Peter: my reputation will be at stake if I'm left all alone," said he, laughing.

The sentry opened the door, and whether boy or girl, a more interesting face I never beheld; the hair was cut close, and I could not tell whether the surgeon's suspicions were correct.

"You wish to speak—holy St Patrick!" cried O'Brien, looking earnestly at her features; and O'Brien covered his face and bent over the table, exclaiming, "My God, my God!"

In the meantime the colour of the young person fled from her countenance, and then rushed into it again, alternately leaving it pale and suffused with blushes. I perceived a trembling over the frame, the knees shook and knocked together, and had I not hastened, she—for a female it was—would have fallen on the deck. I perceived that she had fainted; I therefore laid her down on the deck, and hastened to obtain some water. O'Brien ran up and went to her.

"My poor, poor girl!" said he, sorrowfully. "O! Peter, this is all your fault."

"All my fault! how could she have come here?"

"By all the saints who pray for us—dearly as I prize them, I would give up my ship and my commission, that this could be undone."

As O'Brien hung over her, the tears from his eyes fell upon her face, while I bathed it with the water I had brought from the dressing-room. I knew who it must be, although I had never seen her. It was the girl to whom O'Brien had professed love, to worm out the secret of the exchange of my uncle's child; and as I beheld the scene I could not help saying to myself, "Who now will assert that evil may be done that good may come?" The poor girl showed symptoms of recovering, and O'Brien waved his hand to me, saying, "Leave us, Peter, and see that no one comes in."

I remained nearly an hour at the cabin-door, by the sentry, and prevented many from entering, when O'Brien opened the door, and requested me to order his gig to be manned and then to come in. The poor girl had evidently been weeping bitterly, and O'Brien was much affected.

"All is arranged, Peter; you must go on shore with her, and not leave her till you see her safe off by the night coach. Do me that favour, Peter—you ought indeed," continued he, in a low voice, "for you have been partly the occasion of this."

I shook O'Brien's hand and made no answer—the boat was reported ready, and the girl followed me with a firm step. I pulled on shore, saw her safe in the coach without asking her any question, and then returned on board.

"Come on board, sir," said I, entering the cabin with my hat in my hand, and reporting myself according to the regulations of the service.

"Thank you," replied O'Brien: "shut the door, Peter. Tell me, how did she behave? What did she say?"

"She never spoke, and I never asked her a question. She seemed to be willing to do as you had arranged."

"Sit down, Peter. I never felt more unhappy, or more disgusted with myself in all my life. I feel as if I never could be happy again. A sailor's life mixes him up with the worst part of the female sex, and we do not know the real value of the better. I little thought when I was talking nonsense to that poor girl, that I was breaking one of the kindest hearts in the world, and sacrificing the happiness of one who would lay down her existence for me, Peter. Since you have been gone, it's twenty times that I've looked in the glass just to see whether I don't look like a villain. But, by the blood of St Patrick! I thought woman's love was just like our own, and that a three months' cruise would set all to rights again."

"I thought she had gone over to France."

"So did I; but now she has told me all about it. Father M'Dermot and her mother brought her down to the coast near here to embark in a smuggling boat for Dieppe.* When the boat pulled in-shore in the night to take them in, the mother and the rascally priest got in, but she felt as if it was leaving the whole world to leave the country I was in, and she held back. The officers came down, one or two pistols were fired, and the boat shoved off without her, and she, with their luggage, was left on the beach. She went back to the next town with the officers, where she told the truth of the story, and they let her go. In Father M'Dermot's luggage she found letters, which she read, and found out that she and her mother were to have been placed in a convent at Dieppe; and, as the convent was named in the letters,—which she says are very important, but I have not had courage to read them yet,— she went to the people from whose house they had embarked, requesting them to forward the luggage and a letter to her mother—sending everything but the letters, which she reserved for me. She has since received a letter from her mother, telling her that she is safe and well in the convent, and begging her to come over to her as soon as possible. The mother

* *Father M'Dermot: Apparently, Marryat forgot his character's name. M'Dermot is the priest formerly called Father O'Toole.*

took the vows a week after she arrived there, so we know where to find her, Peter."

"And where is the poor girl going to stay now, O'Brien?"

"That's all the worst part of it. It appears that she hoped not to be found out till after we had sailed, and then to have, as she said, poor thing! to have laid at my feet and watched over me in the storms; but I pointed out to her that it was not permitted, and that I would not be allowed to marry her. O Peter! this is a very sad business," continued O'Brien, passing his hand across his eyes.

"Well, but, O'Brien, what is to become of the poor girl?"

"She is going home to be with my father and mother, hoping one day that I shall come back and marry her. I have written to Father M'Grath, to see what he can do."

"Have you then not undeceived her?"

"Father M'Grath must do that, I could not. It would have been the death of her. It would have stabbed her to the heart, and it's not for me to give that blow. I'd sooner have died—sooner have married her, than have done it, Peter. Perhaps when I'm far away she'll bear it better. Father M'Grath will manage it."

"O'Brien, I don't like that Father M'Grath."

"Well, Peter, you may be right; I don't exactly like all he says myself; but what is a man to do?—either he is a Catholic, and believes as a Catholic, or he is not one. Will I abandon my religion, now that it is persecuted? Never, Peter: I hope not, without I find a much better, at all events. Still I do not like to feel that this advice of my confessor is at variance with my own conscience. Father M'Grath is a worldly man; but that only proves that he is wrong, not that our religion is—and I don't mind speaking to you on this subject. No one knows that I'm a Catholic except yourself: and at the Admiralty they never asked me to take that oath which I never would have taken, although Father M'Grath says I may take any oath I please with what he calls heretics, and he will grant me absolution. Peter, my dear fellow, say no more about it."

I did not; but I may as well end the history of poor Ella Flanagan at once, as she will not appear again. About three months afterwards, we received a letter from Father M'Grath, stating that the girl had arrived safe, and had been a great comfort to O'Brien's father and mother, who wished her to remain with them altogether; that Father M'Grath, had told her that when a man took his commission as captain it was all the same as going into a monastery as a monk, for he never could marry. The poor girl believed him, and thinking that O'Brien was lost to her for ever, with the advice of Father M'Grath, had entered as a nun in one of the religious houses in Ireland, that, as she said, she might pray for him night and day. Many years afterwards, we heard of her—she was well, and not unhappy; but O'Brien never forgot his behaviour to this poor girl. It was a source of continual regret; and I believe, until the last day of his existence, his heart smote him for his inconsiderate conduct towards her. But I must leave this distressing topic, and return to the *Rattlesnake*, which had now arrived at the West Indies, and joined the Admiral at Jamaica.

CHAPTER XLIII

Description of the Coast of Martinique—Popped at for peeping—No heroism in making oneself a target—Board a miniature Noah's Ark, under Yankee colours—Capture a French slaver—Parrot soup in lieu of mock turtle.

WE FOUND ORDERS at Barbadoes to cruise off Martinique, to prevent supplies being furnished to the garrison of the island, and we proceeded there immediately. I do not know anything more picturesque than running down the east side of this beautiful island—the ridges of hill spreading down to the water's edge, covered with the freshest verdure, divided at the base by small bays, with the beach of dazzling white sand, and where the little coasting vessels employed to bring the sugar from the neighbouring estates were riding at anchor. Each hill, at its ajutment towards the sea, crowned with a fort, on which waved the tricolour—certainly, in appearance, one of the most war-like flags in the world.

On the third morning we had rounded the Diamond Rock, and were scudding along the lee-side of the island just opening Fort Royal bay, when hauling rather too close round its eastern entrance, formed by a promontory called Solomon's Point, which was covered with brushwood, we found ourselves nearer than agreeable to a newly constructed battery. A column of smoke was poured along the blue water, and it was followed by the whizzing of a shot, which passed through our boom mainsail, first cutting away the dog-vane, which was close to old Swinburne's head, as he stood on the carronade, conning the brig. I was at dinner in the cabin with O'Brien and the first lieutenant.

"Where the devil have they got the brig now?" said O'Brien, rising from his chair, and going on deck.

We both followed; but before we were on deck, three or four more shot passed between the masts. "If you please, sir," said the master's mate in charge of the deck, whose name was O'Farrell, "the battery has opened upon us."

"Thank you very much for your information, Mr O'Farrell," replied O'Brien; "but the French have reported it before you. May I ask if you've any particular fancy to be made a target of, or if you think that his Majesty's brig Rattlesnake was sent here to be riddled for nothing at all? Starboard the helm, quarter-master."

The helm was put up, and the brig was soon run out of the fire; not, however, until a few more shot were pitched close to us, and one carried away the foretopmast backstay.

"Now, Mr O'Farrell," replied O'Brien, "I only wish to point out to you that I trust neither I nor anyone in this ship cares a fig about the whizzing of a shot or two about our ears when there is anything to be gained for it, either for ourselves or for our country; but I do care a great deal about losing even the leg or the arm, much more the life of any of my men, when there's no occasion for it; so, in future, recollect it's no disgrace to keep out of the way of a battery when all the advantage is on their side. I've always observed that chance shots pick out the best men. Lower down the mainsail, and send the sailmakers aft to repair it."

When O'Brien returned to the cabin I remained on deck, for it was my afternoon watch; and although O'Farrell had permission to look out for me, I did not choose to go down again. The bay of Fort Royal was now opened, and the view was extremely beautiful. Swinburne was still on the carronade; and as I knew he had been there before, I applied to him for information as to the *locale*. He told me the names of the batteries above the town, pointed out Fort Edward and Negro Point, and particularly Pigeon Island, the battery at the top of which wore the appearance of a mural crown.

"It's well I remember that place, Mr Simple," said he. "It was in '94 when I was last here. The sodgers had 'sieged it for a whole month, and were about to give it up, 'cause they couldn't get a gun up on that 'ere hill you see there. So poor Captain Faulkner says, 'There's many a clear head under a tarpaulin hat, and I'll give any chap five doubloons that will hitch up a twenty-four pounder to the top of that hill.' Not quite so easy a matter, as you may perceive from here, Mr Simple."

"It certainly appears to me to have been almost impossible, Swinburne," replied I.

"And so it did to most of us, Mr Simple; but there was one Dick Smith, mate of a transport, who had come on shore, and he steps out, saying, 'I've been looking at your men handling that gun, and my opinion is, that if you gets a butt, crams in a carronade, well woulded up, and fill it with old junk and rope-yarns, you might parbuckle it up to the very top.'* So Captain Faulkner pulls out five doubloons, and gives them to him, saying, 'You deserve the money for the hint, even if it don't succeed.' But it did succeed, Mr Simple; and the next day, to their surprise, we opened fire on the French beggars, and soon brought their boasting down. One of the French officers, after he was taken prisoner, axed me how we had managed to get the gun up there; but I wasn't going to blow the gaff, so I told him, as a great secret, that we got it up with a kite, upon which he opened all his eyes, and crying 'sacre bleu!' walked away, believing all I said was true; but a'n't that a sail we have opened with the point, Mr Simple?"

It was so, and I reported it to O'Brien, who came up and gave chase. In half an hour we were alongside of her, when she hoisted American colours, and proved to be a brigantine laden up to her gunwale, which was not above a foot out of the water. Her cargo consisted of what the Americans called notions; that is, in English, an assorted cargo. Half-way up her masts down to the deck were hung up baskets containing apples, potatoes, onions, and nuts of various kinds. Her deck was crowded with cattle, sheep, pigs, and donkeys. Below was full of shingle, lumber, and a variety of different articles too numerous to mention. I boarded her, and asked the master whither he was bound?

* Parbuckle: A rope used to move an object up or down an inclined plane.

"Why," replied he, "I am bound for a market—nowise particular; and I guess you won't stop me."

"Not if all's right," replied I; "but I must look at your log."

"Well, I've a notion there's no great objection to that," replied he; and he brought it up on deck.

I had no great time to examine it, but I could not help being amused at the little I did read, such as—"Horse latitudes—water very short—killed white-faced bullock—caught a dolphin, and ate him for dinner—broached molasses cask No. I, letter A. Fine night— saw little round things floating on the water—took up a bucket full—guessed they were pearls—judge I guessed wrong, only little Portuguese men-of-war—threw them overboard again—heard a scream, guessed it was a mermaid—looked out, saw nothing. Witnessed a very strange rippling ahead—calculated it might be the sea-serpent—stood on to see him plain, and nearly ran on Barbuda. Hauled off again—met a Britisher—treated *politely*."

Having overhauled his log, I then begged to overhaul his men to ascertain if there were any Englishmen among his crew. This was not pleasing, and he grumbled very much; but they were ordered aft. One man I was satisfied was an Englishman, and told him so; but the man as well as the master persisted to the contrary. Nevertheless, I resolved to take him on board for O'Brien to decide, and ordered him into the boat.

"Well, if you will use force, I can't help it. My decks an't clear as you see, or else—I tell you what, Mr Lieutenant, your vessel there will be another *Hermione*, I've a notion, if you presses true-blooded Yankees; and, what's more, the States will take it up, as sure as there's snakes in Virginny."

Notwithstanding this remonstrance, I took them on board to O'Brien, who had a long conversation with the American in the cabin. When they returned on deck he was allowed to depart with his man, and we again made sail. I had the first watch that night, and as we ran along the coast I perceived a vessel under the high land in what the sailors called the *doldrums;* that is, almost becalmed, or her sails flapping about in every direction with the eddying winds. We steered for her, and were very soon in the same situation, not more than a quarter of a mile from her. The quarterboat was lowered down, and I proceeded to board her; but as she was large and rakish, O'Brien desired me to be careful, and if there was the least show of resistance to return. As I pulled up to her bows they hailed me in French, and desired me to keep off, or they would fire. This was quite sufficient; and, in obedience to my orders, I returned to the brig and reported to O'Brien. We lowered down all the quarter-boats, and towed round the brig's broadside to her, and then gave her half a dozen carronades of round and grape. Hearing great noise and confusion on board after we had ceased firing, O'Brien again sent me to know if they had surrendered. They replied in the affirmative, and I boarded her. She proved to be the *Commerce de Bordeaux*, with three hundred and thirty slaves on board, out of five hundred embarked from the coast, bound to Martinique. The crew were very sickly, and were most of them in their hammocks. Latterly, they had been killing parrots to make soup for them; a few that were left, of the grey species, spoke remarkably well. When they left the coast they had nearly one thousand parrots on board.

O'Brien perceiving that I had taken possession, sent another boat to know what the vessel was. I desired the surgeon to be sent on board, as some of the men and many of the poor slaves were wounded by our shot. Of all the miserable objects, I know of none to be compared to the poor devils of slaves on board of a slave vessel: the state of suffocation between decks—the dreadful stench arising from their filth, which is hardly ever cleared away—the sick lying without help, and looked upon by those who are stronger with the utmost indifference—men, women, and children, all huddled and crowded together in a state of nudity, worn to skin and bone from stench, starvation, and living in an atmosphere that none but a negro could exist in. If all that occurs in a slave-ship were really known, I think it would be acknowledged that to make the slave trade piracy would be nothing more than a just retribution; and this is certain, that unless it be made piracy, it never will be discontinued.

By daylight the vessel was ready, and O'Brien determined to take her to Dominica, so that the poor devils might be immediately sent on shore. We anchored with her, in a few days, in Prince Rupert's Bay, where we only had twenty-four hours to obtain some refreshments and arrange about our prize, which I hardly need say was of some value.

During the short time that I was on shore, purchasing some

fowls and vegetables for O'Brien and our own mess, I was amused at witnessing a black sergeant drilling some of his regiment of free negroes and mulattoes. He appeared resolved to make the best appearance that he could, for he began by saying, "You hab shoe and 'tocking, stand in front—you hab shoe no 'tocking, stand in centre—you hab no shoe no 'tocking, stand in um rear. Face to mountain—back to sea-beach. Why you no 'tep out, sar?—you hangman!"

I was curious to count the numbers qualified for the front rank: there were only two mulattoes. In the second rank there were also only two. No shoe and no 'tocking appeared to be the fashion. As usual, we were surrounded by the negroes; and although we had been there but a few hours, they had a song composed for us, which they constantly repeated:—

> *"Don't you see the* Rattlesnake
> *Coming under sail?*
> *Don't you see the* Rattlesnake
> *With prizes at um tail?—*
> Rattlesnake *hab all the money—ding, ding—*
> *She shall have all that's funny, ding, ding!"*

———ᴓᴓᴓ———

CHAPTER XLIV

Money can purchase anything in the new country—American information not always to be depended upon—A night attack; we are beaten off—It proves a cut up, instead of a cut out—After all, we save something out of the fire.

THE NEXT MORNING we weighed anchor, and returned to our station off Martinique. We had run within three miles of St Pierre's when we discovered a vessel coming out under jury-masts. She steered directly for us, and we made her out to be the American brigantine which we had boarded some time before. O'Brien sent a boat to bring the master of her on board.

"Well, captain," said he, "so you met with a squall?"

"I calculate not," replied he.

"Why, then, what the devil have you been about?"

"Why, I guess I sold all my cargo, and, what's more, I've sold my masts."

"Sold your masts! who did you sell them to?"

"To an almighty pretty French privateer lying in St Pierre's, which had lost her spars when she was chased by one of your brass-bottomed sarpents; and I've a notion they paid pretty handsomely too."

"But how do you mean to get home again?"

"I calculate to get into the *stream*, and then I'll do very well. If I meet a nor-wester, why then I'll make a signal of distress, and some one will tow me in, I guess."

"Well," replied O'Brien, "but step down into the cabin and take something, captain."

"With particular pleasure," replied this strange mortal; and down they went.

In about half an hour they returned on deck, and the boat took the American on board. Soon afterwards, O'Brien desired Osbaldistone and myself to step down into the cabin. The chart of the harbour of St Pierre's lay on the table, and O'Brien said, "I have had a long conversation with the American, and he states that the privateer is at anchor in this spot" (pointing to a pencil-mark on the chart). "If so, she is well out, and I see no difficulty in capturing her. You see that she lies in four fathoms water, and so close under the outer battery, that the guns could not be pointed down upon the boats. I have also inquired if they keep a good look-out, and the American says that they feel so secure that they keep no look-out at all; that the captain and officers belonging to her are on shore all night, drinking, smoking, and boasting of what they will do. Now the question is, whether this report be correct. The American has been well-treated by us, and I see no reason to doubt him; indeed, he gave the information voluntarily, as if he wished to serve us."

I allowed Osbaldistone to speak first: he coincided with O'Brien. I did not: the very circumstance of her requiring new masts made me doubt the truth of his assertion as to where she lay; and if one part of his story was false, why not the whole? O'Brien appeared struck with my argument, and it was agreed that if the boats did go away, it should be for a reconnoissance, and that the attempt should only be made, provided it was found that the privateer lay in the same spot pointed out by the American master. It was, however, decided that the reconnoissance should take place that very night, as, allowing the privateer to be anchored on the spot supposed, there was every probability that she would not remain there, but haul further in, to take in her new masts. The news that an expedition was at hand was soon circulated through the ship, and all the men had taken their cutlasses from the capstern to get them ready for action. The fighting boats' crews, without orders, were busy with their boats, some cutting up old blankets to muffle the oars, other making new grummets.* The ship's company were as busy as bees, bustling and buzzing about the decks, and reminding you of the agitation which takes place in a hive previous to a swarm. At last, Osbaldistone came on deck, and ordered the boats' crews to be piped away, and prepare for service. He was to have the command of the expedition in the launch—I had charge of the first cutter—O'Farrell of the second, and Swinburne had the charge of the jolly-boat. At dusk, the head of the brig was again turned towards St Pierre's, and we ran slowly in. At ten we hove-to, and about eleven the boats were ordered to haul up, O'Brien repeating his orders to Mr Osbaldistone, not to make the attempt if the privateer were found to be anchored close to the town. The men were all mustered on the quarter-deck, to ascertain if they had the distinguishing mark on their jackets, that is, square patches of canvas sewed on the left arm, so that we might recognize friend from foe—a very necessary precaution in a night expedition; and then they were manned, and ordered to shove off. The oars were dropped in the water, throwing out a phosphorescent light, so common in that climate, and away we went. After an hour's pulling, Osbaldistone lay on his oars in the launch, and we closed with him.

"We are now at the mouth of the harbour," said he, "and the most perfect silence must be observed."

"At the mouth of the harbour, sir!" said Swinburne; "I reckon we are more than half-way in; we passed the point at least ten minutes ago, and this is the second battery we are now abreast of."

To this Osbaldistone did not agree, nor indeed did I think that Swinburne was right; but he persisted in it, and pointed out to us

* Grummets (or grommets): Rings of rope used to secure the upper edge of a sail to its stay.

the lights in the town, which were now all open to us, and which would not be the case if we were only at the mouth of the harbour. Still we were of a different opinion, and Swinburne, out of respect to his officers, said no more.

We resumed our oars, pulling with the greatest caution; the night was intensely dark, and we could distinguish nothing. After pulling ten minutes more, we appeared to be close to the lights in the town; still we could see no privateer or any other vessel. Again we lay upon our oars, and held a consultation. Swinburne declared that if the privateer lay where we supposed, we had passed her long ago; but while we were debating, O'Farrell cried out, "I see her," and he was right—she was not more than a cable's length from us. Without waiting for orders, O'Farrell desired his men to give way, and dashed alongside of the privateer. Before he was half-way on board of her, lights flew about in every direction, and a dozen muskets were discharged. We had nothing to do but to follow him, and in a few seconds we were all alongside of her; but she was well pre-pared, and on the alert. Boarding nettings were triced up all round, every gun had been depressed as much as possible, and she ap-peared to be full of men. A scene of confusion and slaughter now occurred, which I trust never again to witness. All our attempts to get on board were unavailing; if we tried at a port, a dozen pikes thrust us back; if we attempted the boarding nettings, we were thrown down, killed or wounded, into the boats. From every port, and from the decks of the privateer, the discharge of musketry was incessant. Pistols were protruded and fired in our faces, while occa-sionally her carronades went off, stunning us with their deafening noise, and rocking the boats in the disturbed water, if they had no other effect. For ten minutes our exertions never ceased; at last, with half our numbers lying killed and wounded in the bottom of the boats, the men, worn out and dispirited at their unavailing attempts, sat down most of them on the boats' thwarts, loading their muskets, and discharging them into the ports. Osbaldistone was among the wounded; and perceiving that he was not in the launch, of whose crew not six remained, I called to Swinburne, who was alongside of me, and desired him to tell the other boats to make the best of their way out of the harbour. This was soon communicated to the survi-vors, who would have continued the unequal contest to the last man, if I had not given the order. The launch and second cutter shoved off—O'Farrell also having fallen; and, as soon as they were clear of the privateer, and had got their oars to pass, I proceeded to do the same, amidst the shouts and yells of the Frenchmen, who now jumped on their gunwale and pelted us with their musketry, cheering, and mocking us.

"Stop, sir," cried Swinburne, "we'll have a bit of revenge"; so saying, he hauled-to the launch, and wending her bow to the privateer, directed her carronade—which they had no idea that we had on board, as we had not fired it—to where the Frenchmen were crowded the thickest.

"Stop one moment, Swinburne; put another dose of canister in." We did so, and then discharged the gun, which had the most murderous effect, bringing the major part of them down upon the deck. I feel convinced, from the cries and groans which followed, that if we had had a few more men, we might have returned and captured the privateer; but it was too late. The batteries were all lighted up, and although they could not see the boats, fired in the direction where they supposed us to be; for they were aware, from the shouting on board the vessel, that we had been beaten off. The launch had but six hands capable of taking an oar; the first cutter had but four. In my own boat I had five. Swinburne had two besides himself in the jolly-boat.

"This is a sorry business, sir," said Swinburne; "now, what's best to be done? My idea is, that we had better put all the wounded men into the launch, man the two cutters and jolly-boat, and tow her off. And, Mr Simple, instead of keeping on this side, as they will expect in the batteries, let us keep close in-shore, upon the near side, and their shot will pass over us."

This advice was too good not to be followed. It was now two o'clock, and we had a long pull before us, and no time to lose: we lifted the dead bodies and the wounded men out of the two cutters and jolly-boat into the launch. I had no time for examination, but I perceived that O'Farrell was quite dead, and also a youngster of the name of Pepper, who must have smuggled himself into the boats. I did, however, look for Osbaldistone, and found him in the stern-sheets of the launch. He had received a deep wound in the breast, apparently with a pike. He was sensible, and asked me for a little water, which I procured from the breaker which was in the launch, and gave it to him. At the word water, and hearing it poured out from the breaker, many of the wounded men faintly called out for some. Having no time to spare, I left two men in the launch, one to steer and the other to give them water, and then taking her in tow, pulled directly in for the batteries, as advised by Swinburne, who now sat alongside of me.

As soon as we were well in-shore, I pulled out of the harbour, with feelings not by any means enviable. Swinburne said to me in a low voice, "This will be a hard blow for the captain, Mr Simple. I've always been told, that a young captain losing his men without bringing any dollars to his admiral, is not very well received."

"I am more sorry for him than I can well express, Swinburne," replied I; "but—what is that a-head—a vessel under weigh?"

Swinburne stood up in the stern of the cutter, and looked for a few seconds. "Yes, a large ship standing in under royals—she must be a Frenchman. Now's our time, sir; so long as we don't go out empty-handed, all will be well. Oars, all of you. Shall we cast off the launch, sir?"

"Yes," replied I; "and now, my lads, let us only have the vessel, and we shall do. She is a merchantman, that's clear (not that I was sure of it). Swinburne, I think it will be better to let her pass us in-shore; they will all be looking out of the other side, for they must have seen the firing."

"Well thought of, sir," replied Swinburne.

We lay on our oars, and let her pass us, which she did, creeping in at the rate of two miles an hour. We then pulled for her quarter in the three boats, leaving the launch behind us, and boarded. As we premised, the crew were on deck, and all on the other side of the vessel, so anxiously looking at the batteries, which were still firing occasional random shot, that they did not perceive us until we were close to them, and then they had no time to seize their arms. There were several ladies on board; some of the people protected them, others ran below. In two minutes we had possession of her, and had put her head the other way. To our surprise we found that she mounted fourteen guns. One hatch we left open for the ladies, some of whom had fainted, to be taken down below; the others were fastened down by Swinburne. As soon as we had the deck to ourselves, we manned one of the cutters, and sent it for the launch; and as soon as she was made fast alongside, we had time to look about us. The breeze freshened, and, in half an hour, we were out of gun-

shot of all the batteries. I then had the wounded men taken out of
the launch, and Swinburne and the other men bound up their
wounds, and made them as comfortable as they could.

—⟡⟡⟡—

CHAPTER XLV

Some remarkable occurrences take place in the letter of marque—Old friends with im-
proved faces—The captor a captive; but not carried away, though the captive is, by the
ship's boat—The whole chapter a mixture of love, war, and merchandise.

WE HAD HAD POSSESSION of the vessel about an hour,
when the man who was sentry over the hatchway told me
that one of the prisoners wished to speak with the English commanding officer, and asked leave to come on deck. I gave permission, and a gentleman came up, stating that he was a passenger; that
the ship was a letter of marque, from Bordeaux; that there were
seven lady passengers on board, who had come out to join their
husbands and families; and that he trusted I would have no objection to put them on shore, as women could hardly be considered as
objects of warfare. As I knew that O'Brien would have done so, and
that he would be glad to get rid of both women and prisoners if he
could, I replied "Most certainly"; that I would heave-to, that they
might not have so far to pull on shore, and that I would permit the
ladies and other passengers to go on shore. I begged that they
would be as quick as possible in getting their packages ready, and
that I would give them two of the boats belonging to the ship, with a
sufficient number of French seamen belonging to her to man the
boats. The Frenchman was very grateful, thanked me in the name of
the ladies, and went down below to impart the intelligence. I then
hove-to, lowered down the boats from the quarters, and waited for
them to come up. It was daylight before they were ready, but that I
did not care about; I saw the brig in the offing about seven miles off,
and I was well clear of the batteries. At last they made their appearance, one by one coming up the ladder, escorted by French gentlemen. They had to wait while the packages and bundles were put
into the boats. The first sight which struck them with horror was the

many dead and wounded Englishmen lying on the decks. Expressing their commiseration, I told them that we had attempted to take the privateer, and had been repulsed, and that it was coming out of the harbour that I had fallen in with their ship and captured it. All the ladies had severally thanked me for my kindness in giving them their liberty, except one, whose eyes were fixed upon the wounded men, when the French gentleman went up to her, and reminded her that she had not expressed her thanks to the commanding officer.

She turned round to me—I started back. I certainly had seen that face before—I could not be mistaken; yet she had now grown up into a beautiful young woman. "Celeste," said I, trembling. "Are you not Celeste?"

"Yes," replied she, looking earnestly at me, as if she would discover who I was, but which it was not very easy to do, begrimed as my face was with dust and gunpowder.

"Have you forgotten Peter Simple?"

"Oh! no—no—never forgot you!" cried Celeste, bursting into tears, and holding out her hands.

This scene occasioned no small astonishment to the parties on deck, who could not comprehend it. She smiled through her tears, as I told her how happy I was to have the means of being of service to her. "And where is the colonel?" said I.

"There," replied she, pointing to the island; "he is now general, and commands the force in the garrison. "And where is Mr O'Brien?" interrogated Celeste.

"There," replied I; "he commands that man-of-war, of which I am the second lieutenant."

A rapid exchange of inquiries took place, and the boats were stopped while we were in conversation. Swinburne reported that the brig was standing in for us, and I felt that in justice to the wounded I could no longer delay. Still I found time to press her hand, to thank her for the purse she had given me when I was on the stilts, and to tell her that I had never forgotten her, and never would. With many remembrances to her father, I was handing her into the boat, when she said, "I don't know whether I am right to ask it, but you could do me such a favour."

"What is it, Celeste?"

"You have allowed more than one-half of the men to pull us on shore; some must remain, and they are so miserable—indeed it is hardly yet decided which of them are to go. Could you let them all go?"

"That I will, for your sake, Celeste. As soon as your two boats have shoved off, I will lower down the boat astern, and send the rest after you; but I must make sail now—God bless you!"

The boats then shoved off, the passengers waving their handkerchiefs to us, and I made sail for the brig. As soon as the stern-boat was alongside, the rest of the crew were called up and put into her, and followed their companions. I felt that O'Brien would not be angry with me for letting them all go: and especially when I told him who begged for them. The vessel's name was the *Victorine*, mounting fourteen guns, and twenty-four men, with eleven passengers. She was chiefly laden with silks and wine, and was a very valuable prize. Celeste had time to tell me that her father had been four years in Martinique, and had left her at home for her education; and that she was then coming out to join him. The other ladies were all wives or daughters of officers of the French garrison on the island, and the gentlemen passengers were some of them French officers; but as this was told me in secrecy, of course I was not bound to know it, as they were not in uniform.

As soon as we had closed with the brig, I hastened on board to O'Brien; and as soon as a fresh supply of hands to man the boats, and the surgeon had been despatched on board of the prize, to superintend the removal of the wounded, I went down with him into the cabin, and narrated what had occurred.

"Well," said O'Brien, "all's well that ends well; but this is not the luckiest hit in the world. Your taking the ship has saved me, Peter; and I must make as flourishing a despatch as I can. By the powers but it's very lucky that she has fourteen guns—it sounds grand. I must muddle it all up together, so that the admiral must think we intended to cut them both out—and so we did, sure enough, if we had known she had been there. But I am most anxious to hear the surgeon's report, and whether poor Osbaldistone will do well. Peter, oblige me by going on board, and put two marines sentry over the hatchway, so that no one goes down and pulls the traps about; for I'll send on shore everything belonging to the passengers, for Colonel O'Brien's sake."

The surgeon's report was made—six killed and sixteen wounded. The killed were, O'Farrell and Pepper, midshipmen, two seamen and two marines. The first lieutenant, Osbaldistone, was severely wounded in three places, but likely to do well; five other men were dangerously wounded: the other ten would, in all probability, return to their duty in less than a month. As soon as the wounded were on board, O'Brien returned with me to the prize, and we went down into the cabin. All the passengers' effects were collected; the trunks which had been left open were nailed down: and O'Brien wrote a handsome letter to General O'Brien, containing a list of the packages sent on shore. We sent the launch with a flag of truce to the nearest battery; after some demur it was accepted, and effects landed. We did not wait for an answer, but made all sail to join the admiral at Barbadoes.

The next morning we buried those who had fallen. O'Farrell was a fine young man, brave as a lion, but very hot in his temper. He would have made a good officer had he been spared. Poor little Pepper was also much regretted. He was but twelve years old. He had bribed the bow-man of the second cutter to allow him to conceal himself under the fore-sheets of the boat. His day's allowance of spirits had purchased him this object of his ambition, which ended so fatally. But as soon as the bodies had disappeared under the wave, and the service was over, we all felt happier. There is something very unpleasant, particularly to sailors, in having a corpse on board.

We now sailed merrily along, the prize keeping company with us; and, before we reached Barbadoes, most of the men were convalescent. Osbaldistone's wounds, were, however, very severe; and he was recommended to return home, which he did, and obtained his promotion as soon as he arrived. He was a pleasant messmate, and I was sorry to lose him; although, the lieutenant appointed in his room being junior to me, I was promoted to be first lieutenant of the brig. Soon after Osbaldistone went home, his brother broke his neck when hunting, and Osbaldistone came into the property. He then quitted the service.

We found the admiral at Barbadoes, who received O'Brien and his despatch very well. O'Brien had taken two good prizes, and that was sufficient to cover a multitude of sins, even if he had committed any; but the despatch was admirably written, and the admiral, in his letter to the Admiralty, commented upon Captain O'Brien's successful and daring attack; whereas, if the truth had been known, it was

Swinburne's advice of pulling up the weather shore, which was the occasion of our capturing the *Victorine;* but it is very hard to come at the real truth of these sort of things, as I found out during the time that I was in his Majesty's service.

———⁊∕∕∕⊱———

CHAPTER XLVI

O'Brien tells his crew that one Englishman is as good as three Frenchmen on salt water—They prove it—We fall in with an old acquaintance, although she could not be considered as a friend.

OUR NEXT CRUISE was on the coast of Guinea and Gulf of Mexico, where we were running up and down for three months, without falling in with anything but West Indiamen bound to Demerara, Berbice, and Surinam, and occasionally chasing a privateer; but in the light winds they were too fast for us. Still we were useful in protecting the trade, and O'Brien had a letter of thanks from the merchants, and a handsome piece of plate upon his quitting the station. We had made sail for Barbadoes two days, and were within sight of the island of Trinidad, when we perceived six sail on the lee-bow. We soon made them out to be three large ships and three schooners; and immediately guessed, which afterwards proved to be correct, that they were three privateers, with West India ships which they had captured. We made all sail, and at first the three privateers did the same; but afterwards, having made out our force, and not liking to abandon their prizes, they resolved to fight. The West Indiamen hauled to the wind on the other tack, and the three privateers shortened sail and awaited our coming. We beat to quarters, and when everything was ready, and we were within a mile of the enemy, who had now thrown out the tri-coloured flag, O'Brien ordered all the men aft on the quarter-deck, and addressed them: "Now, my men, you see that there are three privateers, and you also see that there are three West Indiamen, which they have captured. As for the privateers, it's just a fair match for you—one Englishman can always beat three Frenchmen. We must lick the privateers for honour and glory, and we must re-capture the ships for profit, because you'll all want some money when you get on shore again. So you've just half-a-dozen things to do, and then we'll pipe to dinner."

This harangue suited the sailors very well, and they returned to their guns. "Now, Peter," said O'Brien, "just call away the sail-trimmers from the guns, for I mean to fight these fellows under sail, and out-manoeuvre them, if I can. Tell Mr Webster I want to speak with him."

Mr Webster was the second lieutenant, a very steady, quiet young man, and a good officer.

"Mr Webster," said O'Brien, "remember that all the foremost guns must be very much depressed. I prefer that the shot should strike the water before it reaches them, rather than it should go over them. See that your screws are run up at once, and I will take care that no broadside is thrown away. Starboard, Swinburne."

"Starboard it is, sir."

"Steady; so—that's right for the stern of the leeward vessel."

We were within two cable lengths of the privateers, who still remained hove-to within half a cable's length of each other. They were very large schooners, full of men, with their boarding netting triced up, and showing a very good set of teeth: as it afterwards proved, one mounted sixteen, and the other two fourteen, guns.

"Now, my lads, over to the lee guns, and fire as they bear, when we round to. Hands by the lee head-braces, and jib-sheet, stretch along the weather braces. Quarter-master abaft, tend the boom-sheet. Port hard, Swinburne."

"Port it is, sir," replied Swinburne; and the brig rounded up on the wind, shooting up under the sterns of the two weathermost schooners, and discharging the broadsides into them as the guns bore.

"Be smart and load, my lads, and stand by the same guns. Round in the weather head-braces. Peter, I don't want her to go about. Stand by to haul over the boom-sheet, when she pays off. Swinburne, helm amidships."

By this time another broadside was poured into the schooner, who had not yet returned our fire, which, having foolishly remained hove to the wind, they could not do. The brig had now stern way, and O'Brien then executed a very skilful manoeuvre: he shifted the helm, and made a stern board, so as to back in between the two weather schooners and the one to leeward, bracing round at the same time on the other tack.

"Man both sides, my lads, and give them your broadsides as we pass."

The men stationed at the starboard guns flew over, and the other side being again loaded, we exchanged broadsides with the leeward and one of the windward schooners, the brig continuing her stern way until we passed ahead of them. By the time that we had re-loaded, the brig had gathered headway, and again passed between the same two schooners, exchanging broadsides, and then passing astern of them.

"Capital, my lads—capital!" said O'Brien; "this is what I call good fighting." And so it was; for O'Brien had given two raking broadsides, and four others, receiving only two in return, for the schooners were not ready for us when we passed between them the last time.

The smoke had now rolled away to leeward, and we were able to see the effect of our broadsides. The middle schooner had lost her main-boom, and appeared very much cut up in the hull. The schooner to leeward did not appear to have suffered much; but they now perceived their error, and made sail. They had expected that we should have run in between them, and fought broadside to broadside, by which means the weathermost schooner would have taken a raking position, while the others engaged us to windward and to leeward. Our own damages were trifling—two men slightly wounded, and one main shroud cut away. We ran about half a mile astern from them; then with both broadsides ready, we tacked, and found that, as we expected, we could weather the whole of them. This we did; O'Brien running the brig within biscuit-throw of the weather schooner, engaging him broadside to broadside, with the advantage that the other two could not fire a shot into us without standing a chance of striking their consort. If he made more sail, so did we; if he shortened, so did we; so as to keep our position with little variation. The schooner fought well; but her metal was not to be compared with our thirty-two pound carronades, which ploughed up her sides at so short a distance, driving two ports into one. At last her foremast went by the board, and she dropped astern. In the meantime the other schooners had both tacked, and were coming up under our stern to rake us, but the accident which happened to the one we had engaged left us at liberty. We knew that she could not escape, so we tacked and engaged the other two, nearing them as fast as we could. The breeze now sprang up fast, and O'Brien put up the helm and passed between them, giving them both a raking broadside of grape and cannister, which brought the sticks about their ears. This sickened them; the smallest schooner, which had been the leewardmost at the commencement of the action, made all sail on a wind. We clapped on the royals to follow her, when we perceived that the other schooner, which had been in the middle, and whose main-boom we had shot away, had put her helm up, and was crowding all sail before the wind. O'Brien then said, "Must not try for too much, or we shall lose all. Put her about, Peter, we must be content with the one that is left us."

We went about, and ranged up to the schooner which had lost her foremast; but she, finding that her consort had deserted her, hauled down her colours just as we were about to pour in our broadside. Our men gave three cheers; and it was pleasant to see them all shaking hands with each other, congratulating and laughing at the successful result of our action.

"Now, my lads, be smart;—we've done enough for honour, now for profit. Peter, take the two cutters full of men, and go on board of the schooner, while I get hold of the three West Indiamen. Rig something jury forward, and follow me."

In a minute the cutters were down and full of men. I took possession of the schooner, while the brig again tacked, and crowding all sail stood after the captured vessels. The schooner, which was the largest of the three, was called the *Joan d'Arc*, mounting sixteen guns, and had fifty-three men on board, the remainder being away in the prizes. The captain was wounded very badly, and one officer killed. Out of her ship's company, she had but eight killed and five wounded. They informed me, that they had sailed three months ago from St Pierre's, Martinique, and had fallen in with the other two privateers, and cruised in company, having taken nine West Indiamen since they had come out. "Pray," said I to the officer who gave the information, "were you ever attacked by boats when you laid at St Pierre's?" He replied, yes; and that they had beaten them off. "Did you purchase these masts of an American?" He replied in the affirmative; so that we had captured the very vessel, in attempting to cut out which, we had lost so many men.

We were all very glad of this, and Swinburne said, "Well, hang me if I didn't think that I had seen that port-hole before; there it was that I wrenched a pike out of one of the rascal's hands, who tried to stab me, and into that port-hole I fired at least a dozen muskets. Well, I'm d——d glad we've got hold of the beggar at last."

We secured the prisoners below, and commenced putting the schooner in order. In half an hour, we had completed our knotting and splicing, and having two of the carpenters with us, in an hour we had got up a small jury-mast forward, sufficient for the present. We lowered the mainsail, put try-sails on her, and stood after the brig, which was now close to the prizes; but they separated, and it was not till dark that she had possession of two. The third was then hull down on the other tack, with the brig in chase. We followed the brig, as did the two re-captured vessels, and even with our jury up, we found that we could sail as fast as they. The next morning, we saw the brig hove-to, and about three miles a-head, with the three vessels in her possession. We closed, and I went on board. Webster was put in charge of the privateer; and, after lying-to for that day to send our prize-masters and men on board to remove the prisoners, we got up a proper jury-mast, and all made sail together for Barbadoes. On my return on board, I found that we had but one man and one boy killed and six wounded, which I was not aware of. I forgot to say that the names of the other two privateers were *L'Etoile* and *La Madeleine.*

In a fortnight we arrived with all our prizes safe in Carlisle Bay, where we found the admiral, who had anchored but two days before. I hardly need say that O'Brien was well received, and gained a great deal of credit for the action. I found several letters from my sister, the contents of which gave me much pain. My father had been some months in Ireland, and returned without gaining any information. My sister said that he was very unhappy, paid no attention to his clerical duties, and would sit for days without speaking. That he was very much altered in his appearance, and had grown thin and care-worn. "In short," said she, "my dear Peter, I am afraid that he is fretting himself to death. Of course, I am very lonely and melancholy. I cannot help reflecting upon what will be my situation if any accident should happen to my father. Accept my uncle's protection I will not; yet, how am I to live, for my father has saved nothing? I have been very busy lately, trying to qualify myself for a governess, and practise the harp and piano for several hours every day. I shall be very, very glad when you come home again." I showed the letters to O'Brien, who read them with much attention. I perceived the colour mount into his cheeks, when he read those parts of her letters in which she mentioned his name, and expressed her gratitude for his kindness towards me.

"Never mind, Peter," said O'Brien, returning me the letters; "to whom is it that I am indebted for my promotion, and this brig, but to you—and for all the prize-money which I have made, and which, by the head of St Patrick, comes to a very dacent sum, but to you? Make yourself quite easy about your dear little sister. We'll club your prize-money and mine together, and she shall marry a duke, if there is one in England deserving her; and it's the French that shall furnish her dowry, as sure as the *Rattlesnake* carries a tail."

—◦◦◦—

CHAPTER XLVII

I am sent away after prizes, and meet with a hurricane—Am driven on shore, with the loss of more than half my men—Where is the Rattlesnake?

IN THREE WEEKS we were again ready for sea, and the admiral ordered us to our old station off Martinique. We had cruised about a fortnight off St Pierre's, and, as I walked the deck at night, often did I look at the lights in the town, and wonder whether any of them were in the presence of Celeste, when, one evening, being about six miles off shore, we observed two vessels rounding Negro Point, close in-shore. It was quite calm, and the boats were towing ahead.

"It will be dark in half-an-hour, Peter," said O'Brien, "and I think we might get them before they anchor, or, if they do anchor, it will be well outside. What do you think?"

I agreed with him, for in fact, I always seemed to be happier when the brig was close in-shore, as I felt as if I was nearer to Celeste, and the further we were off, the more melancholy I became. Continually thinking of her, and the sight of her after so many

years' separation, had changed my youthful attachment into strong
affection. I may say that I was deeply in love. The very idea of going
into the harbour, therefore, gave me pleasure, and there was no mad
or foolish thing that I would not have done, only to gaze upon the
walls which contained the constant object of my thoughts. These
were wild and visionary notions, and with little chance of ever ar-
riving to any successful issue; but at one- or two-and-twenty we are
fond of building castles, and very apt to fall in love, without considering our prospect of success. I replied, that I thought it very possible, and wished he would permit me to make the attempt, as, if I
found there was much risk, I would return.

"I know that I can trust you, Peter," replied O'Brien, "and it's a
great pleasure to know that you have an officer you can trust: but
haven't I brought you up myself, and made a man of you, as I
promised I would, when you were a little spalpeen, with a sniffling
nose, and legs in the shape of two carrots? So hoist out the launch,
and get the boats ready—the sooner the better. What a hot day this
has been—not a cat's-paw on the water, and the sky all of a mist.
Only look at the sun, how he goes down, puffed out to three times
his size, as if he were in a terrible passion. I suspect we shall have
the land breeze off strong."

In half an hour I shoved off with the boats. It was now quite
dark, and I pulled towards the harbour of St Pierre. The heat was
excessive and unaccountable; not the slightest breath of wind
moved in the heavens or below; no clouds to be seen, and the stars
were obscured by a sort of mist: there appeared a total stagnation in
the elements. The men in the boats pulled off their jackets, for, after
a few moments' pulling, they could bear them no longer. As we
pulled in, the atmosphere became more opaque, and the darkness
more intense. We supposed ourselves to be at the mouth of the
harbour, but could see nothing—not three yards ahead of the boat.
Swinburne, who always went with me, was steering the boat, and I
observed to him the unusual appearance of the night.

"I've been watching it, sir," replied Swinburne, "and I tell you,
Mr Simple, that if we only know how to find the brig, that I would
advise you to get on board of her immediately. She'll want all her
hands this night, or I'm much mistaken."

"Why do you say so?" replied I.

"Because I think, nay, I may say that I'm sartin, we'll have a hurricane afore morning. It's not the first time I've cruised in these latitudes. I recollect in '94—"

But I interrupted him: "Swinburne, I believe that you are right. At all events, I'll turn back: perhaps we may reach the brig before it comes on. She carries a light, and we can find her out." I then turned the boat round, and steered, as near as I could guess, for where the brig was lying. But we had not pulled out more than two minutes before a low moaning was heard in the atmosphere—now here, now there—and we appeared to be pulling through solid darkness, if I may use the expression. Swinburne looked around him and pointed out on the starboard bow.

"It's a-coming, Mr Simple, sure enough; many's the living being that will not rise on its legs to-morrow. See, sir."

I looked, and dark as it was, it appeared as if a sort of black wall was sweeping along the water right towards us. The moaning gradually increased to a stunning roar, and then at once it broke upon us with a noise to which no thunder can bear a comparison. The oars were caught by the wind with such force that the men were dashed forward under the thwarts, many of them severely hurt. Fortunately we pulled with tholes and pins, or the gunwale and planks of the boat would have been wrenched off, and we should have foundered. The wind soon caught the boat on her broadside, and, had there been the least sea, would have inevitably thrown her over; but Swinburne put the helm down, and she fell off before the hurricane, darting through the boiling water at the rate of ten miles an hour. All hands were aghast; they had recovered their seats, but were obliged to relinquish them and sit down at the bottom, holding on by the thwarts. The terrific roaring of the hurricane prevented any communication, except by gesture. The other boats had disappeared; lighter than ours, they had flown away faster before the sweeping element; but we had not been a minute before the wind before the sea rose in a most unaccountable manner—it appeared to be by magic. Of all the horrors that ever I witnessed, nothing could be compared to the scene of this night. We could see nothing, and heard only the wind, before which we were darting like an arrow—to where we knew not, unless it was to certain death. Swinburne steered the boat, every now and then looking back as the waves increased. In a few minutes we were in a heavy swell, that at one minute bore us all aloft, and at the next almost sheltered us from the hurricane; and now the atmosphere was charged with showers of spray, the wind cutting off the summits of the waves, as if with a knife, and carrying them along with it, as it were, in its arms. The boat was filling with water, and appeared to settle down fast. The men baled with their hats in silence, when a large wave culminated over the stern, filling us up to our thwarts. The next moment we all received a shock so violent, that we were jerked from our seats. Swinburne was thrown over my head. Every timber of the boat separated at once, and she appeared to crumble from under us, leaving us floating on the raging waters. We all struck out for our lives, but with little hope of preserving them; but the next wave dashed us on the rocks, against which the boat had already been hurled. That wave gave life to some and death to others. Me, in Heaven's mercy, it preserved: I was thrown so high up that I merely scraped against the top of the rock, breaking two of my ribs. Swinburne, and eight more, escaped with me, but not unhurt: two had their legs broken, three had broken arms, and the others were more or less contused. Swinburne miraculously received no injury. We had been eighteen in the boat, of which ten escaped: the others were hurled up at our feet; and the next morning we found them dreadfully mangled. One or two had their skulls literally shattered to pieces against the rocks. I felt that I was saved, and was grateful; but still the hurricane howled—still the waves were washing over us. I crawled further up upon the beach, and found Swinburne sitting down with his eyes directed seaward. He knew me, took my hand, squeezed it, and then held it in his. For some moments we remained in this position, when the waves, which every moment increased in volume, washed up to us, and obliged us to crawl further up. I then looked around me; the hurricane continued in its fury, but the atmosphere was not so dark. I could trace, for some distance, the line of the harbour, from the ridge of foam upon the shore; and, for the first time, I thought of O'Brien and the brig. I put my mouth close to Swinburne's ear, and cried out, "O'Brien!" Swinburne shook his head, and looked up again at the offing. I thought whether there was any chance of the brig's escape. She was certainly six, if not seven miles off, and the hurricane was not direct on the shore. She might have a drift of ten miles, perhaps; but what was that against such tremendous power? I prayed for those on board of the brig, and returned thanks for my own preservation. I was, or soon should be, a prisoner, no doubt; but what was that? I thought of Celeste, and felt almost happy.

In about three hours the force of the wind subsided. It still blew a heavy gale, but the sky cleared up, the stars again twinkled in the heavens, and we could see to a considerable distance.

"It's breaking now, sir," said Swinburne, at last; "satisfied with the injury it has done—and that's no little. This is worse than '94."

"Now, I'd give all my pay and prize-money if it were only daylight, and I could know the fate of the poor *Rattlesnake*. What do you think, Swinburne?"

"All depends upon whether they were taken unprepared, sir. Captain O'Brien is as good a seaman as ever trod a plank; but he never has been in a hurricane, and may not have known the signs and warnings which God in His mercy has vouchsafed to us. Your flush vessels fill easily—but we must hope for the best."

Most anxiously did we look out for the day, which appeared to us as if it never would break. At last the dawn appeared, and we stretched our eyes to every part of the offing as it was lighted up, but we could not see the brig. The sun rose, and all was bright and clear; but we looked not around us, our eyes were directed to where we had left the brig. The sea was still running high, but the wind abated fast.

"Thank God!" ejaculated Swinburne, when he had directed his eyes along the coast, "she is above water, at all events!" and looking in the direction where he pointed, I perceived the brig within two miles of the shore, dismantled, and tossing in the waves.

"I see her," replied I, catching my breath with joy; "but—still—I think she must go on shore."

"All depends upon whether she can get a little bit of sail up to weather the point," replied Swinburne; "and depend upon it, Captain O'Brien knows that as well as we do."

We were now joined by the other men who were saved. We all shook hands. They pointed out to me the bodies of our shipmates who had perished. I directed them to haul them further up, and put them all together; and continued, with Swinburne, to watch the brig. In about half an hour we perceived a triangle raised, and in ten minutes afterwards a jury-mast abaft—a try-sail was hoisted and set. Then the shears were seen forward, and in as short a time another try-sail and a storm-jib were expanded to the wind.

"That's all he can do now, Mr Simple," observed Swinburne; "he must trust to them and Providence. They are not more than a mile from the beach—it will be touch and go."

Anxiously did we watch for more than half an hour; the other men returned to us, and joined in our speculations. At one time we thought it impossible—at another, we were certain that she would weather the point. At last, as she neared us, she warped ahead: my anxiety became almost insupportable. I stood first on one leg, and then on the other, breathless with suspense. She appeared to be on the point—actually touching the rocks—"God! she's struck!" said I.

"No!" replied Swinburne;—and then we saw her pass on the other side of the outermost rock and disappear.

"Safe, Mr Simple!—weathered, by God!" cried Swinburne, waving his hat with joy.

"God be thanked!" replied I, overcome with delight.

—⟨∂⟩—

CHAPTER XLVIII

The devastation of the hurricane—Peter makes friends—At destroying or saving, nothing like British seamen—Peter meets with General O'Brien, much to his satisfaction—Has another meeting still more so—A great deal of pressing of hands, "and all that," as Pope says.

NOW THAT THE BRIG was safe, we thought of ourselves. My first attention was directed to the dead bodies, and as I looked at their mangled limbs, I felt grateful to Heaven that I had been so miraculously spared. We then cast our eyes along the beach to see if we could trace any remnants of the other boats, but in vain. We were about three miles from the town, which we could perceive had received considerable damage, and the beach below it was strewed with wrecks and fragments. I told the men that we might as well walk into the town and deliver ourselves up as prisoners; to which they agreed, and we set forward, promising to send for the poor fellows who were too much hurt to accompany us.

As soon as we climbed up the rocks, and gained the inland, what a sight presented itself to us! Trees torn up by the roots in every direction—cattle lying dead—here and there the remains of a house, of which the other parts had been swept away for miles. Everything not built of solid masonry had disappeared. We passed what had been a range of negro huts, but they were levelled to the ground. The negroes were busily searching for their property among the ruins, while the women held their infants in their arms, and the other children by their sides. Here and there was the mother wailing over the dead body of some poor little thing which had been crushed to death. They took no notice of us. About half a mile further on, to our great delight, we fell in with the crews of the other boats, who were sitting by the side of the road. They had all escaped unhurt; their boats, being so much more buoyant than ours, had been thrown up high and dry. They joined us, and we proceeded on our way. On our road we fell in with a cart blown over, under the wheel of which was the leg of the negro who conducted it. We released the poor fellow; his leg was fractured. We laid him by the side of the road in the shade, and continued our march. Our whole route was one scene of desolation and distress; but when we arrived at the town, we found that there it was indeed accumulated. There was not one house in three standing entire—the beach was covered with remnants of bodies and fragments of vessels, whose masts lay forced several feet into the sand, and broken into four or five pieces. Parties of soldiers were busy taking away the bodies, and removing what few valuables had been saved. We turned up into the town, for no one accosted us or even noticed us; and here the scene was even more dreadful. In some streets they were digging out those who were still alive, and whose cries were heard among the ruins; in others they were carrying away the dead bodies. The lamentations of the relatives—the howling of the negroes—the cries of the wounded—the cursing and swearing of the French soldiers, and the orders delivered continually by officers on horseback, with all the confusion arising from crowds of spectators, mingling their voices together, formed a scene as dreadful as it was novel. After surveying it for a few minutes, I went up to an officer on horseback, and told him in French, that I wished to surrender myself as a prisoner.

"We have no time to take prisoners now," replied he; "hundreds are buried in the ruins, and we must try to save them. We must now attend to the claims of humanity."

"Will you allow my men to assist you, sir?" replied I. "They are active and strong fellows."

"Sir," said he, taking off his hat, "I thank you in the name of my unfortunate countrymen."

"Show us, then, where we may be most useful."

He turned and pointed to a house higher up, the offices of which were blown down. "There are living beings under those ruins."

"Come, my lads," said I; and sore as they were, my men hastened with alacrity to perform their task. I could not help them myself, my side was so painful; but I stood by giving them directions. In half an hour we had cleared away, so as to arrive at a poor negro girl, whose cries we had distinctly heard. We released her and laid her down in the street, but she fainted. Her left hand was dreadfully shattered. I was giving what assistance I could, and the men were busy clearing away, throwing on one side the beams and rafters, when an officer on horseback rode up. He stood and asked me who we were. I told him that we belonged to the brig, and had been wrecked; and that we were giving what assistance we could until they were at leisure to send us to prison.

"You English are fine brave fellows," replied he, and he rode on.

Another unfortunate object had been recovered by our men, an old white-headed negro, but he was too much mangled to live. We brought him out, and were laying him beside the negro girl, when several officers on horseback rode down the street. The one who was foremost, in a general's uniform, I immediately recognized as my former friend, then Colonel O'Brien. They all stopped and looked at us. I told who we were. General O'Brien took off his hat to the sailors, and thanked them. He did not recognize me, and he was passing on, when I said to him in English, "General O'Brien, you have forgotten me, but I shall never forget your kindness."

"My God!" said he, "is it you, my dear fellow?" and he sprang from his horse and shook me warmly by the hand. "No wonder that I did not know you; you are a very different person from little Peter Simple, who dressed up as a girl and danced on stilts. But I have to thank you, and so has Celeste for your kindness to her. I will not ask you to leave your work of charity and kindness, but when you have done what you can, come up to my house. Anyone will show it to you; and if you do not find me you will find Celeste, as you must be

aware I cannot leave this melancholy employment. God bless you!"
He then rode off, followed by his staff.

"Come, my lads," said I, "depend upon it we shall not be very
cruelly treated. Let us work hard, and do all the good we can, and
the Frenchmen won't forget it."

We had cleared that house, and went back to where the other
people were working under the orders of the officer on horseback. I
went up to him, and told him we had saved two, and if he had no
objection, would assist his party. He thankfully accepted our services.

"And now, my lads," said Swinburne, "let us forget all our
bruises, and show these French fellows how to work."

And they did so: they tossed away the beams and rafters right
and left with a quickness and dexterity which quite astonished the
officer and other inhabitants who were looking on, and in half an
hour had done more work than could have been possibly expected.
Several lives were saved, and the French expressed their admiration
at our sailors' conduct, and brought them something to drink, which
they stood much in need of, poor fellows. After that they worked
double tides, as we say, and certainly were the means of saving
many lives which otherwise would have been sacrificed.

The disasters occasioned by this hurricane were very great, owing to its having taken place at night, when the chief of the inhabitants were in bed and asleep. I was told that most of the wood
houses were down five minutes after the hurricane burst upon
them. About noon there was no more work for us to do, and I was
not sorry that it was over. My side was very painful, and the burning heat of the sun made me feel giddy and sick at the stomach. I
inquired of a respectable looking old Frenchman which was the general's house. He directed me to it, and I proceeded there, followed
by my men. When I arrived, I found the orderly leading away the
horse of General O'Brien, who had just returned. I desired a sergeant, who was in attendance at the door, to acquaint the general
that I was below. He returned, and desired me to follow him. I was
conducted into a large room, where I found him in company with
several officers. He again greeted me warmly, and introduced me to
the company as the officer who had permitted the ladies who had
been taken prisoners to come on shore.

"I have to thank you, then, for my wife," said an officer, coming up, and offering his hand.

Another came up, and told me that I had also released his. We then entered into a conversation, in which I stated the occasion of my having been wrecked, and all the particulars; also, that I had seen the brig in the morning dismasted, but that she had weathered the point, and was safe.

"That brig of yours, I must pay you the compliment to say, has been very troublesome; and my namesake keeps the batteries more upon the alert than ever I could have done," said General O'Brien. "I don't believe there is a negro five years old upon the island who does not know your brig."

We then talked over the attack of the privateer, in which we were beaten off. "Ah!" replied the aide-de-camp, "you made a mess of that. He has been gone these four months. Captain Carnot swears that he'll fight you if he falls in with you."

"He has kept his word," replied I; and then I narrated our action with the three French privateers, and the capture of the vessel; which surprised and, I think, annoyed them very much.

"Well, my friend," said General O'Brien, "you must stay with me while you are on the island; if you want anything, let me know."

"I am afraid that I want a surgeon," replied I; "for my side is so painful that I can scarcely breathe."

"Are you hurt then?" said General O'Brien, with an anxious look.

"Not dangerously, I believe," said I, "but rather painfully."

"Let me see," said an officer, who stepped forward; "I am surgeon to the forces here, and perhaps you will trust yourself in my hands. Take off your coat."

I did so with difficulty. "You have two ribs broken," said he, "and a very severe contusion. You must go to bed, or lie on a sofa, for a few days. In a quarter of an hour I will come and dress you, and promise you to make you all well in ten days, in return for your having given me my daughter, who was on board of the *Victorine* with the other ladies." The officers now made their bows, and left me alone with General O'Brien.

"Recollect," said he, "that I tell it you once for all, that my purse, and everything, is at your command. If you do not accept them freely, I shall think you do not love us. It is not the first time, Peter, and you repaid me honourably. However, of course, I was no party to that affair; it was Celeste's doing," continued he, laughing. "Of course, I could not imagine that it was you who was dressed up as a woman, and so impudently danced through France on stilts. But I must hear all your adventures by-and-by, Celeste is most anxious to see you. Will you go now, or wait till after the surgeon comes?"

"Oh, now, if you please, general. May I first beg that some care may be taken of my poor men; they have had nothing to eat since yesterday, are very much bruised, and have worked hard; and that a cart may be sent for those who lie maimed on the beach?"

"I should have thought of them before," replied he: "and I will also order the same party to bury the other poor fellows who are lying on the beach. Come, now—I will take you to Celeste."

—◆◆◆—

CHAPTER XLIX

Broken ribs not likely to produce broken hearts—O'Brien makes something very like a declaration of peace—Peter Simple actually makes a declaration of love—Rash proceedings on all sides.

I FOLLOWED THE GENERAL into a handsomely furnished apartment, where I found Celeste waiting to receive me. She ran to me as soon as I entered; and with what pleasure did I take her hand, and look on her beautiful expressive countenance! I could not say a word—neither did Celeste. For a minute I held her hand in mine, looking at her; the general stood by regarding us alternately. He then turned round, and walked to the window. I lifted the hand to my lips, and then released it.

"It appears to be a dream, almost," said Celeste.

I could not make any reply, but continued to gaze upon her—she had grown up into such a beautiful creature. Her figure was perfect, and the expression of her countenance was so varied—so full of intellect and feeling—it was angelic. Her eyes, suffused with tears, beamed so softly, so kindly on me, I could have fallen down and worshipped her.

"Come," said General O'Brien; "come, my dear friend, now that you have seen Celeste, the surgeon must see you."

"The surgeon," cried Celeste, with alarm.

"Yes, my love; it is of no consequence—only a couple of ribs broken."

I followed General O'Brien out of the room, and as I came to the door I turned round to look at Celeste. She had retreated to the sofa, and her handkerchief was up to her eyes. The surgeon was waiting for me; he bandaged me, and applied some cooling lotion to my side, which made me feel quite comfortable.

"I must now leave you," said General O'Brien; "you had better lie down for an hour or two, and then, if I am not back, you know your way to Celeste."

I lay down as he requested; but as soon as I heard the clatter of the horse's hoofs, as he rode off, I left the room, and hurried to the drawing-room. Celeste was there, and hastened to inquire if I was much hurt. I replied in the negative, and told her that I had come down to prove it to her; and we then sat down on the sofa together.

"I have the misfortune never to appear before you, Celeste, except in a very unprepossessing state. When you first saw me I was wounded; at our next meeting I was in woman's clothes; the last time we met I was covered with dirt and gunpowder; and now I return to you wounded and in rags. I wonder whether I shall ever appear before you as a gentleman?"

"It is not the clothes which make the gentleman, Peter. I am too happy to see you to think of how you are dressed. I have never yet thanked you for your kindness to us when we last met. My father will never forget it."

"Nor have I thanked you, Celeste, for your kindness in dropping the purse into the hat, when you met me, trying to escape from France. I have never forgotten you, and since we met the last time, you have hardly ever been out of my thoughts. You don't know how thankful I am to the hurricane for having blown me into your presence. When we cruised in the brig, I have often examined the town with my glass, trying to fancy that I had my eye upon the house you were in; and have felt so happy when we were close in shore, because I knew that I was nearer to you."

"And, Peter, I have often watched the brig, and have been so glad to see it come nearer, and then so afraid that the batteries would fire at you. What a pity it is that my father and you should be opposed to each other—we might be so happy!"

"And may be yet, Celeste," replied I.

We conversed for two hours, which appeared to be but ten minutes. I felt that I was in love, but I do not think that Celeste had any idea at the time that she was—but I leave the reader to judge from the little conversation I have quoted, whether she was not, or something very much approaching to it.

The next morning I went out early to look for the brig, and, to my great delight, saw her about six miles off the harbour's mouth, standing in for the land. She had now got up very respectable jurymasts, with topgallants for topsails, and appeared to be well under command. When she was within three miles of the harbour she lowered the jolly-boat, the only one she had left, and it pulled inshore with a flag of truce hoisted at the bows. I immediately returned to my room, and wrote a detailed account of what had taken place, ready to send to O'Brien when the boat returned, and I, of course, requested him to send me my effects, as I had nothing but what I stood in. I had just completed my letter when General O'Brien came in.

"My dear friend," said he, "I have just received a flag of truce from Captain O'Brien, requesting to know the fate of his boats' crews, and permission to send in return the clothes and effects of the survivors."

"I have written down the whole circumstances for him, and made the same request to him," replied I; and I handed him my letter. He read it over and returned it.

"But, my dear lad, you must think very poorly of us Frenchmen, if you imagine that we intend to detain you here as a prisoner. In the first place, your liberation of so many French subjects, when you captured the *Victorine*, would entitle you to a similar act of kindness; and, in the next place, you have not been fairly captured, but by a visitation of Providence, which, by the means of the late storm, must destroy all national antipathies, and promote that universal philanthropy between all men, which your brave fellows proved that they possess. You are, therefore, free to depart with all your men, and we shall still hold ourselves your debtors. How is your side to-day?"

"Oh, very bad, indeed," replied I; for I could not bear the idea of returning to the brig so soon, for I had been obliged to quit Celeste

very soon after dinner the day before, and go to bed. I had not yet
had much conversation with her, nor had I told General O'Brien
how it was that we escaped from France. "I don't think I can possibly go on board to-day, but I feel very grateful to you for your
kindness."

"Well, well," replied the general, who observed my feelings, "I
do not think it is necessary that you should go on board to-day. I
will send the men and your letter, and I will write to Captain
O'Brien, to say that you are in bed, and will not bear moving until
the day after to-morrow. Will that do?"

I thought it but a very short time, but I saw that the general
looked as if he expected me to consent; so I did.

"The boat can come and return again with some of your
clothes," continued the general, "and I will tell Captain O'Brien that
if he comes off the mouth of the harbour the day after to-morrow, I
will send you on board in one of our boats."

He then took my letter and quitted the room. As soon as he was
gone I found myself quite well enough to go to Celeste, who waited
for me, and I told her what had passed. That morning I sat with her
and the general, and narrated all my adventures, which amused the
general very much. I did not conceal the conduct of my uncle, and
the hopes which I faintly entertained of being able, some day or
another, to discover the fraud which had been practised, or how
very unfavourable were my future prospects if I did not succeed. At
this portion of my narrative the general appeared very thoughtful
and grave. When I had finished, it was near dinner-time, and I
found that my clothes had arrived with a letter from O'Brien, who
stated how miserable he had been at the supposition of my loss, and
his delight at my escape. He stated that on going down into the
cabin, after I had shoved off, he, by chance, cast his eyes on the
barometer, and, to his surprise, found that it had fallen two inches,
which he had been told was the case previous to a hurricane. This,
combined with the peculiar state of the atmosphere, had induced
him to make every preparation, and that they had just completed
their work when it came on. The brig was thrown on her beam ends,
and lay there for half an hour, when they were forced to cut away
the masts to right her. That they did not weather the point the next
morning by more than half a cable's length; and concluded by saying, that the idea of my death had made him so unhappy that, if it

had not been for the sake of the men, it was almost a matter of indifference to him whether he had been lost or not. He had written to General O'Brien, thanking him for his kindness; and that, if fifty vessels should pass the brig, he would not capture one of them, until I was on board again, even if he were dismissed the service for neglect of duty. He said, that the brig sailed almost as fast under jury-masts as she did before, and that, as soon as I came on board, he should go back to Barbadoes. "As for your ribs being so bad, Peter, that's all bother," continued he; "I know that you are making arrangements for another sort of *rib*, as soon as you can manage it; but you must stop a little, my boy. You shall be a lord yet, as I always promised you that you should. It's a long lane that has no turning—so good-bye."

When I was alone with Celeste, I showed her O'Brien's letter. I had read the part of it relative to his not intending to make any capture while I was on shore to General O'Brien, who replied, "that under such circumstances he thought he should do right to detain me a little longer; but," said he, "O'Brien is a man of honour, and worthy of his name."

When Celeste came to that part of the letter in which O'Brien stated that I was looking after another rib, and which I had quite forgotten, she asked me to explain it; for, although she could read and speak English very well, she had not been sufficiently accustomed to it to comprehend the play upon words. I translated, and then said, "Indeed, Celeste, I had forgotten that observation of O'Brien's, or I should not have shown you the letter; but he has stated the truth. After all your kindness to me, how can I help being in love with you? and need I add, that I should consider it the greatest blessing which Heaven could grant me, if you could feel so much regard for me as one day to become my wife! Don't be angry with me for telling you the truth," continued I, for Celeste coloured up as I spoke to her.

"Oh, no! I am not angry with you, Peter; far from it. It is very complimentary to me—what you have just said."

"I am aware," continued I, "that at present I have little to offer you—indeed, nothing. I am not even such a match as your father might approve of, but you know my whole history, and what my desires are."

"My dear father loves me, Peter, and he loves you too, very

much—he always did, from the hour he saw you—he was so pleased with your candour and honesty of character. He has often told me so, and very often talked of you."

"Well, Celeste, tell me,—may I when far away, be permitted to think of you, and indulge a hope, that someday we may meet never to part again?" And I took Celeste by the hand, and put my arm round her waist.

"I don't know what to say," replied she; "I will speak to my father, or perhaps you will; but I will never marry anybody else, if I can help it."

I drew her close to me, and kissed her. Celeste burst into tears, and laid her head upon my shoulder. When General O'Brien came I did not attempt to move, nor did Celeste.

"General," said I, "you may think me to blame, but I have not been able to conceal what I feel for Celeste. You may think that I am imprudent, and that I am wrong in thus divulging what I ought to have concealed, until I was in a situation to warrant my aspiring to your daughter's hand; but the short time allowed me to be in her company, the fear of losing her, and my devoted attachment, will, I trust, plead my excuse."

The general took one or two turns up and down the room, and then replied, "What says Celeste?"

"Celeste will never do anything to make her father unhappy," replied she, going up to him and hiding her face in his breast, with her arm round his neck.

The general kissed his daughter, and then said, "I will be frank with you, Mr Simple. I do not know any man whom I would prefer to you as a son-in-law; but there are many considerations which young people are very apt to forget. I do not interfere in your attachment, which appears to be mutual; but, at the same time, I will have no promise and no engagement, you may never meet again. However, Celeste is very young, and I shall not put any constraint upon her; and at the same time you are equally free, if time and circumstances should alter your present feelings."

"I can ask no more, my dear sir," replied I, taking the general by the hand; "it is candid—more than I had any reason to expect. I shall now leave you with a contented mind, and the hopes of one day claiming Celeste shall spur me to exertion."

"Now, if you please, we will drop the subject," said the general.

"Celeste, my dear, we have a large party to dinner, as you know. You had better retire to your room and get ready. I have asked all the ladies that you liberated, Peter, and all their husbands and fathers; so you will have the pleasure of witnessing how many people you made happy by your gallantry. Now that Celeste has left the room, Peter, I must beg that, as a man of honour, you do not exact from her any more promises, or induce her to tie herself down to you by oaths. Her attachment to you has grown up with her unaccountably, and she is already too fond of you for her peace of mind, should accident or circumstances part you forever. Let us hope for the best, and depend upon it that it shall be no trifling obstacle which will hinder me from seeing you one day united."

I thanked the general with tears; he shook me warmly by the hand as I gave my promise, and we separated.

How happy did I feel when I went into my room, and sat down to compose my mind and think over what had happened. True, at one moment the thought of my dependent situation threw a damp over my joy; but in the next I was building castles, inventing a discovery of my uncle's plot, fancying myself in possession of the title and property, and laying it at the feet of my dear Celeste. Hope sustained my spirits, and I felt satisfied for the present with the consideration that Celeste returned my love. I decked myself carefully, and went down, where I found all the company assembled. We had a very pleasant, happy party, and the ladies entreated General O'Brien to detain me as a prisoner—very kind of them—and I felt very much disposed to join in their request.

—◦◦◦—

CHAPTER L

*Peter Simple first takes a command, then three West Indiamen, and twenty prisoners—
One good turn deserves another—The prisoners endeavour to take him, but are themselves taken in.*

THE NEXT DAY I was very unhappy. The brig was in the offing
waiting for me to come on board. I pointed her out to Celeste
as we were at the window, and her eyes met mine. An hour's conversation could not have said more. General O'Brien showed that he
had perfect confidence in me for he left us together.

"Celeste," said I, "I have promised your father—"

"I know what has passed," interrupted she; "he told me everything."

"How kind he is! But I did not say that I would not bind myself,
Celeste."

"No! but my father made me promise that you should not—that
if you attempted, I was immediately to prevent you—and so I
shall."

"Then you shall keep your word, Celeste. Imagine everything
that can be said in this—" and I kissed her.

"Don't think me forward, Peter, but I wish you to go away
happy," said Celeste; "and therefore, in return, imagine all I could
say in this—" and she returned my salute.

After this we had a conversation of two hours; but what lovers
say is very silly, except to themselves, and the reader need not be
troubled with it. General O'Brien came in and told me the boat was
ready. I rose up—I was satisfied with what had passed, and with a
firm voice I said, "Good-bye, Celeste; God bless you!" and followed
the general, who, with some of his officers, walked down with me to
the beach. I thanked the general, who embraced me, paid my adieus
to the officers, and stepped into the boat. In half an hour I was on
board of the brig, and in O'Brien's arms. We put the helm up, and in
a short time the town of St Pierre was shut out from my longing
sight, and we were on our way to Barbadoes. That day was passed
in the cabin with O'Brien, giving him a minute detail of all that had
passed.

When we anchored once more in Carlisle Bay, we found that the hurricane had been much more extensive in the Windward Islands than we had imagined. Several men-of-war were lying there, having lost one or more of their masts, and there was great difficulty in supplying the wants of so many. As we arrived the last, of course we were last served; and, there being no boats left in store, there was no chance of our being ready for sea under two or three months. The *Joan d'Arc* schooner privateer was still lying there, but had not been fitted out for want of men; and the admiral proposed to O'Brien that he should man her with a part of his ship's company, and send one of his lieutenants out to cruise in her. This was gladly assented to by O'Brien, who came on board and asked me whether I should like to have her, which I agreed to, as I was quite tired of Barbadoes and fried flying fish.

I selected two midshipmen, Swinburne, and twenty men, and having taken on board provisions and water for three months, I received my written instructions from O'Brien, and made sail. We soon discovered that the masts which the American had sold to the schooner, were much too large for her; she was considerably overmasted, and we were obliged to be very careful. I stood for Trinidad, off which island was to be my cruising ground, and in three weeks had recaptured three West Indiamen, when I found myself so short of hands, that I was obliged to return to Barbadoes. I had put four hands into the first vessel, which, with the Englishmen, prisoners, were sufficient, and three hands into the two others; but I was very much embarrassed with my prisoners, who amounted to nearly double my ship's company remaining on board. Both the midshipmen I had sent away, and I consulted with Swinburne as to what was best to be done.

"Why, the fact is, Mr Simple, Captain O'Brien ought to have given us more hands; twenty men are little enough for a vessel with a boom mainsail like the one we have here; and now we have only ten left; but I suppose he did not expect us to be so lucky, and it's true enough that he has plenty of work for the ship's company, now that he has to turn everything in afresh. As for the prisoners, I think we had better run close in, and give them two of our boats to take them on shore. At all events, we must be rid of them, and not be obliged to have one eye aloft, and the other down the hatchway, as we must now."

This advice corresponded with my own ideas, and I ran in-shore, gave them the stern-boat, and one of the larger ones, which held them all, and sent them away, leaving only one boat for the schooner, which we hoisted up in the starboard chess-tree. It fell a dead calm as we sent away the prisoners; we saw them land and disappear over the rocks, and thought ourselves well rid of them, as they were twenty-two in number, most of them Spaniards, and very stout ferocious-looking fellows. It continued calm during the whole day, much to our annoyance, as I was very anxious to get away as soon as I could; still I could not help admiring the beauty of the scenery—the lofty mountains rising abruptly from the ocean, and towering in the clouds, reflected on the smooth water, as clear as in a looking-glass, every colour, every tint, beautifully distinct. The schooner gradually drifted close in-shore, and we could perceive the rocks at the bottom, many fathoms deep. Not a breath of wind was to be seen on the surface of the water for several miles round, although the horizon in the offing showed that there was a smart breeze outside.

Night came on, and we still lay becalmed. I gave my orders to Swinburne, who had the first watch, and retired to my standing bed-place in the cabin. I was dreaming, and I hardly need say who was the object of my visions. I thought I was in Eagle Park, sitting down with her under one of the large chestnut trees, which formed the avenue, when I felt my shoulder roughly pushed. I started up— "What is the matter? Who's that—Swinburne?"

"Yes, sir. On with your clothes immediately, as we have work on hand, I expect." And Swinburne left the cabin, and I heard him calling the other men who were below. I knew that Swinburne would not give a false alarm. In a minute I was on deck, and was looking at the stern of the schooner. "What is that, Swinburne?" said I.

"Silence, sir. Hark! don't you hear them?"

"Yes," replied I; "the sound of oars."

"Exactly, sir; depend upon it, those Spaniards have got more help, and are coming back to take the vessel; they know we have only ten hands on board."

By this time the men were all on deck. I directed Swinburne to see all the muskets loaded, and ran down for my own sword and pistols. The water was so smooth, and the silence so profound, that Swinburne had heard the sound of the oars at a considerable distance. Fortunate it was, that I had such a trusty follower. Another might have slumbered, and the schooner have been boarded and captured without our being prepared. When I came on deck again, I spoke to the men, exhorted them to do their duty, and pointed out to them that these cut-throat villains would certainly murder us all if we were taken, which I firmly believe would have been the case. The men declared that they would sell their lives as dearly as they could. We had twenty muskets, and the same number of pistols, all of which were now loaded. Our guns were also ready, but of no use, now that the schooner had not steerage-way.

The boats were in sight, about a quarter of a mile astern, when Swinburne said, "There's a cat's-paw flying along the water, Mr Simple; if we could only have a little wind, how we would laugh at them; but I'm afraid there's no such luck. Shall we let them know that we are ready?"

"Let every one of us take two muskets," said I: "when the first boat is under the counter, take good aim, and discharge into one of the boats; then seize the other musket, and discharge it at the other boat. After that we must trust to our cutlasses and pistols; for if they come on, there will be no time to load again. Keep silence, all of you."

The boats now came up full of men; but as we remained perfectly quiet, they pulled up gently, hoping to surprise us. Fortunately, one was a little in advance of the other; upon which I altered my directions, and desired my men to fire their second musket into the first boat, as, if we could disable her, we were an equal match for those in the other. When the boat was within six yards of the schooner's counter, "Now!" said I, and all the muskets were discharged at once, and my men cheered. Several of the oars dropped, and I was sure we had done great execution; but they were laid hold of by the other men, who had not been pulling, and again the boat advanced to the counter.

"Good aim, my lads, this time," cried Swinburne; "the other boat will be alongside as soon as you have fired. Mr Simple, the schooner has headway, and there's a strong breeze coming up."

Again we discharged our ten muskets into the boat, but this time we waited until the bow-man had hooked on the planeshear with his boat-hook, and our fire was very effective.* I was surprised to find that the other boat was not on board of us; but a light breeze had come up, and the schooner glided through the water. Still she was close under our counter, and would have been aboard in a minute. In the meantime, the Spaniards who were in the first boat were climbing up the side, and were repulsed by my men with great success. The breeze freshened, and Swinburne ran to the helm. I perceived the schooner was going fast through the water, and the second boat could hardly hold her course. I ran to where the boat-hook was fixed on the planeshear, and unhooked it; the boat fell astern, leaving two Spaniards clinging to the side, who were cut down, and they fell into the water. "Hurrah! all safe!" cried Swinburne; "and now to punish them."

The schooner was now darting along at the rate of five miles, with an increasing breeze. We stood in for two minutes, then tacked, and ran for the boats. Swinburne steered, and I continued standing in the bows, surrounded by the rest of the men. Starboard a little, Swinburne."—"Starboard it is."

"Steady—steady: I see the first boat, she is close under our bows. Steady—port—port—port a little—port. Look out, my lads, and cut down all who climb up."

Crash went the schooner onto the boat, the men in her in vain endeavouring to escape us. For a second or two she appeared to right, until her further gunwale was borne down under the water; she turned up, and the schooner went over her, sending every soul in her to their account. One man clung on to a rope, and was towed for a few seconds, but a cutlass divided the rope at the gunwale, and with a faint shriek he disappeared. The other boat was close to us, and perceived what had been done. They remained with their oars poised, all ready to pull so as to evade the schooner. We steered for her, and the schooner was now running at the rate of seven miles an hour. When close under our bows, by very dexterously pulling short round with their starboard oars, we only struck her with our bow; and before she went down many of the Spaniards had gained the deck, or were clinging to the side of the vessel. They fought with

* *Planeshear (or planksheare): A continuous planking that covers the timbers around a vessel's hull.*

desperation, but we were too strong for them. It was only those who had gained the deck which we had to contend with. The others clung for a time, and, unable to get up the sides, one by one dropped into the water and went astern. In a minute, those on deck were lying at our feet, and in a minute more they were tossed overboard after their companions; not, however, until one of them struck me through the calf of the leg with his knife as we were lifting him over the gunwale. I do not mean to say that the Spaniards were not justified in attempting to take the schooner; but still, as we had liberated them but a few hours before, we felt that it was unhandsome and treacherous on their part, and therefore showed them no quarter. There were two of my men wounded as well as myself, but not severely, which was fortunate, as we had no surgeon on board, and only about half a yard of a diachylum plaster in the vessel.*

"Well out of that, sir," said Swinburne, as I limped aft. "By the Lord Harry! it might have been a *pretty go.*"

Having shaped our course for Barbadoes, I dressed my leg and went down to sleep. This time I did not dream of Celeste, but fought the Spaniards over again, thought I was wounded, and awoke with the pain of my leg.

—◈◈◈—

CHAPTER LI

Peter turned out of his command by his vessel turning bottom up—A cruise on a mainboom, with sharks en attendant—Self and crew, with several flying fish, taken on board a negro boat—Peter regenerates by putting on a new outward man.

WE MADE BARBADOES without any further adventure, and were about ten miles off the bay, steering with a very light breeze, and I went down into the cabin, expecting to be at anchor before breakfast the next morning. It was just daylight, when I found myself thrown out of my bed-place on the deck, on the other side of the cabin, and heard the rushing of water. I sprang up, I

* *Diachylum plaster: An adhesive lead plaster used in treating wounds.*

knew the schooner was on her beam-ends, and gained the deck. I was correct in my supposition: she had been upset by what is called a white squall, and in two minutes would be down. All the men were up on deck, some dressed, others, like myself, in their shirts. Swinburne was aft; he had an axe in his hand, cutting away the rigging of the main-boom. I saw what he was about; I seized another, and disengaged the jaw-rope and small gear about the mast. We had no other chance; our boat was under the water, being hoisted up on the side to leeward. All this, however, was but the work of two minutes; and I could not help observing by what trifles lives are lost or saved. Had the axe not been fortunately at the capstern, I should not have been able to cut the jaw-rope, Swinburne would not have had time, and the main-boom would have gone down with the schooner. Fortunately we had cleared it; the schooner filled, righted a little, and then sank, dragging us and the main-boom for a few seconds down in its vortex, and then we rose to the surface.

The squall still continued, but the water was smooth. It soon passed over, and again it was nearly calm. I counted the men clinging to the boom, and found that they were all there. Swinburne was next to me. He was holding with one hand, while with the other he felt in his pocket for a quid of tobacco, which he thrust into his cheek. "I wasn't on deck at the time, Mr Simple," said he, "or this wouldn't have happened. I had just been relieved, and I told Collins to look out sharp for squalls. I only mention it, that if you are saved, and I am not, you mayn't think I was neglectful of my duty. We arn't far from the land, but still we are more likely to fall in with a shark than a friend, I'm thinking."

These, indeed, had been my thoughts, but I had concealed them; but after Swinburne had mentioned the shark, I very often looked along the water for their fins, and down below to see if they were coming up to tear us to pieces. It was a dreadful feeling.

"It was not your fault, Swinburne, I am sure. I ought to have relieved you myself, but I kept the first watch, and was tired. We must put our trust in God; perhaps, we may yet be spared."

It was now almost calm, and the sun had mounted in the heavens: the scorching rays were intolerable upon our heads, for we had not the defence of hats. I felt my brain on fire, and was inclined to drop into the water, to screen myself from the intolerable heat. As the day advanced so did our sufferings increase. It was a dead calm, the sun perpendicular over us, actually burning that part of our bodies which rose clear of the water. I could have welcomed even a shark to relieve me of my torment; but I thought of Celeste, and I clung to life. Towards the afternoon I felt sick and dizzy; my resolution failed me; my vision was imperfect; but I was roused by Swinburne, who cried out, "A boat, by all that's gracious! Hang on a little longer, my men, and you are saved."

It was a boat full of negroes, who had come out to catch flying fish. They had perceived the spar on the water, and hastened to secure the prize. They dragged us all in, gave us water, which appeared like nectar, and restored us to our fleeting senses. They made fast the boom, and towed it in-shore. We had not been ten minutes on our way, when Swinburne pointed to the fin of a large shark above the water. "Look there, Mr Simple." I shuddered, and made no answer; but I thanked God in my heart.

In two hours we were landed, but were too ill to walk. We were carried up to the hospital, bled, and put into cots. I had a brain fever, which lasted six or seven days, during which O'Brien never left my bedside.* My head was shaved, all the skin came off my face like a mask, as well as off my back and shoulders. We were put into baths of brandy and water, and in three weeks were all recovered.

"That was but an unlucky schooner from beginning to end," observed O'Brien, after I had narrated the events of my cruise. "We had a bad beginning with her, and we had a bad ending. She's gone to the bottom, and the devil go with her; however, all's well that ends well, and, Peter, you're worth a dozen dead men yet; but you occasion me a great deal of trouble and anxiety, that's the truth of it, and I doubt if I shall ever rear you, after all."

I returned to my duty on board of the brig, which was now nearly ready for sea. One morning O'Brien came on board and said, "Peter, I've a piece of news for you. Our gunner is appointed to the *Araxes*, and the admiral has given me a gunner's warrant for old Swinburne. Send for him on deck."

Swinburne was summoned, and came rolling up the hatchway. "Swinburne," said O'Brien, "you have done your duty well, and

---

* *Brain fever: A commonly diagnosed illness (defined as an inflamation of the brain) in the nineteenth century and rampant in Victorian novels.*

you are now gunner of the *Rattlesnake*. Here is your warrant, and I've great pleasure in getting it for you."

Swinburne turned the quid in his cheek, and then replied, "May I be so bold as to ax, Captain O'Brien, whether I must wear one of them long tog, swallow-tailed coats—because, if so, I'd prefer being a quarter-master?"

"A gunner may wear a jacket, Swinburne, if he likes; when you go on shore you may bend the swallow-tail, if you please."

"Well, sir, then if that's the case, I'll take the warrant, because I know it will please the old woman."

So saying, Swinburne hitched up his trousers, and went down below. I may here observe that Swinburne kept his round jacket until our arrival in England, when the "old woman," his wife, who thought her dignity at stake, soon made him ship the swallow-tail; and, after it was once on, Swinburne took a fancy to it, and always wore it, except when he was at sea.

The same evening, as I was coming with O'Brien from the governor's house, where I had dined, we passed a building, lighted up. "What can that be?" observed O'Brien; "not a dignity ball—there is no music." Our curiosity induced us to enter, and we found it to be fitted up as a temporary chapel, filled with black and coloured people, who were ranged on the forms, and waiting for the preacher.

"It is a Methodist meeting," said I to O'Brien.*

"Never mind," said he, "let us hear what is going on."

In a moment afterwards the pulpit was filled, not by a white man, as we had anticipated, but by a tall negro. He was dressed in black, and his hair, which it was impossible to comb down straight, was plaited into fifty little tails, well tied at the end of them, like you sometimes see the mane of a horse; this produced a somewhat more clerical appearance. His throat was open and collar laid back; the wristbands of his shirt very large and white, and he flourished a white cambric handkerchief.

"What a dandy he is!" whispered O'Brien.

I thought it almost too absurd when he said he would take the liberty to praise God in the 17th hymn, and beg all the company to

---

* *This distasteful passage continues the criticism of several groups begun earlier in the novel, including Methodists, clerics, and Blacks imitating Europeans.*

join chorus. He then gave out the stanzas in the most strange pro-
nunciation.

"Gentle Jesus, God um lub," &c.

When the hymn was finished, which was sung by the whole congre-
gation, in the most delightful discord,—everyone chose his own
key—he gave an extempore prayer, which was most unfortunately
incomprehensible, and then commenced his discourse, which was
on *Faith.* I shall omit the head and front of his offending, which
would, perhaps, hardly be gratifying although ludicrous. He reminded me of a monkey imitating a man; but what amused me
most was his finale, in which he told his audience that there could
be no faith without charity. For a little while he descanted upon this
generally, and at last became personal. His words were, as well as I
can recollect, nearly as follows:—

"And now you see, my dear bredren, how unpossible to go to
heaven, with all the faith in the world, without charity. Charity
mean, give away. Suppose you no give—you no ab charity; suppose
you no ab charity—you no ab faith; suppose you no ab faith—you
all go to hell and be damned. Now den, let me see if you ab charity.
Here, you see, I come to save all your soul from hell-fire; and hell-
fire dam hot, I can tell you. Dere you all burn like coal, till you turn
white powder, and den burn on till you come black again; and so
you go on, burn, burn, sometime white, sometime black, for ebber
and ebber. The debil never allow Sangoree to cool tongue. No, no
cocoa-nut milk,—not a lilly drap of water; debil see you damned
first. Suppose you ask, he poke um fire, and laugh. Well, den, ab you
charity? No, you ab not. You, Quashee, how you dare look me in the
face? You keep shop—you sell egg—you sell yam—you sell pepper
hot—but when you give to me? Eh! nebber, so help me God. Suppose you no send—you no ab charity, and you go to hell. You black
Sambo," continued he, pointing to a man in the corner, "ab very
fine boat, go out all day, catch fly-fish, bring um back, fry um, and
sell for money; but when you send to me? not one little fish ebber
find way to my mouth. What I tell you 'bout Peter and 'postles—all
fishermen; good men, give 'way to poor. Sambo, you no ab charity;
and 'spose you no repent this week, and send one very fine fish in
plantain leaf, you go to hell, and burn for ebber and ebber. Eh! so

you will run away, Massa Johnson," cried he out to another, who was edging to the door; "but you no run away from hell-fire: when debil catch you, he hold dam tight. You know you kill sheep and goat ebery day. You send bell ring all 'bout town for people to come buy; but when you send to me? nebber, 'cept once, you gave me lilly bit of libber. That not do, Massa Johnson; you no ab charity; and suppose you no send me sheep's head to-morrow morning, dam you libber, that's all. I see many more, but I see um all very sorry, and dat they mean to sin no more, so dis time I let um off, and say noting about it, because I know plenty of plantain and banana (pointing to one) and oranges and shaddock (pointing to another), and salt fish (pointing to a fourth), and ginger-pop and spruce beer (pointing to a fifth), and a straw hat (pointing to a sixth), and ebery-thing else, come to my house to-morrow. So I say no more 'bout it; I see you all very sorry—you only forget. You all ab charity, and all ab faith; so now, my dear bredren, we go down on our knees, and thank God for all this, and more especially that I save all your souls from going to the debil, who run about Barbadoes like one roaring lion, seeking what he may lay hold of, and cram into his dam fiery jaw."

"That will do, Peter," said O'Brien; "we have the cream of it, I think."

We left the house, and walked down to the boat. "Surely, O'Brien," said I, "this should not be permitted?"

"He's no worse than his neighbours," replied O'Brien, "and perhaps does less harm. I admire the rascal's ingenuity; he gave his flock what, in Ireland, we should call a pretty broad hint."

"Yes, there was no mistaking him: but is he a licenced preacher?"

"Very little licence in his preaching, I take it; no, I suppose he has had a *call*."

"A call!—what do you mean?"

"I mean that he wants to fill his belly. Hunger is a call of nature, Peter."

"He seems to want a good many things, if we were to judge by his catalogue; what a pity it is that these poor people are not better instructed."

"That they never will be, Peter, while there is what may be called free trade in religion."

"You speak like a Catholic, O'Brien."

"I am one," replied he. And here our conversation ended, for we were close to the boat, which was waiting for us on the beach.

The next day a man-of-war brig arrived from England, bringing letters for the squadron on the station. I had two from my sister Ellen which made me very uncomfortable. She stated that my father had seen my uncle, Lord Privilege, and had had high words with him; indeed, as far as she could ascertain of the facts, my father had struck my uncle, and had been turned out of the house by the servants; that he had returned in a state of great excitement, and was very ill ever since; that there was a great deal of talk in the neighbourhood on the subject, people generally highly blaming my father's conduct, thinking that he was deranged in his intellect—a supposition very much encouraged by my uncle. She again expressed her hopes of my speedy return. I had now been absent nearly three years, and she had been so uncomfortable that she felt as if it had been at least ten. O'Brien also received a letter from Father M'Grath, which I shall lay before the reader:

"MY DEAR SON,—Long life, and all the blessings of all the saints be upon you now and for evermore! Amen. And may you live to be married, and may I dance at your wedding, and may you never want children, and may they grow up as handsome as their father and their mother (whoever she may hereafter be), and may you die of a good old age, and in the true faith, and be waked handsomely, as your own father was last Friday s'ennight, seeing as how he took it into his head to leave this world for a better. It was a very dacent funeral-procession, my dear Terence, and your father must have been delighted to see himself so well attinded. No man ever made a more handsome corpse, considering how old, and thin, and haggard he had grown of late, and how gray his hair had turned. He held the nosegay between his fingers, across his breast as natural as life, and reminded us all of the blessed saint, Pope Gregory, who was called to glory some hundred years before either you or I was born.

"Your mother's quite comfortable; and there she sits in her ould chair, rocking to and fro all day long, and never speaking a word to nobody, thinking about heaven, I dare to say; which is just what she ought to do, seeing that she stands a very pretty chance of going there in the course of a month or so. Divil a word has she ever said since your father's departure, but then she screamed and yelled enough to last for seven years at the least. She screamed away all her senses anyhow, for she has done nothing since but cough, cough, and fumble at her pater-nosters—a very blessed way to pass the remainder of her days, seeing that I expect her to drop every minute like an over-ripe sleepy pear. So don't think any more about her, my son, for without you are back in a jiffy, her body will be laid in consecrated ground, and her happy, blessed soul in purgatory. *Pax vobiscum.* Amen! amen!

"And now having disposed of your father and your mother so much to your satisfaction, I'll just tell you that Ella's mother died in the convent at Dieppe, but whether she kept her secret or not I do not know; but this I do know, that if she didn't relieve her soul by confession, she's damned to all eternity. Thanks be to God for all his mercies. Amen! Ella Flanagan is still alive, and, for a nun, is as well as can be expected. I find that she knows nothing at all about the matter of the exchanging the genders of the babbies—only that her mother was on oath to Father M'Dermot, who ought to be hanged, drawn, and quartered instead of those poor fellows whom the government called rebels, but who were no more rebels than Father M'Grath himself, who'll uphold the Pretender, as they call our true Catholic king, as long as there's life in his body or a drop of whiskey left in ould Ireland to drink his health wid.* Talking about Father M'Dermot puts me in mind that the bishop has not yet decided our little bit of a dispute, saying that he must take time to think about it. Now, considering that it's just three years since the row took place, the old gentleman must be a very slow thinker not to have found out by this time that I was in the right, and that Father M'Dermot, the baste, is not good enough to be hanged.

"Your two married sisters are steady and diligent young women, having each made three children since you last saw them. Fine boys, every mother's son of them, with elegant spacious features, and famous mouths for taking in whole potatoes. By the powers, but the offsets of the tree of the O'Briens begin to make a noise in the land,

* *The Pretender: James, the son of Stuart King James II (1685–88). His baptism into the Catholic faith in 1688 precipitated the so-called "Glorious Revolution" in which James II was forced from the throne. The followers of James III were known as Jacobites, while his foes labeled him the Pretender.*

anyhow, as you would say if you only heard them roaring for their bit of suppers.

"And now, my dear son Terence, the real purport of this letter, which is just to put to your soul's conscience, as a dutiful son, whether you ought not to send me a small matter of money to save your poor father's soul from pain and anguish—for it's no joke that being in purgatory, I can tell you; and you wouldn't care how soon you were tripped out of it yourself. I only wish you had but your little toe in it, and then you'd burn with impatience to have it out again. But you're a dutiful son, so I'll say no more about it—a nod's as good as a wink to a blind horse.

"When your mother goes, which, with the blessing of God, will be in a very little while, seeing that she has only to follow her senses, which are gone already, I'll take upon myself to sell everything, as worldly goods and chattels are of no use to dead people; and I have no doubt but that, what with the furniture and the two cows, and the pigs, and the crops in the ground, there will be enough to save her soul from the flames, and bury her dacently into the bargain. However, as you are the heir-at-law, seeing that the property is all your own, I'll keep a debtor and creditor account of the whole; and should there by any over, I'll use it all out in masses, so as to send her up to heaven by express, and if there's not suffi- cient, she must remain where she is till you come back and make up the deficiency. In the meanwhile I am your loving father in the faith,

"URTAGH M'GRATH."

—◦◦◦—

CHAPTER LII

Good sense in Swinburne—No man a hero to his valet de chambre, or a prophet in his own country—O'Brien takes a step by strategy—O'Brien parts with his friend, and Peter's star no longer in the ascendant.

O'BRIEN WAS SORRY for the death of his father, but he could not feel as most people would have done, as his father had certainly never been a father to him. He was sent to sea to be got rid of, and ever since he had been there, had been the chief support of

his family; his father was very fond of whiskey, and not very fond
of exertion. He was too proud of the true Milesian blood in his veins
to do anything to support himself, but not too proud to live upon
his son's hard-earned gains. For his mother O'Brien felt very much;
she had always been kind and affectionate, and was very fond of
him. Sailors, however, are so estranged from their families when
they have been long in their profession and so accustomed to vicissi-
tudes, that no grief for the loss of a relation lasts very long, and in a
week O'Brien had recovered his usual spirits, when a vessel brought
us the intelligence that a French squadron had been seen off St
Domingo. This put us all on the *qui vive.** O'Brien was sent for by
the admiral, and ordered to hasten his brig for sea with all possible
despatch, as he was to proceed with despatches to England forthwith. In three days we were reported ready, received our orders,
and at eight o'clock in the evening made sail from Carlisle Bay.
"Well, Mr Swinburne," said I, "how do you like your new situation?"

"Why, Mr Simple, I like it well enough; and it's not disagreeable
to be an officer, and sit in your own cabin; but still I feel that I
should get on better if I were in another ship. I've been hail-fellow
well met with the ship's company so long, that I can't top the officer
over them, and we can't get the duty done as smart as I could wish:
and then at night I find it very lonely stuck up in my cabin like a
parson's clerk, and nobody to talk to; for the other warrants are
particular, and say that I'm only acting, and may not be confirmed,
so they hold aloof. I don't much like being answerable for all that lot
of gunpowder—it's queer stuff to handle."

"Very true, Swinburne; but still, if there were no responsibility,
we should require no officers. You recollect that you are now provided for life, and will have half-pay."

"That's what made me bite, Mr Simple. I thought of the old
woman, and how comfortable it would make her in her old age; and
so, d'ye see, I sacrificed myself."

"How long have you been married, Swinburne?"

"Ever since Christmas '94. I wasn't going to be hooked carelessly, so I nibbled afore I took the bait. Had four years' trial of her

* Qui vive: *Alert.*

first, and, finding that she had plenty of ballast, I sailed her as my own."

"How do you mean by plenty of ballast?"

"I don't mean, Mr Simple, a broad bow and square hulk. You know very well that if a vessel has not ballast, she's bottom up in no time. Now, what keeps a woman stiff under her canvas is her modesty."

"Very true; but it's a rare commodity on the beach."

"And why, Mr Simple? because liquor is more valued. Many a good man has found it to be his bane; and as for a woman, when once she takes to it, she's like a ship without a rudder, and goes right before the wind to the devil. Not that I think a man ought not to take a nor-wester or two, when he can get them. Rum was not given by God Almighty only to make the niggers dance, but to make all our hearts glad; neither do I see why a woman is to stand out neither; what's good for Jack can't hurt Poll; only there is a medium, as they say, in all things, and half-an-half is quite strong enough."

"I should think it was," replied I, laughing.

"But don't be letting me prevent you from keeping a look-out, Mr Simple.—You, Hoskins, you're half-a-point off the wind. Luff you may.—I think, Mr Simple, that Captain O'Brien didn't pick out the best man, when he made Tom Alsop a quarter-master in my place."

"Why, he is a very steady, good man, Swinburne."

"Yes, so he is; but he has natural defects, which shouldn't be overlooked. I doubt if he can see so far as the head of the main-sail."

"I was not aware of that."

"No, but I was. Alsop wants to sarve out his time for his pension, and when he has sarved, you see if, when the surgeons examine him, they don't invalid him, as blind as a bat. I should like to have him as gunner's mate, and that's just what he's fit for. But, Mr Simple, I think we shall have some bad weather. The moon looks greasy, and the stars want snuffing. You'll have two reefs in the topsails afore morning. There's five bells striking. Now I'll turn in; if I didn't keep half the first, and half the morning watch, I shouldn't sleep all the night. I miss my regular watch very much, Mr Simple— habit's everything—and I don't much fancy a standing bed-place, it's so large, and I feel so cold of my sides. Nothing like a hammock, after all. Good-night, Mr Simple."

Our orders were to proceed with all *possible* despatch; and O'Brien carried on day and night, generally remaining up himself till one or two o'clock in the morning. We had very favourable weather, and in a little more than a month we passed the Lizard. The wind being fair, we passed Plymouth, ran up Channel, and anchored at Spithead.

After calling upon the admiral, O'Brien set off for town with his despatches, and left me in command of the ship. In three days I received a letter from him, informing me that he had seen the First Lord, who had asked him a great many questions concerning the station he had quitted; that he had also complimented O'Brien on his services. "On that hint I spake," continued O'Brien; "I ventured to insinuate to his lordship, that I had hoped I had earned my promotion; and as there is nothing like *quartering on the enemy*, I observed that I had not applied to Lord Privilege, as I considered my services would have been sufficient, without any application on his part. His lordship returned a very gracious answer: said that my Lord Privilege was a great ally of his, and very friendly to the government; and inquired when I was going to see him. I replied, that I certainly should not pay my respects to his lordship at present, unless there was occasion for it, as I must take a more favourable opportunity. So I hope that good may come from the great lord's error, which, of course, I shall not correct, as I feel I deserve my promotion—and you know, Peter, if you can't gain it by *hook*, you must by *crook*." He then concluded his letter; but there was a postscript as follows:

"Wish me joy, my dear Peter. I have this moment received a letter from the private secretary, to say that I am *posted*, and appointed to the *Semiramis* frigate, about to set sail for the East Indies. She is all ready to start; and now I must try to get you with me, of which I have no doubt; as, although her officers have been long appointed there will be little difficulty of success, when I mention your relationship to Lord Privilege, and while they remain in error as to his taking an interest in my behalf." I rejoiced at O'Brien's good fortune. His promotion I had considered certain, as his services had entitled him to it; but the command of so fine a frigate must have been given upon the supposition that it would be agreeable to my uncle, who was not only a prime supporter, but a very useful member, of the Tory Government. I could not help laughing to myself, at the idea of O'Brien obtaining his wishes from the influence of a person who probably detested him as much as one man could detest another; and I impatiently waited for O'Brien's next letter, by which I hoped to find myself appointed to the *Semiramis;* but a sad *contretemps* took place.

O'Brien did not write; but came down two days afterwards, hastened on board the *Semiramis,* read his commission, and assumed the command before even he had seen me; he then sent his gig on board of the *Rattlesnake,* to desire me to come to him directly. I did so, and we went down into the cabin of the frigate. "Peter," said he, "I was obliged to hasten down and read myself captain of this ship, as I am in fear that things are not going on well. I had called to pay my respects at the Admiralty, previous to joining, and was kicking my heels in the waiting-room, when who should walk up the passage, as if he were a captain on his own quarter-deck, but your uncle, Lord Privilege. His eye met mine—he recognised me immediately—and, if it did not flash fire, it did something very like it. He asked a few questions of one of the porters, and was giving his card, when my name was called for. I passed him, and up I went to the First Lord, thanked him for the frigate; and having received a great many compliments upon my exertions in the West India station, made my bow and retired. I had intended to have requested your appointment, but I knew that your name would bring up Lord Privilege's; and, moreover, your uncle's card was brought up and laid upon the table while I was sitting there. The First Lord, I presume, thought that his lordship was come to thank him for his kindness to me, which only made him more civil. I made my bow and went down, when I met the eye of Lord Privilege; who looked daggers at me as he walked up-stairs—for, of course, he was admitted immediately after my audience was finished. Instead of waiting to hear the result of the explanation, I took a post-chaise, and have come down here as fast as four horses can bring me, and have read myself in— for, Peter, I feel sure, that if not on board, my commission will be cancelled; and I know that if once in command, as I am now, I can call for a court-martial, to clear my character if I am superseded. I know that the Admiralty *can* do anything, but still they will be cautious in departing from the rules of the service, to please even

Lord Privilege. I looked up at the sky as soon as I left the Admiralty portico, and was glad to see that the weather was so thick, and the telegraph not at work, or I might have been too late. Now I'll go on shore, and report myself to the admiral, as having taken the command of the *Semiramis*."

O'Brien went on shore to report himself, was well received by the admiral, who informed him, that if he had any arrangements to make, he could not be too soon, as he should not be surprised if his sailing orders came down the next morning. This was very annoying, as I could not see how I should be able to join O'Brien's ship, even if I could effect an exchange, in so short a time. I therefore hastened on board of the *Semiramis*, and applied to the officers to know if any of them were willing to exchange into the *Rattlesnake;* but, although they did not much like going to the East Indies, they would not exchange into a brig, and I returned disappointed. The next morning, the admiral sent for O'Brien, and told him confidentially, for he was the same admiral who had received O'Brien when he had escaped from prison with me, and was very kind to him, that there was some *hitch* about his having the *Semiramis*, and that orders had come down to pay her off, all standing, and examine her bottom, if Captain O'Brien had not joined her. "Do you understand what this means?" said the admiral, who was anxious to know the reason.

O'Brien answered frankly, that Lord Privilege, by whose interest he had obtained his former command, was displeased with him; and that, as he saw him go up to the First Lord, he had no doubt but that his lordship had said something to his disadvantage, as he was a very vindictive man.

"Well," said the admiral, "it's lucky that you have taken the command, as they cannot well displace you, or send her into dock without a survey, and upon your representation."

And so it proved; the First Lord, when he found that O'Brien had joined, took no further steps, but allowed the frigate to proceed to her intended destination. But all chance of my sailing with him was done away, and now, for the first time, I had to part with O'Brien. I remained with him the whole time that I could be spared from my duties. O'Brien was very much annoyed, but there was no help. "Never mind, Peter," said he, "I've been thinking that perhaps it's all for the best. You will see more of the world, and be no longer in leading-strings. You are now a fine man grown up, big enough and ugly enough, as they say, to take care of yourself. We shall meet again; and if we don't, why then, God bless you, my boy, and don't forget O'Brien."

Three days afterwards, O'Brien's orders came down. I accompanied him on board; and it was not until the ship was under weigh, and running towards the Needles with a fair wind, that I shook hands with him, and shoved off. Parting with O'Brien was a heavy blow to me; but I little knew how much I was to suffer before I saw him again.

CHAPTER LIII

I am pleased with my new captain—Obtain leave to go home—Find my father afflicted with a very strange disease, and prove myself a very good doctor, although the disorder always breaks out in a fresh place.

THE DAY AFTER O'Brien had sailed for the East Indies, the dockyard men came on board to survey the brig, and she was found so defective as to be ordered into dock. I had received letters from my sister, who was overjoyed at the intelligence of my safe return, and the anticipation of seeing me. The accounts of my father were, however, very unsatisfactory. My sister wrote, that disappointment and anxiety had had such an effect upon him, that he was deranged in his intellects. Our new captain came down to join us. He was a very young man, and had never before commanded a ship. His character as lieutenant was well known, and not very satisfactory, being that of a harsh, unpleasant officer; but, as he had never been first lieutenant, it was impossible to say what he might prove when in command of a ship. Still we were a little anxious about it, and severely regretted the loss of O'Brien. He came on board the hulk to which the ship's companies had been turned over, and read his commission. He proved to be all affability, condescension, and good-nature. To me, he was particularly polite, stating that he should not interfere with me in carrying on the duty, as I must be so well acquainted with the ship's company. We thought that those who gave us the information must have been prejudiced or mistaken in his character. During the half hour that he remained on board, I stated, that now that the brig was in dock, I should like very much to have an opportunity of seeing my friends, if he would sanction my asking for leave. To this he cheerfully consented, adding, that he would extend it upon his own responsibility. My letter to the Admiralty was therefore forwarded through him, and was answered in the affirmative. The day afterwards, I set off by the coach, and once more embraced my dear sister.

After the first congratulations were over, I inquired about my father; she replied, that he was so wild that nobody could manage him. That he was melancholy and irritable at the same time, and was certainly deranged, fancying himself to be made of various substances, or to be in a certain trade or capacity. That he generally remained in this way four or five days, when he went to bed, and slept for twenty-four hours, or more, and awoke with some new strange imagination in his head. His language was violent, but that, in other respects, he seemed to be more afraid of other people, than inclined to be mischievous, and that every day he was getting more strange and ridiculous. He had now just risen from one of his long naps, and was in his study; that before he had fallen asleep he had fancied himself to be a carpenter, and had sawed and chopped up several articles of furniture in the house.

I quitted my sister to see my father, whom I found in his easy-chair. I was much shocked at his appearance. He was thin and haggard, his eye was wild, and he remained with his mouth constantly open. A sick-nurse, who had been hired by my sister, was standing by him.

"Pish, pish, pish, pish!" cried my father; "what can you, a stupid old woman, know about my inside? I tell you the gas is generating fast, and even now I can hardly keep on my chair. I'm lifting—lifting now; and if you don't tie me down with cords, I shall go up like a balloon."

"Indeed, sir," replied the woman, "it's only the wind in your stomach. You'll break it off directly."

"It's inflammable gas, you old Hecate!—I know it is.* Tell me,

* Hecate: In Greek mythology, the goddess of sorcery and witchcraft.

will you get a cord, or will you not? Hah! who's that—Peter? Why you've dropped from the clouds, just in time to see me mount up to them."

"I hope you feel yourself better, sir," said I.

"I feel myself a great deal lighter every minute. Get a cord, Peter, and tie me to the leg of the table."

I tried to persuade him that he was under a mistake; but it was useless. He became excessively violent, and said I wished him in heaven. As I had heard that it was better to humour people afflicted with hypochondriacism, which was evidently the disease under which my father laboured, I tried that method. "It appears to me, sir," said I, "that if we could remove the gas every ten minutes, it would be a good plan."

"Yes—but how?" replied he, shaking his head mournfully.

"Why, with a syringe, sir," said I; "which will, if empty, of course draw out the gas, when inserted into your mouth."

"My dear Peter, you have saved my life: be quick, though, or I shall go up, right through the ceiling."

Fortunately, there was an instrument of that description in the house. I applied it to his mouth, drew up the piston, and then ejected the air, and re-applied it. In two minutes he pronounced himself better, and I left the old nurse hard at work, and my father very considerably pacified. I returned to my sister, to whom I recounted what had passed; but it was no source of mirth to us, although, had it happened to an indifferent person, I might have been amused. The idea of leaving her, as I must soon do—having only a fortnight's leave—to be worried by my father's unfortunate malady, was very distressing. But we entered into a long conversation, in which I recounted the adventures that had taken place since I had left her, and for the time forgot our source of annoyance and regret. For three days my father insisted upon the old woman pumping the gas out of his body; after that, he again fell into one of his sleeps, which lasted nearly thirty hours.

When he arose, I went again to see him. It was eight o'clock in the evening, and I entered with a candle. "Take it away—quick, take it away; put it out carefully."

"Why, what's the matter, sir?"

"Don't come near me, if you love me; don't come near me. Put it out, I say—put it out."

I obeyed his orders, and then asked him the reason. "Reason!" said he, now that we were in the dark; "can't you see?"

"No, father; I can see nothing in the dark."

"Well, then, Peter, I'm a magazine, full of gunpowder; the least spark in the world, and I am blown up. Consider the danger. You surely would not be the destruction of your father, Peter?" and the poor old gentleman burst into tears, and wept like a child.

I knew that it was in vain to reason with him. "My dear father," said I, "on board ship, when there is any danger of this kind, we always *float* the magazine. Now, if you were to drink a good deal of water, the powder would be spoiled, and there would be no danger." My father was satisfied with my proposal, and drank a tumbler of water every half-hour, which the old nurse was obliged to supply as fast as he called for it; and this satisfied him for three or four days, and I was again left to the company of my dear Ellen, when my father again fell into his stupor, and we wondered what would be his next fancy. I was hastily summoned by the nurse, and found my poor father lying in bed, and breathing in a very strange manner. "What is the matter, my dear sir?" inquired I.

"Why, don't you see what is the matter? How is a poor little infant, just born, to live, unless its mother is near to suckle it, and take care of it?"

"Indeed, sir, do you mean to say that you are just born?"

"To be sure I do. I'm dying for the breast."

This was almost too absurd; but I gravely observed, "That it was all very true, but unfortunately his mother had died in childbirth, and the only remedy was to bring him up by hand."

He agreed with me. I desired the nurse to make some gruel with brandy, and feed him; which she did, and he took the gruel just as if he were a baby. I was about to wish him goodnight, when he beckoned to me, and said, "Peter, she hasn't changed my napkin." This was too much, and I could not help laughing. I told the nurse what he said, and she replied, "Lord bless you, sir, what matter? if the old gentleman takes a fancy, why not indulge him? I'll fetch the kitchen table-cloth." This fit lasted about six days; for he went to sleep, because a baby always slept much: and I was in hopes it would last much longer: but he again went off into his lethargic fit, and, after a long sleep, awoke with a new fancy. My time had nearly expired, and I had written to my new captain, requesting an extension of leave, but I received an answer stating that it could not be granted, and requesting me to join the brig immediately. I was rather surprised at this, but of course was compelled to obey; and, embracing my dear sister once more, set off for Portsmouth. I advised her to humour my father, and this advice she followed; but his fancies were such, occasionally, as would have puzzled the most inventive genius to combat, or to find the remedy which he might acknowledge to be requisite. His health became certainly worse and worse, and his constitution was evidently destroyed by a slow, undermining, bodily and mental fever. The situation of my poor sister was very distressing; and I quitted her with melancholy forebodings.

I ought here to observe that I received all my prize-money, amounting to £1560, a large sum for a lieutenant. I put it into the funds, and gave a power of attorney to Ellen, requesting her to use it as her own. We consulted as to what she should do if my father should die, and agreed that all his debts, which we knew to amount to three or four hundred pounds, should be paid, and that she should manage how she could upon what was left of my father's property, and the interest of my prize-money.

——⟨ℓℓℓℓ⟩——

CHAPTER LIV

We receive our sailing orders, and orders of every description—A quarter-deck conversation—Listeners never hear any good of themselves.

WHEN I ARRIVED at Portsmouth, I reported myself to the captain, who lived at the hotel. I was ushered into his room to wait for him, as he was dressing to dine with the admiral. My eyes naturally turned to what lay on the table, merely from the feeling which one has to pass away the time, not from curiosity; and I was much surprised to see a pile of letters, the uppermost of which was franked by Lord Privilege. This, however, might be merely accidental; but my curiosity was excited, and I lifted up the letter, and found that the second, the third, and indeed at least ten of these were franked by my uncle. I could not imagine how there could be any intimacy between him and my uncle, and was reflecting upon it when Captain Hawkins, for that was his name, entered the room. He was very kind and civil, apologized for not being able to extend my leave, which, he said, was because he had consulted the admiral, who would not sanction the absence of the first lieutenant, and had very peremptorily desired he would recall me immediately. I was satisfied: he shook my hand, and we parted. On my arrival on board the hulk, for the brig was still in dock, I was warmly received by my messmates. They told me that the captain had, generally speaking, been very civil, but that, occasionally, the marks of the cloven foot appeared.

"Webster," said I, to the second lieutenant, "do you know any-thing about his family or connections?"

"It is a question I have asked of those who have sailed with him, and they all say that he never speaks of his own family, but very often boasts of his intimacy with the nobility. Some say that he is a *bye-blow* of some great man."

I reflected very much upon this, and connecting it with the nu-merous franks of Lord Privilege, which I saw on the table, had my misgivings; but then I knew that I could do my duty, and had no reason to fear any man. I resolved, in my own mind, to be very correct, and put it out of the power of anyone to lay hold of me, and then dismissed the subject. The brig was repaired and out of dock, and for some days I was very busy getting her ready for sea. I never quitted her; in fact, I had no wish. I never had any taste for bad company and midnight orgies, and I had no acquaintance with the respectable portion of the inhabitants of Portsmouth. At last the ship's company were removed into the brig: we went out of har-bour, and anchored at Spithead.

Captain Hawkins came on board and gave me an order-book, saying, "Mr Simple, I have a great objection to written orders, as I consider that the articles of war are quite sufficient to regulate any ship. Still, a captain is in a very responsible situation, and if any accident occurs he is held amenable. I therefore have framed a few orders of my own for the interior discipline of the vessel, which may probably save me harmless, in case of being *hauled over the coals;* but not with any wish that they should interfere with the comforts of the officers, only to guard against any mischance, of which the *onus* may fall upon myself."

I received the order-book, and the captain went ashore. When I went down into the gun-room, to look through it, I at once perceived that if rigidly conformed to, every officer in the ship would be rendered uncomfortable; and if not conformed to, I should be the party that was answerable. I showed it to Webster, who agreed with me, and gave it as his opinion that the captain's good nature and amiability were all a blind, and that he was intending to lay hold of us as soon as it was in his power. I therefore called all the officers together, and told them my opinion. Webster supported me, and it was unanimously agreed that the orders should be obeyed, although not without remonstrance. The major part of the orders, however, only referred to the time that the brig was in harbour; and, as we were about to proceed to sea, it was hardly worth while saying anything at present. The orders for the sailing of the brig came down, and by the same post I received a letter from my sister Ellen, stating that they had heard from Captain Fielding, who had immediately written to Bombay, where the regiment was stationed, and had received an answer, informing him that there was no married man in the regiment of the name of Sullivan, and no woman who had followed that regiment of that name. This at once put an end to all our researches after the wet-nurse, who had been confined in my uncle's house. Where she had been sent, it was of course impossible to say; but I gave up all chance of discovering my uncle's treachery; and, as I thought of Celeste, sighed at the little hope I had of ever being united to her. I wrote a long letter to O'Brien, and the next day we sailed for our station in the North Sea.

The captain added a night order-book to the other, and sent it up every evening, to be returned in the morning, with the signature of every officer of the night watches. He also required all our signatures to his general order-book, that we might not say we had not read them. I had the first watch, when Swinburne came up to me. "Well, Mr Simple, I do not think we have made much by our exchange of captains; and I have a shrewd suspicion we shall have squalls ere long."

"We must not judge too hastily, Swinburne," replied I.

"No, no—I don't say that we should; but still, one must go a little by looks in the world, and I'm sure his looks wouldn't help him much. He's just like a winter's day, short and dirty; and he

walks the deck as if planks were not good enough for his feet. Mr
Williams says, he looks as if he were 'big with the fate of Cato and of
Rome': what that means, I don't know—some joke, I suppose, for
the youngsters are always joking. Were you ever up the Baltic, Mr
Simple? Now I think of it, I know you never were. I've seen some
tight work up there with the gun-boats; and so we should now with
Captain O'Brien; but as for this little man, I've an idea 'twill be more
talk than work."

"You appear to have taken a great dislike to the captain, Swinburne. I do not know whether, as first lieutenant, I ought to listen to
you."

"It's because you're first lieutenant that I tell it you, Mr Simple. I
never was mistaken, in the main, of an officer's character, when
I could look him in the face, and hear him talk for half-an-hour; and
I came up on purpose to put you on your guard: for I feel convinced, that towards you he means mischief. What does he mean by
having the greasy-faced sergeant of marines in his cabin for half-an-
hour every morning? His reports as master of arms ought to come
through you, as first lieutenant; but he means him as a spy upon all,
and upon you in particular. The fellow has begun to give himself
airs already, and speaks to the young gentlemen as if they were
beneath him. I thought you might not know it, Mr Simple, so I
thought it right to tell you."

"I am much obliged to you, Swinburne, for your good wishes;
but I can do my duty, and why should I fear anything?"

"A man may do his duty, Mr Simple; but if a captain is determined to ruin him, he has the power. I have been longer in the
service than you have, and have been wide awake: only be careful of
one thing, Mr Simple; I beg your pardon for being so free, but in no
case lose your temper."

"No fear of that, Swinburne," replied I.

"It's very easy to say 'no fear of that,' Mr Simple; but recollect,
you have not yet had your temper tried as some officers have. You
have always been treated like a gentleman; but should you find
yourself treated otherwise, you have too good blood in your veins
not to speak—I am sure of that. I've seen officers insulted and irritated, till no angel could put up with the treatment—and then for an
unguarded word, which they would have been *swabs* not to have
made use of, sent out of the service to the devil."

"But you forget, Swinburne, that the articles of war are made for the captain as well as for everybody else in the ship."

"I know that; but still, at court-martials captains make a great distinction between what a superior says to an inferior, and what an inferior says to a superior."

"True," replied I, quoting Shakespeare:

" 'That's in the captain but a choleric word,
Which in the soldier is rank blasphemy.' "*

"Exactly my meaning—I rather think," said Swinburne, "if a captain calls you no gentleman, you mus'n't say the same to him."

"Certainly not, but I can demand a court-martial."

"Yes; and it will be granted: but what do you gain by that? It's like beating against a heavy gale and a lee tide—thousand to one if you fetch your port; and if you do, your vessel is strained to pieces, sails worn as thin as a newspaper, and rigging chafed half through, wanting fresh serving: no orders for a re-fit, and laid up in ordinary for the rest of your life. No, no, Mr Simple, the best plan is to grin and bear it, and keep a sharp look-out; for depend upon it, Mr Simple, in the best ship's company in the world, a spy captain will always find spy followers."

"Do you refer that observation to me, Mr Swinburne?" said a voice from under the bulwark. I started round, and found the captain, who had crept upon deck, unperceived by us, during our conversation. Swinburne made no reply; but touched his hat and walked over to leeward. "I presume, Mr Simple," said the captain, turning to me, "that you consider yourself justified in finding fault, and abusing your captain, to an inferior officer, on his Majesty's quarter-deck."

"If you heard the previous conversation, sir," replied I, "you must be aware that we were speaking generally about court-martials. I do not imagine that I have been guilty of any impropriety in conversing with an officer upon points connected with the service."

"You mean then to assert, sir, that the gunner did not refer to me when he said the words, 'spy captain.' "

* *Slightly misquoted from Shakespeare's* Measure for Measure, *Act II, Scene 2, lines 130–131: "That in the captain's but a choleric word, / Which in the soldier is flat blasphemy."*

"I acknowledge, sir, that as you were listening unperceived, the term might appear to refer to you; but the gunner had no idea, at the time, that you were listening. His observation was, that a spy captain would always find spy followers. This I take to be a general observation; and I am sorry that you think otherwise."

"Very well, Mr Simple," said Captain Hawkins—and he walked down the companion ladder into his cabin.

"Now a'n't it odd, Mr Simple, that I should come up with the intention of being of service to you, and yet get you into such a scrape? However, perhaps it is all for the best; open war is preferable to watching in the dark, and stabbing in the back. He never meant to have shown his colours; but I hit him so hard, that he forgot himself."

"I suspect that to be the case, Swinburne; but I think that you had better not talk any more with me to-night."

"Wish I hadn't talked quite so much, as things have turned out," replied Swinburne. "Good-night, sir."

I reflected upon what had passed, and felt convinced that Swinburne was right in saying that it was better this had occurred than otherwise. I now knew the ground which I stood upon; and forewarned was being forearmed.

—◦◦◦—

CHAPTER LV

We encounter a Dutch brig of war—Captain Hawkins very contemplative near the capstan—Hard knocks, and no thanks for it—Who's afraid?—Men will talk—The brig goes about on the wrong tack.

A T DAYLIGHT the next morning we were off the Texel, and could see the low sand-hills; but we had scarcely made them out, when the fog in the offing cleared up, and we made a strange vessel. The hands were turned up, and all sail made in chase. We made her out to be a brig of war; and as she altered her course considerably, we had an idea that she was an enemy. We made the private signal, which was unanswered, and we cleared for action; the brig making all sail on the starboard tack, and we following her—she bearing about two miles on our weather bow. The breeze was not steady; at one time the brig was staggering under her top-gallant sails, while we had our royals set; at another we would have hands by the top-gallant sheets and topsail halyards, while she expanded every stitch of canvas. On the whole, however, in an hour we had neared about half a mile. Our men were all at their quarters, happy to be so soon at their old work. Their jackets and hats were thrown off, a bandana handkerchief tied round their heads, and another, or else their black silk handkerchiefs, tied round their waists. Every gun was ready, everything was in its place, and every soul, I was going to say, was anxious for the set-to; but I rather think I must not include the captain, who from the commencement, showed no signs of pleasure, and anything but presence of mind. When we first chased the vessel, it was reported that it was a merchant-man; and it was not until we had broad daylight, that we discovered her to be a man-of-war. There was one thing to be said in his favour—he had never been in action in his life.

The breeze now fell light, and we were both with our sails set, when a thick fog obscured her from our sight. The fog rolled on till we met it, and then we could not see ten yards from the brig. This was a source of great mortification, as we had every chance of losing her. Fortunately, the wind was settling down fast into a calm, and about twelve o'clock the sails flapped against the mast. I reported twelve o'clock, and asked the captain whether we should pipe to dinner.

"Not yet," replied he; "we will put her head about."

"Go about, sir?" replied I, with surprise.

"Yes"; said he, "I'm convinced that the chase is on the other tack at this moment; and if we do not, we shall lose her."

"If she goes about, sir," said I, "she must get among the sands, and we shall be sure of her."

"Sir," replied he, "when I ask your advice, you will be pleased to give it. I command this vessel."

I touched my hat, and turned the hands up about ship, convinced that the captain wished to avoid the action, as the only chance of escape for the brig was her keeping her wind in the tack she was on. " 'Bout ship—'bout ship!" cried the men. "What the hell are we going about for?" inquired they of one another, as they came up the ladder. "Silence there, fore and aft!" cried I. "Captain

Hawkins, I do not think we can get her round, unless we wear—the
wind is very light."

"Then wear ship, Mr Simple."

There are times when grumbling and discontent among the
seamen is so participated by the officers, although they do not show
it, that the expressions made use of are passed unheeded. Such was
the case at present. The officers looked at each other, and said nothing; but the men were unguarded in their expressions. The brig
wore gradually round; and when the men were bracing up the
yards, sharp on the other tack, instead of the "Hurrah!" and "Down
with the mark!" they fell back with a groan.

"Brace up those yards in silence, there," said I to the men.

The ropes were coiled down, and we piped to dinner. The captain, who continued on deck, could not fail to hear the discontented
expressions which occasionally were made use of on the lower deck.
He made no observation, but occasionally looked over the side, to
see whether the brig went through the water. This she did slowly
for about ten minutes, when it fell a perfect calm—so that, to use a
common sea phrase, he gained little by his motion. About half-past
one, a slight breeze from the opposite quarter sprung up—we
turned round to it—it increased—the fog blew away, and, in a quarter of an hour, the chase was again visible, now upon our lee beam.
The men gave three cheers.

"Silence there, fore and aft," cried the captain, angrily. "Mr Simple, is this the way that the ship's company have been disciplined
under their late commander, to halloo and bawl whenever they
think proper?"

I was irritated at any reflection upon O'Brien, and I replied, "Yes,
sir; they have been always accustomed to express their joy at the
prospect of engaging the enemy."

"Very well, Mr Simple," replied he.

"How are we to shift her head?" inquired the master, touching
his hat: "for the chase?"

"Of course," replied the captain, who then descended into his
cabin.

"Come, my lads," said Swinburne, as soon as the captain was
below, "I have been going round, and I find that your *pets* are all in
good fighting order. I promise ye, you sha'n't wait for powder.
They'll find that the *Rattlesnake* can bite devilish hard yet, I ex-

pect."—"Ay, and without its *head*, too," replied one of the men, who was the Joe Miller of the brig.* The chase, perceiving that she could not escape—for we were coming up with her, hand over hand, now shortened sail for action, hoisting Dutch colours. Captain Hawkins again made his appearance on the quarter-deck, when we were within half a mile of her.

"Are we to run alongside of her or how?" inquired I.

"Mr Simple, I command her," replied he, "and want no interference whatever."

"Very well, sir," replied I, and I walked to the gangway.

"Mr Thompson," cried the captain, who appeared to have screwed up his courage to the right pitch, and had now taken his position for a moment on one of the carronades; "you will lay the brig right—"

Bang, bang—whiz, whiz—bang—whiz, came three shots from the enemy, cleaving the air between our masts. The captain jumped down from the carronade, and hastened to the capstern, without finishing his sentence. "Shall we fire when we are ready, sir?" said I; for I perceived that he was not capable of giving correct orders.

"Yes—yes, to be sure," replied he, remaining where he was.

"Thompson," said I to the master, "I think we can manage, in our present commanding position, to get foul of him, so as to knock away his jib-boom and foretopmast, and then she can't escape. We have good way on her."

"I'll manage it, Simple, or my name's not Thompson," replied the master, jumping into the quarter-boat, conning the vessel in that exposed situation, as we received the enemy's fire.

"Look out, my lads, and pour it into her now, just as you please," said I to the men.

The seamen were, however, too well disciplined to take immediate advantage of my permission; they waited until we passed her, and just as the master put up his helm, so as to catch her jib-boom between our masts, the whole broadside was poured into his bow and chess-tree. Her jib-boom and fore-topgallant went down, and she had so much way through the water, that we tore clear from her, and rounding to the wind shot a-head. The enemy, although in

* *Joe Miller: According to Oliver Warner's note, a joker; from a popular book,* Joe Miller's Joke Book.

confusion from the effects of our broadside, put up his helm to rake us; we perceived his manoeuvre, and did the same, and then, squaring our sails, we ran with him before the wind, engaging broadside to broadside. This continued about half an hour, and we soon found that we had no fool to play with. The brig was well fought, and her guns well directed. We had several men taken down below, and I thought it would be better to engage her even closer. There was about a cable's length between both vessels, as we ran before the wind, at about six miles an hour, with a slight rolling motion. ˙

"Thompson," said I, "let us see if we cannot beat them from their guns. Let's port the helm and close her, till we can shy a biscuit on board."

"Just my opinion, Simple; we'll see if they won't make another sort of running fight of it."

In a few minutes we were so close on board of her, that the men who loaded the guns could touch each other with their rammers and sponges. The men cheered; it was gallantly returned by the enemy, and havoc was now commenced by the musketry on both sides. The French captain, who appeared as brave a fellow as ever stepped, stood for some minutes on the hammocks; I was also holding on by the swifter of the main-rigging, when he took off his hat and politely saluted me. I returned the compliment; but the fire became too hot, and I wished to get under the shelter of the bulwark. Still I would not go down first, and the French captain appeared determined not to be the first either to quit the post of honour. At last one of our marines hit him in the right arm: he clapped his hand to the part, as if to point it out to me, nodded, and was assisted down from the hammocks. I immediately quitted my post, for I thought it foolish to stand as a mark for forty or fifty soldiers. I had already received a bullet through the small of my leg. But the effects of such close fire now became apparent: our guns were only half manned, our sides terribly cut up, and our sails and rigging in tatters. The enemy was even worse off, and two broadsides more brought her mainmast by the board. Our men cheered, and threw in another broadside. The enemy dropped astern; we rounded to rake her; she also attempted to round to, but could not until she had cleared away her wreck, and taken in her foresail, and lowered her topsail. She then continued the action with as much spirit as ever.

"He's a fine fellow, by God!" exclaimed Thompson; "I never saw a man fight his ship better: but we have him. Webster's down, poor fellow!"

"I'm sorry for it," replied I; "but I'm afraid that there are many poor fellows who have lost the number of their mess, I think it useless throwing away the advantage which we now have. He can't escape, and he'll fight this way for ever. We had better run a-head, repair damages, and then he must surrender, in his crippled state, when we attack him again."

"I agree with you," said Thompson; "the only point is, that it will soon be dark."

"I'll not lose sight of him, and he cannot get away. If he puts before the wind, then we will be at him again."

We gave him the loaded guns as we forged a-head, and when we were about half a mile from him, hove-to to repair damages.

The reader may now ask, "But where was the captain all this time?" My answer is, that he was at the capstern, where he stood in silence, not once interfering during the whole action, which was fought by Thompson, the master, and myself. How he looked, or how he behaved in other points during the engagement, I cannot pretend to say, for I had no time to observe him. Even now I was busy knotting the rigging, rousing up new sails to bend, and getting everything in order, and I should not have observed him, had he not come up to me; for as soon as we had ceased firing he appeared to recover himself. He did not, however, first address me; he commenced speaking to the men.

"Come, be smart, my lads; send a hand here to swab up the blood. Here, youngster, run down to the surgeon, and let him know that I wish a report of the killed and wounded."

By degrees he talked more, and at last came up to me, "This has been rather smartish, Mr Simple."

"Very smart indeed, sir," replied I, and then turned away to give directions. "Maintop there, send down the hauling line on the starboard side."

"Ay, ay, sir."

"Now then, my lads, clap on, and run it up at once."

"Maintop, there," hailed the captain, "be a little smarter, or by G——d, I'll call you down for something." This did not come with a good grace from one who had done nothing, to those who were working with all their energy. "Mr Simple," said the captain, "I wish you would carry on duty with less noise."

"At all events, he set us that example during the action," muttered the Joe Miller; and the other men laughed heartily at the implication. In two hours, during which we had carefully watched the enemy, who still lay where we left him, we were again ready for action.

"Shall I give the men their grog now, sir?" said I to the captain; "they must want it."

"No, no," replied the captain; "no, no, Mr Simple, I don't like what you call *Dutch* courage."

"I don't think he much does; and this fellow has shown plenty of it," said the Joe Miller, softly; and the men about him laughed heartily.

"I think, sir," observed I, "that it is an injustice to this fine ship's company to hint at their requiring Dutch courage." (Dutch courage is a term for courage screwed up by drinking freely.) "And I most respectfully beg leave to observe, that the men have not had their afternoon's allowance; and, after the fatigues they have undergone, really require it."

"I command this ship, sir," replied he.

"Certainly, sir, I am aware of it," rejoined I. "She is now all ready for action again, and I wait your orders. The enemy is two miles on the lee quarter."

The surgeon here came up with his report.

"Good heavens!" said the captain, "forty-seven men killed and wounded, Mr Webster dangerously. Why, the brig is crippled. We can do no more—positively, we can do no more."

"We can take that brig, anyhow," cried one of the seamen from a dozen of the men who were to leeward, expecting orders to renew the attack.

"What man was that?" cried the captain.

No one answered.

"By G——d! this ship is in a state of mutiny, Mr Simple."

"Will *soon* be, I think," said a voice from the crowd, which I knew very well; but the captain, having been but a short time with us, did not know it.

"Do you hear that, Mr Simple?" cried the captain.

"I regret to say that I did hear it, sir; I little thought that ever

such an expression would have been made use of on board of the
Rattlesnake." Then, fearing he would ask me the man's name, and to
pretend not to have recognised it, I said, "Who was that who made
use of that expression?" But no one answered; and it was so dark,
that it was impossible to distinguish the men.

"After such mutinous expressions," observed the captain, "I certainly will not risk his Majesty's brig under my command, as I
should have wished to have done, even in her crippled state, by
again engaging the enemy. I can only regret that the officers appear
as insolent as the men."

"Perhaps, Captain Hawkins, you will state in what, and when, I
have proved myself insolent. I cannot accuse myself."

"I hope the expression was not applied to me, sir," said Thompson, the master, touching his hat.

"Silence, gentlemen, if you please. Mr Simple, wear round the
ship."

Whether the captain intended to attack the enemy or not, we
could not tell, but we were soon undeceived; for when we were
round, he ordered her to be kept away until the Dutch brig was on
our lee quarter: then ordering the master to shape his course for
Yarmouth, he went down into the cabin, and sent up word that I
might pipe to supper and serve out the spirits.

The rage and indignation of the men could not be withheld.
After they went down to supper they gave three heavy groans in
concert; indeed, during the whole of that night, the officers who
kept the watches had great difficulty in keeping the men from vent-
ing their feeling, in what might be almost termed justifiable mutiny.
As for myself, I could hardly control my vexation. The brig was our
certain prize; and this was proved, for the next day she hauled
down her colours immediately to a much smaller man-of-war,
which fell in with her, still lying in the same crippled state; the
captain and first lieutenant killed, and nearly two-thirds of her
ship's company either killed or wounded. Had we attacked her, she
would have hauled down her colours immediately, for it was our
last broadside which had killed the captain. As first lieutenant, I
should have received my promotion, which was now lost. I cried for
vexation when I thought of it as I lay in bed. That his conduct was
severely commented upon by the officers in the gun-room, as well
as by the whole ship's company, I hardly need say. Thompson was

for bringing him to a court-martial, which I would most gladly have done, if it only were to get rid of him; but I had a long conversation with old Swinburne on the subject, and he proved to me that I had better not attempt it. "For, d'ye see, Mr Simple, you have no proof. He did not run down below; he stood his ground on deck, although he did nothing. You can't *prove* cowardice, then, although there can be no great doubt of it. Again, with regard to his not renewing the attack, why, is not a captain at liberty to decide what is the best for his Majesty's service? And if he thought, in the crippled state of the brig, so close to the enemy's coast, that it wasn't advisable, why, it could only be brought in as an error in judgment. Then there's another thing which must be remembered, Mr Simple, which is, that no captains sitting on a court-martial will, if it be possible to extricate him, ever prove *cowardice* against a brother captain, because they feel that it's a disgrace to the whole cloth."

Swinburne's advice was good, and I gave up all thoughts of proceeding; still it appeared to me, that the captain was very much afraid that I would, he was so extremely amiable and polite during our run home. He said, that he had watched how well I had behaved in the action, and would not fail to notice it. This was something, but he did not keep his word: for his despatch was published before we quitted the roadstead, and not the name of one officer mentioned, only generally saying, that they conducted themselves to his satisfaction. He called the enemy a corvette, not specifying whether she was a brig or ship corvette; and the whole was written in such a bombastic style, that anyone would have imagined that he had fought a vessel of superior force. He stated, at the end, that as soon as he repaired damages, he wore round, but that the enemy declined further action. So she did—certainly—for the best of all possible reasons, that she was too disabled to come down to us. All this might have been contested; but the enormous list of killed and wounded proved that we had had a hard fight, and the capture of the brig afterwards, that we had really overpowered her. So that, on the whole, Captain Hawkins gained a great deal of credit with some; although whispers were afloat which came to the ears of the Admiralty, and prevented him from being posted—the more so, as he had the modesty not to apply for it.

―—*ᴗᴗᴗ*―—

CHAPTER LVI

Consequences of the action—A ship without a fighting captain is like a thing without a head—So do the sailors think—A mutiny, and the loss of our famous ship's company.

URING OUR STAY at Yarmouth, we were not allowed to put our foot on shore, upon the plea that we must repair damages, and proceed immediately to our station; but the real fact was, that Captain Hawkins was very anxious that we should not be able to talk about the action. Finding no charges preferred against him, he re-commenced his system of annoyance. His apartments had windows which looked out upon where the brig lay at anchor, and he constantly watched all our motions with his spy-glass, noting down if I did not hoist up boats, &c., exactly at the hour prescribed in his book of orders, so as to gather a list of charges against me if he could. This we did not find out until afterwards.

I mentioned before, that when Swinburne joined us at Plymouth, he had recommended a figure-head being put on the brig. This had been done at O'Brien's expense—not in the cheap way recommended by Swinburne, but in a very handsome manner. It was a large snake coiled up in folds, with its head darting out in a menacing attitude, and the tail, with its rattle appeared below. The whole was gilded, and had a very good effect; but after the dockyard men had completed the repairs, and the brig was painted, one night the head of the rattlesnake disappeared. It had been sawed off by some malicious and evil disposed persons, and no traces of it were to be found. I was obliged to report this to the captain, who was very indignant, and offered twenty pounds for the discovery of the offender; but had he offered twenty thousand he never would have found out the delinquent. It was, however, never forgotten; for he understood what was implied by these manoeuvres. A new head was carved, but disappeared the night after it was fixed on.

The rage of the captain was without bounds: he turned the hands up, and declared that if the offender was not given up, he would flog every hand on board. He gave the ship's company ten minutes, and then prepared to execute his threat. "Mr Paul, turn the hands up for punishment," said the captain, in a rage, and descended to his cabin for the articles of war. When he was down below, the officers talked over the matter. To flog every man for the crime of one was the height of injustice, but it was not for us to oppose him; still the ship's company must have seen, in our countenances, that we shared their feelings. The men were talking with each other in groups, until they all appeared to have communicated their ideas on the subject. The carpenters, who had been slowly bringing aft the gratings, left off the job; the boatswain's mates, who had came aft, rolled the tails of their cats round the red handles; and every man walked down below. No one was left on the quarter-deck but the marines under arms, and the officers. Perceiving this, I desired Mr Paul, the boatswain, to send the men up to rig the gratings, and the quarter-masters with their seizings. He came up, and said that he had called them, but that they did not answer. Perceiving that the ship's company would break out into open mutiny, if the captain persisted in his intention, I went down into the cabin, and told the captain the state of things, and wished for his orders or presence on deck.

The captain, whose wrath appeared incapable of reflection, im-mediately proceeded on deck, and ordered the marines to load with ball-cartridge. This was done; but, as I was afterwards told by Thompson, who was standing aft, the marines loaded with powder, and put the balls into their pockets. They wished to keep up the character of their corps for fidelity, and at the same time not fire upon men whom they loved as brothers, and with whom they coin-cided in opinion. Indeed, we afterwards discovered that it was a *marine* who had taken off the *head* of the snake a second time.

The captain then ordered the boatswain to turn the hands up. The boatswain made his appearance with his right arm in a sling.— "What's the matter with your arm, Mr Paul?" said I, as he passed me.

"Tumbled down the hatchway just now—can't move my arm; I must go to the surgeon as soon as this is over."

The hands were piped up again, but no one obeyed the order. Thus was the brig in a state of mutiny. "Mr Simple, go forward to the main hatchway with the marines, and fire on the lower deck," cried the captain.

"Sir," said I, "there are two frigates within a cable's length of us; and would it not be better to send for assistance, without shedding blood? Besides, sir, you have not yet tried the effect of calling up the carpenter's and boatswain's mates by name. Will you allow me to go down first, and bring them to a sense of their duty?"

"Yes, I presume you know your power; but of this hereafter."

I went down below and called the men by name.

"Sir," said one of the boatswain's mates, "the ship's company say that they will not submit to be flogged."

"I do not speak to the ship's company generally, Collins," replied I; "but you are now ordered to rig the gratings, and come on deck. It is an order that you cannot refuse. Go up directly, and obey it. Quarter-masters, go on deck with your seizings. When all is ready, you can then expostulate." The men obeyed my orders; they crawled on deck, rigged the gratings, and stood by. "All is ready, sir," said I, touching my hat to the captain.

"Send the ship's company aft, Mr Paul."

"Aft, then, all of you, for punishment," cried the boatswain.

"Yes, it is *all of us for punishment*," cried one voice. "We're all to flog one another, and then pay off the *jollies.*"*

This time the men obeyed the order; they all appeared on the quarter-deck. "The men are all aft, sir," reported the boatswain.

"And now, my lads," said the captain, "I'll teach you what mutiny is. You see the two frigates alongside of us. You had forgotten them, I suppose, but I hadn't. Here, you scoundrel, Mr Jones"—(this was the Joe Miller)—"strip, sir. If ever there was mischief in a ship, you are at the head."

"Head, sir," said the man, assuming a vacant look; "what head, sir? Do you mean the snake's head? I don't know anything about it, sir."—"Strip, sir!" cried the captain in a rage; "I'll soon bring you to your senses."

"If you please, your honour, what have I done to be tied up?" said the man.

"Strip, you scoundrel!"—"Well, sir, if you please, it's hard to be flogged for nothing." The man pulled off his clothes, and walked up to the grating. The quarter-masters seized him up.

"Seized up, sir," reported the scoundrel of a sergeant of marines who acted as the captain's spy.

The captain looked for the articles of war to read, as is necessary

* Marines.

previous to punishing a man, and was a little puzzled to find one, where no positive offence had been committed. At last, he pitched upon the one which refers to combination and conspiracy, and creating discontent. We all took off our hats as he read it, and he then called Mr Paul, the boatswain, and ordered him to give the man a dozen. "Please, sir," said the boatswain, pointing to his arm in a sling, "I can't flog—I can't lift up my arm."—"Your arm was well enough when I came on board, sir," cried the captain.

"Yes, sir; but in hurrying the men up, I slipped down the ladder, and I'm afraid I've put my shoulder out."

The captain bit his lips; he fully believed it was a sham on the part of the boatswain (which indeed it was) to get off flogging the men. "Well, then, where is the chief boatswain's mate, Miller?"

"Here, sir," said Miller, coming forward: a stout, muscular man, nearly six feet high, with a pig-tail nearly four feet long, and his open breast covered with black, shaggy hair.

"Give that man a dozen, sir," said the captain.

The man looked at the captain, then at the ship's company, and then at the man seized up, but did not commence the punishment.

"Do you hear me, sir?" roared the captain.

"If you please, your honour, I'd rather take my disrating—I—don't wish to be chief boatswain's mate in this here business."

"Obey your orders, immediately, sir," cried the captain; "or, by God, I'll try you for mutiny."

"Well, sir, I beg your pardon; but what must be, must be. I mean no disrespect, Captain Hawkins, but I cannot flog that man—my conscience won't let me."

"Your *conscience*, sir!"

"Beg your pardon, Captain Hawkins, I've always done my duty, foul weather or fair; and I've been eighteen years in his Majesty's service, without ever being brought to punishment; but if I am to be hung now, saving your pleasure, and with all respect, I can't help it."

"I give you but one moment more, sir," cried the captain; "do your duty." The man looked at the captain, and then eyed the yard-arm. "Captain Hawkins, I will *do my duty*, although I must swing for it." So saying he threw his cat down on the quarter-deck, and fell back among the ship's company.

The captain was now confounded, and hardly knew how to act:

CHAPTER LVI   *393*

to persevere appeared useless—to fall back was almost as impossible. A dead silence of a minute ensued. Every one was breathless with impatience, to know what would be done next. The silence was, however, first broken by Jones, the Joe Miller, who was seized up. "Beg your honour's pardon, sir," said he, turning his head round; "but if I am to be flogged, will you be pleased to let me have it over? I shall catch my death a-cold, naked here all day." This was decided mockery on the part of the man, and roused the captain.

"Sergeant of marines, put Miller and that man Collins, both legs in irons, for mutiny. My men, I perceive that there is a conspiracy in the ship, but I shall very soon put an end to it: I know the men, and, by God, they shall repent it. Mr Paul, pipe down. Mr Simple, man my gig; and recollect, it's my positive orders that no boat goes on shore." The captain left the brig, looking daggers at me as he went over the side; but I had done my duty, and cared little for that; indeed, I was now watching his conduct as carefully as he did mine.

"The captain wishes to tell his own story first," said Thompson, coming up to me. "Now, if I were you, Simple, I would take care that the real facts should be known."

"How's that to be done," replied I; "he has ordered no communication with the shore."

"Simply by sending an officer on board of each of the frigates to state that the brig is in a state of mutiny, and request that they will keep a look-out upon her. This is no more than your duty as commanding officer; you only send the message, leave me to state the facts of my own accord. Recollect that the captains of these frigates will be summoned, if there is a court of inquiry, which I expect will take place."

I considered a little, and thought the advice good. I despatched Thompson first to one frigate, and then to the other. The next day the captain came on board. As soon as he stepped on the quarter-deck he inquired how I dare disobey his orders in sending the boats away. My reply was that his orders were, not to communicate with the shore, but that, as commanding officer, I considered it my duty to make known to the other ships that the men were in a state of insubordination, that they might keep their eyes upon us. He *kept his eyes* upon me for some time, and then turned away without reply. As we expected, a court of inquiry was called, upon his representations to the admiral. About twenty of the men were examined, but so much came out as to the *reason why* the head of the snake had been removed—for the sailors spoke boldly—that the admiral and officers who were appointed strongly recommended Captain Hawkins not to proceed further than to state that there were some disaffected characters in the ship, and move the admiral to have them exchanged into others. This was done, and the captains of the frigates, who immediately gave their advice, divided all our best men between them. They spoke very freely to me, and asked me who were the best men, which I told them honestly, for I was glad to be able to get them out of the power of Captain Hawkins; these they marked as disaffected, and exchanged them for all the worst they had on board. The few that were left ran away, and thus, from having one of the finest and best organised ship's companies in the service, we were now one of the very worst. Miller was sent on board of the frigate, and under surveillance: he soon proved that his character was as good as I stated it to be, and two years afterwards was promoted to the rank of boatswain. Webster, the second lieutenant, would not rejoin us, and another was appointed. I must here remark, that there is hardly any degree of severity which a captain may not exert towards his seamen, provided they are confident of, or he has proved to them, his courage; but if there be a doubt, or a confirmation to the contrary, all discipline is destroyed by contempt, and the ship's company mutiny, either directly or indirectly. There is an old saying, that all tyrants are cowards; that tyranny is in itself a species of meanness, I acknowledge: but still the saying ought to be modified. If it is asserted that all mean tyrants are cowards, I agree; but I have known in the service most special tyrants, who were not cowards: their tyranny was excessive, but there was no meanness in their dispositions. On the contrary, they were generous, open-hearted, and, occasionally, when not influenced by anger, proved that their hearts, if not quite right, were not very much out of their places. Yet they were tyrants; but, although tyrants, the men forgave them, and one kind act, when they were not led away by the impetuosity of their feelings, obliterated a hundred acts of tyranny. But such is not the case in our service with men who, in their tyranny, are mean; the seamen show no quarter to them, and will undergo all the risk which the severity of the articles of war renders them liable to, rather than not express their opinion of a man whom they despise. I do not like to mention names, but I could point out specimens of brave tyrants, and of cowardly tyrants who have existed, and do even now exist in our service. The present regulations have limited tyranny to a certain degree, but it cannot check the *mean* tyrant; for it is not in points of consequence, likely to be brought before the notice of his superiors, that he effects his purpose. He resorts to paltry measures—he smiles that he may betray—he confines himself within the limit that may protect him; and he is never exposed, unless by his courage being called in question, which but rarely occurs; and when it does occur it is most difficult, as well as most dangerous, to attempt to prove it. It may be asked why I did not quit the ship, after having been aware of the character of the captain, and the enmity which he bore to me. In reply, I can only say that I did often think of it, talked over the subject with my messmates, but they persuaded me to remain, and, as I was a first lieutenant, and knew that any successful action would, in all probability, insure my promotion, I determined, to use a nautical expression, to rough it out, and not throw away the only chance which I now had of obtaining my rank as commander.

—————

CHAPTER LVII

News from home not very agreeable, although the reader may laugh—We arrive at Portsmouth, where I fall in with my old acquaintance, Mrs Trotter—We sail with a convoy for the Baltic.

I HAD WRITTEN to my sister Ellen, giving her an account of all that had passed, and mentioning the character of the captain, and his apparent intimacy with my uncle. I received an answer from her, telling me that she had discovered, from a very communicative old maiden lady, that Captain Hawkins was an illegitimate son of my uncle, by a lady with whom he had been acquainted about the time that he was in the army. I immediately conceived the truth, that my uncle had pointed me out to him as an object of his vengeance, and that Captain Hawkins was too dutiful and too dependent a son not to obey him. The state of my father was more distressing than ever, but there was something very ludicrous in his fancies. He had fancied himself a jackass, and had brayed for a week, kicking the old nurse in the stomach, so as to double her up like a hedgehog. He had taken it into his head that he was a pump; and, with one arm held out as a spout, he had obliged the poor old nurse to work the other up and down for hours together. At another time, he had an idea that he was a woman in labour, and they were obliged to give him a strong dose of calomel, and borrow a child of six years old from a neighbour, to make him believe that he was delivered. He was perfectly satisfied, although the child was born to him in cloth trousers, and a jacket with three rows of sugar-loaf buttons. Ay, said he, it was those buttons which hurt my side so much. In fact, there was a string of strange conceptions of this kind that had accumulated, so as to drive my poor sister almost mad; and sometimes his ideas would be attended with a very heavy expense, as he would send for architects, make contracts, &c., for building, supposing himself to have come to the title and property of his brother. This, being the basis of his disease, occurred frequently. I wrote to poor Ellen, giving her my best advice, and by this time the brig was again ready for sea, and we expected to sail immediately. I did not forget to write to O'Brien, but the distance between us was so great that I knew I could not obtain his answer probably for a year, and I felt a melancholy foreboding how much I required his advice.

Our orders were to proceed to Portsmouth, and join a convoy collected there, bound up the Baltic, under the charge of the *Acasta* frigate, and two other vessels. We did not sail with any pleasure, or hopes of gaining much in the way of prize-money. Our captain was enough to make any ship a hell; and our ship's company were composed of a mutinous and incorrigible set of scoundrels, with, of course, a few exceptions. How different did the officers find the brig after losing such a captain as O'Brien, and so fine a ship's company! But there was no help for it, and all we had to do was to make the best of it, and hope for better times. The cat was at work nearly every day, and I must acknowledge that, generally speaking, it was deserved; although sometimes a report from the sergeant of marines of any good man favoured by me, was certain to be attended to. This system of receiving reports direct from an inferior officer, instead of through me, as first lieutenant, became so annoying, that I resolved, at all risk, to expostulate. I soon had an opportunity, for one morning the captain said to me, "Mr Simple, I understand that you had a fire in the galley last night after hours."

"It is very true, sir, that I did order a stove to be lighted; but may I inquire whether the first lieutenant has not a discretionary power in that point? and further, how it is that I am reported to you by other people? The discipline of this ship is carried on by me, under your directions, and all reports ought to come through me; and I cannot understand upon what grounds you permit them through any other channel."

"I command my own ship, sir, and shall do as I please in that respect. When I have officers I can confide in, I shall, in all probability, allow them to report to me."

"If there is anything in my conduct which has proved to you that I am incapable, or not trustworthy, I would feel obliged to you, sir, if you would, in the first place, point it out;—and, in the next, bring me to a court-martial if I do not correct it."

"I am no court-martial man, sir," replied he, "but I am not to be dictated to by an inferior officer, so you'll oblige me by holding your tongue. The sergeant of marines, as master-at-arms, is bound to report to me any deviation from the regulations I have laid down for the discipline of the ship."

"Granted, sir; but that report, according to the custom of the service, should come through the first lieutenant."

"I prefer it coming direct, sir;—it stands less chance of being garbled."

"Thank you, Captain Hawkins, for the compliment." The captain walked away without further reply, and shortly after went down below. Swinburne ranged up alongside of me as soon as the captain disappeared.

"Well, Mr Simple, so I hear we are bound to the Baltic. Why couldn't they have ordered us to pick up the convoy off Yarmouth, instead of coming all the way to Portsmouth? We shall be in tomorrow with this slant of wind."

"I suppose the convoy are not yet collected, Swinburne; and you recollect there's no want of French privateers in the channel."

"Very true, sir."

"When were you up the Baltic, Swinburne?"

"I was in the old *St George*, a regular old ninety-eight; she sailed just like a hay-stack, one mile ahead and three to leeward. Lord bless you, Mr Simple, the Cattegat wasn't wide enough for her; but she was a comfortable sort of vessel after all, excepting on a lee-shore, so we used always to give the land a wide berth, I recollect. By the by, Mr Simple, do you recollect how angry you were because I didn't peach at Barbadoes, when the men *sucked the monkey?*"

"To be sure I do."

"Well, then, I didn't think it fair then, as I was one of them. But now that I'm a bit of an officer, I just tell you that when we get to Carlscrona there's a method of *sucking the monkey* there, which, as first lieutenant, with such a queer sort of captain, it is just as well that you should be up to. In the old *St George* we had seventy men drunk one afternoon, and the first lieutenant couldn't find it out nohow."

"Indeed, Swinburne, you must let me into that secret."

"So I will, Mr Simple. Don't you know there's a famous stuff for cuts and wounds, called balsam?"

"What, Riga balsam?"

"Yes, that's it; well, all the boats will bring that for sale, as they did to us in the old *St George*. Devilish good stuff it is for wounds, I believe; but it's not bad to drink, and it's very strong. We used to take it *inwardly*, Mr Simple, and the first lieutenant never guessed it."

"What! you all got tipsy upon Riga balsam?"

"All that could; so I just give you a hint."

"I'm much obliged to you, Swinburne; I certainly never should have suspected it. I believe seamen would get drunk upon any-thing."

The next morning we anchored at Spithead, and found the con-voy ready for sea. The captain went on shore to report himself to the admiral, and, as usual, the brig was surrounded with bumboats and wherries, with people who wished to come on board. As we were not known on the Portsmouth station, and had no acquaintance with the people, all the bumboats were very anxious to supply the ship: and, as this is at the option of the first lieutenant, he is very much persecuted until he has made his decision. Certificates of good conduct from other officers were handed up the side from all of them; and I looked over the books at the capstern. In the second book the name struck me; it was that of Mrs Trotter, and I walked to the gangway out of curiosity, to ascertain whether it was the same personage who, when I was a youngster, had taken such care of my shirts. As I looked at the boats, a voice cried out, "O, Mr Simple, have you forgot your old friend? don't you recollect Mrs Trotter?" I certainly did not recollect her; she had grown very fat, and, although more advanced in years, was a better-looking woman than when I had first seen her, for she looked healthy and fresh.

"Indeed, I hardly did recollect you, Mrs Trotter."

"I've so much to tell you, Mr Simple," replied she, ordering the boat to pull alongside; and, as she was coming up, desired the man to get the things in, as if permission was quite unnecessary. I did not counter-order it, as I knew none of the others, and, as far as honesty was concerned, believed them all to be much on a par. On the strength, then, of old acquaintance, Mrs Trotter was admitted.

"Well, I'm sure, Mr Simple," cried Mrs Trotter, out of breath with climbing up the brig's side; "what a man you've grown,—and such a handsome man, too! Dear, dear, it makes me feel quite old to look at you, when I call to mind the little boy whom I had charge of in the cockpit. Don't you think I look very old and ugly, Mr Simple?" continued she, smiling and smirking.

"Indeed, Mrs Trotter, I think you wear very well. Pray, how is your husband?"

"Ah, Mr Simple, poor dear Mr Trotter—he's gone. Poor fellow! no wonder, what with his drinking, and his love for me—and his jealousy—(do you recollect how jealous he was, Mr Simple?)—he wore himself out at last. No wonder, considering what he had been accustomed to, after keeping his carriage and dogs with everybody, to be reduced to see his wife go a *bumming.* It broke his heart, poor fellow! and, Mr Simple, I've been much happier ever since, for I could not bear to see him fretting. Lord, how jealous he was—and all about nothing! Don't you want some fresh meat for the gun-room? I've a nice leg of mutton in the boat, and some milk for tea."

"Recollect, Mrs Trotter, I shall not overlook your bringing spirits on board."

"Lord, Mr Simple, how could you think of such a thing? It's very true that these common people do it, but the company I have kept, the society I have been in, Mr Simple! Besides, you must recollect that I never drank anything but water."

I could not exactly coincide with her, but I did not contradict her.

"Would you like the Portsmouth paper, Mr Simple?" taking one out of her pocket; "I know gentlemen are fond of the news. Poor Trotter used never to stir from the breakfast table until he had finished the daily paper—but that was when we lived in very different style. Have you any clothes to wash, Mr Simple,—or have any of the gentlemen?"

"I fear we have no time, we sail too soon," replied I; "we go with the convoy."

"Indeed!" cried Mrs Trotter, who walked to the main hatchway and called to her man Bill. I heard her give him directions to sell nothing upon trust, in consequence of the intelligence of our immediate sailing.

"I beg your pardon, Mr Simple, I was only desiring my head man to send for your steward, that he might be supplied with the best, and to save some milk for the gun-room."

"And I must beg your pardon, Mrs Trotter, for I must attend to my duty." Mrs Trotter made her courtesy and walked down the main ladder to attend to *her duty,* and we separated. I was informed that she had a great deal of custom, as she understood how to manage the officers, and made herself generally useful to them. She had been a bumboat-woman for six years, and had made a great deal of money. Indeed, it was reported, that if a *first lieutenant* wanted forty or fifty pounds, Mrs Trotter would always lend it to him, without requiring his promissory note.

The captain came on board in the evening, having dined with the admiral, and left directions for having all ready for unmooring and heaving short at daylight. The signal was made from the frigate at sunrise, and before twelve o'clock we were all under weigh, and running past St Helen's with a favourable wind. Our force consisted of the *Acasta* frigate, the *Isis* ship, sloop, mounting twenty guns, the *Reindeer,* eighteen, and our own brig. The convoy amounted to nearly two hundred. Although the wind was fair, and the water smooth, we were more than a week before we made Anholt light, owing to the bad sailing and inattention of many of the vessels belonging to the convoy. We were constantly employed repeating signals, firing guns, and often sent back to tow up the sternmost vessels. At last we passed the Anholt light, with a light breeze; and the next morning the main land was to be distinguished on both bows.

—*꿍꿍*—

CHAPTER LVIII

How we passed the Sound, and what passed in the Sound—The captain overhears again a conversation between Swinburne and me.

I WAS ON the signal-chest abaft, counting the convoy, when Swinburne came up to me. "There's a little difference between this part of the world and the West Indies, Mr Simple," observed he. "Black rocks and fir woods don't remind us of the Blue Mountains of Jamaica, or the cocoa-nut waving to the sea-breeze."

"Indeed not, Swinburne," replied I.

"We shall have plenty of calms here, without panting with the heat, although we may find the gun-boats a little too warm for us; for, depend upon it, the very moment the wind goes down, they will come out from every nook and corner, and annoy us not a little."

"Have you been here before, with a convoy, Swinburne?"

"To be sure I have; and it's sharp work that I've seen here, Mr Simple—work that I've an idea our captain won't have much stomach for."

"Swinburne, I beg you will keep your thoughts relative to the captain to yourself; recollect the last time. It is my duty not to listen to them."

"And I should rather think to report them also, Mr Simple," said Captain Hawkins, who had crept up to us, and overheard our conversation.

"In this instance there is no occasion for my reporting them, sir," replied I, "for you have heard what has passed."

"I have, sir," replied he; "and I shall not forget the conversation."

I turned forward. Swinburne had made his retreat the moment that he heard the voice of the captain. "How many sails are there in sight, sir?" inquired the captain.

"One hundred and sixty-three, sir," replied I.

"Signal for convoy to close from the *Acasta*," reported the midshipman of the watch.

We repeated it, and the captain descended to his cabin. We were then running about four miles an hour, the water very smooth, and Anholt lighthouse hardly visible on deck, bearing N.N.W. about twenty miles. In fact, we were near the entrance of the Sound, which, the reader may be aware, is a narrow passage leading into the Baltic Sea. We ran on, followed by the convoy, some of which were eight or ten miles astern of us, and we were well into the Sound, when the wind gradually died away, until it fell quite calm, and the heads of the vessels were laid round the compass.

My watch was nearly out, when the midshipman, who was looking round with his glass on the Copenhagen side, reported three gun-boats, sweeping out from behind a point. I examined them and went down to report them to the captain. When I came on deck, more were reported, until we counted ten, two of them large vessels, called praams.* The captain now came on deck, and I reported them. We made the signal of enemy in sight, to the *Acasta,* which was answered. They divided—six of them pulling along shore towards the convoy in the rear, and four coming out right for the brig. The *Acasta* now made the signal for "Boats manned and armed to be held in readiness." We hoisted out our pinnace, and lowered down our cutters—the other men-of-war doing the same. In about a quarter of an hour the gun-boats opened their fire with their long thirty-two pounders, and their first shot went right through the hull of the brig, just abaft the fore-bits; fortunately, no one was hurt. I turned round to look at the captain; he was as white as a sheet. He caught my eye, and turned aft, when he was met by Swinburne's eye, steadily fixed upon him. He then walked to the other side of the deck. Another shot ploughed up the water close to us, rose, and came through the hammock-netting, tearing out two of the hammocks, and throwing them on the quarter-deck, when the *Acasta* hoisted out pennants, and made the signal to send our pinnace and cutter to the assistance of vessels astern. The signal was also made to the *Isis* and *Reindeer.* I reported the signal, and inquired who was to take the command.

"You, Mr Simple, will take the pinnace, and order Mr Swinburne into the cutter."

* *Praams (or prams): Flat-bottomed boats used primarily to transport cargo between ship and shore.*

"Mr Swinburne, sir!" replied I; "the brig will, in all probability, be in action soon, and his services as a gunner will be required."

"Well, then, Mr Hilton may go. Beat to quarters. Where is Mr Webster?"* The second lieutenant was close to us, and he was ordered to take the duty during my absence.

I jumped into the pinnace, and shoved off; ten other boats from the *Acasta* and the other men-of-war were pulling in the same direction, and I joined them. The gun-boats had now opened fire upon the convoy astern, and were sweeping out to capture them, dividing themselves into two parts, and pulling towards different portions of the convoy. In half an hour we were within gunshot of the nearest, which directed its fire at us; but the lieutenant of the *Acasta,* who commanded the detachment, ordered us to lie on our oars for a minute, while he divided his force in three divisions, of four boats each, with instructions that we should each oppose a division of two gun-boats, by pulling to the outermost vessel of the convoy, and securing ourselves as much as possible from the fire, by remaining under her lee, and be in readiness to take them by boarding, if they approached to capture any of our vessels.

This was well arranged. I had the command of one division, for the first lieutenants had not been sent away from the *Isis* and *Reindeer,* and having inquired which of the divisions of gun boats I was to oppose, I pulled for them. In the meantime, we observed that the two praams, and two gun-boats, which had remained behind us, and had been firing at the *Racehorse,* had also divided— one praam attacking the *Acasta,* the two gun-boats playing upon the *Isis,* and the other praam engaging the *Rattlesnake* and *Reindeer;* the latter vessel being in a line with us, and about half a mile further out, so that she could not return any effectual fire, or, indeed, receive much damage. The *Rattlesnake* had the worst of it, the fire of the praam being chiefly directed to her. At the distance chosen by the enemy, the frigate's guns reached, but the other men-of-war, having only two long guns, were not able to return the fire but with their two, the carronades being useless.

One of the praams mounted ten guns, and the other eight. The last was opposed to the *Rattlesnake,* and the fire was kept up very

---

* *Again, due to the rapid nature of Marryat's publications, he forgot details from his narrative. Webster had already departed the ship at Yarmouth (see chapter LVI).*

smartly, particularly by the *Acasta* and the enemy. In about a quarter of an hour I arrived with my division close to the vessel which was nearest to the enemy. It was a large Sunderland-built ship. The gun-boats, which were within a quarter of a mile of her, sweeping to her as fast as they could, as soon as they perceived our approach, directed their fire upon us, but without success, except the last discharge, in which, we being near enough, they had loaded with grape. The shot fell a little short, but one piece of grape struck one of the bow-men of the pinnace, taking off three fingers of his right hand as he was pulling his oar. Before they could fire again, we were sheltered by the vessel, pulling close to her side, hid from the enemy. My boat was the only one in the division which carried a gun, and I now loaded, waiting for the discharge of the gun-boats, and then, pulling a little ahead of the ship, fired at them, and then returned under cover to load. This continued for some time, the enemy not advancing nearer, but now firing into the Sunderland ship, which protected us. At last the master of the ship looked over the side, and said to me, "I say, my joker, do you call this *giving me assistance*? I think I was better off before you came. Then I had only my share of the enemy's fire, but now that you have come, I have it all. I'm riddled like a sieve, and have lost four men already. Suppose you give me a spell now—pull behind the vessel ahead of us. I'll take my chance."

I thought this request very reasonable, and as I should be really nearer to the enemy if I pulled to the next vessel, and all ready to support him if attacked, I complied with his wish. I had positive orders not to board with so small a force (the four boats containing but forty men, and each gun-boat having at least seventy), unless they advanced to capture, and then I was to run all risks.

I pulled up to the other vessel, a large brig, and the captain, as soon as we came alongside, said, "I see what you're about, and I'll just leave you my vessel to take care of. No use losing my men, or being knocked on the head."

"All's right—you can't do better, and we can't do better either."

His boat was lowered down, and getting in with his men, he pulled to another vessel, and lay behind it, all ready to pull back if a breeze sprang up.

As was to be expected, the gun-boats shifted their fire to the deserted vessel, which our boat lay behind; and thus did the action in our quarter continue until it was dark, the gun-boats not choosing to advance, and we restricted from pulling out to attack them. There was no moon, and, as daylight disappeared, the effect was very beautiful. In the distance, the cannonading of the frigate, and other men-of-war, answered by the praams and gun-boats, reinforced by six more, as we afterwards found out—the vivid flashing of the guns, reflected by the water, as smooth as glass—the dark outlines of the numerous convoy, with their sails hanging down the masts, one portion of the convoy appearing for a moment, as the guns were discharged in that direction, and then disappearing, while others were momentarily seen—the roar of the heavy guns opposed to us—the crashing of the timbers of the brig, which was struck at every discharge, and very often perforated—with the whizzing of the shot as it passed by;—all this in a dark yet clear night, with every star in the heavens twinkling, and, as it were, looking down upon us, was interesting as well as awful. But I soon perceived that the gun-boats were nearing us every time that they fired, and I now discharged grape alone, waiting for the flash of the fire to ascertain their direction. At last I could perceive their long, low hulls, not two cables' length from us, and their sweeps lifting from the water. It was plain that they were advancing to board, and I resolved to anticipate them if possible. I had fired ahead of the brig, and I now pulled with all my boats astern, giving my orders to the officers, and laying on our oars in readiness. The gun-boats were about half a cable's length from each other, pulling up abreast, and passing us at about the same distance, when I directed the men to give way. I had determined to throw all my force upon the nearest boat, and in half a minute our bows were forced between their sweeps, which we caught hold of to force our way alongside.

The resistance of the Danes was very determined. Three times did I obtain a footing on the deck, and three times was I thrown back into the boats. At last we had fairly obtained our ground, and were driving them gradually forward, when, as I ran on the gunwale to obtain a position more in advance of my men, I received a blow with the butt end of a musket—I believe on the shoulder—which knocked me overboard, and I fell between the sweeps, and sunk under the vessel's bottom. I rose under her stern; but I was so shook with the violence of the blow, that I was for some time confused; still I had strength to keep myself above water, and paddled, as it appeared, away from the vessel, until I hit against a sweep which had fallen overboard. This supported me, and I gradually recovered myself. The loud report of a gun close to me startled me, and I perceived that it was from the gun-boat which I had boarded, and that her head was turned in the direction of the other gun-boat. From this, with the noise of the sweeps pulling, I knew that my men had succeeded in capturing her. I hallooed, but they did not hear me, and I soon lost sight of her. Another gun was now fired; it was from the other gun-boat retreating, and I perceived her pulling in-shore, for she passed me not twenty yards off. I now held the sweep with my hands, and struck out off the shore, in the direction of the convoy.

A light breeze rippled the water, and I knew that I had no time to lose. In about five minutes I heard the sound of oars, and perceived a boat crossing me. I hailed as loud as I could—they heard me, laid on their oars—and I hailed again—they pulled to me, and took me in. It was the master of the brig, who, aware of the capture of one gun-boat, and the retreat of the other, was looking for his vessel; or, as he told me, for what was left of her. In a short time we found her, and, although very much cut up, she had received no shot under water. In an hour the breeze was strong, the cannonading had ceased in every direction, and we had repaired her damages, so as to be able to make sail, and continue our course through the Sound.

Here I may as well relate the events of the action. One of the other divisions of gun-boats had retreated when attacked by the boats. The other had beaten off the boats, and killed many of the men, but had suffered so much themselves, as to retreat without making any capture. The *Acasta* lost four men killed, and seven wounded; the *Isis*, three men wounded; the *Reindeer* had nobody hurt; the *Rattlesnake* had six men killed, and two wounded, including the captain; but of that I shall speak hereafter.

I found that I was by no means seriously hurt by the blow I had received: my shoulder was stiff for a week, and very much discoloured, but nothing more. When I fell overboard I had struck against a sweep, which had cut my ear half off. The captain of the brig gave me dry clothes, and in a few hours I was very comfortably asleep, hoping to join my ship the next day; but in this I was disappointed. The breeze was favourable and fresh, and we were clear of the Sound, but a long way astern of the convoy, and none of the headmost men-of-war to be seen. I dressed and went on deck, and immediately perceived that I had little chance of joining my ship until we arrived at Carlscrona, which proved to be the case. About ten o'clock, the wind died away, and we had from that time such baffling light winds, that it was six days before we dropped our anchor, every vessel of the convoy having arrived before us.

—◦◦◦—

CHAPTER LIX

The dead man attends at the auction of his own effects, and bids the sale to stop—One more than was wanted—Peter steps into his shoes again—Captain Hawkins takes a friendly interest in Peter's papers—Riga balsam sternly refused to be admitted for the relief of the ship's company.

AS SOON as the sails were furled, I thanked the master of the vessel for his kindness, and requested the boat. He ordered it to be manned, saying, "How glad your captain will be to see you!" I doubted that. We shook hands, and I pulled to the *Rattlesnake*, which lay about two cables' length astern of us. I had put on a jacket, when I left the brig on service, and coming in a merchantman's boat, no attention was paid to me; indeed, owing to circumstances, no one was on the look-out, and I ascended the side unperceived. The men and officers were on the quarter-deck, attending the sale of dead men's effects before the mast; and every eye was fixed upon six pair of nankeen trousers exposed by the purser's steward which I recognized as my own. "Nine shillings for six pair of nankeen trousers," cried the purser's steward.

"Come, my men, they're worth more than that," observed the captain, who appeared to be very facetious. "It's better to be in his trousers than in his shoes." This brutal remark created a silence for a moment. "Well, then, steward, let them go. One would think that pulling on his trousers would make you as afraid as he was," continued the captain, laughing.

"Shame!" was cried out by one or two of the officers, and I recognised Swinburne's voice as one.

"More likely if they put on yours," cried I, in a loud, indignant tone.

Everybody started, and turned round; Captain Hawkins staggered to a carronade: "I beg to report myself as having rejoined my ship, sir," continued I.

"Hurrah, my lads! three cheers for Mr Simple!" said Swinburne.

The men gave them with emphasis. The captain looked at me, and without saying a word, hastily retreated to his cabin. I perceived, as he went down, that he had his arm in a sling. I thanked the men for their kind feeling towards me, shook hands with Thompson and Webster, who warmly congratulated me, and then with old Swinburne, (who nearly wrung my arm off, and gave my shoulder such pain as to make me cry out,) and with the others who extended theirs. I desired the sale of my effects to be stopped; fortunately for me, it had but just begun, and the articles were all returned. Thompson had informed the captain that he knew my father's address, and would take charge of my clothes, and send them home, but the captain would not allow him.

In a few minutes, I received a letter from the captain, desiring me to acquaint him in writing, for the information of the senior officer, in what manner I had escaped. I went down below, when I found one very melancholy face, that of the passed-midshipman of the *Acasta,* who had received an acting order in my place. When I went to my desk, I found two important articles missing; one, my private letter-book, and the other, the journal which I kept of what passed, and from which this narrative has been compiled. I inquired of my messmates, who stated that the desk had not been looked into by anyone but the captain, who, of course, must have possessed himself of those important documents.

I wrote a letter containing a short narrative of what had happened, and, at the same time, another on service to the captain, requesting that he would deliver up my property, the private journal, and letter-book in his possession. The captain, as soon as he received my letters, sent up word for his boat to be manned. As soon as it was manned, I reported it, and then begged to know whether he intended to comply with my request. He answered that he should not, and then went on deck, and quitted the brig to pull on board of the senior officer. I therefore determined immediately to write to the captain of the *Acasta,* acquainting him with the conduct of Captain Hawkins, and requesting his interference. This I did immediately, and the boat that had brought me on board not having left the brig, I sent the letter by it, requesting them to put it into the hands of one of the officers. The letter was received previous to Captain Hawkins' visit being over, and the Captain of the *Acasta* put it into his hands, inquiring if the statement were correct. Captain Hawkins replied that it was true that he had detained these papers, as there was so much mutiny and disaffection in them, and that he should not return them to me.

"That I cannot permit," replied the captain of the *Acasta*, who was aware of the character of Captain Hawkins; "if, by mistake, you have been put in possession of any of Mr Simple's secrets, you are bound in honour not to make use of them; neither can you retain property not your own." But Captain Hawkins was determined, and refused to give them to me.

"Well, then, Captain Hawkins," replied the captain of the *Acasta*, "you will oblige me by remaining on my quarter-deck till I come out of the cabin."

The captain of the *Acasta* then wrote an order, directing Captain Hawkins immediately to deliver up *to him* the papers of mine in his possession; and coming out of the cabin, put it into Captain Hawkins' hands, saying, "Now, sir, here is a written order from your superior officer. Disobey it, if you dare. If you do, I will put you under arrest, and try you by a court-martial. I can only regret, that any captain in his Majesty's service should be forced in this way to do his duty as a gentleman and a man of honour."

Captain Hawkins bit his lip at the order, and the cutting remarks accompanying it. "Your boat is manned, sir," said the captain of the *Acasta*, in a severe tone. Captain Hawkins came on board, sealed up the books, and sent them to the captain of the *Acasta*, who redirected them to me, on his Majesty's service, and returned them by the same boat. The public may therefore thank the captain of the *Acasta* for the memoirs which they are now reading.

From my messmates I gained the following intelligence of what had passed after I had quitted the brig. The fire of the praam had cut them up severely, and Captain Hawkins had been struck in the arm with a piece of the hammock-rail, which had been shot away shortly after I left. Although the skin only was razed, he thought proper to consider himself badly wounded, and giving up the command to

Mr Webster, the second lieutenant, had retreated below, where he remained until the action was over. When Mr Webster reported the return of the boats, with the capture of the gun-boat, and my supposed death, he was so delighted, that he quite forgot his wound, and ran on deck, rubbing his hands as he walked up and down. At last, he recollected himself, went down into his cabin, and came up again with his arm in a sling.

The next morning he went on board of the *Acasta,* and made his report to the senior officer, bringing back with him the disappointed passed-midshipman as my successor. He had also stated on the quarter-deck, that if I had not been killed, he intended to have tried me by a court-martial, and have turned me out of the service; that he had quite enough charges to ruin me, for he had been collecting them ever since I had been under his command; and that now he would make that old scoundrel of a gunner repent his intimacy with me. All this was confided to the surgeon, who, as I before observed, was very much of a courtier; but the surgeon had repeated it to Thompson, the master, who now gave me the information. There was one advantage in all this, which was that I knew exactly the position in which I stood, and what I had to expect.

During the short time that we remained in port, I took care that *Riga balsam* should not be allowed to come alongside, and the men were all sober. We received orders from the captain of the *Acasta* to join the admiral, who was off the Texel in pursuance of directions he had received from the Admiralty to despatch one of the squadron, and we were selected, from the dislike which he had taken to Captain Hawkins.

—◦◦◦—

CHAPTER LX

An old friend in a new case—Heart of oak in Swedish fur—A man's a man all the world over, and something more in many parts of it—Peter gets reprimanded for being dilatory, but proves a title to a defence—Allowed.

WHEN WE WERE about forty miles off the harbour, a frigate hove in sight. We made the private signal: she hoisted Swedish colours, and kept away a couple of points to close with us. We were within two miles of her when she up courses and took in her top-gallant sails. As we closed to within two cables' lengths, she hove-to. We did the same; and the captain desired me to lower down the boat, and board her, ask her name, by whom she was commanded, and offer any assistance if the captain required it. This was the usual custom of the service, and I went on board in obedience to my orders. When I arrived on the quarter-deck, I asked in French, whether there was anyone who spoke it. The first lieutenant came forward, and took off his hat: I stated that I was requested to ask the name of the vessel and the commanding officer, to insert it in our log, and to offer any service that we could command. He replied that the captain was on deck, and turned round, but the captain had gone down below. "I will inform him of your message—I had no idea that he had quitted the deck"; and the first lieutenant left me. I exchanged a few compliments and a little news with the officers on deck, who appeared to be very gentlemanlike fellows, when the first lieutenant requested my presence in the cabin. I descended—the door was opened—I was announced by the first lieutenant, and he quitted the cabin. I looked at the captain, who was sitting at the table: he was a fine, stout man, with two or three ribands at his button-hole, and a large pair of moustachios. I thought that I had seen him before, but I could not recollect when: his face was certainly familiar to me, but, as I had been informed by the officers on deck, that the captain was a Count Shucksen, a person I had never heard of, I thought that I must be mistaken. I therefore addressed him in French, paying him a long compliment, with all the necessary *et ceteras.*

The captain turned round to me, took his hand away from his

forehead, which it had shaded, and looking me full in the face, replied, "Mr Simple, I don't understand but very little French. Spin your yarn in plain English."

I started—"I thought that I knew your face," replied I; "am I mistaken?—no, it must be—Mr Chucks!"

"You are right, my dear Mr Simple: it is your old friend, Chucks, the boatswain, whom you now see. I knew you as soon as you came up the side, and I was afraid that you would immediately recognize me, and I slipped down into the cabin (for which apparent rudeness allow me to apologise), that you might not explain before the officers."

We shook hands heartily, and then he requested me to sit down. "But," said I, "they told me on deck that the frigate was commanded by a Count Shucksen."

"That is my present rank, my dear Peter," said he; "but as you have no time to lose, I will explain all. I know I can trust to your honour. You remember that you left me, as you and I supposed, dying in the privateer, with the captain's jacket and epaulettes on my shoulders. When the boats came out, and you left the vessel, they boarded and found me. I was still breathing; and judging of my rank by the coat, they put me into the boat, and pushed on shore. The privateer sank very shortly after. I was not expected to live, but in a few days a change took place, and I was better. They asked me my name, and I gave my own, which they lengthened into Shucksen, somehow or another. I recovered by a miracle, and am now as well as ever I was in my life. They were not a little proud of having captured a captain in the British service, as they supposed, for they never questioned me as to my real rank. After some weeks I was sent home to Denmark in a running vessel; but it so happened, that we met with a gale, and were wrecked on the Swedish coast, close to Carlscrona. The Danes were at that time at war, having joined the Russians; and they were made prisoners, while I was of course liberated, and treated with great distinction; but as I could not speak either French or their own language, I could not get on very well. However, I had a handsome allowance, and permission to go to England as soon as I pleased. The Swedes were then at war with the Russians, and were fitting out their fleet; but, Lord bless them! they didn't know much about it. I amused myself walking in the dockyard, and looking at their motions; but they had not thirty men in the fleet who knew what they were about, and, as for a man to set them going, there wasn't one. Well, Peter, you know I could not be idle, and so by degrees I told one, and then told another—until they went the right way to work; and the captains and officers were very much obliged to me. At last, they all came to me, and if they did not understand me entirely, I showed them how to do it with my own hands; and the fleet began to make a show with their rigging. The admiral who commanded was very much obliged, and I seemed to come as regularly to my work as if I was paid for it. At last, the admiral came with an English interpreter, and asked me whether I was anxious to go back to England, or would I like to join their service. I saw what they wanted, and I replied that I had neither wife nor child in England, and that I liked their country very much; but I must take time to consider of it, and must also know what they had to propose. I went home to my lodgings, and, to make them more anxious, I did not make my appearance at the dockyard for three or four days, when a letter came from the admiral, offering me the command of a frigate if I would join their service. I replied, (for I knew how much they wanted me,) that I would prefer an English frigate to a Swedish one, and that I would not consent unless they offered something more; and then, with the express stipulation that I should not take arms against my own country. They then waited for a week, when they offered to make me a *Count*, and give me the command of a frigate. This suited me, as you may suppose, Peter; it was the darling wish of my heart—I was to be made a gentleman. I consented, and was made Count Shucksen, and had a fine large frigate under my command. I then set to work with a will, superintended the fitting out of the whole fleet, and showed them what an Englishman could do. We sailed, and you of course know the brush we had with the Russians, which, I must say, did us no discredit. I was fortunate to distinguish myself, for I exchanged several broadsides with a Russian two-deck ship, and came off with honour. When we went into port I got this riband. I was out afterwards, and fell in with a Russian frigate, and captured her, for which I received this other riband. Since that I have been in high favour, and now that I speak the languages, I like the people very much. I am often at court when I am in harbour; and, Peter, I am *married*."

"I wish you joy, count, with all my heart."

"Yes, and well married too—to a Swedish countess of very high family, and I expect that I have a little boy or girl by this time. So you observe, Peter, that I am at last a gentleman, and, what is more, my children will be noble by two descents. Who would have thought that this would have been occasioned by my throwing the captain's jacket into the boat instead of my own? And now, my dear Mr Simple, that I have made you my confidant, I need not say, do not say a word about it to anybody. They certainly could not do me much harm, but still, they might do me some; and although I am not likely to meet anyone who may recognize me in this uniform and these moustachios, it's just as well to keep the secret, which to you and O'Brien only would I have confided."

"My dear count," replied I, "your secret is safe with me. You have come to your title before me, at all events; and I sincerely wish you joy, for you have obtained it honourably; but, although I would like to talk with you for days, I must return on board, for I am now sailing with a very unpleasant captain."

I then, in a few words, stated where O'Brien was; and when we parted, I went with him on deck, Count Shucksen taking my arm, and introducing me as an old shipmate to his officers. "I hope we may meet again," said I, "but I am afraid there is little chance."

"Who knows?" replied he; "see what chance has done for me. My dear Peter, God bless you! You are one of the very few whom I always loved. God bless you, my boy! and never forget that all I have is at your command if you come my way."

I thanked him, and saluting the officers, went down the side. As I expected, when I came on board, the captain demanded, in an angry tone, why I had stayed so long. I replied, that I was shown down into Count Shucksen's cabin, and he conversed so long, that I could not get away sooner, as it would not have been polite to have left him before he had finished his questions. I then gave a very civil message, and the captain said no more: the very name of a great man always silenced him.

CHAPTER LXI

Bad news from home, and worse on board—Notwithstanding his previous trials, Peter forced to prepare for another—Mrs Trotter again; improves as she grows old—Captain Hawkins and his twelve charges.

NO OTHER EVENT of consequence occurred until we joined the admiral, who only detained us three hours with the fleet, and then sent us home with his despatches. We arrived, after a quiet passage, at Portsmouth, where I wrote immediately to my sister Ellen, requesting to know the state of my father's health. I waited impatiently for an answer, and by return of post received one with a black seal. My father had died the day before from a brain fever; and Ellen conjured me to obtain leave of absence, to come to her in her state of distress. The captain came on board the next morning, and I had a letter ready written on service to the admiral, stating the circumstances, and requesting leave of absence. I presented it to him, and entreated him to forward it. At any other time I would not have condescended, but the thoughts of my poor sister, unprotected and alone, with my father lying dead in the house, made me humble and submissive. Captain Hawkins read the letter, and very coolly replied, "that it was very easy to say that my father was dead, but he required proofs." Even this insult did not affect me; I put my sister's letter into his hand—he read it, and as he returned it to me, he smiled maliciously. "It is impossible for me to forward your letter, Mr Simple, as I have one to deliver to you."

He put a large folio packet into my hand, and went below. I opened it: it was a copy of a letter demanding a court-martial upon me, with a long list of the charges preferred by him. I was stupefied, not so much at his asking for a court-martial, but at the conviction of the impossibility of my now being able to go to the assistance of my poor sister. I went down into the gun-room and threw myself on a chair, at the same time tossing the letter to Thompson, the master. He read it over carefully, and folded it up.

"Upon my word, Simple, I do not see that you have much to fear. These charges are very frivolous."

"No, no—that I care little about; but it is my poor sister. I had

written for leave of absence, and now she is left, God knows how
long, in such distressing circumstances."

Thompson looked grave. "I had forgotten your father's death,
Simple: it is indeed cruel. I would offer to go myself, but you will
want my evidence at the court-martial. It can't be helped. Write to
your sister, and keep up her spirits. Tell her why you cannot come,
and that it will all end well."

I did so, and went early to bed, for I was really ill. The next
morning, the official letter from the port-admiral came off, acquainting me that a court-martial had been ordered upon me, and that it
would take place that day week. I immediately resigned the command to the second lieutenant, and commenced an examination into
the charges preferred. They were very numerous, and dated back
almost to the very day that he had joined the ship. There were
twelve in all. I shall not trouble the reader with the whole of them,
as many were very frivolous. The principal charges were—

1. For mutinous and disrespectful conduct to Captain
Hawkins, on such a date, having, in a conversation with an
inferior officer on the quarter-deck, stated that Captain Hawkins was a spy, and had spies in the ship.

2. For neglect of duty, in disobeying the orders of Captain
Hawkins on the night of the ——— of ———.

3. For having, on the ——— of ———, sent away two
boats from the ship, in direct opposition to the orders of Captain Hawkins.

4. For having again, on the morning of the ——— of
———, held mutinous and disrespectful conversation relative
to Captain Hawkins with the gunner of the ship, allowing the
latter to accuse Captain Hawkins of cowardice, without reporting the same.

5. For insulting expressions on the quarter-deck to Captain Hawkins on his rejoining the brig on the morning of the
——— of ———.

6. For not causing the orders of Captain Hawkins to be
put in force on several occasions, &c. &c. &c.

And further, as Captain Hawkins' testimony was necessary in
two of the charges, the king, on *those charges*, was the prosecutor.

Although most of these charges were frivolous, yet I at once perceived my danger. Some were dated back many months, to the time before our ship's company had been changed: and I could not find the necessary witnesses. Indeed, in all but the recent charges, not expecting to be called to a court-martial, I had serious difficulties to contend with. But the most serious was the first charge, which I knew not how to get over. Swinburne had most decidedly referred to the captain when he talked of spy captains. However, with the assistance of Thompson, I made the best defence I could, ready for my trial.

Two days before my court-martial I received a letter from Ellen, who appeared in a state of distraction from this accumulation of misfortune. She told me that my father was to be buried the next day, and that the new rector had written to her, to know when it would be convenient for the vicarage to be given up. That my father's bills had been sent in, and amounted to twelve hundred pounds already; and that she knew not the extent of the whole claims. There appeared to be nothing left but the furniture of the house; and she wanted to know whether the debts were to be paid with the money I had left in the funds for her use. I wrote immediately, requesting her to liquidate every claim, as far as my money went, sending her an order upon my agent to draw for the whole amount, and a power of attorney to him to sell out the stock.

I had just sealed the letter, when Mrs Trotter, who had attended the ship since our return to Portsmouth, begged to speak with me, and walked in after her message, without waiting for an answer. "My dear Mr Simple," said she, "I know all that is going on, and I find that you have no lawyer to assist you. Now I know that it is necessary, and will very probably be of great service in your defence— for when people are in distress and anxiety, they have not their wits about them; so I have brought a friend of mine from Portsea, a very clever man, who, for my sake, will undertake your cause, and I hope you will not refuse him. You recollect giving me a dozen pair of stockings. I did not refuse them, nor shall you refuse me now. I always said to Mr Trotter, 'Go to a lawyer'; and if he had taken my advice he would have done well. I recollect, when a hackney-coachman smashed the panel of our carriage—'Trotter,' says I, 'go to a lawyer'; and he very politely answered, 'Go to the devil!' But what was the consequence!—he's dead and I'm bumming. Now, Mr Simple, will you oblige me?—it's all free gratis for nothing—not for nothing, for it's for my sake. You see, Mr Simple, I have admirers yet," concluded she, smiling.

Mrs Trotter's advice was good; and although I would not listen to receiving his services gratuitously, I agreed to employ him; and very useful did he prove against such charges, and such a man as Captain Hawkins. He came on board that afternoon, carefully examined into all the documents and the witnesses whom I could bring forward, showed me the weak side of my defence, and took the papers on shore with him. Every day he came on board to collect fresh evidence and examine into my case.

At last the day arrived. I dressed myself in my best uniform. The gun fired from the admiral's ship, with the signal for a court-martial at nine o'clock; and I went on board in a boat, with all the witnesses. On my arrival, I was put under the custody of the provost-marshal. The captains ordered to attend pulled alongside one after another, and were received by a party of marines, presenting their arms.

At half-past nine the court was all assembled, and I was ushered in. Courts-martial are open courts, although no one is permitted to print the evidence. At the head of the long table was the admiral, as president; on his right hand, standing, was Captain Hawkins, as prosecutor. On each side of the table were six captains, sitting near to the admiral, according to their seniority. At the bottom, facing the admiral, was the judge-advocate, on whose left hand I stood, as prisoner. The witnesses called in to be examined were stationed on his right; and behind him, by the indulgence of the court, was a small table, at which sat my legal adviser, so close as to be able to communicate with me. The court were all sworn, and then took their seats. Stauncheons, with ropes covered with green baize, passed along, were behind the chairs of the captains who composed the court, so that they might not be crowded upon by those who came in to listen to what passed. The charges were then read, as well as the letters to and from the admiral, by which the court-martial was demanded and granted: and then Captain Hawkins was desired to open his prosecution. He commenced with observing his great regret that he had been forced to a measure so repugnant to his feelings; his frequent cautions to me, and the indifference with which I treated them; and, after a preamble composed of every falsity that could be devised, he commenced with the first charge, and stating himself to be the witness, gave his evidence. When it was finished, I was asked if I had any questions to put. By the advice of my lawyer, I replied, "No." The president then asked the captains composing the court-martial, commencing according to their seniority, whether they wished to ask any questions.

"I wish," said the second captain who was addressed, "to ask Captain Hawkins whether, when he came on deck, he came up in the usual way in which a captain of a man-of-war comes on his quarter-deck, or whether he slipped up without noise?"

Captain Hawkins declared that he came up as he *usually did*. This was true enough, for he invariably came up by stealth.

"Pray, Captain Hawkins, as you have repeated a good deal of conversation which passed between the first lieutenant and the gunner, may I ask you how long you were by their side without their perceiving you?"

"A very short time," was the answer.

"But, Captain Hawkins, do you not think, allowing that you came up on deck in your *usual* way, as you term it, that you would have done better to have hemmed or hawed, so as to let your officers know that you were present? I should be very sorry to hear all that might be said of me in my supposed absence."

To this observation Captain Hawkins replied, that he was so astonished at the conversation, that he was quite breathless, having, till then, had the highest opinion of me.

No more questions were asked, and they proceeded to the second charge. This was a very trifling one—for lighting a stove, contrary to orders; the evidence brought forward was the sergeant of marines. When his evidence in favour of the charge had been given, I was asked by the president if I had any questions to put to the witness. I put the following:—

"Did you repeat to Captain Hawkins that I had ordered the stove to be lighted?"—"I did."

"Are you not in the custom of reporting, direct to the captain, any negligence, or disobedience of orders, you may witness in the ship?"—"I am."

"Did you ever report anything of the sort to me, as first lieutenant, or do you always report direct to the captain?"

"I always report direct to the captain."

"By the captain's orders?"—"Yes."

The following questions were then put by some of the members of the court:—

"You have served in other ships before?"—"Yes."

"Did you ever, sailing with other captains, receive an order from them to report direct to them, and not through the first lieutenant?" The witness here prevaricated.

"Answer directly, yes or no."—"No."

The third charge was then brought forward—for sending away boats contrary to express orders. This was substantiated by Captain Hawkins' own evidence, the order having been verbal. By the advice of my counsel, I put no questions to Captain Hawkins, neither did the court.

The fourth charge—that of holding mutinous conversation with the gunner, and allowing him to accuse the captain of unwillingness to engage the enemy—was then again substantiated by Captain Hawkins, as the only witness. I again left my reply for my defence; and only one question was put by one of the members, which was, to inquire of Captain Hawkins, as he appeared peculiarly unfortunate in overhearing conversations, whether he walked up as usual to the taffrail, or whether he *crept up*. Captain Hawkins gave the same answer as before.

The fifth charge—for insulting expressions to Captain Hawkins, on my rejoining the brig at Carlscrona—was then brought forward, and the sergeant of marines and one of the seamen appeared as witnesses. This charge excited a great deal of amusement. In the cross-examination by the members of the court, Captain Hawkins was asked what he meant by the expression, when disposing of the clothes of an officer who was killed in action, that the men appeared to think that his trousers would instil fear.

"Nothing more, upon my honour, sir," replied Captain Hawkins, "than an implication that they were alarmed lest they should be haunted by his ghost."

"Then, of course, Mr Simple meant the same in his reply," observed the captain sarcastically.

The remainder of the charges were then brought forward, but they were of little consequence. The witnesses were chiefly the sergeant of marines, and the spy-glass of Captain Hawkins, who had been watching me from the shore.

It was late in the afternoon before they were all gone through;

and the president then adjourned the court, that I might bring forward my own witnesses, in my defence, on the following day, and I returned on board the *Rattlesnake.*

—————

CHAPTER LXII

A good defence not always good against a bad accusation—Peter wins the heart of his judges, yet loses his cause, and is dismissed his ship.

THE NEXT DAY I commenced my defence, and I preferred calling my own witnesses first, and, by the advice of my counsel, and at the request of Swinburne, I called him. I put the following questions:—"When we were talking on the quarter-deck, was it fine weather?"—"Yes, it was."

"Do you think that you might have heard anyone coming on deck, in the usual way, up the companion ladder?"

"Sure of it."

"Do you mean, then, to imply that Captain Hawkins came up stealthily?"

"I have an idea he pounced upon us as a cat does on a mouse."

"What were the expressions made use of?"

"I said that a spy captain would always find spy followers."

"In that remark were you and Mr Simple referring to your own captain?"—"The remark was mine. What Mr Simple was thinking of, I can't tell; but I *did* refer to the captain, and he has proved that I was right." This bold answer of Swinburne's rather astonished the court, who commenced cross-questioning him; but he kept to his original assertion—that I had only answered generally. To repel the second charge I produced no witnesses; but to the third charge I brought forward three witnesses to prove that Captain Hawkins's orders were that I should send no boats on shore, not that I should not send them on board of the men-of-war close to us. In answer to the fourth charge, I called Swinburne, who stated that if I did not, he would come forward. Swinburne acknowledged that he accused the captain of being shy, and that I reprimanded him for so doing. "Did he say that he would report you?" inquired one of the captains. "No, sir," replied Swinburne, " 'cause he never meant to do it." This was an unfortunate answer.

To the fifth charge, I brought several witnesses to prove the words of Captain Hawkins, and the sense in which they were taken by the ship's company, and the men calling out "Shame!" when he used the expression.

To refute the other charges I called one or two witnesses, and the court then adjourned, inquiring of me when I would be ready to commence my defence. I requested a day to prepare, which was readily granted; and the ensuing day the court did not sit. I hardly need say that I was busily employed, arranging my defence with my counsel. At last all was done, and I went to bed tired and unhappy; but I slept soundly, which could not be said of my counsel, for he went on shore at eleven o'clock, and sat up all night making a fair copy. After all, the fairest court of justice is a naval court-martial— no brow-beating of witnesses, an evident inclination towards the prisoner—every allowance and every favour granted him, and no legal quibbles attended to. It is a court of equity, with very few exceptions; and the humbler the individual, the greater the chance in his favour.

I was awoke the following morning by my counsel, who had not gone to bed the previous night, and who had come off at seven o'clock to read over with me my defence. At nine o'clock I again proceeded on board, and in a short time the court was sitting. I came in, handed my defence to the judge-advocate, who read it aloud to the court. I have a copy still by me, and will give the whole of it to the reader.

"MR PRESIDENT AND GENTLEMEN,—After nearly fourteen years' service in his Majesty's navy, during which I have been twice made prisoner, twice wounded, and once wrecked; and, as I trust I shall prove to you, by certificates and the public despatches, I have done my duty with zeal and honour; I now find myself in a situation in which I never expected to be placed—that of being arraigned before and brought to a court-martial for charges of mutiny, disaffection, and disrespect towards my superior officer. If the honourable court will examine the certificates I am about to produce, they will find that, until I sailed with Captain Hawkins, my conduct has always been supposed to have been diametrically opposite to that which is now imputed to me. I have always been diligent and obedient to command; and I have only to regret that the captains with whom I have had the honour to sail are not now present to corroborate by their oral evidence the truth of these documents. Allow me, in the first place, to point out to the court, that the charges against me are spread over a large space of time, amounting to nearly eighteen months, during the whole of which period Captain Hawkins never stated to me that it was his intention to try me by a court-martial; and, although repeatedly in the presence of a senior officer, has never preferred any charge against me. The articles of war state expressly that if any officer, soldier, or marine has any complaint to make he is to do so upon his arrival at any port or fleet where he may fall in with a superior officer. I admit that this article of war refers to complaints to be made by inferiors against superiors; but, at the same time, I venture to submit to the honourable court that a superior is equally bound to prefer a charge, or to give notice that the charge will be preferred, on the first seasonable opportunity, instead of lulling the offender into security, and disarming him in his defence, by allowing the time to run on so long as to render him incapable of bringing forward his witnesses. I take the liberty of calling this to your attention, and shall now proceed to answer the charges which have been brought against me.

"I am accused of having held a conversation with an inferior officer on the quarter-deck of his Majesty's brig *Rattlesnake*, in which my captain was treated with contempt. That it may not be supposed that Mr Swinburne was a new acquaintance, made upon my joining the brig, I must observe that he was an old shipmate, with whom I had served many years, and with whose worth I was well acquainted. He was my instructor in my more youthful days, and has been rewarded for his merit, with the warrant which he now holds as gunner of his Majesty's brig *Rattlesnake*. The offensive observation, in the first place, was not mine; and, in the second, it was couched in general terms. Here Mr Swinburne has pointedly confessed that *he* did refer to the captain, although the observation was in the plural; but that does not prove the charge against me—on the contrary, adds weight to the assertion of Mr Swinburne, that I was guiltless of the present charge. That Captain Hawkins has acted as a spy, his own evidence on this charge, as well as that brought

forward by other witnesses, will decidedly prove; but as the truth of
the observation does not warrant the utterance, I am glad that no
such expression escaped my lips.

"Upon the second charge I shall dwell but a short time. It is true
that there is a general order that no stoves shall be alight after a
certain hour; but I will appeal to the honourable court, whether a
first lieutenant is not considered to have a degree of licence of judgment in all that concerns the interior discipline of the ship. The
surgeon sent to say that a stove was required for one of the sick. I
was in bed at the time, and replied immediately in the affirmative.
Does Captain Hawkins mean to assert to the honourable court, that
he would have refused the request of the surgeon? Most certainly
not. The only error I committed, if it were an error, was not going
through the form of awaking Captain Hawkins, to ask the permission, which, as first lieutenant, I thought myself authorized to give.

"The charge against me, of having sent away two boats, contrary
to his order, I have already disproved by witnesses. The order of
Captain Hawkins was, not to communicate with the shore. My reasons for sending away the boats—" (Here Captain Hawkins interposed, and stated to the president that my reasons were not
necessary to be received. The court was cleared, and, on our return,
the court had decided, that my reasons ought to be given, and I
continued.) "My reasons for sending away these boats, or rather it
was one boat which was despatched to the two frigates, if I remember well, were, that the brig was in a state of mutiny. The captain
had tied up one of the men, and the ship's company refused to be
flogged. Captain Hawkins then went on shore to the admiral, to
report the situation of his ship, and I conceived it my duty to make
it known to the men-of-war anchored close to us. I shall not enter
into further particulars, as they will only detain the honourable
court; and I am aware that this court-martial is held upon my conduct, and not upon that of Captain Hawkins. To the charge of again
holding disrespectful language on the quarter-deck, as overheard by
Captain Hawkins, I must refer the honourable court to the evidence,
in which it is plainly proved that the remarks upon him were not
mine, but those of Mr Swinburne, and that I remonstrated with Mr
Swinburne for using such unguarded expressions. The only point of
difficulty is, whether it was not my duty to have reported such
language. I reply, that there is no proof that I did not intend to

report it; but the presence of Captain Hawkins, who heard what was said, rendered such report unnecessary.

"On the fifth charge, I must beg that the court will be pleased to consider that some allowance ought to be made for a moment of irritation. My character was traduced by Captain Hawkins, supposing that I was dead; so much so, that even the ship's company cried out *shame*. I am aware, that no language of a superior officer can warrant a retort from an inferior; but, as what I intended to imply by that language is not yet known, although Captain Hawkins has given an explanation to his, I shall merely say, that I meant no more by my insinuations, than Captain Hawkins did at the time, by those which he made use of with respect to me.

"Upon the other trifling charges brought forward, I lay no stress, as I consider them fully refuted by the evidence which has been already adduced; and I shall merely observe, that, for reasons best known to himself, I have been met with a most decided hostility on the part of Captain Hawkins, from the time that he first joined the ship; that, on every occasion, he has used all his efforts to render me uncomfortable, and embroil me with others; that, not content with narrowly watching my conduct on board, he has resorted to his spy-glass from the shore; and, instead of assisting me in the execution of a duty sufficiently arduous, he has thrown every obstacle in my way, placed inferior officers as spies over my conduct, and made me feel so humiliated in the presence of the ship's company, over which I have had to superintend, and in the disciplining of which I had a right to look to him for support, that, were it not that some odium would necessarily be attached to the sentence, I should feel it as one of the happiest events of my life that I were dismissed from the situation which I now hold under his command. I now beg that the honourable court will allow the documents I lay upon the table to be read in support of my character."

When this was over, the court was cleared, that they might decide upon the sentence. I waited about half an hour in the greatest anxiety, when I was again summoned to attend. The usual forms of reading the papers were gone through, and then came the sentence, which was read by the president, he and the whole court standing up with their cocked hats on their heads. After the preamble, it concluded with saying, "that it was the opinion of that court that the charges had been *partly* proved, and therefore, that Lieutenant Peter Simple was dismissed his ship; but, in consideration of his good character and services, his case was strongly recommended to the consideration of the Lords Commissioners of the Admiralty."

———◦◦◦———

CHAPTER LXIII

Peter looks upon his loss as something gained—Goes on board the Rattlesnake *to pack up, and is ordered to pack off—Polite leave-taking between relations. Mrs Trotter better and better—Goes to London, and afterwards falls into all manner of misfortunes by the hands of robbers, and of his own uncle.*

I HARDLY KNEW whether I felt glad or sorry at this sentence. On the one hand, it was almost a deathblow to my future advancement or employment in the service; on the other, the recommendation very much softened down the sentence, and I was quite happy to be quit of Captain Hawkins, and free to hasten to my poor sister. I bowed respectfully to the court, which immediately adjourned. Captain Hawkins followed the captains on the quarter-deck, but none of them would speak to him—so much to his disadvantage had come out during the trial.

About ten minutes afterwards, one of the elder captains composing the court called me into the cabin. "Mr Simple," said he, "we are all very sorry for you. Our sentence could not be more lenient, under the circumstances: it was that conversation with the gunner at the taffrail which floored you. It must be a warning to you to be more careful in future, how you permit anyone to speak of the conduct of your superiors on the quarter-deck. I am desired by the president to let you know that it is our intention to express ourselves very strongly to the admiral in your behalf; so much so, that if another captain applies for you, you will have no difficulty in being appointed to a ship; and as for leaving your present ship, under any other circumstances I should consider it a matter of congratulation."

I returned my sincere thanks, and soon afterwards quitted the guard-ship, and went on board of the brig to pack up my clothes, and take leave of my messmates. On my arrival, I found that Captain Hawkins had preceded me, and he was on deck when I came up the side. I hastened down into the gun-room, where I received the condolements of my messmates.

"Simple, I wish you joy," cried Thompson, loud enough for the captain to hear on deck. "I wish I had your luck; I wish somebody would try me by a court-martial."

"As it has turned out," replied I, in a loud voice, "and after the communication made to me by the captains composing the court, of what they intend to say to the Admiralty, I agree with you, Thompson, that it is a very kind act on the part of Captain Hawkins, and I feel quite grateful to them."

"Steward, come—glasses," cried Thompson, "and let us drink success to Mr Simple."

All this was very annoying to Captain Hawkins, who overheard every word. When our glasses were filled—"Simple, your good health, and may I meet with as good a messmate," said Thompson.

At this moment, the sergeant of marines put his head in at the gun-room door, and said, in a most insolent tone, that I was to leave the ship immediately. I was so irritated, that I threw my glass of grog in his face, and he ran up to the captain to make the complaint; but I did not belong to the ship, and even if I had, I would have resented such impertinence.

Captain Hawkins was in a great rage, and I believe would have written for another court-martial, but he had had enough of them. He inquired very particularly of the sergeant whether he had told me that I was to leave the ship directly, or whether, that Captain Hawkins desired that I should leave the ship immediately; and finding that he had not given the latter message (which I was aware of, for had he given it, I dare not have acted as I did); he then sent down again by one of the midshipmen, desiring me to leave the ship immediately. My reply was, that I should certainly obey his orders with the greatest pleasure. I hastened to pack up my clothes, reported myself ready to the second lieutenant, who went up for permission to man a boat, which was refused by Captain Hawkins, who said I might go on shore in a shore-boat. I called one alongside, shook hands with all my messmates, and when I arrived on the quarter-deck, with Swinburne, and some of the best men, who came forward; Captain Hawkins stood by the binnacle, bursting with rage. As I went over the planeshear, I took my hat off to him, and wished him good-morning very respectfully, adding, "If you have any commands for my *uncle*, Captain Hawkins, I shall be glad to execute them."

This observation, which showed him that I knew the connection and correspondence between them, made him gasp with emotion. "Leave the ship, sir, or by God I'll put you in irons for mutiny," cried he. I again took off my hat, and went down the side, and shoved off.

As soon as I was a few yards distant, the men jumped on the carronades and cheered, and I perceived Captain Hawkins order them down, and before I was a cable's length from her, the pipe "all hands to punishment"; so I presume some of the poor fellows suffered for their insubordination in showing their good will. I acknowledge that I might have left the ship in a more dignified manner, and that my conduct was not altogether correct; but still, I state what I really did do, and some allowance must be made for my feelings. This is certain, that my conduct after the court-martial, was more deserving of punishment, than that for which I had been tried. But I was in a state of feverish excitement, and hardly knew what I did.

When I arrived at Sally Port, I had my effects wheeled up to the Blue Posts, and packing up those which I most required, I threw off my uniform, and was once more a gentleman at large. I took my place in the mail for that evening, sent a letter of thanks, with a few bank notes, to my counsel, and then sat down and wrote a long letter to O'Brien, acquainting him with the events which had taken place.

I had just finished, and sealed it up, when in came Mrs Trotter. "Oh my dear Mr Simple! I'm so sorry; and I have come to console you. There's nothing like women when men are in affliction, as poor Trotter used to say, as he laid his head in my lap. When do you go to town?"

"This evening, Mrs Trotter."

"I hope I am to continue to attend the ship?"

"I hope so too, Mrs Trotter, I have no doubt but you will."

"Now, Mr Simple, how are you off for money? Do you want a little? You can pay me by-and-by. Don't be afraid. I'm not quite so poor as I was when you came down to mess with Trotter and me, and when you gave me the dozen pair of stockings. I know what it is to want money, and what it is to want friends."

"Many thanks to you, Mrs Trotter," replied I; "but I have sufficient to take me home, and then I can obtain more."

"Well, I'm glad of it, but it was offered in earnest. Good-bye, God bless you! Come, Mr Simple, give me a kiss; it won't be the first time."

I kissed her, for I felt grateful for her kindness; and with a little smirking and ogling she quitted the room. I could not help thinking, after she was gone, how little we know the hearts of others. If I had been asked if Mrs Trotter was a person to have done a generous action, from what I had seen of her in adversity, I should have decidedly said, No. Yet in this offer she was disinterested, for she knew the service well enough to be aware that I had little chance of being a first lieutenant again, and of being of service to her. And how often does it also occur, that those who ought, from gratitude or long friendship, to do all they can to assist you, turn from you in your necessity, and prove false and treacherous! It is God alone who knows our hearts. I sent my letter to O'Brien to the admiral's office, sat down to a dinner which I could not taste, and at seven o'clock got into the mail.

When I arrived in town I was much worse, but I did not wait more than an hour. I took my place in a coach which did not go to the town near which we resided; for I had inquired and found that coach was full, and I did not choose to wait another day. The coach in which I took my place went within forty miles of the vicarage, and I intended to post across the country. The next evening I arrived at the point of separation, and taking out my portmanteau, ordered a chaise, and set off for what had once been my home. I could hardly hold my head up, I was so ill, and I lay in a corner of the chaise in a sort of dream, kept from sleeping from intense pain in the forehead and temples. It was about nine o'clock at night, when we were in a dreadful jolting road, the shocks proceeding from which gave me agonizing pain, that the chaise was stopped by two men, who dragged me out on the grass. One stood over me, while the other rifled the chaise. The post-boy, who appeared a party to the transaction, remained quietly on his horse, and as soon as they had taken my effects, turned round and drove off. They then rifled my person, taking away everything that I had, leaving me nothing but my trousers and shirt. After a short consultation, they ordered me to walk on in the direction in which we had been proceeding in the chaise, and to hasten as fast as I could, or they would blow my brains out. I complied with their request, thinking myself fortunate to have escaped so well. I knew that I was still thirty miles at least from the vicarage; but ill as I was, I hoped to be able to reach it on foot. I walked during the remainder of the night, but I got on but slowly. I reeled from one side of the road to the other, and occasionally sat down to rest. Morning dawned, and I perceived habitations not far from me. I staggered on in my course.

The fever now raged in me, my head was splitting with agony, and I tottered to a bank near a small neat cottage, on the side of the road. I have a faint recollection of someone coming to me and taking my hand, but nothing further; and it was not till many months afterwards, that I became acquainted with the circumstances which I now relate. It appears that the owner of the cottage was a half-pay lieutenant in the army, who had sold-out on account of his wounds. I was humanely taken into his house, laid on a bed, and a surgeon requested to come to me immediately. I had now lost all recollection, and who I was they could not ascertain. My pockets were empty, and it was only by the mark on my linen that they found that my name was Simple. For three weeks I remained in a state of alternate stupor and delirium. When the latter came on, I raved of Lord Privilege, O'Brien, and Celeste. Mr Selwin, the officer who had so kindly assisted me, knew that Simple was the patronymic name of Lord Privilege, and he immediately wrote to his lordship, stating that a young man of the name of Simple, who, in his delirium called upon him and Captain O'Brien, was lying in a most dangerous state in his house, and, that as he presumed I was a relative of his lordship's he had deemed it right to apprise him of the fact.

My uncle, who knew that it must be me, thought this too favourable an opportunity, provided I should live, not to have me in his power. He wrote to say that he would be there in a day or two; at the same time thanking Mr Selwin for his kind attention to his poor nephew, and requesting that no expense might be spared. When my uncle arrived, which he did in his own chariot, the crisis of the fever was over, but I was still in a state of stupor, arising from extreme debility. He thanked Mr Selwin for his attention, which he said he was afraid was of little avail, as I was every year becoming more deranged; and he expressed his fears that it would terminate in chronic lunacy. "His poor father died in the same state," continued my uncle, passing his hand across his eyes, as if much affected. "I have brought my physician with me, to see if he can be moved. I shall not be satisfied unless I am with him night and day."

The physician (who was my uncle's valet) took me by the hand, felt my pulse, examined my eyes, and pronounced that it would be very easy to move me, and that I should recover sooner in a more airy room. Of course, Mr Selwin raised no objections, putting down all to my uncle's regard for me; and my clothes were put on me, as I lay in a state of insensibility, and I was lifted into the chariot. It is most wonderful that I did not die from being thus taken out of my bed in such a state, but it pleased Heaven that it should be otherwise. Had such an event taken place, it would probably have pleased my uncle much better than my surviving. When I was in the carriage, supported by the pseudo-physician, my uncle again thanked Mr Selwin, begged that he would command his interest, wrote a handsome cheque for the surgeon who had attended me, and getting into the carriage, drove off with me still in a state of insensibility— that is, I was not so insensible, but I think I felt I had been removed, and I heard the rattling of the wheels; but my mind was so uncollected, and I was in a state of such weakness, that I could not feel assured of it for a minute.

For some days afterwards, for I recollect nothing about the journey, I found myself in bed in a dark room and my arms confined. I recalled my senses, and by degrees was able to recollect all that had occurred, until I laid down by the roadside. Where was I? The room was dark, I could distinguish nothing; that I had attempted to do myself some injury, I took for granted, or my arms would not have been secured. I had been in a fever and delirious, I supposed, and had now recovered. I had been in a reverie for more than an hour, wondering why I was left alone, when the door of the apartment opened. "Who is there?" inquired I.

"Oh! you've come to yourself again," said a gruff voice; "then I'll give you a little daylight."

He took down a shutter which covered the whole of the window, and a flood of light poured in, which blinded me. I shut my eyes, and by degrees admitted the light until I could bear it. I looked at

the apartment: the walls were bare and whitewashed. I was on a
truckle-bed. I looked at the window—it was closed up with iron
bars.—"Why, where am I?" inquired I of the man, with alarm.
"Where are you?" replied he; "why, in Bedlam!"

—◦◦◦—

CHAPTER LXIV

*As O'Brien said, it's a long lane that has no turning—I am rescued, and happiness pours
in upon me as fast as misery before overwhelmed me.*

THE SHOCK WAS too great—I fell back on my pillow insensible.
How long I lay, I know not, but when I recovered the keeper
was gone, and I found a jug of water and some bread by the side of
the bed. I drank the water, and the effect it had upon me was sur-
prising. I felt that I could get up, and I rose: my arms had been
unpinioned during my swoon. I got on my feet, and staggered to the
window. I looked out, saw the bright sun, the passers-by, the houses
opposite—all looked cheerful and gay, but I was a prisoner in a
madhouse. Had I been mad? I reflected, and supposed that I had
been, and had been confined by those who knew nothing of me. It
never came into my head that my uncle had been a party to it. I
threw myself on the bed, and relieved myself with tears. It was
about noon that the medical people, attended by the keepers and
others, came into my apartment. "Is he quite quiet?" "O Lord! yes,
sir, as quiet as a lamb," replied the man who had before entered. I
then spoke to the medical gentleman, begging him to tell why, and
how, I had been brought here. He answered mildly and soothingly,
saying that I was there at the wish of my friends, and that every care
would be taken of me; that he was aware that my paroxysms were
only occasional, and that, during the time I was quiet, I should have
every indulgence that could be granted, and that he hoped that I
soon should be perfectly well, and be permitted to leave the hospital. I replied by stating who I was, and how I had been taken ill. The
doctor shook his head, advised me to lie down as much as possible,
and then quitted me to visit the other patients.

As I afterwards discovered, my uncle had had me confined upon the plea that I was a young man who was deranged with an idea that his name was Simple, and that he was the heir to the title and estates; that I was very troublesome at times, forcing my way into his house and insulting the servants, but in every other respect was harmless; that my paroxysms generally ended in a violent fever, and it was more from the fear of my coming to some harm, than from any ill-will towards the poor young man, that he wished me to remain in the hospital, and be taken care of. The reader may at once perceive the art of this communication: I, having no idea why I was confined, would of course continue to style myself by my true name; and as long as I did this, so long would I be considered in a deranged state. The reader must not therefore be surprised when I tell him that I remained in Bedlam for one year and eight months. The doctor called upon me for two or three days, and finding me quiet, ordered me to be allowed books, paper, and ink, to amuse myself; but every attempt at explanation was certain to be the signal for him to leave my apartment. I found, therefore, not only by him, but from the keeper, who paid no attention to anything I said, that I had no chance of being listened to, or of obtaining my release.

After the first month, the doctor came to me no more: I was a quiet patient, and he received the report of the keeper. I was sent there with every necessary document to prove that I was mad; and, although a very little may establish a case of lunacy, it requires something very strong indeed to prove that you are in your right senses. In Bedlam I found it impossible. At the same time I was well treated, was allowed all necessary comforts, and such amusement as could be obtained from books, &c. I had no reason to complain of the keeper—except that he was too much employed to waste his time in listening to what he did not believe. I wrote several letters to my sister and to O'Brien, during the first two or three months, and requested the keeper to put them in the post. This he promised to do, never refusing to take the letters; but, as I afterwards found out, they were invariably destroyed. Yet I still bore up with the hopes of release for some time; but the anxiety relative to my sister, when I thought of her situation, my thoughts of Celeste and of O'Brien, sometimes quite overcame me; then, indeed, I would almost become frantic, and the keeper would report that I had had a paroxysm. After six months I became melancholy, and I wasted away. I no longer attempted to amuse myself, but sat all day with my eyes fixed upon vacancy. I no longer attended to my person; I allowed my beard to grow—my face was never washed, unless mechanically, when ordered by the keeper; and if I was not mad, there was every prospect of my soon becoming so. Life passed away as a blank—I had become indifferent to everything—I noted time no more—the change of seasons was unperceived—even the day and the night followed without my regarding them.

I was in this unfortunate situation, when one day the door was opened, and, as had been often the custom during my imprisonment, visitors were going round the establishment, to indulge their curiosity, in witnessing the degradation of their fellow-creatures, or to offer their commiseration. I paid no heed to them, not even casting up my eyes. "This young man," said the medical gentleman who accompanied the party, "has entertained the strange idea that his name is Simple, and that he is the rightful heir to the title and property of Lord Privilege."

One of the visitors came up to me, and looked me in the face. "And so he is," cried he to the doctor, who looked with astonishment. "Peter, don't you know me?" I started up. It was General O'Brien. I flew into his arms, and burst into tears.

"Sir," said General O'Brien, leading me to the chair, and seating me upon it, "I tell you that *is* Mr Simple, the nephew of Lord Privilege; and I believe, the heir to the title. If, therefore, his assertion of such being the case is the only proof of his insanity, he is illegally confined. I am here, a foreigner, and a prisoner on parole; but I am not without friends. My Lord Belmore," said he, turning to another of the visitors who had accompanied him, "I pledge you my honour that what I state is true; and I request that you will immediately demand the release of this poor young man."

"I assure you, sir, that I have Lord Privilege's letter," observed the doctor.

"Lord Privilege is a scoundrel," replied General O'Brien. "But there is justice to be obtained in this country, and he shall pay dearly for his *lettre de cachet*.* My dear Peter, how fortunate was my visit to this horrid place! I had heard so much of the excellent ar-

* Lettre de cachet: *A letter with an official seal.*

rangements of this establishment, that I agreed to walk round with Lord Belmore; but I find that it is abused."

"Indeed, General O'Brien, I have been treated with kindness," replied I; "and particularly by this gentleman. It was not his fault."

General O'Brien and Lord Belmore then inquired of the doctor if he had any objection to my release.

"None whatever, my lord, even if he were insane; although I now see how I have been imposed upon. We allow the friends of any patient to remove him, if they think that they can pay him more attention. He may leave with you this moment."

I now did feel my brain turn with the revulsion from despair to hope, and I fell back in my seat. The doctor, perceiving my condition, bled me copiously, and laid me on the bed, where I remained more than an hour, watched by General O'Brien. I then got up, calm and thankful. I was shaved by the barber of the establishment, washed and dressed myself, and, leaning on the general's arm, was let out. I cast my eyes upon the two celebrated stone figures of Melancholy and Raving Madness, as I passed them; I trembled, and clung more tightly to the general's arm, was assisted into the carriage, and bade farewell to madness and misery. The general said nothing until we approached the hotel where he resided, in Dover Street, and then he inquired, in a low voice, whether I could bear more excitement.

"It is Celeste you mean, general?"

"It is, my dear boy; she is here"; and he squeezed my hand.

"Alas!" cried I, "what hopes have I now of Celeste?"

"More than you had before," replied the general. "She lives but for you; and if you are a beggar, I have a competence to make you sufficiently comfortable."

I returned the general's pressure of the hand, but could not speak. We descended, and in a minute I was led by the father into the arms of the astonished daughter.

I must pass over a few days, during which I had almost recovered my health and spirits, and had narrated my adventures to General O'Brien and Celeste. My first object was to discover my sister. What had become of poor Ellen, in the destitute condition in which she had been left I knew not; and I resolved to go down to the vicarage, and make inquiries. I did not, however, set off until a legal adviser had been sent for by General O'Brien, and due notice given to Lord Privilege of an action to be immediately brought against him for false imprisonment.

I set off in the mail, and the next evening arrived at the town of ———. I hastened to the parsonage, and the tears stood in my eyes as I thought of my mother, my poor father, and the peculiar and doubtful situation of my dear sister. I was answered by a boy in livery, and found the present incumbent at home. He received me politely, listened to my story, and then replied that my sister had set off for London on the day of his arrival, and that she had not communicated her intentions to anyone. Here, then, was all clue lost, and I was in despair. I walked to the town in time to throw myself into the mail, and the next evening joined Celeste and the general, to whom I communicated the intelligence, and requested advice how to proceed.

Lord Belmore called the next morning, and the general consulted him. His lordship took great interest in my concerns, and, previous to any further steps, advised me to step into his carriage, and allow him to relate my case to the First Lord of the Admiralty. This was done immediately; and, as I had now an opportunity of speaking freely to his lordship, I explained to him the conduct of Captain Hawkins, and his connection with my uncle; also the reason of my uncle's persecution. His lordship, finding me under such powerful protection as Lord Belmore's, and having an eye to my future claims, which my uncle's conduct gave him reason to suppose were well founded, was extremely gracious, and said that I should hear from him in a day or two. He kept his word, and, on the third day after my interview, I received a note, announcing my promotion to the rank of commander. I was delighted with this good fortune, as was General O'Brien and Celeste.

When at the Admiralty, I inquired about O'Brien, and found that he was expected home every day. He had gained great reputation in the East Indies, was chief in command at the taking of some of the islands, and, it was said, was to be created a baronet for his services. Everything wore a favourable aspect, excepting the disappearance of my sister. This was a weight on my mind I could not remove.

But I have forgotten to inform the reader by what means General O'Brien and Celeste arrived so opportunely in England. Martinique had been captured by our forces about six months before, and the whole of the garrison surrendered as prisoners of war. General O'Brien was sent home, and allowed to be on parole; although born a Frenchman, he had very high connections in Ireland, of whom Lord Belmore was one. When they arrived, they had made every inquiry for me without success; they knew that I had been tried by a court-martial, and dismissed my ship, but after that, no clue could be found for my discovery.

Celeste, who was fearful that some dreadful accident had occurred to me, had suffered very much in health; and General O'Brien, perceiving how much his daughter's happiness depended upon her attachment for me, had made up his mind that if I were found we should be united. I hardly need say how delighted he was when he discovered me, though in a situation so little to be envied.

The story of my incarceration, of the action to be brought against my uncle, and the reports of foul play relative to the succession, had in the meantime been widely circulated among the nobility; and I found that every attention was paid me, and I was repeatedly invited out as an object of curiosity and speculation. The loss of my sister also was a subject of much interest, and many people, from goodwill, made every inquiry to discover her. I had returned one day from the solicitor's, who had advertised for her in the newspapers without success, when I found a letter for me on the table, in an Admiralty enclosure. I opened it—the enclosure was one from O'Brien, who had just cast anchor at Spithead, and who had requested that the letter should be forwarded to me, if anyone could tell my address. I tore it open.

"MY DEAR PETER,— Where are, and what has become of, you? I have received no letters for these two years, and I have fretted myself to death. I received your letter about the rascally court-martial; but perhaps you have not heard that the little scoundrel is dead. Yes, Peter; he brought your letter out in his own ship, and that was his death-warrant. I met him at a private party. He brought up your name—I allowed him to abuse you, and then told him he was a liar and a scoundrel; upon which he challenged me, very much against his will; but the affront was so public, that he couldn't help himself. Upon which I shot him, with all the good-will in the world, and could he have jumped up again twenty times, like Jack-in-the-Box, I would have shot him every time. The dirty scoundrel! but there's an end of him. Nobody pitied him, for everyone hated him; and the admiral only looked grave, and then was very much obliged to me for giving him a vacancy for his nephew. By-the-by, from some unknown hand, but I presume from the officers of his ship, I received a packet of correspondence between him and your worthy uncle, which is about as elegant a piece of rascality as ever was carried on between two scoundrels; but that's not all, Peter. I've got a young woman for you who will make your heart glad—not Mademoiselle Celeste, for I don't know where she is—but the wet-nurse who went out to India. Her husband was sent home as an invalid, and she was allowed her passage home with him in my frigate. Finding that he belonged to the regiment, I talked to him about one O'Sullivan, who married in Ireland, and mentioned the girl's name, and when he discovered that he was a countryman of mine he told me that his real name was O'Sullivan, sure enough, but that he had always served as O'Connell, and that his wife on board was the young woman in question. Upon which I sent to speak to her, and telling her that I knew all about it, and mentioning the names of Ella Flanagan and her mother, who had given me the information, she was quite astonished; and when I asked her what had become of the child which she took in place of her own, she told me that it had been drowned at Plymouth, and that her husband was saved at the same time by a young officer, 'whose name I have here,' says she; and then she pulled out of her neck your card, with Peter Simple on it. 'Now,' says I, 'do you know, good woman, that in helping on the rascally exchange of children, you ruin that very young man who saved your husband, for you deprive him of his title and property?" She stared like a stuck pig, when I said so, and then cursed and blamed herself, and declared she'd right you as soon as we came home; and most anxious she is still to do so, for she loves the very name of you; so you see, Peter, a good action has its reward sometimes in this world, and a bad action also, seeing as how I've shot that confounded villain who dared to ill-use you. I have plenty more to say to you, Peter; but I don't like writing what, perhaps, may never be read, so I'll wait till I hear from you; and then, as soon as I get through my business, we will set to and trounce that scoundrel of an uncle. I have twenty thousand pounds jammed together in the

Consolidated, besides the Spice Islands, which will be a pretty penny; and every farthing of it shall go to right you, Peter, and make a lord of you, as I promised you often that you should be; and if you win you shall pay, and if you don't then d——n the luck and d——n the money too. I beg you will offer my best regards to Miss Ellen, and say how happy I shall be to hear that she is well; but it has always been on my mind, Peter, that your father did not leave too much behind him, and I wish to know how you both get on. I left you a *carte blanche* at my agent's, and I only hope that you have taken advantage of it, if required; if not, you're not the Peter that I left behind me. So now, farewell, and don't forget to answer my letter in no time. Ever yours,

"TERENCE O'BRIEN."

This was indeed joyful intelligence. I handed the letter to General O'Brien, who read it, Celeste hanging over his shoulder, and perusing it at the same time.

"This is well," said the General. "Peter, I wish you joy, and Celeste, I ought to wish you joy also at your future prospects. It will indeed be a gratification if ever I hail you as Lady Privilege."

"Celeste," said I, "you did not reject me when I was pennyless, and in disgrace. O my poor sister Ellen! If I could but find you, how happy should I be!"

I sat down to write to O'Brien, acquainting him with all that had occurred, and the loss of my dear sister. The day after the receipt of my letter, O'Brien burst into the room. After the first moments of congratulation were past, he said, "My heart's broke, Peter, about your sister Ellen: find her I must. I shall give up my ship, for I'll never give up the search as long as I live. I must find her."

"Do, pray, my dear O'Brien, and I only wish—"

"Wish what, Peter? shall I tell you what I wish?—that if I find her, you'll give her to me for my trouble."

"As far as I am concerned, O'Brien, nothing would give me greater pleasure; but God knows to what wretchedness and want may have compelled her."

"Shame on you, Peter, to think so of your sister. I pledge my honour for her. Poor, miserable, and unhappy she may be—but no—no, Peter. You don't know—you don't love her as I do, if you can allow such thoughts to enter your mind."

This conversation took place at the window; we then turned round to General O'Brien and Celeste.

"Captain O'Brien," said the general.

"Sir Terence O'Brien, if you please, general. His Majesty has given me a handle to my name."

"I congratulate you, Sir Terence," said the general, shaking him by the hand: "what I was about to say is, that I hope you will take up your quarters at this hotel, and we will all live together. I trust that we shall soon find Ellen: in the meanwhile we have no time to lose, in our exposure of Lord Privilege. Is the woman in town?"

"Yes, and under lock and key; but the devil a fear of her. Millions would not bribe her to wrong him who risked his life for her husband. She's Irish, general, to the back bone. Nevertheless, Peter, we must go to our solicitor, to give the intelligence, that he may take the necessary steps."

For three weeks, O'Brien was diligent in his search for Ellen, employing every description of emissary without success. In the meanwhile, the general and I were prosecuting our cause against Lord Privilege. One morning, Lord Belmore called upon us, and asked the general if we would accompany him to the theatre, to see two celebrated pieces performed. In the latter, which was a musical farce, a new performer was to come out, of whom report spoke highly. Celeste consented, and after an early dinner, we joined his lordship in his private box, which was above the stage, on the first tier. The first piece was played, and Celeste, who had never seen the performance of Young, was delighted. The curtain then drew up for the second piece. In the second act, the new performer, a Miss Henderson, was led by the manager on the stage; she was apparently much frightened and excited, but three rounds of applause gave her courage, and she proceeded. At the very first notes of her voice I was startled, and O'Brien, who was behind, threw himself forward to look at her; but as we were almost directly above, and her head was turned the other way, we could not distinguish her features. As she proceeded in her song, she gained courage, and her face was turned towards us, and she cast her eyes up—saw me—the recognition was mutual—I held out my arm, but could not speak—she staggered, and fell down in a swoon.

" 'Tis Ellen!" cried O'Brien, rushing past me; and making one spring down on the stage, he carried her off, before any other person could come to her assistance. I followed him, and found him with Ellen still in his arms, and the actresses assisting in her recovery. The manager came forward to apologise, stating that the young lady was too ill to proceed, and the audience, who had witnessed the behaviour of O'Brien and myself, were satisfied with the romance in real life which had been exhibited. Her part was read by another, but the piece was little attended to, everyone trying to find out the occasion of this uncommon occurrence. In the meantime, Ellen was put into a hackney-coach by O'Brien and me, and we drove to the hotel, where we were soon joined by the general and Celeste.

——∽∾∾—

CHAPTER LXV

It never rains but it pours, whether it be good or bad news—I succeed in everything, and to everything, my wife, my title, and estate—And "All's well that ends well."

I SHALL PASS over the scenes which followed, and give my sister's history in her own words.

"I wrote to you, my dear Peter, to tell you that I considered it my duty to pay all my father's debts with your money, and that there were but sixty pounds left when every claim had been satisfied; and I requested you to come to me as soon as you could, that I might have your counsel and assistance as to my future arrangements."

"I received your letter, Ellen, and was hastening to you, when—but no matter, I will tell my story afterwards."

"Day after day I waited with anxiety for a letter, and then wrote to the officers of the ship to know if any accident had occurred. I received an answer from the surgeon, informing me that you had quitted Portsmouth to join me, and had not since been heard of. You may imagine my distress at this communication, as I did not doubt but that something dreadful had occurred, as I knew, too well, that nothing would have detained you from me at such a time. The new vicar appointed had come down to look over the house, and to make arrangements for bringing in his family. The furniture he had previously agreed to take at a valuation, and the sum had been appropriated in liquidation of your father's debts. I had already been permitted to remain longer than was usual, and had no alternative but to quit, which I did not do until the last moment. I could not leave my address, for I knew not where I was to go. I took my place in the coach, and arrived in London. My first object was to secure the means of livelihood, by offering myself as a governess; but I found great difficulties from not being able to procure a good reference, and from not having already served in that capacity. At last I was taken into a family to bring up three little girls; but I soon found out how little chance I had of comfort. The lady had objected to me as too good-looking—for this same reason the gentleman insisted upon my being engaged.

"Thus was I a source of disunion; the lady treated me with harshness, and the gentleman with too much attention. At last her ill-treatment and his persecution, were both so intolerable, that I gave notice that I should leave my situation."

"I beg pardon, Miss Ellen, but you will oblige me with the name and residence of that gentleman?" said O'Brien.

"Indeed, Ellen, do no such thing," replied I; "continue your story."

"I could not obtain another situation as governess; for, as I always stated where I had been, and did not choose to give the precise reason for quitting, merely stating that I was not comfortable, whenever the lady was called upon for my character, she invariably spoke of me so as to prevent my obtaining a situation. At last I was engaged as teacher to a school. I had better have taken a situation as housemaid. I was expected to be everywhere, to do everything; was up at daylight, and never in bed till past midnight; fared very badly, and was equally ill paid; but still it was honest employment, and I remained there for more than a year; but, though as economical as possible, my salary would not maintain me in clothes and washing, which was all I required. There was a master of elocution, who came every week, and whose wife was the teacher of music. They took a great liking to me, and pointed out how much better I should be off if I could succeed on the stage, of which they had no doubt. For months I refused, hoping still to have some tidings of you; but at last my drudgery became so insupportable, and my means so decreased, that I unwillingly consented. It was then nineteen months since I had heard of you, and I mourned you as dead. I had no relations except my uncle, and I was unknown even to him. I quitted the situation, and took up my abode with the teacher of elocution and his wife, who treated me with every kindness, and prepared me for my new career. Neither at the school, which was three miles from London, nor at my new residence, which was over Westminster Bridge, did I ever see a newspaper. It was no wonder, therefore, that I did not know of your advertisements. After three months' preparation I was recommended and introduced to the manager by my kind friends, and accepted. You know the rest."

"Well, Miss Ellen, if anyone ever tells you that you were on the stage, at all events you may reply that you wasn't there long."

"I trust not long enough to be recognised," replied she. "I recollect how often I have expressed my disgust at those who would thus consent to exhibit themselves; but circumstances strangely alter our feelings. I do, however, trust that I should have been respectable, even as an actress."

"That you would, Miss Ellen," replied O'Brien. "What did I tell you, Peter?"

"You pledged your honour that nothing would induce Ellen to disgrace her family, I recollect, O'Brien."

"Thank you, Sir Terence, for your good opinion," replied Ellen.

My sister had been with us about three days, during which I had informed her of all that had taken place, when, one evening, finding myself alone with her, I candidly stated to her what were O'Brien's feelings towards her, and pleaded his cause with all the earnestness in my power.

"My dear brother," she replied, "I have always admired Captain O'Brien's character, and always have felt grateful to him for his kindness and attachment to you; but I cannot say that I love him. I have never thought about him except as one to whom we are both much indebted."

"But do you mean to say that you could not love him?"

"No, I do not; and I will do all I can, Peter—I will try. I never will, if possible, make him unhappy who has been so kind to you."

"Depend upon it, Ellen, that with your knowledge of O'Brien, and with feelings of gratitude to him, you will soon love him, if once you accept him as a suitor. May I tell him—"

"You may tell him that he may plead his own cause, my dear brother; and, at all events, I will listen to no other until he has had fair play; but recollect that at present I only *like* him—like him *very much*, it is true; but still I only *like* him."

I was quite satisfied with my success, and so was O'Brien, when I told him. "By the powers, Peter, she's an angel, and I can't expect her to love an inferior being like myself; but if she'll only like me well enough to marry me, I'll trust to after-marriage for the rest. Love comes with the children, Peter. Well, but you need not say that to her—divil a bit—they shall come upon her like old age, without her perceiving it."

O'Brien having thus obtained permission, certainly lost no time in taking advantage of it. Celeste and I were more fondly attached every day. The solicitor declared my case so good, that he could raise fifty thousand pounds upon it. In short, all our causes were prosperous, when an event occurred, the details of which, of course, I did not obtain until some time afterwards, but which I shall narrate here.

My uncle was very much alarmed when he discovered that I had been released from Bedlam—still more so, when he had notice given him of a suit, relative to the succession to the title. His emissaries had discovered that the wet-nurse had been brought home in O'Brien's frigate, and was kept so close that they could not communicate with her. He now felt that all his schemes would prove abortive. His legal adviser was with him, and they had been walking in the garden, talking over the contingencies, when they stopped close to the drawing-room windows of the mansion at Eagle Park.

"But, sir," observed the lawyer, "if you will not confide in me, I cannot act for your benefit. You still assert that nothing of the kind has taken place?"

"I do," replied his lordship. "It is a foul invention."

"Then, my lord, may I ask you why you considered it advisable to imprison Mr Simple in Bedlam?"

"Because I hate him," retorted his lordship,—"detest him."

"And for what reason, my lord? his character is unimpeached, and he is your near relative."

"I tell you, sir, that I hate him—would that he were now lying dead at my feet!"

Hardly were the words out of my uncle's mouth, when a whizzing was heard for a second, and then something fell down within a foot of where they stood, with a heavy crash. They started—turned round—the adopted heir lay lifeless at their feet, and their legs were bespattered with his blood and his brains. The poor boy, seeing his lordship below, had leaned out of one of the upper windows to call to him, but lost his balance, and had fallen head foremost upon the wide stone pavement which surrounded the mansion. For a few seconds the lawyer and my uncle looked upon each other with horror.

"A judgment!—a judgment!" cried the lawyer, looking at his client. My uncle covered his face with his hands, and fell. Assistance now came out, but there was more than one to help up. The violence of his emotion had brought on an apoplectic fit, and my uncle, although he breathed, never spoke again.

It was in consequence of this tragical event, of which we did not know the particulars until afterwards, that the next morning my solicitor called upon me, and put a letter into my hand, saying, "Allow me to congratulate your lordship." We were all at breakfast at the time, and the general, O'Brien, and myself jumped up, all in such astonishment at this unexpected title being so soon conferred upon me, that we had a heavy bill for damages to pay; and had not Ellen caught the tea-urn, as it was tipping over, there would, in all probability, have been a doctor's bill into the bargain. The letter was eagerly read—it was from my uncle's legal adviser, who had witnessed the catastrophe, informing me, that all dispute as to the succession was at an end by the tragical event that had taken place, and that he had put seals upon everything, awaiting my arrival or instructions. The solicitor, as he presented the letter, said that he would take his leave, and call again in an hour or two, when I was more composed. My first movement, when I had read the letter aloud, was to throw my arms round Celeste, and embrace her—and O'Brien, taking the hint, did the same to Ellen, and was excused in consideration of circumstances; but, as soon as she could disengage herself, her arms were entwined round my neck, while Celeste was hanging on her father's. Having disposed of the ladies, the gentlemen now shook hands, and though we had not all appetites to finish our breakfasts, never was there a happier quintette.

In about an hour my solicitor returned, and congratulated me, and immediately set about the necessary preparations. I desired him to go down immediately to Eagle Park, attend to the funeral of my uncle, and the poor little boy who had paid so dearly for his

intended advancement, and take charge from my uncle's legal adviser, who remained in the house. The "dreadful accident in high
life" found its way into the papers of the day, and before dinner-
time a pile of visiting cards was poured in, which covered the table.
The next day a letter arrived from the First Lord, announcing that he
had made out my commission as post-captain, and trusted that I
would allow him the pleasure of presenting it himself at his dinner
hour, at half-past seven. Very much obliged to him, the "fool of the
family" might have waited a long while for it.

While I was reading this letter, the waiter came up to say that a
young woman below wanted to speak to me. I desired her to be
shown up. As soon as she came in, she burst into tears, knelt down,
and kissed my hand.

"Sure, it's you—oh! yes—it's you that saved my poor husband
when I was assisting to your ruin. And an't I punished for my
wicked doings—an't my poor boy dead?"

She said no more, but remained on her knees, sobbing bitterly.
Of course, the reader recognises in her the wet-nurse who had exchanged her child. I raised her up, and desired her to apply to my
solicitor to pay her expenses, and leave her address.

"But do you forgive me, Mr Simple? It's not that I have forgiven
myself."

"I do forgive you with all my heart, my good woman. You have
been punished enough."

"I have, indeed," replied she, sobbing; "but don't I deserve it all,
and more too? God's blessing, and all the saints' too, upon your
head, for your kind forgiveness, anyhow. My heart is lighter." And
she quitted the room.

She had scarcely quitted the hotel, when the waiter came up
again. "Another lady, my lord, wishes to speak with you, but she
won't give her name."

"Really, my lord, you seem to have an extensive female acquaintance," said the general.

"At all events, I am not aware of any that I need be ashamed of.
Show the lady up, waiter."

In a moment entered a fat, unwieldly little mortal, very warm
from walking; she sat down in a chair, threw back her tippet, and
then exclaimed, "Lord bless you, how you have grown! Gemini, if I
can hardly believe my eyes; and I declare he don't know me."

"I really cannot exactly recollect where I had the pleasure of seeing you before, madam."

"Well, that's what I said to Jemima, when I went down in the kitchen. 'Jemima,' says I, 'I wonder if little Peter Simple will know me.' And Jemima says, 'I think he would the parrot, marm.' "

"Mrs Handycock, I believe," said I, recollecting Jemima and the parrot, although, from a little thin woman, she had grown so fat as not to be recognisable.

"Oh! so you've found me out, Mr Simple—my lord, I ought to say. Well, I need not ask after your grandfather now, for I know he's dead; but as I was coming this way for orders, I thought I would just step in and see how you looked."

"I trust Mr Handycock is well, ma'am. Pray is he a bull or a bear?"

"Lord bless you, Mr Simple, my lord, I should say, he's been neither bull nor bear for these three years. He was obliged to *waddle*. If I didn't know much about bulls and bears, I know very well what a *lame duck* is, to my cost. We're off the Stock Exchange, and Mr Handycock is set up as a coal merchant."

"Indeed!"

"Yes; that is, we have no coals, but we take orders, and have half-a-crown a chaldron for our trouble. As Mr Handycock says, it's a very good business, if you only had enough of it. Perhaps your lordship may be able to give us an order. It's nothing out of your pocket, and something into ours."

"I shall be very happy, when I return again to town, Mrs Handycock. I hope the parrot is quite well."

"Oh! my lord, that's a sore subject; only think of Mr Handycock, when we retired from the 'Change, taking my parrot one day and selling it for five guineas, saying, five guineas were better than a nasty squalling bird. To be sure, there was nothing for dinner that day; but, as Jemima agreed with me, we'd rather have gone without a dinner for a month, than have parted with Poll. Since we've looked up a little in the world, I saved up five guineas, by hook or by crook, and tried to get Poll back again, but the lady said she wouldn't take fifty guineas for him."

Mrs Handycock then jumped from her chair, saying, "Good morning, my lord; I'll leave one of Mr Handycock's cards. Jemima would be so glad to see you."

As she left the room, Celeste laughingly asked me whether I had
any more such acquaintances. I replied, that I believed not; but I
must acknowledge that Mrs Trotter was brought to my recollection,
and I was under some alarm, lest she should also come and pay me
her respects.

The next day I had another unexpected visit. We had just sat
down to dinner, when we heard a disturbance below; and, shortly
after, the general's French servant came up in great haste, saying
that there was a foreigner below, who wished to see me: and that he
had been caning one of the waiters of the hotel, for not paying him
proper respect.

"Who can that be?" thought I: and I went out of the door, and
looked over the banisters, as the noise continued.

"You must not come here to beat Englishmen, I can tell you,"
roared one of the waiters. "What do we care for your foreign
counts?"

"Sacré canaille!" cried the other party, in a contemptuous voice,
which I well knew.*

"Ay, canal!—we'll duck you in the canal, if you don't mind."

"You will!" said the stranger, who had hitherto spoken French.
"Allow me to observe—in the most delicate manner in the world—
just to hint, that you are a d——d trencher-scraping, napkin-
carrying, shilling-seeking, up-and-down-stairs son of a bitch—and
take this for your impudence!"

The noise of the cane was again heard; and I hastened down-
stairs, where I found Count Shucksen thrashing two or three of the
waiters without mercy. At my appearance, the waiters, who were
showing fight, retreated to a short distance, out of reach of the cane.

"My dear count," exclaimed I, "is it you?"

"My dear Lord Privilege, will you excuse me? but these fellows
are saucy."

"Then I'll have them discharged," replied I. "If a friend of mine,
and an officer of your rank and distinction, cannot come to see me
without insult, I will seek another hotel."

This threat of mine, and the reception I gave the count, put all to
rights. The waiters sneaked off, and the master of the hotel apologised. It appeared that they had desired him to wait in the coffee-

* Sacré canaille!: What a scoundrel!

room until they could announce him, which had hurt the count's dignity.

"We are just sitting down to dinner, count; will you join us?"

"As soon as I have improved my toilet, my dear lord," replied he; "you must perceive that I am off a journey."

The master of the hotel bowed, and proceeded to show the count to a dressing-room. When I returned up-stairs—"What was the matter?" inquired O'Brien.

"Oh, nothing!—a little disturbance in consequence of a foreigner not understanding English."

In about five minutes the waiter opened the door, and announced Count Shucksen.

"Now, O'Brien, you'll be puzzled," said I; and in came the count.

"My dear Lord Privilege," said he, coming up and taking me by the hand, "let me not be the last to congratulate you upon your accession. I was running up the channel in my frigate when a pilot-boat gave me a newspaper, in which I saw your unexpected change of circumstances. I made an excuse for dropping my anchor at Spithead this morning, and I have come up post, to express how sincerely I participate in your good fortune." Count Shucksen then politely saluted the ladies and the general, and turned round to O'Brien, who had been staring at him with astonishment. "Count Shucksen, allow me to introduce Sir Terence O'Brien."

"By the piper that played before Moses, but it's a puzzle," said O'Brien. "Blood and thunder! if it a'n't Chucks!—my dear fellow, when did you rise from your grave?"

"Fortunately," replied the count, as they shook each other's hands for some time, "I never went into it, Sir Terence. But now, with your permission, my lord, I'll take some food, as I really am not a little hungry. After dinner, Captain O'Brien, you shall hear my history."

His secret was confided to the whole party, upon my pledging myself for their keeping it locked up in their own breasts, which was a bold thing on my part, considering that two of them were ladies. The count stayed with us for some time, and was introduced everywhere. It was impossible to discover that he had not been bred up in a court, his manners were so good. He was a great favourite with the ladies; and his moustachios, bad French, and waltzing—an accomplishment he had picked up in Sweden—were quite the vogue. All the ladies were sorry when the Swedish count announced his departure by a P.P.C.

Before I left town I called upon the First Lord of the Admiralty, and procured for Swinburne a first-rate building—that is to say, ordered to be built. This he had often said he wished, as he was tired of the sea, after a service of forty-five years. Subsequently I obtained leave of absence for him every year, and he used to make himself very happy at Eagle Park. Most of his time was, however, passed on the lake, either fishing or rowing about; telling long stories to all who would join him in his water excursions.

A fortnight after my assuming my title, we set off for Eagle Park, and Celeste consented to my entreaties that the wedding should take place that day month. Upon this hint O'Brien spake; and, to oblige *me*, Ellen consented that we should be united on the same day.

O'Brien wrote to Father M'Grath; but the letter was returned by post, with *"dead"* marked upon the outside. O'Brien then wrote to one of his sisters, who informed him that Father M'Grath would cross the bog one evening when he had taken a very large proportion of whisky; and that he was seen out of the right path, and had never been heard of afterwards.

On the day appointed we were all united, and both unions have been attended with as much happiness as this world can afford. Both O'Brien and I are blessed with children, which, as O'Brien observed, have come upon us like old age, until we now can muster a large Christmas party in the two families. The general's head is white, and he sits and smiles, happy in his daughter's happiness, and in the gambols of his grandchildren.

Such, reader, is the history of Peter Simple, Viscount Privilege, no longer the fool, but the head of the family, who now bids you farewell.

ABOUT THE EDITORS

The Heart of Oak Sea Classics book series is edited by DEAN KING, author of *A Sea of Words: A Lexicon and Companion for Patrick O'Brian's Seafaring Tales* (Henry Holt, 1995; second edition, 1997) and *Harbors and High Seas: An Atlas and Geographical Guide to the Aubrey-Maturin Novels of Patrick O'Brian* (Holt, 1996), and editor, with John B. Hattendorf, of *Every Man Will Do His Duty: An Anthology of Firsthand Accounts from the Age of Nelson, 1793–1815* (Holt, 1997).

Comments on or suggestions for the Heart of Oak Sea Classics series can be sent to Dean King c/o Henry Holt & Co., 115 West 18th St., New York, NY 10011 or E-mailed to him at DeanHKing@aol.com.

The series' scholarly advisors are JOHN B. HATTENDORF, Ernest J. King Professor of Maritime History at the U.S. Naval War College, and CHRISTOPHER McKEE, Samuel R. and Marie-Louise Rosenthal Professor and Librarian of the College, Grinnell College, author of, most recently, *A Gentlemanly and Honorable Profession: The Creation of the U.S. Naval Officer Corps, 1794–1815* (Naval Institute Press, 1991).

LOUIS J. PARASCANDOLA is an Assistant Professor of English at Long Island University's Brooklyn Campus where he teaches British and African American literatures. He holds a Ph.D. in English from the CUNY Graduate School. His publications include *"Puzzled Which to Choose": Conflicting Sociopolitical Views in the Works of Captain Frederick Marryat* (Peter Lang Publishing Co., 1997) and *"Winos Can Wake Up the Dead": An Eric D. Walrond Reader* (Wayne State University Press, 1998).